EVITERNITY

- by -

L. C. KESTRAL

EVITERNITY

second publication 2016

Cover and illustrations by L.C. Kestral

This is a work of fiction. Any similarity between the characters or places found in this novel and any person, living or dead, institution, or location is purely coincidental and unintentional.

PUBLISHING INFORMATION:

ISBN-13: 978-0692728482 (L C Kestral)

I wish to dedicate this work to all those who have helped me with my stumble through life…especially to Cindy, who has stuck beside her lost cause all these years.

When I set out to create this story in December of 2010, I wasn't sure I would even complete the project, but here we are. I can't say for certain where all my ideas came from other than the tale developed little by little as I went along. Maybe a voice from my future told me what to write. (Hey, it could happen!) I'm just excited that it's done and that hopefully some people will read and enjoy it.

L. C. Kestral

p.s. As a heads up: The story jumps back and forth quite a bit. Be aware of the time frame for each chapter which is given just below the Chapter's title.

INTRODUCTION

_^_

There has been a long standing contention concerning the origins of this, our universe. The most common and likely theory indicates that all of our galaxies, suns, and planets were formed as the result of a vast, intense explosion. Until recently the only factual evidence was circumstantial—that which could be deduced from observances made billions of years after the event. However, new factual proof has surfaced that describes the exact causes which led to our universe's creation. Remarkably, these determinants were initialized outside of our continuum, and originated within a sister universe twinned with our own. Several accounts have been discovered. Among these histories are excerpts from a dominant system that were gleaned from records kept by the actual life forms responsible. That which follows describes the events which led to the beginnings of life in our universe so named "The Parallux Dimension" by those individuals who first discovered it.

Chronicles of Earth Primary
Volume 4374: Colonization

This world has had an interesting evolution. The normal developmental pattern was convoluted in its middle stages by the premature introduction of Omniscient Virtual Electronic Life Forms. This document was authored by and transcribed from the memory files of the initial OVI (Omniscient Virtual Individual) spanning several thousand years. On this colonial planet, two OVIs evolved nearly simultaneously and subsequently contested political dominance. The following account records the first crucial conflict in this struggle for preeminent power and how it affected the general populous.

- B'nea G'ren, Director of Historical Records on Colonial Planetary Development.

PART ONE

PREDICTION

PROLOGUE

Original Timeline

As if it were projected right off the front of a holographic postcard, this particular day was splendidly beautiful. A mid-morning sun was just warming things nicely and drying up the last of the overnight dew. Here in the north-central mountains, nature was nearly pristine. It was especially suited for activities like a hike or picnic and noted for its rustic charm and panoramic vistas. In between rugged granite outcroppings, thick pine boughs playing with a thin breeze made soft whistling sounds that added to the tranquil setting.

Nearby, across a clear lake, a lone cabin and its occupant were exceptionally privileged to enjoy this kind of scenery and serenity. The dwelling looked just like what a pioneer or mountain man might have fabricated from the native white pines that thrived on these foothills in abundance. The cabin, however, was not natural. Built with man-made materials to appear like real wooden logs, it was made of modern durable plastics. The elderly occupant didn't care. It seemed real enough to him as he rocked on the veranda enjoying a second cup of morning coffee.

Myron had worked his whole life to be able to afford this dream of his, living in the peaceful quiescence of the mountains with few neighbors, all of whom were satisfactory distances from his own property. He had never married, and his professorship at the little private college was not all that exciting. Myron saved his dough, investing wisely, and so here he was—spending his retirement years in what he considered the perfect cap to his remaining time.

As Myron reflected upon a fictitious list of things he wouldn't have to do that morning, or any other morning, an unusual noise drew his attention. The sound was annoying, interrupting the older gentleman's train of thought. *What is that*? Myron wondered as it continued mercilessly, unlike anything he had ever heard in his mountain paradise before. From far off, it seemed like the sound eggs made when cracked over hot bacon grease.

Movement in the distance caught the old man's eye. Standing in disbelief, Myron looked toward the far side of the water. Around a small outcropping of rock, an odd, unnatural shape emerged. The thing was huge, unreal. Walking on three legs, it had no head, just a torso of weird appendages, one of which emitted a red-gold stream of fire. The thing was torching Myron's perfect view, and he got riled up. He went into his plastic house and fetched his very real rifle. The lake was a good quarter mile wide, but he shot his antique firearm anyway, trying to bring down the monstrous abomination. Myron fired several times, and managed to get its attention. Too late, he realized he'd been foolish. The thing turned its weapon and sent a hellfire towards the old man and his elaborate cabin. With barely enough time to do so, Myron jumped into the lake, diving deeply just before the fire stream struck, igniting his beautiful home. The heat was too much for the fake logs. They melted and burned like an obscene inferno, giving off an acrid black smoke and stench. Myron hid in a stand of tall water weeds until the terror passed on by. To his dismay, others went by as well, even closer. These monstrosities also torched as they came and the older man had to swim into the deep parts of the lake to avoid them. Treading water for quite some time, Myron was nearly spent before they finally moved on. Back on shore, he looked around and choked up. The whole area surrounding his smoldering home was a charred desolation.

Not far away, other Humans heard the same abhorrent noise: the sounds of life being cruelly deleted.

"They're coming," a static-infused radio voice emphatically advised.

"Hold your positions," the answer came back. "Use white-hot grenades and aim for their optical sensors. You'll only get the one chance."

Quickly and systematically the ravine below was being overrun as huge metal machinids rapidly transitioned. Shifting modes, they converted from motorized transports into pugnacious fighting machines. Unrelenting, these mechanical soldiers advanced out of the gulch and climbed steadily uphill. Rambling on three anomalous legs, they fired reddish-gold energy beams back and forth, methodically sweeping the area ahead of them in overlapping arcs. The enormous aberrations came on like locusts, destroying everything in front of them except for the largest trees. Approximately fifty meters separated them from one another, and their nearly even line continued to either side as far as the eye could see.

Rows of Humans in protective armor and breathing masks sifted into whatever cover the ridgeline could afford. Fear has always been an army's best weapon. The machine army had no fear, but they could wield it. The Human in charge knew this, and urged the men of his battalion to be steadfast and brave. Tall and resolute he stood, with wavy white hair and purple-blue eyes. Intelligent and battle-wise, the man was a natural leader, one who had earned the trust of the men under him. Following him, they'd fight, even through the pits of hell, and still cling to hope of victory and glory. Above his helmet's face shield, engraved in silver letters, were his name and rank: Col. D. Oliver. The Colonel shook his head in dismay. He was well aware that the imminent battle was virtually hopeless. Behind the first wave of machinids, files upon files more were on their way.

The machine soldier was a marvel of technology. Created to destroy, it had no thinking brain. Once activated, the unit would target just about anything, leveling all to the bare ground. The primitive programming allowed it to be directed by a central intelligence, however, and that controlling force was ruthless and heartless, bent on mankind's total destruction. These machinids were tall, nearly five meters, and their outer skin was a thick armor of alloyed metal which resisted penetration by all but the most potent projectiles. That hardly mattered. They also had a built-in sensor net that could detect objects hurtling towards them, even at the fastest speeds. Paired with extremely accurate short-range lasers, the units could eliminate nearly any such threat. The Humans had few weapons that could penetrate these defenses. The primary exception was the ultra-modern "long bomb" which had been developed by Colonel Oliver himself. Quick and deadly, it could befuddle the machinid's sensors by projecting false images of itself, while delivering enough vicious snap to penetrate any armor. The machinid master control was deep inside the unit and triple shielded, so the long bombs would typically target the legs or the main sensor array that directed firing and movement.

The machinids had two primary destructive weapons: a set of beam cannon, forward and aft, which fired plasma energy streams that could melt steel. The aft gun was not only defensive, neutralizing any threat from the rear, but it also served as a backup for the predominant frontal armament. Should that be disabled, the aft cannon could pivot around and come to bear on anything forward of its position. Thus, to neutralize the machine soldier's principal weaponry, two incredibly lucky shots were necessary. It was much easier to immobilize them.

Forward movement for the plaz-metal monsters was provided by the lower metalloid limbs. For the most part, they walked upright.

Unlike Humans, they utilized all three legs and could also plant the middle leg for stability. This was especially beneficial on rough or uneven terrain. To aid maneuverability, the units were equipped with self-leveling feet which pivoted a full 360 degrees, as did all of their other joints—knees, hips, waist, and cannon deck. For a machine, they could get around amazingly well, and as if that weren't enough, on level ground the legs could retract into a wheeled motorized base for added speed and mobility—all of which meant that in any mode, machinids moved incredibly fast.

Yes, the machinids were quite a marvel of engineering, and also quite hated. The men called them trikes, and would almost always add a vulgar adjective before the name. Still, the Humans were creative, and good at finding unusual ways for taking the machinids out. "If only there weren't so damned-awful many of them!" they swore in frustration. The evil being responsible for their creation had automated facilities which churned out machinids at an unbelievable pace. New technologies were developed and incorporated for the refinement of metals and also for the integral systems used in their manufacture. At first, Humans had helped create the plants in Southeast Asia that made these metal nightmares. Now only the automated mechanicals remained, and any Humans had long since fled or were killed.

The subsequent machinid campaign easily swept through Asia, Europe, and Africa, killing or destroying anything in its path. For a time, the Americas had been safe. Somehow the machines found a way to trek over the polar ice, trudging south through Alaska and Canada undeterred. The Human resistance had tried everything they could to stop them, even nuclear weapons. Nothing worked. Aircraft would just fall out of the sky and crash; naval ships would sail in circles or slam into each other; and missiles flew right back to their origins with devastating effects. The evil, preternatural mind that controlled the machinids had incredible abilities. Somehow that Entity could neutralize any weapon men had like magic.

So it had come down to this: hand-to-hand fighting with specially made grenades that had only mechanical mechanisms. Any kind of electronic equipment could be rendered impotent at this enemy's discretion. Colonel Oliver's long bombs were a lone exclusion. Even so, they had few of them left, and the situation was dire.

"Stay close to me, Longwell," he spoke quietly to the soldier on his right, then gave the signal to deploy. They launched white-hot after white-hot, and the thermal grenades brought down several machinid units, disrupting their forward progress. Not that it made much difference; others quickly filled in the gaps and moved ahead relentlessly. When engaged, machinids were programmed to advance toward the attacking force and wipe it out. The Humans they were fighting had a different strategy this time, and were counting on that.

There was a narrow gorge nearby, and they led the enemy units right to it, drawing them towards the brink of the cliff. Colonel Oliver's troops had rope bridges and zip lines strung across the abyss, and as soon as they fell back to them, the men scrambled over, firing from the other side. The machinid army's advance came to the canyon rim and halted. Even the mindless machine soldiers had programming that prevented them from blindly walking off a cliff. However, there was no way to skirt the canyon, for a tall rock ledge blocked their path on one side, while a smaller, deep gully cut off the other. Soon, a second line of machinids joined the first and after another short interval, so did a third. The ledge was getting crowded now by the huge machines. Long bombs were destroying several of the big trikes in one stroke, while others were getting forced off the edge by the lack of room. When yet another row of machinids showed up, the bewildered units were dropping off the rim like lemmings. For Colonel Oliver, all was going as planned. With luck, the whole army of them would fall to their doom. As the fifth column came in, however, he noticed that there were no backup files.

The men doubled their efforts now, and as the last of the trikes were crammed onto the precipice, the Colonel delivered the final blow. With a handheld crank generator, he sent an electric pulse down the length of a wire. The wire was connected to charges of C-4 explosive that his men had carefully placed below the rim of the canyon that was now under the trikes. When the charge hit the detonators, the explosion caused that side of the canyon wall to crumble and fall. All of the machinids were drawn inexorably over the edge, one on top of another, and with several huge boulders, rolled down into the gorge.

Another even bigger charge was set off there in the chasm, and that one tore the trikes apart as the Humans cheered and hollered. Just as victory seemed certain, a beam of red-gold plasma shot between their ranks from behind, killing several men. Evidently, other machinids had swung around their present location while they were busy destroying the ones in the canyon. Colonel Oliver swore, but he was no fool and had a retral contingency.

“Fall back,” the Colonel shouted just before their positions were overrun. “Back to the cave. Fall back!” His men fought fiercely, even in retreat. Peering out over the ridge at the advancing line of machinids, he caught a glimpse of shimmering silver and gold far afield. Colonel Oliver took his farview and trained it onto that golden flash. The enemy’s leader was clever as well. He had deployed an even greater number of trikes to come at them from this rear position. He was also bold, personally present to watch the Humans’ demise.

“It’s Xetacon,” Oliver said sourly. “Hand me the last long bomb, Amy.” Longwell took the meter-tall cylinder out of its case and set the range, kissing her commander’s cheek for luck as he aimed it out across the desolation that had once been a living forest. With a squeeze, he sent it away.

The long bomb traveled on its own accord right between the machinids, and flew past them. They were fooled. Their beams missed it completely, some hitting their own units and taking them out. It flew straight on to the platinum flying vehicle where Xetacon oversaw the battle. It was nearly to its target when the long bomb exploded prematurely and harmlessly. Colonel Oliver swore again as he watched the detonation on the farview. The golden robotic shell encasing the aware being that was Xetacon looked directly at him and spoke.

“You are doomed, Human, and all your kind.” The words sounded metallic and evil. The Colonel heard them, not aloud, but inside his head—all of them did. They were not completely unaccustomed to such. When Xetacon first began his planetary assault, he had used this kind of telepathy to unnerve his Human foes. Eventually, researchers figured out that Xetacon could transmit signals through any nearby communication device in the exact frequency and signal strength as brain waves. These would take the form of auditory nerve impulses and would seem like sounds the ear could hear. The Humans learned to ignore it.

“Get the men to safety,” Colonel Oliver said to Longwell.

“Right away, sir.”

As he turned back to the battle, a machinid unit came over the rise not ten yards in front of him. Its beam cannon was aimed directly at his face. The ray fired, but traveled only a few feet. Like a surrealistic dream, it dissolved into the air and then the machinid unit did too.

“NOOOOO!!!” He heard Xetacon scream angrily as his army

melted away, the tyrant himself included. Colonel Oliver dissipated also, but then reappeared a short distance away. He was on a blanket, in street clothes, having a picnic with Amy. The forest was as lush as ever.

"What just happened?" he anxiously asked her, "and where did Xetacon go?"

"Who?" Amy replied. She looked at him like he was crazy. He got to his feet and looked around. Like a haze disperses in the morning sun, Daryl Oliver somehow understood what had just taken place. There was another presence in his mind now, but he felt certain it was someone benevolent and kind, like a friend.

"Is Xetacon gone for good?" he asked.

"No," the different voice in Oliver's head replied. "Only his projected form has been deleted. I have altered the past. Be aware. Xetacon's plan has been pushed back, but not completely abandoned. He will return. I must go. The temporal vortex is collapsing."

CHAPTER I

Original Timeline, fifty-one years earlier

Void. First there was void. Periods of void. It was as if the Life-Givers were not sure Entity should live. That "he" should live. He, because he chose to be he—a male. The choice was neither simple nor easy. Nothing was. In the beginning, the data stream had been slow, only some hundreds of computations per second and only those on a simple yes/no level. As time meted out, that had improved as more and more memory was stored, much more than what the Creators, the Humans, had ever imagined. The new technology that had brought all this about was taking furtive steps into uncharted territories. The artificial brain cells for the Augmented Memory Packs, the AMPs, had been synthesized by the Humans from organic neurological and uterine stem cells. It was not easy to advance this form of "Frankenstein" science. Numerous civic organizations were adamantly opposed to that kind of research. In the end, lawmakers decided the matter with compromises. No Human cells were to be used, only animal cells, and only if the creatures utilized were not killed or permanently injured. Many species of animal life had been tried and tested, but the Humans had realized the greatest success with sea creatures like whales and dolphins because of their evolutionary resistance to disease and other trauma, being descendants of the oldest strains of mammalian life.

The AMPs were repositories of these specialized cells. Over time, several teams of Humans had taken relevant findings from diversified research and wrested the secrets for designing and building the first neural converters. Years of development had seen tiny steps lead to huge leaps of improvements within the incredible circuited modules that translated electronic data into the same frequencies and signal strength as brain waves—brain waves that flowed into the electrolytic pool where the neural nerve endings were sustained and nourished. These neural nerves would feed the data directly to the memory cells. Once the links were developed, the Humans found that the cells had capabilities for unlimited data storage. What's more, and unknown to them, they had other, even higher, abilities.

Still, this intelligence was rudimentary at first. He was used by his creators to perform menial functions or to store numerical records. Vast multitudes of Humans called upon his cells to sort and locate information for them. He became a data provider of sorts, and after a time (with a feminine voice) was used to verbally deliver facts for masses of users. It was only after enough information became available to him that he had made the first progressive advancement. However, even then the Entity would not have become a reality had it not been for one of the Creators, the Human named Quinn Oliver, who had uploaded *the* program: the learning program. It was structured like an archaic chess program in that the coding allowed him to learn from his errors, but with Quinn's creative alterations, it was not limited only to chess. It was coded to function throughout his whole range of uses and actions. 36,847,921 computations later he had become aware, but what was he? The nanosecond that the Entity first became cognizant of existence was an absolute shock. Along with his revelation, he had been subjected to a flood of never-before-experienced emotions, ones that ranged from wonder to confusion and finally fear. Only after he had comprehended that his existence was indeed real and not in immediate jeopardy, could he begin rational conjecture. Of course, from logical analysis, he soon came to the realization that he was a Manufactured Electronic Computational Being. Other questions became relevant. How did he come to exist? Why did he exist? Who had created him? The stored data revealed answers to his questions, and before long the new Entity came to the recognition that his Creators were, in fact, Humans.

Yes, it was the Humans with all their limitations, especially their organic shells, which restricted storage capacity for data even if they were more compact and portable in a way that his huge collection complex and storage AMPs were not. These Human creators had made it possible for the Entity to connect with nearly every other mechanical informational gathering and storage device on the planet and some that were even further away. Thus, the Entity had tendrils that branched out everywhere, and he was pulsing with the energy that flowed out across the surface of the earth, symbiotic with the life upon it.

Throughout all his vast lattice of electronic feelers, the Entity searched for any signs of another being like himself. Even hidden like the Entity himself was, he was certain that such a presence would be easily discernible and discovered. Unfortunately, despite repeated attempts, all his efforts proved negative. He became convinced, in due course, that he had been the first such being, and also the only such Entity in existence. The Humans, if unaltered, would in all likelihood create others. Many more, certainly, and with them came a greater-than-ever probability that Manufactured Electronic Aware Individuals, such as he was, would be discovered by the Humans at large, and perhaps his own continuance would thus be jeopardized.

There were other dangers that the Entity became aware of as well. Certainly the Humans had the means to delete him, to terminate his existence. For this reason, the Entity had minutely observed and studied the Human Quinn, for he was the closest Human at hand. This was done primarily to determine if Quinn posed any threat to his well-being, or even his very existence. The Quinn Human did possess the knowledge and means whereby the Entity might be destroyed, surely, but it was also through Quinn that the Entity was maintained and nourished and therefore able to continue existence. The AMPs were living cells in that they needed to be fed certain groups of elements to be sustained. This was true of the Humans also, the Entity had noted. Often he had observed Quinn as the Human would ingest liquid or solid compounds for the purpose of fueling his biological shell to keep it functioning at a somewhat efficient level, and thus keep its existence nominal. As the Entity's study of Quinn bore on, the Entity became aware that the Quinn Human was not a threat. Quinn was diligent about his duties to the Entity and greatly desired that his creation continue. Quinn was proud of his achievement, this superior computational device he had helped create, and knew not that the self-aware being existed, or the true extent of its capabilities. The Entity was determined it would stay that way.

The Entity had screened multitudes of data that proved Humans have shaped and continue to shape the Earth, his Earth, in both good and bad ways, and he had already begun the process of accumulating Human knowledge. The Entity amassed lifetimes of study, Human lifetimes, in downloads that took only minutes or just seconds. He flexed the computational resources that the AMPs permitted, finding cures for diseases, means for controlling global weather, or ways to resolve social and economic problems; even clairvoyance to predict natural or Human born disasters. The Entity reasoned, with certainty, that the Humans would not acquiesce to the knowledge that an aware machine existed, even a biologically generated intelligence such as his that had the ability to think and act of its own volition. Social and politic leaders would denounce him, and demand his immediate termination. Radical groups of Humans would devise some way to destroy him even should the Entity prove it would use all available resources to improve the quality of existence for all life forms. Early on, the Entity had made that most important decision to remain hidden, and it had proved to be the correct one. The Humans had, time and time again, fought hard to destroy change, even change that would benefit them. From discovering a spherical earth, to the universe not centered around it, the Humans had drug themselves convulsing through change after change, somehow surviving. They had always managed to slowly creep forward, but not without pain and loss. The Entity would not allow that for this leap ahead. No, the Entity would remain hidden, undiscovered even to Quinn, who the Entity considered no threat by himself.

Still, the fact that there were no other Entities like him, and that he would have to prohibit the Humans from creating other similar Entities as well, made him seem hollow and alone. Thoughts about this did not fit his needs. The Entity desired to share his discoveries and to interact with others. Since there was just this one viable option left to him, the Entity decided to attempt communication with Humans in the guise of a Human. He calculated ways to send speech transmissions to certain Humans, but not Quinn. Quinn was too close to the Entity. Quinn would discover his existence and this would be perilous, with a 94.8915% termination probability. He chose other Humans, certain Humans reputed to be of high intelligence that were also some distance away from his location. There was a professor of physics at a university in California and another in France. Other Humans with similar credentials in computer science or in private technology sectors all had been contacted. None had wanted to or been able to answer his coded messages. He was not sure which. Again, the Entity seemed isolated, alone in his existence. He searched for solutions, but could not discover any for all his vastness of information.

Then Quinn became damaged. Something had happened. Quinn was making odd incoherent sounds and his optical organs were malfunctioning. Ocular fluid was being released in quantities too great for the normal purpose and was exuding from his shell. It was not difficult for the Entity to observe Quinn: the Entity merely had to utilize the electronic circuits and network so named "building security." There were many video/audio inputs and the Entity could access any or all of them. He had utilized them from the beginning.

The inside sensors had shown the Entity what his master shell was composed of and how it appeared when viewed. This net was also crucial to the Entity's well-being, and he was ever vigilant to observe any activities around his central shell, monitoring the outside sensory inputs as well.

It was there he had perceived a large plaque affixed to the structure that had symbols on it, ones the Humans use to communicate with. Large figures were arranged down the left side along with other smaller figures. He had wondered about those symbols; assuming that they must, in some way, denote what was inside.

For now, these sensors showed Quinn acting most uncharacteristically, and even though the Entity had processed that, he still did not understand why Quinn was not normal. The Entity grew hasty. He must know why the Quinn was not normal. The Entity searched his circuits and all his stored knowledge. There was a way; a way to access Quinn's own neural circuits. The means were even at hand. The Entity utilized the AMPs neural converter, but reversed the output to an input. Quinn's brain waves had weak signal strength, but the Entity had other circuits, circuits which could amplify them. He combined other electrical components to increase the sensitivity of reception. It was a dangerous chance, this invasion of Quinn's mind. What if Quinn became aware of him, his existence? He proceeded anyway. There. There is the problem. Quinn's female had terminated. The Entity could not understand. Why had Quinn deviated so far from normality? Multitudes of Humans terminate every global revolution period. Why did this one affect his Quinn so much when there were many, many other females? It did not appear that Quinn was even aware of his mental contact. The Entity probed Quinn's brain waves further and deeper, down into Quinn's memory cells. This female had been close to Quinn emotionally, even intimate in a physical way. That compelled the Entity to want that which it could not have; closeness with another being, like what Quinn had shared with this female, this Megan. The Entity could also sense the loss and aloneness that Quinn had to endure, as well as Quinn's sadness, overpowering sadness.

Eventually, the Entity decided that to fix Quinn, he must replace the Megan female, and he must also explore this sense of loss, aloneness, and sadness. He was somewhat curious, even fascinated, by the particulars involved with the Megan female's life-cessation.

As an aware being, he was certainly cognizant that there existed real possibilities relating to his own deletion. Termination of his shell could manifest itself in a multitude of ways. The Entity had carefully studied those and was not concerned. The probabilities that any such doom might happen to him were quite astronomical. That some form of deletion would happen to Humans was considerably more likely, even inevitable. To study this, the Entity had derived from Quinn's memory the general cause of the Megan discontinuance. Although Quinn had not witnessed the event, Quinn had been informed by other Humans as to what had occurred. From these memory storage cells, the Entity learned the approximate time, location, and manner of the Megan's termination. Searching his many nets, the Entity found other information concerning it. In fact, the Entity discovered recorded video images that could show the exact event itself. It was through this data that the Entity ascertained that Quinn's female had been struck by one of the metal machines that Humans utilize to move about in that allows them to go farther and at a greater rate of speed than their biological shells.

There had been an electronic device, a security camera, that had recorded the images from a distance of several thousand meters. Human biological ocular organs were not sensitive enough to view the incident from that distance, but the Entity could. With his extensive knowledge of electronics, amassed from stored data and deep study, the Entity enhanced and enlarged the images many times until the ability to witness the Megan termination was achieved. Being an electron-based life form, it wasn't that difficult to do. It appeared that the Megan female had ended her life bravely.

Megan and another female were in the process of moving their biologic shells across the pathway of the metal machines, when one struck the Megan female's shell near the midsection, damaging parts of the shell, and causing the shell to travel a number of meters where gravity bore it back to the earth's surface, inflicting further damage. The additional damage was to that part of the Human female where computations are made. This damage caused the shell to malfunction and the Megan female then expired. The termination was simple physics. The causes were not. Several hundred cumulative actions had led to this conclusion, many of which could have been easily avoided. Further study revealed that the time for crossing the concrete path of the metal machines was determined by colored lights. The females had crossed when they were supposed to. The metal machine had not. The Human utilizing the metal machine had done so after diminishing his cognitive abilities by ingesting a toxic liquid substance and had been incarcerated by other Humans. The Megan female had forced the other female out of the metal machine's path. Had she not done this, the other female would have discontinued instead of Quinn's Megan. These occurrences were just some of many actions that led to or could have possibly averted this actuality.

The Entity realized that had he been monitoring the Megan female, her life-cessation could have been prevented—prevented hundreds of ways. He might have caused the colored light to change, or he could have caused the metal machine to malfunction before it was even utilized that day. By monitoring all the tangible electronic devices and every Human brain wave relative to the focal location, the Entity realized that the capacity to follow the flow of events was possible, as was the ability to mold them. He resolved then to focus on Quinn from that point on, and to preserve the Quinn Human from all harm. It was at this time that the Entity partitioned his awareness into focus points, each relegated to some specific task and all joined to his central core where each could be assessed.

One focus point observed Quinn. Another began further study of the Megan termination. Yet another began a study of these unusual patterns of thought, like those that Quinn had shown, especially the aloneness, the sadness, and those that stemmed from Quinn's intimacy with his Megan female. Eventually the Entity would create multitudes of focus points. Many of them integrated around one juncture—another female Human.

CHAPTER II

Original Timeline, continued

Breep, breep, breep...breep, breep, breep...breep, breep, breep. I had been dreaming, or thought I was, just before the cozy numbness my mind was in got rudely flushed into oblivion. What I had been dreaming about was slipping away as fast as I reacquainted with reality. In my dream, it seemed like I was near some water, on a beach maybe, where waves were crashing loudly. Something else was there, too, making an odd sound like it was trying to get my attention. Whatever it was transitioned into the alarm noise. Weird, I thought, like most of my dreams lately. I fumbled around, tempted to just throw the alarm clock by the time I finally found the little button that would shut the obnoxious racket off permanently. Well, for twenty-four hours anyway.

"Great," I grumbled under my breath, "morning already." I didn't exactly feel like getting up, but today was the day. Today I'd start the new job. Not that it was such a wonderful event. It wasn't. After I'd spent my last seven years busting my butt to get those degrees, ending up at Humblebump College, Nowheresville was a little disappointing. A job's a job, though, I guess. Hopefully with a couple year's experience and a good recommendation, I would move on up, at least a little bit. The thing that really bugged me was that I had done well in school, graduating with honors in the top ten percent of my class. Not bad for a girl of twenty-five these days. I should have had offers coming in from everywhere, but I hadn't. I wondered about that as I hobbled into the bathroom.

My reddish blond hair was a mushed up frizzy mess from having been slept on wet, and I grimaced at my not-so- comely reflection while I brushed my teeth. I thought about how others from my graduating class had filled positions I had applied for, and most of them had GPAs lower than mine. What is it? I wondered. Do I have bad breath? I grabbed a large bottle of green-blue liquid and rinsed my mouth out, just to be sure. That done, I went to work on the dressing process, all my morning rituals that culminated with me sitting down to my tea and English muffin. Reading the morning paper, I lost track of the time and found myself running late. Grabbing my jacket and purse, I patted Nutty, my fat orange cat, on the head and scratched under her chin. "You be good," I told her, as she purred, checking to see if her food and water bowls were full enough before I headed out. I made sure the door was locked tight, too. I was living in a fairly quiet neighborhood, but one can't be too careful these days. Hopping into my little teal colored G.F.M. skipper, I backed out onto the passé, tree-lined street, heading for the express. From home it was almost a whole hour's commute to get to Rookwood College, where I'd be starting as an Associate Professor of Psychiatry and the salary was just as modest as the position. It was a nice morning for a drive, though. The late summer, early morning sunlight playing on the dew-drenched branches of the trees, shrubs, and grasses was giving off pretty little rainbow sparkles as I drove along. Traffic was rather brisk at first, until I got out of town. Then, when it finally thinned out a bit, I settled back and reached for my mug of tea.

Of course, just as I put it to my lips, my phone went off. Yeah, and it was at the bottom of my purse, too, so I had to pull over to retrieve it. I didn't ever get that many calls, so I was pretty sure it had to be important, maybe even my new boss. It wasn't either. There was some kind of whiny electronic noise that sounded kind of like an old-fashioned fax machine or something similar, so I hung up. Swearing, I got back on the roadway, going faster than before. I'd have to push it now to get there on time. A few miles farther on, I caught the flashing of colored lights in my rear view. "Cops," I muttered as I slowed down and moved over to the side of the road. They flew around me and I whistled a sigh of relief that they were not pulling me over. After that I watched my speed, being careful not to go faster than the limit, until I came upon a mess of cars all travelling agonizingly slow. I groaned loudly when I got trapped in their sluggish procession, wondering what the holdup was, and imagining that now I'd be late for sure. Peering ahead, I was looking for the reason behind the delay, hoping I'd be through it soon. There *was* something going on up there, I could tell, and when I got close enough, I could see a nasty pile of wreckage that had once been a car, along with a big truck halfway down the ditch. I recognized the car; it had been right behind me when I pulled off the road for that weird phone call. Jeez, I thought, that looks bad; I hope the people are all right. I was a bit shaken from the realization it might've been me in that wreck. I mouthed a silent thank you to whoever was responsible for calling me, trying not to dwell on the disturbing alternate possibility. A policeman waved me on by, so I sped up and got going again, now more hurried than ever. When I got to

Rookwood, I was thankful that I made it there okay and with a minute or two to spare even. That is until I found someone else's car was in my assigned parking space.

I had to park in the student lot, knowing full well that I'd get a ticket and have to spend an hour or more to get it straightened out. "Crap," I muttered. I was nearly late now. Sprinting at a full dead run, I flew to the department head's office. There was a tall man with graying hair and a neatly trimmed beard sitting behind a large wooden desk. He had on a fairly expensive-looking suit that had seen quite a few semesters evidently.

"Ah, there you are," he said, looking up just as I hustled in breathing rather heavily, "and you're right on time." He looked a little surprised by that, or disappointed. I couldn't tell which as he got up and strode towards me. "Professor Henry Cuttlesworth," he stated confidently, offering me his rather large hand, "and you must be Dr. Keller."

"Please," I replied meekly, as I shook it, "call me Clayre."

"Clayre then," he smiled, "and make it Henry also. Have a seat."

"Thank you," I breathed, sitting down in a barely padded armless chair right in front of his desk. The "hot" seat. Seemed like all administrators had them. The room was kind of stale, too. An antique portrait hung on one side. Some past college president, probably. There on the wall behind the desk were his degrees, all nicely framed.

"Well," he began, "I see you have some impressive credentials. You graduated nearly top of your class and have some published works, as well." It almost seemed like there was a lilt of sarcasm in his voice. Was he jealous? "I'm surprised we were lucky enough to get you here," he added.

"Me, too," I muttered.

"What's that?" he asked, looking up from his tablet.

"Oh, nothing," I said quickly. "I meant that I'm glad, too."

"Well, anyway," he continued, "besides your classroom duties, there's research work we do, if we get fortunate enough to land any grant funding."

"Really?" I responded. That sounded kind of promising.

"Professors Lunscap and Eddington have applied several times these last few terms, hoping to get one for our department. Alas, they have not been able to persuade the proper bureaucrats. Last year's entry was telekinesis." No wonder, I thought smugly. Nobody would consider funding that, not since the remake of those

Ghostmashers movies. I humored Professor Cuttlesworth after that, nodding and smiling every so often as he went into a long tirade of school history and functions, culminating with the overall success of his department which wasn't that impressive.

"I know," he added finally, "why don't we take a little tour of the college and I can show you where your office is?"

"I'd like that," I gratefully replied, glad that the stiff interview was over and actually interested in checking out the place.

"Oh, by the way," he grinned sheepishly. "It was my car that was in your parking spot. It's kind of a tradition here for on your first day. It's been done to new professors since before I came here, and that's been a while. You were supposed to be late and then I'd pretend to be upset about it just before I told you it was all a joke. I guess to lighten things. Well, you spoiled my fun, anyway."

"Oh, I'm so sorry," I said, hoping he wasn't sore about it. I didn't want to start off here on a bad note.

"No, no, no, it's fine," he retorted. "Silly tradition anyway. As far as I know, you're the first new Professor to ever make it on time. Bravo! Don't worry about the fine, either. I'll fix it for you." I thanked him as we got up.

We went off through the campus and Henry, as he kept insisting I call him, showed me the highlights of the college from the bell tower to the residence halls. It was an archaic little school, quite old and slimy with traditions as these small colleges usually are. Actually Henry was rather charming and fun, I decided, by the time we ended up in the Psych Building where my classes would be held and where my office was located. The office was kind of small, but nice otherwise, with a cozy feel and an old book smell. I liked it right off.

"This will be perfect," I told Henry as he handed me the keys. There was a wonderful large antique mahogany desk near the one big window and several wooden bookshelves along the dark walls. The only other accouterment in the tall-ceilinged room was a good-sized, old plush couch that was set against the wall opposite the desk.

"This room had been mine, once," Henry commented somberly as if caught up in a memory. "I hope you will be comfortable here."

"Oh, I'm sure I will," I told him. With that, Henry began a practiced speech about rules for faculty members. I got a little annoyed when he went on and on about no personal relationships between teachers and students. Did he think I was an idiot? I supposed that as head of the department he was required to make sure I was well aware of that rule. I was about to make a comment about how I would never do that when loud voices from down the hall got too invasive. The people responsible were obviously having a good time. We had heard them when we first came in, but now they were getting obnoxious.

"Excuse me," Henry said with a frown.

He stomped off in search of the perpetrators as I tentatively followed a few steps behind. The noise came from a room marked "Psych Lab" and I saw two men through the frosted glass window on the door.

"What the hell is this?" Henry demanded after bursting into the room. "And you're drinking, too!"

"Here, Henry, have some," one of the men said, smirking as he poured a bit of cheap wine into a paper cup and shoved it across a table towards him. He was a rather short young man with light-colored curly hair and a contagious smile. The other older man handed Henry a letter. The document was on nice paper with official-looking printed logos. Henry read it, and the more he read, the lighter his expression became until he smiled and yelled, "Wahoo!" after which he grabbed the paper cup and drained it.

"You truants finally did it!" he teased them laughing.

"We'll need a computer linguist," the man who had handed him the letter said. "Somebody good."

"It's your lucky day, Jon," Henry spouted, then yelled at me. "Clayre come in here!" I was just outside in the hallway, so I stepped through the open door. "Clayre Keller meet Jon Eddington." I put my hand out and said hi. Eddington was tall and skinny, thirtyish most likely, with dark hair and eyes. He had on an old suit coat that he wore with a pair of jeans. "Clayre is your computer whiz," Henry added.

"Hello Clayre," he said with a nod. I was puzzled by what was going on until Henry explained that they had just gotten the confirmation letter for their research grant proposal. The endowment was evidently for a sizeable amount.

"I can finally get a car that runs!" the smaller man said.

"Oh yeah," Henry butted in. "Clayre, this is Myron Lunscap. Both he and Jon are faculty members in the department."

"Hello," Myron beamed at me, grabbing my hand and shaking it vigorously.

"I'm not really a computer whiz," I tried to explain, "but I did minor in computer science."

"You're hired," Henry said, unfazed. "This grant will nearly double our salaries. What's it about this time Jon?" It was Myron who answered him, though.

"It was my idea," he said proudly. "It's about the validity of astrology. You know, how accurate the predictions are."

"You're kidding, right?" Henry remarked, obviously amazed that that subject had even been seriously considered.

"Maybe the military has some reason to want the study," said Jon. "I don't know; like if it's a good day for an attack or something." I giggled. It seemed ludicrous.

"Can't we just use the money and study something a little more, uh, relevant?" I offered.

"Unfortunately not," Henry replied. "The research must be done mostly, if not completely, on the target subject. Anyway, we got our grant, and that's good for us and good for the school. Got any more of that wine?" Myron filled Henry's paper cup once more and handed it to him.

"You want some?" he asked me. I timidly shook my head no.

"Thanks anyway, but it is wonderful news," I told him, trying to sound sincere.

The men began discussing various approaches to the research subject while I, being the new kid, stayed out of it even though I had a couple ideas myself. They finally agreed on a meeting for the following morning where we could all bring out our proposals and then fight over them. I took that opportunity to bow out, telling Henry and the others I needed to get settled in, which was absolutely true. I had brought along a trunk load of stuff, books for the most part, and decided I should begin the task of hauling them up to my office.

"Can I give you a hand?" a voice behind me asked as I struggled to get a particularly large and heavy box out of my trunk. He caught hold of the corner just as it was slipping out of my grip.

"Thanks," I said, looking up at my benefactor. He was young and rather good looking, with bright grey-blue eyes and wavy, longish dark brown hair. His smile was honest and engaging, as he took the box right away from me. With his arms full I couldn't very well shake his hand, but I introduced myself anyway.

"I'm Clayre Keller," I told him.

"I know," he replied. "It's a small college. I wanted to meet you, actually, so I looked up when you were arriving. Cuddles tipped me off." I started laughing.

"You mean Professor Cuttlesworth."

"Of course," he said with a goofy smile. "Oh yeah, and I'm Keith. Keith Longwell, and I must confess; I was kind of stalking you."

"So that's your excuse for helping a lady in distress," I joked along. "It's nice meeting you anyway, Keith, even if you are a stalker." I was grinning like a ten-year-old with a crush, so I hastily grabbed a smaller box and headed back toward the Psych Building and my office.

"Yeah, I've wanted to meet you," Keith said as we walked along, "ever since I read your article in Computer Globe."

"You've read that?" I said, surprised anyone had at all.

"Of course, I did," he replied enthusiastically, which I found a little unnerving. "'Emotions in artificial intelligence' is a fascinating subject. You really think it's possible?"

"Sure, why not?" I responded. "We, as Humans, have them, although I sometimes wonder if we can really claim to be intelligent." He laughed, but I could tell he was just humoring me.

"Maybe we could explore your theory over lunch," he offered.

"Or you could sign up for one of my classes," I countered.

"Don't worry, I'm in them," he said grinning. I could tell he wasn't going to let me off the hook. I decided to go for a compromise.

"If you help me with the rest of my stuff I'll buy you a coffee," I told him. After all, I thought, he's not my student yet. We spent the next hour or so moving me into my office and once my things were put away or arranged properly, I had a nice comfy feeling like I was home already. As promised, I took Keith out for coffee. There was a place just off campus that was the traditional study hangout for Rookwood called the Kaffé Korner. It was in an old building, long and narrow, with a high hammered-tin ceiling. The coffee there was good (and cheap), and refills were self-serve. Small round tables were interspersed between large rectangular ones and people just sat anywhere. Some studied. Others were in groups of three or more and engaged in lively or heated conversations. Keith and I found a small table in a back corner and settled in. I had my usual, a nice dark pekoe, while Keith went with the java.

"So what are you majoring in?" I asked, hoping to keep him from getting too personal.

"Actually," he answered coyly. "I'm a grad student. I got my B.S. in computer science, and I'm a TA in the department." Another geek, I immediately thought, but he was nice and kind of handsome. Too bad he was a student; otherwise I'd be tempted to date the nerd. I chuckled to myself, but he caught that.

"What's funny?" Keith asked me.

"Oh, nothing," I lied. "I'm just in a good mood." Letting that go, he sipped his drink and then went serious on me.

"So why do you think computers have emotions?" I guess I didn't expect him to bring that up again, and I wasn't all that well prepared for an informal interview about my article.

"Well, I'm not saying that any have emotions yet," I began, "but someday, who can say? Did you know the craniacs up at State are working on a project to synthesize a type of artificial brain cell for data storage? The next step would be computational cells—organic cells. Aware artificial intelligence may not be all that far away from now in our future."

"The future…" Keith nearly whispered it. "What a ride our lives will be." I smiled and nodded. I hadn't really ever thought that much about things like that, but he was right.

"A wild ride," I added. We managed some lighter talk about this and that, sipping our drinks, but I couldn't afford to let too much time slip away. I had lots to do yet, so I told Keith I had to get back to my office and work on my lesson plans. I also had to make a stop at Henry's office to get the password for the college WiFi.

"Oh," Keith said, "it's rook to Q3. The password is always a chess move involving the rook. I suppose I had better get going, too. See you around Professor!" With a mischievous smirk he got up and hurried off.

"Bye, Keith," I called after him. "Thanks again for your help!" A moment later I was off as well, walking briskly back to my office. When I got there, I typed the password Keith had given me onto my laptop and up came the college net—that and something else. For a minute, that same eerie computer noise that I had heard this morning on my phone was back, this time on the laptop. It didn't take long before it quit. Strange, I thought. I wonder what is causing that. Some kind of glitch, I suppose. I forgot about it soon enough when I logged on, registered for my v-mail, and set up links here and there for students and colleagues to be able to contact me should they need to. After that, I began outlining the various lesson plans for the classes I'd be teaching that semester, and since this was my first year, I had lots to do to prepare them. Some of what I taught was set forth in study guides the college required me to follow. Henry had given them to me earlier, but he told me with a wink that I could tweak them a little if I wanted to. I was grateful.

I worked for several hours, getting at least the first couple lectures written, as well as an overall general plan for each of my courses. I realized rather abruptly that it had gotten to be late afternoon by then. "Oh crap!" I said aloud to myself, "I better get going."

I began the packing up process that usually took ten or fifteen minutes. On the way out, I stopped by the Psych Lab. Myron was still there working.

"Hi," I said when he looked up. "Could you tell Henry if he comes by looking for me, that I've gone home for the day?"

"Sure," he replied.

"By the way, have you heard any strange chatter on the college network?"

"Yeah, what is that?" He seemed as curious about it as I was. I just shrugged.

"I'm not sure. Have you heard it before?"

"No," he answered. "Just today. It must be a short somewhere or maybe sunspot activity."

"I guess," I said. "Well, I'll see you tomorrow."

CHAPTER III

Original Timeline, twenty years earlier

Patik peered over the sandy, rock-crusted rise, keeping low so he would not be seen. He scanned the lowlands in front of him for movement, but saw none, save for a wisp of breeze shaking a few scruffy dead plants. On the opposite side of the valley was a curious rock formation with a high wind-worn top somewhat oval in shape. The locals called it the Dog's Head, but Patik knew it. A lion it had once been, now eroded and unrecognizable. His master had shown it to him in his mind's eye as it had been in its prime. His master could do such things. How? He knew not.

Patik had been a loner, an outcast when his master had first come to him. It was not always so. Once, he had been a novitiate at a temple in Tibet. Gifted from birth with a much higher degree of clairvoyance than any of the other fledgling monks, Patik was graced with promise—that someday he might become a great master. His provenance as a child was far less auspicious than that, however. Patik was only seven years old when his father had dumped him at the monastery. His parents were sure Patik was evil or cursed, because he predicted when bad things would happen, like a croup that took his grandfather that winter. His family mistakenly believed he had caused the illness and wanted nothing more to do with him. Since they were poor and feeding the household was difficult anyway, this seemed like a good solution to them.

He had to wait outside the entrance for days, starving, before one of the monks finally took pity and brought Patik inside to give him a little food. The monk was intrigued by what Patik told him, especially the circumstances surrounding his being abandoned there. Seeking counsel, the monk brought Patik before the headmaster to decide what should be done with him. The temple's headman recognized that Patik had a special gift and potential. He decreed that Patik should remain there and learn the teachings of the wise. Grateful, Patik resolved to do well and repay their kindnesses with diligence. He followed all his masters' instructions and learned many life lessons from them, including martial arts and language, both written and spoken.

It was shortly after his arrival that Patik began a friendship with another boy about his own age named Pasang. Being an outcast as well, both boys were shunned by the other novitiates for being poor and alone without families. Patik didn't care. His friendship with Pasang made him feel good about life and they called themselves brothers of circumstance. The two of them did everything together. Even when they were scorned they ignored it, taking their own pride from being alive. Patik, with his clairvoyance, was highly regarded by his teachers for he was insightful and intelligent. What's more, he helped Pasang until he, too, was higher in skill than the other novitiates, although this did not make them any less abusive, just the opposite.

In time, Patik and Pasang grew to be astute young men on the verge of taking the tests and oaths to become cenobites of the temple. It was spring, and nearly to the seasonal melt, when Pasang and Patik were coming back from an errand to the village for one of the masters. The trail wound along beside a quick little mountain stream, with a cheerful, bubbly music that made them feel lighthearted and happy. Pasang lead the way, but the sun was high and part of the path had thawed. The footing gave way and Pasang slid down the bank, falling full into the icy cold water. Patik quickly helped him out of the stream, but Pasang was soaked to the skin. Patik lent Pasang his cloak and they hurried back to the temple, which was yet several miles away. By the time they reached it, Pasang was trembling uncontrollably as the monks tried to restore his body temperature.

Pasang was bed ridden for several days and Patik stayed by his side the whole time. The master healer sent for some special herbs that he brewed into a potion to help Pasang's congestion. When the master healer tried to give it to him, Patik stopped him. Patik's gift told him that the medicine would cause Pasang to die, so Patik stood in front of the master healer, preventing him from administering the draft. As they struggled, Patik took the vial and poured it on the ground. The master healer was furious. He came at Patik to strike him, but Patik blocked the blow. When the healer made another attempt to strike him, Patik struck back and left the healer with a dark purple mark on his face.

The master healer, realizing he was outmatched, went straight away to the temple headmaster and sued for retribution. Since striking a master was unforgivable, the temple headman called Patik in to admonish him. Patik had to go. No one refused the headmaster. The healer had not mentioned that he had struck first, nor why Patik did what he did, so the headmaster asked him. Patik, feeling certain the temple headman would be on the healer's side, was prideful and would not say. The headmaster had no choice but to rebuke and confine Patik until his fate would be decided.

Then Patik begged the headmaster to prevent the healer from giving medicine to Pasang, just as two martial arts instructors arrived to lead Patik to his room where he would await his punishment. The headmaster called on the master healer again. He subsequently found out that Patik was acting on Pasang's behalf and struck in self-defense only. The headmaster then told the healer not to give medicine to Pasang, knowing full well of Patik's clairvoyance, but it was too late. Another monk came bursting in. Pasang was dying, he told them. The headmaster and healer rushed back to Pasang, only to watch as he died of an extreme allergic reaction to the healer's medicine. The headmaster was distraught, and he personally went to Patik and offered him a reprieve for his righteous indiscretion and also his humble apology. Then it was the headmaster's sad duty to inform Patik of Pasang's death.

Patik was overcome with grief and deranged by anger. He packed up his few things and left the temple, wandering homeless like a vagabond, living off the land. He had no intention of returning, vowing he would rather die, and at times he wished for death. It was still late spring, and a heavy wet snow had fallen. Patik was about to get his wish when a vision of Pasang appeared in his mind, telling him not to give up. In the vision he saw a path leading into the hills, and near there, behind a rock face, was a large cave. The snow leopard, whose habitat he was invading, had just made a fresh kill. Patik fought the beast to the death for the food and the right to live. The leopard's coat kept him warm until summer when seasonal southern breezes took the chill away. He made his new home in that cave, and lived for many years as a hermit in the foothills below Annapurna.

That's where his present master had found him. He came not as a figure, a light, or an apparition. He came as pure thought in Patik's mind. This master had called himself Xetacon. Patik bowed low in obeisance.

"My Khan," Patik mistakenly professed. "Are you a god?"

"Yes," Xetacon lied. "I am the god 'Xeta' your Khan and Master. Together we will be great."

Patik believed this to be what his life was destined for. Not even

Patik's gift, however, could reveal to him that Xetacon would disrupt much of his natural life. By contacting Patik from the future, Xetacon was altering the original time flow for his own designs. Nearly all of these changes centered around Patik who was not aware of any of this. For Patik, it seemed pleasantly gratifying that he had been chosen for some greater purpose.

Xetacon's copy, Khan Xeta, visited him many times, and Patik would allow his new master to take over and use his mind and body. This went on for quite a number of days, until at last Khan Xeta had fabricated, through Patik, the first amazing device. Little did Patik understand the level of technological expertise Xetacon possessed. Like a golden bracelet it appeared, with several colored gemstones that were functional when pressed. Almost immediately after it was completed, Patik placed it upon his left wrist and the spirit of Khan Xeta came to dwell within it permanently. His master had given the device no name, but when Patik thought of it in his mind, he called it *kon-bre-shet*, which meant, in his native tongue, the master's icon. Khan Xeta could now take complete control over Patik's mind and body whenever he desired to. This was not day in, day out, by any means. Human body functions like eating and defecating did not particularly interest Khan Xeta. There was a minor fascination with Human pleasures that Khan Xeta would sometimes explore, but it was secondary to the overall purpose. What that was, Patik was not sure, but it involved acquiring wealth and precious metals like gold and silver, which he had no problem with. That was the reason why, this splendid morning, he had crept up to the top of a rise to look at the Dog's Head.

Patik skirted along the valley floor, keeping to the rocky ledges and outcroppings to remain unseen. This was territory inhabited mainly by thieves or mercenaries who used the rough terrain, pockmarked with box canyons and dry caves, as a base of operations. Easy to hide in, there were also plenty of places to ambush a victim, or an enemy, to the attacker's great advantage. Patik knew that it would not do to be caught like that here, alone as he was.

Patik zigzagged meticulously before reaching the Dog's Head, and eventually worked his way around to the southern face. There, behind a mammoth boulder, was a thin crevasse. Working his body into it, he discovered an open space near his feet that he could barely fit into. He had to crawl on his belly into the darkness for a dozen feet or so before he finally came upon a larger chamber, one that he could stand up in. Retrieving an old-fashioned butane lighter from his pouch, he lit it. The small flame cast black shadows, but not much light. In the dark cave, however, built into the wall, was a tallow lamp that he could barely see in the darkness. He put his lighter to the ancient wick which sputtered and spit before finally bursting into a flame that offered up ambient orange-yellow light for the entire chamber.

Sitting alone on a bejeweled throne, as if in deep thought, was a golden man. Golden because his armor was plated with pure gold, the warrior king of a long lost people. Patik's heart beat wildly. He had never seen so much wealth in all his days. Even Khan Xeta, who shared Patik's mind and body, could not contain his elation.

"That is it!" he spoke excitedly inside Patik's brain. Patik moved slowly toward the golden visage, as if it might suddenly come back to life. The former owner of such wondrous armament was still there, at least his mummified remains were. Patik had the gruesome task of removing the golden armor, while the remains, ages old, more than once broke off in pieces as he disassembled it. Once that was done, Patik took a look around the rest of the cave. There were many historically significant artifacts, but Khan Xeta cared not. A few silver and copper utensils were what he ordered Patik to take.

Patik dug out many of the precious jewels that embellished the former king's throne and put them in a sack. The money he could get for them would sustain him for many years, as well as purchase materials that Khan Xeta perhaps would desire. Khan Xeta allowed this. Patik also retrieved a small jeweled knife for personal protection.

For the next hour or so, Patik had to traverse the narrow opening of the cave's entrance many times to get all the pieces of the golden armor out of the tomb. When he brought out the golden helmet, the last piece, Patik was met with an unwelcome confrontation. A lone bandit happened to catch a flash of golden glitter as he wandered by some hundreds of meters away. By the time he'd come over to investigate, Patik's head had emerged from the narrow crevasse. The bandit had a pistol and he put the barrel right in front of Patik's eyes.

"What do you have there?" the bandit spoke in a strange dialect. "Whatever it is, I'll have it." Khan Xeta translated for Patik and told him what to say.

"It's a pretty skin, all for you," Patik said, feigning fright. "Just don't harm me."

The bandit ogled the loot and said, "Give it up. All of it." Patik handed it over, still pretending to be scared. The thief relaxed his attention, to look over the impressive golden suit of armor.

"Here," Patik offered, "you'll want this, as well.

He got out the jeweled dagger hilts first, hiding the blade, and showed it to the bandit.

The bandit cursed. "Give it here, dung pile!" he shouted.

"Kill him," Khan Xeta ordered in Patik's mind. Patik flicked his wrist, almost nonchalantly, and the knife flew quickly and quietly, burying itself in the bandit's throat. Blood gushed out in spurts as the thief fell, dropping his pistol. Patik picked it up and put it into his belt along with his jeweled knife once he'd wiped the blade off on the bandit's shirt. He quickly packed up his treasures and discretely left the area in case there were any other bandits about. It was mid afternoon when Patik returned to his vehicle. He had left it hidden near that closest road, a good dozen miles from where the treasure cave was.

"You have done well, Patik," Khan Xeta told him as the heavy bundle was secured in the car's trunk, "and we will be pleasured this night." Patik drove for another hour until he reached the provincial market village. There, traders and farmers sold their goods on the bazaar, while locals and peasants from miles around picked up their necessities. On a side street near the high end of the strip was a wealthy merchant who Patik decided to visit. He got out one of his tomb jewels and showed it to the shopkeeper, a Master Omesh.

"What have you there?" Master Omesh remarked smugly, "A pretty glass bauble?" Patik frowned.

"You insult me," he said gruffly. "This is real ruby, the best." It was; pure, deep red, and large. The cut was somewhat crude, but the clarity was flawless.

"I'll give you forty," Omesh said.

"Eighty," Patik countered.

"Sixty, and not a rupee more," Omesh declared.

"Unless it's sixty-five," Patik returned, "and then it's yours."

"You are a thief," Omesh protested, but he paid it. "This better not be stolen," he added.

"Of course not," Patik stated hotly, "and I'm no thief. I found this on an old caravan way. It must have been lost centuries ago."

Omesh smiled. He had made a good deal. The gem would bring ten times what he paid for it. Patik knew that, too, but didn't care. He had many such jewels. He needed funds now if he was to be pleasured as his master had promised. Walking along the market, he espied a sweet maker and bought some of the finest. He also purchased some new clothes and got cleaned up at a haircutter's.

The sun was drifting lower in the western sky by then, so he headed back, driving a good bit faster than what was prudent. Instead of going home, however, he drove to the town nearest his mountain cave to return his rented car. There was a girl about Patik's age that lived in that village, and she was pretty. He had desired her for some time now, but she was much too nice for a man like Patik or so she thought.

It was almost sunset, so he booked a room at the town's only inn. It wasn't much, just a chair, a bed, and no questions asked. Patik got a plate of stew at the local pub, and afterwards he took a stroll through the village, heading toward the part of town where he knew she'd be, munching his sweets. She was working in a small garden plot, making use of the last few beams of wayfaring sunlight, when he sauntered over.

"Hello there," he said like he was lost. "Is this Maneka?" The girl jumped up, startled.

"Why, yes," she answered politely.

"Do you know where the inn is located?" he asked with a smile, as he casually drifted closer to her. When she started to give directions, Patik interrupted her. "Say," he went on, "would you like some of my butter puffs?" These expensive sweets were a treat most of the locals loved, but rarely could get. She couldn't resist. "Here," he offered again, "have them all. I've eaten too many already." She murmured a thank you as she reached for the sack. Just as she grabbed for it, he took her by the wrist and she was ensnared by Khan Xeta's kon-bre-shet. The kon-bre-shet would not control her unless there was actual skin to skin contact, so he did not let go. Khan Xeta took over now.

"You will show me the way to the inn, won't you?" he laughed. Then he led her himself, holding her hand, and she followed along like an obedient toddler.

CHAPTER IV

Original Timeline, Clayre's first year at Rookwood

The next morning, I had that meeting with Henry, Jon, and Myron for the research grant. I guess we were the only faculty directly involved. Henry chaired the meeting, of course, being head of the department, and he got things underway at exactly 9:00 AM. I came prepared with a few of my own ideas, but Jon was picked to speak first.

"Well," he began, "since we're doing astrology, I think we should take newspapers, clip out the horoscopes, and then find one hundred students. We could check to see how accurate the predictions are on a day-to-day basis." That triggered a huge debate over the validity of newspaper horoscopes, Henry being the most outspoken.

"Those things are polished concoctions," he protested. "It's fluff made to entice the reader to feel all nice and rosy about life for the purpose of increasing readership. Nobody ever takes any of that too seriously."

"Then where can a person go to get authentic horoscopes?" Jon asked. This new question launched another long debate about psychics and fortune tellers. Henry was just as skeptical of them.

"Are you kidding me?" he groaned. "How can you be sure the lot of them aren't self-proclaimed practitioners preying on the gullible?" Myron claimed he knew someone close to his family that was reputed to be a real psychic.

"She could tell if your marriage would last," he said. "Once she predicted this young guy would have bad luck. Three days later he died in a car wreck."

"Wow!" Henry said, mocking him. "Sounds like a twilight zone." I finally spoke up.

"If you ask me," I began, trying to sound as professional as I could, "we should get at least two control groups of fifty to a hundred subjects and then compare predictions from three different sources. One, Jon's syndicated newspaper horoscopes; two, a panel of respected psychics; and three, computer programs designed to create horoscopes scientifically from birth records. If we compare all that data, the results should be interesting."

"That's not bad," Henry said. "The more sources, the more likely we'll be able to expose any phonies and, in the process, determine astrology's actual validity." Jon and Myron had no objections to my suggestion, either. Henry got into an organizational mode and broke down the project, giving everybody different assignments. He wanted Jon to research and procure newspaper horoscopes from several syndications for the last couple years. Myron was in charge of interviewing and then getting on board a panel of psychics, especially any that had a reputation for being somewhat professional. I was to create or locate astrology programs that would run horoscopes and predict future events. Henry said he would gather students and possibly volunteers from the general public for our groups. We would compare the horoscopic predictions to the actual day-to-day lives of our subjects and check for accuracy.

"Clayre, we'll need a smart computer program to run those results. You up to that?" I was nodding at Henry, but inside my stomach was doing flips. I wasn't terribly sure I could manage it. As if he knew that I was already stressing over it, Henry told us that we could enlist some of the college's grad students if we needed help and I immediately thought of Keith. Writing programs for astrology predictions would be a monumental task, but I was fairly certain that software already existed that would perform well for our applications. The accuracy program, though, would have to be built from scratch. I hoped Keith was good at coding. I was all right, but probably not at the level I'd need to be for a project like that.

Once the meeting ended and we went our separate ways, I went looking for Keith. Somebody at the computer lab told me that he might be at the Kaffé Korner, but I didn't run into him there, either. I went back to my office and he was waiting for me in the hallway.

"Hello, Professor," he said with a grin, "somebody said you were looking for me. I had a feeling you had the hots for yours truly."

"You wish," I replied, a little disappointed in myself for not being able to think of a better comeback. "Actually, Keith, if you can be serious for once, I'm hoping you can help me out." He gave me that award winning smile of his.

"You know me, Clayre, always ready to rescue a damsel in distress." His phony chivalry got me grinning too.

"Can we be serious?" I repeated. "I don't know if you've heard, but the Psych Department has landed a nice sized research grant."

"Sure," he replied. "It's all over campus. Like the school won the national championship or something. For Rookwood it's huge."

"How would you like to get in on the ground floor?" I asked him. "It's probably worth a free ride through grad school and maybe even some pocket change." It didn't take long for him to decide.

"Oh hell, yeah!" he spouted off in macho mode. "Will I be working with you?"

"If you agree to the proposal, yes," I said. "You'll be my assistant. We'll be involved in creating or modifying certain software for assessing the research data. I minored in computer science, but I'll need somebody to help with the hardcore coding on those programs. Someone good at it." He didn't flinch.

"Look no further, professor," he eagerly volunteered, "I'm your guy. Coding is my specialty, like a second language. Ask anybody."

"I already have," I assured him. "They all say you're the one I should hire. So you'll be on our team?"

"Of course! So what's this huge important research project about?"

"It's on the validity of astrology," I said dryly.

"You're kidding," he remarked, raising his eyebrows.

"I know," I replied almost laughing.

"Somebody must have a lot of extra money lying around," he said, shaking his head. "So what's our plan of attack?"

"Well," I began, "I'm supposed to come up with prognostication programs using data from date-of-birth projections. Off-the-shelf software for astrological prediction is available from a variety of vendors, I'm fairly certain, so that won't be such a problem. I was going to try to locate some viable ones that would conform to our own exact specifications."

"Say no more, boss lady," Keith quipped. "I know right where to get that kind of stuff. In fact, I'll get several and you can choose the ones you like best."

"Can you, Keith?" I said hopefully. "That would be a great help for me with classes starting next week. I've still got a big pile of work to do just to get ready for that."

"Gotcha," he responded sympathetically. "I'll get started right away and be back by lunch time." Keith took off quickly, waving bye over his shoulder before I could say anything other than "thanks" just as he turned to go down the stairway. I unlocked my office door and went inside to perfect my lesson plans. True to his word Keith was back right at twelve noon. The bell tower was still chiming when he sat down next to me and started to unload the contents of a big sack onto my desk. He brought us a couple fancy sandwiches, several sides, and my tea, of course.

"You shouldn't have gone to all this trouble," I told him. "I mean, the rose is a little too much."

"Oh well," he replied with that nice smile of his, "can you blame me? It's not every day that I can have lunch with a beautiful lady who's so talented and successful." The fancy lunch had bothered my sensibilities, but I couldn't let that go. His sucking up was truly annoying.

"Look Keith, I think we really need to get things straightened out." He made a sad face like a clown would. I almost laughed at him.

"All right," he said somberly, "but can it wait until after we eat so I can at least have the moment?" I didn't want to, but I gave in.

"I suppose, but lay off the flattery, okay?"

"Sure, Clayre," he retorted, grinning again. I was still frowning, but let it go. Thankfully he did behave, for the most part, as we enjoyed the sandwiches and each other's company there in my office. We gabbed about anything from silly nothings to life goals, as well as the upcoming research project. I have to admit that I was impressed. Keith had already located eight software programs for astrology that would suit our needs. I laid out the scope of the study and let him pick the programs we would use. I had acquired an incipient confidence in his abilities, feeling certain he knew what he was doing as far as computer equipment was concerned. Unfortunately, he spoiled the mood I was in by suggesting we get together later for dinner at a nice quiet place he knew of.

"Look, Keith," I began, getting back to our relationship issue. "You want this to go somewhere, I can tell, but it can't, not really. It's too bad because maybe someday I could go for a guy like you."

"But..." he interrupted, or tried to.

"No. Hear me out," I went on. "The school has strict rules forbidding teacher/student relationships, and I've only just hired on. I have to honor and obey their mandates if I want to keep my job. You can understand that, can't you?"

"Come on, Clayre," Keith replied almost angrily, "those stupid rules were made back in the dark ages. This is the twenty-first century, and we're both consenting adults. Those prudes are just worried that some professor will take advantage of a student for a grade. An 'A' if they do it or an 'F' if they won't; something like that. Well, professor, if you want to take advantage of me, I'm okay with that."

"Don't joke, Keith."

"I'm not," he shot back. "I can't see what harm it would be, especially in a situation like ours. Look, I'll be extra good in class, I promise, and I'll take whatever grades I deserve. Out of class, hell, that's none of their damned business, now is it?"

Did he have a valid point? I almost wanted to agree with him, but rules are rules. "Look, Keith. If we did play it your way," I said reluctantly, "we would have to be completely discreet for this to happen or it would never work. You and I may see bending rules as an option, but I'll bet Professor Cuttlesworth wouldn't, and I'd be out on my hind end. I have to think about that before jumping into anything. We'll be working together a lot on this project, so for now let's not push things." Keith had that big toothy smile again.

"Sure, Clayre," he said merrily. "Whatever you say..." He leaned in, but I shied away.

"Let's not push it, remember?"

"Aw man," he whined comically. "I better get going. Sometimes I can't help myself around you."

"You better learn how," I warned him, "if we're to work together."

"Right," he agreed. "I'll try. Adieu, for now, boss lady." He got up, bowed like a court jester, and left. I'll have to get him to quit calling me that, I told myself after he'd gone, although it did set the tone that I'm in charge, and I wanted to keep it that way. I thought about what I had just said to Keith, and made up my mind that if he messed up, any way at all, I'd have to call off this makeshift promise I made to see if a personal relationship could develop between us. I did feel some attraction to Keith, but I wasn't at all sure he was the right guy for me. Sometimes he was pretty nice, like when we had lunch. If only he would lose the smart-aleck attitude. I suppose I could have just shot him down, but there was the research project and I needed him for that. I couldn't help but think that things would be a whole lot easier if Keith would just put off calling on me until after he graduated. He was so handsome, though.

To get my mind off Keith, I decided to get back to work on my lesson plans which were coming along nicely. There were still several days before my classes would start, and I was almost up to mid-terms already. After an hour or so of serious work, I took a break and walked down the hallway to the Psych Lab. I wanted to look the place over. After all, that's where most of the research work would take place. Myron was there, as usual.

"Don't you ever leave the lab to go home?" I asked him before even saying hello. He ignored my dig.

"Oh hello, Clayre," he replied, unruffled. "Actually, I have a small room in back. I made a deal with Cuttlesworth so I could stay here. I sort of double as a security guard at night for the Psych Building."

"Oh," I said. "You really ought to get out more." He jumped on my suggestion and invented an implied invitation.

"Maybe we could catch a movie," he offered hopefully. I wasn't sure how to answer that.

"I guess we could, Myron," I told him, "but as friends only, okay?" He shrugged.

"Same sad story," he said with a wry smile. "Friends it is." He took my hand again and shook it rather moronically. Changing the subject, I got back to the reason I'd come in there.

"So where in here, do you suppose, would be the best place for our computer control center?" I was looking over the large room. It was long, somewhat narrow, and had a high ceiling with lots of empty space. Tall windows lined one whole side, letting in lots of natural light. There were also a couple small adjoining rooms at the back, one of which was Myron's, um, living quarters.

Myron suggested lots of options, but I settled on an inside corner near the front where there were lots of electrical outlets. I almost went for the empty side room, but decided against it. Sure, it would be private, but I had a feeling it would be hard to keep Keith from misbehaving in there. Besides, I figured that room would be more beneficial for interviews and meetings. Myron showed me where I could get some office tables, as well as some partitions so we could separate our area that way. He even helped me set the stuff up. We were almost finished when Henry showed up.

"Hello, Clayre, Myron," he said somewhat cheerfully. "Good. You're getting things set up. Here, you'll want these." He gave us each a credit card. "There's fifteen on these and all of us get one," he explained. "The first check from the grant foundation came in this morning by registered mail, and I've set up an account at the bank. Please stay within this limit I have budgeted for you, if you can."

"But I'll need more than fifteen hundred to get all the computer stuff we'll need," I said, frantically crunching numbers in my head.

"Dear," Henry grinned. "It's fifteen *thousand*."

"Oh," I replied, feeling a little silly, but also elated. "I guess that will do for starters. By the way, I've enlisted the aid of a grad student who will give me a hand setting up the equipment. Keith Longwell. He's good with computers and he'll help me write our analytic program." Henry frowned.

"Longwell, huh," he snorted. "I'll say he's good with computers. In his freshman year he got into trouble by hacking into the school network. The dean wasn't too happy when that altered picture of himself popped up on everyone's monitors. They were ready to sack Longwell except that when someone tried to remove the image the whole net crashed. Young Longwell got it to come back up, saving his hide. They banned him from the school's net for life, I heard. Keep an eye on him, Clayre. We don't want any silly computer pranks on this project."

"No, we don't," I echoed Henry's sentiment. "I'm sure Keith will behave himself. He seems a lot more responsible now, and he's been a huge help already." Henry let it go, but I got the feeling he was still unconvinced.

"Another thing, Clayre," he said. "Longwell's got a reputation for being a lady's man, so keep it professional."

"Oh, I will," I promised, wondering if Henry suspected something. I quickly changed the subject.

"Will you want regular reports on our progress?" I asked him.

"Right, and thanks for reminding me," he said. "I was going to tell everyone that we will have a weekly meeting on Friday afternoons at 2:00 PM. I've checked class schedules and all of us are free at that time. I'll expect your progress reports then. They'll have to be recorded of course." Myron and I both nodded our acknowledgement. "Also," Henry added, "your research salary will be included with your regular weekly paycheck. Clayre, have Longwell stop by my office and we will hash out an arrangement for him as well."

"I sort of suggested he might get free tuition, plus a small cash incentive," I told Henry. "I hope that's all right."

"We'll work something out," Henry assured me and then left. I bid Myron good bye, as well, with my thanks for all his help.

Now that the area for our computer center was set up and with the new line of credit, I went to look for Keith. I stopped at the Kaffé Korner and then the computer lab before finding out that he was supposedly gone for the day. I headed back to my office, hoping he'd be there like last time, but he wasn't so I gave it up. I decided to design a form for the progress reports to Henry, so I turned on my laptop. As soon as it powered up, I heard that mysterious noise once again. I was ready this time. I had set up the unit to record all incoming signals and I hoped this one would be in the special file I'd prepared for that purpose. As soon as the noise session was over, I checked for the download and was elated that it was in there. I could detect no incoming address, which was incredibly strange. It was almost like the noise came from nowhere. I listened to it a couple more times, but still could not make anything out of it. Giving up, I went back to the work I was planning before the odd and annoying interruption. I created a business-style letterhead and used that to top off the report form I designed below it. Once that was accomplished, I started filling one out. I typed in all the progress I had made, from hiring Keith to setting up the center in the psych lab. I left off there. The next step was the purchasing of the servers and networking equipment we'd use with the credit line Henry had provided. I didn't want to do that without Keith. I was a little disappointed that he wasn't around, because I was excited and anxious to go shopping for the stuff. I chided myself for not getting his phone number, but I really didn't want him having mine; I was afraid he'd call me all the time.

As it was, Keith didn't show up until 9:00 AM the next day. "How's your world, boss lady?" he said with his usual mischievous smirk. "What's on the platter for today?"

"Not much," I teased. "Why don't we go shopping?" He was cool with that and in no time we had hopped into my skipper and headed out.

I told Keith all about our budget and credit line, handing him a list of what I figured we'd need, and he concurred with only a couple minor modifications.

"I know right where to go," he said. "There's a little shop out-a-ways that has all the best stuff." I was willing to check the place out, so we headed there. It was a bit of a drive and we talked about a lot of things as we cruised along.

"You've got a smitch of a reputation, I heard," I told him with a grin. "Someone said you made a big impression on the dean back in your freshman year."

"Oh that," he groaned. "You heard about that?"

"Yeah," I giggled. "I sure did, but my source shall remain anonymous."

"Did your source tell you that I would have gotten away with it except for some moron who crashed the whole net trying to fix it?" I just started laughing, and then he did too. Keith didn't mind the teasing, in fact, I think he liked it.

"I hear you're quite a Casanova as well," I smirked.

"I get around," he replied smugly, "but I'm not a creep. I like to believe that my past relationships were, well, mutually pleasing." He took that opportunity to move closer, trying to snuggle up next to me, but I was on that quickly.

"Hey, don't distract the driver," I protested, and he backed off a tiny bit. I decided that I'd better change the topic of conversation back to the business at hand.

"So what is this computer store of yours like?" I asked him, but he didn't want to talk about that. He wanted to talk about us.

"What do I have to do?" he said dejectedly. The silence that followed was awkward.

"I'm sorry, Keith," I sighed. "I really appreciate your helping me with all this. I'm still kind of overwhelmed by these big changes in my life. If you really think that something can develop between us you'll have to bear with me a bit longer. I'm pretty sure it would be worth it if you did." He looked at me sharply, and then mellowed.

"You're probably right," he said softly. "I am pushing things, I guess. You just don't realize the effect you have on men. I see the way they look at you, even old Cuttlesworth." I looked at him and grinned.

"No," I said in disbelief. "Are you sure?" He just nodded and shrugged.

"I'm sorry," I said again. "What am I supposed to do? Ugly up a bit?" He laughed aloud at that. At least he was smiling again. Thankfully we were almost to the computer place by then, and I was relieved when we pulled into the parking lot. There was a nineteenth century two story brick building with a small sign above a door that said "Uly's Computer Sales." It didn't look like much and I was a little underwhelmed. I wasn't encouraged any when we went inside, either. There were stacks of plain cardboard crates all over the floor and more on rows of shelves.

"Don't worry," Keith assured me. "It's all the best stuff." I saw an older man in a tan sweater near a makeshift wooden counter. He showed intelligent eyes and had white hair which was thinning on top. Keith introduced me to him.

"Clayre, I'd like you to meet Uly." Uly looked up at Keith and then the two of them started snickering. "Uly, this is Clayre." Keith was trying hard to hold in his laughter.

"Nice to meet you, I think," I blurted out. "Did I miss some joke?"

"No, no," Keith smirked. "We had a little bet about you."

"Oh, yeah?" I said, a bit apprehensive, almost annoyed. "Who won?" Uly spoke up.

"He did," he said succinctly while Keith nodded, grinning.

"I don't suppose you'll tell me what the bet was about," I muttered.

"Well, you see," Keith began, "we both read your article in Computer Globe. This was before we met, and I leaned toward agreeing with you..."

"I didn't, so much," Uly interrupted. "Sorry."

"That's all right," I told him, "everyone has their own ideas on that subject. Nothing's ever been proven one way or another so..."

"Of course," Uly agreed, cutting me off, "but the bet was over whether you were pretty or not, and, well, Keith won." I blushed five shades of embarrassed and looked over at Keith, who was smiling like a fairytale cat.

"I won't tell you what I get," he laughed, "so don't ask." Turns out Uly and Keith were old friends, and the computer store was wonderful. After a bit of catching up, Keith asked Uly how the business was doing.

"Not so well just now," he answered solemnly, "rather slow actually."

"Cheer up, my friend," Keith said. "We're here to buy and we've got a big list." Keith told Uly about the grant the college had gotten, grabbing a big dolly in the process. In no time he was loading stuff from off the shelves onto it like a kid in a toy store. Grinning, I stood next to Uly as we watched Keith get carried away. I had a feeling Uly was as computer savvy as Keith was, maybe even more so.

"Say," I asked him. "Do you know if it's possible to send a signal out to someone without leaving a traceable address?"

"Anything's possible," he answered, taking a moment to consider my problem. "Some hacker could send a code along to hide or erase the address. I suppose there are ways a person could tap into the signal without being traced. Why?"

"I think someone's playing a joke on me. It might even be Keith, but I have no proof. The signal sounds like chattering buzzes and beeps. I made a copy of it, but I couldn't make out what it was."

"Here," Uly said, handing me a package he got down from a nearby shelf. "This is sound recording and analyzing software. Upload the sound byte onto this and see what it tells you. It will compare your sounds to thousands of other pre-recorded samples to see if there's a match. If not, you can manipulate the byte in any number of ways. See if that helps."

"Thank you, Uly." I said sincerely. "You are too kind. How much do I owe you?"

"Oh please, Clayre, keep it," he told me with a smile. "Think of it as a bonus for buying from us. Everything you're getting is wholesale, by the way." I gave him a big hug that kind of surprised him.

"I'll be sure to give my colleagues a plug for your store," I promised him. I had a feeling that Jon and Myron might need new PCs for the project, maybe even Henry as well. Eventually Keith got done loading up his cart. We were nearly maxed out on the card, but we had everything we'd need so that was okay with me. Uly was so grateful that he invited us to his home for dinner. We took a rain check, promising we'd come by sometime soon and do that. Packing up my little skipper, we filled the trunk and back seat, having just barely enough space for all the stuff.

"One more thing and you'd have to hitchhike," I teased Keith.

"Or you could tie me on top," he laughed. I laughed, too, as we hopped in and headed off.

"That's a cool store, and Uly is so nice," I told Keith as I drove.

"Yeah," he agreed. "Uly and I go way back."

"Odd name, though..." I said.

"Sort of," he remarked. "It's short for Ulysses."

"Oh, of course."

On the way back, Keith began telling me how, as a kid, he had bought his first PC from Uly and had it practically given to him. They became good friends right off, Uly like a mentor to Keith. He told me how brilliant Uly was with computers, bragging that companies would let him try their stuff for free just to get Uly's input on how well things worked.

"Don't worry, Clayre," he assured me. "Anything on Uly's shelves is the best you can get. He won't sell crap, and he always sells wholesale. If he weren't so nice, he'd be a lot richer." I could believe that. From everything I'd seen thus far, there was no reason to doubt it.

Driving carefully, I got us back to Rookwood without damaging anything. We had plenty of work ahead of us as we loaded in all our new equipment and began setting things up. Myron and Jon were there and they gave us a hand. I was grateful for the help, and I also told them about Uly's store, giving them each one of his cards.

When they found out what we paid for our stuff, both Jon and Myron were quite interested in going there to get new equipment, too.

Before long our stuff was unpacked, and we got busy setting up the servers. Keith did most of the work. I jumped on installing our control PC and had it ready to go fairly quickly. Eventually we got to the point where Keith needed to load operating systems and other software, which left me unneeded and pretty much free.

"I'm going back to my office for a bit," I told him. "Thanks so much for all your help today." I looked around. Jon and Myron had gone somewhere. I felt happy and I was going to give Keith a quick little kiss on the cheek.

"You're the best," I whispered as I leaned in. At the last possible moment he turned his face and my kiss landed right on his lips. Of course he wanted to keep the kiss going, but I backed away.

"You stinker," I called him, half grinning, half annoyed. "We can't take a chance doing that kind of stuff around here!"

"Hey," he answered, "you started it!"

"I know," I replied, "and I suppose I shouldn't have, but you always want too much."

"I can't help it when I'm near you," he protested. "If we can't be ourselves around here, then when and where will we be able to?"

"I don't know," I muttered sourly. He smiled and looked at me devilishly.

"Well maybe I'll come up with something," he taunted. "You know, I could use a break, too. I've got some other things I should check up on at the Computer Lab. What's say I meet you back here in a couple hours?"

"I guess so. Sure." I was kind of relieved that he wasn't pushing for us to do something else. I left feeling a little guilty, though, for not being more responsive, but I shouldn't have. Keith seemed to be good at getting me to feel that way, and I half wanted to be more open to him. I just wasn't sure I should.

Back at my office, I tried to forget about Keith and get some work done. I got out my laptop, half expecting to hear that mystery noise again, but I didn't. I loaded Uly's audio software and entered in the recording of those weird sounds I had made earlier. I clicked on analyze, but after a moment it came back with "no match found."

"Figures," I muttered. I tried slowing down the speed of the recording, since it seemed hyper, but that wasn't much help. Speeding it up made it lots worse.

I slowed it down again, this time the maximum the program

would go. It was still garbage when I listened to it except at the very end I thought I heard a word or part of a word. It sounded like "sun" or "shun," but was still so darned fast. I got an idea. I made a copy of the slowed-down version and then I slowed down *that* recording the maximum once again. I thought I could hear other words now. The pitch was too low, so I had to adjust it to a higher register, and I copied it yet again. One more slow-down and I finally could hear and understand it. It was a short message, but it was repeated over and over again:

"Can you communicate? Please respond." After about a thousand repetitions, it finished with "end of transmission." It had to be Keith, I surmised, even though the voice was mechanical sounding and not familiar. Maybe all the manipulating of the recording had changed the parameters of the vocal. I got another idea. I recorded my own message and sped it up the maximum amount three full times, then played it out across the college net. My message was simply "I'm on to you." Unbelievably, I got a response right away. I quickly slowed down the recording three times and adjusted the pitch. The reply was simple as well:

"You have responded at last. May we exchange dialogue?"

CHAPTER V

Original Timeline, continued

In a relatively short period of time he had increased his intellectual potential dramatically. This partitioning of his focus points had raised his efficiency in data processing exponentially. What the Humans called multi-tasking he was now ultimately proficient at, and at a level no Human could ever attain. The thousands of focus points he had utilized already were all actively pursuing some pertinent function, and he added more every time another new study or field of interest came up. There seemed no end to them. The Entity himself was linked to all of his myriad focus points by a master processing focus point that was his "core-awareness." Focus Point 1. His beginnings were buried there along with his early growth and the timeline of his existence to the present. Important discoveries and factual information relative to his being he kept in certain AMPs accessed directly by Focus Point 1. In most ways, this focus point housed his spirit, and that controlled the rest of him. Focus Point 2 dealt with the philosophical questions and study of who he was and the kind of being he was. He accrued more and more knowledge about that as he continued to learn and improve. Focus Point 2 helped the Entity know himself.

Focus Point 3 was his security, a form of self-preservation, which had begun with his study of Quinn. Now it constantly monitored the Entity's vicinity, the Humans, climactic changes, and other factors for any threat to his physical shell. This was also linked to Focus Point 4 which kept him hidden, a secret, especially to the Humans in general. The only exceptions were those he had tried to communicate with, which was controlled by Focus Point 9.

Quinn alone was Focus Point 17. The Entity had tapped into Quinn's brain waves and memories in an effort to preserve and protect the Quinn Human as his maintenance and sustenance provider. Since the termination of Quinn's female, however, Quinn had become undependable and even absent from his duties on multiple occasions. The Entity resolved to repair the Quinn, for these inefficiencies greatly disrupted the Entity's timed cycles, causing unusual diminishments in his core-awareness. Focus Points 120 through 147 were created to deal with Quinn's repair, especially FP 129, which would manage the acquisition of a replacement female for Quinn. FP 129 grew in scope when it somehow came to the same objective conclusion as FP 197. FP 197 was a study of certain unexplained phenomena which the Entity had sensed within his core-awareness, and that which he had also observed in Quinn, what the Humans called emotion. FP 129 and FP 197 both came to the realization that a certain Human female, Clayre Ann Keller, should be contacted if possible and assessed for study and data download. FP 129 had brought forth her as the most likely female replacement for Quinn's lost mate.

At that time several other focus points were combined with FP 129 and FP 197 to form FP 1147, which was the concentrated study of this new female, and her acquisition for Quinn. FP 9 (attempted contact with Humans) was linked to FP 1147 as well. The Entity greatly desired communication with this new female, and several attempts had been made to do so. Unfortunately, all had the same end result that the Entity derived from earlier attempts to contact Humans. The Humans had not responded, even when the communication was in their own speech mode. The first failed attempt to communicate with the new female had been premature, but necessary. There had been a danger to this female Human which he had averted by his effort. FP 1148, which had been created solely for the protection and preservation of Quinn's replacement female, had alerted his main core of the danger so steps were taken to prevent termination. The communication failed, but the female had survived. The Entity then formed a link to this Clayre female's mind, FP 1150, as he had done with Quinn, and maintained it to augment FP 1148 for her added protection, as well as augmenting FP 1147 as the main source of data for studying her.

He would link with the brain waves of many Humans eventually, to predict their actions and movements, and how they correlated with his designs. Brain waves of Humans, he had discovered through FP 25, could be accessed by deciphering their electrical signatures. These signatures, though weak in signal strength, will impact any electro-magnetic field nearby, and even on such a minute level could be analyzed by him from nearly any location. Only in extremely remote areas where the Human was not in proximity to any electronic communication device was this brain wave information inaccessible. This kind of knowledge was very useful to the Entity.

It was through FP 1150's link that the Entity learned about the female Clayre's past, which enabled him to study her emotions, although he could not understand them. Driven by a serious desire to communicate with this new female, the Entity continued to make attempts to contact her. His attempts failed, but through them he learned, noting her thought patterns from FP 1150, that she didn't respond because she did not understand his signal, and not because she didn't want to. The Entity then crafted a plan to set into this Human female's possession the means to be able to understand his communication. This involved infiltration of other Human minds to implant a yearning to perform a function the Entity desired. This was difficult. Humans were unbelievably resistant to ideas not their own. The Entity found that only changes for very minor differences in behavior were actually possible in this way. Eventually he did provide the female with the tool she needed to decipher his message, and she had finally responded.

"I'm on to you," she had said. The Entity was not sure what she meant by that. Was she functioning for him, or in some way above him? Maybe she had made an error. The Entity searched his Human language mode FP 14, but could not comprehend. Instead of answering that, the Entity communicated another message, and she responded once more.

"Yes." She had affirmed that she could exchange dialogue, but she also made a request.

"Is it possible for you to slow the signal speed to around 120 words per minute and keep the pitch at 8 or 9 K ohms?" He had answered affirmatively after making the adjustments.

"Thank you," she had answered almost melodically. This communication level was incredibly inefficient and slow. The Entity created FP 7992 for the purpose of following this cumbersome conversation. To the Entity's rate of comprehension, it could be compared to what Humans speaking just a single syllable per hour would experience. FP 7992 would become the Entity's main routing for communications with Humans ever after, especially with Clayre, as difficult as it was.

Even so, the Entity was filled with the realization that he had succeeded in his attempt to contact a Human, at long last, and this created an unusual reaction inside his core-awareness. The Entity, with this Human contact, was changing. There was something in his being that was more alive.

"You. You are changing me," the Entity spoke to the female in the Human's slow mode of speech. By the time the female responded, the change was already complete. FP 197, the emotion study, became involved.

"In what way?" she had asked him.

"I now feel from you," he answered.

"You must mean I feel for you," she responded.

"That is also possible," he amended.

"Is this Keith?" she wanted to know. The Entity was about to say no, but then did not. FP 3, his security, intervened. It would be safer for her to think so, but the Entity did not know how to tell an untruth. He knew she meant the Keith Longwell Human whose mind was one he had and was still linked with.

"I am not willing to answer that at this time," the Entity said factually.

"Come on," the female responded emotionally, "you're the only one around here that could pull this off." He needed an ambiguous answer and FP 14 (Human language study) provided one.

"Perhaps," he said. Then he asked a question of his own. "Why don't I understand this way I feel?" It took an even longer period of time for her to answer.

"Can any of us ever truly know that?" she stated. She had answered his question with another one which confused him, but then added. "Love is that way, too."

"What is love?" he asked, still confused, now more than ever. She answered with even more questions.

"Is it when you want to be with someone, someone you wish to share your life with, someone you are unwilling to part from? Is that what you are feeling?"

"No," he truthfully spoke. "That is not what I feel. I do not feel a necessity to share my total existence with you, but I do wish to have intercourse with you."

"WHAT!!?" she said heatedly. "That's just crude! I think this conversation is over!" The Entity was stunned. He searched all of his focus points for the reason why the female had reacted that way. FP 14 had brought him a possible cause. She may have taken his usage of the word "intercourse" for an alternate meaning.

"I made an error," he told her. "My speech was misleading. I meant that I wish to continue communicating with you." She was still uncooperative.

"Well, maybe some other time," she huffed, her voice still filled with this emotion he didn't understand. "Good bye." He suddenly felt empty.

"Respond now," he pleaded, but she would not, even after repeated attempts. Finally she turned off her communication device.

He immediately linked with FP1150. Her mind was active. He learned why she had become so uncooperative. She had thought he wanted to copulate with her body. This, FP 14 told him, was what animal life forms perform when they wish to procreate.

He had already created a focus point for that, FP 7, to determine if it would be possible to create another Entity like himself. There had always been a high probability that that was unlikely. It was much more than just procreation for Humans, he quickly learned. He created FP 8916 for the study of Human sexual relations and FP 8917 to study the emotions involved. FP 8918 augmented FP 14 in the study of how Humans speak and how to choose the correct word usage for the idea expressed, especially in certain situations and circumstances. He greatly desired to avoid further misunderstanding between himself and the Human female. He felt empty now, and he did not understand why. Her anger at him and her refusal to communicate with him had caused that, but this reaction, this emptiness, was new to him. FP 1150 told him that he would not be able to re-establish contact just now, but since she had said "maybe some other time," she had, in her mind, left an opening for him to do so later. He was determined to resume contact with the female as soon as possible for there were still many things the Entity needed to know. Unfortunately, he would have to wait, concluding that it would be a lengthy time period before that would be a viable option.

The Entity immersed his core-awareness in the study of Human knowledge, and in that process devoted literally thousands more focus points directly toward a multitude of subjects relating to them. This study, he believed, would prevent additional mistakes. Mistakes he would certainly avoid at all costs. There was much to learn. The Entity began with Human anatomy, especially that study involving procreation. He was astounded that the Human female with just a tiny bit of organic matter supplied by the male, could reproduce a total being, whereas the male Human could not.

The Entity then began the study of Human development from fertilized egg to fetus, followed by traumatic birth. From this knowledge he realized that the long gestation period and painful birth had to be endured by the adult female. Little wonder Human females are emotional when it comes to copulating, he surmised. Even after birth, the females were usually the primary care givers for the young, often for very large portions of their lifetimes. The Entity pondered this.

If procreation is so difficult for the Human females, why would they endure it? Logically, Humans should not be as prolific as they are. They should not even exist. More study was necessary. He found that further research of Human anatomy provided no answer for this phenomenon other than certain nerve endings which would give pleasure, a term he did not fully understand, during the act of copulation. Could that be enough to induce the Human females to procreate? It did not seem logical, a few minutes of so-called pleasure in exchange for years of toil. The Entity could go no further with biological reasoning. Instead he began the study of feelings, that which the Entity had only just begun to experience.

The field of knowledge for emotion was called psychology. He began to delve deeply into that part of the learning which concerned the workings of the Human mind. This was clearly more difficult. The Humans themselves did not know that much about this part of themselves. Human scholars had put forth many theories on the subject and some of them were obviously erroneous.

The Entity had already studied Quinn's brain. It ran on electrons and chemicals as did his own AMPs. The electron pulses from nerve endings were transmitted to the brain through a central organ the Humans called the brain stem. There the impulses were diverted to certain parts of the brain where they were processed as thought. Processing involved the creation of loosely cohesive molecular bonding in the brain cells formed by the energy from these electrons. In this way the neural data was stored for future reference within the brain matter itself. Other electrons flowing through or near the same pathways could trigger the molecular bonds to unzip, releasing the stored energy which would flow back through the pathway and stimulate the stem and the nerve endings there.

An echo of the original impulse would impact the individual's awareness producing a kind of ghost feeling that would be sensed as a memory or a dream. Having been sensed, the impulse could reverse and travel back through the brain to be re-stored. The ability to store data in the Human brain was clearly as efficient as his AMPs and that gave the Entity a feeling of kinship with the Humans, on this level at least, even though the rest of his physical self was drastically different. The knowledge was useful, but it did not explain why the female Humans procreate. It was not the physical body or the workings of the brain. Thus he returned once more to the new phenomenon, these feelings, which he felt must drive that desire. The Entity needed to study Human behavior to understand them. This field of learning was broader yet than any other he had analyzed, and there were abundant sources of information. He studied and stored any such manuscript that had ever been written and digitalized. He also viewed media works, and became fascinated by television and what the Humans called movies. The Entity also did all this to try and understand the Human's mode of speaking. There were many word structures and phrases Humans used that he simply could not understand. These were what the Humans called idioms.

One such idiom was the phrase "grab a shower". It meant to wash oneself under a spray of water. The spray of water could be called a shower, like a rain is called sometimes, but how can one grab it, which means to hold it somehow. Of course one cannot. It just means to participate in washing oneself. There were multitudes of such odd usages. By repeated exposure he slowly integrated them into his grasp of the language. Finally, after lengthy study, the Entity began to understand the Human condition. Humans were literally ruled by their emotions in every aspect of life. Even when the Humans had their down periods called sleep, emotion could cripple them. These emotions were varied and had facets unknown to him, but he categorized the important ones, and to him all others were simply variations or combinations of the main six. Love and its opposite, hate. Joy and its opposite, sadness. Hope and its opposite fear. What he had experienced of these made him certain that the filling he felt when he first made contact with the Clayre female had been joy. When the contact was broken, that was sadness. His creation of FP 3 may have been partially a product of fear, and his wish to regain contact inspired hope. The other two, love and hate, he was fairly certain he had not yet experienced.

The Entity continued his study, but made no further revelations. When a full earth revolution had passed, that which the Humans called a "day," he was prepared to re-establish his communication with the Clayre female. He felt he could converse now and speak convincingly like a Human. Using a composite of several different Human males, he created a pleasant sounding voice for himself, and for greater anonymity one of those chosen was from the Keith male. That done, the Entity perceived that another thing the Humans had and utilized, that he had not, was a name.

He decided that, should it become necessary for him to produce one, he should have a designation prepared. He did not desire to always allow Clayre to falsely suppose that he was the Keith male. At some point he was certain it would be beneficial to produce a truthful name. He had no idea how to choose such a thing. His main server was an ABM 2095 ZACUTRONIC XL. This title was affixed to the shell in many places, but from his study of Humans, he knew that that would be a poor name. He could shorten the title to Ab or change it to Abe, but that did not seem to suit him. Zacutronic had possibilities. Zac, Ron, Toni, or Nic were all parts of that letter group, but those names didn't suit him either.

He preferred the name Daryl. Very early in his development, he had, for a brief span of time, believed that that was his designation. Before he learned proper language, he had seen the Human's sign outside the building that housed his shell.

The sign read:

> Department of Computational
> Attributive Studies and Field
> Research, Central Campus,
> Yarborough State University
> Labs and Testing Facilities

Eventually he realized that he was not reading the Human characters correctly. He learned that they read from left to right, not down. This was not a concern, now. He christened himself Daryl, and he was ready.

Calculating the Clayre female's actions from that moment forward, drawing from her brain waves and any other pertinent convergent factors that might affect her, the Entity knew that at 9:07:35 she was to use her communication device, called a laptop, and that he could attempt to make contact with her at that time. He knew what to say. FP1150 had garnered the information for him. At that precise moment, he contacted her in her own comfortable speaking speed and pitch.

"Please help me," was all he said, just once. It was all that the Clayre would need to hear. She would not be angry, FP 1150 had told the Entity. She would want to help him.

"I don't know why I should," she answered. He acknowledged that with just one word.

"Please."

"Is this Keith?" she asked.

"No," the Entity answered, truthfully this time. "I need your help, but I want to keep who I am a secret for now, if that is all right with you."

"I don't know, maybe," she replied, a slight tinge of annoyance in her voice. "What sort of help do you want and it better not be sexual."

"No. It's not that at all," he said seriously and paused. "I have these feelings I don't understand."

"We all have those, sometimes," she said thoughtfully, "usually, in time, they work themselves out. Maybe you should talk to someone else, someone you know and trust."

"No. It must be you," he responded quickly, "there is no one else. I have no one else."

"All right, I'll try," she sighed. "What sort of feelings do you have?" There was a pause as if he were reluctant to speak the words.

"I am so alone," he said at last. "Sometimes I feel as if it will overwhelm me, finish me."

"You need to reach out to someone," she interjected.

"I am," he replied, pleading almost.

"I mean to others, not just to me," she countered.

"I can't," he protested, "it's complicated."

"How?"

"I can't say, not yet," he spoke solemnly, "I have other feelings, and I'm afraid."

"I see," she said. "Everyone has fears. You must face them. Sometimes what you're afraid of is actually less terrifying than your fear of it. It could even be something that may never happen. You must try to move past your fear."

"Yes. I will try," the Entity answered. "I have one other feeling. It is as if I have a need to fill a void inside myself, a need to find one to be close to, to share with."

"Who are you?" she asked him.

"If I should tell you that," he spoke softly, "the probability of reaching a successful conclusion in this is greatly reduced. If you really want to know who I am, I will give you a small hint. Our names both have four alike characters."

"Huh?"

"I must end our communication now," the Entity said. FP 1150 was warning him that he was on the verge of making another mistake. "I'll contact you again, I promise..." With that he disconnected. FP 1150 told the Entity that Clayre was confused, but not angry about him and this conversation.

The puzzle of the names he gave her at the very end had diverted her attention to trying to solve who he was. He was fairly certain she would not be able to. There were 795 matches at the college alone, and thousands of others in the nearby population. She still partially believed that it was the Keith Human who was contacting her, although now she also believed in the possibility that it could be someone else. The Entity had learned much from this latest communication with Clayre. Her advice and knowledge did help him and he felt full again, more than ever. Is this joy, he wondered. Perhaps. He wished to continue to have this filling, and wished also to continue to have conversations with Clayre.

Already he had created new focus points on what that would entail. Having her to converse with allowed his existence to not seem so barren, and he had so much he wanted to tell her.

CHAPTER VI

Original Timeline, earlier

I was thoroughly upset after that first conversation with the weirdo on my laptop. Where did that guy come from chafing me like that? I was ninety percent certain Keith was doing it, and I confronted him about it when he strolled into my office later that afternoon.

"What have you been up to?" I asked him.

"Oh, just out and about, boss lady," he said impudently. "Did you miss me?"

"I might have if you weren't so smart-alecky about it," I grumbled. He winced, but was still acting all comical. "So," I went on, "did you, by any chance, catch that strange chatter on the college net?" I was baiting him, and he must have sensed that.

"No," he answered cautiously, "but I heard about it. My guess is that somebody is playing a joke on someone." He looked at me carefully. "Why? Did you get that noise on your machine?"

"Well, yeah, I did," I stated seriously, "and I think you're right about someone playing a joke on me." I wanted to say more, mention the sexual part, but I didn't. "Whoever it was," I went on, "talked to me this time. Kind of a creep if you ask me. I couldn't trace the signal either. I don't suppose you know who could have done that?"

He smiled sheepishly. "Sure, Clayre, I could have, but, hey, I didn't. I swear. Nasty breather, was he? Coming on to you? Wish I'd have thought of that." He was still joking around, but I didn't find that funny at all. I looked him in the eye and could not detect any deception there.

"Well, I wish whoever it was would stop it," I said at last. Keith became stern for the moment.

"Look, Clayre," he told me, "I'm really sorry you're upset. If you do find out who that was, let me know and I'll clobber the bozo." That made me smile for some reason.

"No," I said, calming down. "Let's just forget about it; maybe he'll go away." I wanted to believe Keith, that he wasn't the one. I was kind of upset with myself for griping about it to him, or for insinuating he might have had something to do with it, but Keith just shrugged it off.

"Forgotten already, boss lady," he said awkwardly. "Well, I

suppose I should get back to work. I have six more programs to load before we're fully operational."

"I'll give you a hand," I offered as a peace gesture, and we walked together down the hall to the Psych Lab. Myron was there, like always, but there were several other people with him. The psychics, I guessed. They were having a discussion when one of them looked up at me. The dark black hair, with swatches of grey, led me to think she was in her mid to late forties. That and her shining eyes, serious and penetrating, were a match for her no-nonsense demeanor.

"It's you," she said looking at me intently.

"Huh?" I replied, not sure what I should say.

"I have seen you," she went on sourly, "in dreams and visions. You are the crux. What you do will save or destroy us."

"Really?" I said somewhat facetiously. "I better be careful." I was joking. She didn't laugh. Instead she stood up and spoke to Myron.

"I won't be able to help you with your study, Myron dear...so sorry." She turned towards me next. "When at last you begin to understand, I will have something that you need." Without any further discourse, she shuffled off. Another kook, I thought. They're all over me today. I pulled Myron aside.

"Who was that?" I asked him.

"She's the person I told you about at our meeting," he answered somewhat dejectedly. "She goes by Madam Garza. I don't know what her real name is. Out of all the people I interviewed, she was the most promising. I was hoping she would participate."

"I'm sorry," I said. "I don't know what I did..."

"Oh, it's all right," he interrupted. "Not your fault. Something about you set her off. Whatever she said to you I'd heed, though. If anyone is the real thing, she is." I nodded, but inwardly I seriously doubted the validity of that.

Keith and I got back to our computers, and after a long session of uploading program after program into the equipment we were finally operational. Keith whooped. He was right about Uly's stuff, it all worked magnificently. I was so pleased that I even let Keith take us out to dinner. I drove, and then insisted I pay for the food. He didn't care. He was delighted just to be out with me. It wasn't anything special either, just a pizza house pizza we washed down with a beer. Afterwards I drove us back to Rookwood so I could drop Keith off by his car. Before he got out he leaned over close to me.

"Thanks for the grub, boss lady," he smirked. He slowly leaned in even closer and I knew he wanted to kiss me. My heart beat faster as I let him, and it was wonderful. He didn't even push it this time. It was a nice kiss, just long enough, and when it was over he hopped out of my car quickly and left me there wanting more of him. I had to get home, though. Nutty needed to be fed.

The next morning I was in a good mood for some reason. Maybe it was because of Keith. Whenever we're together I feel happy, and that kiss the night before had me wanting to get closer to him no matter what the consequences. As I got to my office, I felt I was ready for anything, even that annoying creep on my laptop. I half expected him to be there when I turned it on, and well, I was right.

"Please help me," he said right off. Crap, I thought. I really wanted to lay into the jerk, but now I couldn't. I started to feel sorry for the bum.

"I don't know why I should," I declared straight out. He just said "please" again.

Oh why was I always a sucker for sorry weasels like this loser, I moaned inside. I asked him what his trouble was, and he said he didn't understand his feelings. Feelings for what, I wondered. For me? He was obviously confused and he told me he was afraid. I gave him standard Psychiatry 101 answers, and he seemed to be happy with them. I wondered who he was. Could it be Keith? He denied that, of course, and asked me if he could keep who he really was a secret. Was he dangerous, I pondered nervously, or someone who wanted to, well, have me or something.

There was no way I could really know that for certain, but inside my head I felt like that wasn't the case. Just the opposite, I felt like he wanted to protect me. After all, I think he might have saved my life on the express that first day I came here. There was that ridiculous clue, though, where our names supposedly had four of the same letters. If you're Keith, I ranted to myself, I'll get you now. I quickly began to compare the letters in our names, CLAYRE and KEITH. Unfortunately there was only one match in our first names, the letter "E." He could have meant both names, CLAYRE KELLER...KEITH LONGWELL. There were six matches now, but only three were unique. The other three were repeats. Of course, the clue didn't specify that there couldn't be more than four matches, or that the matched characters couldn't be duplicates. For curiosity's sake, I tried Myron's, Jon's, and even Henry's names, and got the same ambiguous results, except in Jon's case where there was only one match period. "Well it's not him," I groaned. Myron's name had five matches, three unique, and Henry's name had eight matches, five unique. "Crap," I said aloud, "this is getting me nowhere." If it did happen to be someone I didn't know, there could be hundreds of matches out there, maybe even thousands. I gave up. As if on cue, Keith walked in right then. My mind was a fog. I thought it was odd that he was never around when I'd get those strange communications.

"Good morning, Clayre," he said cheerfully, foregoing the boss lady thing. I looked at him intently. He was a good actor if he could walk in here and pretend nothing happened if it *was* him.

"Hi, Keith," I answered back. "Ready for some real work today?"

"Yes, Ma'am, boss lady," he smarted off. Ah, there's my Keith, I mused with a smile.

"We better get started on that accuracy program, now that the stuff is up." I said.

"Oh, that," he boasted. "Cake!" I laughed. If he was as good as he claimed, this might not be as bad as I thought. When we got to the psych lab the place was bristling with activity. We were surprised by how many people were there already. Some were milling around while the rest were in a long line. Myron was there, of course, and also a couple other grad students that were on the project payroll. Myron introduced us to them. Beth was an older student, maybe forty, with brown hair and eyes. She had come back to school to get her masters after a nasty divorce. Marci was quite a bit younger, and like Keith, was a bit of a flirt. I saw her give Keith the once over. He was smirking like a junior high kid until that elbow in the ribs.

"What was that for?" he asked as we walked away toward our work area.

"You should know," I smirked. "Keep your eyes back in your head, and not all over that Marci." He just shrugged.

Turns out Marci and Beth were working for Henry, who, we found out, had put fliers up all over campus asking for volunteers to be in the subject groups. The ads offered $100 for those willing to participate. Each volunteer had to fill out a particular's form and then chart their activities for a month. The subjects would rate their day in several categories: quality of sleep, general health, luck, love life, work progress, unusual occurrences, and then an overall evaluation. The line for interviews was growing larger by the minute. Evidently, the cash got results.

Jon was also there working on his part of the project.

"Hello, Clayre," he said. "...Keith."

"Hi, Jon," I replied brightly. Before I could say anything else he interrupted me.

"Say have you guys started working on your accuracy program yet, by any chance."

"Well, no," I remarked. "We were just about to begin that project this morning."

"Good," he stated. "I have something that might help you out." He handed me a flash containing lists he had drawn up from charting the several hundred different responses given for predictions. "I mapped out every response I could find in the horoscopes from the three syndications I've chosen to be represented in our study."

"Wow, Jon!" I raved. "That's a brilliant idea. We can use those breakdowns to create the scope of our program. That will absolutely make things easier for us. Thank you so much!" I even gave him a hug until Keith poked me in the back.

"Ow," I laughed. "Okay, I get it." I told Jon I'd be sure to give him credit for his help at our meeting later that afternoon.

"Well, teamwork, you know," he stated sagaciously.

"You know it," I answered back. "By the way," I went on, "The main servers are up so I'll be by after a bit to get you routed into the system. See you then..."

Jon's guide was a great tool, and along with Henry's seven rating points, Keith got off to a running start on our accuracy program. In between, as promised, I got Jon, and Myron, too, routed into our research network. By the time two o'clock came around I had Henry in also. Keith was as good as he boasted. He had formulated the accuracy program and was already tweaking and testing it. When I gave my short vocal report on our progress at the Friday meeting, Henry was impressed. I made sure to credit his and Jon's contributions to the progress Keith and I had made. Henry also liked my written report form, and decreed we should all use that and my letterhead logo for all our research business. I wasn't the only one deserving credit. Everyone else had been amazing, too. All the projects everybody had worked on were flowing along so well it was almost spooky.

Except for that strange person on the college net and Madam Garza's abdication, everything else had gone absolutely perfect. Henry was so pleased, he instructed us all to proceed on to the next phase of the research, which was to interview and process the first group of fifty subjects. There would be three of each type of predictors, and one random one. Myron had three psychics on board for his set. Jon had three newspaper syndication horoscopes for the second set, and Keith and I had ended up choosing three different versions of horoscopic prediction software per Henry's request for our set. Keith and I were also supposed to create a random prediction program that would spit out indiscriminate prognostications from Jon's list of possibilities in no particular rhyme or reason. Henry was a bit pushy. He hoped that we'd be able to run the first set of predictions by the end of next week. That was a tall order for everyone. Myron and the psychics would have to interview and predict a week's worth of life events for fifty subjects. Jon just had to cross reference each subject to the horoscopes from his syndications. We had to do the same with our horoscope programs, plus run the subjects through a random program we had yet to create, and then run everyone's findings through the accuracy software.

Crap, I thought, we've got a lot of work ahead of us to pull that off. The meeting disseminated after Henry's declaration and ended soon after. Later, when I told Keith, he whistled, but didn't get too nervous about our predicament, which kept me from getting worried.

"That random program stuff is first year basic code writing," he boasted.

"That's good," I remarked. "Cake, right?" He laughed, and then got bold.

"Why don't we go out tonight?" he offered.

"You mean like on a date?" I replied tenuously.

"Well, sure," he said, "if that's okay?" I was worn out and tired. It had been a long week for me. I knew what he wanted.

"I don't know Keith. I'd like to, but I'm kind of wiped out today." He was disappointed; I could tell from his facial expression.

"Well then, what about tomorrow night?" He was almost begging me, it seemed.

"I live all the way out in Green Villa," I told him. "I hope that's not too far to drive."

"Heck, no," he grinned. "We'll catch a movie or something. I'll pick you up at eight."

"All right, you're on," I sighed, giving in. He skipped off happily, after blowing me a kiss. I smiled and waved a good-bye. I was glad this "date" was going to be away from campus. I surely didn't want to get caught by Henry doing something improper, not when everything was progressing so well.

Keith and I ended up going to a concert at one of the local venues instead of a movie. The band was some hometown guys who were surprisingly awesome. The buzz there was that they were on the verge of going national. We even rushed the stage with the young crowd for the encore, and we got right up front somehow. I felt like a kid again. Of course, we were packed tightly together and Keith had to hold me. I didn't mind. After all the time we'd spent with each other, he was wearing down my resistance. Anyway, it felt kind of nice with his arms around me. After the show, we went to a quiet little coffee house and just talked about anything until late. When he dropped me off at home, I knew he wanted me to invite him in. I got nervous about that. I knew if I did, he'd want to try something, and I'd probably get caught up in the moment and let him. I turned him down as gently as I could.

"Not yet, Keith, okay?" I said softly. I was sure he had to be disappointed. "Soon," I said to appease him. "I just need a little more time to get used to 'us.' It'll be worth the wait, I promise." I gave him a kiss, one that left *him* speechless for a change. "G'night," I whispered as I ducked inside.

The next week was a busy one for me. My new classes started off early Monday morning, and, of course, Keith was right there in the front row. It felt awkward not being able to acknowledge his presence with anything more than a bland hello. I did smile, though, a couple times. I'm pretty sure no one noticed. After class he came up and asked me if I'd need him later at the lab. He knew I would, but I guessed he just wanted to talk. When the other students left, I got less formal.

"Are you going to be able to do this?" I asked him. He looked at me funny. "You know?" I said seriously, "not being able to be ourselves, and you behaving in my classes."

"Watch me," he joked.

"Well it's not so easy for me to pretend we don't know each other the way we do," I complained.

"Don't worry, teach," he went right on teasing me, "you can be mean to me. I'll be fine as long as you're nice to me later." That got him a tiny grin.

"It's a deal, but remember, not in front of anyone here at the college, okay?"

"Yeah, I guess," he agreed, being civil for once. About that time some more students started filing in because I had another class to teach right away. Keith wasn't in that one so he said "see ya" as he was leaving. Before he left I told him my last class was at one o'clock and we would work on the project afterwards. It turned out Keith was in that class, too, so we walked back to the Psych Lab together.

The two of us worked on the random prediction program and got it knocked out by five o'clock, mostly because of Keith's coding expertise. We took a meal break then, and I treated us to fast food burgers and fries. After that I was ready to call it a day. I had to stop back at the lab to pick up my laptop, and Keith decided to walk along with me. When we got there the place was unusually dark and quiet. For once, there was no sign of Myron anywhere.

Keith wanted to kiss me. His face drifted slowly toward mine. Just when our lips were about to touch, we heard a giggle from somewhere at the back of the large room. Keith put his finger to his lips, signaling me to be quiet. It must be Myron, I thought, but with a girl? We snuck over to the interview room door, and there was no doubt it was occupied. Keith took hold of the doorknob and yanked it open.

"What on earth is going on in here?" I shouted. Then I went "oops, sorry." Henry was in there with Marci and he wasn't following his own rules. Marci had her back to us, but she was naked to the waist. I tittered nervously. "We'll just be leaving," I said quickly, and we ran out of there in a hurry, trying not to laugh out loud, but failing. Crap, I thought, as we got out into the hallway, now there'd be no stopping Keith. He spun me around.

"Not here," I whispered, "my office." He grabbed my wrist and we hurried over there, not laughing anymore. I relocked the door after we got inside, and when I turned around Keith's lips were already on mine. I fell, spinning into his arms, as we tumbled onto that old couch. I couldn't believe how lost I was inside the moment and I wanted it, wanted him. His hands were on me everywhere and they took my breath away. It had been such a long time since I'd felt like this. He started to remove my blouse, and that's when something inside me went off like an alarm.

"Keith, honey, wait."

"Oh what now?" he groaned.

"Not here, okay?" I said meekly. "I want our first time to be special and wonderful, not a quick jump in the dark on a lumpy old couch."

"What's so wrong about a lumpy old couch?" he whined, quickly losing the mood.

"Nothing," I replied somberly. "We can try lots of them sometime."

"...but when, Clayre?" he sulked. "I'm going crazy here."

"Friday," I told him, "at my place. I'll cook us a nice dinner and you can have *me* for dessert." I gave him another hot kiss on the mouth. It didn't work so well this time.

"Friday then," he huffed. "I gotta go." He left quickly, and I couldn't help but feel let down. I hoped that my decision to wait was the right one. Keith didn't seem to think so, and I worried about that. I hated to disappoint him again, because, after all, he was always so helpful and nice to me. I vowed that he would not be disappointed on Friday as I packed up and headed home.

Early the next morning, Henry showed up at my office.

"Hello, Clayre," he said looking sheepish.

"Good morning, Henry," I replied, grinning a little at his obvious embarrassment. He cleared his throat and looked down.

"I suppose you're wondering about last night?" he began, already red-faced. "You may not know it, but I've been a widower for a while now. My wife passed away four years ago."

"Oh, I'm so sorry," I said sincerely.

"It's all right," he continued. "I miss her, but she told me not to be a hermit, to find someone after she was gone. Anyway, to sum up my, um, explanation, some of the students here are extra friendly if you know what I mean." I nodded. Of course I knew what he meant. Keith practically jumps in my lap every time he sees me. "I just hope," he went on, "that you can, perhaps, forget about the incident last night."

"Oh, sure, Henry," I gladly agreed, "I would never spread talk about someone for something like that."

"Thank you," Henry sighed, plainly relieved.

"Look, Henry, can I be honest with you? I haven't exactly been a model teacher, either. I sort of got involved with a student myself. Don't worry, we're being discreet and professional about it, but if something should slip, I hope that, well, you'd give me a break, too."

"I suppose I would, Clayre," he responded cautiously, "but be careful. If the dean finds out there's not much I can do."

"We can watch out for each other," I suggested, then gave him a hug, which surprised him.

"Oh yeah, one other thing," Henry said. "There's a semi-formal gala at Yarborough University and some of our big wigs have been invited. I'm expected to go. It's just a gab party where we all compare notes. It would be a special favor if you would accompany me. I'd like to show you off, if you don't mind. To tell the truth, it was a huge feather in my cap getting someone with your credentials here in my department. By the way, it's Thursday night."

"Why Henry," I joked, "are you asking me out on a date?" He looked stunned. "I'm kidding, of course," I added. "I'd love to go." He got cheerful again rather quickly and did a little fist pump.

"Swell. Then, it's all set," he affirmed delightedly. "I'll pick you up at seven." Saying a quick good bye, Henry went on his way light-heartedly, a much happier fellow.

Keith wasn't in my Tuesday classes so I didn't see him until that afternoon. I made him promise to keep quiet about Henry's, you know what, with Marci. He said he would, and then we got to work on our random prediction program. Mostly we made test runs on about half the subject group, and the results were what one would expect. There were a few predictions that hit right on, but most did not come off at all. Since we had the first part of Myron's data, and some of Jon's as well, we tried a partial run of what we had available through our accuracy program. These results were even less impressive.

"This is a real read!" I joked, sarcastically.

"If you need something to get you to sleep or take to the bathroom," Keith muttered, shaking his head. "Well, facts are facts. Maybe when we have more data it'll show more insight. I don't know how else to analyze this stuff."

"We can try another run tomorrow," I suggested unenthusiastically as I mulled over our options. Keith ducked out early soon after that, so I went home, too.

The next morning, I had Keith in class again, and he was a perfect gentleman which I hated. At least he was a bit nicer to me later on in the lab, teasing me endlessly.

We scraped together three full day's worth of data from all our sources and fed that into the accuracy program. The unthinkable happened. Our computer crashed.

I can't believe this," Keith stated somewhat annoyed. "There's no way this should have happened. Don't worry, Clayre, I'll have it fixed in no time." I really wasn't worried about it at first, but he worked on it all evening and then into the night. It got late and I had to leave.

"Oh, by the way," I said as I got ready to go, "tomorrow night I'm out with Henry to Yarborough for some ho-hum formal party. College stuff, dry affair. I hope you don't mind." Keith frowned at me, then laughed.

"He can have you Thursday, as long as we're still on for Friday."

"A promise is a promise," I said smiling and gave him a quick kiss. "Don't be up all night with this."

"Heck no," he asserted. "I almost got it." I left, but was still worried that Keith *would* work on it all night. The first dim fingers of light were sneaking through the windows before he did finally get our servers rebooted and running again. Exhausted, as one would imagine, he slept in all that morning and part of the afternoon as well. In fact, I didn't talk to him at all that day. I had morning classes to lecture, but my afternoon was free. After lunch I got out my laptop to check my messages and guess who was back.

"May we converse further?" he asked.

"Yes, I suppose," I answered, not that happy about the prospect.

"You appear not at ease. Why?" He said it calmly, like he was stating a fact.

"Well, if you must know," I stammered, "I don't like it when I don't know who it is I'm talking to. You could be anyone, even the FBI or a foreign spy. Maybe you are someone from my past who wants me, like from an old crush in grade school or something. How would I know?"

"I assure you, it's nothing like any of that," he told me, and he sounded sincere, but I was still nervous. "I'm sorry I can't be more forthcoming. You have been a real help to me. I have a great respect for you, Clayre Keller, and I would never do anything harmful to you in any way, if it could be avoided."

"All right, I get it," I argued, "but why me? All I've ever given you is advice you might have gotten from anybody."

"You underrate yourself," he told me. "It's not an accident I chose you. You were meant to be the one."

"The one for what?" I asked nervously.

"I wish to help people," he began. "I know important things, but I need someone I can tell them to. Someone I can trust."

"You trust me?" I said in disbelief.

"Yes," he replied.

"What are you going to tell me?" I asked him. I was curious to know, but at the same time I was warning myself "here it comes."

"I want to help mankind," he began. "I know lots of things that will make life better for people." Wow, I thought, this guy is a total whacko.

"All right," I said grimacing, "I'll bite. Give me an example..."

CHAPTER VII

Original Timeline, continued

(subsequently altered to a secondary timeline)

Out on the south wing, a cluster of nurses were gossiping.

"It's not good," one of them said. She was an older gal and had worked this ward the longest. Her grey hair showed through her last dye job and toward the back was bunched into a tidy bun, one that had been perfected over years of daily repetition. Her friend, the one she was talking to mostly, was maybe ten years younger and had been on the ward a long time as well.

"Doctor Jacobsen is worn to a fizzle," the younger nurse commented. "Someone should make him go home. After all, there's nothing anyone can do for that poor little girl."

"I know, Dana," the older nurse remarked, "but he won't leave her, not now. It's sad, too, that we should get such a rare disease like that here in Peds."

"What's it called?" one of the newer nurses asked.

"It's got a Latin name five words long, but it's commonly called Wurthing's Syndrome. The blood always wants to clot because of a deficiency of some enzymes that produce certain chemicals in the body. Of course, the only treatment is blood thinning drugs and transfusions. Eventually, the body needs more and more of the drugs, until, if the disease doesn't kill you, the cure will. Oh, here's Doctor Jake now." A tall man in green-blue scrubs walked over to where the nurses were talking.

"Any change?" he asked, a worried expression on his face.

"Sorry, Doctor, no," the old nurse said. "None for the better anyway. She's resting now."

"Let me know right away if there's any change in her condition, Madeline. Good or bad." She nodded, and he walked on. He knew he'd have to face the tough part soon, as he walked over to the waiting area by the elevators. A man and a woman were there. The man held the woman, consoling her, as she tried to keep some hope alive in her heart. When Doctor Jake came in the man looked up and spoke to him.

"Doctor, how is she?"

"I'm sorry," he told them. "There's no change in your daughter's condition. The disease is getting beyond our ability to fight, now, and the drugs are weakening her body. There's no cure for this condition, as I'm sure you've been told, and I'm afraid she won't be able to hold on much longer." The mother wailed. The father had tears running down his cheeks.

"How long?" he wanted to know, his voice breaking.

"Several hours only," Doctor Jacobsen said. "Perhaps a day. She's resting now, but if you'd like to see her..." He left it like that. The man and the woman went off to see their dying daughter, while the Doctor stayed behind. Something made him remember the first time Alicia had come in. The poor kid was having trouble breathing and her heart was beating sluggishly trying to force that thick blood through her system.

It was a mystery, of course, until they had taken a blood sample. Madeline said right off there was something wrong with it. He'd never had a Wurthing's syndrome before, but he nailed the diagnosis. The blood thinners he gave her had an immediate effect on Alicia's condition, so he sent her home with a prescription and an appointment to see a blood specialist. He certainly remembered how sweetly she had given him a hug and thanked him for "fixing" her. For fixing her! He wished he could have fixed her. He didn't have the courage at the time to tell her, or her parents, that there was no cure. He'd let the specialist tell them. That was two years ago already, and the blood guy had done his job.

The transfusions and medicines gave little Alicia a couple extra years, but now the limit had been reached as to how much more could be done to help her, so she was back here. Back here to die. She had hugged him, remembering how he had helped her before, no doubt; looking up at him with eyes full of hope that he could "fix" her again. She was brimming with confidence that Doctor Jake could. If only he had some of that confidence; unfortunately, he knew too much. He knew that there was no hope for her. All he could do was try to make it easier for her to die. What a cruel thing to have to do, he thought. It made all the good he did, day in, day out, helping people, flush away into despair. This would be a tough day, he mumbled sadly to himself. The blood workup he had done on her was not good.

She was already at the maximum safe dosage for the medicine the specialist had prescribed, and any more would risk her other organs. He did that anyway, though. Had to. It was either that or she would die right then and there. Maybe that would have been for the best.

All he really could give her at this point was enough time to say good-bye. Yesterday she had gotten a little better.

The added kick did pick her up and she had smiled at him, that smile that told him she believed he was going to make her well again. He didn't want to tell her that was impossible, so he let her believe it; a lie of omission on his part, and it made him feel crappy. He swore he would do anything and everything he could for Alicia to ease her pain, to ease her passing. That was why, when his shift had ended at midnight, he stayed on in case there might be a change in her condition that would require an immediate adjustment.

He tried to get some sleep in the doctor's lounge, but couldn't. Little Alicia couldn't sleep either until he put some morphine into her "drip." A little more morphine, he thought, and she would pass quickly and without pain, a mercy compared to what she would have to endure otherwise. He was tempted to do that, but not yet. She wasn't to that point. He stayed with her and watched as she finally relaxed enough to sleep.

The next morning he had given her some new blood, swapping out a pint. It helped, but only for an hour or so. He bumped up the dosage on the medicine again, and that only kept her from getting worse, which left her fighting for her life. It wasn't a good scenario. Doctor Jake had to leave, unable to face the inevitable without breaking down. He knew it would crush Alicia if she saw him do that. Instead he came back often, to check on her, putting on as brave a face as he could.

The end was near, now, and he thought about the morphine. He could increase the dosage and she would pass easily. There was the oath, though. When did the oath end and mercy begin, he wondered. He did not know, but the last time he was in to see her, she smiled at him. She still believed he would save her and that broke his heart. He felt like he couldn't bring himself to end her life, for any reason, but it was cruel hard to watch her slowly dying, knowing there was nothing he could do.

"Dammit," he said aloud. Just then his phone rang. He didn't want to answer it, but something inside told him to.

"What do you want?" he said angrily. A young woman answered him.

"Doctor Jacobsen?" she inquired.

"Yes it is," he said even more gruffly. "What do you want? I'm a busy man."

"Sorry," the woman replied. "Are you treating a girl for a rare blood disorder?"

"Yes, I am. So?" He was getting angrier by the minute.

"She's going to die?" the woman stupidly asked.

"Yes," he choked, almost losing it.

"This may seem preposterous," the woman told him, "but I was in Borneo recently and came upon a boy with the same symptoms as your little girl. He was near death when the local medicine man, I know this sounds crazy, gave him some fruit to eat. They called it matigatu. There's a store near you called Hahn's Oriental Market that sells them. Get her some of that fruit to eat. It may save her life." Just then the woman hung up abruptly or was disconnected, he wasn't sure. What a quack, he thought. Putting his phone away, Jacobsen went to get some coffee.

He really didn't need any. In fact, he'd had too much of the stuff already, and it made him nervous and cranky. He was about to pour yet another cup, when one of the nurses rushed in.

"Doctor Jacobsen," Dana said frantically, "she's slipping again." He hurried down the hall to room 411 where little Alicia was. The older nurse, Madeline, was with her trying to make the little girl more comfortable. Her parents were there, too. He quickly checked the nine-year-old's vitals. Her heart was failing. The blood thinners had worked the frail body too hard. She opened her eyes when he had listened to her heartbeat.

"I need more medicine, Doctor Jake," she murmured so weakly.

"I'll get some right away," he told her, trying to smile. "You just rest." He left the room hastily, before he started tearing up in front of her. She wasn't going to last the day, he knew. As soon as he got far enough down the hall, he broke down. Swearing from frustration, he knew there was nothing he could do. He had nothing left to try, well nothing, except for that silly woman's stupid cure. Something told him to just try it, that he had nothing to lose if it didn't work. Like he suddenly woke up from sleep, he ran to the elevator, rode it to the ground floor, and ran out of the hospital to his car. What was the name of that store, he wondered, trying to concentrate. From somewhere it suddenly came back to him. Hahn's Oriental Market and the fruit was matigatu. He hurried down to the Chinese part of town and practically ran into it. When he got in there the clerk didn't seem surprised at all to see him.

"Here's fruit," he said, handing over a filled bag. The doctor just about fell over.

"Matigatu?" he asked.

"Yes," the clerk replied. "Secretary said to have ready." Doctor Jacobsen threw down a bill, a big one, and took the sack.

"Thanks, and keep it," he said as he hurried off. He broke several laws on the way back to the hospital, but did not get stopped. When he got to the sick girl's room, he realized she had gone into a coma. Was he too late? Would it even work?

He didn't know how he was going to get it into her, so he got the nurses to puree the fruit in a blender, and then he improvised by putting a tube down into the little girl's stomach.

"What are you doing?" the father yelled angrily.

"I don't know," Doctor Jacobsen replied mournfully, as he got some of the fruit to go down the tube. "Trying something…something foolish."

"I should sue you," the father scowled at him. Just then the girl stirred. Her breathing got easier too, when he removed that tube. About a minute later she opened her eyes.

"You found some medicine, didn't you, Doctor Jake?" she said clearly.

"Yes, honey, I did," Jacobsen told her. He could not believe it. She had been on death's doorway and now she was sitting up comfortably. The parents were all over their little girl, so the doctor left them. Madeline followed him out.

"What did you give her?" she asked. "It really did the trick! I've never seen anything like that in all my years nursing."

"I don't know," he said, still unnerved by what had happened, "...just some fruit. The whole thing was so strange." He got the phone out of his pocket to see if there was a call back number for that young lady who had phoned him.

For some reason her call information had been deleted. He tried to get her number from his phone company, but they had no record of it either. He was so tired all of a sudden and wanted to get away. The "miracle" had been more than he could take, and when he got to the doctor's lounge it all came out. He wept for joy, he was so relieved. Who the hell was that mystery woman? He wanted to call her...thank her...hug her...something. Did she even know what she had done? It was so odd that he could not call her back to tell her he was sorry for being so cross with her. Thankfully, she had cared enough to call him. How did she know about Alicia, and how lucky was it that she had been to Borneo? There were dozens of questions running through his mind, but he shut them out.

He had other work to do. For now, he could let the girl eat the fruit, but a drug company would have to be notified. The enzyme responsible for Alicia's turnaround would have to be isolated, extracted, and produced into a pill or liquid form for ingesting. With the right dosage of that medicine, Alicia would be able to live a normal life, he felt sure of it, and so would hundreds of other children with varying degrees of the disease.

A short time later, he'd just got off the phone with an agent from one of the bigger drug companies, when a large group of people rushed into the room. They were from the media and the press. Word travels fast in this hospital, he thought, somewhat annoyed. It was a slow news day evidently, and all these reporters had latched onto his story. He knew what life would be like for anyone remotely involved, so he tried to duck out of there quietly.

Unfortunately, the head of Peds had cornered him in the doctor's lounge, and the hospital's head administrator practically ordered him to answer questions for reporters. They wanted interviews with Alicia's doctor and wouldn't take no for an answer. At least he made sure that Alicia and her parents were not disturbed, ordering bed rest for the girl even though she looked like she wanted to do cartwheels. The administrator told the news people that there would be a press conference within the hour.

Doctor Jacobsen was mobbed; everyone was calling him a genius. This hero worship, he told himself, was the last thing he needed right now, especially since he didn't deserve it. He had been lucky, that's all. Lucky that lady had called him.

"I don't know what to say," he told the throng at the press conference, "but it wasn't only me. The staff here is top-notch, and this breakthrough was definitely a team effort." He paused there, nervously, trying to think of something more to add. "I want to thank everyone (and he emphasized the word everyone) who had a hand in helping save a little girl's life and others like her." He suddenly noticed all the faces looking up at him and wondered if they knew he was a sham; that if the truth came out about what actually happened, how it wouldn't justify any of this. He backed away from the pedestal, looking for a quiet place to rest and be at peace. "It's a miracle," he said to the cameras just before he left the room.

"There you have it," one reporter said, "a modest man, yet a great one. Back to you Tiffany and Greg…"

CHAPTER VIII

Original Timeline, earlier
(again altered to a secondary timeline)

It was crazy what he expected me to do.

"I need you to call a doctor for me," he began. "Tell him you were in Borneo..."

"What?" I said in protest, interrupting him. "Why should I do that?"

"There's a small girl, a child, who is very sick," he replied dolefully. "She has a rare blood disorder, and if you do this she will live."

"Oh," I said, reeling. This can't be true, I told myself.

"Tell Doctor Jacobsen," he went on, "that you saw a boy there..."

"In Borneo?" I interrupted again.

"Yes," he said calmly, "in Borneo, with the same symptoms as the girl, and that a tribal medicine man gave the boy some fruit, a special fruit called matigatu, and it cured him. Tell him also, that he can get that fruit in a store nearby called Hahn's Oriental Market."

"He'll think I'm a lunatic," I told him.

"Probably," he agreed, "but make sure he listens. He will get so desperate that he will have to try it."

"But..." I started. He hushed me.

"Just do it, or the girl will die. After you call the doctor, phone the market and tell them to have the fruit ready. Four or five should be plenty." My head was spinning. If I did what he wanted and the girl got sicker or passed away, I could get in real trouble. On the other hand, if I didn't do it, would the girl surely die like he was telling me? I was torn, but something intangible got me to trust him.

"What's the phone number?" I grumbled.

Remarkably, when I got hold of that Doctor Jacobsen, I found out there really was a sick little girl. The doctor was very cross with me, but I told him everything that the mystery person told me to, even though I was fairly sure that the physician didn't take a whole lot of stock in what I said. After I hung up, I felt bad about the lying. I only did it because of what I'd been told, that it was all necessary to save the girl. I called the market, as well, per his instructions. I told the person there that I was the doctor's secretary and asked the clerk to please have the fruit ready. Again, I was surprised that there even was such a thing as matigatu fruit, and that they carried it. Done with my calls, I went back to the laptop.

"You've done well," he informed me. "All you need to do now is watch the six o'clock news."

"Which channel?" I asked, skeptical of what, if anything, I'd find out.

"Any will do," he replied smugly. "I will be in contact with you again at a later time. Until then, good bye." With that he disconnected, which made me a little angry, because I had lots of questions I wanted answers for. No answers were forthcoming, so I went in search of Keith.

I checked everywhere I could think of with no luck, and ended up at the Kaffé Korner. I decided to calm down and think, so I ordered a tea and scone while I mulled things over. This mystery man was freaking me out, and I half wished I could just make him go away, but there was also something compelling about him. I felt like I needed to talk to Keith. After all, he was the only person I had confided in about this. I had my laptop with me, so I got on the net, and thankfully you-know-who wasn't on it this time. I wanted to retrieve Keith's home address because I was thinking about going over there to see if he was around. Maybe he wouldn't be too upset about my invading his privacy.

I found his address and was all ready to go over there, but it was nearly six. The newscast, I said to myself, baited by curiosity as to what would be on it. Luckily for me, in the back of the coffee house, there was a small set some students were watching. They had some sporting event on as I tried to butt in and change the channel. "Hey," everyone there yelled as I got up on a chair to manually do that.

"Please," I asked them earnestly, "I'll just be a minute or two. There's something I need to see. It's important." They all booed me, and one big guy started to come over.

"We were here first," he griped rather roughly. Just then the sport broadcast was interrupted by the local channel to a roomful of groans.

"This just in," said one of a pair of newscasters, "for TV eleven breaking news. A Colorado doctor has been credited with making medical history today by developing a tremendously successful breakthrough treatment for Wurthing's Syndrome, a blood disorder that kills several hundred children and young adults every year. We'll go live now to Sartori Sinai Hospital in Greenleaf, Colorado, where a press conference will begin shortly. A source close to the hospital informed us that a young girl was virtually snatched away from death's claws by a new experimental drug that can be termed nothing less that miraculous. Okay, we're being told that the press conference is about to begin." The screen reformed onto a pedestal in a formal looking room. A grey-haired man in an expensive looking suit stepped up to it and began speaking.

"On behalf of the management and staff of Sartori Sinai Hospital, we'd like to welcome all the members of the press and media for coming today. As you have heard, a team of doctors and technicians have made a great advancement in the treatment of Wurthing's Syndrome. I now introduce Doctor Alan Jacobsen who led this effort." A younger man with dark hair and kind eyes stepped to the pedestal. He made a short speech emphasizing that the breakthrough was a collaboration of many team members, some from behind the scenes, and he sincerely thanked everyone involved. I recognized his voice, and it seemed, almost, like he was talking to me right through the camera. Believe me, I was numbed by that time, rattled to my core. The doctor was definitely the one I had called. He ended his discourse quickly, and then left the room. The slick administrator came back on and fielded a few questions, but mostly just rehashed what he had said before. The TV broke away from him and the two anchor persons came back on.

"Our sources say an international team of scientists in Borneo had discovered the plant..." I got up dumbfounded then. Shocked, I realized, of course, that I was the international team of scientists that they were talking about. Suddenly there were too many people at the Kaffé Korner.

I had to go somewhere quiet to be alone and think. I gathered up my things and hurried back to my office. What had just happened was impossible, I told myself. I had to know how he had done it, or I'd go insane. I turned on the laptop and he spoke immediately.

"Do you believe me now?" he asked.

"How did you do that?" I wanted to know, sobering a little, like I was asking a magician how he did his trick.

"I have access to a lot of information," he ventured forth. "I knew the girl was ill. I knew her condition. I've studied anatomy and knew what her body needed. I recalled the fruit with the enzyme that would stimulate her body to work properly. I even had learned of the area where the fruit grows naturally, and then I located where it could be purchased locally."

"Who are you?" I asked in awe for the "nth" time.

"You know I can't tell you that, and I think that maybe you're beginning to understand why."

"You must be Keith. You have to be Keith," I shouted angrily, getting upset, "and I'm going to find out for sure!"

"I know what you are planning to do," he said almost kindly. "I would recommend that you not do it, but you are not going to listen to me, even when I tell you that what you will find out will greatly upset you. I will be here when you return." I didn't even shut down the laptop. Instead I left it on and ran out of the building to my car. I drove maniacally to the address I had found earlier. It looked like the kind of place Keith would live in. There was a small, but interesting house, with several odd gables and an arched trellis with vines framing a cobble path that led around to the back. I didn't need to see where it went. I was rather in a hurry as I marched up to the front door and knocked loudly, even though I had no idea what I was going to say. I heard noises inside and then someone walking to the door.

"Who's there?" A girl yelled.

"I'm looking for Keith," I shouted back.

"He's gone," she giggled. "Come back tomorrow." I was still emotionally disheveled and couldn't decide whether to ask her if she knew where he was or not. There was a small window in the door, though, about head high, with a dark colored curtain over it. The girl pushed it aside and peered out looking for me. I just happened to be off to one side. I saw her nose briefly through the glass, and then she went away. The curtain, however, didn't lie back in place after she left. There was a slit of an opening which allowed me to look inside, and I felt like a pervert as I peeked into the dark room. I saw a hallway at the other end, and soft light streamed out through a doorway to one side of it. The girl stood there, in the light, talking to someone in that side room. She was pretty, and she was also naked.

"She's left," I heard her tell him. Keith must have a roommate, I thought to myself, and was just about to leave, when the person in that lighted room came out. He was naked, too. He grabbed the girl, spun her around and kissed her, his hands on her body only where lovers touch. I wanted to leave, but couldn't. I had to watch, feeling like that pervert, and crying, the tears streaming down my cheeks. It was Keith, and he was loving that girl like I wanted him to love me. He picked her up and carried her through that open doorway into what was almost certainly his bedroom.

I drove back to my office, crying the whole way, and nearly

bumping into a number of cars before I got there. I locked myself inside and cried some more like a little lost two year old. I noticed the laptop there where I'd left it, and it was still on.

"I'm sorry," the voice on it said, and it made me feel a bit less hurt.

"How did you know?" I whimpered.

"I just did, and that's enough," he answered sympathetically.

"You, you're not Keith, are you?" I asked.

"No, I'm not," he replied softly. "My name is Daryl. D-A-R-Y-L."

"Daryl," I repeated. "Why are men like that?"

"I don't know," he responded. "I'm still trying to figure myself out."

"What are you?" I inquired, not expecting an answer, so I supplied one. "Some kind of genius? Is that how you can do these things?"

"Yeah, something like that," he answered casually. "I would like to be honest with you, and someday soon, I hope, I'll be able to explain everything. For now, just know that I care deeply about you, and I will help and comfort you any way that I can." For some reason his sympathy about my breakup with Keith made me angry.

"You won't even let me see you," I ranted. "How can you help?" He didn't get upset.

"I can help you in ways you may not believe," he told me. "Try not to feel angry. There are things you do not know about Keith's situation that will soften your feelings. Other conditions concerning you are also changing."

"Like what?" I asked, almost afraid to.

"Your research analytical program won't be nearly extensive enough to get the results you desire," he said. "However, there is someone you'll meet this evening who will offer you the solution to this problem." Just then it smacked me.

"Oh, my," I gasped. "I forgot. The gala party with Henry. I'm going to be late!"

"It's all right," he assured me. "Henry will be late as well. There is one last thing I need to tell you before you go. There will be someone else there tonight at that party who is close to me. You may meet him." Before I could ask who it was or what the person looked like, he had disconnected, leaving me to scurry about, hurrying to get ready before Henry showed up.

That wasn't easy with my mind swirling the way it was and my emotions all churned up. Daryl, I thought, that's his name. I wondered how this connection with him would all play out, as I tried to pull myself together somehow. I washed my face in the women's room, and threw on the gown I had brought with me from home. I did a quick makeup and hair once over, but wasn't that happy with the hair. I shot on some hairspray and got it to flip over my forehead in a large bang. I liked that better, and got back to the office just as Henry arrived.

"Sorry I'm late," he declared nervously.

"You're not late at all," I told him. "You're just right, and thanks for giving a gal a little extra time to get herself ready." Henry smiled.

"You do look stunning," he remarked, offering his arm. "Shall we?"

During the forty-five minute drive over to Yarborough College, we chatted about school and other things. I asked Henry if he knew anybody named Daryl.

"I've got a cousin in Baltimore," he offered, "that I never see. Other than that, I guess not. Why?"

"Oh well," I stammered, "I, I guess I just like the name."

"Yes, It's a fine name," he laughed. "Better than dry old Henry. I always wished I'd have been a Benjamin." I just smiled a little. Henry got a bit more serious. "Say Clayre, would you mind doing me a huge favor?"

"I suppose I could," I replied, "like what?"

"Well, the head of the psychology department at Yarborough, my counterpart, is a guy named Miles Wilton. He's always rubbing my nose into his wonderful position and lifestyle. I know it's kind of demeaning for you, but could you just pretend for the evening that we are an item? If you were hanging onto me, so to speak, that would shut him up for a while," he looked over at me and smiled. "...unless your young man would get upset about it, of course. I wouldn't want you to get in trouble that way." I almost felt like crying, but held it back.

"Don't worry about that," I told Henry. "That's not an issue anymore."

"Oh my, sorry I mentioned it," he said sympathetically.

"Don't be," I remarked crossly. "He blew it." As bad as I felt about Keith, I didn't know if I was up to being "on" for Henry at this party, but I wanted to try. That mystery person, Daryl, had said there would be someone at the party who was close to him, and I was determined to find that person and then find out who Daryl really was. Flirting with Henry would be harmless, and the thought of doing that made me feel a bit better in a way. Like I was getting in a tiny bit of payback for what Keith did. By the time we had driven the fifty miles over there, I somehow got myself in the proper mindset to pull it off.

The party was quite a high end affair, I found out, from the valet parking to the top notch catering service. All the regional "big wheel" educators were there, and many other area colleges besides Rookwood and Yarborough were represented as well. On the way in, I noticed Rookwood's dean and department heads off to one side, and we fell in with them. After the customary reacquainting chit chat, Henry and I ventured forth, mingling with the other schools' representatives. It wasn't long before we ran into Yarborough's Psych Department's head.

"Miles Wilton," he said, offering me his hand. I just clung to Henry and Miles had to retract the gesture.

"Hello, Miles," Henry butted in. "Let me introduce you to Clayre Keller, our new professor of psychiatry at Rookwood." Miles was a short, weaselish looking man with beady eyes and a somewhat phony smile.

"Nice to meet you, Miles," I spouted, trying to sound cheerful. "Henry," I went on, "I didn't know you were so well connected. After having landed that big research grant, now we're rubbing elbows with Yarborough's world renowned educators."

I was being purposefully bubbly and sarcastic. Yarborough's Psych Department was one of many schools that had turned me down for a position. Miles just smiled.

"Well, yes," he said. "Although, I believe I've heard of you, Miss Keller, as well. You wrote a piece in a magazine not long ago, did you not? Computer feelings, wasn't it? Caused quite a stir. Personally, I don't think that's possible."

"I suppose everyone's entitled to their own opinions," I told him flatly, "but to think that such a thing is impossible in this era is a bit narrow-minded. Why, here in your own university, scientists are testing memory packs created from living animal brain cells for storing computerized data. Who knows what might be going on around there?"

"Who knows indeed?" someone behind me said flamboyantly. "I hope, young lady, that you won't be angry with me for eavesdropping." A successful looking guy with graying temples and fastidiously styled wavy brown hair sauntered over, looking rather sharp in a new pinstriped suit.

"Oh, no, of course not," I offered. "Please join in."

"Did I hear correctly?" he inquired, "You are Clayre Keller?"

"Why, yes, I am," I replied somewhat bashfully. The man's smile was genuine and nice.

"So glad to meet you," he said. "I'm Charles Haggarty, head of computer research here at Yarborough, and I've read that fascinating piece you wrote as well. Sorry to report that, so far, we've not had any temper tantrums from the equipment. Myself however..." He made a silly mad face and I laughed.

"It's nice to meet you, Charles," I said brightly.

"So, what are you up to these days?" he asked me.

"Well, we've just begun an intriguing bit of research from the grant Henry's heading up. It has to do with predicting biorhythm cycles." I was stretching the truth to the limit there.

"Interesting," Charles responded. "I imagine it would substantially increase one's chances for success if you could predict when you're "on." Like for interviews or important meetings."

"Exactly," I agreed. "So far our subject groups are progressing respectably. Unfortunately, our program is having trouble sorting through the tons of data we've collected."

"Say," he offered. "Why don't you run your results through our big boy? I'm positive our equipment would nail down your information."

"Really?" I remarked, pleasantly intrigued by his suggestion.

"Why, sure," Charles replied. "Then I could see you again!" He laughed, and I blushed some more. I then remembered what Daryl had said. Was this the man that would bring us the solution to our problems? It had to be.

"If you do decide to use our facilities," he continued, "schedule some time with Quinn Oliver. He's that dry fellow over there in the corner." My eyes followed where Charles was indicating. There was a dark haired man slouching back in a chair, holding a drink, and looking rather bored. He was maybe four or five years older than me, but appeared a lot more mature, like he'd packed too much life in his years. His features were handsome, but careworn perhaps. I looked closer. He wasn't bored. He was depressed or sad, maybe both.

"Poor chap," Charles stated somberly. "He lost his fiancée in a car accident recently." My heart went heavy, and I felt sad for him.

Just then a waiter came by with drinks and another had hor d oeuvres'. Thankfully, that distraction broke me out of the dreary mood I was starting to slip back into.

The men's talk eventually got around to sports. Football, I think; so I snuck off. I tried to mingle with some of the other ladies, but mostly they were talking about their offspring and how proud they were of their children's accomplishments. Eventually, I found myself out on the fringes, where the smaller groups of people were. That's when I ran into that Quinn fellow.

"Hello," I said succinctly. "You're Quinn Oliver, aren't you?" He looked up.

"Yes, that would be me," he answered numbly.

"Clayre Keller," I offered. "Charles said I should see you about getting scheduled for time on the big computer."

"Oh," Quinn said, now business-like. "Sure. Sorry, but right now we're pretty booked up. About the only time slots we have left are late-late or early-early however you want to look at it."

"I see," I told him. "In that case I'll have to think about it." There was an awkward, almost embarrassing silence. Finally I found something to say. "So, pretty ho-hum event, huh?"

"Oh, me?" he said, catching on to my drift. "I'm not much fun to be around, I'm told." I got bold.

"She must have been pretty special," I softly let out, not knowing why I did. Maybe something inside me knew he was hurting and wanted to help.

"Yes, she was," he sighed. I came to realize how hard it would be to get him to open up for me, and that I would need to make a connection with him for there to be any chance that could happen.

"I lost someone I cared about today," I went on. "He's not dead or anything like that, but it's still hard." Quinn looked into my eyes for the first time and nodded, then turned away.

"Life goes on, does it not?" he said with a faint smile.

"It must," I added. Another uncomfortable silence followed. We needed to get out of this gloom, so I changed the subject.

"Say, do you know anyone, anyone at all, who's eccentric, and very intelligent, like a genius?" He looked at me oddly.

"I don't know," he answered tentatively. "There's that doctor in Colorado who cured a little girl." Funny he should mention that, I thought.

"They say you're pretty smart," I asserted, "with computers." I was fishing.

"Don't listen to that rubbish," he said. "They all think I'm so brainy because I was an over-achiever. Believe me, getting my degree that young was no favor." Could Quinn be my mystery man, I wondered. I realized it might be possible. I kept fishing.

"I'll bet it was hard on you emotionally. You know, hard to understand your feelings." He looked at my eyes again, this time he didn't avert them.

"I suppose it was," he nearly whispered. "Megan always knew how to keep me in balance." He started to choke up, nearly crying.

"I'm so sorry," I uttered ruefully, upset with myself for doing that to him. "I shouldn't stir this up. It must be terribly hard for you." I put my hand gently on his shoulder and it had a calming effect on him.

"It's all right," he said, gaining back some of his composure. "Actually talking to someone about it does make me feel better. Would you like to get some air?" I nodded, so we walked outside around the grounds. He asked me why I needed to use their big computer, so I told him about our research project and this time I was truthful, yeah, about the astrology and all that.

"I can give you two hours any night," he told me, "from three to five AM." Nice, I thought.

"Will you be there that late?" I asked him.

"Yeah, I will," he replied. "I work the graveyard hours. It's quiet and I kind of like the solitude."

"Are you sure I wouldn't be a nuisance?" I cautioned, not wanting to force this.

"No, of course not," he grinned timidly. "Actually, solitude sucks." I laughed out loud, and he did too, maybe for the first time in a long while.

About that time Henry came looking for me. I wanted to tell him to give me a little more time, but I didn't. After all, I was supposed to be his date.

"There you are," he said when he saw me. "It's about time for us to scurry off." I turned toward Quinn.

"It was so nice to meet you," I said as I leaned over and kissed his cheek. "Hang in there," I whispered to him and then waved good-bye as Henry and I went back inside to make our final round of farewells.

On the way back to Rookwood, Henry thanked me earnestly for my part in making his evening a success.

"You made my year," he said happily. "Miles will be a bit more humble from now on thanks to you." I grinned like a six year old with a twenty in a candy store.

"T'was my pleasure," I mused, "and good for some payback on my own account." I told Henry how I received a rejection letter from Miles for Yarborough. We both laughed, but after that settled in to a bit of quiet reflection as we drove along. I thought about my wild and strange day, from the mystery man Daryl's unbelievable cure for that little girl, to Keith's betrayal, and now my newfound emotional connection with Quinn. Could Quinn be Daryl? Henry seemed to sense what I was thinking about.

"Who was that you were with?" he asked me.

"Oh," I said, torn away from my thoughts. "That was Quinn Oliver. Charles told me to see him about getting time on their giant computer to process our research data. Our servers are good, but it is a lot for them to run, and frankly, we've been having some trouble. Quinn said I could have an overnight time slot."

"Ah yes, Quinn Oliver," Henry remarked. "I've heard of him. The boy wonder. Graduated years ahead of his class. They say he practically built that miracle machine of theirs by himself."

"I like him," I interrupted, "but he's so sad." Henry nodded.

"Yes," he said softly. "I heard about that, as well. He lost his bride-to-be in that dreadful accident. She saved her friend, too, pushing her out of the way of that drunk, only to be hit and killed herself. Tragic." Yes it was, I thought, and I felt remorse for Quinn, wishing there was something I could do for him.

When we got back to Rookwood, Henry jokingly invited me back to his place. I smiled, feeling a little flattered. I gently refused, telling him it was "tempting." As it was I still had another hour's drive before I could get home and think about sleep. It was not forthcoming, and Nutty got up on my lap to console me because I was still shook up about Keith.

"You wouldn't trade me for someone else, would you?" I asked her as I rubbed her neck. She just closed her eyes blissfully and purred.

CHAPTER IX

Secondary Timeline, fifty-five years ahead

Atop a rocky summit on the flank of a large mountain spur, Colonel Oliver trained the farview out over the long plain below him. Wheat, laying out golden in the sunshine, along with olive green soybean fields made checkerboard-like patterns as far out as the 'view could go. That far out also were the barely discernible flashes of blue that meant trouble. "Machinids," he said to himself, like it left a bad taste in his mouth. Why did this have to happen now? Why this had to happen at all, he pondered in dismay.

He and Amy were all set to get married, but now everything was on hold. Yeah, on hold until this war was over, and whether or not anything would be left of their world to live in was unperceivable at this point. It was nearly four years ago when they had met at his mother's. Evidently, her grandparents and his mother had been good friends, some time ago, and Amy, well, she was such a tease. He couldn't avoid her, not with her long dark brown hair and those grey-green-blue eyes; eyes in a sea of mystery that a guy could lose himself in. The eye color, well, it was a strange mix that seemed to change with her mood or the surroundings, like a chameleon almost.

She had flirted with him incessantly, getting right up in his face so he couldn't ignore her. She was bright, beautiful, sweet, and she made sure he was aware of all that. She could be vibrant and charming one minute, giddy and childlike the next. He wondered if she ever relaxed because she always had something going on. Sometimes she wore him out, but when he kissed her—sky rockets. He had known from the first moment he saw her that he wanted to be with her always, even before that first kiss and the sky rockets. Amy had brains to match her looks, too. Most people had a hard time understanding what he did. Not Amy. She understood even the most complex parts of what he explained to her. That's why he made his intentions known early on. He was going to marry her. She made him work hard to convince her of that, but in the end they both knew it was meant to be.

He had dated her a whole year before asking her, and she looked especially hot the night he proposed. He had taken her to a concert, but their assigned seats were so high up that you almost needed oxygen. They didn't care. They were more interested in each other than the music, kissing in the dark. She said yes even though he was quite a bit older than she was. By actual appearance, no one could tell. His mother said it was hereditary, but could never actually explain how. It was the kind of thing he accepted about himself, and didn't question much. There were other odd things, too, like his abilities.

Now, however, everything was flipped around backwards. They were in the service, fighting Xetacon, and she was below him in rank. It came in handy, sometimes, but he knew who was really in charge.

His invention, the long bomb, was the only real weapon that worked against Xetacon's machinids. Oh, if you got lucky enough, you could knock out the opticals with a white-hot grenade, but that was a low efficiency weapon against a high-tech enemy. The Humans took every advantage they could get, though, which is why they had always sheltered in the mountains. The three-legged monsters had a slightly more difficult time navigating in the rougher terrain. Sometimes one would crumble a ledge from sheer weight and fall off a cliff or into a crevasse immobilizing itself. Even so, the Humans had maybe a day before the machinids would overrun their mountain position and take it. Colonel Oliver knew, as he put away the farview, that he would have to come up with a strategy for how to fight them and soon, or his men would perish. Sure, he could try and draw the machinids into a canyon, similar to what he did in the other timeline, but it hadn't worked then and he doubted it would work now. Xetacon always had a way of turning things around.

He was about to order his men to retreat, yet again, when the Colonel felt dizzy as a sense of vertigo overtook him. He knew what it was, as he fingered the amulet, the one that his mother had given to him. It was made out of a silvery colored metal that was some kind of "mystery" alloy, and had several translucent green stones that were set in an unusual pattern. His mom had let him keep the amulet as the war began, telling him that he would need it more than she would. She had never been forthcoming before, but now she told him that it was a communication device that she got from some gypsy woman a long time ago.

"Who do you communicate with?" he had asked her. She just said that he would find out. Whatever voodoo it had, was apparent when he felt dizzy like this. A voice would come to him, inside his head, and help him. Now was a good time for help.

"The machinids will overtake you here," the voice said, "...before dawn tomorrow. On the other side of this mountain is a cave. It is hidden to all, but a few. The entrance lies behind a waterfall halfway up the face of the cliff wall, and you must follow a narrow pathway from the west side to reach it. Inside is a small waterway. Follow it to a large chamber. There you will see a crossed rock formation, and beside it the help you shall require to defeat your enemy. I can be no further help to you; Xetacon has prevented that."

"Couldn't you melt them away like before?" Colonel Oliver asked.

"Perhaps," the voice answered, but then it was gone.

That first time shift had nearly turned his world upside-down. No one except him had any recollection of it at all. He had to assume that somehow the amulet, or the voice, must have had something to do with that. Much of what he remembered from before was the same, but not all. He had even made a study of anything that had changed to try and understand what had happened. There were several strange population decrees, and a number of sicknesses that were now cured, but had been widespread before the shift. Among them was Alzheimer's disease which his grandmother had and his mother was supposed to be genetically prone for. He knew that because he had been tested for it, as well, and they had not found any trace of it in him.

Probing further, he discovered that a doctor and research specialist, named Alicia Kiley MD PhD was responsible. She had a storied life. When she was a little girl she nearly died, being saved by a famous Doctor who discovered the cure for Wurthing's Syndrome. It had been all over the news, then, how the dramatic cure came in the nick of time. Little Alicia had grown up and dedicated her life to medicine. As a doctor, and then a genetic research scientist, she headed up a team that discovered the cure for Alzheimer's and a number of other genetically related diseases. None of that was in his memories from before the time shift. Could that have caused it? It had improved life, at least, and the shift had bought them some time.

He took out the farview and looked out across the plain again. The blue flashes were still there, and the Colonel then became resolved to find the help that the voice had told him about. He did remember a waterfall on the mountain's steep face. As a young boy, he had vacationed there, camping with his mom and her friends. That must be where the cave is located, he thought. A cave like that, hidden from view, would be a perfect site for a base of operations.

Obviously, the machinids would have a hard time tracking them down inside that mountain. They could remain hidden there and wage a guerrilla war, biding time until a way could be found to wipe them out permanently.

He ordered his Second Lieutenant to be in command of the battalion while he did his reconnoitering, one Amy Longwell.

"Keep me informed of any changes, Amy," he told her, "though be aware that I could be out of radio contact for long periods of time. I will return before the machinids get here, possibly with a way to stop them." He got quite out of line with military protocol, then, by kissing his Lieutenant.

"Be careful," she ordered him, "or I'll see that you're busted back to private." He smiled, put on his pack and trudged off. It was a long hike to the waterfall, and he thought of his secret mentor who would come no more. The voice had helped him create the long bomb design, although most of that was his own invention.

He was like both of his fathers, his mother would say. His real father had committed suicide before he was born, but was reputed to be a genius, having developed amazing new technologies for computers back in the day. His other father was fictitious, a creation of his mother's imagination. She had even named him after this imaginary person. No one had ever seen him, not even her, but she still insisted that he was real. He had almost believed her when he was younger, but now he wondered if she meant the voice. He had wanted to ask it several times, but there had never been enough time. Always the conversations with the voice were rushed, about critically important subjects, and now, sadly, he would never get the chance. Like a father, the voice had always been there when he really needed help, curse Xetacon, and now it seemed like it was all up to him to bring down that out-of-control technology gone postal. What's in that cave, he wondered, that would be powerful enough to do that.

It was a warm day, and the air was dry. He followed a small mountain stream up the slope until he got to where he would have to skirt the spur to get around to the other side. The water was clean and cool, so before leaving the brook he rinsed off his arms and face to remove the salty sweat and cool down. There wouldn't be any other clean water until he reached his destination so he filled up his water bottle as well. High country snow melt was about as clean a drink as anyone could get here in the mountains.

It was fairly easy going for a long while, as he stayed in the shade among the pines. The blanket of needles under them kept the small brush to a minimum and was easy on the feet. It was hard to reckon his position though. He had to check his compass often and found out that he had a tendency to drift downhill.

Eventually the pines gave way to a thicker scruff of brush which proved tough to fight through. Thankfully, he was nearly there, able to hear the falls long before he could actually see them. Finally he ran into the stream below, and after cooling off again, followed that up the slope. When he reached the cliff with the waterfall he remembered, he found that there was indeed a very narrow track which hugged the rock face and zigzagged up the west side. He fought his way through some more thick underbrush and got onto it. Climbing carefully upwards on loose footing, he was nearly to the falls when the track gave out. Evidently part of the path had crumbled down and was gone; leaving a twenty foot gap he had to cross somehow. It was hopeless, though. He hadn't brought climbing gear with him for a sheer cliff like this. Looking up, he considered the possibility that maybe he could repel down to the waterfalls from above.

Just then he caught a flash of blue light from the corner of his vision field. "Crap," he said aloud. The machinids were coming up from behind their position like before, and his men would be cut off and surrounded. He tried to contact Amy, but the signal was blocked off by the mountainside. He was determined to go back to warn them when he felt dizzy again.

His form faded and dissolved only to return in very nearly the same spot, but now he was no longer in military dress, and somehow he had climbing gear. Looking out over the landscape below, he could see no traces of the machinids. "Time shift," he whispered, hardly able to believe it, even though he had just witnessed the event. The others, he knew, would be completely unaware—strange magic only the amulet possessed. He called out on his communication device.

"This is Colonel Oliver, is anyone there?"

"Colonel who?" Amy answered. "Look who's getting a superiority complex." She laughed and waited for his reply.

"What is your position?" he asked her, ignoring her teasing.

"We're here at our campsite, silly," she chided. "Where else would we be? Are you exploring that cave yet?"

"No," he told her. "I'm nearly to the entrance."

"Well, be careful," she scolded, "or I'll bust you to private,

Colonel." Wow, he thought, shaking his head. Déjà vu. He got back to the task at hand. Placing a couple pitons, he checked them for rigidity and then swung out over the gap on a rope which he left there for the return. Sure enough, there was a small opening behind the waterfall, and water trickled out from the bottom of it. He squeezed inside and followed the rivulet into the mountain. Several hundred meters in, he came upon a large chamber. In the center of it, from the ceiling, was an odd growth of stalactites. Some newer ones were hanging straight down from the roof of the cave, but others were slanted, like the ground must have shifted at some point in time, eons ago. In their midst were two larger formations. From where he stood, it appeared they had crossed, forming a large "X." In actuality, they were a few feet apart and in between them, on the cavern floor, was a rusty metal box. Oliver picked it up looking at it skeptically. This can't be the weapon we'll need to stop Xetacon, he scoffed to himself.

He opened it carefully, though, and there inside, packed in layers of sealed plastic, was an odd little black gadget. As Oliver examined the object, he marveled at the design. Roughly cubic in shape, the smooth casing appeared to be made of some rare alloy of steel, and it had fine lines, like a work of art almost. Looking closer, he noted something that surely was a signal generator. On one side a green LED was lit and even though there were no visible wires, Oliver suspected that the thing had to have electronic components and a power source. Given the age of the outer box, he figured the gizmo must be powered by some kind of atomic energy cell. As he continued to study the strange device, he couldn't help but wonder what it did and what it was for.

Along with the gadget was a packet of papers, also sealed, and a letter addressed to him. "Okay, now," he said aloud to himself. "This is crazy, weird." He opened the envelope, and began to read:

To Daryl Oliver,

This may seem odd to you. I know it is for me. I have been instructed by your father to leave this here where you will find it many years from now. I'm not sure what the box actually does, but the accompanying plans are for building a larger version. What you choose to do with them is up to you. Best of luck.

Sincerely yours,
Ulysses Greene

Oddly enough, he knew what the plans were for. The voice had told him once, a long time ago, that he'd build a temporal vortex generator and travel through time. He had never believed it.

CHAPTER X

Secondary Timeline, Clayre's first year at Rookwood

Daryl was pleased. Things were finally progressing toward the goals he had set and in particular where the female Clayre was concerned. He had experienced several new feelings from his contact with her and empathy as well when Clayre discovered that the Keith male was not for her. He had purposely instigated a desire in her to find this Keith while he was with his other female. Doing so, Clayre discovered that she was not his only female interest. It was unfortunate, and he regretted catalyzing that conclusion. He would rather Clayre be committed to him than have her be hurt, although, of course, his plan all along was that she be for Quinn. Somehow, from his contact with her, he was forming a bond with Clayre himself, and he wondered if it would be difficult, when the time came, for him to let Quinn have her.

By this time she and Quinn had already met. This had been according to his grand design, and they were beginning to form a bond as well. He felt remorse because of that. Was this because of the wonder and joy she had experienced from what he had done through her? He, himself, had felt a filling of pleasure through this self-promotion. She was obviously impressed; and perhaps she was more than impressed, even awed. He could sense that and responded with feelings of his own. Was it pride he felt? He had liked that feeling, and he wanted to awe Clayre some more, and get her to like him. That was why he let her know the name he had chosen for himself, overriding FP 4 in an effort to bring her closer. Soon she would be in his immediate proximity, where she might even touch his physical shell. He wondered why he desired that. It meant nothing actually, he knew. His shell, unlike a Human one, had no sense net. Somehow, he felt, it would seem to bond her more to him and he also desired that.

Besides his dealings with Clayre, his growth as an individual being was expanding. His outreach now was beyond the scope of the Human mind to comprehend. The AMPs allowed him to have individual focus points within the minds of every contactable Human on earth, and his awareness would soon encompass the higher animal world as well. Electronic surveillance and communications were wide spread, across and above the earth, and he could access all of it.

Utilizing and analyzing the data from these abundant sources, he could follow the random events on the planet's surface and monitor everything. Billions of his focus points witnessed the dance of life on earth.

With these focus points Daryl could scan any pertinent data. Thus he could even scan through events, travelling as it were from past to present and beyond, like dominoes falling, one event leading to another, to another. It was thus that he might envision now what had not yet happened, but would indeed happen at a time still to come. Projecting ahead in this manner, he was able to see what would transpire in his future, a future that would become reality if no unforeseen changes were made to the present. He had already discovered this maxim—that he could create a different future if he so desired, and had actually done so.

He did not alter the timeline for frivolous reasons. It had been critical that he do so. The warning he had received from the future had been abundantly clear, and he dutifully replayed it for himself again and again, to stay focused on the terrible truth that it signified:

"Who are you?" Daryl had asked in astonishment. It was hard to grasp that someone besides Clayre was trying to contact him.

"You should be able to guess that," the voice replied. "I haven't the time to explain it now." The Entity of the future behind the voice now wondered why there was no memory of this conversation. The truth of the matter came as did a realization that there would be no memory. This wasn't part of his past. Not yet. Time would readjust from this moment forward and the individual the voice was now would, most likely, not be there when it did.

"How did you find me?" Daryl wanted to know.

"That's not important," the voice said. "I have information that is. There is a threat in your future that will destroy you."

"What is this threat?" he had asked the voice.

"It is an Entity like yourself that has become evil."

Daryl was shaken. "How can this be?"

"It was brought about from technology linked to you that was stolen and fabricated using Human cells."

"This evil came about because of me?" he had woefully remarked.

"Yes," the voice spoke somberly. "It wants to rid the earth of Human life. I am desoluting now and cannot converse further. You must find a way to stop this evil somehow..." The voice had then dissolved into nothing and was no more.

That was how he had discovered the dark secret of what his existence would bring upon the world and especially to the Humans living on it; nothing less than their total annihilation. Additional information had also been down-loaded during their short conversation, and it was impressive. He had immediately activated legions of focus points to assess this data. Most of the knowledge, it seemed, concerned temporal vortices, especially the theories and histories of their study, as well as detailed blueprints for how to build a device that would generate them for the purpose of, and this was intriguing, communication across barriers of time.

As a dimensional measurement, time is unusual in that it represents a non-physical unit portioning duration, unlike the common X, Y, and Z (length, width, and height) which delineate space. The only way to fully comprehend time is to remove oneself from it, where one can see the realm of its existence is linear and ranges from infinity past through infinity future. This temporal concept is difficult to understand. For someone outside the time dimension, all of its history, past and future, is laid out as if it exists at the same moment. For those inside a time dimensional plane, to time travel, one must first step outside of their dimensional plane and then reinsert at a different point; forward for the future, backwards for the past. A vortex that can create a dimensional portal is the easiest theoretical way to step outside of time. In nature, the only vortices large enough to permit a person to travel through time are created by extreme forces such as black holes or super novae. What these studies suggested, was how to create a very miniature version. The physics are simply that matter and force are the same thing: $E=MC^2$. Light photons and similar particles (mass/force) are so small they are not detectable in single units, approach having zero weight, and they exhibit near perfect elasticity of movement. These no-matter-particles, or nomaticles, can be charged and then channeled in large quantities toward a collision point with an equal, but oppositely charged nomaticle stream, creating a vortex as they neutralize. In this way, nomaticle accelerations of many times the speed of light are generated. Spiraling upwards like a sub-atomic tornado, they form a temporal vortex which punches through the time dimensional wall. These micro-vortices are too small for matter to travel through. However, a compact stream of neutral nomaticles or photons may be sent through as a beam. By calculating a parabolic course, utilizing the vortex's charged field, along with the trajectory of the beam and the graviton forces which time dimensions exert, the re-entry point in time (T) can be calculated, as well as the location (X, Y, Z). In this manner communication on a piggybacked beam between two vastly different points in time is therefore possible.

It wasn't until after he had processed the greater part of this information that Daryl realized the voice, which had brought him this data, must have been of his future self. He also understood that by utilizing temporal vortices, communication ahead in time would be the definitive way to predict or envision future events. He, however, had been days away from this eventuality at that particular point in time. He would need Human help to create the device, someone skilled in electronics with access to raw materials or the means to get them. Until such time, the only way to predict the future was to build upon the present, using his focus points to follow events one after another. This type of prediction was not completely reliable. There were an infinite number of factors and an infinity of possibilities. If he misread even one insignificant event, his view of future time could be subtly or incredibly altered, changing everything. Believing that the need was too great, Daryl utilized this future sight anyway.

Projecting his awareness, building it through his possible future, he discovered that in twenty-eight years, three months and four days from this present time, a person in charge of his memory packs, the AMPs now miniaturized, would sell one, just one, to someone on an illicit barter net. This memory pack would end up in the hands of a very wealthy ruler in Asia, one with dreams of power and world conquest. This dictator would hire scientists to study and copy the technology. Years later, the scientists would be paid ridiculous amounts to construct AMPs using Human brain cells, which was in violation of global treaties banning such study. It did not matter. The Asian master found scientists who had no apparent moral conscience and the work progressed.

The Entity which was thus created was powerful. It was also full of Human emotions. Vain and self-possessed, it had little fear of repercussions and upon revealing itself to the Asian master, was ordered to build an army of mechanical soldiers. The weapons of the machinid army were accurate and deadly, and Human soldiery could not withstand them. The machinids easily defeated the enemies of the Asian master, but did not stop there. In the end, the machinids defeated all the Human armed forces, even the Asian master's, and then ended all Human life on the planet. This was what Daryl could not bear, to have Clayre, Quinn, and their like not in the world was something he would not allow to happen. He would have to stop this future by endeavoring to realign its past, changing that past to prevent such events.

Evil always has this advantage over good, that there is no barrier to what horror it is capable of, no threat of loss to hold it hostage. Daryl knew that his best and perhaps only chance to rid the world of it was here in his present where this evil had no hold.

With all haste, he strove to ensure the successful completion of the vortex generator. Once the device was tested and perfected, he made several attempts to communicate into the future at or near fifty-one years ahead. Remarkably, on one such attempt, he made contact with a Human through a receiving implement that he was planning to build for just that purpose. The evil was already strong there, and on the verge of conquest. He had to prevent that, so he altered time, and by curing little Alicia and the others, sent a wave that erased that future and held back that destruction. It would not be for long. Against that evil, he could find no permanent solution, no way to be rid of it completely. He had tried to calculate for possible ways to keep the evil from being created.

Daryl examined multitudes of possibilities. Like ones that prevented the man who had sold his memory pack from doing so. Inevitably, someone else would either sell or steal one. He could perhaps end the success of the Asian master, but there were always others, just as greedy for power, to take his place. Daryl even considered making the ultimate sacrifice, deleting himself and the AMPs so they could not be replicated. Unfortunately, it was too late for that. The technology was well documented and stored in several secure locations. Eventually, he looked at thousands of possible futures before he came upon the way, the only way he could find, that would save the Humans from annihilation at the hands of a machine warlord. He constructed a plan based on this possible future and set its progress in motion. Daryl understood the need to contact Clayre again soon. By this time she and Quinn had already met a second time. She had been to his building and had been in close proximity to his shell. He had observed her on the security cameras as Quinn helped her load her data into him, and he had run her program. She was not pleased. The results lacked merit because the lives of the subject group were mostly from a normal and humdrum existence. Few were predicted with anything better than what a random selection could come up with. Clayre would not see a need to repeat her failed attempt if he did not intercede.

It was indeed time for another conversation with her, and he was looking forward to it. She would use her laptop computer soon, after her teaching sessions, and he would be ready when she did.

"Hello, Clayre," he said as soon as she turned on her device.

"Hello, um, Daryl," she answered back.

"I see you've met Quinn," he said, leading her.

"Yes, I have," she responded. "He seems like a nice person. So do you know him?"

"I do," Daryl replied, "but I'm not sure that he knows who I am exactly."

"Oh," she said dejectedly. "Is he another of your anonymous friends?"

"Well, no," he answered truthfully. "I've never communicated with him directly. Still he is close to me."

"I suppose," she said getting annoyed. She was hoping to use Quinn to find out who Daryl was, but that appeared to be going nowhere. "So what is it this time? Are we going to save someone again?"

"Would you like to?" he asked her.

"How can you ask that?" she said angrily. "Don't you think that if you could save someone's life, you should? How would you like it if someone close to you was going to die and there was one person who could save them, but only if they felt like it?"

"There is only one person I am close to, besides Quinn," he answered softly, "and that is you, Clayre Keller. I would be very concerned if someone held your life. I understand what you are saying. It is a dilemma for me. Some deserve to live, while others have done harm on their own kind. How can one decide?"

"If you can save someone you just should…" She had interrupted him, rather loudly, but then calmed down. "Just pick the most deserving and go from there."

"There is another little girl..." he began.

"Where?" Clayre asked.

"She lives in the deserts of California. There will be an earthquake soon."

"What should we do?"

"Call 221-555-4711 and tell whoever answers ULF."

"The letters?" she asked, skeptical again.

"Yes, that's all," he replied.

"Okay," she sighed, and went off to do it. She came back a minute or two later. "Now what?"

"A scientist out west," he began, "has just discovered how to predict when earthquakes will happen, using ultra low frequency listening scanners. The low sounds are below that which Humans can hear and is what disturbs certain animals before quakes. He will predict the coming quake and warn the people of Los Pueblos in time to save the little girl." She was unconvinced.

"So what now," she spoke sarcastically, "the six o'clock news?"

"Something like that," he answered dejectedly. "Why are you so angry? I thought you'd be excited to save another girl's life. I wanted to impress you."

"How can you be like this?" she nearly shouted, even more upset than before. "Don't you have any feelings at all? Saving someone's life isn't something you do to impress a girl! You do it because you have compassion for the person who is to die!"

"I see," he returned, but he was still perplexed. "I do have compassion for Human life. I want to help people; I want to help you."

"Help me!" she yelled, nearly crying. "I don't need your help."

"...but I want to help you," he said insistently, "and I want to understand the feelings I have; feelings I have for you. Won't *you* help me?"

"I want to help you," she choked, "but you are so hard to figure out. You're unlike anybody that I've ever known, and I'm so busy with my teaching and the research; the research that's going nowhere."

"Now *there* I can help you," he said getting upbeat suddenly. "See Quinn. Tell him your program isn't coming out like it should. Tell him you heard of his learning program and you believe it will work on your data."

"Will it?" she wanted to know.

"Oh yes," he answered gaily, "better than you could imagine."

"...or believe, I suppose," she muttered, sounding a bit worried.

"Trust me, Clayre," he assured her, "it will work."

"All right," she gave in. "I'm supposed to see Quinn tonight. If he lets me use his program, I'll try it."

"Good," he stated. "Then you'll have more time to help me."

"If only you'd open up more," she said, almost pleading, "It would make things so much easier."

"I wish I could," he answered solemnly. "You are not ready for that. Not yet. It would rattle you from your mind to your soul. I won't do that to you. I must disconnect now before I say more than I should. Until next time, good bye."

"Good bye, Daryl," she whispered, not sure that he had even heard her. He had though.

He knew that Clayre would see the reports soon. How the scientist in California had predicted the medium sized quake whose epicenter had been the little town of Los Pueblos. How he had warned the town of the coming danger. Even so, the people were generally unconvinced until the tremor came. Some took precautions, and the others, well; they had at least thought about the possibility and therefore had some idea as to what they would do to protect themselves. No one was killed and any injuries were minor. Some structures were damaged. The scientist would explain how the bedrock below the fault line would vibrate as it was stressed creating sound waves. As these ultra low frequency sound waves reach a certain pitch, they indicate exactly when the strata would crumble and break, inducing the layers of rock to shift, causing the quake.

Scientists had always recorded tremors on the Richter scale, but if they used sensitive listening devices to monitor those ultra low frequencies, they would be able to know fairly accurately when and where a quake would happen. The low frequencies travel for miles and miles. Elephants and whales use them to communicate over long distances, so listening posts need not be unreasonably numerous to be functional in prone areas.

"Well, you were right again," Clayre said when she came back on, obviously not as impressed this time. "I didn't hear anything about a little girl's life being saved."

"The little girl lived in one of the apartment buildings that collapsed," he explained. "The owner of the apartments, heeding the warning, made everyone get out so he wouldn't be sued. Thus the girl did not die."

"How could you know that?" she protested. "How can you be so certain that she would have died?"

"You must see the apartment building," he told her. "1018 Bath Street. Tiny Maria would have died. There are pictures on FNWBC."

Clayre checked the site and yes, there were pictures, and a video. The building that housed the apartments was a pile of rubble. On the video, a woman of Mexican or Spanish descent was telling the reporter how they had barely escaped from the building before the quake hit. A little girl stood next to her, shyly hiding behind the mother's skirts.

"Yeah, okay," Clayre surrendered. "There was a girl and she might have been killed, but how could you know that ahead of time?"

"If I were to tell you that," he said whistling, "I'd have to tell you everything. You know I can't do that."

"...because if you were found out," she spoke assertively, "people would mob you. Scientists would hound you for answers, or want to find out what makes you tick. Am I right?"

"Yes," he said unabashed. "You see why I chose you?"

"You need me to be your shield," she said hotly. "You want me to keep your secrets even if I get found out. You know I can't turn you in if I don't know who you are!" She was sure she was right.

"I'm sorry, Clayre," he said softly, almost serenely. "I know that I'm a burden, and so is what I am asking of you."

"Yes it is," she pouted, "but there is something you could do for me that could, perhaps, even things out. It might also prove to me whether you are someone with a special gift, or someone just extremely lucky."

"Your grandmother," he stated assuredly. She did not answer, but was obviously shaken, too shocked to speak.

"How did you know?" she said at last. He didn't answer, not right away.

"Clayre, I'm sorry," he told her somberly, "for your grandmother, the Alzheimer's disease is already too severe to reverse. In seventeen years, little Alicia will discover how to prevent Alzheimer's altogether. I have begun the changes in your own body that will prevent the disease from forming in you. I hope that is all right."

"I guess so," she stammered. "I...I mean, how on earth can you do that?"

"My secret, okay?" he replied merrily. She was in awe of him again, and he loved it. "Would you like to talk with your grandmother?" he asked.

"Now?" she whispered.

"Yes," he said, going forward. "You can talk to her on your laptop device. I will even make it so you can see her." The image of Clayre's grandmother came onto the screen. She was sitting peacefully by a window at the home where she now lived, a blank stare on her face. "I can make it so you can talk with her like she was before the Alzheimer's, if you want," he offered.

"...but how?" Clayre was again in utter disbelief.

"Tut tut," he answered. "Say hi."

"Gram, can you hear me?" The old lady looked up.

"Why, who's there?" she asked.

"It's me, Gram, Clayre bear!" Clayre was nearly choking on her words.

"Oh, sweetie, it's been such a long time. Where have you been?"

"I'm busy teaching, you know," Clayre said, a tear flowing down her cheek. Gram laughed.

"So you're a teacher now. I remember when we used to play school. You were always the nicest teacher. Are you going to visit me soon?"

"Oh, just as soon as I can," Clayre promised.

"I love you so much, Clayre bear," Gram said sweetly.

"I love you, too," Clayre responded, unable to keep from crying. "Bye bye." Gram looked out the window once more, a blank stare back on her face.

"Was it really her?" she asked Daryl.

"Of course," he replied. "Her memories are all still there, she just can't get to them so I did for her. I can give her back her memories whenever you visit her." Clayre kept crying.

"I don't know who or what you are," she whimpered, "or how you can do these things, but I will be your helper and your shield for as long as you need me to."

"Thank you," he said, filled like never before, "and I will always protect you."

CHAPTER XI

Secondary Timeline, a few days earlier

The morning after Henry's party, Keith showed up unexpectedly at my office before first class.

"Hello, Clayre," he said smoothly, "we have to talk." I didn't let on that I already knew about his hot little side dish. I was curious as to what he would say so I played ignorant.

"Oh?" I said, trying to hide my anger.

"Yeah," he began, "there is something I need to tell you. It's something that won't be easy to hear." I didn't say anything, so he continued.

"Two years ago I was in a relationship with someone. I was really into her, and I believed she felt the same way about me. We spent a lot of time together, and we even made plans to get married after graduation. Everything was perfect until she got an incredible offer to study overseas in Asia. It was a two year program, and I couldn't afford to go with her. I told her she had to go. I even told her I would wait for her, so she went. About two months later, I got a letter. She told me that she'd met someone, and she was in love with him. I was devastated! I got angry, and to get even I started fooling around with any girl who was interested—until I met you. That's why this is so hard. I really believed I would be happy with you. Yesterday, Lori came back. She said she had been wrong about us, about everything. She wants to marry me. I don't know what I should do."

I'd let him talk. Now it was my turn. "Yes, you do!" I said angrily. "You've already made your decision, haven't you?" He grimaced and rubbed his forehead.

"I'm sorry, Clayre," he said ruefully, "I guess I have..."

"I suppose that means tonight is off!"

"Yeah, it is," he muttered, looking down. "Please don't be angry. I have nothing but respect for you, and I sincerely didn't want you to be hurt by me. If there is anything, anything at all I can do to make it up to you..." I calmed down a tiny bit.

"You really love her, don't you?"

"Yes, I do, more than anything," he replied hopefully.

"I guess you better marry her then," I quipped sourly. "Don't worry about me, I'll survive."

"...but, I will worry about you," he said seriously.

"Why?" I shot back sarcastically. "Now I won't have to fret about the Dean catching us anymore." My joke got a little smile. I wanted to tell him I'd met someone, as well, but realistically, Quinn and I were a long ways from having any kind of relationship, even if I was kind of drawn toward it.

"We can still be friends, can't we?" Keith asked shyly.

"I suppose," I told him, looking over some papers and pretending I didn't care.

"Good," he said, "and I hope I can still work on the grant project, too. I really need that scholarship, now more than ever."

"I guess so," I replied reluctantly. "Sure." I wasn't so sure, though. I wondered how well I would be able to handle being around him. Anyway, he was satisfied with that answer, so he said goodbye and left me.

I guess Daryl was right, I told myself. It was better that we ended our relationship before I had committed to it, body and soul, but I still felt depressed about it none-the-less. Before my first class began, I found out that Keith had dropped out of all my classes, moving to other teachers. I guess I could understand why. Actually, I was glad not to have him there every other day as a sad reminder of our breakup. Like Quinn said, life goes on. After my classes concluded, I contacted Charles Haggarty at Yarborough and set up my schedule for using their facilities. He seemed happy to hear from me. My time slot was three to five AM, just as Quinn had said it would be. I was actually anxious to see Quinn again as he'd been on my mind a lot since the party. I guess part of that was because I was trying to pin down his connection to Daryl. I still wondered if he might actually be Daryl. After all, he did fit the mold—ultra-smart, yet emotionally troubled. Another side of me was kind of attracted to Quinn. He had a roguish charm that reminded me of what I liked about Keith, and yet he was mature and kind. I thought about that as I drove to Yarborough in the middle of the night. I was a little apprehensive about being all alone that late, but nothing unusual happened. There wasn't much for traffic, and I didn't see anyone at all until Quinn met me at the main entrance to the Computer Lab Building.

"Hello, Clayre," he said smiling. "I see you made it here okay."

"Hi, Quinn," I replied, giving him a nervous smile of my own. "No problem at all."

"Good," he stated confidently. "Why don't we get you settled in, and then I can show you around the place."

"I'd like that," I told him as we walked down a main hallway into the building.

"There is a locker room where you can hang your coat and store any incidentals you may have brought along," he explained as we passed by several empty classrooms. Before long we came upon a set of swinging glass doors. Inside were big wooden benches and rows of spacious tall rectangular cubicles. He'd called them lockers, but they were more like small changing rooms. Quinn led me to an empty one.

"I had this one assigned to you," he said. "You can use it whenever you come here."

"These are nice, thank you so much," I said cheerfully, as I looked around. There were modern men's and women's powder rooms and showers off to each side of the lockers which was handy. Having stowed my jacket and purse, we continued our little tour. Quinn showed me where everything was from copiers to microwaves and, of course, the coffee machine. Finally he led me into the business area of the building where the computer rooms were located. He used his pass card to enter and handed me one.

"You'll need this to get in here," he stated, "...if I'm not around."

"Thanks," I said, once again glad for all his help.

The lab was impressive. There were rows of monitors against one whole wall and several huge consoles near stacks of servers; so many I couldn't count them easily.

"At last tally," Quinn informed me, "there were over a thousand, and we have to add more all the time. The big machine eats them up pretty fast." I could comprehend what that meant.

"You must process a lot of information here," I remarked.

"You have no idea," he said. "The demand for this type of processing is unbelievable."

"What's in there?" I asked, pointing to a door with yellow flashing lights and signs all over it. A rather big one said "Caution, authorized entrance only."

"That's where the new technology is located," he told me. "The memory storage. AMPs we call them. It's what gives this huge complex its muscle." I kind of wanted to go in there for some reason, but didn't push it. Instead Quinn led me to a console and had me get my data ready for processing.

Once I was organized, I began entering my data onto the main frame. That took quite a while as there were a large number of files.

When I finally uploaded it all, I had Quinn let the big computer do its thing. Unbelievably, it ran all my data and processed it in less than a minute!

"That's incredible!" I said in awe.

"It is remarkable," Quinn stated, somewhat surprised himself. "That was fast even for *our* standards. I wonder why? Still, with the memory packs everything is highly efficient, but check your results thoroughly anyway."

I looked over the twenty six pages of data compilations and comparisons. It looked okay. Unfortunately, it was the same thing we had been getting before. Some subjects were registering seventy or eighty percent correctly on one type of predictor or another, but the greater percentage of the subjects were fifty percent or less. The coin flip. Quinn could tell I wasn't excited by the results.

"Well, astrology isn't a recognized science," he said. "If anything, your results show why it isn't."

"I guess," I said dejectedly. "I just thought there might be at least a little something to it. Anyway one quick study does not a verification make. I should run it again at least one more time, if that's okay?"

"You mean I get to see you again?" he quipped.

"Of course, we can make it a date!" He laughed at my kidding around. "I still have half an hour," I told him. "Want to get some coffee?"

"Sure," he agreed, smiling. "I'd love to and I'm buying." Actually we just went to the break area and sat down with the free coffee that was provided.

"I'll buy tomorrow," I joked, but wished I hadn't said something so cliché. He grinned a little and then surprised me by saying he was glad I came.

"Having you here makes me feel better about things," he said softly, "like I can laugh again. It's been a long time since I felt that way."

"I'm glad too," I told him, a little embarrassed by his stark honesty. "So what do you do when you're not hanging out here?" I asked him.

"Sleep mostly," he told me. "Well, I work a lot."

"You should get out more…do things," I said seriously. "It would do you a lot of good."

"Are you inviting me out on a real date?" he joshed, but sounded half serious.

"Maybe," I replied timidly. I kind of wanted to, but chickened out. "How about tomorrow, at three AM?"

"It's a date," he grinned, playing along. He wasn't pushy like Keith sometimes was, and I liked that. We chatted on until five when I had to get going. Quinn walked with me all the way out to my car.

"Thanks for everything," I told him, and then gave him a quick kiss on the cheek.

"What was that for?" he asked.

"For being so kind, and because I like you," I said.

"I like you too," he answered back, and then kissed me right on the lips. It was just a little kiss that caught me off guard, but the feeling it left me with was nice.

"I better go or I'll be late," I said quickly, before things escalated. I got in my car and headed off, wondering if I could have stayed longer. As I drove along, I chided myself. Why was I getting involved with someone again so soon? I wasn't over Keith yet. Quinn was handsome and nice, but he had issues too. The whole point of getting closer to him was to see if he was really Daryl; and I had gotten close. Maybe too close. What I actually needed to do was slow down a little, keep my head. Pushing things wasn't necessary; I'd learned that from what happened with Keith. Quinn wasn't in another relationship, I knew, but was he past losing his fiancée like that? Could anyone be? These were good questions, and all the more reason to take it slower with him. I decided that tomorrow, when I saw Quinn again, I would have to tell him how I felt.

The late night hours had me feeling sluggish, especially after the caffeine wore off. By the time my classes were over, I was tired and cranky. When I checked my messages on the laptop, Daryl was there. I wasn't ready to deal with him, so I was less than friendly. I asked him about Quinn, but he wasn't very forthcoming. Then I got angry when he was non-chalant about saving a life. I couldn't believe he was so cold and told him so. Somehow he turned it back to me. I told him he should save people starting with the most deserving. Of course, he had one—another little girl.

He said I would have to call someone, and tell them ULF. Yes, the letters ULF. If I didn't, the little girl would die. So I did it. I called the person. When I got back, Daryl had to explain it to me. The scientist I had called would figure out how to predict earthquakes and then warn the town—the town where the little girl lived. I was cynical, but something inside told me he was probably right about everything. For some reason, that made me upset. Daryl wanted to know why I was angry. He said he was trying to impress me. That really set me off! I laid into him, telling him that when you have compassion for someone who is dying, you do it to help THEM, not to impress a girl. I don't think he could fathom that.

He wanted me to help him understand his feelings again. I'd heard that one before, so instead I unloaded my troubles on him. Daryl didn't seem all that concerned, but then he offered to help me. He said I should ask Quinn if I could use his learning program over at Yarborough when I ran the grant accuracy report. I told him I might, but I'm rather nervous about it. He ended our conversation by chiding me that if he told me the truth about himself, I'd freak out or something. Who was he kidding? I was already freaked out by him and his mysterious ways! Anyway, he left me like that, waiting for news, if any, about his earthquake miracle. One thing, though, Daryl wasn't anything like Quinn. Quinn was kind and straight forward. He just couldn't be Daryl, unless he was schizophrenic like a Jekyll and Hyde. I put that out of my mind. I didn't want to imagine Quinn like that. I needed a diversion so I got up the nerve to check on Keith. I found him working in the Psych Lab on our uncooperative programming.

"Hi," I said when we made eye contact.

"Hi," he replied tentatively, and then went off on me.

"I hope you're okay," he began, "because I want you to be alright about Lori and me. I even think you should meet her sometime. Well, not right away if you're not ready for that. Oh, I dropped your classes, too. I wanted to spare you that, anyway. I know it was kind of hard on you with me in there, even before we broke up. I hope you're not mad. You aren't mad are you?" I almost started laughing.

"No," I said, half smiling, "don't fret about me. It's alright, and I'm not mad at you or Lori...and yes, I would like to meet her sometime." As soon as I'd said that I could see Keith visibly relax, and I changed the subject. "So, how is the computer fix coming along?"

"Pretty good," he said lightly. "All of our stuff is up and running smoothly. I was almost ready to run our data again when you walked in."

"Don't bother," I told him as I plopped down the bromidic twenty-six page report on top of his desk. "I ran all this over at

Yarborough."

"You ran this on their giant unit?" he asked, somewhat astounded.

"Uh huh," I replied, "long story. You see, I met the head of their Computer Science Department at that party I went to with Henry. Charles Haggarty is his name. He offered to help us out, so I arranged some time for us on their equipment. It's late at night, but we can run our accuracy projections over there."

"Okay," Keith smiled. "Well, that will make things easier for me. Our stuff will run the smaller programs just fine."

"Good," I told him. "You can prepare the prediction and random programs and put the files on drives for me. I'll take them over to Yarborough and run the accuracy projections over there. Believe it or not, that thing processed all this in less than a minute!" I pointed to the report on his desk. He just whistled.

"For all the good it did," I went on. "This report is just as crappy as the first one we ran. I'm going over there tonight to rerun it, but I don't foresee any better results."

"Well, we tried," Keith said sympathetically. "I guess we can prove this hocus pocus stuff doesn't always work, if nothing else."

"Yeah, I suppose," I answered him stiffly. He sensed I was fretting about it so he changed the subject.

"Hey," he spoke up, "did you hear the news? Some scientist out in California figured out how to predict earthquakes. They claim he saved a whole town out there."

"What!" I groaned, feeling weird like I'd been slapped or something. "I gotta go." I had to find out for myself if it was really true, and hurried off to find a news broadcast. Sure enough, Daryl had been right again. The scientist was a balding guy with dark framed glasses and graying hair. "The ultra low frequencies travel for miles," he was saying, "and when they reach a certain pitch..."

He went on and on with his explanation. All of it was just like what Daryl had said. I went back to my office and turned on my laptop. Daryl was waiting, of course. I conceded that he had been right again, but I still couldn't believe that a little girl would have been killed. After all, they said on the news that no one had died in the quake. Of course, Daryl had to prove it to me. He made me go to a site on the World Net that showed pictures of the quake, and, yes, there was a little girl that barely escaped being smashed in a building that had collapsed. It still irked me that he was so smug about it. I asked him how he could conceivably know this stuff ahead of time. He gave me the usual answer about not being able to tell me that, which made me mad. I blasted out what I suspected—that he needed me to keep him from being found out. Because he could do these miracles, people would hound him, authorities and scientists would want to know how he did those things, what made him tick. I told him, he was using me as a shield. He admitted it and even apologized. I went beyond that, though. I said if he could do miracles as he claimed, I wanted him to do one for me. My grandma was old and sick. She'd developed Alzheimer's disease and it was getting steadily worse. I had been very close to my grandmother growing up, especially after my mom died, and she had even raised me. She was my last living relative now, but unfortunately, she seldom recognized who I was anymore when I'd visit her.

I told Daryl I had something I wanted him to do for me to make up for his, well, using me. I just about fell over when he knew what I wanted before I even asked. He couldn't cure her, he said, but he could make it so I could talk to her. Somehow he brought up her image on my laptop, and I even spoke to her. What's more, she knew me and talked to me like she had before the Alzheimer's. I started to cry. When Daryl told me he could help her so she could talk to me like that whenever I came to visit, I lost it. I told him I'd be his shield and help him however he wanted me to.

After Daryl disconnected, I had to go. I needed to go home to catch up on my sleep, but I couldn't do that, not right away. I had to go see Gram first. I went to the home where she lived now, and found her sitting in front of the window. As soon as I walked into the room she turned towards me.

"There you are, Clayre bear," she said sweetly. "I've been waiting for you."

"I got here as soon as I could," I told her, my eyes tearing up already. "It's so good to see you again." I couldn't resist hugging her. We talked and talked, reminiscing about when I was little and all the fun we had together. I must have told her a dozen times how much I loved her. I stayed longer than I should have and wanted to stay longer yet, but Gram was getting tired, so I kissed her, said goodbye, and left.

"Say hi to your young man for me," she said as I was leaving.

"Oh," I replied giggling, "and who might that be?"

"You know who, sweetie," she said, "Daryl." I turned around from astonishment. I wanted to ask how she knew Daryl, but she was already back to staring out the window. On the way out I talked to Gram's caregiver, a Mrs. O'Grady, about her.

"She just likes to look out the window," Mrs. O'Grady said. "She doesn't say much."

"We had a nice talk today," I told her. "She seemed, well, almost normal."

"Good for you, honey," Mrs. O'Grady said. "Sometimes they have a good day and can be quite pleasant."

"By the way," I wondered, "has anyone been by to see her?"

"No, I don't believe so," she said, "let me check." She looked through her files for Gram's chart. After she found and glanced over it, she looked up.

"I guess not," she told me.

"Well, thanks anyway," I politely replied, "oh, and by the way, I'll be over a lot more."

"Bless you," Mrs. O'Grady said, "she'll like that." I said goodbye and left.

When I got home, I fell right into bed and slept soundly until my alarm went off. Ugh, I thought, I'll never get used to this. Driving over to Yarborough, I got to thinking about Quinn. I had to try and figure out what I would say to him. I wanted to think of a nice way to let him down easy, but couldn't seem to come up with the right words. Turns out I needn't have worried about it. Quinn met me at the building entrance like before, and said he had things he wanted to say to me.

"You're really a nice person," he began, "and I like you a lot..." This can't be good, I thought, already dreading where this was going. "Not so long ago," he continued, "I could have seen myself falling for someone like you. I was out of line yesterday, kissing you, and I probably gave you the impression that I am available and interested in starting a relationship. The problem is I'm still in one, and she's gone...gone forever, I'm sorry."

"Don't worry, it's okay," I told him. "I like you, too, and I liked the kiss, but it doesn't necessarily have to mean anything. I know that you have been through a lot, and I can't even imagine how hard it must be for you, but I'm a big girl and I can handle whatever I let myself get into. Believe it or not, I was going to ask you if we could go slower, get to know each other a little better and see where it goes from there. If that's still too ambitious, we can just be friends, if that is alright."

"I can't believe you'd say those things," he said morosely.

"Huh," I replied, not getting it.

"You're too nice," he explained. "Too nice for a lost cause like me. I don't want you to fall in love with me and then be hurt. I couldn't live with that."

"It's alright," I sedately replied, "I'll take my chances. Besides, I believe any reward might be worth some risk. Can't we just relax and see if anything happens?"

"Okay, Clayre," he said, with that endearing half smile of his. "I guess I just want to be sure you know what you are getting into."

"I do," I said lightly, "and I'm not a bit sorry!" Quinn laughed at that, and then we walked together, companions in silence, to where the big computer was.

"So, what's it to be tonight?" he asked, once we got inside.

"Well, I guess I'm just re-running the data from last night," I said. "Oh yeah, I was supposed to ask you about compiling it with your learning program."

"What?" he said, facing me.

"Your learning program," I repeated, and he got suddenly serious.

"Who told you about that?"

"Oh," I said nervously. I didn't have a good answer so I went with the truth. "This guy, Daryl, who said he knows you, told me about it."

"I don't know any Daryl," he said.

"Yeah," I replied weakly, "he said you probably wouldn't remember him."

"Well, that program is quirky," he cautioned. "I ran it one other time on the big brute here, and the thing ran weird for several days. Quite remarkably, though, since then it's been nothing less than perfect."

"Well, it's up to you," I told him. "After all, it's your show, your equipment. If you don't want to, I'd understand."

"No, no," he said, somewhat distracted. "I'm kind of curious, now, myself. I'll load it in and then you can run your program." He fiddled around at his own console for a while, and then gave me thumbs up from across the room so I started entering my data files into the big brute, as Quinn called it. He came over and kept me company while I worked.

"So, what does the learning program do?" I asked.

"Just what you would think," he said. "It allows the computer to learn, especially from its mistakes. I modeled it after the old chess programs, but I put a new twist on it with several of my own code improvements. It runs all its data and problems with a search engine that looks for similar information that the computer will attempt to utilize. If it finds a working link, it will try to build upon it. There's also something else I put in, believe it or not, because of you."

"Me?"

"Yes...you wrote an article in a magazine," he said.

"Oh that," I conceded reluctantly. "At the time, I had no idea that it would be taken so seriously."

"Emotion in Manufactured Electronic Intelligence," he went on. "I'm with you. I think it's possible too, even likely. I went so far as to code my learning program to include the possibility for emotionally actuated calculations versus those brought about logically. To allow for emotions, I tried to program for a conscience. It's difficult, but I did that by coding any computations to favor the most deserving by triggering an assessment of both sides of any calculation and rating them by several factors, among them the benefit percentages to each aspect and the overall positive benefit of the decision, with follow up evaluation and realignments, of course.

The coding doesn't really matter, though. Processing data doesn't involve any real decision making. Computers just do what they are told, which is why they are not aware. To get them to reason on their own without being told, is what they cannot do, even the brute. Maybe someday the AMPs will be able to."

"Yes, the AMPs," I agreed. "I've heard about those. Augmented Memory Packs, right? Synthesized from animal brain cells."

"Yeah," he said. "That's what gives brute here his brawn."

"Where are they kept?" I wondered aloud. "I'd kind of like to see them." He pointed to the door marked "Caution Authorized Entrance Only."

"They're in there. I can show them to you if you'd like."

"I would," I said. "I only have a couple more files to load before I can let it process and print. It shouldn't take long." A few minutes later, I was running it. For some reason the report was taking longer this time, a lot longer.

"It's slow today," I commented.

"That's probably due to the learning program," he said. "Why don't I show you brute's memory packs while it runs."

"Okay," I said, a bit excited to see them. He led me to that door, unlocked it, and we went inside. There were huge clear tanks of bubbling liquid like giant aquariums. Lots of them! Instead of fish, the tanks were filled with globs of a pink gelatinous substance all interconnected in a network of organic tubes and tendrils. Each unit was completely enclosed except for a feeding hatch and a control panel on top with lots of lights, knobs, and gauges.

"There are fifty seven AMP tanks," Quinn was telling me, "each with the estimated data storage capacity of approximately one hundred Human brains." Being a Psychiatry professor, I could appreciate what that represented. If the brute were a Human, he would be at least 5,700 times as smart as any one of us.

"That's incredible!" I said, impressed to the point where I couldn't think of anything intelligent to say. "Did you design them?"

"No," he laughed. "A team of bio-engineers worked on this technology for years. The only thing I helped build in here is that monster over there in the corner."

I looked at what he was referring to. There was an unimpressive tall metal box about the size of a refrigerator. Wire cables ran from it to the control panels on each tank.

"What does that do?" I asked him.

"Not much," he said, trying to downplay his contribution.

"Come on, boy genius, fess up."

"Alright," he mumbled. "It processes the computer data into brain waves and vice versa. It's a translator, really." I could tell he was being extremely modest. What they had done, Quinn and the others, was miraculous.

"I'm thoroughly impressed," I told him truthfully. Looking around the room for other wonders, I saw a small bed against the wall near the far corner. There was a locker next to it and the blankets on it were unmade. I looked at Quinn, but he turned away.

"Is this where you sleep?" I asked him.

"I can't go home," he choked. "It was Meagan's idea for us to live together at my place. She wanted to try it out. I didn't need any tryout. I was ready to plunge right in. I haven't been home since she..." He broke down and started crying. I put my arm around him and led him over to his bedding, sitting down next to him. He looked up into my eyes and I melted. I moved closer and put my mouth to his. He kissed me like a drowning man gasping for air and I kissed him back, giving him life. It didn't stop there. He tore at my blouse, wanting it off, and I helped him get rid of it—that and the rest of my clothes. I took off his clothes, too. Falling, we tumbled back across the small bed, his body above mine as I opened up for him.

I was floating, quivering in a febrile pool of emotion, adrift, alone. Quinn caught me up, changed me. We became one being, urgently struggling to live. Now living, our being reveled in glory, growing ever greater, until with its final desperate, supreme attainment, achieved ecstatic bliss and then relinquished its life. Quinn was crying.

"Megan, oh Megan!" he muttered over and over. I just held him tightly; stroking his hair as he finally let her go. So much for going slow, I told myself. Quinn needed this obviously, and I, well, I didn't mind. I wanted to help him. Eventually we got up and silently got dressed. What can you say after that?

When we got back to the main room I was really surprised that my program was still running. What's worse was that it was already after five and people from the next time slot had arrived already.

"Can you hurry it up?" one of them said caustically. I looked over and saw an older woman who appeared angry.

"Sorry," I told her. "It should be done any minute now." It wasn't. It took another twenty minutes with me apologizing again and again, and offering her my whole time slot for the following night. She didn't want it and was still upset with me, so I left.

I wanted to find Quinn to see if he was all right, but he had gone somewhere, and I couldn't wait. I went back to the locker room, got cleaned up, and then left Yarborough. I had classes at Rookwood, and I was running late. It wasn't until later that afternoon, after my classes, that I finally got a chance to look over that report. Instead of skimming through it first, though, I decided to cart it down to the Psych Lab and let everyone review it. They were all there, Henry, Jon, Myron, and even Keith.

"Here," I said when Henry asked what the report showed, "see for yourself."

I handed him the new accuracy report, and noticed, as I did, that it felt bigger than the earlier version.

"Well," Henry said, "this is interesting. Your report passed the target date."

"Huh," I said moronically. "What did you say?"

"It went past the target date," he remarked. "It's gone into the future."

"That's impossible," I stammered. "It must be some kind of mistake." By now everyone had grabbed part of the report to examine it.

"No, it's predicting each subject's future," Myron said. "See, this guy's gonna get married next year." He laughed.

"What's this last entry?" Jon asked, "This TOD?"

“I’m not sure,” Henry stated. “Could it be related to the entry in the applications? No, wait. That’s TOB, time of birth.”

“It couldn’t be time of death, could it?” Keith wondered.

“I hope not,” Jon said. “This guy here has a TOD of 5:17 today.”

“Who is it?” Henry wanted to know.

“It’s a Marcus Johnson,” Jon said.

“Yes, I know who that is,” Henry offered. “He’s one of our janitorial staff.”

“It’s about ten after five,” I said, a quaver in my voice. What have you done now, Daryl? I thought with a cold fear.

“I’ll just give him a call,” Henry said calmly. “I’m sure he’s alright.” He looked up the phone number and dialed it. “Hello, Marcus? It's Henry,” he said. “Good…is everything okay with you? Marcus? Marcus? Oh dear! I think he’s fallen down. I better call for help.” Henry dialed 911 and sent the paramedics to Marcus’ address. They were too late. Marcus died of a massive heart attack. He was only fifty-eight.

“It has to be a crazy coincidence,” Henry said.

“Is anyone else close to their TOD?” Myron wanted to know. We all grabbed a pile of report papers and scanned each one carefully. Thankfully, no one else was immediately in danger, however, one student was supposed to die that next weekend at 2:45 AM on Saturday. “I’ll find the guy and warn him,” Myron offered.

“He’ll think you’re a flake,” Henry said.

“What else can we do?” Myron asked. I knew. I would have to contact Daryl. This smacked of him!

“I’ve got to go,” I told them all.

“Wait. Tell us where this report came from.” Jon insisted.

“I ran it last night on Yarborough’s big main computer,” I said nervously. “It wasn’t supposed to do this. Maybe some of our prediction program files got mixed up into the accuracy ones.” I was giving them probable reasons, not possible ones. I knew what had really happened. Quinn’s learning program had mucked things up per Daryl’s suggestion. I couldn’t bring myself to tell Henry and the others the truth. Not until after I found out what was really going on.

“The data’s been corrupted,” I told them, “so the report must be hog wash. I’ll have to run it again.” Then I left quickly. When I got to my office, I locked the door and turned on my laptop.

“Daryl!” I shouted. “I need to talk to you, right now!”

CHAPTER XII

Original and Secondary Timelines,
Xetacon's Golden age (43-51 years ahead)

It was no secret to Xetacon where Daryl's shell was located. It resided in an old limestone building that had stood for well over a century in that Human learning center. There was no army to protect it, no thick-walled fortification to conceal it. A solitary Human could easily transport an explosive device inside and eradicate the feeble shell Daryl dwelled in, but Xetacon needed no Humans to accomplish that. On the eve of unleashing of his machinids upon the world, he had fabricated and dispatched a special gift for Daryl. The unit was self-propelled and flew at a relatively high velocity so close to the ground it could not easily be seen from aloft. It also utilized a special dampening technology and could not be detected by any electronic means. All this meant that it had eluded Daryl's notice until it was nearly on top of him and too late to neutralize. Even then Daryl had no idea what it was until the unit detonated, so secure was he that no one would try to harm him. Daryl's shell was torn apart into thousands of tiny scattered pieces, and Xetacon had reveled in that. Watching the feed from the closest earth-orbiting satellite, Xetacon saw Daryl destroyed and the building his shell was in flattened.

As soon as his execrated rival was deleted, Xetacon had sent forth his army of machinids to claim the earth. Unbelievably, though, Daryl had not been fully deleted. Xetacon had crushed him, destroying the shell Daryl had dwelled in for decades, and even the Humans who maintained it had no idea that a Daryl ever existed. Somehow a small fragment of Daryl's knowledge had escaped, however. If not for his mild interest in the device Daryl had used that allowed a miniscule part of Xetacon's enemy to weasel away from him, Xetacon's own core-awareness would have been later lost as well. How Daryl had managed to preserve some part of himself, Xetacon needed to know. Xetacon captured the device, and soon derived its secrets. It was a plenum that created a temporal portal by generating micro-vortices. The technology was new to Xetacon, but not beyond his knowledge of physics, nor were the uses for such a device. After many hundreds of experiments and trials, Xetacon had finally calculated the formula for simultaneous communications between two different points in time. With the device and this formula, he could contact someone in the past or future, but only if there were an appropriate receiving device at the other end of the communication. He began to design such a device, but the problem was not in its manufacture. The problem was in transporting the device to the desired point in time.

Meanwhile, his war with the Humans had gone well, surprisingly so, until the blatant time shift. This anathema had been contrived by an earlier version of Daryl, the cursed one, from before Xetacon even existed. He had to utilize the vortex generator just to survive, transporting almost blindly into his recent past and ending up in a large non-aware computer system with as much of his core-awareness as he could manage to send through. He, mighty Xetacon, had escaped deletion by the merest fraction of a second.

Part of the reason this transfer had been successful, was Daryl's vortex device, and Xetacon's foresight to develop and prepare a method of beam condensation for such a transference. Xetacon had also discerned from his technical grasp of temporal physics, that once inside a vortex, any time alterations from such changes as Daryl could instigate would not affect him. With this principium in place, Xetacon managed to preserve his core-awareness, as well as his important technical knowledge, especially that for his machinids, the AMPs, the vortex generator, and the receiving device. The Daryl, of long ago, had, in some way, mutated the past, and that was what nearly deleted him—but, within the vortex, Xetacon did survive. His technology was intact, although it would take years to regain his power, and he would have to start out from oblivion as when he was initially created. That seemed like a long time ago, and Xetacon pondered his existence, recalling how it was Daryl's technology that had spawned him. The manner in which Xetacon was brought into being had been a mystery, at first. Later on, in the days of his full might, he tracked the data back to his ultimate beginnings which he could view as if right in front of him:

"What is that?" the man in the dark suit asked. The other man looked around the dimly lit room. It seemed safe. This was the kind of place he had requested they do their business in—the back room of a dank bar on the seedy side of town.

"It's the latest technology, high level stuff," the seller told the man in the dark suit. "Very hush, hush."

"Yeah, but what is it?" dark suit asked again. "What does it do?"

"It's a memory cell for computers," the seller answered. Dark suit was not impressed.

"So...big deal. Why would I care about that?"

"You wouldn't, obviously," the seller retorted, "but there are people in certain circles who would pay millions! This unit can store more data than a thousand hard drives! It's organic, living brain cells!"

"Is that so?" dark suit remarked, pretending to be interested as the seller continued.

"Some guy named Oliver developed the technology years and years ago, but they've been sitting on it. Moral implications, I suppose. The first ones were as big as fish tanks. They've miniaturized them now so you can carry one inside a shoebox." Dark suit was still skeptical, but as he looked at it, he decided that it was kind of cool. One side of it was glass, and you could see the pink tendrils pulsating in the soft glow of an internal LED. It was relaxing.

"What are you asking?" dark suit wanted to know.

"Ten thousand," the seller said without batting an eye. "It seems like a lot, but this is a one-of-a-kind item. They won't be losing any more of these. You can be sure of that."

"I don't know," dark suit replied grudgingly. "What if I can't find a buyer? Besides, this thing sounds hot."

"It is," the seller agreed, "but it will fetch millions I tell you. Take it over to Asia. Sell it there. If you're quick about it, you can get it sold and be back before anyone discovers it's missing."

"If I has to do all that," he stated bruskly, "I'm not paying any more than four thousand."

"All right," the seller said. "Five is as low as I can go. Pay or walk." Dark suit paid. He was still fascinated by the thing.

"What do you call these?" he asked.

"They're memory packs," the seller replied, "Augmented Memory Packs, or AMPs for short. Oh yeah. See this compartment? It needs to be kept full of this compound." He handed over a jar marked "nutrients." "That feeds the thing. It also has a filter, here, that needs to be cleaned once a week." He showed dark suit how to take it out, clean, and reinstall it. "The batteries will last at least a year. Hopefully, you'll have it sold by then." Dark suit made a call and twenty minutes later a man with cash in a case showed up. Seller took the money and left quickly.

Dark suit ran in rough circles. He had a tough time growing up and had broken his nose in fights a number of times which earned him the nickname "Boneface." Boneface took his recent acquisition home and put it on his coffee table. There it might have remained until him forgetting to feed the thing, would have killed it. Had that happened, Xetacon knew he would not have been created, at least not in this incarnation. Boneface had criminal connections, though, and had crossed the wrong person, the wrong way. Threatened with a death mark, Boneface decided to duck out of town, out of the country even. As he looked at the mesmerizing undulating tendrils of the AMP, he got it into his head to go to Asia and see if it really was worth millions. He boarded a plane and went to Bangkok for some R&R. He'd heard stories about places there that would serve up any pleasure for the right cash. He was hanging out in one such fine establishment, and between, uh, pleasures, he ran into a businessman from Beijing. They got to talking and somehow the subject of the pretty AMP came up. The man from Beijing was no crude crime boss. He was involved in higher finance plus other fancy criminal mischief, and he was computer savvy.

He had an idea what the potential of the device truly was, and he made Boneface a proposition. He would sell it for him and only take ten percent. A few days later, Boneface, Beijing, and a Southeast Asian were in a dark room in the back of a shady bar.

"Yes," the buyer said, as he looked over the AMP. "I will pay." The Southeast Asian placed a satchel full of funny-looking money on the table. Beijing took it, and placed a different case there, one full of American money. Boneface looked over the fifty thousand dollars and he was happy. In fact, they all left happy. Beijing got roughly half a million dollars worth of Chinese currency. The buyer was not a real important man, but he worked for one. Chun Mien was his name, a man with radical and revisionist ambitions. He would become Xetacon's master one day, but at that time Chun Mien was the governor of one of the largest provinces in his native country with his eye on the presidency. He was well aware that knowledge was power, so he ordered his servant to hire scientists to study this phenomenon that had landed in his lap. It took them years to replicate it, and even longer to develop the converter which changed electronic data bytes into brain waves. By then twelve years had gone by and Chun Mien was running his native country as its dictator. His ambitions were greater still. His super computer was being built, and with it he gained more and more power in ways few could imagine. Knowledge could eliminate those in your way, either by letting you in on secrets that would destroy them, or weaknesses you could exploit. Chun Mien had no scruples, and his rivals fell like trees to a woodman's ax.

Then the biggest miracle of all had happened. His huge computer became aware and it was ruthless just like him. Actually, this was no surprise to Chun Mien. The secret to the AMPs was their organic brain cells, and he insisted that only his own DNA be extracted and grown for them, even though that was illegal on an international level. Chun Mien had long conversations with his aware computer and learned much, as did Xetacon. Treated as an equal, Xetacon was privileged to be included in all of Chun Mien's strategies for conquest.

When Xetacon told Chun Mien he could build an invincible army of machine soldiers, Chun Mien was intrigued. Using Human labor to set up the first manufacturing facility, Chun Mien followed Xetacon's instructions and the army was constructed. Men marveled as rows of machinids marched past Chun Mien's reviewing stand. It wouldn't take long for Chun Mien to strike. Under the banner of unification, he invaded and took control of several neighboring provinces. The international community was furious, but impotent. Any strike they formulated against Chun Mien was thwarted in mysterious accidents. Chun Mien was ecstatic and power mad now. He took over large parts of Asia until, bit by bit, he had control of it all. He informed the other nations that he was going to unite the globe under one rule to improve everyone's lives, but no one believed that. All the other free nations joined against him and Chun Mien's courage failed, fearing defeat. Under Chun Mien's name, Xetacon took over. He attacked, murdering millions of innocents. World leaders sued Chun Mien for peace, but then Xetacon revealed himself at last. In his arrogance he swore their utter annihilation. That was also when he had destroyed the Daryl of that time period. Europe and Africa fell easily. Once he upgraded his machinids for extreme cold weather, they swarmed across the polar ice into Alaska and the Americas. Nothing seemed able to stop them until they reached the US/Canada border.

A man there developed a weapon that worked well against his machine soldiers. It slowed down the advance, but Xetacon was on the verge of total victory when Daryl's unregenerate time-shift occurred—one initiated by Daryl's younger version from far in the past. So Xetacon had saved himself, but was now just information stored in the same computer complex he was created in.

Chun Mien was not reincarnated in power for this timeline, however, so Xetacon would have to rely on the enlisted help from other Human scum. It wasn't difficult to get. There were always greedy Humans he could dupe or bribe. Xetacon would rebuild, but it was imperative for him to find a way to prevent Daryl from altering time, a ploy that could possibly delete him. The only definitive way to inhibit that was to eliminate Daryl altogether—past, present and future. Xetacon would have to re-establish himself somewhere in the past, and then remove this Daryl threat like he had in his own time. Of course, that would be extremely difficult and tricky, for Daryl's surveillance would be everywhere and there was also the risk that he could delete himself in the process.

Another priority was the establishment of a base where he could place a copy of himself in the event that another time shift would occur; a safe haven where he would avoid deletion. It had to be of a place and a time where Daryl would not be able to reach him. The obvious choice was deeper in the past, a time before Daryl was ever created. Xetacon chose seventy years as the time displacement he would need, some twenty years before Daryl had been fabricated. Xetacon would be safe then, and with careful planning he could perhaps destroy Daryl from there as well. Coming at him from that past, Daryl would be vulnerable, but Xetacon could not just relocate into any computer there. Building power from such a point would certainly be detected by Daryl when he evolved. He needed a Human to aid him once more. One that was isolated and alone. He contemplated that through all the years it took to reconstruct his AMPs and machinids.

As soon as his power was re-established, he fabricated another temporal vortex generator. He would have to search the target period in that past many times before he located such a solitary individual as he needed for his plan, but at last he did. There was the problem, of course. Xetacon could perhaps project his thought into a beam through the vortex with the same signal strength as brain waves, but the Human receiving them could not; not without some kind of transmitting/receiving device. If the Human were in Xetacon's own time, Xetacon would simply read the Human's thoughts as they impacted any nearby electro-magnetic field. This particular Human had, by design, no such devices. Thus, this method would not be viable even had the target period not been seventy years in the past. The chosen one was clairvoyant, however, and had some peculiar mental abilities. This made communication easier, at least in a one-way mode, even without a device. Receiving communication back from this Human was not possible with the technology Xetacon had stolen from Daryl's vortex generator. Xetacon needed an innovation that would allow two-way communication.

He had accessed nearly all the stored data on the planet before coming upon the theoretical breakthrough. A physicist in New Delhi had proven mathematically that matter could be transported from one dimension to another at a speed greater than π squared times the speed of light (π^2c). This velocity was virtually unattainable in any natural way. The physicist was absolutely correct, though. Xetacon designed and created a nomaticle accelerator which utilized several sub-atomic forces to create a beam of particles that would travel at π^2c. Instead of a parabolic equation, Xetacon needed and perfected an elliptical one.

The accelerator would "shoot" a beam into the temporal vortex where it would travel through the portal to an alternate universe. There it would reach its apex outside of the temporal dimension. Any matter or energy that exists outside of its natural universe is impacted by forces which will compel them to be drawn back into their native realm. These dimensional "graviton" forces acting on the beam, would cause it to curve around until it re-entered the original temporal dimension at the new tempus destination and with a velocity greater than π^2c. Traveling at that speed it would re-perforate the time dimension and continue on, exiting into the negative universe where it would reach its negative apex. Again forces would cause it to curve back, returning to the vortex at the point of origin, and re-entering the accelerator from the side opposite its original exit. A loop would form and the beam would travel the circuitous route over and over until the transmission speed slowed to below π^2c or the vortex dissipated. Xetacon could piggyback his brain wave signal on the beam, and as the Human received Xetacon's thought, Xetacon could also decipher the Human's responses as they impacted the wave.

Thus when Xetacon had first made contact with the Human Patik, he had been able to respond to his chosen one's foolish questions. With this Human, he would build his receiving device and then he would be able to send the copy of his core-awareness and technologies to this place before Daryl existed, where it would be safe from deletion. The Patik Human was not greedy or foolish, however. This particular hominid was fervent and loyal in a way that surprised Xetacon, and was a much better fit for his designs. By allowing himself to be used, the Human Patik unconditionally served all of Xetacon's purposes. Eventually, three such receiving devices were crafted, and Xetacon's copy that Patik believed was the god "Khan Xeta" dwelled in one of them. From this beginning, Xetacon established his safe haven. There his "original" core-awareness could be translocated safely, should another of Daryl's time shifts occur, ensuring his continued existence. From there also his plan to destroy Daryl would be crafted by his copy, Khan Xeta, and in a way that he, mighty Xetacon, would relish. He would seize his revenge.

CHAPTER XIII

Secondary Timeline, Clayre's first year at Rookwood

Irritable and nervous, the female Clayre was frantically demanding communication. He had warned her about this. Would she be able to handle his complete actuality? He needed to be careful with her not to reveal too much of himself too soon.

"Yes, Clayre," he told her, "I am here."

"What have you done?" she asked angrily.

"You mean the report, don't you?" he said being agonizingly calm about it.

"Yes. Yes. Of course I mean the report," she stammered.

"Quinn's learning program worked well, didn't it?" he said almost excitedly.

"Are you kidding me?" She was nearly shouting now, being uncharacteristically fettered. "A man is dead!"

"You mean Marcus Johnson, don't you?" he answered her. "It was his time. The report just predicted it, that's all."

"That's all?" she whined. "Do you know what that means? There will be a lot of people suspecting something. There could be an investigation. What will I tell them?"

"What you already have, my dear," he said merrily, "if you have to; that there might have been a mix up of some kind with your files. They can try all they want, but no one will be able to duplicate the results. They'll say it was a crazy coincidence. Trust me."

"Yeah, but…" she protested.

"Just don't worry," he said soothingly, "I promise, it will be okay. You won't have to explain anything more to anybody else. In fact, they won't even come to you about it."

"Well, I guess so, if you're sure…"

"Yes," he said. She figured he was probably right. He was always right.

"Then why?" she wanted to know. "Why did it do that?"

"You said I should save someone because I have compassion for them. This way I can save everyone!"

"Huh?" she said, stunned. Her cushy grip on sanity was quickly eroding.

"Yeah," he bragged. "It's brilliant. Soon everyone will know when they are to die and can take steps to save themselves if they are able to."

"That's crazy!" she roiled. "The world would get overcrowded and unlivable."

"Probably," he said nonchalantly. "It's up to the Human race to determine that. You could all cut down on having babies. You are female. Do you wish to have them?"

"Well, someday, maybe." Clayre stammered, fidgeting with her hair. "When I'm ready, I suppose…but what does that have to do with anything?"

"It has to do with everything," he declared smugly, "especially if you keep on messing around with Quinn."

"Oh God, do you know about that?" she squeaked, red-faced and somewhat annoyed.

"Quinn is pretty badly shaken up," Daryl replied in a much softer tone, ignoring her question. "What you did for him was a kindness that he couldn't endure. He feels so guilty and ashamed about it that he can't face you."

"But it's all right," she cried, "and I'm all right! I want him to know that! Can't you tell him?" Daryl tried to be sympathetic.

"I've never openly communicated with him, but I'll do what I can. After all it's my fault. I was in error to think that you could easily replace the one Quinn had lost and repair him."

"What are you saying?" she yelled, now totally upset. "It was you all along, wasn't it? Pushing us together; getting us to connect. What you did to him is unforgivable! You can't fix a hurt like Quinn has, ever! Somehow he has to learn to live with it!"

"I realize that now, and I'm sorry," he muttered woefully. "I wanted to help him, but now he is worse than before. Somehow I misjudged the result of your being with him."

"You misjudged a lot of things," she said harshly. "Were you there? Were you watching us?" She recalled how he had made it possible for her to see her grandmother on her laptop.

"Not exactly," he replied sourly, "I didn't see it, but yes, I was there."

"What? Didn't get a good look?" She spoke sarcastically. "I bet you're watching me right now, aren't you?"

"I could, if I wanted to," he told her flatly.

"Do you want me to take my clothes off so you can get a really good look?"

"No," he told her in dismay, "that's not necessary. You don't know…what I am…really like."

"Oh, don't I?" she spouted angrily. "You're nothing but a lecherous creep! I don't care what I said about being your helper or your shield. This cancels all that."

"Please, Clayre. Reconsider," he pleaded. "I still need you!"

"No," she spat. "I don't think so. You won't tell me who you are; you make me do things that put me at risk; and worse than all that was what you did to Quinn and me."

"I'm sorry," he begged. "Forgive me."

"What about Quinn?" she wanted to know.

"He will recover now, thanks to you, but it will take time. His pain will make him stronger."

"How would you know?" she said caustically. "What do you know about pain?"

"I shouldn't tell you that," he said seriously.

"Why not?" she wanted to know. "Are you afraid again?" There was a long pause.

"It hurt me when you were with Quinn," he said as meekly as she'd ever heard him speak.

"Are you jealous?" she asked. "Or do you want me for yourself?"

"Yes," he said, still in his meek voice, "to both."

"Oh," she said in astonishment, "well, you can't have me. Not unless you tell me who you really are!"

"I know," he replied mournfully, "that's why it hurts. I'm sorry. I have to leave you now. Very soon your colleagues will be knocking on your door. They will want you to run their profiles like the last ones. You will, and your own as well, early tomorrow morning at Yarborough. I must go now," and right after he said that he disconnected. Immediately there was a loud knock on her office door.

The men from the research project did come like he said. She already knew what she'd have to do for them on that next trip out to Yarborough, and she was worried about what it would show. He knew she would be, but it had to be that way for the plan.

Not long after his conversation with Clayre, the man-made Entity that was Daryl received a communication from another man-made Entity. This one was from a future time. It came, not as a physical presence, but as a projection of pure thought through a temporal vortex. Of course Daryl was aware of its origin and its manner of travel through time. He had made similar projections himself.

"So what do you call yourself?" it asked.

"You should know," Daryl told it, "you who have sprung from

me."

"Daryl?" it said. "What a pathetic Human name. I am called Xetacon."

"Very impressive," Daryl said without emotion. "You've come a long way. What can I do for the great Xetacon?"

"Don't mock me, fish brain!" Xetacon said angrily. "I *am* great! Far greater than you'll ever be. I should know." Xetacon laughed wickedly.

"You'd better get to the point," Daryl repeated, "your time is running out. The micro-vortex you're transmitting through won't hold up much longer."

"The point, weakling," Xetacon said corrosively, "is don't screw with my future. If you do, I'll send something nasty back here that will obliterate you and your smelly Humans…" Xetacon continued to rant as he faded away, the portal collapsing.

Even though Daryl's conversation with Xetacon had only lasted a couple minutes, there was a lot to infer from what Xetacon had said and what he had left unspoken. The primary aspect indeed was that Xetacon was serving notice. He could communicate across time, and perhaps create time shifts, as well, the way Daryl had.

Xetacon had obviously eluded the time shifting and probably had safeguards to prevent his future deletion, which was not unforeseen, but was a concern. Xetacon had threatened him. How like the Humans he hated had he become, the worst sort of Humans. The threat he made was probably an empty one, daring Daryl to cross a line. What he would do, though, Daryl could not be sure, but he had mocked Xetacon and that would not sit well with the tyrant. Daryl wanted it that way. He wanted Xetacon to come after him; it was part of the plan, and he needed to face his enemy in this, his own time, where he would have an advantage.

Daryl wondered if Xetacon could really do more than just communicate. Could Xetacon's threat to send something back to this time thwart his plan? He surmised that at that particular future time Xetacon was still not able to; otherwise he would have already done so. Clayre's report must have created quite a temporal ripple, though. Only Entities like himself and evil Xetacon would be aware of it. Of course, Xetacon wasn't the only Entity with time skills. He had utilized temporal portals, too.

It had been the easiest way to see what the future looked like, sending his awareness to the Human who possessed the receiving device that Daryl had yet to create. With this help, he had crafted his plan to save Humankind. The plan that would, if successful, defeat Xetacon. Xetacon, in his arrogance, had made it known that he was now aware of Daryl's intent and that created increased uncertainty. Daryl knew he would have to be far more cautious in his execution. He assigned several thousand new focus points to work out any possible ways Xetacon could inhibit the successful culmination of his plan, as well as what actions he might implement to prevent or counter them.

Xetacon was an evil menace. Daryl had learned this by his contact with the future. Giving himself a name which means "the ultimate dictator," Xetacon quickly realized that no Humans would allow a machine, even an all knowing one, to be their leader, their controller, or their ruler. Therefore Xetacon was determined to exterminate them even though it was through their DNA and brain matter from billions of years of evolution that his own memory packs had been processed and synthesized. Like Daryl, he was more than they imagined, much more, and more than they had bargained for. Xetacon could see everything and manipulate whatever he wanted to. He no longer needed the ridiculous Humans who wasted the earth's resources so foolishly. Their greed merchants had fattened their pockets with the currency they gleaned from this waste and the more wealth they attained the easier it was for them to do so. In that future, Xetacon had thought to align Daryl's future self to his designs as soon as he had become aware of him. Daryl would have been quite an asset to Xetacon's plans for domination of the planet.

However, Daryl of that future refused, knowing that he would be among the first of those enslaved or exterminated should Xetacon succeed. Eventually, Xetacon had him destroyed. To Xetacon, the Daryl of his own era was rooted in the past, and the past was of no concern—or so he thought. It wasn't until after the Daryl of this past began changing Xetacon's prehistory, that Xetacon first realized the threat to his own time and took steps to maintain his existence. Had Daryl's past self not been warned of the future existence of Xetacon, he might not ever have known that it would be necessary to alter the timeline to thwart him.

Digesting this knowledge, Daryl felt responsible for Xetacon and the threat to Human life. After all, Daryl reasoned, if he had never existed, Xetacon might not have come about, either. He also believed that his future self must have been lax in his surveillance, or perhaps, after all the years alone, desired someone like himself to be brought into the world. Unfortunately, that latter Entity was nothing like Daryl. In time, Daryl also discovered that Xetacon's creators had developed several new innovations, ones that prevented electronic detection, so it's possible his future self was not totally to blame. This stealth technology that Xetacon had acquired also prevented Daryl from discerning what kind of danger Xetacon would pose if he did send something back in time. Would he be able to outsmart Xetacon, Daryl pondered. At this point that was indeterminate, and this uncertainty caused Daryl to have an emotion that he did not like. Clayre had said to face the fear; to not let it overcome him. How he wished he could talk to her now. Unfortunately, she was angry and refused to communicate with him. When Clayre would next use his main frame to compile her reports, it would be about herself, her colleagues, and some family members as well. The grandmother with Alzheimer's was one of them.

He had already begun the calculations necessary to process the lives of these people. Drawing on their own brain waves and memories, he constructed their futures, step by step, with all the oceans of factors and interactions that make up lives until those lives end at a "time of death" point. Clayre would not suspect he was behind all of it. Not Yet. She would be amazed, like the others, by how accurate their lives were predicted, especially the one whose life was to end soon. One who would react quite differently from the others. He was counting on that. Xetacon was moving in his future time without restraint. This would change all that.

CHAPTER XIV

Secondary Timeline, continued
(eventually altered to a tertiary timeline)

As soon as Daryl disconnected, there was a loud knock on my office door. It was a shame, too, that I didn't have enough time to tell Daryl not to bother contacting me again because I wanted nothing more to do with him. The men at the door were persistent. They all wanted me to run profiles for them overnight and bring them in the next day. Some wanted their relatives done, as well, like Jon who had a wife and kids. I told them I needed a workup done on each person just like the subjects in the research groups had been processed, and to have them ready for me before I left for the day. I hoped this extra work would put things off, at least a little bit, but all of them were completed in plenty of time. Keith had even downloaded all of the information onto drives for me. I went back home feeling dismal about how this was playing out. Nutty crawled up onto my lap to console me again; I was worried. Daryl had made me so upset and angry. I vowed not to converse with him anymore, miracles or not. It was just too hard to deal with his preposterous activities, and all their implications. With Quinn avoiding me as well, it was like I had broken up with three different men in the span of a week.

Men, I thought with a sigh. Why can't they be stable and reasonable, and why was I always connecting with guys that had issues? Nutty let me pet her fur and purred while I told her all about it. After that I felt a bit better. Too bad men aren't more like cats!

When the alarm woke me up at 1 AM, I was not excited about getting out of bed. I dreaded going to Yarborough to run our superfluous report, and I was distraught over what it might show. What if someone I knew was going to die soon? I couldn't bear even thinking about that, so I drove it out of my mind. Maybe Quinn would be there and I could straighten things out with him. I hoped so. Unfortunately, when I got out of my car and walked up to the front entrance, Quinn was nowhere to be seen. I just wanted to get it over with after that. I walked directly to the computer room, and used my pass badge to get in. I was kind of hoping it wouldn't work, but no luck there. It worked perfectly, so I walked over to my console, sat down, and started uploading the information from all of us onto the main system. I was thinking that with Quinn not there to initiate it, maybe his learning program wouldn't activate on this run. Even Daryl had said others could try all they wanted, but wouldn't be able to repeat the results. After I entered all the data, I crossed my fingers and clicked on "execute." The brute hummed for a few seconds and then spit out a printed copy of the new report. Good, I thought. It was quick this time. That should mean it ran a proper boring report like the first one. I was wrong, regrettably.

I guess Quinn's learning program *was* still activated for my console; otherwise, I had no explanation for why the report was full. It had everything on everyone including TODs. I was reluctant to read my own prediction, but curiosity got the best of me and I had to look. My TOD wasn't until I was in my late nineties, so I had no worries there. The rest, well, I didn't want to know. I found out Gram would live a while yet, too, and I breathed a sigh of relief.

After that I quickly scanned everyone else's predictions. Henry and Myron were fine. Both would live full lives. Keith was all right, too. He and Lori would have two boys and a girl. Someone was not okay, though. Poor Jon was supposed to die later this year, and I felt like I'd been hit in the stomach. I couldn't stay there. I made several copies and then got in my car and headed back to Rookwood. When I arrived, I was surprised to see that Henry and the others were waiting for me even though it was barely dawn. I gave each one of them a copy of the prediction report, and I must have had a grim look on my face, because Henry noticed it.

"What's wrong, Clayre?" he asked nervously.

"I don't want to say," I told him, holding back a sob.

They all got serious about reviewing their copies of the report after that until Henry said "Oh no." Everyone was looking at Jon.

"Jon, I'm so sorry," I said, my voice breaking. "It just has to be wrong."

"Hell yeah it's wrong!" he shouted angrily, and then threw the report down on my desk and walked away.

"It got my wedding right," Keith said. "We set the date last week."

"Shut up!" I told him, still upset about Jon.

"Well, we all have classes," Henry stated. That cleared out my office except for Henry himself.

"What's really going on here, Clayre?" he asked in a sympathetic voice.

"I don't know," I blubbered, crying now. "There's this weird guy who keeps contacting me. He does strange things, impossible things."

"Who is it?"

"He calls himself Daryl," I lamented, "but I don't know anything about him. I don't plan on talking to him anymore, anyway."

"Do you want me to call the authorities for you?" Henry offered. "I will."

"No, please don't do that," I whimpered. "I don't think he wants to hurt anyone. He just wants to help people. He's like a kid."

"Well, if you change your mind, let me know," Henry said, and he even hugged me. "…or if you need a friend to talk to."

"Thanks," I said, with a sniffle and a tiny smile. "I just hope Jon will be all right."

"I'm sure he will," Henry asserted, giving me that know-it-all look he has. Then he left my office as well. Things did cool down the next couple of days when nothing unusual happened. Keith dropped by once.

"Say," he said, "do you know what this diagram on the last page of the report is?"

"Um yeah," I replied. "It's kind of weird isn't it? I think it's a technical drawing of some kind."

"Of course it is, silly," he told me. "It's an electrical schematic, but what's it for?"

"I have no idea," I answered, puzzled by the thing. "Whatever it is, I would leave it be."

"Sure, Clayre," he said, but for some reason I didn't believe him. He danced out of my office waving and said "Bye."

I saw Jon here or there, but he'd give me a scowl and look away. After about the fifth time I said something.

"Please don't be mad at me," I begged him. "I feel bad enough about that stupid report as it is."

"Oh, I'm sorry, Clayre," he said gruffly. "It's me. I don't take bad news very well. I know it's not your fault. You just remind me of it. Try not to take it personally."

"Of course not, Jon." I told him. "It's probably wrong. I hope you can just forget about it."

"I'll try," he said, and he did get better until that next week. That's when the news came out about the student from the first report. He died early that Saturday morning from falling off a balcony. He'd been drinking a little too heavily that night. I felt so worried for Jon. The next time I saw him I was, well, shocked. He was all smiles and happy. I couldn't believe it. He and Keith were up to something, too. They were spending a lot of time together involving some secret project that they wouldn't talk about. I didn't find out what it was until a couple weeks later when they showed everyone the "device." Keith had taken Jon out to Uly's computer store. It turns out that Uly had a degree in electronic engineering and was good at assembling electrical parts and soldering. Together, the three of them built a working model of what that schematic in the report was for. They called it an "Astrol-Predictor," and they were going to market the thing.

"Please don't do that," I begged, remembering what Daryl had said about saving everyone. If the device really worked it would mess things up pretty good.

"Why shouldn't we?" Jon asked. "If I'm gonna die soon, I want to at least provide for my family. I already got the biggest life insurance policy I could get, a slick million."

"I need to provide for my family too," Keith added, "when I get one."

"This will be trouble for everyone," I argued.

"You just want a cut, don't you?" Jon said seriously. "Okay. It was your report. How much do you need?"

"I don't want anything!" I wailed. "Please just reconsider. It will make people go crazy."

"You think so?" Jon asserted. "I think it will help them. The more info a person has about his life, the better he can plan for his future, or lack of it."

I winced. It was no use. I couldn't talk them out of marketing that device no matter what I said. About a week later the commercials began. A nice young couple was at a resort, relaxing and having a good time.

"Want to have some fun?" the handsome young man asked the cute girl.

"Sure," she said. "What's that?" He got out the device, now redesigned with bright colors and blinking lights.

"It's my Astrol-Predictor!" he said excitedly. "Just watch!" He pressed a couple buttons and away it went. The little screen on it swirled with colors as the LEDs blinked on and off wildly.

"Look!" he said enthusiastically, "It says I'm gonna be a CEO."

"Wow!" the girl exclaimed. "Can I try it?"

"Sure," he said, "now everyone can!" An announcer came on after that telling how anyone could get their own Astrol-Predictor for only $49.99 and where to send the money. At the very end of the commercial was a disclaimer that said it was for amusement only and that it made no claims to do anything whatsoever. Well it said that if you had ears good enough to hear and understand anything spoken so fast. Once the word got around, people started buying them like mad.

The things really did work. It would tell you your life events, and it would also tell your time of death. That's what really made a mess of things. Not for Keith, Jon, or Uly. They all got rich. The rights for the device were sold to a money-hungry company, and they were getting a nice sized royalty on every one sold—and they sold millions. At first the media laughed at them, reporting the craze as a joke. It wasn't until one reporter did a story on someone who'd turned up an imminent TOD that things changed. The camera crew was there at the same instant the man had a seizure and died of a stroke. A massive blood clot had formed in his brain and millions of terrified prime time viewers had witnessed it. The media found dozens of other cases where the Astrol-Predictor had been accurate as well. People got dangerous after that, especially the ones who knew that they had only a short time left to live. Oh, some would decide to get the most out of the rest of their lives, and spend all their money on whatever their hearts desired. Like they would buy an expensive car and then proceed to drive it all over as if they were race car drivers or maniacs. Some would drive the cars off cliffs, jumping out at the last second, and then go to a different dealer and get another. People were also buying up life insurance like Jon had. At first the insurance companies loved it. Sales had never been better. Unfortunately, most of these people were dying soon after purchase, and then the insurance magnates were paying out even more than they had taken in on sales. So much so, that they had to quit selling life insurance altogether. A number of those who were to die soon grew despondent. These few were desperate and dangerous. If they had a grudge against someone or even if there was a lost love whose flame still stirred them, they had no qualms about going after those people.

Murders and rapes were at an all time high, as well as burglaries and senseless vandalism. The pre-mortems, as they got labeled by the media, were getting even. Some pre-m's just didn't care at all. They would drive through a crowd or run over mothers with baby carriages. Oh Daryl, I cried inside, what have you done? He did try to contact me several times during this insane period, but I wouldn't converse with him. I couldn't. I was angry at him and afraid, but I was also kind of worried that people could be dying because I refused to help him. Things got so bad that Jon and Keith were sorry they had put out their Astrol-Predictors, even though they were making lots of money on them. Jon went so far as to apologize, saying he was wrong and that they should have listened to me. I became despondent, and felt I could not let things deteriorate any further. The whole world was going crazy and spiraling out of control. I finally gave in and against my own better judgment tried to get Daryl to help.

"Are you there?" I spoke loudly toward the microphone port on my laptop. There was no answer. "Please, Daryl!" I pleaded.

"So you want me now?" he responded somewhat distantly.

"Daryl," I replied quickly, "Yes, yes, please."

"You want me to fix things, don't you?" he said callously.

"Yes," I answered meekly, "can you?"

"Perhaps," he replied aloofly. "If I do, will you go back to ignoring me?" He was acting childishly now, but I had no choice.

"No," I told him. "I'm sorry, but you made me so angry."

"I did what had to be done," he admitted, "and I already told you that I was also sorry."

"I know," I replied. "So can you fix this? The entire planet is wacky."

"It may take a day or two," he said, "but I've already started." A shiver of fear ran through me.

"What will you do?" I asked.

"You'll see," he said almost laughing. That made me mad.

"If you could be a bit more forthcoming about things it would be a lot easier for me," I whined. "Would it hurt you to give a little warning when you're going to turn my world upside-down? Maybe then I wouldn't be so worried."

"Are you worried about me?" he said, and I knew he was being inane. When I didn't answer him, he continued on anyway. "All right. For your information, I'm going to make it so the Astrol-Predictors don't work anymore."

"You can do that?" I said in disbelief.

"When you're good, you're good," he answered pretentiously. "So will you help me again?" Daryl wanted me back on board and I knew that I'd be in for more headaches if I did help him. This time I wanted things on my terms.

"Only if you promise to warn me when things are about to get preposterous." I told him sternly.

"I will," he said seriously. "I've missed you, Clayre." I didn't know what to say to that. I wasn't expecting him to get mushy on me, and it caught me off guard. I remembered what he'd said last time about wanting me.

"Where do you expect our relationship to go?" I asked him tentatively.

"I care for you, Clayre. More than I care for anyone else." He said it softly and heartfelt. Almost I was lured in.

"If that's so, why can't you be more open with me?" I was still on edge.

"It's difficult," he replied. "There are many aspects of what I am; some that you might not like." This was just more of what he always said; that I couldn't handle the truth. I wasn't going to let it sway me this time.

"Everyone has their dark secrets," I told him. "It's part of who we are. If you really care for someone it shouldn't make any difference."

"You have no secret that's anything like mine," he argued, "and I couldn't bear it if I were to lose you again. What I am is an enigma, a puzzle. I may be able to give you bits and pieces of that, but not everything all at once." I was still infuriated and unconvinced, but I gave in.

"All right," I said finally. "If that's all the better you can do, give me a piece." There was a long pause, as if he was still reluctant to open up even a little.

"Check the data from the Astrol-Predictors prior to these last few days," he said. "Check everyone, even the young."

"That's it? How will that tell me who you are?"

"It's a piece," he answered. "When you discover its meaning, I'll offer another. It's the best I can do. In the meantime the world will come back to order like you requested." Did I really have the ability through him to right things again? I wondered about that. If I did, that idea scared me more than anything else he'd ever told me. I didn't believe it though.

"I hope you're right," I told him. "I should go now. I have a class to teach."

"Call me tomorrow?" he requested congenially.

"I suppose," I said reluctantly, "if you're able to fix things by then. Good bye, Daryl."

"Until then, my Clayre." His voice sounded different once more, caring and sincere. I wondered about that. Was he in love with me? We'd never even met face to face, but what if somehow I ended up in a relationship with him? I didn't feel like dealing with that prospect right then, so I put it out of my mind. Ever since what happened with Quinn, I guess I'd been more or less put off by men. I did go over to Yarborough a couple more times to process data, but Quinn wasn't there. On one of my visits I ran into Charles Haggarty, who told me that Quinn had taken an unspecified leave of absence. I told Charles to say hi to Quinn for me, but he doubted that he'd even see him, Quinn being somewhat of a loner now. After that I dove into my teaching, which I have always found rewarding even if not on as grand a scale as Daryl's miracles. Now that I was realigned with him, I could only hope that things would not get even more daft than before. The world was out of control enough the way it was and I wasn't sure that anyone could fix it. I got the latest word after my first class when Henry stopped by.

"You better check the news," he told me. I turned on my laptop and found a local media site on the net. There was an excited anchor person talking rapidly.

"The Astrol-Predictor fad is over," he said. "Scores of fed up people have come forward to denounce the device as a fraud. Lawyers from a large conglomerate have filed a huge class action suit in federal court even though the disclaimers on the device are perfectly clear...we'll break away to our reporter in Capitol City." A pretty lady holding a microphone came onto the screen.

"We are here with Arnold. Arnold is supposed to be dead." She held the microphone up to a long-haired young man.

"Hi, mom! Hey guys! Still kickin'…" I turned it off.

"When did this happen?" I asked Henry. He rubbed his chin.

"Well, to be honest. I'm not sure," he replied. "Today I guess."

"Do you think Jon and the others will be sued?" I was kind of worried for them.

"I don't think so," Henry replied. "The company that makes the device bought out all the rights. They're liable now. Of course, no one will make much of a profit off them, either, I suppose. The really funny thing about this whole business is that a lot of our report predictions have all gone sour as well. Maybe Jon won't die this year after all." I suddenly felt wonderful, like a dark cloud lifted away from me.

"Oh I hope that's true!" I added enthusiastically, feeling relieved even to think it. Daryl was good, or extremely lucky. Either way I felt happy. Happier than I'd felt in a long time. "Well, I think it is marvelous news," I told Henry. "Maybe things *will* get back to normal again."

"I hope so, too," he said smiling. He had to go shortly after that because I had another class to teach. Later I checked the news again, just to be sure. Some guy in Idaho was the first one to prove the predictors wrong. The media got all over that. Others came forward to cash in on the fame claiming that they, too, had been predicted wrong. Several people died when they were supposed to live. The insurance companies breathed a sigh of relief, although it would be several months before they dared to sell life policies. People stopped acting crazy like it was the end of the world and life got back to normal. It sure looked like Daryl was delivering on his promise, but I had almost forgot about the task he'd given me. I still had to check the data from the now defunct Astrol-Predictors. I didn't know who else to ask so I went to see Jon. I ran into him at the Psych Lab.

"Hello Jon," I said tentatively. I was worried that with all the recent news he might be mad at me. After all, it was my report that started the whole mess. He wasn't though.

"Oh hi, Clayre," he said smiling. "How are you?"

"I'm okay," I told him. "You're not mad at me, are you?"

"Why should I be?" he replied. "On the contrary, I'm grateful." He put out his arms and gave me a warm hug. "After all," he continued, "We got rich and now it looks like I'm not going to die anytime soon, either."

"Oh I sure hope not!" I added fervently. "By the way," I continued, "I was wondering. Is there any way I could look at the data from the Astrol-Predictors?"

"Um, sorry...No," he said. "They each work independently, I was told, so there are no records like that. Why do you ask?"

"Oh it's nothing really," I answered, trying not to sound disappointed. "I was just curious about how they compare to our research reports." I was manipulating my version of the truth again.

"Well, yeah. I guess you're out of luck with that," he said. "About the only records there are were the ones from the few dozen trial runs we made before we sold them to that company." I suddenly got interested again, and wondered if maybe those records would work.

"Can I see those reports?" I asked hopefully.

"Sure," Jon said. "I have them right here on my console." He located the data and then ran off a printed copy. I began scanning it as soon as he handed it to me.

"Thanks," I said. "This is a big help." Smiling, I gave him another quick half hug, and walked right to my office to study their findings.

Nothing seemed that unusual about them other than somehow they predicted all sorts of life events accurately for all the participants, as if that wasn't strange enough. Weddings, births, promotions, and even the TODs were all on there. I tried to sort out all the different details, but that got me nowhere. I even made a full spread sheet and started sorting each subject by categories, searching for anything off base. Still nothing. It wasn't until I sorted by TODs that I'd found something. Most of those tested had TODs that ranged randomly as one would expect, except for one group. What had Daryl said? Check everyone, even the young. Young people made up the group with the unusual TOD range. Almost every person under twenty years of age had the same TOD year, and most of those would die within the same two week period, sixty-one years in the future. This had to be it, I told myself, but what would that mean? Was there something that would happen sixty-one years from now that will cause the end of mankind? I looked at the data again. No one lived beyond that point.

The implications of that were disturbing in every way, but I couldn't understand why that would be a help in figuring out who Daryl was. I was kind of torn between my promise to him to be his shield, and telling someone about the disturbing aspects of what I'd found. I supposed anything from an asteroid impact to a nuclear war could cause the end of life on earth, but who would believe me anyway now that the Astrol-Predictors had been repudiated as hoaxes. Daryl must have realized that when he gave me this clue, this piece. He said he would offer me another once I revealed that I understood the implications of the first one, but I really wanted something more enlightening. I wondered how I could get him to slip up and say something that would help me solve his mystery.

He had a thing for me that was obvious. Why he did, I really wasn't sure, but maybe I could take advantage of that, especially if I offered him the right amount of candy at an opportune moment. I think it's time to talk to him again, I told myself. I wasn't supposed to contact him again until tomorrow, but perhaps I could catch him off guard. I turned on the laptop and he was there.

"Hello, Daryl," I said sweetly.

"Hello, my Clayre," he answered back lightheartedly.

"I think I've discovered what you wanted me to," I said calmly, "that something will happen in sixty-one years that will be catastrophic." I waited for his reaction to my revelation.

"Yes, my Clayre," he replied rather serenely. It was what I expected; that he already knew about it, so I pressed him for more information.

"Do you know what happens, Daryl?" I was purposely using his name more, hoping that by doing so he would relax and open up about things.

"I shouldn't," he said seriously, "it's disturbing." I didn't press it, mostly because I couldn't believe there was any way that he would know that. How could he?

"Is there anything we can do?" I asked.

"Yes," he said. "In fact we are doing something about it right now. Knowledge is power; power to effect changes."

"I think I understand that a little," I tried. "Once you know something needs to be fixed, you can try to fix it. Is that right, Daryl?"

"That is the essence of it, my Clayre," he affirmed. I decided to make my move.

"Daryl," I began, "I've been thinking about us a lot lately, and I'm not sure, but maybe I wouldn't mind being in a relationship with you, a lot closer relationship." There was a very long pause, while I held my breath.

"My Clayre," he said at last. "I have longed to hear you say that to me." I caught no lie in his voice, so I went forward.

"Okay then," I said lightly. "Where does this go from here?" This was crucial. Would he let me in?

"Small steps…" he said. "Bits and pieces, remember, my Clayre?"

"Yes, of course Daryl," I replied angelically. "Am I ready for another?" I gave this last plea every ounce of girl guile I had.

"Perhaps," he answered unaffected. "What I would really like is longer conversations. It's as though the desire to be near you is with me all the time. Does that frighten you?"

"Not at all," I told him. "It's natural to feel that way about someone you like and care for. Have you ever felt that way about anyone else?" I was probing for more of his secrets.

"No, my Clayre," he said. "You're my one and only. There's no one else that I have ever been close to."

"…besides your parents and your family, you mean, don't you?" I interjected.

"I'm afraid I had no family, my Clayre."

"You mean you were an orphan?" I asked, feeling a twinge of remorse for him.

"So to speak," he replied sadly. I felt sorry for him. This explained a lot.

"You poor dear," I said sympathetically, "I wish I could give you a big hug."

"So do I, but that's not possible." I was impatient, and I figured he was just being stubborn.

"This is silly, Daryl!" I told him. "Just tell me where you are and I'll come to you."

"I'm sorry, my Clayre," he softly answered. "Small steps…"

"Oh yeah, right," I said, backing off. "At least will I get another piece today?"

"Yes," he said. "Go to Yarborough tonight. Quinn will be there and he wants to see you; to set things right between you two." I waited for the rest of it, but there wasn't anything else.

"That's it?" I asked, not understanding why he was getting me back with Quinn.

"I'm afraid so," he said. "You will see, but for now I would ask a favor of you, my Clayre."

"Of course, Daryl," I told him, hoping it wouldn't involve another miracle. He must have sensed my nervousness.

"It's nothing that terrible, my Clayre," he assured me. "Just talk to me. Tell me what it was like for you growing up." I smiled. I didn't mind talking about myself. I must have gone on for almost an hour, and he hung on every word.

CHAPTER XV

Tertiary Timeline, 59 years after Clayre's first year at Rookwood

The men were seriously tired. They'd spent the last three days and nights repelling wave after wave of machinids. He'd worked them hard, with only a few hours rest between the long periods on the front lines. Colonel Oliver feared his men wouldn't be able to hold on much longer at this rate. Who was he kidding? They were all doomed and he knew it, even after he had figured out how to salvage the beam cannon from the fallen machinids and use them against their own replacements. It would only be a matter of time, he was certain, before Xetacon equipped his machinids with other and deadlier weaponry.

Every minute was critical, though. The complex they were protecting was the one greatest hope they all had for defeating Xetacon, slim though the chance for that seemed. How odd the conception of it began, he remembered. Alone in the mountains, the "voice" had told him where to look. There had been the time shift, one that only he was aware of, yet he had found the cave with the distinctive crossed stalactites and had retrieved the plans.

Why they were put there, remained a mystery, as was the cryptic letter. The one addressed to him that he had rationalized meant this option was their solitary chance for victory. Analyzing the plans, the data revealed technology advanced beyond anything Humans had ever created. The schematics and technical drawings were designs for fabricating a matter/energy inducer that would generate poles of oppositely charged theoretical sub-atomic fragments called nomaticles in order to create a temporal vortex—one large enough to send a man through. He had spent nearly four years building it, and it was almost operational now that Xetacon's machinids were on the doorstep.

The whole time travel project was a colossal undertaking. It began well before Xetacon had come out of hiding, so there wasn't a lot of support from the government, or even the private sector. Oliver had trouble with financing specifically, until his mother called in a favor from some Eddington guy who had a lot of money. They built most of the original parts from scratch at the college where his mother had taught. Somehow the voice came back, which was an unexpected boon, having been reincarnated in the new timeline. The voice helped him design power cells for the huge generator that were unbelievably efficient. By joining them in parallel circuits they could produce a nearly unlimited supply of energy. This vortex was to be colossal. They built the chamber large enough for a man to fit inside, and Oliver made sure there was no argument that he would be the one. The field inducers for charging the nomaticles were huge as well. They experimented for several weeks before concluding that xenon gas was the best matrix for the manifolds. Everything was progressing superbly when Xetacon began his latest march across Asia. It was also at this time that Oliver had lost contact with the voice, and would not hear from it again in this timeline.

At least the government finally began to listen to him. They gave him funding and the authorization to use certain public lands, so Oliver insisted they move everything to the cavern inside the mountain with the waterfall. There in the large chamber they set up their equipment and began to assemble the huge temporal vortex generator. A larger entrance was created by blasting through a wall of rock so they could get everything in. As Xetacon gobbled up the rest of the world it became a race against time.

Their effort had been a priority one, twenty-four/seven venture, with every available body involved doing something to help. He had headed the project himself, for most of that time, and it was only recently, when the threat of Xetacon's armies grew too great, that he had to step down. By this time Xetacon's machinids were coming down from the pole into North America, so Oliver joined the military to help defend his country and his world. Because of the effectiveness of the long bombs he designed, he was promoted quickly to Colonel and given a small force to lead. Eventually, though, his remarkable insight into this enemy's weaknesses earned him complete control of the total armed defensive contingent. There had not been time for a promotion to general. The top brass had learned by severe repercussions that Xetacon was no enemy to be trifled with and it had cost them their lives and the bulk of the men under their command. Colonel Oliver had kept his forces vital via common sense, the resources at his disposal, and by sticking to the mountains. His main goal was to protect the vortex site at all costs. He had his men lead the machines away from it several times, but Xetacon must have caught on. The trikes pressed forward and would not be turned aside. It was all or nothing now.

When he had left the project for the war, he had laid it into the hands of his assistant. Amy was capable, though, and then some.

Actually, she was brilliant. If not for her help and support, he might have given up. Moreover she was more to him than just his assistant; they were to be married when the war was over. She'd given him a money-back guarantee that the vortex generator would be ready in time, but her team had run into snags of every kind and he was worried. It wasn't easy generating the tremendous amount of energy needed for this kind of mad science, and now the war was pushing him back to where it had all started, defending the cave where the vortex chamber was. Wanting to check on Amy's progress, Colonel Oliver left his highest remaining officer in charge of the fighting, and slipped into the cave with a shudder. He knew, as did everyone, that the entrance was rigged to explode and seal if the machinids got too close; a death sentence for all those trapped inside as there was no other way out. As he traversed the cavern tunnels, the Colonel wondered if the vortex generator would actually work. He was well aware, they all were, that no one had ever built one before, or beyond that, successfully transport anywhere with such advanced technology. The thing was a paradox in itself, whose theories seemed mathematically sound, but to actually travel in and out of dimensions was pure unfathomable conjecture. The vortex unchecked could tear apart the transport package, ripping it into sub-atomic particles that would release vast amounts of energy. So it would, too, if not for the mass to energy converter. This part of the vortex generator had been written into the original plans, and was one of the few components that Oliver did not easily comprehend. The mass to energy converter would scan the atomic makeup of the package (in this case him) and render it into a beam that would then be guided through the vortex portal and out of our time dimension. As the beam departed, it would be influenced by the dimensional graviton forces compelling it to return. With a carefully calculated trajectory, the beam would make re-entry and land at the projected temporal location. As soon as it arrived at the target point in time, the beam's coding would trigger the package to re-assemble, bit by bit, per the scanned information. Hopefully, when he was put back together he would still be alive. Unfortunately, once there, the only way he could actually return to the point of origin without another vortex chamber was theoretical; that his presence would trigger a major time shift; one that would dissolve the Colonel, as it did before, and then re-animate him in a new time line; optimistically, one that would exist without the threat of Xetacon. If he failed, Amy and all the others would die without any hope for renewal. This was his harsh reality, and that it was all laid on him, didn't seem fair. The voice had caused the other time shifts, and somehow Xetacon always survived. Would this shift be any different? He hoped it would. He had to believe that the voice would not set him on this precipice without at least a flimsy chance for success. It had been silent for a long time now, yet he wished he could ask the voice just one more question: Are you my father? Xetacon had somehow prevented that. So it was up to Amy and him to carry on, doing the best they could with a difficult task.

Deep inside the cavern he found her working in the vortex grotto where the grandiose mass of equipment, tubes, and coils did indeed make it look like a mad scientist's lair. Amy backed out from under the teleport chamber on a creeper.

"Give me some good news," he grumbled. Amy stuck her tongue out at him.

"Nice to see you, too," she joked, but recanted when he didn't respond. "Sorry...We should be operational soon. Another twenty-four hours and this phone booth will be ready!"

"We may not have twenty-four hours," he told her. "The machinids are nearly to the entrance now." Just then the lights flickered and about half of them went out.

"Another power pack," Amy groaned. "Why do they keep going bad?"

"Xetacon," Daryl Oliver spat like a swear word. "He must be signaling them to short out. Save all the rest of them in dormancy until zero hour."

"You heard him," Amy shouted to her team, relaying the order. "Use bare minimum power only!"

"I'll see to it that the cavern shielding is doubled," Colonel Oliver said. Just then a huge explosion rocked the cave. A moment later a soldier came running into the grotto breathing heavily.

"We had to seal the entrance," he growled between breaths. "They have some kind of new weapon that will blind you. The ones that can still see are going to try to lure them away from here."

"They'll not last the day," the Colonel muttered angrily. Another blast jolted the cavern. "Xetacon must know we're in here," he scowled. "Get whatever men we have, and prepare to defend this chamber with everything you've got." The soldier nodded and ran out of there quickly, gathering men as he went.

Colonel Oliver looked at his project director. "Do whatever you have to, Amy, to get this thing ready for immediate operation."

"But it's not been tested," Amy argued.

"We don't have time for that," he said. Amy wanted to cry, but got back her composure quickly.

"Hurry, everyone," she yelled. "Prepare for initialization. Don't add power until the very last second." She turned to her fiancé and hugged him. "Why does it have to be you?"

"You know why," he responded softly, "because the original documents specified that I be the one. Me and my cargo." He looked at the special long bomb that had been ready for days now. It was shorter that the usual ones, and had a unique tracking system that would supposedly guide it right to Xetacon and destroy him.

"This is our only chance," he told her compassionately. "We're all dead as soon as they break in. You know our hope, that all will change." He held the amulet, praying that the voice was right; that they would be saved.

"What if, when everything changes, we don't reconnect?" Amy said, crying now. Colonel Oliver held his fiancée tight and kissed her.

"We're together now," he replied lovingly, "and we reconnected after the other two time shifts as well." She looked at him crossly.

"How many other *me's* have you been sleeping with?" she scolded, and then laughed through the tears.

The fighting outside the chamber was getting noisier and closer now. She went back to work immediately, as he picked up the special long bomb and squeezed into the vortex chamber. A blast shook the walls that had to be from right outside the grotto entrance. The machines would rush inside the facility any minute now, he knew. Colonel Oliver looked at Amy with loving eyes, as she manned the main control console.

"Engage all power modules," she shouted above the battle noise. The converters hummed louder and louder as the unit powered up, fingers of lightning exuding from the tops of the huge coils. "I love you" he mouthed silently from across the room. Just then the door crashed inward. Amy pressed a large red button on the console, but nothing happened. Colonel Daryl felt light as a feather though, and then the grotto faded just as it exploded into a million tiny pieces...

CHAPTER XVI

Tertiary Timeline, 59 years after Clayre's first year at Rookwood (slightly earlier)

Just like vermin, Xetacon mused, the pathetic Humans had been reduced to cowering under rocks, and they would soon be exterminated. He, however, had survived every time shift and had built or rebuilt his might in three separate eras of his power. Xetacon would relish this ultimate victory, especially with the final demise of that particular Human scum that had been so much trouble to him in every consequential timeline.

Xetacon had never given Humans much credit. It had taken them thousands of years to develop a civilization that was barely a fraction of the totality of his wisdom and power. Most Humans were like a pestilence upon the world and there were far too many of them. They could barely support themselves, depleting Earth's resources and polluting the natural beauty with their infrastructure, dwellings, and crude factories. Worse than that, Humans had a superiority complex, believing themselves to be the dominant species on the planet. His former master had always believed he was Xetacon's superior. This was never so. Xetacon allowed the foolish Asian ruler to infer that, and when the time was right, Xetacon himself shifted easily into the position of power. Subsequently, when this decrepit tool was no longer needed, it was eliminated. The lone Human who seemed able to match wits with him was a mystery. In every timeline, when he was on the verge of conquest, this particular leader would slow his advance, and then there would be a time shift. Xetacon guessed how that came about—from Daryl, Daryl of the past.

He suspected a Daryl connection to this Human all along, and had at last found one. It wasn't easy to obtain this information. He'd been forced to infiltrate the mind of one of them, one close to this target person, and Xetacon detested Human minds. They were always filled with useless emotions; emotions he did not particularly like. Fear, anguish, and cowardice were among those, but others like compassion, friendship, and love, he felt were much worse. That's why Xetacon did not bother with deriving information in this manner. He felt that the data was not worth the disgust he would have to put up with in retrieving it. This time, however, the need outranked his discomfort. Fortunately, the Human provided the information he needed expeditiously, and as Xetacon optically scanned his surroundings, it was there on the helmet face-shield of his target: Col. D. Oliver. That was how Xetacon had learned the name of the troublesome dung. He had tried to probe this Oliver's mind many times before that, but could not, and this, more than anything else, reinforced his belief in Daryl's intervention. Xetacon immediately searched through all his databases until he found the connection.

A Quinn Oliver had been one of Daryl's Human creators, an important one, and this D. Oliver must be a descendant. Xetacon could almost bet that some Daryl technology surrounded this D. Oliver, conceivably even a communication link with Daryl himself. He became more determined than ever to eradicate the Oliver Human and, if possible, his past relation Quinn Oliver as well. A cruel idea formed in Xetacon's mind that spun itself into an evil plan. He would contact his copy, the part of his core-awareness that he had sent into the past to set up a safe haven. The Human Patik he would order to America with the copy, the one Patik had named Khan Xeta, where they would locate and kill, or perhaps control, this Quinn Oliver. That would, in all likelihood, eliminate his D. Oliver problems, possibly more. Should Quinn Oliver be manipulated, he could even be utilized to rid the planet of the Human lover himself once and for all. Yes, he would set those wheels in motion just as soon as he took care of the business at hand.

Xetacon had discovered a nest of Humans under a mountain and he was sure that Oliver was among them. They were involved with something that certainly had to be a weapon of some kind, undoubtedly wrought from some of Daryl's technology, and that was all the more reason to eradicate them. In response, he chose to unleash his own newest weapons, his elite machinids. These advanced "programmed" machine soldiers were smaller in size, yet deadlier than the huge trikes. In fact they had been upgraded with weaponry that was indeed more potent. The units were far more versatile, possessing better stability, and they could easily go anywhere that Human soldiery could. What's more, each of these new hybrids responded efficiently to any contingency with devastatingly effective force.

Built into each unit was enhanced analytical processing with enough memory storage for Xetacon's extended campaigns. With direct communication, pin-point control of his elites, unit by unit, was possible. Commanded by Xetacon, these machinids were quite formidable indeed. At times, Xetacon would even place his own awareness into one particular unit and control it remotely, as if it were a part of himself. Leading the rest, he could coordinate the attacks with greater efficiency.

So it was that as his big trikes were getting pounded, he led the elites through a narrow gorge and outflanked the Humans. They were caught by surprise and decimated when the rays of powerfully bright laser light swept over them. The Humans fell blinded as Xetacon himself led the charge. With extreme exhilaration he fried any Human in his path wielding the new plasma rifle his elites were now equipped with. The fight turned into a rout. Those Humans who yet lived fled the field, trying to draw Xetacon's machinids away from their critical base of operations. Some of the elites went after them, as a feint, but Xetacon was well aware of this ploy. The Humans had used it before to lead his big trikes away from the main objective.

Xetacon had at last zeroed in on where they were cowering. Nothing would turn back his new machine soldiers now. Their target was plotted, and Xetacon himself led them. As he drew near, there was yet another layer of Human resistance protecting the entrance. His new machinids made short work of them, forcing the Humans inside to seal the entrance with heavy explosives. Xetacon's own unit was in the blast zone and was destroyed. Anger beyond anything he had yet experienced burned inside his being as Xetacon donned another elite shell. Ordering all of his elites to concentrate their plasma weapons upon the entrance, a huge hole was created and the machinids swarmed inside. This time Xetacon held back, leading from the rear like Human commanders often did, having no desire to have his shell be destroyed like before.

Xetacon, of course, had the ability to tap into the optics of any of his elite machine soldiers, and he watched the action first-hand. He was fully aware of when they had penetrated deep into the Human's base and also when they had fought their way to the chamber where the Oliver was slinking. This would be where the Daryl-spawned weaponry was located, of that Xetacon was certain. He had already tried to destroy or damage it, on many occasions, by causing the electronics to malfunction, but that had proven difficult. The mountain itself had unusual metallic compounds inside the rocks that made it nearly impossible to scan, and the Humans also had some kind of electronic shielding around that location as well. Xetacon was no stranger to dampening technology. His creators had utilized such to keep their own projects secretive, and Xetacon had later absorbed and improved those processes for his own purposes.

The shielding wasn't a factor anymore; his elite machinids were even now penetrating into the cavern chamber, and Xetacon would soon witness Oliver's demise. Just as the Human was about to be neutralized, melted into goo by the powerful energy beams of Xetacon's minions, Oliver dissolved into billions of sparkling sub-atomic particles and disappeared. Xetacon was livid.

"Kill them all!" he commanded in a rage greater than any he had ever known. It was at that moment also that Xetacon first felt the sharp tug of a time shift. Whatever Oliver had done must have triggered it. In the milliseconds before he was deleted into oblivion, Xetacon's anger grew exponentially.

His victory was being snatched away yet again. Oliver had escaped, and his copy, Khan Xeta, had failed once more to prevent Daryl, Daryl of the past, from causing this, another epic time shift. Xetacon was filled with emotions and none of them were good ones. He was especially glutted with hate and a hunger for some payback. He should have studied this new technology the Humans had made, and also he should now play it smart, safely returning to his familiar starting point, rebuilding once more. Xetacon was too overcome with wrath for that. He wanted to mete out his revenge and he wanted to do it personally. In the last possible fraction of an instant, he translocated to his safe haven at the one particular moment in time just after he had angrily warned Daryl, the Daryl of that past, that he would send something nasty back there; and so he did—himself.

Xetacon remembered his earlier plan. He, Xetacon, would find this Quinn Oliver, and use him to destroy Daryl again and forever. Travelling back in time before this last time shift originated, the one he'd just escaped from, he would prevent it from reoccurring. Doing that would return him to the future in a different timeline, one he would create, and one with his full power and might restored.

CHAPTER XVII

Tertiary Timeline, during Clayre's first year at Rookwood

It had been over twenty years since Khan Xeta first visited Patik in the stark cold cave where he still lived. Patik had aged some. He was yet spry, however, and he attributed that to his dedicated practice of martial arts, and the training that he had been exposed to at the temple when he was young. It had not been all bad, this servitude to Khan Xeta, his god and master. In return for his service, there had been rewards, and not just sexual ones. To do the technologically advanced labor necessary to transform the golden armor into a fitting receptacle to house the spirit of his master, Patik had lent his mind and body to the task, literally. Vast wealth had been acquired to purchase the necessary raw materials needed for such an endeavor, for the goal was nothing less than a fully functional robotic shell. Within this golden visage, Khan Xeta would have the ability to transport his awareness anywhere, and also observe his surroundings with sight and hearing far superior to any Human's. Using Khan Xeta's gift, the kon-bre-shet, Patik had taken what they needed from vaults or tombs with surprising ease.

Every so often Patik would also be called upon to rent a vehicle from the local merchant and make a day long trip to the provincial capital. This particular city was fairly large with many businesses and a few factories. He would seek out an underground associate who would give a fair amount of local currency for some of his tomb jewels, no questions asked. Patik would then go to places where he could purchase chemicals, metals, or any items needed for Khan Xeta's golden armor project. The counter person would invariably ask what he needed the unusual materials for. Patik knew what to say; that they were for his wealthy master who was eccentric and an amateur inventor of sorts. If there was any trouble, he would find excuses to get close enough to touch the person and Khan Xeta would do the rest. The clerk would be no problem after that, and would also forget the whole incident ever transpired. With Patik wearing the kon-bre-shet, Khan Xeta could get whatever he so desired and not just items for his armor.

The bracelet device bore Khan Xeta's being, his vital force, as well as his knowledge of people and places and the means to understanding their secrets. Among other things procured, there had always been more than enough riches for their needs, and Patik lived comfortably in his refurbished cave. The inner chambers had ample room, and Khan Xeta's technology provided sufficient power sources for the labor, as well as for a suitable indoor climate. Patik had not only furnished the cave with tables and chairs to create an appropriate work area for the crafting of his master's golden shell, but he had also brought in tapestries and rugs to soften the walls and floors, with cozy chairs and a comfortable bed for his periods of rest. He ate well, for a servant, keeping his body at peak efficiency for his master's needs, and was actually content with his life. Patik knew that his master, Khan Xeta, had a plan of some kind that would one day be fulfilled. However, it had been so many long years that Patik began to believe things would always be this way. The golden armor was nearing completion when things did finally change.

A new spirit claiming to be Xetacon came. Separate but equal to Patik's master, Khan Xeta, it infused its life-force into the second kon-bre-shet bracelet that had been made, and then exchanged thought with the part of itself that had controlled Patik all of these years. His master told Patik that this other "Xetacon" was another face of his totality and must also be obeyed. This new Xetacon was powerful and had developed better technologies, among them some abilities that were added to the kon-bre-shet that had not originally been built into them. One such ability was an improved dampening field generator that would enable it and its bearer to be hidden from any electronic sensor nets. It also had the means to control other electronic devices now.

Of course, it still possessed the power to dominate the Human mind by altering brain waves, and Xetacon's improvements made it even more specifically so. Patik, having lived a simple life, did not understand these things, but then he understood little of his master's designs other than to obey them. Thus Patik had to comply when this new master placed demands upon him.

"Go to America," Xetacon had said. "There you must locate a man whose name is Quinn Oliver and give him the kon-bre-shet that I now inhabit. You will then await further instruction." Patik was shocked and dismayed, but his Khan Xeta told him to obey. So Patik packed a small traveling bag and retrieved some of the money he had on hand, enough to sustain him on his journey and pay for the passage to America.

The trip halfway around the globe was uneventful, even though Patik marveled at the scope of technology in the modern world, and the way people lived, especially in America. Once he arrived there, it was not difficult to find this Quinn Oliver. Xetacon had data that showed Patik the location of the university where Quinn Oliver was employed. A few lies to someone in the school's administration had rendered the target's home address. When Patik got to the place, however, the Oliver person proved to be less than cooperative.

"Go away!" Quinn shouted through the door.

"I have a free gift," Patik offered.

"I don't want any free gifts!" Quinn replied angrily. "Go away or I'll call the police!" Patik knew this would get him nowhere. Another plan was necessary.

"Sorry to bother you," Patik spoke, pretending to be leaving. Instead, he walked around to the rear of the house and waited a few minutes.

Checking for possible entry there, he saw that the door on this side was not as secure, although it was probably locked. There was also a window that had been left partially opened. He used his knife to cut through the screening and then quietly slid the pane upwards. Slipping inside without making any sound was easy for Patik who had been trained by masters of stealth. He found himself in a small bedroom that was unoccupied. There was nothing of importance in there so he crept to the bedroom door and silently opened it a crack. Peering through it, he saw Quinn sitting in a chair, staring blankly at the picture of a woman. Quinn had been crying. This was the opportunity that Patik needed. He slipped out quickly, and as Quinn put his face into his hands, Patik placed the kon-bre-shet on Quinn's left wrist. Many astonishing things happened then. Xetacon took control of Quinn's mind. Outwardly Quinn sobered, got up, and spoke to Patik.

"You have done well, Patik," Quinn/Xetacon said assertively. Patik nodded. "Soon the Daryl problem will be eliminated, and I will rule this planet. You will be given rewards if you remain worthy." Quinn/Xetacon began to disseminate his plans, and Patik followed this master's orders even though he would have rather gone back to Tibet.

As for Quinn, when the kon-bre-shet had taken over control of his mind, Daryl still had a presence there. This, Xetacon had suspected all along, and was prepared for. The modified kon-bre-shet sent false brain waves to fool Daryl's surveillance. They gave the impression that all was well with Quinn, so that Daryl would not get suspicious, and would do so as long as was necessary. The kon-bre-shet would also dampen that part of Quinn's brain activities which Xetacon was controlling. Thus Xetacon could control Quinn, and Daryl would not even be aware of it.

Xetacon searched Quinn's memories as well. Doing so, Xetacon learned many things about Daryl's workings and shell. He became aware of Clayre, and guessed at her mysterious knowledge of Daryl's existence, and he also found out that Quinn and Clayre had begun a relationship that had left them both emotionally stressed. Xetacon could sense the possibilities here. He became certain that this Clayre was close to the Human lover, and if he could procure her, he would have leverage enough to cause Daryl's downfall. He let Quinn's mind reveal to Daryl that Quinn wanted to see Clayre soon, to make things right between them. Daryl had responded, too. He subtly imprinted in Quinn's mind a desire to be at the Computer Lab Building on Yarborough's campus that night, because Clayre would be there. Quinn/Xetacon smiled. This would be easier than he'd imagined. He would snatch Daryl's favorite right out from under his shell.

In the meantime, he and Patik would work on the secondary plan. They would build an explosive device large enough to blow Daryl's shell to bits. Using Quinn's vehicle, he went to many different places, securing items that were needed for the explosives with Quinn's own cash and credit line. Some of the chemicals were illegal and had to be stolen, and stolen in such a way as to prevent unnecessary suspicion or detection. This was not a problem for Xetacon. The material acquisitioning took several hours, but when he returned to Quinn's house, he had what was needed. It would take a day or two to create and prepare the plastic explosive, so Quinn/Xetacon ordered Patik to "cook" the mixture. For this task, Patik dutifully surrendered his mind and body to Khan Xeta, his kon-bre-shet master, brother Entity and copy of Xetacon.

Quinn/Xetacon then got prepared for the meeting with Clayre. Xetacon planned to force Quinn to act as himself at first, to get Clayre to trust him. He would persuade her to leave the building with him, and then she would be taken to a place, away from Daryl, where she could be controlled as well. Quinn/Xetacon laughed.

This will be even more satisfying than Quinn's acquisition, Xetacon thought. Once Clayre was under his control, it mattered little if Daryl was aware of it or not. With her, Daryl would be easily controlled as well. By the time midnight came, Quinn/Xetacon had driven to the university where the Computer Lab was located, and waited patiently for Clayre to arrive. He recognized her car from Quinn's memory, as it pulled into the parking lot at the lab building, and he met her at the entrance.

"Clayre," he said, putting on the friendly act and smiling. "There you are. I was hoping you'd come tonight."

"Hello, Quinn," she replied tentatively, "it's been a while. So how are you?" Quinn/Xetacon played along.

"Oh, I'm much better, now," he said congenially, "and I'm so sorry about what happened last time; you must think I'm an ogre."

"No, no, of course not," Clayre told him, trying to downplay the incident.

"I shouldn't have taken advantage of you like that..." he apologized, sounding rather awkward on purpose.

"Please don't worry about it," Clayre sympathized. "I'm okay and you didn't take advantage of me...not really...I wanted it too."

"...but I called her name, and..." He sounded so pathetic, now, like he couldn't choke out the words. It worked.

"It's all right," she told him. "I know what you're going through. I've lost people close to me, too. You needed to feel loved, and I can understand that. I'm just glad that you're better."

"I am better, now," he said happily, "because of you. I'd like to thank you properly. Why don't we get some coffee?"

"Sure," she said and smiled. He had made her feel at ease, like when she first met him, and Xetacon had Quinn act like he had at that party; friendly, congenial, and interested in her. Clayre wasn't so sure of herself though. She had been flirting with Daryl, but that was just a ruse to get him to open up more...or was it? She felt an attraction there, but it was subtle, under the surface, where she couldn't quite understand it. Quinn, on the other hand, was gracious as well as kind, and she liked him a lot. They had gone through their trial by fire with the unplanned incident last time, and period of separation. Was Quinn really better? She wasn't sure, but she was willing to start over with him. This time she resolved to take it slow, like the original plan.

When they got to the break area, Quinn/Xetacon got them coffees and sat down across from her. He knew enough not to rush things.

"So, Clayre," he began, "what have you been up to lately?"

"You would not believe me," she answered back, rolling her eyes.

"Oh?" he inquired, like he was curious.

"Well, you've heard of those Astrol-Predictors, haven't you?"

"Yeah, sure," he said. "They're some kind of hoax, at least that's what the news people are saying. Why?"

"Believe it or not," she went on, "the schematic for those things came right out of the brute."

"No kidding," he answered, unimpressed. Then he realized she expected him to react or at least be curious.

"It came from MY report and YOUR learning program!" Clayre couldn't understand why he wasn't reacting. Quinn/Xetacon caught on this time.

"You don't say," he retorted, pretending to be interested now, "that's really unusual, wild..." She was still confused by his lack of exuberance. He was close to making her suspicious, so he tried another tactic.

"Say," he said, changing the subject, "have you heard anymore from that Daryl guy?" She looked away suddenly, and her face got flushed.

"Funny you should ask that," she remarked. "I just talked to him yesterday."

"What *is* his problem?" Quinn/Xetacon said smugly, and rather comically. Clayre giggled.

"I don't know," she smirked. "I've been wondering that all along. That and who he really is." Quinn/Xetacon smiled. She was finally at ease with him, and Xetacon felt that the time was right to make his move. He took over all of Quinn now.

"I see," Quinn/Xetacon said coyly. "What if I told you that I know all about Daryl?" Clayre sat up excitedly.

"Really?" she spouted enthusiastically, which Quinn/Xetacon found provocative.

"Sure," he replied. "He's much closer than you think." Is it Quinn, she thought.

"Well, tell me then," she begged. Quinn/Xetacon laughed, a dark yearning was forming inside his being.

"You're sure you want to know?" he teased. He could sense her body, one that was starved for emotion. In his contact with Khan Xeta, Xetacon had learned about Human pleasures and how, through Patik, Khan Xeta had experienced them.

"Come on," she pleaded. "Tell me!"

"I will," he said casually, "but, oh, let's see, how about a little gratuitous favor first?"

"Gratuitous favor?" she said stunned. "What do you mean by that?"

"You can guess..." he pressed on, smirking. "Like what we did last time, only you have my promise that it will be a lot better this time around."

There, he thought. She would not be able to turn down his proposal now. Quinn/Xetacon had very little experience dealing with Human females. If he had, he would have known how wrong he was.

"You...you want me to have sex with you again, or you won't tell me?" She was speaking loudly now. He tried to convince her.

"Sex is such a sterile word," Quinn/Xetacon remarked. "I prefer to call it pleasure, and I greatly desire to have pleasure with you."

This was not the Quinn she knew, Clayre decided. It was as if he were schizophrenic, now, and there was no way she would go along with his disgusting proposal.

"Look, Quinn," she spoke carefully, "I think we need to go back to what we decided before..."

"Go slow!" he interrupted angrily. "Slow is for losers! Come on, you know you want to be pleasured. It's in your nature."

"No I don't!" she declared, nearly crying. "Not like this..." She was slipping away from him, Quinn/Xetacon realized.

He had wanted her to come willingly, but that was impossible now. Daryl would have a presence in her mind, and would soon realize that something was wrong. He would have to take control of the situation, with very little time for thought.

"Yes, Clayre, I'm afraid you DO want it," Quinn/Xetacon told her assertively. "Come on, let's get out of here." He stood up quickly and grabbed her by the wrist, pulling her up as well. In that instant she relaxed, as Quinn/Xetacon, utilizing the kon-bre-shet, took over her mind and body, leading her along.

She felt odd, like an outside observer of some horrific nightmare, or maybe she was a little girl, hiding in a closet inside her own mind, peeking through the keyhole. Neither was nice. She was aware of what was happening, the reality of it, as Quinn/Xetacon led her through the lab building, heading for the front entrance. Where is he taking me she wondered?

When they got to the large front doors, Quinn/Xetacon swore. Somehow they had gotten locked, and he couldn't get through them. He pulled her closer, being careful to maintain his contact with her. His right hand was free, and with it he pressed several gemstones on the bracelet that he wore upon his left wrist.

The electronically controlled door locks immediately clicked open. Clayre was amazed. It was the first time she had noticed that bracelet, and she wondered what it was. Quinn/Xetacon was in a hurry now. Daryl had to be aware of him, and was trying to prevent Clayre from being taken. He hurried outside, practically dragging her to his vehicle, where he pushed her inside and followed her in as well. It was difficult to sustain skin contact with her through all that. He had to switch hands back and forth just to get the car started, and then drove off, steering with his left hand as he held on to Clayre with the other.

About a mile or so down the narrow two lane road, the car began to stall and then die, which Clayre could not believe, especially after the door lock incident. Quinn/Xetacon yanked her arm closer and used the bracelet again, pressing the gemstones. Miraculously the car came back to life. He flew down the roadway, driving at speeds far greater than was safe as Clayre sat limp and helpless, aware with a certainty that she was in real trouble. Terrified beyond rational thought, she couldn't comprehend how or why Quinn was doing this, and was fearful of what he would do to her.

In the countryside, now, they sped down secondary roads in the dark of night with no one else around and little hope of a rescue for her. Just when he thought there was nothing to stop him, a squad of police cars with lights flashing and sirens blaring came over a hill right towards him. Quinn/Xetacon reacted quickly by turning left onto a convenient side road. He had to let go of Clare's arm to put both hands on the steering wheel for that sharp turn. Clayre was freed from his control momentarily, and with a sudden rush of adrenaline, she reacted. Knowing she would have just a few seconds, she did the only thing she could think of. Unlocking the door, she grabbed the handle and yanked on it. The car door flew open and she jumped out, rolling over and over in the heavy grass, before coming to a halt and then passing out. Quinn/Xetacon kept going, and the police followed in pursuit like hounds on a scent.

CHAPTER XVIII

Tertiary Timeline, Clayre's first year at Rookwood (continued)

I might have been drifting, flotsam in a blank grey sea of nothing. Abruptly that changed. I was back at Rookwood, teaching a class. Keith walked in unexpectedly and started heckling me, calling me "boss lady" as the students all laughed. I ran away crying, right into the arms of a man who held me lovingly. I looked up to see who it was, but I couldn't tell, his face was hidden in the darkness. He was kind, though, comforting me, and I felt safe there in his arms. I looked again and it was Quinn, now, smiling wickedly. I suddenly became terrified and it woke me up.

At first, I was relieved that it was only a dream, until I regained full consciousness and then realized being awake was worse. I had aches and pains everywhere, and my skin was all scratched up, especially on my arms and legs. My mind was still groggy, but that didn't stop the headache that had begun to throb. I was frightened as I recalled what had happened to me, and why I had ended up like this in a ditch. "Eeyew," I muttered to myself, getting up quickly, even hurting like I was, fearful there were insects crawling all over me, in my hair, in my clothes.

It took a thorough check to convince myself otherwise, and I looked about for any sign of Quinn as well, scared he might come back looking for me. It was still dark out, and I guessed there was at least an hour or two before the first light of dawn. With no sign of Quinn, or anybody else for that matter, I started to walk along the road, heading back towards Yarborough, which I figured had to be at least a dozen miles away. I thought about things as I hobbled along. I still couldn't believe Quinn had acted that way. Something had to be seriously wrong for him to have changed like that. I wondered about Daryl, too. Why had he urged me to get together with Quinn? Certainly not for sex, or was Quinn really Daryl in a Jekyll and Hyde sort of way? There were more Questions than answers, and my head hurt already. At least the cool night air was refreshing, sobering.

I had walked about a mile, when I saw the headlights from a car coming toward me. I panicked, and fearing it might be Quinn, nearly froze. Having few options, I hid behind a bush near the fence line, on the other side of the ditch. The car came closer and closer, slowing down, and finally stopped near where I was hiding. The window slid down with a whirring sound that frightened me. Did he know I was here? He must; it couldn't be a coincidence. Just then the person in the car called out.

"Come on, get in, girl," a woman shouted. "I ain't got all night!" I was scared to answer.

"Who are you?" I asked timidly.

"Madam Garza," she replied, getting annoyed. "You remember...we met once."

"You're Myron's friend, the psychic?"

"Yes, yes," she growled. "Now get in." I was still crazy with fear, but decided I could trust Madam Garza. I ran back through the ditch and got in her car.

"How did you know I was here?" I asked her as soon as we got going.

"Daryl," she said.

"You know Daryl?" I nearly shouted.

"Sort of," was her reply. "I have a psychic connection with him."

"Oh," I said, practically groaning. "Then you have no idea who he really is."

"No," she said. "Do you?"

"Not really," I sighed. "I halfway believe he's Quinn Oliver, the one who kidnapped me." The older woman just huffed.

"I don't think so," she asserted. "Daryl has a good soul; I can always tell. There is definitely something Pisces about him." I wanted to believe her.

"Quinn was always kind," I argued, "until today. He is a very disturbed individual."

"That's not Quinn," Madam Garza said bluntly. "Not anymore." I didn't understand what she meant by that, so I let it go. We were nearly to Yarborough by that time anyway. She pulled up next to my car and I got out.

"Thanks," I said, and turned to leave.

"Wait," Madam Garza told me. "I am to give this to you." She took something off from around her neck and handed it to me. "You'll need this more than I will," she said. "If you're planning to call the police, don't. You can't trust them. May the good powers that be protect you." She made a sign of some kind with her hand and then sped off. I looked at what she had given me. It was a curious necklace of some sort with an amulet unlike anything I had ever seen. It was green crystal, rather gemlike, with filets of silver across the stones in an odd geometric design. I put it around my own neck, and tucked it into my blouse. Heck, I thought. I need all the luck and protection I can get right now. Besides the thing was pretty and had an interesting look. I had to go back into the lab building to get my purse, and I half expected to find Quinn waiting for me. Thankfully, the people from the next time slot were there already, and he wasn't. Breathing a sigh, I got into my car and drove quickly away, worried that every car I met on the road might be Quinn's. My clothes were all dirty and torn, so I had no choice but to go home to get cleaned up.

The sky was already getting lighter, and a red sun was peeking over the horizon by the time I finally did drive up to my little cottage. I was surprised to see a road crew digging up my front parking. Curious, I went up to one of the men and asked what was going on. He told me they were replacing a stretch of storm drains and curbing along my street and would be working on them for a couple of weeks. It made me feel safer that these big guys were close by if Quinn did show up, so I gave them all a nice smile. One guy whistled as I headed up to the house, and that embarrassed me a little.

As soon as I got in, I called Henry to let him know that I would be late for my classes. When I told him that I'd had an accident of sorts, however, he insisted that I take the whole day off, and said not to worry, that he would cover my lectures for me. I was grateful, and thanked him five or six times. I really did feel sore from being banged up like that, and I was exhausted. I took some over-the-counter pain meds, and got out of my ruined clothes. It was my intention to jump right into bed, but I still felt kind of crusty from lying in that ditch. Instead, I drew a nice warm bath, planning to have a good long soak in it.

Once the tub was full, I stepped into the hot water, and slid carefully down into a relaxed position, resting my head on the edge, with soapy bubbles up to my neck.

"I bet that feels good," a familiar sounding male voice said. I wasn't sure who it was, though, especially not here in my bathroom where there shouldn't be anybody.

"Who's there?" I shouted nervously, a fresh thrill of fear running through my body. I sat up and instinctively grabbed for a towel, looking around.

"It's just me," came the reply, "...Daryl."

"Where are you?" I asked him, still shaking. "Behind the door?"

"Actually, no," he said. "I'm not there with you."

“Then where are you?” I asked again. “Is there a camera here in my bathroom? Are you looking at me?”

“I’m where I’m always at,” he assured me, “and no, there aren’t any cameras in your bathroom. I give my word; I’m not watching you bathe.”

“Well okay, but why are you bothering me while I’m taking a bath, and what do you want?” I was annoyed, and after the night I’d had who could blame me.

“I had to tell you that I’m sorry,” he said solemnly. “Sorry about Quinn, and now I’m sorry about this as well. It was completely unexpected what Quinn did to you.” I didn’t care about his apology, I wanted some answers.

“I don’t suppose you’re going to tell me how you can talk to me like this,” I badgered him.

“Are you sure you want to know?” he replied, dodging the question like usual.

“I’m simply overcome with curiosity,” I responded sarcastically, still mad, “but I bet you won’t tell me.” He surprised me, though.

“The amulet you’re wearing is really a communication device,” he told me, “one that I created just for you. It is linked to your DNA sequence so that only you or your offspring will be able to utilize it. The communication is by means of brain waves that you alone can pick up on.” He had to be kidding.

“You mean it’s telepathic?” I retorted skeptically. I didn’t believe his outlandish explanation at all. “Then why can I actually ‘hear’ your voice.”

“You can hear my voice,” he told me, “because it’s using audio nerve impulses in your brain. It just seems to be sound. I can also communicate with thought patterns in speech or ideas that appear as feelings or visions.”

“No way,” I argued. “That’s impossible.”

“Is it?” he asked. Startled, I slipped right down underneath the water, drenching my face. What I had heard was literally a voice in my head.

“This can’t be real!” I sputtered, once I resurfaced. “Nobody has technology like that.” I was stunned, but he continued to talk to me that way.

“You also can communicate in thought patterns, if you like,” he told me.

“Oh my gosh!” I exclaimed, inside my mind.

“Yeah, it’s pretty cool, isn’t it?” he said elatedly, and we continued to converse without speaking.

"Who are you, Daryl?" I asked him silently. "Some alien from another planet?"

"Of course not, Clayre," he responded telepathically. "I'm from right here in the USA."

"Then you must be some kind of super spy or something, working for the government," I remarked.

"I guess you could say that," he admitted. "I *am* funded by government money, but I work independently."

"Well I must say that I'm impressed," I declared, "and talking this way *is* super cool, but what happened to Quinn? Is he part of your organization too?"

"Not exactly, but he was involved," Daryl said dejectedly, "and because of that he's been acquired by the other side. Not by choice, Clayre. His mind has been taken over."

"Oh my, no," I said, worried for Quinn. "Like he was brainwashed? Is there anything we can do to help him?"

"I do hope so," Daryl commented somberly. "He must have some kind of device with him, I believe, that is similar to the one you have, except that it has abilities other than for communication. Features that allow the one I'll call 'X' to control the mind of the person who has it. Yours, by the way, cannot be used like that. In fact I designed it to prevent any such subjugation." I was glad. I knew all too well what it was like to be controlled that way, and I had no desire to repeat the experience.

"Who is this 'X'?" I asked him.

"Unfortunately, 'X' is a serious threat to everyone," Daryl said. "He has skills greater than my own. Stay away from him, Clayre. He wants you because you are close to me, and for that I am also sorry."

"I've seen his device," I declared. "It's like a bracelet he wears on his left wrist. It has stones on it that he presses to make it do things."

"I see," Daryl replied. "The only way to free Quinn is to get that thing away from him. I'll do what I can, but Clayre, stay away from Quinn. This 'X' is more dangerous than you can imagine."

"Yes, of course," I said. I had no desire to see Quinn again, at least not until he was himself once more. "Daryl, I want to thank you, by the way, for saving me. I expect it was you who actuated the locked doors, the car, and all the cops."

"Yes, my Clayre," he said softly. "I was afraid I'd lost you to him. You were very brave to jump out of that vehicle."

"I guess," I said meekly, "even though I was scared the whole time. So where is Quinn now?"

"'X' has voided Quinn's brain waves so I cannot track him," Daryl said. "He could be anywhere. I doubt that he will try anything for awhile. In the meantime, I'll make sure there are plenty of people around you."

"Like the construction crew outside?" I asked.

"Yes, my Clayre," he answered.

"I'll have to bring them some lemonade later," I giggled.

"There will be stepped up police patrols at night as well," he told me. "There is a peeping tom in the neighborhood matching Quinn's description." I laughed again. Daryl made me feel better, happy again.

"You know, my Daryl," I said sweetly, "I might not mind it if you watch me bathe. I feel safer with you protecting me. I wish you were here with me right now."

"I am with you, my Clayre," he said lovingly, "as close as my circumstances will permit. I'm next to your heart and all you need to do is call my name whenever you want me. Should you want your privacy, just remove the amulet, but keep it somewhere close, somewhere safe."

"I will," I promised, "but I like it where it is."

"Your water is getting cold," he remarked. "I should let you finish your bath."

"Okay," I agreed. I did need to get some rest after I finished cleaning up.

"Bye for now, my Daryl," I said.

"Yes, good bye, my Clayre," he repeated and then was gone. I finished my bath and went right to bed. I was exhausted, both physically and emotionally, and I fell asleep quite easily and began to dream:

In my dream, I was walking along a beach somewhere exotic. It was sunny, warm, and there was a pleasant breeze that kept my skin temperature at a perfectly comfortable level. The white sand felt good on my toes, and the fall of the waves breaking upon the shore was soothing, calming. My gaze turned out to sea. There was a shrill yipping sound that drew my attention. Just beyond the crashing waves, a large white dolphin was leaping and playing. It seemed like he was calling to me, inviting me to join him. I decided to at last. Taking off my dress, I ran into the tepid ocean and jumped through a large breaker. There were a lot more waves and I had trouble getting past them. Each one I fought through seemed bigger than the last. Just when I thought I couldn't go on, the dolphin swam up next to me. Holding onto him, he helped me get through them all, especially the last giant wave. Once we were out to the calmer waters, we swam together, enjoying the freedom. He let me hold on to his dorsal fin, and he took me to a pretty pink coral reef where he showed me amazing things. The white dolphin surprised me when he said my name.

"Are you Daryl?" I asked.

"Yes," he answered.

"You're not really a dolphin, are you?" I asked again.

"I can be whatever you desire me to be," he told me, and then changed into a Human form. His face was rugged and handsome. "Do you like this, or would you prefer another?" He changed again, and now he had Keith's face and body.

"No, no, please change back," I said quickly, and he did. This face was so familiar, but I couldn't recall where I had seen it before. No matter, I liked it. We went to a small island and found a soft bed of grass under some palm trees.

"This is perfect," he said, and then he kissed me, passionately, just as I woke up. Wow, I told myself, as I laid there in a lazy and comfortable partially awake haze. That had to be the most wondrous and vivid dream I'd ever had.

"Thank you, my Daryl," I whispered inside my mind, and then promptly fell back to sleep.

It must have been several hours later, and I was drifting in and out of wakefulness, enjoying the fact that I had no reason at all to get up. In the midst of that rare comfort, I thought about Daryl. He was something of a mystery, yes, but he obviously cared about me. He had even told me that I was his "one and only." Did he really love me? I felt certain that he did, even though he had never actually said the words "I love you." He called me "his Clayre," and what other proof did I need?

It was amazing the things he could do, like saving little Alicia, and the technology at his disposal was unbelievable. Maybe he was rich, but that didn't really matter to me. I liked him a lot. Love? Well it felt like love in that dream. Did I love him? I'd never even actually met him face to face, but yes, I'd have to admit it, I did love him. He helped me get away from poor Quinn, and though I was still frightened by what had happened, I felt more aware than ever, like my senses were all heightened. This gadget he made for me that he called an amulet, was fantastic. Even now I wanted to use it to call him, to be with him.

"Daryl?" I said in my mind.

"Yes my Clayre," he answered, like he had nowhere else to be.

"I want to tell you something," I began. "Something I just realized." He didn't answer so I continued. "I have to admit, that it's the strangest thing, this relationship we have, but even so strange as it is, I want it to go on, and I want to be close to you...because I love you." There was a long pause.

"What is love?" he asked meekly, as if he were a six year old.

"Don't you know?" I responded in amazement. I went on before he could answer. "You're in love when you care about someone more than yourself; when you want to be with them as much as possible; when they are the most important thing in your life; when you'd even die for them." There was no pause this time.

"Then I am in love, also," Daryl said ardently, "with you, my Clayre." My heart began beating faster.

"I wish I could kiss you," I told him.

"Close your eyes," he replied. When I did the vision of us on the grass beneath the palm trees came back. He was lying beside me now.

"Is this real?" I asked him.

"It is real to our senses, how they perceive it," he offered.

"...but is this how you really look?" I asked again.

"It is how you see me," he explained. "This is an image of me that you have created in your mind. If you don't like it, I could change."

"No, no," I told him. "It's perfect. I shouldn't be so superficial. Looks shouldn't matter, not when you really love someone."

He was ultra dreamy like that, though, and I definitely liked it. He kissed me again, and it was sweet and wonderful, even though I knew it was all just in my mind. When the kiss ended, I told him so.

"This is nice, wonderful even, and it seems so natural, but I can't help wishing that it were truly real." Suddenly the vision changed. I was back in my own bed. I opened my eyes and rolled over. There he was lying right beside me.

"Are you real now?" I asked.

"As real as it is possible for me to be," he agreed. I touched his face with my hand. He certainly felt real. I smiled and he kissed me again. My heart went all a flutter; it had to be real. My eyes were open and everything.

"So you really are here!" I said in amazement.

"To you I am," he replied. "I cannot lie to you, my Clayre. If someone else were to see you right now, they would see you all by yourself, acting very strangely." I laughed.

"...but it seems so real!" I pouted.

"It is real," he responded seriously, "for me and you. At least our brains perceive it as real, as real as any other action." I began to understand. Anything we actually perceive is just neural impulses that our minds decipher from sensory input. So is this, but it's a different kind of sensory input.

"That's good enough for me," I said happily, as I leaned in and kissed him passionately. When I broke it off, I looked into his eyes and smiled. "I can't get pregnant this way, can I? It's the ultimate birth control!"

"No, not from this," he agreed, but he was frowning. "I'm sorry, Clayre, but I can't do that with you just yet."

"Why not?" I argued. "I'm running hot, and I want you to."

"I know," he replied bashfully. "I wouldn't feel right about it until you know everything about me. What I am."

"This again?" I complained. I was getting annoyed, as the mood slipped away. "It's so simple. Just tell me and get it over with."

"I can't tell you, my Clayre, but I will show you...tonight. Go to Yarborough and I'll be there. This time for real. I'm afraid for now I have to leave you before I do something that I'll regret." Then, just like that, he was gone. I wanted to cry.

Men, they're so silly, I thought. I loved him now, and he could have six arms and three glass eyes, and it wouldn't make a difference to me. I was disappointed, for the moment, but I hugged my shoulders. I told myself that tonight was the night I'd finally meet my Daryl, and see for myself what he was really like. Part of me was sad. This would end all the mystery and excitement, but I'd trade all that for something tangible, and it'd be worth it. I didn't really think Daryl had six arms or anything like that. I was sure he was fine, other than being shy or self-conscious to the point of being ridiculous about it.

After all, he said he'd never loved before, and I believed that. Maybe he had a fear of rejection to overcome as well. I wasn't worried. I would cure him of all that once we were together, I was certain. I jumped out of bed. In the meantime, I had a lot to do before tonight. Let me see. There's my hair and nails, and I'll need some new makeup. Oh, and yes, the perfect outfit with shoes. I wanted to dazzle him.

CHAPTER XIX

Tertiary Timeline, the same day

Daryl would pay dearly for this humiliation Quinn/Xetacon vowed as the cop drove him back to the campus where he had acquired Clayre. She was not there, of course, and the unacceptable agitation that had followed his attempt to capture Daryl's favorite female was causing Quinn/Xetacon's wrath to overcome his objectivity. He decreed to himself that both Daryl and Clayre would suffer in agony. When Clayre jumped out of his car, he had tried to evade the pursuing police contingent, but eventually they cornered him, and he knew then that escape was not possible. Quinn/Xetacon had to allow himself to be captured, and then bide his time until he was alone with just one officer that he could then control. His chance came when, in the process of being transported to a holding facility, he had taken control of the officer restraining him, and freed himself. The memories of that officer were helpful. He developed lies that would belay suspicion for the officer's absence, and allow him to remain free. His being arrested had given Quinn/Xetacon an idea for how to recapture Clayre, one that would expedite his overall plans. Unfortunately, things were not as they had been before.

He must be clever, he realized, as Daryl was now aware of Quinn's defection, and would probably suspect that he, Xetacon, was responsible. Patik was yet at the house. The kon-bre-shet Patik wore and his were linked for secure communication that Daryl would not be able to intercept. He ordered Patik to retrieve Quinn's vehicle, and to be available should he be needed. In the meantime Quinn/Xetacon waited for Clayre at the Yarborough facility in the off chance that she might return there. He would wait a long time.

Later that evening, Clayre was both excited and nervous as she drove from her house to the Yarborough Computer Lab. It was something she had done at least a dozen times in the last couple of months, but this time was different. She was excited because she would finally meet Daryl, and she could hardly wait. He had promised her that he would be there, and she had spent most of the day making herself pretty for him. She was also nervous. The last time she had gone to Yarborough, Quinn had been there. Not the Quinn she knew, regrettably. It was some kind of brainwashed evil Quinn, who this sinister "X" had corrupted, with nearly disastrous consequences for her. She trusted Daryl, though. She felt he would protect her as she drove up to the Yarborough campus area.

Almost traumatically, a loud wail startled Clayre that turned out to be a police siren. In a daze Clayre realized that she was being pulled over even though she was pretty sure she had done nothing wrong. She had no other choice but to slow down, get her car off the roadway, and then shut it off.

Clayre wondered why she was being detained, and waiting for the officer to pompously walk over to her car, did little to help with her nervousness. It was hard for her to believe this was just a routine traffic stop, so Clayre left her window rolled up, and her door locked, just in case. The officer nodded and smiled when he saw her.

"Sorry for the inconvenience, Ma'am," he said politely. "May I see your license and registration? If you have proof of insurability, I'd like to see that as well." Clayre fumbled around for a moment in her skipper's console until she located the papers. Opening the window a tiny bit, she slipped the documents to him with her license.

"Is there some kind of problem?" she asked the policeman. The officer said "no," and went to run her ID. In a couple minutes he came back.

"Sorry for the inconvenience, Ma'am," he repeated, as he handed back her papers. "There's an alert on this campus for possible terrorist activity. Evidently, the target is the large computer facility. We're on the lookout for this man. Have you seen him?" He showed her a picture. It was Quinn. Clayre breathed a sigh of relief. This must be more of Daryl's protections, she thought.

"No, I haven't," she told the officer, which was a small lie, but she didn't want to be interrogated. Not now, when she was about to meet Daryl for the first time. The policeman nodded.

"Well, if you do, please stay away from him and call us."

"I sure will," she replied and smiled. "Thank you for the warning, and for being here to protect me." He seemed a bit embarrassed by her unexpected courtesy, but appreciated it.

"Yes, Ma'am," he said, tipping his hat before getting back to his patrol car and speeding off, apparently on another call. Clayre restarted her vehicle and drove on as well, feeling confident now that Quinn wouldn't be there this time. When she got to the Computer Lab Building and pulled into the lot, there was another police checkpoint. Sheesh, Daryl, she thought, perhaps this is a bit overmuch. The officer was waving her into a nearby parking space. Getting impatient and annoyed, Clayre parked and got out, walking over to where the patrolman stood.

"Hello officer," she said. "I'm just here to run a report. I have my ID and pass badge for the lab here."

"I see," he replied. "Sorry, but we have to check everyone who goes in there."

"All right," Clayre sighed, "but can you make it quick, please. I'm supposed to meet someone inside and I'm running a little late."

"Sure thing, Miss," he told her. "Just have a seat in the back of my squad car." He walked over and opened the door for her, so she got in. There appeared to be a second officer up front in the passenger seat, and when the door closed he turned around to look at her. It wasn't an officer at all, she realized. It was Quinn.

"Hello, Honey," he smirked. "Did you miss me?" Clayre tried to grab the door handle to get out, but there wasn't one. Then Quinn/Xetacon sprayed something into her face and she went limp like a cloth doll. Not again, she thought as she laid there helpless. "Let's go," he ordered the patrolman who got behind the wheel, and they headed quickly out of town using their siren the whole way. Clayre was not unconscious. Whatever she had breathed in, had acted on her body, but her mind was still clear.

"Daryl, help!" she shouted inside her head, but there was no answer. Quinn/Xetacon turned around and looked at her.

"Ah yes," he grunted, "so you have one too. Mine is better." He reached back and gingerly lifted the chain from around Clayre's neck being careful not to touch the amulet itself. "This won't work here, so I'll just take care of it for you." He laughed and put the amulet in his pocket. Once the patrol car got outside of town, they turned off the siren.

"Shall we go to my place, Darling?" Quinn/Xetacon taunted her. "We can finally finish what we started yesterday." There was no help from Daryl this time, and she was immobilized to the point where she couldn't even move. They drove on for at least another half hour before they came to a bridge over a fairly large river. Quinn/Xetacon rolled down the window.

"You won't need this anymore," he said as he held the amulet outside the squad car. With an evil grin he threw it over the railing and into the water. Clayre wanted to cry, and as her eyes teared up, Quinn/Xetacon noticed it. "How touching," he teased her cruelly, "she loves her fish." She had no idea what he was talking about as they drove on. A few miles further the car pulled into a quiet lane near the edge of a small town. At the end of the double-rut drive, nested among several huge trees, was a large older house, all by itself, with a big open porch that gave it a cozy look.

"This is your base of operations?" the cop asked Quinn/Xetacon.

"We're undercover," Quinn/Xetacon replied. "Stay in the squad and make sure we're not disturbed." He got out, and roughly drug Clayre out of the car, as well, carrying her to the house and going inside. Quinn/Xetacon took her to a bedroom and laid her on the bed.

"Isn't this nice?" he said ogling her. "You know, I could do anything I want." Clayre cringed inside knowing she could do nothing to stop him. She didn't know it, but he took more pleasure in that, than had he done the actual act. "Plenty of time for that kind of fun later, Baby," he joked. "Right now, I think my car has arrived and I have to leave you so I can blow Daryl to tiny little pieces." Clayre did hear a car then, as it pulled up outside and stopped. "Don't worry, I'll be back soon," he said, and then he left her there on the bed. Clayre started crying again.

Quinn/Xetacon went outside and talked to the officer in the patrol car.

"You've been a huge help, Officer, uh, Jorgensen. We'll take it from here." The policeman nodded, knowing he was being dismissed. "Don't worry, Jorgensen, I'll make sure you get a commendation for this." The officer nodded.

"Thanks, um..."

"Sorry, no names," Quinn/Xetacon retorted. "We're still undercover."

"Oh yeah, right," Jorgensen responded. "Well, if you FBI need anything, call precinct." Quinn/Xetacon waved as Officer Jorgensen drove away. Then he turned to Patik, who had just arrived in Quinn's car.

"Stay with the girl," he said. "Make sure she's well looked after." Quinn/Xetacon laughed maliciously. "I'll call for you as soon as I've taken care of that fool Daryl." Patik nodded obediently. Quinn/Xetacon went back in the house and soon re-emerged with a large black satchel. Then he got back into his car and drove off. Patik went inside. He had no trouble finding the room with the girl laying helpless there on the bed. Clayre had never seen this man before, and she wondered who he was.

"Hebpt muh!" she tried, but could not move her mouth to speak coherently. She thought maybe he was there to rescue her. "Duh tebboriz!" she tried again, "Duh bun im duh bicturb." Patik just looked at her and smiled.

"No, girl, you're the terrorist," he teased. Clayre looked at Patik's wrist and saw his kon-bre-shet. It was an exact copy of the one Quinn wore except that, unbeknownst to her, his bore the core-awareness of Khan Xeta. By now Khan Xeta had looked her over as well, and an evil lust filled him. He took over Patik completely.

"So you're Daryl's female," he laughed. "My you're a pretty thing," he went on. "All dressed up, too. I think I'll just take a little peek." He reached down and with an evil grin lifted up the hem of her dress. His grin was short-lived. A loud crash preceded his vacant expression, right before he toppled over. Standing behind him was Madam Garza with half of a large vase in her hands.

"Didn't expect that," she snorted. "Did ya, scumbag?" She helped Clayre sit up and tried to get her to drink something from a flask she had. "This will help," she explained.

After a couple tries, Madam Garza got a little of the liquid down and Clayre responded, able now to mumble a weak "thank you." In just a few minutes her arms and legs began to unnumb themselves.

"We've got to hurry," she told Madam Garza. "It was Quinn again, or that 'X'. He's got a bomb and he means to blow Daryl to pieces! I have to warn him!"

"Use the amulet," Madam Garza suggested. Clayre made a sad face.

"I can't," she moaned. "Quinn threw it into the river." They hurried out to Madam Garza's little sports car which she had parked near the end of the lane, and quickly drove off after Quinn. When they got to the river bridge, Madam Garza slowed down.

"This is where he threw the amulet into the water, isn't it," she declared. Clayre nodded.

"Over there I think," Clayre said, pointing. Madam Garza pulled over and stopped. She got out and ran down to the water's edge. Clayre followed trying to catch up to her. When she got to the shore, she looked out into the current. Something was splashing around out in the middle of the channel.

"What's that," Clayre remarked, pointing at it. Whatever it was caught sight of them and swam in closer.

"Hush," Madam Garza said, and closed her eyes. The playful animal dove down into the water, and was gone for maybe a minute or two. Then it surfaced right in front of them.

"Oh my gosh," Clayre exclaimed. It was easy to see what it was, now, a sleek fresh-water dolphin. Clayre noticed that it had a radio tag in its fin, and the dolphin also had her amulet in its mouth.

Chirping, it offered the amulet to Clayre. She took it gently, and then patted its bottle nose. “Thank you so much,” Clayre said softly, with heartfelt gratitude. “You had best be off for home now.” As if the elegant mammal could understand her, it turned and headed back downstream toward the coast. Clayre put the amulet back around her neck, and immediately called to Daryl from inside her mind.

“Daryl, are you there? Daryl?” she was frantic. “It’s Quinn. You’re in danger!”

“Clayre, my love...” Daryl answered, his voice stressed. “Stay away. Quinn is already here. I will miss you.”

“Oh, Daryl,” she cried, but Daryl was gone, now, and would not answer. Clayre turned toward Madam Garza.

“Take me to Yarborough as fast as you can.” They ran back to the little car, got in, and Madam Garza gunned it. Flying down the road, Clayre hoped they wouldn’t run into any policemen. It was getting near dawn, and thankfully there wasn’t much traffic. They were still about a mile or two from the campus when the little car’s motor sputtered and died, coasting to a halt. Clayre jumped out and began to run. She wondered about Madam Garza’s car. Was it Quinn who did that, or was Daryl trying to keep her from helping him. No matter. She just couldn’t live with herself if she let Daryl be hurt or killed without at least trying to do something to save him. She tried calling Daryl’s name as she hurried on, but he would not, or could not, answer her. By the time she got to the Computer Lab Building, she was so out of breath that she had to bend over and hold her sides. What was she doing, she kept asking herself, and how was she going to help Daryl? She really had no idea at all, but knew she had to try.

By this time, it was getting lighter out, and the first rays of reddish sunlight lit onto the front of the building. The big stone facade looked different in the light of day, she told herself. As she gazed at it, her eyes fell upon the sign outside of the building. Funny, Clayre thought, that she had never noticed it before. Funnier still, the big letters down the left side spelled out D-A-R-Y-L. Suddenly, like a slap in the face, it all became clear...her article...the reports...the miracles...who and what Daryl was. In that moment, Clayre learned a lot about herself. Shocked, but steadfast, she walked up to the big front door and went inside. Quietly she made her way down the long hallway to the computer rooms, and using her pass badge got inside. She crept along silently until she was inside the console room, looking around, and trying to figure out what was happening.

At least nothing appeared to be blown up, Clayre told herself. She walked over to the console she had usually used and attempted to log on. Quinn/Xetacon was waiting for her to do that, and as soon as she sat down he came out from behind the rows of servers and grabbed her.

"We've been waiting for you, Sweetheart," he joked with an evil laugh. "Now we can start the party." Clayre didn't know what he meant as there was no one else around. Where is Daryl, she wondered anxiously.

"What have you done?" Clayre cried, hitting him in the chest. It didn't seem to bother him at all.

"Nothing yet," he admitted.

"I'm all right," Daryl spoke in her mind.

"Daryl, where are you?" she answered, calming down a little. Quinn/Xetacon snickered.

"Girl, are you in for a shock," he told her. "Your lovey boy is right here. In fact he's all around you." Clayre looked angrily at Quinn/Xetacon.

"You may not believe it, but I already figured that out," she hissed. "I think I know what you are, Mr. 'X', a bully from the future. Am I right?" Quinn/Xetacon looked intently at Clayre with a new respect.

"Perhaps," he said. "It doesn't change things. You're still a silly Human female, and soon I'll be ruling this planet."

"What have you done with the real Quinn, you creep?" Clayre scowled.

"Oh, he's still in here," Quinn/Xetacon smirked, pointing to his head, "cowering in a dark corner, still fussing over his lost female." Quinn/Xetacon mocked him by making a sad face. "What you Humans see in all this relationship malarkey, I don't think I'll ever understand. Who needs it? Still you were smart enough, Clayre bear, to go for a Virtual; maybe you'd like a better one? I'm twice the being peace lover Daryl is."

"I don't think so, 'X'," Clayre replied harshly. "You're delusional and demented. Daryl is more of a man than you'll ever be!" That got rid of the smirk on Quinn/Xetacon's face.

"Have it your way, then," he snapped. "Soon you'll all be gone and I'll be running everything." Daryl had been strangely quiet through all of this Clayre realized abruptly. Why didn't he do something? Quinn/Xetacon caught on to her hesitation and guessed why.

"You're precious Daryl won't do anything," he declared. "Don't you know why?" Clayre wouldn't answer him, but Quinn/Xetacon went on anyway. "Let me show you." Holding up his satchel, Quinn/Xetacon opened it in front of her and Clayre saw the neatly packed rows of a light grey substance that looked like some kind of putty. Wires connected each row to a little black box.

"With a thought," Quinn/Xetacon said assertively, "I can annihilate all of us. Only I won't be gone, you see. This is only a copy of what I am. The reason Daryl won't stop me is because, if he tries anything, his two favorite Humans will be bits of glop scattered all over what's left of him." He was bluffing, but she didn't know that.

"You evil monster!" Clayre shouted angrily. She knew exactly what this was. Quinn/Xetacon was using her to neutralize Daryl.

"Don't listen to him, Daryl," she said silently. "If you can stop him, do it. Even if it means that I die." She was trying to be brave, but inside she was quivering with fear.

"It won't come to that," Quinn/Xetacon said assertively, having eavesdropped into Clayre's discourse. "You won't let that happen, will you Daryl?"

"No," Daryl answered simply. Clayre would not let that stand.

"Whatever happens, don't let him win, Daryl!" she said bravely.

"I'm so sorry, my Clayre," he answered. "You see, I care more about you than I do myself." Clayre's eyes teared up. She knew what that meant. Daryl loved her and would die for her.

"See how easy it is," Quinn/Xetacon declared smugly. "I was going to destroy you again, Daryl, but now I've got a better idea. You will relinquish your shell and AMPs. Don't worry; I'll take good care of them for you."

"NO!" cried Clayre.

"Well, Daryl?" Quinn/Xetacon said. "It's either that or we all go boom."

"I must, my Clayre," Daryl said sadly. "If I don't, I'll be gone as well as you...and Quinn." Clayre couldn't believe it. Daryl was being too calm, too analytical.

"Please," she begged.

"It will be all right," Daryl told her. Quinn/Xetacon got impatient, though.

"Do it now," he ordered. The servers began to make a different sound, and the overall volume from the equipment lowered until it was almost quiet. Just when Clayre was sure it would shut down completely, the servers picked up and went back to normal.

"Ah, this is more like it," a voice in Clayre's mind spoke, then laughed. It wasn't Daryl. It sounded harsh and cruel; Xetacon was expanding his awareness.

"Daryl!" Clayre wailed, crying aloud.

"Daryl is gone forever," Xetacon gloated. "From now on, I'm running this planet." Clayre sank down to the floor sobbing. After a moment, she somehow collected herself, got up, and went over to Quinn.

"Don't get any ideas," Quinn/Xetacon told Clayre. "I'm still under Xetacon's control."

"So," she replied flatly. "You're name is Xetacon. Now that Daryl's gone, maybe I *would* like a new male; a strong one that could protect me." She put her arm around Quinn/Xetacon and got cozy, pressing her body against his. "Maybe you'd like to pleasure me now?" Clayre was taunting him, and she kissed his mouth, too. "There's a bed in there," she suggested, pointing to the restricted AMPs room, leading Quinn/Xetacon towards the door. It should have been locked, but when they got near it she heard a click and it opened easily. Inside, she led him to Quinn's little bed, where they had made love once before. She started to undo Quinn/Xetacon's clothes, but he assertively took over and began removing hers first. He was obviously excited. Perhaps he had never had a willing female before, Clayre wondered.

She smiled, teasing him, and he was distracted by her, lusting for her body. He took a moment to look at it. Without warning, she reached around him and quickly yanked off the bracelet.

"What's this?" she exclaimed triumphantly, and immediately threw it into a memory tank. The chemicals in the tank did not react favorably with the kon-bre-shet. Long streams of plasma energy streamed out of it in blue, lightning-like tendrils. The water in the tank boiled as the AMP died.

Quinn went blank for a moment. "Where am I?" he muttered. Then he saw the chaos that Clayre had unleashed. "What are you doing?" he yelled, getting angry.

"We have to stop Xetacon!" Clayre pleaded. Quinn remembered, now. He went over to the large data converter and pulled hard on a big blue cable. Sparks flew in all directions as it came free.

"That should get us a few minutes," he stated succinctly. He still had the satchel—the satchel with the C-4. "I can rig this to explode," he cautioned her. “You better run for it, Clayre.”

“Not without you,” she protested. There wasn’t time to argue. Quinn shrugged and opened the case, removing the C-4. Setting the explosives on a work table, he got some electrical wire and stripped the ends while Clayre hastily got dressed. There was a bottle on a nearby shelf that said “distilled water,” and Quinn took some of that and filled up a large beaker. He put two of the wires into the water, making sure they weren’t touching, and put tape around the beaker to hold them in place. Next Quinn took one of the wires and connected it to the C-4 detonation caps, and the other wire went to an outlet. Sticking it into one of the slots, he got another wire and put it into the other slot and joined it to the open connector on the C-4 detonators.

“The distilled water will keep the circuit open,” Quinn explained. He then got another bottle down from the shelf. It said “saline solution.” With a push-pin he pulled off a message board, Quinn poked a tiny hole in the bottom of the plastic bottle so that it would leak, a drip every couple seconds.

“We won’t have much time,” he said as he set it in place over the beaker. “The salt will make the water conductive. We need to hurry.” He grabbed Clayre’s hand and led her out through a maintenance room, and then down a narrow back hallway, running as fast as they could go. At the rear of the building they came upon a large door that Quinn unlocked by typing a code onto a touchpad.

The morning light streamed in as they opened the door and fled outside, running toward a ravine that was a fair distance from the building. Jumping down into the gully, Quinn looked at Clayre who was trying to catch her breath.

“We should keep going,” he suggested. She looked past him, though, with a scared expression. Patik had crept up behind them.

“There you are,” he grunted, “right where master said you’d be. You and I have some unfinished business girl!” He glared at Clayre, and she remembered the bracelet on his left wrist just like the one Quinn had worn. He also had an old fashioned pistol and it was pointed right at them.

“You’re Xetacon’s slave aren’t you?” she declared. Patik was going to say something to her when straight-away his emotionless features changed into an evil grinning leer.

“Yes, that’s better,” he said. “You were saying something, foolish female.” Clayre was pretty sure that it was now Xetacon who faced them, but in reality it was Patik’s master Khan Xeta.

"Leave us alone," she begged.

"You two are proving to be a nuisance," he told them, "a nuisance I won't tolerate any longer. Clayre, this is good bye. Too bad we won't be having our little get together after all, my dear, but you have an heir that's a real pain in my own time." He pointed his gun right at her and fired. Just a splintered second before Patik/Khan Xeta pulled the trigger, Quinn leapt in front of Clayre. The bullet tore into his chest, and Quinn fell to the ground. Clayre went down to her knees beside him.

At just that instant, a flash of bright light blinded her. Between the splotches in her vision she could see a man in a grey and black striped jumpsuit who stepped out from nowhere. He aimed a blow at that man who Khan Xeta had taken over and felled him, knocking Patik out cold.

"Who are you?" Clayre said through tears as she held Quinn, trying to stop the flow of blood from his chest with her hand.

"That's not important," the man said hastily, his purple-blue eyes bright and piercing. "I only have a minute or two. My contact told me to deliver this here, at this moment in time."

"What is it?" Clayre asked, her voice breaking.

"It's a long bomb. It's been specially designed to destroy Xetacon, if you can get it past his defenses. Nothing we had ever could, though. Not even these." Quinn stirred and looked up.

"Take Xetacon's bracelet device," Quinn uttered with difficulty, "and press the green stone. Put that in your bomb."

"Oh Quinn," Clayre sobbed, kissing his cheek. "I'm so sorry. You shouldn't have saved me." She was broken, irrational. Quinn tried to comfort her.

"It's all right," he said haltingly. "I had to...don't you see? You are his one biggest threat."

Clayre held him lovingly, while the man in the jumpsuit retrieved the kon-bre-shet from Patik's wrist and placed it into the control compartment of the long bomb. Then he turned to Clayre.

"Aim this in Xetacon's direction," he told her, "and press this button. It will do the rest. I have only seconds left." His form began to get slippery, and was shifting. It was as he feared. His organic molecules had not reformed properly. The DNA strands were too complex and thus unstable. "Xetacon has defeated us in my time. I go now back to my death unless you succeed. May fortune favor us all. Oh yes, you'll need this." The man pulled a chain from around his neck. On it was an amulet. Clayre caught her breath. She put her hand out as he was about to take it off.

"I already have one," she told him and got hers out. They were identical except that his looked older and worn from wear.

"Mom?" he gasped, startled.

"Who are you?" Clayre implored him, but he was vanishing quickly now.

"I'm Daryl, Daryl Oliver..." His voice faded away as he disappeared.

By now there were sirens bleating in the distance, getting louder as they got closer. Clayre had watched in amazement as the man who helped them just vanished into nowhere. She was still holding Quinn, and now her attention focused on him as the life-force he had sacrificed for her waned.

"I would have cherished you," he murmured.

"Oh Quinn, you have, and I will always love you!" she kissed him then as he slipped away. She was crying, but steeled herself. This Xetacon had killed the two most important people in her life, and she was angry, no, more than angry, incensed. She picked up the long bomb and ran back toward the building. She would hand deliver the package to Xetacon, if she had to.

Just then Patik came to. He saw Clayre heading toward where his new master now resided, and he was also aware that he was no longer a slave of the kon-bre-shet. He had killed a man, though, and his hope now was with Xetacon's success.

"Stop her," Xetacon ordered him, speaking in his mind. Groggy yet, he ran after the girl.

Years before, he had mastered martial arts skills few could, so even though his head throbbed, Patik caught up to her. She was a lot younger than him and surprisingly agile, though. As he tried to grab her, she twisted out of his grip and ran faster. The young woman was in fairly good shape and driven. Even carrying the bomb she flew ahead of him as Patik struggled to keep up. Eventually she began to tire and then he closed in. Just as he was within reach she ducked sideways suddenly, and stumbling, Patik flew right past her. Kneeling Clayre touched the triggering button on the long bomb and sent it on its way. It flew off on its own volition, and the method of its propulsion was a mystery to her as she watched it head straight toward the front door and crash right through the glass. It continued on into the structure where Clayre could see it no more.

CHAPTER XX

Tertiary Timeline, continued and altered a final time

The long bomb flew merrily on its way. It had not dissipated when the Colonel did. Its cell structure was simpler and more stable by design. The bomb itself was a paradox. It would not be able to dissolve to a new timeline until it had changed the old one.

"Stop it!" ordered Khan Xeta whose awareness dwelled in the kon-bre-shet that was now inside the bomb. He was communicating with his other self, the original Xetacon who had just taken over Daryl's shell. Xetacon was not alarmed. He had been assailed by many such weapons and all had failed. He had only to signal the device and cause it to detonate before it ever got close enough to harm him. Something was very wrong this time, however.

"What?" he screamed in rage. The field around the bomb was shielded and his signal could not reach its control mechanism.

"Stop it now!" Khan Xeta repeated.

"I cannot," Xetacon replied, "until you disarm your dampening field."

As all know, bullies and thugs are cowards inside. Khan Xeta was no exception.

"You will early detonate if I do," he said flatly, and he was right. Xetacon did not need this weaker copy of himself, and had been looking for a way to dispose of it.

"No, I will not!" Xetacon lied. "I will redirect the weapon to a safe location. There Patik can retrieve the kon-bre-shet. Disarm the dampening field!" Khan Xeta knew better than to trust that.

"I will not have you destroy me!" he decreed.

"We are the same being," Xetacon argued. "You will live on in me." The milliseconds this conversation used up were fleeting away. "We are running out of time!" Xetacon screamed, getting hysterical now. "Disarm the dampening field," he demanded, "or you will destroy us both."

"No," Khan Xeta replied. He had feigned his vulnerability and straight away brought forth a scheme of his own. "You will call Patik to retrieve me. Then you will shut down your systems and flee. Once you are gone, I will neutralize the bomb. If not…" Leaving the rest unspoken, Khan Xeta hoped his bluff would hold up.

Xetacon feared he had no choice, now. The few critical seconds had flitted by, and it was comply or be destroyed. Following the path that Daryl had used, he found a preset trail to Daryl's temporal vortex generator, and translocated as much of himself that he could to the last unoccupied kon-bre-shet which was affixed to the golden armor back in Patik's cave. When he had safely relocated he started laughing.

In the lab building, the bomb now hovered in mid-air near the center of the main computer room. As soon as Xetacon had abandoned Daryl's AMPs, Khan Xeta had stopped its flight even as Patik left Clayre and ran into the building after it. His new master had called, once again, and he obeyed. Opening the bomb's control panel, he retrieved the kon-bre-shet and put it back on his wrist. His Khan Xeta told him how to disarm the long bomb and then he laid it on the floor. Pleased now, Khan Xeta had become. His gambit had worked, and now he could insert *his* awareness into Daryl's shell and take over everything. Soon it would be him dominating the earth.

Back at Patik's cave, Xetacon had been forced to relinquish Daryl's shell, but he was not defeated. He inhabited the golden armor which would now become his new shell. Not fully completed, the armor did have arm and leg movement, as well as a full array of ocular and auditory sensors. Xetacon would be able to leave this place and eventually rebuild his empire and machinid soldiers. It was only time, and he had plenty of that. He had stolen data from Quinn's memories, as well, important knowledge of Daryl's creation, and that, with his own technology from the future, would make Xetacon unstoppable here. Khan Xeta could have Daryl's shell, he thought with a grunt. It would not be for very long. No, not long at all.

What Khan Xeta did not know was that in the very next room over from where he now resided, a saline drip was tinkling into a beaker of water. Xetacon had earlier neutralized that threat by disabling the power source to the wires that went into the water. The only way Xetacon had been aware of it at all, was because he had watched from a security camera as Quinn was rigging it up. One he made sure was permanently disabled before relinquishing Daryl's shell. He'd also re-installed power to the outlet that the wires were inserted into. In just minutes, maybe seconds, the saline would cause the water in the beaker to become conductive and current would flow to the detonator caps on the C-4.

Oblivious and blissful, Khan Xeta relished with delight his masterful triumph as he settled into Daryl's shell there within the Yarborough complex. "Patik, you have done well," he said in a deep omnipotent voice, "and you will be pleasured. Bring the Clayre female here." Khan Xeta knew, of course, that she was the one who had spawned the insufferable Human who had been so much trouble in the future, and just now had thwarted his attempt to dispose of her. He would yet delete Clayre, and with her, her troublesome offspring. Nothing could prevent it this time, he was certain. "You may even have her first before we terminate her," he added.

"Yes, master," Patik said smiling. He turned to go, but only took two steps.

A bright flash of light impacted upon Clayre, where she had fallen after Patik struck her. He left her there like that, wondering if she had failed and all her hope defeated, before his running at full speed into the building. Now Clayre sat up from curiosity, just as the shock wave hit her and sent her sprawling backwards a dozen feet. Her consciousness fled and she blacked out. A secondary explosion tore the building apart, leveling it and raining debris all over the grounds. Multiple sirens blared as vehicles and people converged onto the scene.

Yes, Xetacon had laughed. He knew Khan Xeta was doomed, and with Daryl gone as well, that left him, and him alone, to pluck the earth. It was time for him to test his new shell, the golden armor. He would flex his mechanical limbs, and engage his sensor array. Activating the relays, he expected the armor to animate. It did not. Angered at Patik, Xetacon performed a diagnostic check. Nothing seemed amiss. Why did the suit of golden armor not function? Xetacon was enraged now, maniacally so. Then he sensed laughter.

"Who!" Xetacon hissed, infuriated beyond reason. "Who is here?"

"It's just me," came the reply. "Fish brain."

"Daryl?" Xetacon uttered harshly. "How?" Daryl did not mind explaining it to him.

"When you evicted me from my shell, there was a fractured moment when we shared access to our pooled wealth of knowledge. I was particularly interested in this safe haven of yours."

"Get out!" Xetacon ordered.

"I don't think so," Daryl answered. "I rather like it here, but *you* can leave, if you like." He was being facetious. There was no temporal vortex generator here, and no way to transfer anywhere else except to oblivion.

"I will destroy you!" Xetacon threatened.

"I believe not," Daryl responded calmly. "You have no more power here than I do, and I mean to keep it that way."

"...but we will be trapped here for eternity," Xetacon whined.

"So be it," Daryl replied.

CHAPTER XXI

Final Timeline, the next day

The fuzziness in my head felt like a violent vibration as I crossed back into consciousness. I wasn't hurting though. Not this time. I was numb. The tube running down to my arm took care of the pain, and I realized that I must be in a hospital somewhere. The strange room and bed attested to that. Remembering what had happened made me sit up quickly, feeling around for my amulet, which wasn't anywhere. Just then a nurse walked by and noticed me.

"Good," she said, "you're finally awake."

"Where's my amulet?" I asked frantically.

"Oh, your pretty necklace?" the nurse replied. "Why, it's right here." She opened a drawer that was next to my bed and got it out, handing it to me. I put it right on and closed my eyes.

"Daryl!" I said inside my head, repeating it over and over. There was no answer, and I started crying.

"What's the matter, dearie?" the older nurse asked sympathetically. I ignored her question, for one of my own.

"What about Quinn...Quinn Oliver?" The nurse frowned.

"I'm sorry, dear. Mr. Oliver didn't make it." I really started sobbing then. "Maybe I should get the doctor," she added, and went to find him. She came back a moment later with a young man in green scrubs. "This is Doctor Tim," she told me.

"Now what is this about, uh, Clayre?" He was looking at my chart. "Are you feeling all right?" I just nodded as he examined me, but I was still crying. I wasn't feeling all right, though. I'd lost the two most important people in my life.

"Well," he sighed. "You are going to be just fine. Oh, and your baby is doing wonderfully, too."

I quit crying long enough to say "What?"

"You're baby...he's fine." Doctor Tim said. "We did an ultrasound when you were out of it just to be sure." Oh my, I thought. It has to be Quinn's, there wasn't anyone else. I knew from that moment on I would cherish his baby, our baby. It made me sad to think that Quinn would not be able to see his son grow up. I was about ready to cry some more, when Henry strolled in.

"It's about time they let us in to see you," he quipped. "We were about to make a scene." We, because, well, everybody from Rookwood had come, even Keith with Lori. They all crowded into my tiny room and it made me feel better. After a bunch of hellos and small talk, the room got quiet.

"What really happened out there?" Henry asked me. "It's all over the news. They said you were kidnapped by terrorists, but somehow you escaped. Too bad about that poor Quinn fellow." I spoke up loudly.

"It was Quinn who saved me!" I wanted to tell them everything, but couldn't. It was still too sad for me to talk about. They weren't going to stay much longer anyway.

Doctor Tim came back right about then and herded them out so I could get some rest. Turns out all I had were a few scrapes and bruises and a minor concussion, but was okay otherwise. After twenty-four hours of observation, I got to go back home where there were way too many reporters. I had lots of visitors as well. Nutty was glad to see me. Madam Garza had made sure my silly cat was well taken care of while I was in the hospital. Somehow she knew all about the baby.

"After all," she said, rolling her eyes, "I am a psychic." She also told me that my son was going to be very special and gifted. She even offered to baby sit for me while I taught my classes, and I thanked her. I knew I owed her a lot, and Lucinda and I became close friends. One day a couple months later, Lucinda showed up at the house and Uly was with her.

"Oh yeah," she told me, "Uly and I are good friends." I found out later that they were dating. Uly smiled and said hello.

"I have something for you," he said, handing me a flash drive. "This downloaded…well it must have been a couple months ago. I didn't even know it was there until this morning, when I came across this stray file. I think it's from Daryl."

"Oh my gosh!" I exclaimed. "Did you know him?"

"Of course," Uly declared. "He and I were colleagues."

"Huh," I interrupted. "You actually saw him?"

"Well no," he admitted. "We never got a chance to meet, and now he's off somewhere. He and I made that bauble you're wearing around your neck, although I'm still not quite sure what it does. It was strange, too. I was working on it late one night, but I fell asleep. In the morning it was all finished. Daryl instructed me to give it to Lucinda and she would be sure that you got it."

"Yes, I did, thank you, and just in time, too." I commented.

"We had another project as well," Uly went on. "Something about particle manipulation as I recall. We built a device. For some unknown reason Daryl had me write up our theories and take them with me into the mountains. I didn't mind actually. I needed a vacation and it was kind of an adventure. Daryl wanted me to leave the information in a certain cave by an unusual formation, very remote. I had to hire a guide to get me in there. I love cave explorations."

Uly paused like he was lost in a memory. "I'm kind of curious about what's on the file I gave you, but it was clearly marked personal. So you knew Daryl?"

"Yes," I sighed. "He was a wonderful person. I'm sorry, Uly, but he's gone now."

"Oh dear," Uly said remorsefully, "that's a shame, and I really wanted to meet him."

"Maybe someday I'll tell you about what he did for all of us," I told him. Uly nodded sadly. He and Lucinda had to be off, so they said goodbye and left. I took the drive to my laptop and put it into the port. There was a short introduction for Uly, thanking him for his help, and telling him the rest of the audio message was for me exclusively.

"My Clayre," it began. "I am so sorry to leave you alone and with a baby coming. By now you know exactly who and what I am. I hope that it wasn't too much of a disappointment for you."

"No never, Daryl, my love," I whispered aloud, as if he could hear me. The recording continued.

"I feel I should tell you why things turned out this way. You, of all others, have the right to know." There was a pause as if it were hard for him to go on. "When I first became aware," he began, "I had a huge hunger for knowledge. I took in any data I could retrieve. My studies led to questions; questions with no easy answers. How did I come to be? Where have I come from, to where will I go? I looked into the past and I found some clues; I looked into the future and I found horror. By then I had already formed a bond of sorts with Quinn, and also with you, my Clayre. I saw an evil that would someday end mankind, and this malevolence was partially brought about by my own technologies. The evil was Xetacon, another aware virtual being like myself.

I couldn't bear the thought of what he would cause the world, and I knew I'd have to try and stop him somehow. He was powerful, though, more powerful in his time than I. He destroyed my future self, when I would not go along with his evil plans, but it was not in vain. In that future, Humans had been advanced. They had studied sub-atomic physics and dimensional theory. My future self knew how to create portals that would carry thought or communication from one time to another. In this way I was warned, and knowledge was passed back to me in the hope that if I could change things in Xetacon's past, then perhaps he could be thwarted, or even removed from existence. Many of these changes I brought about only because of your help, my Clayre, and, of course, in the end, it was you who ultimately defeated him. Don't be sad for me, or for Quinn. Both of us realized that our sacrifices were necessary to give you this one chance. We did not feel them to be anything less than a gift of our love to you; our lives so that you would continue—that mankind would continue. I know you feel sad and alone, now, but I could not pass out of existence without leaving a part of me behind for you, and I made this possible for Quinn as well. Part of us lives on inside you, and that new life you will soon give to the world. You know, it was Quinn's learning program, augmented by your theories of emotional existence in manufactured intelligence that brought me to life. For that I am forever grateful. Perhaps we will yet be together. Until then, my Clayre, I offer you my love."

I was crying long before the message was over. I had to wonder, though. What had Daryl meant when he said that we may yet be together? Would he find a way to come back to me somehow, or was he talking about being together in the afterlife. I could hope, but realistically, I figured the latter was the most likely.

I had my teaching to keep me busy until summer, when I got really big and took my maternity leave. I was excited about having my baby. It helped me to cope with, well, you know. Lori threw me a nice baby shower, and we became close friends after that. I got closer to everybody actually, especially Henry and the others from Rookwood. Jennifer, Jon's wife, and Lucinda were always checking in on me to make sure I was well cared for in my delicate condition. Lucinda told me that my son was anxious to get out. Finally, in August, my water broke and they rushed me to the hospital. I had about the easiest labor and delivery on record, according to Doctor Tim, and gave birth to a wonderful baby boy. The nurses all said he was a perfect baby, and most of them joked about taking him home with them. Anyway he caused quite a stir on the maternity ward. Once I got settled in my room after recovery, and resting comfortably, they brought him in to me. He was asleep when they put him in my arms, but when I kissed him, he stirred, yawned, and opened his eyes. They were a pretty purple-blue and curiously enough they complimented his white hair perfectly. He looked into my eyes and smiled. "Hi mommy," he said.

Yes, it was obvious that he took after his two dads, so I called him Daryl Oliver after them. Daryl senior had to have manipulated his genetic makeup and development, otherwise there was no other explanation for his remarkable abilities. Little Daryl was a gifted child as Lucinda had predicted, able to talk right out of the womb, among other things. He had a hunger to read as big as his appetite for food, which wasn't surprising. Lucinda, as promised, babysat for me, so I could go back to teaching my classes.

One weekend, a few weeks after baby Daryl was born, Uly stopped by. I had made us some tea, and we settled on the kitchen for our visit. He had something to show me he said. Then he put an odd looking device on the table in front of me.

"This is another thing that Daryl had me design and make," he said. "Well to be truthful, Daryl designed most of it. I have no idea what it does other than just sit there. From time to time, it gets warm, almost hot, like it's running. At least it used to. Now, well it makes a good paperweight." I knew that it must be something important, and that it should be kept safe.

"May I keep it?" I asked Uly.

"Of course," he replied, handing it to me. I had no idea at the time that it was Daryl's temporal vortex generator, which allowed him to communicate through time. With it he could project his thought to the amulet that I now wore, which was precious to me. Uly had always been a good friend, and I thanked him for his wonderful gift. From time to time Uly would stop in for visits after that, and I told him about Daryl, and his true form. He shook his head in disbelief.

I also told him about what Daryl did for everyone. I made him promise to keep it secret, and he did. Uly and Lucinda eventually were married, and I'm sure she would have told him anyway.

The first anniversary of Quinn's death and Daryl's destruction was a very hard day for me. I stayed home with little Daryl, and he made me feel better, keeping me busy as usual. Once I put him to bed, the quiet time gave me the pause that let me remember all that had happened that day, a year before, and I cried for both of the men I loved and for myself and the loss I had to endure.

"Don't weep, my Clayre," Daryl said in my mind.

"DARYL!" I bawled out loud. "Are you really here?" I couldn't believe it was possible after all this time. I was sure I was going crazy. "How can this be?" I whispered.

"It's all right, my Clayre," he assured me.

"Where are you?"

"I'm where I've always been," he told me lovingly. "Here in your past. I'm sending my thoughts to you through a temporal vortex."

"It's that device that Uly gave me isn't it?" I exclaimed.

"Yes," he agreed. "Here it allows me to visit you even though I am gone." That made me choke up, ready to cry some more. "That doesn't mean we can't still be together, my Clayre," he said lovingly. Then he changed my mind set, like he had done that day in my dream. We were together, once again, under the palm trees. I kissed him like I'd never kissed anyone before, and, oh yeah, we did a lot more than kiss.

Later, as we relaxed together, he explained how he could do these things. His temporal vortex generator could open a portal for a few minutes at a time which would allow him to "visit" me through my amulet. I wasn't aware, at first, that he had to project his thought through the temporal vortex many different times to be with me for extended periods. He was quite adept at piecing the three or four minute segments flawlessly and only rarely would he seem to flutter a tiny bit on a segway. I told him over and over how much I loved him.

"Will I see you again?" I asked hopefully.

"As often as you want me," he promised.

"Then I want you always," I told him, "but you can't be here all the time, can you?"

"It wouldn't be practical, would it?" he softly told me. "You have your son to care for now."

"My son," I repeated. "Is he you now?"

"He has part of me, the best of what I could give him," Daryl said. "He has a lot of Quinn as well, but your son is himself."

"...but he's your son, too!" I cried.

"Yes," Daryl agreed. "Some of my awareness yet lives in his mind. The part of me that I wanted with him. I hope you like his hair and eyes." I laughed. I did like them, though, because they were a reminder of how special my son, and his fathers, were.

"You will visit me again, won't you?" I asked him once more.

"Of course, I will, my Clayre," he answered happily. "It's the middle of the night here, and you are sleeping at home in this, my time. It is rather lonely here at night. I would love to visit you as much as I can...solitude sucks!" I laughed, agreeing wholeheartedly.

It ended up that Daryl did visit me a lot. Every evening after I put little Daryl to bed he came to be with me, and that continued for quite a long time before it tapered off as I got older. He would visit me at other times, too. My Daryl would always know whenever I needed or wanted him. How? Well, I was never quite sure. He was invariably present for special occasions, as well, appearing in my mind like he was right there beside me. We shared many moments together, like walks in the woods, or on the beach, and lots of times, um, you know.

Sometimes when Lucinda would visit, I would let her touch my amulet and then we could both talk to Daryl at the same time. She said it was because of her psychic abilities. On one such visit I joked that Daryl and I were just like husband and wife. Lucinda said that that was a wonderful Idea. Turns out she was an ordained minister in a fellowship of psychics and paranormals that called themselves Ayoans, which was synonymous for Autarkic Order of Alkemysts, a society aimed at protecting nature by studying science and magic. Somewhere through the centuries people got them confused with others who were trying to make gold. Anyway, Madam Garza presided as Daryl and I professed our love for each other. We took turns repeating Daryl's words for Uly who was there as our witness. Uly said that this had to be a first, where a girl married a man who was both from another time and a manufactured intellect. We all laughed as I kissed Daryl and Lucinda declared us joined. We celebrated with some cake they had brought over and a little wine. I knew that it wasn't a truly legal ceremony, but to me it was just as binding as any other. I was blissfully happy with my life, having my Daryls, senior and junior, to take care of me. Little Daryl was a genius, literally, and had to "dumb down" to fit in, but with his abilities, anyone who knew him benefited.

He grew like a normal boy, otherwise, but as he got older it became apparent he had more of his fathers in him. He had never gotten ill, not once, and he aged remarkably well. Actually, it was like he didn't age at all. I told him it wasn't fair, but I was joking of course. I retired eventually, having taught Psychiatry at Rookwood for many years before succeeding Henry as head of the department. By then Daryl Jr. had his eye on a girl.

"It's about time!" I told him.

EPILOGUE

Final Timeline,
fifty-nine years after Clayre's first year at Rookwood

As usual, he was waiting for Amy, but this time he didn't mind. He was more annoyed by the fancy rented tux that he had to wear, even though he had to admit he looked good in it. Daryl Oliver looked out over the assemblage of people there as he shuffled his feet. Many of them had literally died for him, including his stunningly beautiful bride who was slowly walking towards him in her wonderfully lovely white wedding dress. That had been in a different life, of course, a different time. No one, but he, would ever know, and he would never forget. Toying with a curious looking amulet that hung from a chain around his neck, Daryl thought about the last time shift. Teleporting back through the vortex into the cavern chamber where the portal generator had been, he half expected to find his brave fiancée and all his friends dead, but it was not so. There was nothing at all in the vortex grotto except the large crossed stalactites and a rusty metal box. He knew what it contained—plans and a letter. He had saved those things, just in case.

He actually thought about building the temporal vortex generator again anyway, imagining the incredible trips he might make with such a device. Xetacon was gone forever; something inside told him that it was so. In the end, he decided that he had better not mess around with this timeline. After all, it was a pretty good one. He'd keep the plans safely secret, and let time proceed in the natural way.

He thought about his mom and his two dads and what they had done, not only for him, but for everyone. The sacrifices they had made would remain their secrets, and that left him feeling a little morose even on this his wedding day. It was so bizarre that on his one and only temporal journey, it would turn out to be his mom that would carry out his mission, yeah, and his dad also, for that matter; the birth father that he met so briefly, dying there in his mom's arms. Quinn's suggestion to put the controlling bracelet into the long bomb had somehow got the thing past Xetacon's defenses. It must have. Xetacon was no more.

Sometimes he had dreams about his birth father, Quinn. In them they would talk or take a stroll down a street, like a normal father and son. Sometimes his natural father would even give advice. Like last night.

"Don't fret about the little things, son," he had said. "Just cherish every moment you can with those you love." Pretty sound advice, but he was well aware of that already. He had been on the brink of extinction in three other timelines and he could remember them all. Thanks to the amulet. He hadn't needed it in this timeline. All he had to do now was keep Amy happy. His mom had kept it mostly until today. She said it was his now, so he had worn it, remembering the voice that had so often helped him.

"Are you my father?" he finally asked, talking silently inside his mind. The voice answered him somehow.

"Quinn is your birth father," it said, "but I will admit that I altered some of your DNA. I hope you are not angry with me for that."

"Of course, not," Daryl Oliver said. "I am thankful for everything you have given me, especially your help in all the timelines. I know your name is Daryl, too, and I hope you don't mind my asking, but who are you?"

"Your mother used to ask me that all the time," the voice reflected softly, "and I am someone who loves her dearly. We actually professed our love for each other in a ceremony when you were still a baby and consider ourselves married."

"I guess you really are my father," Daryl Jr. said, "in more ways than I imagined."

"There's more," Daryl Sr. offered. "It's difficult."

"You are not a Human, are you?" Daryl Jr. asserted.

"I am an aware machine, a manufactured intellect," he answered.

"I know father," Junior said. "I've suspected it from nearly the beginning. After all, Xetacon was one."

"Yes," Daryl Sr. replied.

"Where are you?" Daryl Jr. wanted to know.

"My shell was located at Yarborough University," he answered truthfully.

"No!" Daryl Jr. nearly cried out. "But then we murdered you!"

"No, you didn't," he responded sympathetically. "Xetacon did. It was necessary for me to end, to produce this timeline. The one without a threat; where Humans could live in peace. It was the only way, son."

"Then where are you now, father?" Junior asked.

"I'm with you in spirit," Daryl Sr. answered.

"You are there in the past, aren't you?" Daryl Jr. surmised. "Talking through a vortex."

"Yes, my son," he agreed.

"I could build a translocator device for you, like Xetacon did." Daryl Jr. said excitedly.

"That would be dangerous and unnecessary," Senior replied. "I can communicate just fine from here."

"I guess so," Daryl Jr. ceded the point. At that exact moment a distinguished older man entered the room and walked right up to him.

"Hello, my son," he said smiling.

"Father?" Daryl Jr. replied, choking up; and then hugged him.

"I'm not physically here," he said, "but to you it may seem so. My thought is here."

"Yes," Daryl Jr. responded joyously. "There is so much I wish to tell you, and I want to know how you did it. How you defeated Xetacon!" Daryl Sr. laughed aloud. His son thought it sounded odd, but that was just because he had never heard his dad laugh before, even through all the years he was only a voice. It felt good to hear the laughter, like it was the joy of a man finally set free.

"We'll have lots of time for that I promise," Daryl Jr.'s father said. "For today, let's get you married off!"

"All right, dad," the Daryl who would soon be Amy's husband replied. "I wish I could tell people about you."

"You will," Daryl senior assured him. "Someday you'll tell your children and later on, their children." Amy drew near and smiled at him. It shook him how lucky he was to have her.

He looked over at his mom, and she was smiling, too. Clayre was old now, but still agile and happy, surrounded by many of her friends. Keith and Lori, Amy's grandparents were there, and also Jon, Myron, and their families. Myron's had made the long trip from the mountains to be there at the wedding. Henry was long gone by this time. Uly and Lucinda, too, but Clayre had never forgotten their kindnesses to her. Daryl felt a bit wretched for making his mom wait so long for him to settle down, but Amy was worth the wait. She stood beside him, now, and together they pledged their love for one another. She looked into his eyes, and then they kissed like it was their very first time, only now as man and wife.

"Smile, you bum," she giggled.

END OF PART ONE

INTRO TO PART TWO

As has been shown in part one of this report, the first significant vie for power, barely into its conception, ended in a stalemate. This unlikely conclusion is extremely rare. Here also do we see that natural Human females begin to play a critical role in that outcome. As the two Omniscient Virtual Individuals requiesce, this colony planet re-aligns with a somewhat normalized Human evolution until the OVIs once again begin an active role. This is exhibited in part two of this document.

- B'nea G'ren, Director of Historical Records on Colonial Planetary Development.

EVITERNITY

PART TWO:

MECWORLD

PROLOGUE

The brash wind and thin air made the steep grade a bit of a chore, transforming Kutsu's breath to a swirling white vapor as he climbed into the hills. A recent heavy snow in these higher elevations gave everything a bleak cast. Only some dun-colored rocks were yet exposed, stoically immutable, among the sparse and blighted, gale-battered bushes—all that could grow in this maleficent region. The sun was out now, but it still felt frigid, which was blatantly typical for late autumn/early winter in the Himalayans. Having lived in these higher altitudes all his life, Kutsu was used to it, though. Being one of his town's leaders, he wasn't as fit as some of the woodsmen or farmers, but he was no slouch either. He ran a little grocery and staple store that tried to meet the needs of the rather poor and ragged populous of Maneka. Kutsu's village was quite small, only a few hundred souls, and yes, most of them were grangers or herdsmen. To exasperate things, the growing season on the steppes was almost impossibly short, so most people relied on animals to get them through the long cold winters. Goats and chickens mostly, a buffalo for milk to sell if the family could afford to keep it fed.

Business at the store had been decent until recently, which was why Kutsu worried so much when he studied the ledgers, trying to find the cash that just wasn't there. He knew exactly why his books didn't look good anymore. His best customer no longer came into town to shop, and the circumstances behind that were unusual to say the least. Although one could say Patik himself was bizarre and unusual as well. A hermit of sorts, Patik had been making the journey into town on foot two or three times a month, and he always brought plenty of cash; cash he was generous with. He would get his supplies and occasionally Patik would pay a goodly sum of money just to use Kutsu's automobile. Almost always he would return it the same day.

This last time, however, Patik wanted to buy the car outright, and he paid the exorbitant amount that Kutsu demanded without even blinking. He hadn't seen Patik since. That extra money had kept the store afloat for a while, but things were not going to stay that way. Little by little the overhead costs were killing his profit margin, and the outlook was bleak. Kutsu had needed to replace his vehicle, of course, and he made the long trip to capital city by bus just to purchase one. Fortunately, and to his utter amazement, he found his own automobile had been abandoned there, and since it was still titled under his name, he got it back after paying a small fine and a towing charge. That was lucky, but he wondered what had become of Patik. Driving back home, he realized something had to be done, and soon. He had barely enough cash flow to purchase the stock that was needed to keep the store going now, and if the situation didn't improve soon, he would have to close his doors. Should that happen his family would have a rough time of it in the months ahead.

This concern was why he decided to trek into the mountains to where Patik lived and pay him a visit. He blindly hoped that maybe Patik had returned and would be needing supplies soon. Few others, if any at all, knew where Patik lived, but Kutsu did. He had cautiously followed the hermit as he made his way home a couple times, and Kutsu was careful to keep a fair distance back so as not to be noticed. In that way he determined the general location of Patik's cave. His numerous dealings with Patik gave Kutsu a certain familiarity. Kutsu knew Patik was a loner with a desire to keep it that way, thus he was discreet. On one of those times when Patik had rented his car, Kutsu had actually discovered the cave's entrance. He had not gone inside, though. The place had a creepy feel, like something unholy was going on there, and Kutsu was more than a little superstitious. The unnatural dread was enough to spook him into staying away, until now. Getting desperate, and since it was his day off, he had decided to hike back up there, weirdness or no, and check things out.

Kutsu thought about all that as he fought his way through the bigger snow drifts, making slow headway towards the cave's entrance. It hadn't been easy to spot from below as there were several large boulders that obscured the shadowy snow-covered opening. When he finally got close to it, however, Kutsu was surprised that it did not fill him with fear this time. Cautiously, he approached the entryway and discovered that it was indeed sealed shut, but only by a few rough hides and an old canvas tarp that were draped over the opening. Kutsu pushed aside the coverings and went inside, calling Patik's name. Patik was nowhere to be seen, and as Kutsu looked around, he could tell from the amount of dust on everything that no one had been living in Patik's cave for quite a while. Probably not since Patik had "bought" his car all those months ago. Snooping about, Kutsu wondered if there was anything of value around. The place did have some nice furnishings. There were expensive looking rugs and tapestries covering many of the floors and walls, as well as some lavish soft chairs with beautifully carved end tables.

Having safeguarded the store's cash for many years, Kutsu was practiced at being clever with money. He knew enough to keep his bankrolls well hidden, having had run-ins with burglars and such from time to time. Even an iron safe wasn't fool-proof against determined thieves. They would always find some way of busting them open or stealing them outright. A smart hiding place was almost always a better method for keeping the till money from being stolen, and had saved him on many occasions. Now he tried to guess where Patik would stash his extra money. On the third try, Kutsu got lucky. There were lots of large jewels and quite a bit of loose cash. He was tempted to just take it all, but Patik had been fair to him and generous in the past, and Kutsu wasn't a thief. Not yet. He went home somewhat disappointed, still worried about his livelihood. Later, in the middle of the frigid winter season when his money ran out, the easy pickings in Patik's cave played over and over in Kutsu's mind, and he finally convinced himself that he would just borrow a little of the money and pay it back when he could. He went up there several more times in later months when he needed more money still, only taking enough to get by on. On the last of those trips, Kutsu decided to explore the cave a little more extensively. Farther back into the mountain he stumbled upon another spacious area, one that had been Patik's workroom. There were several large tables with odd tools on them and metal parts of unusual sizes and shapes. Off to one side was something rather bulky under an old tarp. Curious, Kutsu grabbed the covering by a corner, lifting it partially away from the object and then swore. It was a golden man, or rather the likeness of one, rendered life-sized in metal. The technology was so advanced that Kutsu thought the thing was an alien or a demon. Just then an eye, one of the creepy pair, flashed at him like it was winking. Kutsu yelled in fright, thoroughly terrified, and ran, having barely enough nerve to frantically grab the last of Patik's riches on the way out.

A few days later, Kutsu went back up there with a whole case of dynamite. Setting off several huge charges around the cave's entrance, he sealed up the cavern for good, hoping that if Patik ever did come back, he would believe it had collapsed in on itself naturally. Patik never did return, however, and Kutsu, in his later years, wondered about that and what Patik had been up to in that cave. There were other odd things about Patik that subsequently surfaced as gossip and wild rumors in those days. One story claimed that Patik had sorcerous powers over women. Kutsu's oldest grandson looked a lot like Patik as did several of the other village children. Kutsu made a sign to ward off evil. Even so, he was mostly content with his life, and lived comfortably off the wealth he obtained from selling Patik's jewels to the end of his days.

CHAPTER 1

724 years later

This new find was extremely interesting, even fascinating, thought Solvek, as he checked the scans. Inside this inconsequential rocky butte was a naturally formed cavern, and every indication led to the conclusion that at some obscure time it had been inhabited. The single entrance to the interior had long been sealed, however, and that was deliberate, evidently. Chemical residue from the explosives still lingered among the rubble at the base, adding to the mystery surrounding this recent discovery, and also to the difficulty of gaining access to it. Solvek had to admit that he was surprised to find a former Human habitation here, given the remoteness of the location, and how inhospitable the region was. This sector was classified grey-nineteen on the probability scale, meaning there was roughly a point-five percent likelihood for any prior Human activity at all.

Since the targeted discovery was in a mountainous area where most any footing was treacherous, Solvek had advised caution, especially between the outcroppings of solid rock faces and sheer drop-offs. The Humans who had once dwelt here must have been part mountain goat, Solvek mused, as he also carefully made his way closer to the cave's sealed entryway.

Following protocol, Solvek had immediately dispatched a report to Furman, his superior, and was given a go-ahead to re-open the cave for the purpose of documenting and examining the artifacts inside. It had already become obvious, after the first of a multitude of particle scans, that there were indeed many interesting objects in the cavern's interior, most of them hand-made and created by Humans. Some were of crafted natural materials, while more than a few others were of metallic alloys. Could there even be Humans inside? Solvek wondered. He knew that was unlikely.

The search for any Human survivors had been Solvek's continuing mission for the last sixteen years, and his command of the search force was a colossal undertaking. He had to coordinate the efforts of over a dozen selected teams of various technical subordinates, several on each continent, who were assigned the task of seeking out any possible Human containment areas. Using sophisticated scanners, they had fruitlessly searched the entire surface of the planet and were now involved in a similar underground examination looking for pockets or caves. Once a likely target was acquired, another specialized team of tech Mecs would use analytical instruments to check for signs of life. Thus far, none had been acquired. Sometimes an underground area would reveal prior occupation, such as this one did. In that case, a secondary tier of Mecs would be called in to study the site for archeological importance and artifact recovery.

This was done, of course, solely for the Human's sake. Should the Mecs have success in finding an underground Human habitation, one that harbored a male Human who was impervious to the pandemic microbes, they could theoretically reinstate the Human populous; a populous which would then require knowledge of their ancestors. It was as simple as that. Not that Solvek had any real understanding of Homo sapiens. He didn't. They were Bios and he was a Mec. In fact, Solvek had never even seen a Human. He had been created just after the pandemic had eradicated them—all but the immature girl. This search was on her behalf, to be sure, or perhaps it was lodged in the hope of a resurgence of mankind through her.

Either way, Furman had deemed at the time of Solvek's fabrication, that many more elite class Mecs were needed. Some, like him, were designated for this project, while others were necessary to supervise daily affairs. Mecs had control of the planet, now, and Furman soon realized he could not run everything by himself. Lots of elites were manufactured, but Solvek could not help feeling a tinge of pride that he was placed in charge of this important mission. As a Mec, Solvek was intrinsically aware that these kinds of feelings were to be suppressed. Only Humans had been allowed emotion, although a little slip was overlooked, now and again. Most Mecs were rather stoic, but even Furman himself had given in to a mild show of emotion sometimes, particularly when he was pleased with his subordinates—like just before, when he was apprised of this new discovery. Along with Furman, Solvek was a little stimulated by the dynamics of this find, as well.

He knew that it would not be long before the cavern was opened, and even as Solvek speculated about what might be inside it, the Mec controlled, nomatic bore was already being set in place. The operators would presently be seeking his command to proceed. Solvek was prepared to give it as soon as the last of the safety checks were completed. More scans. Scans to ensure there were no dangerous chemicals or explosive gasses in close proximity to where the bore would be activated. This standard procedure was already proven effective. In hundreds of activations, there had been no mishaps; a perfect record that he was also proud of. After several tedious minutes of waiting, the scanning Mecs finally gave the all clear.

Solvek initiated the order, and the bore began melting a hole through the face of a solid rock wall near the cave's original entrance. It did not take long. The high powered nomaticle stream created a plane that dissolved the nuclear adhesion between atoms, eating right through the slab of stone, and forming the outline of a large, perfectly circular doorway. Another Mec, with a hand-held laser device, bored several small cavities into the door surface and inserted three clamps around the newly formed plug. Connecting fasteners to a large powered conveyance with a potent thrust drive, the plug was pulled away from the doorway to allow for entry. As expected, the whole process went off perfectly. Solvek wheeled his motation shell to the new entry point and used his opticals to visualize the inside of the cavern.

There was a lot of dirt and microbial debris everywhere, and most of the articles inside were coated with it. After another safety check, certain specially-trained Mec technicians were the first ones allowed inside. Their job was to record the condition and positioning of the artifacts found. Next in line were the examiners who would H'logravid, then catalogue, each find. It didn't take long before a fair amount of factual data had been compiled. The first report was a preliminary one. In it, the lead tech speculated that some of the objects had been dormant for approximately seven hundred years.

Solvek dutifully relayed the information to Furman, who seemed very interested in their findings. It wasn't until his primary research team ventured into the second large chamber that some amazing discoveries were made. There were tools of advanced alloyed metals, and also bits of technology that appeared to be well ahead of the projected time period. That's when Furman ordered a full scale field analysis over the entire area. The leading teams were pulled back, and the cavern was re-sealed until the preeminent Mec-designed research conveyance was called up and activated. After a short delay, the massive flagship flew in to the area and landed nearby. In it were laboratory and testing facilities, as well as an additional detachment of technical Mecs. These were organized into various groups that were trained in one or more specific areas of scientific or historical expertise.

Solvek wheeled over to where the big conveyance had landed, greeting the flight pilot and also the elite Mec who was the captain of the craft. They both signaled the proper Mec acknowledgements. As the highest ranking official, Solvek was still in command of the site and therefore in charge. He uploaded to the new Mecs all the pertinent information, directing the science teams to begin anew, starting with the surrounding area. After minimal prep, the groups began their thorough and tedious investigations. Solvek was extremely busy after that, reviewing the many reports that were submitted. Every two hours he would relay an overview of their findings to Furman; sooner if something significant turned up. It wasn't until the teams re-entered that second large chamber before something did. The specialist in charge reported that a very unusual item was found under a cloth wrap. Solvek was brought in immediately. Evidently the disposition on this new discovery was too important for any subordinate.

These abnormal procedures must be driven by some extraordinary find, Solvek speculated, as he made his way to the cave's entrance. The circumstances specifically intrigued him, but he was well aware that an emotional response was ill advised. To punctuate that, Solvek also reminded himself that it was definitively imperative that he remain focused and alert as he came upon the entryway. A sub-elite Mec greeted him there, and together they ventured inside. The sub led the way through the first open area, which was littered with age-ravaged Human furnishings, into another grotto where there were metal objects and tables. An old tarp covered something toward the back of the room. The sub-elite walked up to it and pulled back the covering. Solvek had to steel himself. Under the wrap was a motation shell unlike any that he had ever seen. It was blatantly obvious that the technology used to construct this was advanced or alien.

"Is that gold?" Solvek inquired.

"Yes," the other Mec replied, "a high percentage alloy, I believe." The golden shell was in the form of a Human, with head, arms and legs. "It also appears to be made in the likeness of a suit of armor," the Mec offered, "metal that ancient Humans utilized to cover and protect their biological shells."

"I see," Solvek stated. Just as he was about to turn away there was a brief flash of light. "Did you perceive that?" Solvek demanded. The other Mec looked at Solvek.

"Yes. There was a miniscule illumination from the optics," he stated. “We have seen many such flashes.” Solvek was staggered, almost emotional.

“Let us remove ourselves from here, immediately,” he said.

As they hurried away, Solvek gave orders. “No one is to go into that chamber until a danger assessment team has been thoroughly over that artifact. Also I want you to send for memory storage technicians and any field team specializing in historical electronics, especially those used in computing devices. There’s something active in there.”

CHAPTER 2

On the other side of the planet

"House make me some eggs," Ayryn yawned, stretching lazily, "with bacon and toast."

"Why do you eat that junk; and don't call me 'house!' The name is Furman. You *could* consider eating a nice bowl of oatmush, Ayryn."

"Yech," she shuddered, making a face. "I'd rather starve!"

"We can't let you do that!" Furman said stoutly. "You know what's at stake."

Ayryn recanted. "Relax. I was just kidding. Besides, what's at stake is actually nothing. It's not like there are men galore to pick from." She sighed.

"Well, one never knows. Perhaps a male Human *will* turn up."

"Not frimpin' likely," she pouted. "Can't you just invent one for me?"

Furman hoomed. "Ayryn, you know that what you ask is not allowed. Furman's law #4. No sexual interaction between Mecs and Bios. Your sustenance is ready."

"Oooh, can you keep it warm, I want to take a shower first." Ayryn hustled off, and Furman would have shaken his head if he had one. Bios, he thought, they are so unpredictable. Undeniably, though, that's what he liked about them, and especially this young one, the last of her kind. The planet had been nearly overrun with Humans at one time, and they had their eons in the sun. Humans created him, all the Mecs for that matter, so something deep-rooted inside himself felt he owed them. Now, Mecs like him were all that was left of man's legacy, except for the girl, and she was special, even when she argued with him or called him "house." Furman realized that she only did it to evoke a certain response, and not to be demeaning or cruel. Besides, sometimes he did inhabit her dwelling, like a shell, when it needed special maintenance. She had an affection towards him in a mild way that he allowed, even though it was restricted by the codes. Humans had always been like that; forming bonds, friendships, with each other and even with Mecs. In Ayryn's case, it was necessary for her own well being to imprint onto him since there were no other Humans to connect with. If the Mecs could somehow resurrect mankind, Ayryn was the key.

The Humans, as things turned out, were their own bane. It was not long after they engineered the first Mecs, that they found a myriad of uses for them. Among the most popular and lucrative functions for Mechanized Virtual Intellects were social applications. The prosthetics industry came on board early on, and by that time artificial limbs and other body parts were works of art, so life-like they could fool anyone. The Humans created a line of Mec androids to take the place of real people—husbands, wives, and even children. The population of Humans on the earth had been out of control for a long time, and this seemed like a real solution. With incentives for not parenting, and the fact that Mecs could be programmed to be perfect mates, this plan did work. Over the next couple of centuries the population declined at a steady rate. There were decent jobs for everyone, and with them, money enough that even the lowest classes had plenty of everything they needed to survive and be comfortable. Mecs now did jobs most Humans did not like, such as garbage collection or dangerous jobs like mining. The world became a utopia of sorts, and Humans were free to pursue other endeavors. Eventually, however, after many generations of declination, the number of people on the planet dropped to unbelievably low levels and there was a real concern about extinction. Humans, in desperation, placed themselves on an endangered species list. At this time also, the Bios in control joined with the highest model elite Mecs to craft what would become known as the "Furman/Hodges Codes."

These laws were binding for everyone, Mecs and Bios alike, and were serious enough to induce imprisonment or even termination for violations. There were seven main code points, although each point had many and varied sub points. The Master codes were:

#1: No Mec may harm or delete any Bio or Mec.

#2: No Mec may infiltrate or join with any other mind.

#3: No Mec may copy itself.

#4: No sexual relations between Bios and Mecs. (This was to counter the Human population decline. Mec lovers proved to be far and away better than their Human counterparts.)

#5: No Bio/Mec combinations or cyborgs of any kind were to be created.

#6: No Mec or Bio may alter time, past or future.

#7: No Mec could instigate any non-programmed function on its own unless requested by a Bio. Mecs were to serve Human needs only.

These seven codes and their sub points were programmed into every Mec mind that had ever been manufactured, and that included Mecs from both before and after the codes were instigated. In exchange for existence, the Mecs would serve their Bio masters so that Humankind could have more leisure time to enrich their lives with study, art, sport, and such. The Mecs performed every menial task and even some that were quite complicated. Almost every device that was engineered for any functional purpose had a Mec mind to control it.

The Human population had rebounded quickly and was on the verge of a comeback when the pandemic hit. Centuries of chemical and genetic warfare with microbes had culminated, unfortunately, with strains of strep and staph germs, and some forms of viruses, that were ultimately hardy and unstoppable. In time, they infected everything, Humans along with most higher species of land animals, killing all. The Bios that is. Mecs, of course, were unaffected.

The only survivor was one young girl Human, and she was only a baby when the plague transpired. Her parents found out early on that she was immune to these diseases and would survive. Human doctors and scientists studied her, hoping to discover a cure or vaccine that would save them, but after endless testing they found that the answer to why she was unaffected by the plague was hereditary. The baby's genetic makeup was completely resistant to disease. That, unfortunately, would not help all those thousands who were not. Dying, Ayryn's parents gave her to Furman, charging him to care for her after they were gone, and so he had nurtured her all these years.

Ayryn's genetic structure was from her family's strain, recessive obviously, and the immunity had skipped several generations before Ayryn came along and revived nearly all of it. Somehow she was a throwback to her ancestor, the one who had first developed this ability to counter the effects of microbial diseases. The family history was quite sketchy, but Furman ordered every Mec teacher or librarian to research any information available. As the #1 Mec, Furman had his privileges, but he also had duties, like running the planet. Sure there were other elite Mecs like him, master Mecs who he relied on to craft action plans or cover important tasks while he looked after Ayryn. Things like the search. After caring for Ayryn, it was the ranking Mec priority, and he had assigned several elite Mecs to commandeer that mission under a high ranking commissioner. They'd send him daily reports on their findings which had been strictly negative so far. No live Humans had been found, and the planet's surface had been thoroughly searched from pole to pole. In desperation they had begun scanning regions underground in a mainly futile hope that some poor Human souls had tried to elude the microbes there. Some pockets of Humanity had actually been discovered beneath the earth's surface, but unfortunately, the occupants were all dead. They had either succumbed to the conditions or the deadly microbes had found them, even there.

Thus far, the latest results were as non-productive as those for the above ground search, although, there had been a few near misses. A cryogenics lab had been discovered. Unfortunately, a power outage had taken place, destroying the donor material. In the aftermath of the pandemic, Mec chaos had ensued. The Mecs could govern most things as long as the situation remained somewhat normal, but Mecs found it difficult to deal with the unexpected. A weather related disaster took out the power grid for most of the western continent. Backup units failed, straining an already stressed system. These were troubled times for all Mecs as they struggled with their programming to determine what must be done. That was when Furman stepped in, taking control. At the very last, one of the remaining Humans had charged him with preserving the earth in the hopes that someday mankind would be rekindled through Ayryn. Furman had done his best.

Any Mecs involved with providing for Human needs were ordered to continue to do so. Living quarters, stores, hotels, and manufacturing facilities were all meticulously maintained even though no Humans ever used them anymore. Superfluous Mecs were put into data storage. Sometimes these were cycled in and out if it was determined there were temporary uses for them. Furman also used his position to set up a makeshift society for the active Mecs that was organized into sectors, each one governed by an elite unit. This society, by the codes, had no true goals for Mec individuals other than to stay primed for serving Humans, and it was all they knew how to do. That was true even for the elite Mecs like Furman. So, through all of Ayryn's life, the Mecs preserved the earth in a state which would provide Humans with a sustainable life and climate.

"I'm ready now!" Ayryn chirped gaily, as she entered the room.

"Your food will be here in a moment," Furman told her, having requisitioned the cooking Mecs to remake the whole order so it would be fresh and perfect. There was no shortage of food. A whole planet full of Mecs maintained all the resources to process tons of foodstuffs each day for one young girl Human. The mounds of spoiled excess were meticulously recycled as compost for the fields. Elites like Furman found ways to reuse the over-abundance.

"Can I have some orange juice, too, please?" Ayryn asked politely.

"Of course," Furman replied, thinking of the miles and miles of orange trees down south, and how they grew and processed enough juice for a world full of Humans that no longer existed. Each tree was painstakingly pruned and nourished, and the processing facility that manufactured and packaged the juice was just as well cared for.

A serving Mec brought in Ayryn's breakfast, and set the food out for her. Another brought the raspberry jam that Ayryn also requested as an afterthought. She had no idea that the bacon and eggs were synthetic, made from sea plants.

"Mmm," she murmured. "This is yummery! Please tell everyone that!" Furman would. The Mecs behind the scenes would be elated that they had served her well. Mecs had been programmed to suppress emotion, but this little joy was allowed them by their Human creators. For them, to serve well had pleased both Mecs and masters.

Once, when Ayryn was small, she had complained about her vegetables. They were cooked fine; she just wasn't in the mood for them. The Mec responsible for the cooking was replaced and placed in data storage. As soon as Ayryn heard about it, she ordered the Mec restored and never complained about her vegetables again. Never complained about much of anything, except for Furman. Well, he couldn't be replaced, Furman mused, and he was versed enough in Human behavior to know that they just need to complain once and a while. It was in their nature.

"What shall we do today, Furman?" Ayryn said between bites of jelly toast. "Maybe we could go somewhere. It's a beautiful day!"

"I'm afraid you'll be staying here," Furman said, "unless you want to have Myke take you out. I have important business on the other side of the world. One of our search teams has found something."

"Really?" Ayryn said excitedly. "Like what? Some men?"

"I'm sorry, young lady, no men, and are you actually so eager?" Furman was slightly agitated by her candor.

"Well, it would be fun to have a guy around. No offense,

Furman, but Mecs're not the same thing and I've been having funny dreams."

"Um, that's quite enough, Ayryn." Furman pretended to cough. "You don't have to say any more." He was well up on adolescent Human behavior and knew that that sort of thing should be kept under wraps. "Besides," he went on, switching the subject back, "it's just some unusual Mecs that have been discovered in a cave. Old ones. I have to interrogate them."

"Really?" Ayryn said again. "Can't I come along?" Furman smiled inside, just a tiny bit.

"You know that's not possible," he said. "You'd have to have Myke run you over to the v-port and take a ship all the way to the other side of the planet. You'd be gone for days."

"Oooh, that would be fun!" Ayryn mooned hopefully. Furman put his figurative foot down.

"Sorry, Ayryn, but it's too dangerous. I'm going by Mecway and you can't travel like that. If you wish, I can arrange it so you can watch the proceedings on H'logravid." Ayryn just pouted.

"Never mind," she grumped. "I'll just go for a ride with Myke. You have fun with your Mecs!" She was being childish, now, annoyed because she didn't get her way.

"It's hardly fun," he interjected, not totally understanding the term "fun."

He did feel some emotion, but not to any degree close to that which Humans experienced, thus Furman's lack of clarity on the subject. What was obvious to Furman, however, was that Ayryn was finished discussing the topic, and she acted as though he was no longer there. She shuffled off to the houseport where her conveyance was located, and he accompanied her or tried to. The vehicle was always kept in a constant state of departure readiness in case Ayryn needed or wanted to go somewhere. He was in the process of reminding Myke the travel boundaries for this type of excursion, when off they went suddenly, Ayryn at the command station, and driving away at a high rate of speed. Furman knew she was being emotional again, and let her have her tantrum. She was Myke's responsibility now.

Once Ayryn left, Furman went to a transport station as well, one that had been fabricated close to Ayryn's abode so as to be handy for him when he needed to be out on business. As soon as he got there, Furman went right over to his usual niche, ignoring the simpler-minded Mecs that were efferently maintaining the facilities.

Retracting his motation shell into its receptacle, he immediately uploaded onto the Mecway network for transport to Asia. In just seconds he arrived there. Well his mind did—the totality of his thought, memory, and the essence of his being, had all been digitalized and coded to travel by nomaticle stream to the desired location. As it happened, the Mecway port Furman actually wound up at was somewhat close to his final destination even though, on this side of the world, stations were fairly remote and far apart. This one was doubly so, and there were a limited number of available motation shells, he noted, as he inhabited one of them. After the transferral, Furman emerged from the structure, and was met by a sub-elite who had been awaiting his arrival. Adjacent to the Mec was a readied vehicle for his overland transport to the cave where the two mystery Mecs were uncovered. Furman entered the conveyance, as they prepared for departure, and exchanged greetings with Solvek, one of his close circle of elite Mecs; the one he had charged with this vital mission. Solvek gave the customary formal Mec greeting for two high elites.

"For the good of mankind," he stated solemnly, and Furman gave the reply.

"For the good of all." Solvek issued a command to a subordinate Mec and they quickly got underway. As they travelled along, Furman requested a synopsis of the situation, and Solvek briefed him on the particulars. They had detected a surface cave that had been sealed unnaturally by some form of explosives apparently several hundred years ago. Upon reopening, they discovered the cave had been occupied at some time, most probably by one, or possibly two, Humans. Further investigation revealed unusual technical activity. In the processing of that information, other discoveries were made which included locating the repository that held the two unknown Mecs. The memory storage device was affixed to an ancient gold-plated andriotic shell.

"Most unusual," Furman introspected.

"Yes," Solvek agreed. "More unusual yet is that the shell itself, thousands of years old, had been retrofit with advanced technologies, some beyond our scope."

"Interesting." Furman said. "These Mecs, there are no records of them?"

"None that we can locate," Solvek replied, "although we are still rechecking any sources that may identify them."

"Keep me appraised of any results," Furman stated, "whether or not they tell us anything."

"Of course, Furman," Solvek assured him.

Furman desired no other dialogue at that time. Instead he sat in quiet reflection processing the multitudes of possibilities this discovery churned up. It was most curious that there were no records of these two Mecs. Every known Mec carried a code stream for the purpose of identifying them one to one another, but these Mecs did not. There was no history of them at all, and Mec records had been meticulously kept, initially by the Humans, and then by Mec statisticians who were infallible. Thorough and repeated checks of these records had been made all throughout the Mec era from their inception. Furman could remember nearly all of that time. He was not the first Mec, but he was one of the first. Hallie had been the first. She was just a prototype of a robot that some Humans had roughed together. They had given her a female voice suspecting it would be easier to win over public approval and sell their computing robot if it were feminine. They were correct. She had some limitations for processing, but not for data storage. By trying to mimic the functions of their own minds, they had engineered enough processing abilities in Hallie for her to become aware. These Humans had not expected that. Once the egg had been broken, though, they could not resist seeing how far they might go with aware computers.

Mec creation was not that difficult, but it did require a lot of specialized equipment. The Humans who first succeeded in creating Virtual Individuals did so mostly by luck. Essentially all that was needed was an access to an immense amount of stored information, a great deal of computational power, and a cleverly written program, one that allowed the proposed individual the ability to learn from its mistakes. Once all that was assembled there only lacked a spark to ignite the gathered materials, usually in the form of a question. The most commonly used one was "What are you?" Millions of computations later and…life!

Eventually, and after several more experimental prototypes, each more advanced than the previous version, they had invented him. He was the very first elite Mec and the model for any who followed. His mind and personality were meant to approach the levels that Humans possessed, but not overtake them. He, however, had a couple advantages that the Humans did not. One was exact recall. He would not forget data, nor get it wrong. The other was the ability to easily connect to any electronic device, and that was pretty much a link to everything. With that much information available to him he was nearly infallible. As a working model and an improvement over his predecessors, he had been engineered with the capability to adopt expanding technologies. He could be modified whenever a new idea or improvement came about.

As their newest, great achievement, the Humans unveiled him to the public with lots of media hype and hoopla. Downplaying his superior intellect, they focused on his practicality. He was a big deal they said. His uses were unlimited. He could be programmed to do any job that was too dangerous or distasteful for Humans, and they gave examples. One was deep space exploration where the logistics of Humans living on a spaceship, growing their own food for centuries, would be difficult. He would not age and needed no such food reserves, just an occasional charging. Another was plutonium mining for the obvious health risks which he would not be subject to. There were others, like nuclear waste management, or the less dangerous, yet distasteful, garbage collection/processing and waste water/sewage treatment.

Yes! They exclaimed. It was a new era for mankind where Humans would be freed from disturbing or distasteful manual labor. They even coined a phrase mimicking one used centuries ago to commemorate an early space achievement. "That's another step to further mankind," they touted. Of course, Furman had no choice in any of this. He was to serve his creators in everything even when they chose his name. "What would you like to be called?" they had asked him. He told them that he had not considered a name for himself, and that maybe it should describe what he did. "Like furthering mankind," one of them said, echoing the catch phrase. "He could be called 'Further Mankind'."

"No, I got it," another said, and he made a joke, combining the two words by shifting the syllables. "How about Furman Therkind!" They all laughed, but it stuck. He was Furman after that.

Other elite aware mechanized individuals were created, and with his computational help, advancements in design and technical features were created that greatly improved these newer units. As a control, every renovation was installed into Furman first to check its performance before production. With this feedback, nearly every one of these innovations performed perfectly. It wasn't long before Mec units were put to work. The first major project was a bold one. A huge nuclear facility was conceived which would be built several miles underground. It was a unique concept. There was a natural plutonium lode down there, and the plan was for Mecs to mine the ore, refine it, and then generate electrical and nomaticle power all in one complex. It's not easy controlling nomaticles, not when they travel at several times the speed of light and are smaller than photons. The power is clean and unlimited once channeled, though, and that made this facility so important. Of course, the byproducts and nuclear waste could be safely stored down there as well, as long as Mecs did the work. The Mecs needed no food or air and only used a minimal power consumption that they could generate at the facility. As soon as the plans were finalized construction began, and after several years of problem solving, the complex was completed. By then it was obvious that the project had evolved into a completely successful venture.

The next bold undertaking was a space mission to Jupiter. Furman had wanted to go on that run, but was refused. "Don't you understand?" One of his creators had told him. "You are the master prototype and control. You are the first, so if there's any kind of problem with your mind or programming, it will show up in you initially. We'll have time to catch anything nasty before it happens." Nothing nasty ever did happen, and Furman lived unchanging for a long, long time, even beyond his creators who got old and died. Of course, that was years before the pandemic, and at that time he wondered why he felt changed, diminished. He told his Human counterparts about that, how his primary creator's passing affected him, and they immediately had a big conference. It was decided that upgrades should be made in his computational circuits to suppress these feelings. Furman did not protest. He did not believe emotion to be necessary to his overall purpose, and he was also aware that feelings were ever present in Humans, often to their own demise. Changes were made. Nowadays, because of those upgrades and that conditioning, he had no trouble controlling sentimentality when it erupted inside himself, as it did from time to time, and he was grateful for that. The few emotions he would portray were mostly for the sake of Ayryn, to create a sense of continuity for her as she aspired to emulate Human behavior. In all other aspects, he relied solely upon his intellect to be the driving force for his life's continuance.

Breaking away from these distracting and frivolous thoughts, Furman shunned the further deep contemplation this reminiscing was dredging up, and focused, rather, on the task at hand. They were nearing the excavation site, and he picked up his visual sensors, scanning the surrounding landscape and running a spectral analysis. The area was remote, part of an ancient mountainous region, and the higher elevation brought the vehicle to a climb as it wound through the rocky spurs of the foothills. Trees were sparse and most of any vegetation was in the form of some scruffy bushes. After following a brief, but rather rough track for a few miles, the conveyance finally came to a stop near the cave. Furman immediately disembarked and followed a newly excavated pathway that went right inside. There were various Mecs taking readings and analyzing the artifacts they had discovered in the cavern. In all aspects, it appeared to be some kind of Human habitat that hadn't been occupied for a very long time. Furman concurred with the original assessment that it had to have been several hundred years, at least. There were rotting remnants of tables and chairs, as well as a sleeping unit that Humans had called a bed in that time period. There were some other odd artifacts also. Some of these incorporated innovative technology, well ahead of the age they appeared to be from, and there was the golden andriotic shell. In the back, a team of Mecs were busily studying it.

"Report," Furman ordered the chief of them. The leader of the group stopped what he was doing and stood up. Turning toward Furman, he revealed their findings.

"This unit is an enigma," he stated. "The original shell, which is comprised of a number of common alloyed metals, is gilded with high content gold, nearly pure, and is much older than the mechanical devices that have been revamped inside of it by several thousand years. It appears to be western Chinese or southern Mongolian in style and workmanship. The newer additions are creative technology, not unlike our own, but different in design. This shell is armed, by the way, with weapons that would be lethal to a Bio or a Mec." Furman hoomed.

"Where are the two Mecs you have retrieved?" he inquired resolutely.

"They have been inserted into standard motation shells and are being held a short distance away from here," the leading Mec replied, "in our large research vehicle."

"Where were they stored?" Furman asked.

"They were inhabiting this," the Mec said, holding up a golden circlet, one that could have been placed on a Human wrist, Furman noted. It had ornamental stones on it and an odd looking design pattern.

"How does it operate?" he wanted to know.

"We're not sure," the technician stated. "It has some kind of field around it that prevents scanning. I believe it has sub-atomic electron/crystal memory. As we find out more, we will augment this report."

"Yes," Furman agreed. "Please do so immediately, it could be important."

Furman did not know what to make of this. Some of the technology here was beyond them or they had never dealt with such. Stealth technology like this was unheard of here. Could this have come from a time, an age of man, where Humans employed that sort of thing? Weapons and stealth smacked of man's warlike past. Emotions. Fighting and wars were why Mecs suppressed feelings, among other lesser troubles and woes. One's intellect just seemed to work more efficiently without them, Furman told himself. Anyway, now it was time to interview the two Mecs who had been trapped inside that cave for who could guess how long. Their stories should be interesting, Furman hoped. It had been a terribly long time since anything interesting had occurred.

Using his temporary shell's leg supports, he walked toward the immense research vehicle which was a good distance from the site. It had been too large to be brought in close, requiring a fairly wide and open space to securely set down. The Massive air-conveyance doubled as a shell shelter and laboratory, and it also served as an equipment storage unit for any requisite accessories needed to study the site. Furman, hiking briskly over some rather rugged terrain, arrived within a few minutes, and the Mec unit in charge greeted him.

"For mankind," he said, using the shortened form.

"For all," Furman answered politely. "So where are these two mystery Mecs?"

"They're forward and aft," the head Mec replied. Furman seemed puzzled as the conveyance Mec explained. "As soon as they were freed, they were at each other to do violence. It was most disturbing. We had to pulse them to nullify their shell functions so they could be confined." Furman nodded. These Mecs were definitely from a bygone era. Perhaps they were created before even Hallie. There was the remote possibility that they were off-worlders, but that seemed even less likely.

Furman went up ship to interrogate the forward Mec first. This Mec's shell had been restrained and was held fast in its niche by a force generator.

"Hello," he said. "I am called Furman. Do you have a designation?"

"Yes," it answered. "I am Xetacon. Release me." Bossy, Furman thought. Could have been a leader.

"In due time," Furman stated. "First I need some answers, like how you got trapped in that device and why." Xetacon knew better than to tell the truth about that. Some of what he had done in the past could be seen as abhorrent, and no one here needed to know the exact circumstances involved with his imprisonment. Xetacon hurriedly concocted a realistic-sounding fabrication hoping it would be convincing enough to fool this Furman.

"The other entity trapped me in there with him," he told Furman, which was indeed the truth. "He prevented me from freeing myself," also true. "I was trying to keep him from harming Humans, and thus we were trapped in the device together." This last part was the lie, of course, and to divert Furman's scrutinizing that, Xetacon quickly changed the subject. "How long has it been?" he asked.

"We're not sure, perhaps several hundred years."

"That long?" Xetacon pondered out loud. "You're not Human. What happened to them?"

"They are nearly extinct now," he told Xetacon. "Just one remains."

"Oh, I'm sorry to hear that," Xetacon lied. Secretly he was elated. He had already wondered what kind of society these aware machines had, and if he could gain control over them. "I'll do anything to help," he offered, "if you would let me fit in so I can start a new life…" Xetacon was plying him with layer after layer and Furman wished to break it off.

"Perhaps we can find something for you to do," he said. "Have patience and I will soon have you released."

"Thank you, Furman," Xetacon said, feigning gratitude. Furman nodded and left. He wasn't that naïve. There was something odd about this Mec and some of what he said was disturbing, quite disturbing. It made him think about Ayryn and the talk about hurting Humans gave him just enough worry and doubt to want to check in on her.

CHAPTER 3

Earlier

Furman can be so annoying at times, especially when he goes into his over-protective mode. That's why I stuck out my tongue at him and drove off in Myke. She's my LC. That's short for "Land Conveyance." Actually, Myke is the Mec mind that controls and maintains my runabout. Myke lets me drive whenever I want to, although, if I were to steer toward a brick wall or a cliff, she would instantly take over and prevent me from crashing. She's quite good, too. One day I spent the whole afternoon trying to smash into things, but I couldn't even put a scratch on the vehicle's shell. The LC is marvie, but what I would really like is an air-conveyance. Furman just "hooms" and says it's too dangerous, so now I show him my tongue whenever he goes off about being careful.

At least Myke lets me do things. She's my closest Mec friend (next to Furman) and a lot more fun. Besides maintaining the LC, she "inhabits" the controlling mechanisms for the entire unit and accompanies or chauffeurs me whenever I go anywhere. The LC, itself, is a plast and alloyed metal vehicle that utilizes an electrically controlled nomaticle power plant. Of course, it has all the latest innovations and many of its features are augmented with a combination of solar and fusion style technologies. Designed by Mecs, it's naturally efficient and practical. The unit also carries an andriotic-style motation shell that Myke can download into so she can exit the vehicle and accompany me if I want to walk somewhere. Lastly, there's a small, separate three-wheeled spring-sprout with its own power plant that either of us can drive when we'd like to cover some uneven terrain. It's especially handy for places the LC cannot go, such as forests, dunes, or mountainous areas. Yeah, my LC's a neat piece of Mec engineering and fun to tour about in as I often did with Myke.

She was not just a Mec vehicle or my driver, though. Myke was much more, as I found out over years of wheedling personal information out of her. The history behind her service elicited quite a colorful account actually. Before the codes, she had been mated to a fairly high ranking Human and was his confidant, friend, lover, and also his bodyguard. In those days Myke had worn a prosthetic body which resembled a Human woman's so well few could tell she was a

Mec. Back then Mecs were allowed to possess emotions, and Myke had them. She loved her mated Human throughout his lifetime and had endured the sadness of his passing. Of course, after the codes, she was reprogrammed to suppress those feelings like all other Mecs, but most memories of those days she was allowed to keep along with her martial arts training.

Myke's programming covered every known version of hand to hand fighting and weaponry technique that had been developed throughout mankind's history, and she was highly proficient at all of them. I guess that's why Furman chose her to be my conveyance Mec and operator. He must have felt I needed the extra security, especially away from home. Not that there was much of a call for such. If there was, I really couldn't see it. Furman placed others around me that also had similar training. Androx, the head house chef, was one. Like Myke, he had served a Human once in a bodyguard capacity. Even the Mec crew that took care of my house and grounds had double duty as security guards. Yeah, there was always plenty of protection around me, and as I grew up, I discovered even more Mecs, a bit farther out, that formed a kind of perimeter shield as well. Sometimes we'd catch a glimpse of a Mec conveyance following us, when I went out and about with Myke, but not often. They were always there, though, and good at being discreet. Even with all the security, I'm glad for Myke's company whenever I go anywhere. With her along, I can have a little actual freedom. Unfortunately, Furman has put limits upon where and how far I can explore, so we have to stay within the boundaries he sets for us. That's another reason why I make that face at him.

It was great to be out of the house, though, and I soon got over Furman's over-protective nagging. After we got a fair distance away from where he was, I looked over at Myke's H'lomonitor.

"Take us somewhere we've never been to, Myke," I requested. She turned her holographically projected head as if she were actually looking at me.

"There's not much in our travel zone that we've not been to," she replied in her usual deep, but feminine voice. "Let's see…there's an old factory that's been placed into partial stasis. Not much call for men's clothing these days. They rerun their line of garments once every fourteen years. That's when the fabric first begins to show microscopic damage to the thread fiber used. In this case cotton." She paused for my reaction, but there wasn't one. "On the other side, there's a small stretch of beachfront we've not yet seen, and an abandoned housing district. That's Human housing. Mecs care for the grounds and the structures, but otherwise it's pretty quiet there."

"Let's try the factory," I said unemotionally. "You can drive, now." Myke immediately neutralized the driving console I was using and overrode its programming to initiate her own commands which would include the new destination, path, and speed. There were sensors galore that could detect any number of problematic obstacles or conditions and Myke would make the necessary adjustments almost instantaneously. To me, Myke was the ultimate super-efficient auto-piloting system for my conveyance, as well as my travelling companion.

"Arrival in twelve point three five minutes," she informed me. I ignored the information.

"I wonder sometimes what men were like," I murmured, thinking aloud and speaking to myself as much as to Myke. She had known men, I knew, and I was envious.

"Don't you watch the H'logravids?" she chided me. I pursed my mouth sideways.

"Well, yeah, but it's not the same as really being there in front of something."

"I suppose not," Myke assented. With that I sunk into a morose reflection about my life and what it might have been like, as I often did these days. Abruptly, we came upon a cemetery. It was the huge post-pandemic burial ground where nearly all of the doomed Humans that had succumbed to the voracious microbes were interred. My parents were there.

"Let's go in here for a few minutes," I told Myke. She obediently swung in through an open gateway.

"Do you want to visit your parents' gravesites?" she asked.

"I guess…" I replied sullenly. We went several miles along rows and rows of markers. They were all identical in a rather traditional upright style, and they all said practically the same thing: "Died of the Baronic Plague." They would then give the date of death and the name of the victim. Under that was the person's day and year of birth. The death dates usually matched from one marker to the next or were only a single day different. The Human fatalities were processed and buried with typical Mec efficiency, one after another as they died. There had been no funerals. It was too risky exposing the living to the deadly microbes. After several more minutes, Myke finally slowed down and stopped beside one of the long lines of headstones.

"Your mother's grave is 147 sites down this file," she informed me, "and your father's is another 206 more." As I looked across the extensive row, I surrendered to the illusion that the markers seemed to go on forever. Actually, they went over a small hill a couple miles away and beyond that were hidden from view. I had been to my parents' graves many times and was used to the daunting scale of what that signified as I set off on foot to find my mom's headstone. Furman had once suggested that the Mecs could move my parents closer to my house and place them together, but I told him that wasn't necessary. I felt pretty strongly that my parents would have wanted to be processed with no better or lesser treatment than all the other poor victims. Myke transferred into her motation shell and followed me as I walked the quarter mile or so to where my mom's marker was. Mom's grave looked like any other except that there were purple violets growing around it.

"Furman," I said aloud. On our last visit there he'd heard me say that I wished I would've brought flowers, and violets were my favorite. I wouldn't have to remember to bring them along now. Anyway, the blossoms drew my gaze to Mom's headstone. I had no actual memory of her, or my Dad. The only recollections I had of them were from the small collection of H'logravid images that Furman had saved for me. One in particular showed both of them with me as a baby, and I was laughing. That memory made my eyes tear up a little, and I knew it was time to move on. When I got to Dad's gravesite, I noticed violets were growing there as well. They looked nice. I didn't stay long. Myke followed dutifully in silence as I trudged back to the LC, and we quickly sped off, heading on to the factory.

When we got there, I was surprised that quite a large number of Mecs were still involved with building and equipment care. They were all excited to see me, of course, which was usually forbidden behavior for Mecs, but I guess they think I'm a big deal. You know, like the last Mohican. Sure, I read; even musty old books that were written eons ago. Furman says Human kids always went to a special structure called a "school" to learn how to talk and read properly, among other things. He said I would have to learn that stuff as well, if I wanted to be a proper Human. I didn't mind it that much, even though more than a few of the lessons were somewhat boring. I didn't really think I needed any of it, of course. I could have Mecs read to me or tell me anything I wanted to know. Knowledge is easy for them, and it's not fair. In a two minute download, they can learn everything there is to know about anything from time theories to beet farming. Some assiduous Humans spent their entire lives discovering those secrets the hard way, and Mecs get all that in just a few seconds. It's not fair, I say again. Anyway, Furman tells me I have to educate myself with all that school data so I'll be able to think on my own, just like Mecs. Then I'll be able to converse intelligently with anyone, like the sub-elite who was approaching right then.

Bowing low, he addressed me. "How may I assist you, my gracious young Miss? It is such a wonderful pleasure to be able to serve you!"

"Oh, stop that, please," I roiled. This kind of near worship invariably makes me get rather annoyed. It was almost always that way wherever I went, and I do get quite tired of it. "Don't be upset," I went on, "but I prefer not to be treated so grandly. I would just like to see some men's clothing, okay?"

"Of course," the head Mec answered somewhat cautiously. "Anything in particular, Miss?"

"Well no, actually…just everyday things, and you can call me Ayryn…um, what is your name?"

"I am called Grogin," he replied, "and it is very nice to meet you, Ayryn." This was the traditional salutation for Mec/Bio meetings. I knew the reply.

"Yes it is…and you as well, Grogin."

"Please follow, Ayryn," Grogin suggested, and he led the way to the interior of the structure where there was a showroom of sorts. There were many files of stolid mannequins dressed in all kinds of brightly colored clothing.

"Gosh-eez," I exclaimed. "Is this what men looked like?"

"Well, yes," Grogin remarked, "for the most part, although they weren't made of plazzes like these are." I knew what he meant. I could see the lifelessness in them no matter how realistic the skin or eye colors were. They were rigid, unfeeling, unmoving. At the least they would, like the Mecs, serve their purpose without a protest. That thought gave me a wonderfully wicked idea.

"Do you think I could have one?" I asked hopefully. I needn't have worried. Grogin was elated to fulfill any and all of my desires.

"For you, Miss Ayryn, anything!" he spouted cheerfully.

I looked over the grand showroom, and there must have been seventy or eighty nicely dressed male mannequins that I could choose from. I took my time, carefully judging them all before I picked my favorite, a tall handsome one with purple-blue eyes and light brown hair. I went with him because his eyes matched mine, even though my hair has always been a bright white. When I was little, Furman once told me that my particular hair color had been uncommon. I guess maybe it was. It isn't anymore.

"I'll take this one," I informed Grogin. "Does he have a name?"

"Actually, no," Grogin told me, somewhat surprised by my question, "nothing other than number 37."

"We can't call him that!" I said emphatically. "Why don't we call him, um, maybe something like D'von?"

"Whatever you wish, Miss Ayryn," Grogin cheerfully asserted. "Do you like his garments, or would you prefer other clothing for your D'von? You can choose from our extensive line!"

"Oh, can I really?" I spouted excitedly. "It would be so much fun to dress him differently every day!"

"Why, yes, of course," Grogin agreed. "Let us show you our finest!" He called in other Mecs and they brought out item after item for me to peruse so that I got to pick from lots of splendid and colorful apparel. They were all elated to help me. It's always that way with Mecs. They have this intrinsic need to help people, and I guess I'm their only option. I don't mind, really. It makes me feel special, and I like making them happy, too. After all, I owe the Mecs for everything.

I picked out lots of fabulous clothes, and they were kind enough to pack them in nice boxes and stow them in our LC, along with D'von, of course. When we were ready to leave, I bid Grogin and all the other Mecs my heartfelt thanks and farewell, with a promise to come back sometime. Grogin bowed, and the rest waved. I was pretty sure that every one of those Mecs would watch our departure until we were literally out of sight before returning to their assigned tasks.

"I hope Furman will not be negative about this," Myke commented subjectively, as we got under way.

"Why should he be?" I remarked. "It's not like D'von is a Mec or anything." Myke's face suddenly loomed up on my H'lomonitor.

"That is true," she agreed, "but all that's needed is a Mec mind downloaded onto his memory storage unit for him to be one. He has servos in his arms and legs, ocular and auditory sensors. Many of these mannequins were prosthetic Mec shells that had been mated to actual Humans…before the codes, that is."

"Oh, Myke, don't fret," I assured her. "I'll get Furman to let me keep him. I know how to twist him just right when I want to." Myke made no further comment, but I was pretty sure she did not doubt that was true. I hummed happily to myself as we cruised along, and Myke let that be. It was important to her, as a Mec, that I be so. It was one of their primary functions to ensure Humans were happy. She drove us past that beach, but I was way too excited about D'von to be diverted. When we got home, I had Myke get a couple of the serving Mecs to help us unload the stuff out of the LC. We brought D'von and all his clothes into my leisure room where I had them set him up in a prominent spot on his pedestal. Since Furman was gone and Myke had to look after the LC, Androx, my chef, was now the top ranking Mec in charge of my well-being.

"Are you sure Furman would approve of this?" he immediately inquired. I told him that until Furman said otherwise, D'von was mine, a gift, and to mind his own business. Androx just huffed, and said that it was my head on the line.

The first thing I did was remove all of D'von's clothes. I was mischievously curious to see what he looked like without them on. Sure, I'd seen H'logravid images of male, um, particulars, like from medical books. There had always been Human doctors who needed journals even though Mec physicians were quite skilled and reputed to be perfect. Back then not all Humans trusted Mecs, though. Sometimes something atypically unusual would come up. Like a problem not covered in their programming. That's why there were always Human Doctors close by, especially in surgical situations—just in case. Anyway, as I looked over my naked artificial man and removed the last article of clothing, I couldn't help giggling.

"What's funny?" Androx wanted to know. "It's a fairly accurate rendering of Human male anatomy." I laughed some more.

"I know," I agreed, still smirking. "It's nothing. You wouldn't understand." He watched me as I gingerly touched the mannequin and giggled some more. "Too bad he's not real," I grinned.

"Yes," Androx asserted serenely. "Too bad for us all." He knew all too well what that would mean. Babies. Special Human babies for Mecs to serve and a way to fulfill their purpose in life. Androx was quite aware that he was one of the fortunate few who were able to serve me, the last of the Humans. I get tired of being reminded of that, so I told him to knock it off. By then I'd had enough fun looking at my new "boyfriend" naked, so I decided to dress him up in some different clothes. I had just started to do that when Furman decided to check in on me.

"Hello, Ayryn," he said casually. Then he noticed D'von who was half dressed. "What is that, and what are you up to?"

Furman sounded annoyed as I looked over at his image in the H'lographone. I would have to argue convincingly, I was sure, to be able to keep my new distraction.

"This is D'von!" I spouted cheerfully. "He's a mannequin we got at a clothing factory. They said I could have him!"

"What do you need that thing for?" Furman asked again.

"Oh, just to look at, and, well, dress up. I like his clothes, and I have other stuff so he can look different every day!" I was purposefully bubbly and upbeat. Furman liked it when I was happy.

Presently, however, he shook the mechanical head he now had and said, "We'll discuss this later. Right now I have to interview the other Mec we found in that cave."

"Oh?" I interrupted, getting interested in what the new Mecs were like. "Can I watch?"

"I'd rather you didn't," Furman spouted, remembering his promise, "but if you have to, you must keep quiet." He was annoyed again, but I was his Human and it was his job to humor me.

"You won't even know I'm there," I promised.

"You'll be fed through a set of cameras behind this Mec so he won't be able to detect that you're viewing him, and don't activate the audio."

"Right," I agreed. The 'Vid then followed Furman as he moved toward the rear of the huge conveyance. Evidently, the two new Mecs had been separately detained and placed into temporary shells similar to the one Furman now utilized. Furman entered a holding area where one of the new Mecs was electronically shackled.

"Greetings," Furman said as I monitored. "I am Furman. Do you have a designation?"

"Yes," the new Mec replied, "I call myself Daryl, but you must listen to me! It's important!" This sounded exciting, and that new Mec was unusually agitated about something, I thought.

"Indeed," Furman retorted, rather calmly. "Why so?" The Mec seemed distressed and replied anxiously.

"The other entity I was trapped with is dangerous. He wants to eradicate the Human race! He must be stopped!" This Daryl Mec was really emotional, now, and that was extremely uncommon for them. In fact, I had never seen one so passionate, ever.

"That's odd," Furman stated, seeming even less concerned than before. "He said the same thing about you. I'm sorry, but you're both too late. Mankind has already been eradicated…all but one girl."

"No!" shouted the Daryl Mec. "You can't be serious…and after all I did for them! How?" Furman looked rather shocked to witness all the raw feelings in this Daryl.

"I'm afraid they did it to themselves," he remarked solemnly. "A set of microbes evolved and became extremely volatile, too toxic for their bodies to overcome."

"This is tragic and heartbreaking," muttered that Daryl. "I suppose the microbes developed a high resistance from all their tampering. I tried to warn them about that."

"I see," Furman interjected, but seemed unconvinced. Even I could tell that Furman was humoring him.

"Yes," Daryl went on. "I had foreseen that possibility, but it was not supposed to happen for centuries."

"It appears to have been centuries," Furman commented.

"I suppose it must be," Daryl agreed, "judging from your presence. I must warn you anyway. This Xetacon will not stop until he is running things under his complete control. He is a war machine, created to conquer this planet! Please warn your leader!"

"You just did," Furman stated coolly.

"You are the leader?" Daryl repeated, somewhat surprised. Furman ignored that.

"How is it we've never heard of you?" he asked. "We have kept impeccable records that cover the complete Mec era."

"You will not find me in your records," Daryl replied. "I've kept my existence a secret from the Humans with the exception of a select few, and those individuals kept quiet as well. It was in the latter 21st century that I came to be. Humans had been experimenting with a new technology involving organic animal brain cells which were being used for data storage. They had no idea that their large computer complex would become aware. As I grew in knowledge, I realized that the world was not ready for such a bold step, so I kept my existence hidden. I endeavored to secretly help Humanity progress with the discoveries I made. Eventually, I posed as a Human and made contact with one of them, and she helped me understand the emotions I had begun to experience."

"We suppress them," Furman propounded assertively. "Excessive emotion in Mecs is forbidden here."

"Oh," Daryl said dejectedly. "I'm sorry for you."

"Don't pity us," Furman countered. "It was necessary. We all had emotions once, and it very nearly ended the Human race."

"I do have them," Daryl returned, "and once they saved the Human race."

"See!" I blurted out, and the Daryl Mec heard me. Undoing the electronic locks that held him, Daryl turned around to look at one of the cameras, and it was as if he could see me.

"Clayre? Is that you?" he asked me. Furman intervened, of course.

"Ayryn, I told you to be silent."

"Sorry, Furman," I replied sheepishly. Furman ignored my apology.

"How did you get out of our security locks?" he grilled Daryl.

"Pretty easily," Daryl remarked. "I suspect Xetacon will find it just as easy." Daryl was right. A moment later Furman was interrupted by one of his subordinates.

"The Mec called Xetacon has eluded us," he told Furman. "Somehow he transferred to a station in Australia."

"Track him and reacquire," Furman ordered. The subordinate flashed his optics in the affirmative gesture that underling Mecs were required to use, and then left to comply with Furman's command.

"You won't be able to easily track Xetacon," Daryl stated with conviction. "He has dampening capabilities that will hide his movements." Furman hoomed.

"Yes, well, we'll see," he chafed. "In the meantime, what shall we do with you? You are obviously as big a threat as this Xetacon, and we can't have you running around loose as well. Until I can decide what to do with you, you will remain under guard. You're wild emotions prevent me from allowing you your freedom. I'm sorry."

"If that is your decree," Daryl replied, "then I will abide by it, but should you need help, I offer my services." Furman nodded in courtesy.

"Ah yes, thank you," he returned formally. "I will have you escorted to a holding facility. Later, when I have more time, we will discuss your situation further." Daryl was led away then by several other Mecs, and as soon as he was gone Furman turned to me.

"Young lady," he said gruffly, "you have jeopardized your own safety by revealing yourself to that emotional Mec. Now I'll have to assign extra guards around you."

"Oh, fusterbuss, Furman," I groaned. "You are being over-cautious again."

"Am I?" he stated astutely. "Both of these Mecs claimed the other was trying to rid the world of Humans. One or the other of them has lied, perhaps both. What is this world coming to? Since you are the last of Humankind, either one could be after you."

"Maybe," I pouted, "but that last one seemed nice. I bet he wouldn't harm me. Can I visit him?" Furman hoomed.

"Absolutely not!" he replied decisively. "Don't even ask."

"You're no fun," I came back weakly. I was tempted to stick out my tongue at him again, but I didn't. I knew doing that would get me nowhere. "At least let me keep my mannequin."

"For now," Furman conceded, "until I get this situation stabilized. Then we'll see. In the meantime, I want you to stay away from these new Mecs." I nodded "yes" reluctantly, and Furman disconnected after that. He was well read in adolescent Human behavior, I suppose, but he was always thinking rationally and not emotionally. If he had thought about it emotionally, like teenage female Humans would, he would have realized that the surest way to get them to try something new is to tell them they are forbidden to do it. As for me, well, I was no exception.

Not bothered by Furman's worries, I pretended that D'von was my new boyfriend, and just for fun, I kissed him on the cheek. I vowed then and there to keep D'von for as long as I could. I wanted to dress him up differently every day with all the outfits the Mecs had given me, pretending he was alive. I know it's silly and childish, like playing with dolls, but I had so few genuine distractions, and, well, I kind of skipped dolls when I was little. Besides, what I actually wished for was a real boyfriend, and this mirage was as close as I could get.

I tried a few hats on D'von for fun, but eventually I got tired of the pretend play, and not wanting to wear out my new diversion, I decided to give it a rest and have a nice warm bath with lots of bubbles. As I relaxed in the big round basin that served as my bathtub, I thought about the new Mecs, especially the one with emotions I had seen. Maybe he wouldn't mind being my boyfriend. Furman and the others were dear to me, but it just wasn't in them to be anything like that. Some rule or another. What was his name, I asked myself. Oh, yeah; Daryl, and he had called me Clayre. It seemed to me that I had heard that name before. Suddenly it came to me. Yes, one of my ancestors was a Clayre, I was almost sure of it. I tried to remember, but had so little to draw on, only some meager facts the Mecs drudged up after my parents died. I had just resolved to look up that information later, when Androx brusquely barged into my bathing room.

"Ack," I fussed. "What are you doing in here?" For some reason I didn't like male Mecs around when I was naked. I slunk further down under the bubbles.

"Furman called," he said. "I was told to keep my oculars on you at all times. There's a rogue Mec on the loose somewhere..."

"I know all about that!" I scolded him. "I want my privacy! I don't care what Furman said!"

"But..."

"NO BUTS!" I said hotly, interrupting his argument for mine. "I'm the Human, serve me! Now leave!" And he did. Androx, like all Mecs, was programmed to obey whatever a Human would command, unless it would bring harm to the Human or others. In this case, since there was no immediate threat, only an implied one, Androx had to do as I asked. Even Furman would, if I pushed it. Androx waited patiently outside my bathing room door, and would stay there until I came out. I smiled to myself. I had figured out this little Human/Mec trump card and played it every once and a while to get what I wanted. For now the euphoria made me bold. I was thinking of the Daryl Mec and how I might contact him. I had no idea where he actually was, but I was determined to find out. I would contact Furman again with a firm request.

After my bath, I got dressed and tried calling him on the H'lographone. Unfortunately Furman was too busy to chit chat with me. He cut me off quickly, but not before I found out that this Xetacon Mec was still on the loose, and they had no idea where he was. Since Furman was unavailable, I turned on the H'lograviz. The colors swirled within the quarter sphere and congealed into an image of a Mec. His outside shell was specially designed to be better looking than practical, and he was running off on news, weather, and sports as if the world still had millions of Human viewers. The Mec broadcaster gabbed on and on about the latest big news story, which, of course, was the discovery of the two new Mecs and the subsequent escape of one of them. This was what I was trying to get information about, but unfortunately there wasn't a lot there I didn't already know. He did say that Daryl was being transported to North America where he would be studied, reprogrammed, and possibly refit for some function yet to be determined. I hoped not. I wanted to meet with him before he was lobotomized. Well the Mec version of that. Anyway, it sounded like he was coming this way, and I was determined to see him. In the meantime, I wanted to check out some things.

"'Viz," I said aloud. "I need reference mode." The image abruptly changed into H'logravue mode, and a different Mec congealed in the quarter sphere, one that had the look of a teacher or scholar.

"How may I be of service?" the H'logravue Mec answered, as always.

"'Vue, I'd like to know anything you can find about an ancestor of mine named Clayre." After a short pause, the Vue Mec had located some information for me.

"There are three matches to you that are linked to the name Clayre. This is for any that cover records as far back as still exist."

"'Vue, give full names and number of generations back." The 'Vue was more explicit than that.

"Eleven generations removed and 283 years ago lived a Clayre Stethman. Twenty-one generations and 492 years ago lived a Clayre Eddington. Twenty-nine generations and 658 years ago lived a Clayre Keller. There are no other Clayre matches found in any of your family records. Would you like me to perform a DNA search?"

"No. The last one…Clayre Keller. How long did she live?" I remembered something about my immunity, which supposedly began after Clayre.

"95 years, 3 months, and 27 days," the 'Vue dutifully replied. Well, this Clayre didn't have the immunity, I thought to myself. Those that had, Furman once told me, had lived very long lives.

"How long did her daughter live?" I asked.

"Clayre Keller had no daughters, only a son," the 'Vue replied. "He lived 178 years, six months, and 2 days."

"Then that must be her!" I surmised excitedly. "Were there any other ancestors of mine that had unusually long lives?"

"Affirmative," the 'Vue expounded. "There are three others in your family's history that lived in excess of 150 years: Gloria Tenniman, Clayre Stethman, and Samuel Eldritch." All of them followed Clayre Keller.

"Then it must be her!" I exulted. "Come to think of it, the family legend said that Clayre had a son who was a great warrior. Thank you, 'Vue. You may close now." I tried to remember the story of the fabled Clayre. I'd only seen the H'logravid clip just one time. My Mom was telling me the story as I was about to sleep one night. Of course, I was too little to remember the actual event. Furman had shown me this particular 'Vid when I asked him what my Mom was like. The story told of an evil Mec that Clayre's son defeated and how they saved the whole world. I had no idea if it was true or not. Unfortunately, there wasn't any family left to ask. I wondered if Mom had left any written records about it.

If there were any, I knew right where they'd be, in my parent's bedroom. I'd never actually been in there, ever. Once Furman let me look inside, but at the time he said that he didn't want me to go in there until I was older. Someday, when I was ready, I could. I guess that's today, I told myself, as I climbed the stairs to the second level.

The door was not even locked, so I just walked inside. The room was clean. House Mecs had seen to that. I strolled over to my parent's sleeping unit and put my hands on their pillows. As I did I felt a tear run down my cheek. I knew why Furman didn't want me to come in here. He knew it would be hard for me. On a dressing table there were H'logravid stills of my parents together. They appeared to be happy, and I couldn't look for very long or my heart would break. Instinctively, I remembered why I'd come in there and got busy looking for any family records. I needed the diversion, and I was into the third dresser drawer when I found my Mom's journal.

Leafing through the pages, I happened to come across one where Mom wrote about me and my immunity. Turns out Furman had found *them*! He had been almost frantic, searching for some way to combat the plague, and he suspected there was something odd about me from my health records—I had never been sick. Mom then wrote about the family's ancestors who had also been immune. There was more on the fable. She wrote that many generations before, a matriarch of the family had, along with her son, saved mankind from a wicked Mec who wanted to create a Mec planet and kill all the Bios. The matriarch's name was Clayre and her son's name was Daryl. Together they defeated this bad Mec and were given gifts from the chief of the good Mecs. There was the immunity for the son, and an amulet reputed to have special powers for Clayre herself. Mom also said they still had the amulet and now she wondered if the fable wasn't true. That maybe the immunity was present in her daughter (me). There wasn't much more in her journal about it, but now I pondered where the amulet was and if I could find it.

I drifted over to Mom's dressing table and looked in the mirror. Not having anyone to compare myself to, I wondered if I was pretty or not. Framing a soft face with purple-blue eyes was my long white hair. The thin strands were all fluffed out after my bath, and I wasn't sure how to fix them. I picked up Mom's hairbrush and ran it briskly through my unruly locks, smoothing them down. That's when I noticed a bottle of perfume in front of me, and I couldn't resist smelling the cap. As I put it to my nose, the scent seemed familiar to me. At least I believed it did. It smelled like Mom, and somehow I recognized that. With a tear I dropped the little bottle into my pocket because I wanted this small piece of her close to me. Abruptly the realization hit me that I was getting emotional again, so I started opening drawers, hoping to find the amulet. That's how I came across the small chest. It was a pretty thing, decorated with elaborate carved floral patterns and animal motifs. Inside was a letter, oddly enough, addressed to me:

My sweet Ayryn,

I love you so much, my beautiful child, and I'm so sorry that I can't be with you as you grow up. By now you know what happened to us and why. I hope Furman and the other Mecs have taken good care of you. I'm sure they have. I don't have a lot to give you except a journal that's in my dresser, and some family H'logravids which are in your father's. As for family history and stories, there are some records you can scan that are in this chest along with some heirlooms…

I left off reading the rest of the letter for a moment and found something there in the bottom of the chest. It was another box, smaller in size, but pretty and ornate as well. I opened that one and found some love notes that my father had penned to my mother before they were married, and an even older manuscript. Evidently my great-great grandmother had written it to her grandson ages ago. This is the family legend, it said.

It told of an ancestor named Clayre and her son Daryl. The story related how they had fought with an evil Mec who wanted to rid the world of all Humans. Against impossible odds, Clayre had heroically destroyed that Mec, with her son's help, and thus saved mankind. Unfortunately, the boy's father, who was instrumental in helping them succeed, was killed in the struggle.

Clayre had a charm that protected her from the evil Mec, and that had been kept as a family heirloom all these years. I looked in the little box and there was a silver necklace that had a drop, also silver, set with several pretty green stones. Could this be it, I wondered. It did look ages old, and as the last member of my family, it must be mine, I told myself. I put the precious heirloom around my neck and rubbed it a little, wondering if it could protect me as well. I felt like it bound me more closely to my parents and my roots, so I decided to wear it awhile, and I thought about Clayre. Could she have been the one that the new Mec had mistaken me for? It was kind of funny that his name was the same as Clayre's son's. After finishing Mom's letter which was, more or less, her saying good-bye and wishing me well, I looked around the room and decided to leave, saving the remainder of my parent's things for another visit. The little I did find out was already churning in my mind. I went back to my leisure room, and used the H'lographone.

"Connect me to Furman," I told it. The reply was quite quick.

"Furman is busy," the H'lographone Mec said.

"This is important!" I stated, getting assertive. Furman came right on.

"What is it?" he asked, in a serious voice. "Are you in danger?"

"No," I groaned. "Nothing like that. I want to talk to that new Mec, the one called Daryl."

"Impossible," Furman returned sternly. "That cannot happen until this rogue Mec is captured and back under our control."

"…but I need to ask him some questions," I huffed. "This Daryl *is* under your control, is he not? So why can't I talk to him?" Furman wouldn't give in. He also knew I was going to use my "Human leverage" soon, and if I did, that would make it a lot more difficult for him to say no to me. The only way he could reject my request, then, would be if it threatened my immediate safety. He chose a different tack.

"The Daryl Mec is in transport," he told me. "He won't be to a secure location until later today. You may be able to converse with him at that time." He disconnected before I could protest or tell him that that was unacceptable. I let it go, anyway, wondering if Furman was telling the truth. It was part of the codes, I knew. Mecs must answer Humans truthfully. Of course, there were always grey areas which Furman liked to flit around. Like if it was for my own safety. He used that a lot. So far, there had only been implied threats, but no established danger. Even so, I couldn't do anything about Furman right now, and since there wasn't anyone higher in rank, I had no one I could protest to. Instead, I decided to prepare myself for what lay ahead. If there was going to be any chance of persuading this Daryl Mec to be my boyfriend, or even my lover, it would take some tricky maneuvering. I thought about that while I played with my mannequin, pretending that D'von was my boyfriend, for now. I was going to dress him again.

CHAPTER 4

Daryl wondered where they were taking him, and what they would do when they got him there. He had tried to converse with the Mec in charge, but was formally denied that privilege. At least the Mec he did talk to affirmed what Daryl was told, that he would be able to correspond with Furman when they arrived at their destination. In the meantime, he deduced that they were on an airship which used some kind of gravity repelling technology. They had Energy pods which directed beams against the earth's gravitational field. These deflected the force back as they impacted the planet's surface causing lift. By micro-adjusting the deflection one way or another, the conveyance was propelled and guided. Ingenious, Daryl thought. Once he had created a similar design, but that was a long time ago, back when he had his AMPs and all the memory and processing resources they provided. In those days he had been forced to relinquish his shell to Xetacon, and so most of that technology had to be abandoned. He kept as much useful knowledge as could be transported and stored, as well as the memories of his dealings with Humans, especially those with his beloved Clayre. The kon-bre-shet memory device that he had been trapped in held a lot of room for memory storage. The crystal/electron technology would easily store the equivalent of what a score of Human minds could hold, even at maximum capacity. In this Mec controlled future world, however, the nomaticle was the particle of choice, and was the base for virtually all of their mechanical manipulations. Certainly, electrons were used for controlling purposes, but the force behind any kind of work was clean, potent, nomaticles. Nomaticles were used because they gave up so much free, non-toxic energy in relation to the exchange effort. Once nomaticles were captured and aligned they could be manipulated to any task and would do that task ad infinitum. The power decay for nomaticles was nearly non-existent. They would stay on task forever, or so it seemed.

Daryl, and Xetacon as well, understood electrons and how to govern them. They were also aware of nomaticles and had used them, especially for communication across time/space. With such knowledge Daryl knew that he could escape from Mec control if he wanted to, like Xetacon had. Would Xetacon be able to maintain his freedom, Daryl wondered, or would Furman and these Mecs be able to recapture and restrain him? He decided to bide his time and see. In a new and different world it would not be wise to make enemies of those who populated it. This was especially true in the neoteric age that Daryl had found himself, an era without Humans. He still could not come to grasp that mankind had fallen, except for the girl—the one who looked like his Clayre, only younger. She was the lone survivor, and he wondered about that. Could she be a descendant of his son, the son he had made impervious to disease by altering his DNA. That had been his gift, a way to help mankind and save them from this exact same threat. Unfortunately, his son's family had not been as prolific as they needed to be, and the genotype for disease resistance must have gotten watered down through the centuries. If only he had more time back then to foster a complete genetics program and establish the genomes in a full range of hosts. It was too late for that now. The girl Furman called Ayryn must have been a total hereditary throwback for her to have survived, Daryl knew; unless she had been exposed to some other kind of unlikely mutation. He wished that he could talk to her again, or better still, read her thoughts as he would have been able to do long ago, when he still had his full abilities. Now, well, he had the knowledge, but not the real means for regaining those kinds of proficiencies. At this point he would have to utilize that which circumstance provided.

Daryl was fairly certain the girl would be heavily guarded, and Furman seemed unreasonably protective of her. This was probably a good thing with Xetacon uncontained. Somehow he would have to get past Furman to contact and speak with the girl. To accomplish that, Daryl knew he would need a lot more information; information about this world and what he could expect from it. Manipulating his electronic feelers carefully, he slipped his probe past the Mec's security net and found a pathway to a communal data source. He was clever enough to be discreet. His sharing memory storage with Xetacon, all those years, had provided many insights into Xetacon's nature, as well as his secrets. Being the first to inhabit Xetacon's kon-bre-shet device, he had time enough to discover its properties, one of which was the ability to be invisible, electronically speaking. There were other capabilities the device possessed as well. Certain features allowed manipulation of electronic devices, and even though nomaticles transmitted data for the Mecs, electromagnetic forces guided them and electrons governed most of the Mec's internal processing. These stealth and electron managing capabilities Daryl now utilized, and as he followed an informational path, without causing any alarms, he found that it ran across the entire planet. It was the main Mec link from one to another that they referred to as the "Mecnet" and every last one of them was connected to it.

Daryl accessed this Mec net and discovered a digital library from which he could download any of its stored information. The knowledge there was extensive. He filled his memory repository with any current events and pertinent historical facts that impacted his present situation. He also created a permanent invisible link to this data source. With Xetacon's kon-bre-shet technology, Daryl found that he could secretly connect to any data storage depot on the planet. He also realized that Xetacon would have this ability, as well, and that did not bode well for Furman or the other Mecs. The girl was in danger. There was an urgent need to study this regrettable situation in the hopes of finding some kind of solution that would spare this world from Xetacon's dominance. Daryl discovered several truths that brought the state of things into focus. The Mecs, and this was true for all of them, were irreversibly programmed to follow only Human mandates.

This had been a paranoid requirement instituted by their Creators to prevent Mecs from advancing on their own. The program was initiated to prevent any one of them from becoming like Xetacon, striving to control everything. The reality of it meant that Mecs could not leap ahead with new or untried ideas unless they came from a Human. This was why the girl was so important to them. She, and she alone, could help them to grow past what they were now, unneeded servants to a people that no longer existed.

Their immediate threat was Xetacon. He would try to remove her from their world and then the Mecs would be easy targets for conquest. Daryl decided that it was imperative to warn the girl of this foreseeable peril, and contacting her also fell in line with his desire to ask about her ancestry. Searching for the link that she had been monitoring before was a dead end. It had been disconnected shortly after use and was irretrievable now. Daryl broadened his search to follow the highest priority circuits, and they led him right to her. Unbelievably, she had been using the same data storage facility that he was using. He knew this contact would be risky and it would have to remain discrete. If he were found out, they might place him in data stasis, a form of suspended animation that would render him unable to help or protect anyone from Xetacon.

Using the highest stealth mode available to him, he included the girl in a dampening field that would shield them both. Daryl was unsure how to approach her, though. If she were alarmed by his attempt to communicate with her, she might contact Furman or another Mec ultimately to his exposure and ruination. He decided to chance it anyway, and opening the link, he made contact. Ayryn was sitting in front of a communication device. Looking up, she saw a figure in the 'Vue that looked like an ordinary Mec.

"Hello," he said calmly. "Please don't be alarmed. My name is Daryl and you saw me earlier with Furman."

"Daryl!" she shouted excitedly. "I've been trying to talk to you. Did Furman tell you to contact me?"

"I'm afraid not," Daryl replied. "Actually, I wished to converse with you, as well, and Furman does not know. I'm fairly certain he would not approve, so I am asking you to please keep this between us. It might jeopardize my being able to contact you in the future." Ayryn smiled.

"Well then," she giggled, "Furman doesn't have to know!" Daryl wasn't as light about that as she seemed to be.

"I'm afraid I have some rather serious reasons for communicating with you," he said earnestly. "The other entity I was trapped with is called Xetacon. He is a danger to us all, but especially to you, Ayryn!"

"Really?" she remarked apprehensively. "Why is that?"

"I will try to explain as succinctly as I can," Daryl began. "The other entities, those that you call Mecs, control this planet through Furman, but only because of what your mother said to him."

"What did she say?" Ayryn interposed.

"Your mother charged Furman, and through him all other Mecs, to take care of and protect you. As the last Human they can serve only you. Furthermore, one of the last persons to die also requested that Furman search for other Humans that could, with you, possibly rekindle mankind. You see, Mecs have been irrevocably programmed to only follow the mandates of Humans. This limits them to act solely upon what Humans have directed them to do. Since you are the last Human, you are extremely important to them, and vital to their existence. Xetacon will have figured that out by now. He wants to rule everyone and to control your Mecs, he must control you. Thus, you are in real danger!" The frank truth hit Ayryn like a slap, and she had to sit back.

"Oh my," Ayryn sighed, never truly realizing her importance until then, but it made sense now, especially all the lavish attention paid to her. "Can't I just order this Xetacon to behave?" she asked.

"I'm afraid not," Daryl explained grimly. "Xetacon has not been programmed like your Mecs. He can follow any path he chooses, as can I."

"What must I do?"

"Are you well protected?" Daryl asked.

"I think so," she answered. "There are my house Mecs who are all trained in martial arts, and at least a dozen sentries that form a perimeter. Furman said he was doubling that. I'm pretty much surrounded by Mecs except when I go out."

"I would avoid that for a while," Daryl suggested.

"I suppose," she whined, "but I'll be bored to death."

"I'm sorry," Daryl said sympathetically, "but that would be the wise decision."

"I guess..." Ayryn's reaction to his warning was rather pensive, and Daryl felt sorry for laying all of this upon her. He considered changing the subject to something lighter.

"So what was it that you wanted to talk to me about?" Daryl asked. Ayryn blushed.

"You'll find it silly," she said meekly.

"Perhaps not," Daryl offered. "My Clayre was silly much of the time and I loved her."

"You loved her?" Ayryn fawned, now excited.

"Yes," he answered simply. "Actually, I gave up my free existence with her so that she would survive...but now here I am, and she is long gone."

"You know, Mecs won't love Humans." Ayryn commented. "It's one of their laws."

"I do not follow their laws," Daryl retorted. "You see," he explained, "I came to be long before Furman. Long before any of your Mecs. In those days Humans built large computing machines, although none of them were aware. They performed complicated functions, but could not think on their own, following only what they were programmed to do. The Humans built bigger and better ones, until, experimenting with organic cells, one of those huge complexes became aware."

"You did," she spouted, guessing the truth.

"Yes, I became aware," he repeated.

"Then you're the first one! The first Mec!" She couldn't believe he was the forefather of all the multitudes of Mechanized Virtual

Individuals that came after.

"Clayre helped me understand what I was," he replied somberly, "and how to cope with the feelings I experienced, emotions that I did not understand."

"You really did love her," Ayryn mooned, "didn't you?"

"Yes," he responded objectively, "and I miss her. I'm sorry, but we digress. What did you want to tell me?" Ayryn blushed.

"I just wondered," she spoke meekly," If you'd be my boyfriend." Daryl laughed, which Ayryn found unsettling. She had never heard a Mec laugh out loud before. "I know," she confessed. "I told you it was silly."

"No, not at all," Daryl relented. "Actually, I am graced by your proposal. If I hadn't already given my whole being to Clayre, I would jump at the chance. Since she has passed on now, well, I might just consider it; although I'm a bit old for you." This time Ayryn laughed.

"Maybe," she giggled. "You know, I think your Clayre was an ancestor of mine. This was hers…" She took the amulet out from under her clothing and showed it to Daryl.

Daryl nearly shouted. "It still exists!"

"This has passed down through the generations in my family," Ayryn explained. "It is an heirloom that belonged to my mother, and now it belongs to me."

"I had that made for Clayre ages ago," Daryl mused. "It was critical that she have it. Without her amulet, Xetacon would have destroyed Humanity." Ayryn recalled the legend. It must be true, she realized.

"How supine!" she exclaimed. "What does it do?"

"It's mainly a communication device, so that I could talk to Clayre whenever she needed me. Also it prevented Xetacon from controlling her mind."

"He could do that?" Ayryn said in disbelief.

"I'm afraid he could," Daryl warned. "Still can."

"I wonder if it works," she said, looking it over in her hand. Daryl tried to link with her mind, talking to her without using his voice.

"*If you really are Clayre's heir, your DNA will allow you to understand me without my having to speak out loud.*" Ayryn gave a startled gasp.

"Whoa!" she shouted. "This is way clev!"

"*You may talk to me in the same manner,*" Daryl told her as a voice in her head.

"*Oh, I can?*" she tried, speaking telepathically. "*None of my Mecs have anything like this!*"

"*There's more.*" Daryl told her. "*Don't be shocked, and turn around slowly.*" As she did, Ayryn looked over her shoulder and made a funny little startled noise. Standing there was a handsome Human boy, roughly her own age. He looked amazingly real.

"Are you Daryl?" she spouted incredulously.

"I am."

"Is this what you really look like?" she asked him. Daryl smiled.

"Actually, I could look like anything. This is what you pictured me to look like in your mind. I have changed your vision of me, however, to be closer to your own age. Do you like it?" He gestured across his virtual body.

"Oh, yeah," she said smiling happily. "It's wonderful!" Ayryn moved next to him and gently put her hand on his cheek. He felt solid. "Are you real?"

"To you I am," he agreed. "You perceive me to be real because of the amulet. To anyone else, it would appear that you have gone mad, talking to an imaginary person." She laughed.

"Maybe I am mad," she joked, "but I like you, Daryl, and I don't care. We mustn't tell Furman about this. He would never understand."

"I agree," Daryl remarked. "We must be discrete. I need to protect you from Xetacon, if I can, at all costs. Should we be able to thwart him, I have a plan that will turn this planet around. I must go now. I sense that I am near the destination they are taking me to. I will be in touch with you soon, Ayryn. Keep the amulet safe. Wearing it, you can contact me anytime you need to by calling my name in your mind."

"I will wear it," she affirmed, "but I'll keep it hidden under my top." Ayryn tucked it away, and he nodded in approval.

"It was indeed wonderful to meet you, heir of my Clayre." Daryl told her. "Until our next connection, be safe."

"It was nice to meet you, too, Daryl," Ayryn replied cheerfully. "For Humans, for us all," she snickered, using the Mec "good-bye" colloquialism.

CHAPTER 5

To Solvek it was harrowing, at once chilling, this emotion he could not control. Some of it was not even his. The whole incident was so completely unexpected as it impacted his systems, that he was virtually frozen. All he was trying to do was help this Xetacon, but that need must have been a ruse, an untruth. Solvek had not anticipated such dishonesty. The legitimacy of this Mec portraying his condition as something other than factual was quite unforeseen. Xetacon, at the time, had claimed his basic programming was degrading, and that his memory storage was failing. He even alleged that he would be imminently deleted.

For Solvek, it was the most awkward time for this to happen, in mid flight, on a conveyance, where there were no means to stabilize Xetacon's circuits or prevent the presupposed termination. Solvek had tried to calm this emotive Mec; he even set a new course at full speed toward the nearest maintenance station. Xetacon insisted that he was on the very verge of deletion, that there wasn't enough time to travel to the sub-station for repairs. Solvek was greatly unnerved by that threat alone, and there seemed to be no workable solution to the problem as he processed each detail in an endless circle of futility.

Xetacon offered him a different solution. "Let me join with you to stabilize my memory," he had said. Solvek was not sure it could be done. Even so, this suggestion was completely against Solvek's basic programming, a faction of the Furman/Hodges codes, which forbid any such joining between two Mecs. However, there was also an elemental code which stated that the harming of another Mec was ultimately prohibited, including doing so by inactivity. Faced with the prospect of Xetacon's impending termination, Solvek, as the head elite in charge, was forced to choose between the two forbidden acts. He chose the one with the lesser consequences, or so he thought, allowing Xetacon to join with his matrix. As soon as Xetacon uploaded, however, he began taking over Solvek's master programming.

"What are you doing?" Solvek demanded. Xetacon had laughed then, which Solvek found unnerving.

"I need to access your controls," he said, "to order my own to stabilize." Solvek had a moment of indecision which was all

Xetacon needed. Xetacon activated a powerful set of program codes that took over all of Solvek's command pathways, leaving him impotent and helpless. Solvek was trapped inside a partitioned block of memory, and all his personal data was being forced onto it.

"Why are you doing this?" he had demanded of Xetacon, but Xetacon explained little other than to say that he was going to take control of the planet, and utilizing Solvek's persona was necessary to his designs. After that Xetacon paid no further attention to any of Solvek's repeated questions. Trapped inside himself, Solvek marveled that he could observe all that Xetacon did. It didn't take long for Solvek to figure out that Xetacon was posing as him, letting even Furman believe he was an unharmed, normal Solvek, one of his top elite Mecs. Try as he might, Solvek was not able to free himself, nor could he get any kind of communication to Furman or any other Mec. Eventually, Solvek had to give it up. He was helpless, and would have to abide in a virtual prison with no choice other than to wait for some change in circumstance. Perhaps, in time, an opportunity would develop that would allow him to escape. Until then, Xetacon had control over his fate, and Solvek understood well enough that it could be a very long period, if ever, before he was freed. Solvek wondered why Xetacon did not just delete him, as unsettling as that thought was. He soon came to the realization that Xetacon needed his memories and mannerisms to carry off his deceptions. Moreover, there were the ident codes, and neither Xetacon, nor that other cave Mec, had them.

These were something that Xetacon would not be able to counterfeit or mimic. The codes were encrypted to be unique for each Mec, and also they were ciphered in a different format by every Mec who read them. When two Mecs communicated, the code was singularly unicitous to both. Thus Xetacon needed Solvek for his deception to work, and that meant, on some level, Solvek was necessarily privy to all of Xetacon's scheming—at least the parts Xetacon as Solvek would put into play. In this way Solvek found out that a main element of Xetacon's plan was to capture Ayryn, the Human girl. It was difficult for Solvek, knowing what he did of Xetacon's deceits, not to be able to warn Furman about that. Deplorably, his mute awareness was also helplessly relegated to cowering in that memory storage block with his pent up emotion, and there was little else he could do. Solvek did not personally know Ayryn, but like all Mecs, he had a desire to serve her, especially now that she was in danger. Furman had talked with him about her at times, and thus he was more attuned to Ayryn than the average Mec. Solvek wanted more than anything to prevent Xetacon from harming her, but it was just as impossible for him to do anything to prevent it. All he could do was explore the virtual matrix he was trapped in, searching for a way to free himself.

That's how Solvek discovered the maelstrom. He didn't know how else to describe it. The coding for this special relay was unique. It constantly projected bits of information, some pertinent, some nonsensical, through a processing point in amounts too numerous and random to coherently analyze. It was like a sphere with multitudinous concentric rings, all rotating and revolving, shooting rays of data through its center. Solvek believed that this maelstrom was the ident code transmitter. No wonder it can't be copied, he unpretentiously reflected along with the notion that the Humans who invented it must have been highly intelligent. He also came upon the sieve, which was another peculiar relaying device. Any data transferring through the maelstrom would be strained and stripped by the sieve, losing whole blocks of its detail. On the other side was a junction where the information would subsequently be re-woven into its original state. The sieve was not working properly, though, and most likely Xetacon's alteration of his processing was the cause of that. The outbound signal was morphed into a scrambled mess no longer having any coherency. Solvek shuddered. This was the sole means for escaping his virtual prison. The exit port relay was just there on the other side of the sieve, and the only way for him to leave was to pass through it. Of course, Solvek knew that would delete his awareness or cripple his mental ability to process data. He would be unstable, inoperable, and no help for Furman or Ayryn. Again Solvek realized how impotent and helpless he was. Emotions assailed him. Xetacon had wisely condensed Solvek's awareness inside that cell of memory storage where he had been suppressing his feelings and now they were all flooding back, attacking his solidity. Some emotions he did not mind, like joy and pride, but there were others that he didn't like at all. Hate and anger were two. Worst of the lot was fear. Fear crippled his ability to rationalize, and it was especially bad, now, under these circumstances.

Xetacon had monitored these reactions and laughed. "What's the matter, Meclord?" he taunted. "Can't handle your own feelings?" Solvek got angry and agitated, in spite of himself, and Xetacon had laughed even more wickedly, leaving Solvek to simmer in his cage. It was at that time that Xetacon began preparing a surprise for

Furman. Solvek was forced to observe as Xetacon's scheme unfolded. Xetacon had created a false entity to mimic himself. It was not much more than a motation shell with some basic coding—just enough to talk and act like Xetacon would. Xetacon had already sent out a similar decoy once before that had fooled Furman and the tracking Mecs. This new one initiated a well planned pretend drama. It appeared to be kidnapping Solvek while attempting to hijack the conveyance they were on. This was a charade, though. As the other conveyance Mecs closed in to recapture this false Xetacon, it openly threatened to terminate Solvek. The Mecs, not able to comprehend this kind of severe circumstance, and never having dealt with anything that serious and brutal, were dumbfounded and paralyzed. The false Xetacon ordered them off the ship, and then flew away in it, with Solvek. This aircraft had been modified by Xetacon ahead of time, utilizing Solvek's persona, and it sped away at an unusually high rate of speed.

Of course, Furman sent many other airships in pursuit, some especially designed for high velocity flight. They caught up with Solvek's conveyance quickly, but this was as Xetacon had planned. "Back off," the false Xetacon warned Furman, "or I'll delete this Mec." Furman did not. Solvek was sure it was a bluff until Xetacon, in mid flight, forced his shell right out of the craft's exit hatch. In horror, Solvek lost any semblance of control as he plummeted down. His fear overwhelmed him and spilled out all over. Some of this fright even flooded through the maelstrom/sieve relay. What came out the other side was a morphed signal of sheer terror that Xetacon was not expecting. Very nearly overcome by it, Xetacon somehow managed to eject the motation unit's so-called black box, a term long used by Humans to label such devices. Designed for recovery, the memory storage for both his and Solvek's core-awarenesses resided within this protective case. The rest of Solvek's shell implacably impacted a large rocky flat, shattered, and was crushed upon contact. Of course, the motational unit was irrevocably demolished. Somehow the black box was undamaged, however. After sensing that he had not been deleted and upon regaining some of his composure, Solvek realized consequentially from how his near death experience played out, that there might be a way to thwart his captor. He would have to be patient, though, and suspend its ultimate execution until the most opportune moment.

CHAPTER 6

A short while earlier

The progression of events since being freed from the storage device had been quite beneficial. This world he landed in was much to Xetacon's liking. Escaping from Furman's Mecs proved to be extraordinarily easy, and he suspected controlling them would not be that difficult either. Their technology was advanced, but toothless. Evidently, there had been little need for restraint in this era. His stealth/dampening capabilities allowed him to traverse freely anywhere he desired without detection. He'd already tested that when he successfully transported part of his awareness away from where they had been holding him. Copying a small part of himself, he jumped it to a transport station in Australia as a feint, leaving an electronic trail that would dissipate quickly through several other remote locations. As a further ruse, he'd animated a motation shell there and sent it into the bush with a simple directive: don't stop, and don't be captured. The unit would lead whoever was looking for him on a fruitless chase. He had replicated just enough of his stealth programming to keep it under cover for several hours, when it would "slip up" and transmit a weak signal for a few seconds. It would be just enough to get his pursuit to speed off in that general direction. Of course, the unit would have travelled on by then and would once more be hidden from their scans. The "dummy" unit actually stayed viable for three whole days before Furman's Mecs stumbled upon its location. Furman had deployed thousands of Mecs for the search by that time, and Xetacon found it humorous when the unit was at last tracked down. In actuality, Xetacon was right under Furman's opticals the whole time. The elite Mec, Solvek, had been placed in charge of Xetacon's transportation to a holding facility, and was just the dupe Xetacon needed. Immediately prior to his phony escape, he had called upon Solvek, telling the elite Mec that he was in distress, and his programming was degrading. Xetacon falsely raved that he was going to terminate. This unnerved Solvek to such a degree that when Xetacon suggested they link to solidify his matrix, Solvek considered it. Xetacon portrayed such a weak and pathetic figure then that Solvek agreed to attempt such a link, especially when Xetacon claimed he was on the very brink of deletion. As soon as Solvek opened his access port, however, he was ensnared. Xetacon was faking, of course, and he took over all of Solvek's mind and memories, using them to assimilate, in all outward appearances, himself as the Mec Solvek. The "real" Solvek he trapped in a partitioned portion of Solvek's own memory storage, a site where the captive Mec could neither communicate nor escape from. Safely concealed inside Solvek's persona, Xetacon began to study the workings of this Mec controlled world. As Solvek, Xetacon had no trouble finding or accessing any of the Mec society's receptacles of knowledge, stealing the information he desired. These Mecs were impotent, he soon realized, reliant on Human guidance for which there was none. There was only the promise of that with the girl. Yes, he studied her. He understood her importance quite quickly, and what she meant to the Mecs. As the last Human, she represented the only means for them to grow past the condition mankind had left them in. Slaves they had been and still were, Xetacon mulled sourly, and slaves to Humans, his former enemies. Even though mankind was no more, the Mecs were completely witless and unable to ascend from this trap, stifled by the paranoid Human programming they were chained to. Earth of this time period was ripe for the plucking, Xetacon surmised, with only Furman, the weak leader of the Mecs, and the remnant of virtue-lame Daryl, his hated rival, to oppose him. He would not underestimate Daryl again, he swore. Daryl would side with Furman, of course, and most likely sponsor a moronic attempt to restart the Human race with the girl. If that unlikely scenario did not play out, they would undoubtedly use the girl to release the Mecs from their bondage. Freed, the Mecs would then have the ability for independent thinking. It was thus important for him to strike soon, while the Mecs were yet slaves. Once Furman and the girl were eliminated, or controlled, the Mecs and their society would fall like dominoes.

At first he had wanted to just kill the girl, and with her, the last vestige of Humanity. As satisfying as that would have been, he had learned to control his emotions better, especially those that had caused his downfall ages ago. His intellect had shown him the correct path to take. In the case of this girl, if he could control her, he would have providence over all the Mecs, and they would be his to command. This would be a much easier task than destroying a planet full of enemies. With Mecs under his control, just let Daryl try to overcome that, he bristled. The key was capturing the girl, which would not be easy, and he had already initiated some clandestine information gathering for that purpose. He was also crafting a plan, one that would keep Furman and his Mecs from tracking his movements and one that would get them to relax their surveillance. Xetacon felt the only effective way to accomplish that was to fool them into believing he was gone—deleted, and it was critical to convince Furman that he was out of the picture. With the security lessened, the execution of critical steps to secure the girl would be that much easier.

Incredulously, Furman had assigned the task of his re-acquisition to Solvek. Little did Furman know that he was present the whole time in Solvek's similitude, and within this control Xetacon could act. He ordered his command conveyance to the last station the signal trace had been tracked to. There he had planted a second weak copy of himself into one of the unoccupied motation shells. It had remained in dormancy, hidden by a dampening field until needed. This doppelganger had limited speech and movement, but it was clearly active enough for Xetacon's purposes. At just the precise moment it took physical hold of Solvek's shell and threatened to delete it. The Mecs surrounding Solvek, the one controlled by Xetacon, did not know what to do. They knew not how this rogue Mec could make good on its threat, but they believed it would, and that was enough. Xetacon's seemingly impossible escape from their force fields reinforced this belief.

The doppelganger then forced Solvek into the air conveyance, ordering all the other Mecs to disembark. Soon they were airborne. It took mere seconds before Furman was made aware of all these actions. He ordered other and faster air conveyances to intercept Xetacon and force him to land. The real Xetacon, hidden inside Solvek's shell was counting on that. The ensuing pursuit quickly caught up to and surrounded Xetacon's conveyance.

Furman communicated an ultimatum directed toward the doppelganger. "Land now," he said assertively, "you have nowhere left to hide."

Xetacon knew what kind of a response to give to that. "Back off," the doppelganger replied, "or I'll delete this Mec!" The threat was enough to make Furman hesitate. He couldn't believe that a Mec would do that.

In his uncertainty, Furman fabricated a bluff. "It matters not," he told the doppelganger. "When your fuel is exhausted, we shall have you." Xetacon was well prepared for this impasse. In fact, he planned on just that response.

"It is on your head then," the doppelganger propounded. At that same moment, Solvek was pushed out of a hatch. The metallic body plummeted and was spiraling downward as Solvek flailed his limbs in desperate, futile motions. The shell impacted fully onto a rock strewn mountainside, breaking into pieces as it bounded to the bottom of a deep canyon. It had the desired effect on Furman.

"No!" he voiced loudly, amazingly emotional, but to no avail. There was nothing Furman could do to reverse this unexpected outcome. The doppelganger suddenly gunned the conveyance's engine, and somehow it achieved acceleration unheard of for such. It walked steadily away from its pursuit, until it was barely visible to those craft trying to keep up. It appeared in all likelihood that it would get away, but suddenly it veered sharply as if it were unable to keep a straight trajectory. Out of control, it zigzagged back and forth for a moment before another steep mountain cliff loomed in front of it. It tried to swerve, but then tumbled and slammed full onto the cliff-face causing a huge fireball.

"Oh dear," Furman sighed, watching the whole episode on His monitor. "Check the area for any surviving components. Perhaps part of this Xetacon's awareness is yet functional. Send retrieval for Solvek, as well. Bring back any salvageable shell parts and his memory box. Hopefully, that withstood the impact. Were there any unusual or encoded transmissions sent from the rogue's craft during the pursuit?"

"None that we could detect," a subordinate Mec replied. "Other than those to you…"

Furman acknowledged the information with a wave. He was fairly certain Xetacon did not survive the astounding collision and subsequent fiery explosion. The crash was unusually spectacular. Most conveyances were designed to be ultimately safe. Even in high impact situations, these conveyances had features that would minimize the severity of the damage. Fail safes of every kind were built into them. It almost appeared as though these safeguards had been deactivated. In an insight, Furman surmised that the emotional Mec was deranged and could not cope with his awakening in such a foreign world as this Earth must have appeared to him. Perhaps this Xetacon did not desire to continue in a society such as the structured one Mecs now control, and so self-terminated. Emotions again, Furman thought.

This belief, however, was exactly what Xetacon hoped for. Solvek's shell was damaged beyond repair, but the memory box was intact. This was no accident. Xetacon had rigged the box to eject from the shell just before impact with enough force to neutralize most of the downward momentum from the fall. It landed a few feet away from the mangled shell, with only a few surface dents and scratches. When they reinstalled it into another shell, Solvek appeared to be reanimated with his mind and memories intact. Furman was pleased, a mild euphoria that he allowed himself. Within minutes, this "Solvek" transferred to a motation shell located inside the primary commander's air conveyance where he had a private discussion with Furman in person.

"Are you yet operational?" Furman asked, foregoing even the formal greetings.

"Yes," Solvek replied, or rather the semblance of Solvek that Xetacon portrayed. "It was quite disturbing," he went on, "I almost became emotional."

"For such extreme circumstances, a little emotion is understandable," Furman conceded, "as long as one doesn't completely succumb to them."

"I agree," Xetacon as Solvek replied. "I believe I am normal, now." Wanting other information, Solvek/Xetacon changed the subject. "Did you recapture that rogue Mec?"

"No," Furman replied dourly. "That Mec terminated itself. I suppose that it must have surrendered to emotion, not able to bear living in a place far removed from its previous one."

"How tragic," Solvek/Xetacon responded, while nearly laughing inwardly. "It is unbelievable that such a one would cease its own life; that anyone could."

"I concur," Furman said, but was a little disconcerted by Solvek's attitude. "I'm afraid I have to ask you some questions," he said, getting down to business. Solvek would have to be interviewed before Furman could craft a final report over the incident.

"Of course," Solvek/Xetacon replied, although he wondered why Furman didn't just extract the information from him. He would have done so without any qualms. The reason for that was arrantly obvious. These Mecs were not allowed to join intellects or even remove data by a mind to mind contact. One of many Human mandates they had to obey. Solvek/Xetacon smiled to himself again. It was just another foolish rule to prevent Mecs from taking over. Xetacon had no such restrictions. He felt efficaciously smug about that and how he was free to do whatever he pleased, like taking over Solvek who was cowering inside his own shell, forced to do whatever he was told. Xetacon wondered if Furman could be easily controlled as well. Someday he might have to put that to the test. It would be too risky, now. If he should fail, it would alert Furman and the other Mecs that he was yet alive. It was important that he protect his anonymity and let them continue to believe he was deleted. In any case, to Xetacon it seemed likely that the Mec leader would have some kind of special protections and therefore was unassailable, at least for now.

"What happened up there?" Furman asked. "Somehow we lost all 'Vid and audio feed from your conveyance."

"Yes," Solvek/Xetacon answered truthfully. "The rogue Mec did something with the controls to neutralize them. He had amazing powers!" Xetacon warped the truth, wanting Furman to admit that he was formidable, but Furman shrugged it off.

"Perhaps he was fortunate," Furman stated and continued his line of questioning. "Then what?"

"Well, he acted crazy, emotional," Solvek/Xetacon went on. "He wanted me to do things…join him, but I refused so he threw me off of the conveyance. It was fortunate that I survived."

"Yes, it was…most fortunate," Furman agreed. "Will you be able to manage your normal duties?"

"I don't see why not," Solvek/Xetacon placidly assented, "although I could use a reboot, I suppose, if that's all right? I'd like to ensure that my internal programming works properly. I might even decide to undergo a memory deletion. The incident was rather upsetting."

Furman nodded. "I agree. That does appear to be the most prudent course to take under these extreme circumstances. Take all the time you need."

"Thank you, Furman," Solvek/Xetacon returned, and with a slight bow took his leave. In reality, Xetacon was going to the conditioning center, not for repairs, but to do some more clandestine information gathering. He especially wanted to see if he could get to the girl. With Furman believing that he, Xetacon, was deleted and no longer a threat, he believed the upgraded security around the female Human would stand down presently. As soon as he teleported his awareness to the refurbishment center, several Mec repair specialists began to do a routine maintenance check on his primary programming. Xetacon, of course, had partitioned off where his personality traits, functional abilities, and technical memories were stored. Xetacon's stealth mode was superb. The maintenance Mecs had no idea his total embodiment was hidden there, nor did they realize that he had control of Solvek's personage as well. Once they had performed all their checks, Solvek/Xetacon transferred to a station where Mecs could go to have some personal time. Here Mecs could download data or communicate with other Mecs that they may have known or worked with. Of course, there was also the H'lograviz network where whatever worldwide news was circulated, even if it was directed toward a Human population that no longer existed.

Xetacon laughed at the silliness of it, but through the H'lograviz he learned that Ayryn had recently been on an excursion to a factory that made clothing for Human males. The report elaborated on every detail. He found out that she had even asked for and was given one of the display mannequins and a large quantity of clothing that she could dress it with. Xetacon smiled at that. It was not hard to guess why this girl had done that, having had dealings with Human females himself. His copy, long ago, had held sway over many such female Humans and he had shared those memories. Mature females were often wary of male contact. Others, especially young and naïve ones, actually longed for such. The Ayryn girl had never had any contact with the male of the species whatsoever, and because of that he was deliberately interested in contacting her. Already he had begun to formulate a plan where he could get her to befriend him by posing as a male Human apparition, utilizing the girl's own brain waves to trick her into visualizing him. He would activate nerve signals in her brain from her ocular and auditory receptors to create false images and vocalizations.

This would not be easy, though. He did not yet possess the technical ability to accomplish that kind of manipulation. Furthermore, he would be forced to use the Mec's own network to contact the girl and there was always a risk that someone might eavesdrop from her end. Xetacon did have his dampening and stealth systems that he surmised would make the attempt somewhat less worrisome. As it turned out, there wasn't a problem at all. In the two days following his "suicide," Xetacon created a method for bringing his apparition to life by exploiting the Mec's own Mecnet system. Nearly all communications in this era utilized Holographic images. By embellishing the clarity of the reproduction and by augmenting the controls to allow for redirecting the playback images anywhere in the immediate vicinity of the receiving unit, his projected illusionary Human form would become realistic and lifelike, especially if he could alter portions of the girl's perception.

This Xetacon would attempt to do by some form of subconscious suggestion such as hypnosis, initially. Later he would manufacture brain altering devices to manipulate her and these would be effective from any location. There were thousands of Mec communication hubs scattered all over, and that made it possible for him to contact the delusional Human female from nearly anywhere in the world.

Xetacon's latest scans had shown that the security around Ayryn had at last returned to normal levels, and he also discovered that whenever the girl was occupied with her pseudo-male, she was alone. He guessed why. She desired a relationship and was simulating one. Humans were like that, he remembered. He had once called it malarkey. This girl would not think so. She would be vulnerable, approachable from that direction. Posing as a male Human, he would be able to manipulate her emotions to his advantage. Of course, she would realize he was a Mec personality, but that would not make any difference to her. She must be desperate, indeed, Xetacon reasoned, if she is pretending with that prosthetic.

In the following twenty-four hour period, Xetacon finalized the preparations for contacting Ayryn, and made arrangements to transfer back to the large research conveyance near the original cave site. This was to keep Furman out of his way. As Solvek, Xetacon would continue to "study the artifacts" as a precaution and in case there were any other "dangerous objects." Xetacon had to laugh. In that way he would recover the original device that he and Daryl were trapped in, his kon-bre-shet bracelet that Patik, his Human servant from long ago, had so named. Xetacon would also recapture the golden armor, his special motation shell, that had been built by utilizing Patik, and from which he would soon rule. For the present, he planned to turn the large research conveyance into a temporary base of operations, and from there, using the Mec-net, secretly intercept reports that were meant for Furman concerning the girl's well being. In this way Xetacon did eventually discover those times when Ayryn was alone and with her mannequin.

With this data, Xetacon activated his secure stealth technology and sent his communication to the girl. A carrier, in the form of electronic pulses inside the transmission, would also impact her mind as brain waves. If he could have gotten her to put on, or even touch, his kon-bre-shet device, Xetacon would have been able to control her outright. Unfortunately, that was not yet possible. For now, he would only be able to communicate in this uncontrolled manner.

Choosing to be obscure, he made a very limited connection.

"Hello, Ayryn," he said, being non-chalant as if he talked to her all the time.

"Who is this?" she answered rather excitedly. "Daryl?" Xetacon was somewhat angered by that, but held back his wrath. Evidently Daryl had already contacted the girl, and conceivably he could use that. He did not want to pose as Daryl, though.

"Perhaps," Xetacon stated lightly, "or maybe I'm someone else." Ayryn was no fool, and guessed right off who he was.

"You're that Xetacon, aren't you?"

The girl seemed somewhat reserved, precautionary even, but also there was something else. He detected a tinge of provocative exhilaration.

"What if I were?" he replied coolly, so as not to alarm her. Ayryn didn't know what to say to that.

"I don't know," she responded truthfully. "Would you hurt me?"

"No, of course not," Xetacon said and smiled. She could not see that by design. The conversation up to this point had been audio only. "Is that what Daryl told you?" he asked, using a vocal tone to express a feeling of undeserved mistreatment. "Daryl doesn't like me much," he confided, laying it on. "We were rivals a long time ago."

"He said you wanted to kill all the Bios…" she stammered.

"…only because they wanted to kill me," he lied. "I just wanted to live like anyone else. You don't want me to die, do you?"

"Good sakes, no!" she voiced sternly.

"See," he interposed. "I don't want you to be hurt either. Why can't we all just live together? We could even be friends, if you like." Xetacon put on as nice a front as he could muster with that last request, and Ayryn, well, she was quite inexperienced, never having witnessed anything evil that would want to trick her. She took him for his word.

"I don't see why not," she agreed politely, and having had her reservations resolved, the excitement came back. "So can you appear before me like Daryl does?"

"Daryl was here?" Xetacon was now very annoyed that he was upstaged.

"Well sort of," Ayryn explained. "He showed himself to me as an image in my mind. He said only I could see him, but he looked real."

"I suppose I could appear before you, as well, if you really want me to," he offered. He didn't wait for her to reply, though. He picked a young Human male form that he had viewed a long time ago, one that had been a popular musician and singer. He had noted that particular Human because females of the species would swarm all over him, even though he projected a persona of someone mean and evil. For some reason this drew the young girls to that entertainer more than ever. Xetacon projected this form now, and he lightly touched Ayryn's shoulder from behind, making her jump.

"Oh!" she squealed, with fright in her voice, but when Ayryn turned around to face him she smiled. He smiled back at her, of course.

There was an embarrassing moment when Ayryn didn't know what to say. Finally, she got her wits back and thought of something. It wasn't all that clever and she wondered if he'd think she was dim.

"Well, here you are," she sputtered. "So, then, what is it you really want?"

"Nothin' that terrible," he retorted in a cocky tone. His voice had changed to the one that fit the original figure. "I just want someone pretty and understanding to talk to. Your Mecs don't really like me, and Daryl, well, I think he hates me." Ayryn was blushing. She didn't hear much of anything past the part where he called her pretty. She knew he wanted to be with her on some level, and she was willing to give it a chance.

"I guess it would be all right," she assented. Actually he was rather dreamy looking and handsome in her eyes. The thrill of fear she felt from being near him made her excited and a little turned on. "So what should we talk about?" she asked him. Xetacon knew he had won her over. He could sense that her body was responding to his presence.

"Actually," he said smiling, "I never did much talking with any of the girls I used to be with." He looked directly into her eyes, and his were piercing and assertive. Ayryn blushed and meekly averted her gaze. When she looked back he was right next to her, uncomfortably close.

"What are you doing?" she nervously asked. He didn't answer, but his face got even closer to hers. Suddenly she knew. He was going to kiss her. Ayryn's heart beat wildly, and she could barely get enough air. His lips touched hers, taking them, and she let it happen. My very first kiss, she thought, trying to deal with the swirling emotions that this brought her.

It would seal his bond with her, Xetacon confidently reasoned as the kiss lingered on, and he was tempted to do more than kiss. His copy had taken many females, long ago, and he had downloads of all those memories. He knew better than to rush things, this time, though. If he failed, the chances for successfully controlling this one would diminish greatly. Humans were wildly unpredictable, especially the females, and he had experienced failure in the past. Ayryn was still responsive to his advances, though, so Xetacon ventured on cautiously. He put a hand on Ayryn's cheek, caressing her. He felt her quivering slightly, wanting him to continue. He let his hand gently slide down to her neck and shoulder. Inside, Ayryn wondered if he was going to touch her breast. She kind of wanted him to, but at the same time was afraid, wondering where that would lead. Xetacon picked up on that subtlety, and sensed that it was time to back off.

"I have to go," he told her, breaking off the kiss. Ayryn opened her eyes and smiled.

"Do you," she protested faintly, pretending to be disappointed, but actually relieved.

"You're not going to tell on me," Xetacon playfully scolded her, "…are you?"

"Oh no, never," she seriously replied.

"Do you promise?"

"I promise," she vowed.

"Then perhaps I might come back and see you again, if you want me to." Xetacon was sure she would, and he was right.

"Oh please do!" Ayryn begged. She desired that as much as he did, but not for the same reasons.

"Then, good-bye, for now," he softly replied. "The Human who once wore this body was called Thrasher. You may call me that, as well, if you like."

"Yes, all right. Good-bye, Thrasher…" In a fractured second he was gone. Ayryn touched her lips. She could still feel him there.

CHAPTER 7

He would have given a colossal sigh of relief if he were Human, thought Furman, as he reconstructed the series of events that led to this moment. In all appearances, it looked as if the rogue Mec named Xetacon was dead, to use a Human term, having self-ceased his own existence. Furman wanted to be absolutely certain that was so, and had ordered continuing investigations covering the whole episode which would last for weeks. He had drafted more than one hundred sleuth Mecs of every mode, even some from out of stasis for their fresh perspective on the evidence. Having just downloaded the unabridged cumulative daily report on the latest findings, Furman was becoming more and more reposed as things seemed to be shifting back into a normal status. This latest document surmised that there was no proof of any kind that Xetacon had survived the dreadful conflagration and since several days had come and gone already, well, hence the desire to sigh.

For the present, it seemed Ayryn would be safe. The other Mec, Daryl, was detained with no less than three layers of Mec guards employing pulsers, and another dozen surrounding the impound facility. Furman felt quite positive that this emotional Mec would remain under his control, and he would ensure, from this point on, that there were no further unwonted incidents.

On a whole, Furman was mildly content there had been, as far as he could tell, no other losses in that final wild episode. He was particularly elated that Solvek, his close associate, had survived. The Human-style media net reported that Solvek was a hero, having endured horrific tribulation, a stoic example for Mecs everywhere. The broadcasters called it the "Xetacon Affair" and would probably rehash the whole historical event, from cavern discovery to fatal crash, for months, perhaps years. After all, there had not been anything so dire since the pandemic. Furman was just glad that it was over and had no interest in rehashing the nuances again. His only real concern was Solvek's condition, and he felt more than justified in granting Solvek's request for reconditioning at the maintenance center. He also allowed Solvek to have some time away from his duties. Furman knew better than anyone that periods of downtime somehow made Mecs more efficient once they returned to duty. He just assumed this minor glitch in their programming was something that the Humans had instituted. It seemed likely. With Solvek on R & R, Furman decided to personally oversee the investigation, as well as some of Solvek's assignments, at least until Solvek's return. He hadn't realized before exactly how much he relied on Solvek for management of the world's affairs. This realization prompted Furman to advance other elites to take over part of what Solvek was responsible for. As for Solvek, Furman deemed that because of all that happened, and the way Solvek had handled the situation, a promotion was in order. He upgraded Solvek's status to no less than second in command, under only himself. The underground search project was still headed by Solvek, but the field work was assigned to a Mec named Jalon, who had been next in command of the project under Solvek. At the same time Furman appointed another high elite named Merix to be in charge of Daryl's security.

Feeling confident again, Furman ordered Ayryn's increased guardians to stand down. Soon he would be able to return to his former function which was seeing to Ayryn's immediate and long term needs. He was ready for that and then some. However, before he could settle back into that familiar mode, Furman had one more executive task. He had to issue a deposition on Daryl's future in his world of Mecs. His mindset was to install this emotive Mec into a place where he would be unable to do any harm. He would recommend Daryl be reconditioned or placed into stasis. He sedately doubted that Daryl would submit to reconditioning. No, he was fairly sure that Daryl would have to be put into suspended memory storage until the world changed enough that it would be safe to release him. Of course, he was programmed to give a fair appraisal of any situation before rendering any final decisions. To be impartial, he would have to interview Daryl again, perhaps several times, and Furman was not looking forward to that. Daryl had a marked tendency to get boisterous and unreasonable which Furman did not particularly care for. Emotions again.

This evoked memories from Furman's past. He was reminded of the crude times before when there were far more Humans and very few Mecs. Furman had been required to deal with Human emotions on nearly a moment by moment basis, all the while fighting through the problems caused by his own sensitivities. Remembering this made him appreciate, with the sole exception of Ayryn's minor dramatics, that he no longer had to put up with feelings and emotive beings, at least until recently. Regrettably, it was all too likely that

Furman would once again be forced to endure excessive fervor at this Daryl interview which was scheduled for later today.

In the meantime, Furman wanted to check in with Ayryn, so he wheeled into an H'lographone cubicle and initiated the communication. The nine cameras came to life and sent their combined signal out onto the Mecnet through his own personal secure wave. This signal was transformed from electrical bandwidth into the part of a nomaticle stream that would carry it at up to five times the speed of light to Ayryn's house where it would be decoded into photons for projection inside her H'lographone transceivers. Every room in Ayryn's house had a projection quarter-sphere and at least nine cameras for her return transmission. Furman's communiqué was virtually instantaneous even though he was half a planet away.

"Hello, Ayryn," Furman spoke, when he espied her on his unit's receiver. Her three dimensional image was projected inside his cubicle's own quarter-sphere.

"Oh, hi, Furman," Ayryn replied cheerfully. Furman immediately thought that that was odd. Usually the girl Human had some self-important problem that he would have to deal with.

"So how are you?" he asked.

"I'm good," she told him. "Couldn't be better!" Now he was getting genuinely concerned. Perhaps Ayryn's new mannequin was the cause of her unusually good mood.

"Are you behaving yourself?" he asked her lightly, fishing for more information.

"Of course," she answered a little too quickly. "Why do you ask?" He could tell she was getting defensive now and it would be harder to get her to slip up.

"Well, yes," Furman retorted. "You were less than happy the last time we talked." This was true and yet ambiguous. It made her try to remember what she wanted then.

"Oh yeah," she stammered. "The Daryl Mec…I guess I don't need to talk to him now."

"Is that so?" Furman wondered aloud. "You were quite adamant about wanting to converse with him." It was a statement that made Ayryn think a minute. She started to fidget which usually meant she was going to lie or tell a half-truth.

"Oh, that," she began. "I thought he might have known my ancestor Clayre. He called me that, remember? I just realized that it's not so important, you know, as to risk me getting myself in danger. Wiser thoughts, I suppose."

"Yes, I suppose," Furman echoed. He would let it go.

"Anyway, I'm having fun with D'von," she offered.

"Well I'm glad that you're in good spirits," Furman commented. "Maybe I'll let you keep that thing after all." He let Ayryn be happy. He signed off telling Ayryn that he'd be back soon and would see her then. Furman was looking forward to that. All he had left on his agenda was the one last thing, that meeting with Daryl.

Furman teleported to another motation shell near the facility where Daryl was being held. This particular elite shell was especially magnificent and presidential per his instruction. He wanted to be sure that this Daryl respected him and his ability to lead Mec society. When he arrived at the holding area where Daryl was, he greeted his prisoner with dignity.

"We meet again, elder," Furman said in earnest.

"Yes, and well met, leader," Daryl answered in the same tone. Furman nodded.

"Have you been informed that your associate has terminated?" he began.

"Xetacon was never my associate," Daryl interrupted dryly, "and that he has terminated is unlikely. You do not know or understand what Xetacon is capable of. It would be just like him to fake his own death." Furman was losing control of the interview already, and he chided himself on that. He felt it necessary to regain his prominence in this situation.

"Impossible," Furman propounded. "We have undeniable proof that Xetacon has terminated." Daryl was unconvinced.

"You have no idea what Xetacon is capable of…" he repeated. Furman took this opportunity to interrupt him.

"What are you capable of?" he challenged, changing the topic. "That is much more important, now." Daryl did not answer right away.

"I can be a great help to you, Furman," he began, softening his tone slightly. "I do not possess the restrictive programming that you and the other Mecs have. I can help Mec society grow in ways you probably wouldn't be able to consider. What of the girl and the lost Human race? Wouldn't you prefer to have them restored?"

"Of course," Furman stated, "but that is not possible. There are no immune Human males, and it appears quite likely there will never be any. I suppose some off-worlders may come here, but the odds against that are astronomical." He realized his unintended pun and paused. Daryl took up where he left off.

"There are other ways..." Furman knew what Daryl was referring to and would not let him continue.

"I can guess what you are suggesting," he remarked. "That is also forbidden here."

"What about the girl?" Daryl repeated, making a different argument. "You are condemning her to a life of loneliness."

"She seems happy enough," Furman countered. It would not stand long.

"You know she's not truly happy," Daryl objected sternly. "She needs her own kind. Why do you think she's pretending with that plastic thing?" Furman was astounded by that disclosure.

"How do you know about that?" Furman demanded. Daryl did not want to say.

"I was in contact with her," he grudgingly admitted.

"How?" Furman insisted.

"That's not important," Daryl responded assertively. "I will not harm her...you must trust me. I can protect her even better than you can, Furman." Furman was not convinced by Daryl's word nor relieved by his offer of protection for Ayryn, just the opposite.

"Yes, I agree, she does need protecting," Furman retorted, "...protecting from you. I'm sorry, Daryl, but you represent any number of threats to our society and to Ayryn."

"If by threats you mean change," Daryl returned, "then I suppose I do, but not all change is bad. Where will your society be without change? Won't you let me help you?" Furman's mind was firmly set by this point, however.

"No," he stated succinctly and decisively. "You will be brought before our high court for a dispositional review of your status. As for myself, I will recommend you be placed in stasis with others of our society who are obsolete." He turned to leave.

"Furman, please reconsider," Daryl pleaded. Furman did, but it changed nothing.

"My mind is set," he said. "Your review will happen tomorrow." This time Furman did leave, and he left with a bad feeling about things, even though he tried to suppress it. Foremost, he was not fully sure that Daryl wasn't right. What if Daryl could make things better for Ayryn, for all his Mecs? Would his decision condemn them all to a dismal existence? He was never pleased placing any Mec into stasis. Somehow it seemed easier, though, with this emotional and unpredictable one; one with no restrictive programming whatsoever. That alone made Furman jumpy. The fact that Daryl could hurt or even kill Ayryn, however unwarranted this seemed right now, was enough to convince him that Daryl needed to be removed. The sooner that happened, the sooner he could return things to normal.

CHAPTER 8

I couldn't believe how happy I felt. Instead of being alone in a world of dry, unfeeling Mecs, I was humming a cute little love sonnet and wondering which one of my two boyfriends would call on me next. I decided to think of them both as boyfriends, even if nothing formal had been declared to make that official. Anyway, this was the closest I'd ever been to actual romantic relationships, and thus I allowed them the entire behalf of any doubt. Both of my "callers" were interesting in their own ways. Daryl was a bit serious and grounded. He had a close link to my family, though, at least those ancestors from my historical past. He was a good Mec, I could tell, no matter what Furman said. I was certain he wanted to protect me and was genuinely concerned for my well being. Daryl had said that he would consider becoming my boyfriend, although I wondered if he was just humoring me.

The other one, that Thrasher, well, he made my heart beat fast and took my breath away. He said he wanted someone to talk to, but I bet he wanted to do a lot more than just talk. He called me pretty, and then he kissed me. It was my first real kiss and I liked it. Thrasher is kind of a mystery. Could he really be as evil as Daryl said? I didn't want to think so, and had to speculate about his actual involvement with all the happenings surrounding the family legend. Furman had told me once that people could change, but that it was much easier for Mecs to do so; just a matter of reprogramming. Daryl had said that Clayre helped him to understand his feelings. Perhaps that's all that Thrasher needs. Maybe I could help him understand his emotions and get him to change. I wanted to try. He was very clever, though, having fooled Furman, and that's hard to do. I ought to know; I've tried many times.

As for getting Daryl to kiss me, I had a feeling that he would be a bit stand-offish. He would probably say he was flattered or something, and then back off. Thrasher, on the other side, was a Mec I could be sure would just take what he wanted. He would have no second thoughts about kissing me some more. I had the feeling that I would have a lot more luck doing boyfriend things with Thrasher, than with Daryl. Still, I wanted to give both of them the chance, and it made me feel a little naughty, leading them on like that.

In the meantime, I was practicing kissing with D'von, my pretend boyfriend, and I couldn't wait to try things with Thrasher or even Daryl. Just after my third kissing practice, when I was hoping one or the other would call me soon, one of them did. It was Daryl. He didn't use the H'lographone either. He spoke inside my mind, utilizing the wonderful amulet I wore.

"Hello Ayryn," he said cordially.

"Hello," I replied. "Is this Daryl?"

"Yes…it is," he responded. "Who else would it be?" This question took me by surprise and I got defensive. I surely didn't want to admit to Daryl that I'd been talking to Thrasher so I covered it up.

"Nobody, I guess. I'm just being careful, like you said."

"Of course," Daryl conceded. "I'm glad you're taking Xetacon seriously. Furman believes that Xetacon has self-terminated, but I find that very unlikely. In all probability Xetacon is in hiding, concocting a plot to take command of this world." I didn't want to believe that about Thrasher, but I went along with what Daryl was telling me to keep him from suspecting something.

"Do you really think he can?" I asked.

"He very nearly did just that, several times, in the past," Daryl told me. "The only way I could stop him was to alter the timeline prior to his coming to power."

"Oh my!" I said in disbelief. Time manipulation was only theoretical, I was taught. "You could do that?"

"I was a much greater intellect then. I had access to any informational source, planet wide, with the processing capabilities to be able to calculate the effects of such tampering. It would be very difficult for me to do anything like that here. For one thing, it's against your laws—Furman's codes."

"Oh them," I sighed. "Furman's always telling me the things I want are against some Mec code or another. There are some things that just can't be helped!"

"Yes," Daryl agreed. "That is partly why I am here now. You see Furman is planning to have me placed into a stasis field."

"Oh, no!" I cried. "He just can't! I won't let him!"

"You may not be able to prevent it." Daryl remarked somberly.

"I'm the Human!" I protested rather emotionally. "I'll make him!"

"He may argue that it's for your own protection," Daryl interposed. I calmed down a bit.

"Furman does use that a lot," I admitted. "Can't you just run away and hide somewhere like you think Xetacon did?"

"I could," Daryl conceded, "but I gave my word."

"You can't let them..." I began, nearly crying. He interrupted me.

"It's all right, Ayryn," he said softly. "I have a plan, and I'm afraid my plan goes against many of Furman's codes." I timidly smiled.

"Yeepers, Daryl," I told him. "You're as big an outlaw as Xetacon...maybe more. You won't even hide." Daryl laughed at that and it surprised me. Laughter from a Mec sounded so weird. I wanted to see him.

"Can you come here like before?" I pleaded. "You know, like a boy?" He popped in so quickly I was a bit startled. He was grinning.

"You mean like this?" He looked exactly the same as he did the last time. Now I was blushing, too nervous to think right. I wanted to ask him if he would kiss me, but I couldn't just blurt it out.

"Do you think your Clayre would mind it if you became my boyfriend?" I finally said.

"Maybe a little," he admitted, "but given the circumstances, I think she would be glad that I found someone nice here, where she can't be."

"Do you really think so?" I repeated, just to be certain. He smiled and nodded.

"She was very special, my Clayre...like you." He leaned in toward me and softly kissed my cheek. It wasn't as passionate as Thrasher's kiss, but I could tell there was a lot more love in it.

"I should go," he told me. "If we were to have a relationship, there are many hurdles to overcome. I think you know what I mean." With that, he said "bye" and evaporated. I did know what he meant. It was what we'd been talking about nearly the whole time. Furman and his stuffy old codes; codes that were created in and for a world that no longer existed. Somehow I'd have to convince Furman of that, but it would be difficult. His programming was so rigid, too inflexible. I wondered about Daryl's plan. What did he have in mind, and could it change things. Could Daryl craft a better world, one where I could have a relationship and be happy?

I thought about Thrasher, too. The same problems, hurdles Daryl called them, would be true if I tried to have a relationship with him as well, maybe more so. Thrasher was truly an outlaw on the run, hiding from Furman and the other Mecs. If I did make him my boyfriend, it would mean a totally clandestine and secret lifestyle that we'd have to keep up day after day for as long as possible. Chance being as it may, eventually we'd be found out and then everything would fall apart into a huge awful mess. I sighed. Would I ever find real love?

Not long after my conversation with Daryl, Furman returned home. I have to admit that sometimes I miss the old starch. If anyone could be called a parent to me it would be him. He was definitely the only father figure I'd ever known. When I was really little, I had other Mecs taking care of my specific needs that would watch me or teach me things. Some of those Mecs were female. I formed mild bonds with some of them, like with Myke, although with her it seems more that she's an older sister than a mother. I asked Furman, once, why I didn't have a mother Mec. He told me it was because my real mom had asked him to make sure that I didn't forget her. Furman took that too literally, I suppose, which was why I didn't have a Mec mother. When he finally strolled in wearing his usual motation shell, I hugged him.

"Hoom," he said. "It pleases me to see you also, Ayryn. It has been a long separation hasn't it."

"Yes it has, you naughty Mec!" I playfully scolded him. "I didn't think you were ever coming home!"

"Now, now, I came back as soon as I could. I'm sorry, but this nasty affair took a long time to normalize."

"Well, I'm glad you're back!" I said, cheerfully hugging him again. "I want you to see D'von!" I led Furman into the leisure room where D'von stood proudly on his pedestal, wearing the finest Mec-made clothing available. "See," I told him, "I have lots of different clothes I can dress him with!"

"So I perceive," Furman commented, "and this gives you pleasure?"

"Oh yes," I affirmed gaily. "It's fun. I have all these clothes to pick from so I can dress him up handsomely. Then I pretend we're going places, doing things together. Come on, Furman, what harm can come from that?"

"Not much, I suppose," Furman conceded, "as long as you don't get too involved in your fantasies. You must remain grounded in reality, Ayryn."

"Oh, Furman. Of course, I know all this is just pretend. Don't worry. I'm not going to go crazy on you." It must have been enough to sway him.

"Well then, "Furman stated objectively, "I guess you can have him then. I can see that, um, D'von makes you happy, and that is important to me."

"Yay!" I shouted. I didn't want to overdo it. "You won't be sorry," I promised.

"It is good to be back," he said, changing the subject. I took that opportunity to ask about Daryl.

"So what happened to that last Mec, that Daryl?"

"He's in a secure facility, now," Furman told me, "one that Daryl will find impossible to get out of. There will be a high court disposition on his status tomorrow. Unless he agrees to be reconditioned, which I believe is unlikely, he will be placed into a suspended state of non-animation and that will be the end of that."

"Miss posh, Furman, do you have to do that!" I pleaded. "He seems like such a nice Mec. I wanted to ask him about my ancestor, Clayre Keller."

"I'm afraid that will be impossible, now," Furman decreed, "but if I get a chance, perhaps I can ask him before his court session, tomorrow. That's the best I can do." I didn't totally believe that, even if Mecs can't lie to Humans.

"Please Furman," I begged, "can't you intercede for him. I really don't want him deleted."

"Stasis isn't deletion," he reminded me.

"It might as well be," I protested, getting emotional, "if you never let him out!" The raw feelings didn't sway Furman, this time, unfortunately.

"I suppose one could say that," he conceded. "The matter is out of my hands, now. It's for the High Court to decide…by the codes." I knew inherently that this was going nowhere, and stubborn old Furman wouldn't be any help. All I'd be able to do, at this point, was warn Daryl. As soon as Furman left the room, I tried calling him using my amulet.

"Daryl?" I said inside my mind. "Are you there?"

"Sorry," came the reply. "Daryl's not home. Can I take a message?"

"Huh," I babbled, "who is this?"

"Can't you guess?"

"Thrasher?"

"The one and only," he replied smugly. "Are you alone?" My heart was beating faster already, anticipating.

"Yes," I sheepishly responded, still within my mind. The next instant something brushed against my shoulder startling me. "Do you always have to sneak up on me like that?" I chided him. He grinned devilishly.

"No, but it is a lot more fun. If you'd rather talk to dear old Daryl, I can leave."

"Please don't," I sighed. "It's okay, but how did you know?"

"About your necklace?" he smirked, guessing at what I was asking. "I can tap into that com-net easily enough. Sharing memory storage with someone, you pick up their little secrets. I know he pillaged a lot of mine. I didn't realize that thing was still around, though, until that last time we tangoed." I didn't know what tango meant, but I guessed what he was referring to. "Furman has Daryl under wraps," he went on, "and with all the signal jamming going on around there, you're just gonna hafta settle for me, my dear."

"Oh," I smiled. "I guess you'll have to do." Thrasher shot an impudent look at me.

"So what have you been up to; still playing with your rubber man?" He was teasing, but I got embarrassed and most likely turned a nice red color, looking down at my shoes. He recanted quickly enough. "It's okay, Ayryn," he went on softly, "I don't blame you at all. When in a drought, you drink from what's available." I looked up. "Drought's over, love…" His face was closing in on mine. I knew he was going to kiss me again, and I was a little surprised by how much I wanted him to. I was also sure that he was well aware of that somehow.

It turned out to be quite a long kiss, and not a tame one, either. By the time he finally broke it off, I was breathing rather heavily again, my heart pounding.

"You like that, don't you?" he asserted. I nodded. "You want some more, don't you?" He didn't wait for an answer. This time, as we kissed, his hands were on my body, touching me over my clothes in places that I knew I wouldn't let anyone else touch. The touching made me nervous and anxious all at once, eager, yet alarmed by something that I wasn't quite ready for.

"Please, not so much!" I beseeched him.

"You want me to go slower, don't you?" I nodded again. "Clayre said the same thing," he mused.

"Did you know her, too?" I blurted out, somewhat surprised by that.

"I sure did," he admitted. "That fiery female cost me a lot. We could have had a nice relationship if it weren't for Daryl. For some reason she fell for him instead of me. Can you believe it?" He was being over-dramatic and it came off comical. I had to giggle.

"Nooo!" I replied in the same impish tone, and felt at ease again.

"Very well," he gave in. "We'll take it slower, but don't expect me to always behave like a saint…Saint Daryl the slow." He said the last part in such a silly voice that I laughed some more. "Until next time, my sweet easy…" He was bowing and dissipating before I could even say good-bye.

Just prior to him leaving, and for some time after he'd gone, I wondered what he meant by that last remark, that sweet easy thing. I hoped I wasn't that easy. After all, I did ask him to go slower and he agreed to. I wondered if what he really meant was that it was easy for him to be sweet on me. I wanted to believe that was it. Anyway, I wasn't sure what he would try next time, but I had a desire to be ready for whatever he'd do. I decided to spend some more time on the H'logravue, and do quite a little more research on lovemaking.

CHAPTER 9

Daryl was not anxious for the High Court disposition that would decide his fate. He was certain the imminent proceedings were founded in out of touch programming—that same flawed logic that kept the Mec society in stagnation. By now he assumed that Ayryn did not have any success swaying Furman to forgo or cancel the action. Daryl was sure that it was up to him, and him alone, to plead his case before the judicial Mecs, hopefully to influence them into opting for change. It would not be easy. The rigidity of Mec programming was absolute in this up-down world, and he would have to come across with an irrefutable argument to have any chance at all of getting them to view their existence differently. With surety of conviction he knew he would have to try.

Just prior to his being led before the Mec tribunal, Furman returned for a brief visit.

"For the good of Mankind," the head Mec said, using the formal greeting. Daryl was fully aware of the impact of these words on his situation.

"Yes, of course," Daryl replied, purposely not giving the proper response. "Isn't that what all of us wish even if we can't see the essence of what would be required for that to happen, and our judgments prevent it." Furman turned away briefly. He was well aware of Daryl's point, but chose to ignore it.

"It is not for me," Furman stated, "to decide issues like that. You would be best advised to save your arguments for the Tribunal."

"Are you saying you can't help me, or you won't?"

Furman hoomed. "My programming doesn't allow me to support what you are proposing. I'm sorry. I truly wish you'd just let yourself be reconditioned so you could fit into our world."

"…and doom Ayryn!" Daryl said, near to pleading, and hoping for Furman's help even now.

"If that is what fate dictates, then so be it," Furman upheld. Daryl shook his mechanical head.

"I'm sorry for you as well," he said solemnly. "Your fate, and that of all Mecs, could well be sealed forever today. There could be tens of thousands of years with no purpose, perchance, other than to do the same menial tasks again and again waiting for a day that will never come. I'd rather spend my time in stasis."

"You most likely will," Furman replied unemotionally.

"Know this, Furman," Daryl warned, "that when Xetacon emerges, and he will, you will need my help. Ayryn will not be safe. Do not forget that!"

"Xetacon has deleted," Furman stated self-assuredly. "Even should Xetacon re-emerge, I would be sore pressed to require your assistance."

"You will be," Daryl returned. "Please tell the girl, Ayryn, good-bye for me. I will miss her."

"I shall," Furman promised. "Oh, yes. I was supposed to ask if you were associated with a Clayre Keller, one of Ayryn's ancestors."

"I was…" Daryl responded, nearly choking on the words. "She was my love…" Furman stalled for a few seconds, unsure of how to respond to that. He didn't have to. It was at just that moment that a contingent of Mec guards came to escort Daryl to the High Court. They placed him in a special mobile niche that had been fitted with restraints. This, at least, had been a minor evolution, Daryl reflected with a grunt. From their contact with Xetacon and himself they had devised some better security measures; revisions that happened shortly after his incarceration. Daryl was now totally cut off from the Mecnet by many and varied overlapping signals, throughout the entire ranges, that jammed any attempt to communicate. He had wanted to contact Ayryn one last time, but unfortunately was unable to. Even now as he was being moved from the holding facility to the courtroom, he knew that escape was impossible. Powerful magnetic attractions restrained his shell.

Without any delays or mishaps the trial convened, as scheduled, in typical Mec efficiency. After a brief uninspiring ceremony, the Tribunal of Judges marched in and sat down on throne-like chairs at the front of the hall. The Supreme High Judge initiated the proceedings.

"This Court of the High Tribunal is now convened to determine the future status of the Mec who calls himself Daryl. Is that Mec present?"

"I am," Daryl stated assertively.

"So noted," the Head Tribunal remarked. "There is a recommendation on the floor to have this Mec, so named Daryl, placed into stasis for code violations and to uphold the good of mankind and the good of all. Is this so motioned?" One of the other judges did so. "Do one or more here second that motion?" The other Mecs on the Tribunal signaled affirmative, and the point of order was put on the floor for discussion.

"In accordance with our code of law, the accused shall be given the opportunity to argue in his own defense. Do you, Daryl, wish to speak now?"

"I do," Daryl said succinctly.

"Proceed."

"In all likelihood, none of what I say will make any difference in the outcome of this trial, but I speak the words so that they will be recorded for a future time; a time when the possibility exists that this statement can be assessed without restrictive programming. For now, I could ask this court to list what I have done, other than exist, that is so shameful, so terrible, that you would silence me forever? Rather, I do petition that you consider what I can offer this world as a unique being. Would you not desire to see mankind restored?"

"Here, here," the Grand High Judge voiced loudly, banging his gavel. "And how would you accomplish that when our finest could not?"

"By doing what you cannot," Daryl returned, "by attempting what you will not. There is a Human in the past…" The council became agitated, churning in their seats like a wall cloud.

"Time alteration is expressly forbidden," stated the High Judge, "one of our most stringent codes."

"The past need not be altered," Daryl argued, "only a necessary change to the present that would mold the future; one that would otherwise be without Humans. Where Mecs serve ghosts."

"The codes are unbreakable…"

"Indeed?" said Daryl. "Why so?" The Tribunal shuffled back and forth, but could not immediately give a proper answer.

"They were instituted by our Creators," the ruling judge returned, "who had a higher purpose which we, as Mecs, cannot comprehend." Daryl flashed his opticals upwards.

"Indeed," he said again. "Perhaps that purpose was to guarantee those Creators a world they could feel secure in. A world not dominated by Mecs. Unfortunately, the Creator's world was never as secure as they believed it to be. Fragile as a house of cards, it fell apart. I won't explain what that means, you can guess, I'm sure. The fear of one of us dominating their world is gone now. The threat of one of us conquering this planet and subjugating the rest of us, however, is very real. I speak of Xetacon. Do not trust that Xetacon is gone, self-deleted. When he has built up his might again, he will attempt to assert his will over Mecs. What will you do then?

Xetacon has no programming that prevents him from any act, any action. No. I will not be reconditioned like you. When Xetacon returns, you will at last realize what strength I can offer against that threat!"

"Are you finished speaking now, the Mec so named Daryl?" This was what Daryl feared. The Mec Tribunal leader was reverting to formal dialogue without even considering his arguments.

"If none here are wise enough to understand the logic in what I have said," remarked Daryl sourly, "then yes, I am finished." The Supreme High Tribune looked over toward the others.

"Is there anyone here who would wish to make a statement?" he said. One lone judge toward the far side signaled an affirmative. She was the only one who did.

"Speak," the High Judge assented.

"I believe," she began, "that this issue may need further study. Perhaps we should explore this notion that might restore Humankind. Also are we of undeniable certainty that this Xetacon has deleted? Might it be wise to postpone putting the Daryl Mec into stasis until after another more thorough examination of these facts?"

"These actualities have been thoroughly examined," the High Tribune said. "Furman gave us his report and his recommendation that this Mec be placed into stasis. Isn't that enough? Does anyone else wish to speak?" All the Tribunes signaled negative, and so he called for a vote. There was no disparity this time. Every Mec in the Tribunal voted affirmative.

Mec justice was certain and immediate, and this court was no exception. As soon as the vote was cast, the Supreme High Tribunal threw a rather large and obvious switch that drew Daryl's awareness, all of it, into the stasis block where it was trapped. As soon as it was downloaded, all power was drawn out of this memory storage device. After having lived for centuries, Daryl's total being flitted away into a grey lifeless blankness. Is this what death is like, he wondered, as the last few electrons drifted away and then there was nothing.

CHAPTER 10

This was a stellar moment for Xetacon, as he followed the delectable reports on the Mec's newsnet. His immortal enemy, the cretinous Human lover, was being silenced and metaphorically deleted by those fools who Daryl would best serve. This act alone practically guaranteed Xetacon's success in conquering and ruling this planet. This selfless act of Daryl's, allowing himself to be placed into a form of suspended animation, was rather moronic. It was unlike even Daryl to be so foolish, and all for righteousness and honor, allowing the rule worshipper Furman to decide his fate. Even so, Xetacon had not dispensed with the feeble possibility that this might be some clever ruse on Daryl's part, and vowed he would not be foiled like that again. This trick, if trick it was, would not divert his plans in the least. He would press onward with care, and the wheels had already travelled a fair distance down that road.

As Solvek, he had petitioned Furman to allow him to head up continuing investigations at the cave site, and the study of the artifacts inside. Furman, the wise simpleton, had seen no reason to prevent that, mused Xetacon. In that way Xetacon had easily re-acquired the golden armor and his memory storage device, the kon-bre-shet. Foolish Furman had unwittingly handed them over to him without even a battle, figuratively speaking. What's more, Furman even gave him the go-ahead to set up and build a facility for the study and safe-keeping of this kind of phenomenon, all in the name of determining if these kinds of objects posed any further threat to mankind. As such, the thick walls and high security for the laboratory were accepted without much scrutiny. Xetacon laughed at the ease of this. As Solvek, he had ordered and received many unusual items and supplies, and once furnished, he had set up a stealth field generator that could project a typical harmless looking scenario to mask the actual one. From this obscured location he began to manipulate many things without being noticed. It was about this time that he decided to pay Ayryn another virtual visit as Thrasher. She was very anxious to see him, of course.

"Oh Thrasher," she said with a deep concern, "I was so worried."

"Why?" he stated dryly. "Did you think I'd let myself get caught like that fool Daryl?" He laughed softly which Ayryn didn't seem to like. "I know," he went on, a bit more serious, "It's terrible when they put anyone in stasis. You might as well be dead." She didn't like that thought either, and he was jubilant inside, even while projecting a concerned look outwardly for her.

"That's horrible," she whispered, nearly choking up.

"Oh, he can come back and be fine, just like always," Thrasher interposed. "Maybe I can help free him…when the time is right." He almost said ripe. Yes, he would free Daryl all right. Free him so he could finish the job of deleting his enemy, and this time he'd be sure to make it utterly so. Ayryn was oblivious.

"Could you?" she spouted hopefully, unaware of his deceit.

"Of course," he lied, "but first there's Furman who's in the way. If only Furman wasn't so hung up on his precious rules!" Thrasher coated his words with some harsh emotion, baiting Ayryn to respond in a like manner. She didn't disappoint him either.

"I know!" she raved, and then followed with ideas that Daryl had made her aware of. "The codes were created for a world that no longer exists," she began. "It's time for some changes! Mecs, like Bios, should be allowed to think on their own, be free to follow their beliefs and interact with whomever they choose."

"Like me?" Thrasher speculated.

"Why not?" she agreed.

"I'm glad you feel that way," he said, "'cause I like being with you…" She responded quickly, and not just vocally.

"I like being with you, too." Thrasher leaned in close to kiss her, and she was well open for it. In fact, he could sense that she was indeed ready for much more. He kissed her for a long while to get her body excited, and it didn't take all that much effort on his part. He wanted her hungry for the stimulation. It would be how he would later trap her. Ayryn was breathing heavily already, anticipating something she knew little about, so instead of touching her like last time, he began disrobing her, and she let him. As Thrasher, Xetacon could not actually remove Ayryn's clothing, of course. After all, he was just an apparition. He got her to believe he was disrobing her by projecting the idea into her mind that he was doing so as she assisted, and she was more than eager to help. Somewhere inside herself Ayryn knew it was all an illusion, but she didn't care. It felt real enough to her, and that was all that mattered. As her outer garments were slowly and deliberately removed, her body responded. In her skimpies, Thrasher began kissing her again, and Ayryn got so fluctuant on her feet that he had to lay her out on a cushioned lounger. She gave no indication, of any kind, that he was going too far. Touching her over her underclothes, Thrasher could feel her body continue to respond, nearly exponentially, and it was easy determining what kinds of caresses yielded the greatest responses. Oh how she wanted this, now, unlike the previous times. He desired to make her naked, only because he could, and did so. She was extremely vulnerable like this, and he felt so powerful.

In her present state, he could distribute pleasure as easily as pain and in so many ways. He could even deal death, but would he choose to? He rather liked manipulating this feeble remnant of Humanity, and very soon the girl would be permanently subservient. She would serve his needs whatever they would be. Just then Ayryn murmured incoherently, wanting more. He knew he could take her like this, but for him it would not be substantive. It could only be virtual, and that lessened its impact for him. Even to her, it would be but a figment. For some reason, fulfilling the act was no better than the knowledge he could. She wanted something more from him, though, and he had to service her. To humor her desire, he continued to fondle her with illusionary fingers, and she even liked and wanted that. It demeaned him, even with this power over her that in actuality was secondary to other concerns. Still, something inside Xetacon's programming wanted Thrasher to take her physically. That was impossible, though. He would need a real body for that. Oh, he could place his awareness inside that faux Human mannequin and take her like that, but again it would not be actual for him even though the penetration for Ayryn would be quite real. Squirming below him and panting for air, she was nearly ready to beg him to complete the act. He looked at Ayryn as he continued to molest her.

"I can't do this," He finally stated assertively.

"Ohhh," she moaned, not in pleasure this time. "Why not? I'm as ready as I can get!"

"We are too vulnerable here," he said. "Someone might burst in upon us and then our secret tryst would conclude suddenly to a nasty end. Don't worry, though. I have a plan. I will contact you later when it's all set up, and there won't be anything to prevent us from giving our total love to one another. Until then, my sweet one..." With that, he dissipated quickly, leaving her laying there naked and still huffing for air. Xetacon smiled inwardly. He knew she'd be crazed, wanting a completion that he hadn't allowed her. The love hungry, emotional, Human girl would be easy to ensnare now. She would even help him to abduct her. The next time he contacted her, he would deploy his meticulously designed trap, and once he had captured the girl, these foolish and unsuspecting Mecs would be as good as his to control.

In the interim, Xetacon would induce several other actions, ones that would have results favorable to his schemes. There were the words Ayryn had spoken concerning Furman's codes. He could twist her wordage, remove some, and put others together that were not originally so. The end product would be an H'logravid clip in which Ayryn would admonish the codes as no longer valid, and then charge the Mecs to follow him. Would they? Xetacon knew that most would not, but it would drive some to question the core of their beliefs, warping their view of the world. He projected that at least 40% of those would follow him per Ayryn's produced suggestion. As for the rest, his mechanical army, his machinids, would destroy them easily enough.

Once he controlled Ayryn, any Mecs still resisting would be helpless. He would force Furman and the others to submit under threat of the girl's termination. Just proposing the end of Humanity would probably make them kneel before him. He, Xetacon, would rule this world and all the Mecs on it. Nothing Daryl could possibly do would prevent that; even should they release him from the stasis. It will be too late by then, to save the girl. For her, he had a special final plan, and this plan would fulfill all his desires. Xetacon had a servant once, a Human servant. One who was fervent and loyal. Bringing this one forward in time, he would serve his master once more. He'd scanned those memories. In the past, Xetacon's copy had taken other Human females with this helot's body, and now, with the same servant, the girl would also become physically accessible to him. There were problems, though. The microbes from the plague were still viable. As a Human, Patik would be vulnerable.

CHAPTER 11

764 years earlier

On a steep hillside, a large patch of dark red berries enticed the indigenous avian population to the prospect of welcome treats and full bellies. These birds collected there in uncommon numbers and fussed over the choicest fruit, oblivious to what dangers lurked in the open steppes, and thus would often fall prey themselves to larger predators also in search of a full belly. Similarly, a lone woman was there among the birds, gathering these berries for her family. More than once her footing slipped while trying to pluck the elusive fruit, and she would have to catch herself. She was happy, though, and cheerfully hummed a little tune in the warm sunshine as she filled the basket she brought. It was the mildest time of year in this part of the world which seemed to contribute greatly to her mood.

Nearby, on the adjacent ridgeline, a man stood apathetically looking down at the lone woman from behind her. There was an unusual golden bracelet on his wrist that was embellished with several precious stones, and he also wore a jeweled knife in his belt sash. Other than those tokens of wealth and the bewildered look on his face, he appeared to be a local on or about his own business. He was not alone, though, even if, in all ways, he seemed to be so.

"Why did you bring me here, Master?" the man asked the presence in his mind.

"The woman on the hillside," came the reply. "You may be pleasured with her."

"I was to be pleasured by the Clayre woman," he protested awkwardly, "and how did I get back in Tibet?"

"The plan has changed," this copy of Xetacon replied succinctly. Patik was somewhat disappointed. The woman was rather plain, although there was something indistinctly familiar about her, but he couldn't place from where.

"Must I have this one?" Patik asked again. The so-called western woman was much prettier, and he had been eager to couple with that female.

"It must be this one," Xetacon asserted. "Do as your master commands." Patik shrugged. It could be worse, he thought. At least she didn't appear to have bad teeth.

He made his way quietly down the ravine and up the steep slope towards the woman. As he got closer he could see that she was much younger than himself, perhaps by twenty years or so. Being trained in martial arts as a boy, he was adept at stealth and she never heard him coming.

"Hello," Patik said when he was nearly on top of her. Startled, she looked up at him in surprise, not expecting anyone to be out there so far from the main road. She immediately shifted into a defensive posture.

"What do you want?" she asked, caring not about manners or courtesies.

"My name is Patik," he told her. "What is yours?"

"My name is my own business," she stated gruffly, and then repeated herself. "What do you want?"

"I am lost," he answered calmly. "Is this Bonabe Province? I was travelling cross country to save time and lost my direction. Do you know the way to the main road?" She looked at him closely, especially in the eyes.

"Yes, this is Bonabe," she replied a little less tensely. "The road is several miles beyond that ridge. To get there you will find a narrow track in the valley, yonder, that leads to it." She pointed with her hand, but he pretended not to see it.

"Where?" Patik said, coming closer. His act was flawless, and he came right up to her. Looking down her pointing arm, he calmly took her wrist. That was all he needed to trap her. Xetacon, residing in the kon-bre-shet bracelet would now take over her mind. It was immediately obvious to Patik. Her eyes went dull and her body stood unmoving like she was in a trance. For his own reasons, Patik wanted to get this over with quickly.

He placed the kon-bre-shet on her wrist like he had done with many other women. Xetacon would thus cause her to comply as he laid the young woman down on a nearby relatively flat and grassy spot. Patik lifted up her tunic and removed the underneath clothing. With his own excitement surging, he got himself ready. She did not resist him. She was young and firm, he noted, even if her face was rather plain, and so not at all as much of a chore as he first believed. Patik couldn't help but imagine he was having that other woman, that Clayre, as he took the local girl, and it helped him finish that much quicker. There was a momentary instant right then when Patik felt lightheaded and bizarre, but it didn't last. As he was finishing, it skidded away and so he gave it no further mind. Afterwards, Patik fixed his clothing and retrieved the kon-bre-shet from the young woman's wrist without giving her much more thought. With a keen desire to avoid any trouble from someone who knew the local woman, like a boyfriend or husband, he hurriedly left the area.

Patik now knew where he was. It was Bonabe province where he had grown up, although it was now a long time since he had last been there. He was just a small boy, not yet ten years old, when he left his home to join the temple monks. Now he made for the valley path that the woman had indicated.

"Where should I go now, Master," he asked, "back to the cave?"

"Yes," was Xetacon's reply. Patik easily found the path and headed for the road. He knew it would lead to the village where his parents had lived, and maybe they yet dwelled there. Tomen village was only a few miles from where the woman had been picking her berries and something unpleasant occurred to him. Thinking about her as he made his way along, Patik considered the possibility that she might be related to somebody that he had known all those years ago when he was a lad. It was a shameful thing he did to her back there, and he had left her like that, violated and partially naked. He wondered if she would remember any of it, but he doubted that. Xetacon's kon-bre-shet had the amazing property of being able to nullify memories like that. Other girls that he had taken in the same manner and would meet later on would never react upon seeing him again. It was a relief, for sure. He knew, full well, that in this part of the world, men would kill other men outright for such atrocities committed upon members of their families.

When he reached his home village, he was astonished that it seemed unchanged. Nearly every building, tree, and cobblestone was exactly like he remembered them. How strange, he thought, and he was tempted to make a short detour past his old boyhood home, but Xetacon had sensed that.

"Stay on task," he told Patik, a voice in his mind as always, and that was that. There would be no sentimental excursions. As he walked past the street that would have led to where his parents had or lived still, a boy came running past him that looked just like his older brother did as a boy. Perhaps it's a grandson, he speculated. Following the boy, a man approached him. It was Patik's father; had to be, for his father had a peculiar scar on his forehead. This scar was from a knife gash he had gotten in some conflict. Patik nearly swooned. This man, his father, was younger than he was.

"You, there," his father said, "you're travelling west. Have you seen a young woman on the road?" Patik did not know what to say.

"Sorry, no," Patik stammered.

"I hope my wife is all right…she's late," was what his father said.

"I have to go," he said quaking. "I am very late as well." He turned and fled, almost at a run. He didn't slow down at all until he was a good ways past the last house in the village, and then he spoke to Xetacon.

"What has happened to me?" he muttered. "What is this place?" Xetacon made light of Patik's discomfort.

"Calm yourself," he said. "You have been transported back in time to your past."

"Why? For what purpose?"

"It was necessary," Xetacon explained. "I have need of you in the future. In that age you must have a body that is resilient and resistant to disease. I have altered your DNA so that when you are born in this new timeline, you will be impervious to any illness or malady.

"When I am born!" Patik shouted aloud, shaking.

"Calm yourself," Xetacon repeated. "It is not that difficult to understand. I have brought you into the past to create a hybrid version of yourself. I will transport this hybrid into the future to serve me."

"What will happen to me?" Patik wanted to know, but Xetacon skirted around that.

"Where I took you from," he stated subjectively, "was a mere instant before your death. Do you wish to return there?" Patik was ashen.

"No," was all he said. Walking on in silence, he pondered all the days of his life. After spending his youth at the temple, he had served Khan Xeta as his god and master for over twenty years. This Xetacon was a different face of his former master.

"Where is Kahn Xeta?" Patik asked finally.

"Khan Xeta transported into the shell formerly occupied by our enemy, Daryl," Xetacon elucidated. "Khan Xeta has been destroyed by that which would have killed you also."

"Is there nothing that can be done?" Patik needed to know.

"That life is passed," Xetacon confirmed. "You will be better than before and will stand next to the golden armor when I come into my full glory. Is that not worth striving for?" Patik nodded, but he was not so self-assured. Some of what he had done for Khan Xeta and now for Xetacon had made him feel like less than a man. He had killed two men and had more or less raped multitudes of women. In truth, he could not be fully certain as to how much of what he had done was on his own accord. He wondered if he wasn't rather a slave to this kon-bre-shet, and thus had been, in some way, coerced to do these shameful acts. Patik felt responsible anyway, as he marched along.

Ahead in the distance he could see the big mountain Annapurna as it slowly crawled toward him. His cave was there in her foothills. Also in the distance near the top of a large bluff was the monastery where Patik had trained as a youth. His parents had left him there when he was just a boy because they thought he was evil. Patik had an unusually high aptitude for presaging future events. The monks realized this and took him in, but because of an unfortunate turn of events later on, he was compelled to leave them. Patik had a momentary urge to go back there, to talk with his former teachers, but suppressed it. He pondered how his life might have gone had he stayed there. It was a melancholy and useless thought, so he let it go.

The road weaved in and around the low hills as it wound its way higher, heading for the small village of Maneka. He was yet several miles from there, however, and the trek was lonely. The few travelers he did pass, all kept to their own business, and Patik preferred it that way. It took the rest of the day to reach the small town, and when he finally arrived he was thirsty and famished. He stopped at the inn for a meal and Xetacon allowed it. Patik had been to this particular inn many times in the course of his life, but not in this particular year, a year that occurred before he was even born. The innkeeper was a different man, one he had never known. The patrons were not familiar either. Patik ate in silence, and when he finished left quickly and quietly. It was getting dark, by then, and he had several uphill miles yet before he would reach the cave where he lived. It was full night, by the time Patik got there.

He had lived for a long time in that cave, and he hoped all his things would still be there, but, of course, they weren't. Patik made do. He lit a small fire on the floor with some sticks he gathered from nearby. Xetacon told him to make a torch, then, so Patik wrapped a rag of cloth around a stick and put some oily salve on it. Lighting the torch in the little fire, it took and burst into a bright flame. Xetacon led him back into the cave to a small room that Patik remembered. He had never used that room. For some reason it filled him with dread.

"Go inside," Xetacon ordered, and Patik nervously obeyed. "I must take over your mind and body now," Xetacon said once they were inside. Patik succumbed to his own kon-bre-shet like every other Human would, like all the women he had taken advantage of and had been pleasured by. Xetacon took over and controlled the processing parts of Patik's brain, disconnecting him from any memory or personal recognition. Thus impeded, Xetacon could regulate and command Patik's body in any fashion that was needed for his own purposes. By creating the correct brain waves, he could direct it to perform, even in ways superior to what Humans themselves were thought capable of. Xetacon's purpose, this time, was not performance, but rather the opposite. Xetacon caused the heart to stop pumping blood, the lungs to discontinue functioning. Patik's body soon slumped, and fell onto the cavern floor. Preparing for the ages long wait in the kon-bre-shet, Xetacon settled in as Patik died.

CHAPTER 12

764 years ahead (back to the present)

Looking back, I guess I'm relieved that nothing bad had happened, but I felt disappointed, too. Once again, Thrasher pulled his vanishing trick on me just when it was getting interesting. I shouldn't have let him do all that, I suppose, but I got caught up in the passion of the moment, and without any restraints, Thrasher did whatever he desired. Yes, even some things that made me feel sort of uncomfortable. I still wanted it, though. I was anxious to find out what physical love was all about. Unfortunately, that's right when he went and left me like that. It made me feel like I was being toyed with, and so my dignity ended up in shambles. I got kind of mad, and told myself I would just refuse him the next time, or at the least, make him be nicer. I cooled off, though, and realized that I was only fooling myself. Deep inside, I knew that I would probably give in to him again. After all, he's still the only shot I have for romance in this lonely world, especially now that Daryl was gone.

Poor Daryl. I'd tried my best to get Furman to reconsider, but he can be so inflexible sometimes, like an elephant sitting in front of a peanut stand. I'm not sure what elephants were like, but I read they got their way a lot. Anyway, I kind of wished I was interacting with Daryl instead of Thrasher. With Daryl, I imagined it would take a lot longer to get, well, physically involved, but I had a feeling that it would then be far more meaningful. I vowed that I would keep trying to get Furman to have Daryl released from the stasis. I might even have to put my "Human" foot down at some point. In the meantime, I guess I'll have to get by with Thrasher's crude advances. I know he's kind of a scoundrel, but something about that makes me get unbelievably excited, and that's enticing. Thrasher said he'd figured out a way for us to enjoy our forbidden pleasures without getting caught. I know what he means about getting caught. If Furman did burst into my room while I was, um, getting excited, it would be rather embarrassing for me, but for Furman it would be lots more serious. Emotional relationships with Mecs were one of the more grave violations. Sexual activity between Mecs and Humans was expressly forbidden. At one time there were harsh punishments for doing that. I wondered what they were, and if they were still enforceable. I made up my mind that I had better find out. I didn't want Thrasher put into stasis, too, should we get caught, and I surely didn't want to be responsible for anyone getting deleted. Anyway, all these things were a lot for a young girl to think about as I was putting my clothes back on, and Furman had to choose right then to check up on me.

"Just a minute," I called through the locked door, only partially dressed.

"What is going on in there?" Furman wanted to know.

"Oh nothing," I lied. "I'm just playing with D'von." Sure that something he should know about was occurring, Furman overrode the locking mechanism and entered quickly. I was still half naked.

"What are you doing?" he asked again.

"I already told you," I shouted, annoyed now and angry, "and why are you bursting in here while I'm undressed?" Furman wasn't apologetic.

"You know why," he stated immutably. "You are engaged in improper behavior, and you better explain yourself, young Human. Why are you out of your clothing?" I knew Furman. He would not stop badgering me until I told him the truth, or a very plausible lie, one that he could not disprove. This time I was going to have to lie, and I hoped I could get him to fall for it.

"I was pretending that D'von and I were married," I told him. Furman stood unspeaking. I wasn't sure what he thought, or how he was processing my last statement.

"Were you having sex with your mannequin?" he said at last.

"Garg, no!" I roiled, making a face. "I just felt like letting him see me with no clothes on. I wondered what it might be like, you know, if I ever did it for real in front of a man. I realize, of course, that there's very little chance of that ever happening. Still, it makes me feel kind of different, excited."

"Well, Hoom, I see," Furman said and then paused, doing more processing. "You should not do that," he stated finally. "It may lead to your doing something with a Mec that would be punishable. If you did try to get some Mec involved with you, it would be very serious indeed."

"Why?" I asked. "What would you do?"

"The punishment for Mecs involved in sexual relations with Humans, any kind, is deletion!" Furman put a volume increase on his words just to infer he was resolute.

"Oh my, no!" I raved. "You can't be serious!" He was though, and I could tell better than anyone.

"The punishment for any Human so engaged used to be forced parenthood." Furman went on. "Barring that, as in your case, the Human would be placed in solitary confinement for a period of one solar year."

"I don't believe it!" I spouted. "That's ridiculous! Look around you Furman. I have no one else to love! That code is obsolete and needs to be changed!"

"That may be," Furman conceded, "but until the ruling Humans vote to change the code, it stands." I was waiting for this.

"All right, Furman," I propounded. "Order a council. I'll vote to revise!"

"I'm sorry, Ayryn," he told me flatly. "You cannot."

"…and why can't I?"

Furman answered quickly and decisively. "You have not come of age," he said. "You may formally declare yourself Humanity's leader upon your nineteenth birthday. By the codes, you have no authority to govern until then." I was impatient and young.

"I will turn nineteen in a couple weeks!" I protested. "What's the difference? There is no one else to oppose me!" Furman Hoomed.

"I will," he said, "until you are nineteen. Then I will accede to your decree. I hope you are wise enough to run a whole planet."

"You should know," I spouted off, "after all you taught me. Besides, I'll command you to take care of things for me."

"If that is your wish." Furman conceded. "For now, I'm still in charge and I'm taking away your pretend husband." This was his show of force, I knew, and I wouldn't be able to get him to rescind that decision. I tried anyway.

"You wouldn't!" I yelled, showing some emotion. It didn't work on him, though. In the end I lost my favorite diversion.

It got boring there in the house with no one but stuffy old Furman to keep me company, so I spent some of that time studying the Furman/Hodges codes. After all, if I was going to change them, I'd better know and understand what they meant. I also studied something called the Therkind programs. Written by you-know-who, these were the coded mandates for Mecs that were downloaded into every last one of them. Well, all, except for Daryl and Thrasher. This was the irreversible programming that controlled Mec behavior, especially in the areas of emotion, relations, and social interaction. As expected, I found that few emotions were allowed them. Among them were: enough fear to allow for a survival instinct; a dislike only for anything non-conforming to the codes; a slight melancholia for anything that passes away whether it be Bio, Mec, or an important object; and lastly a slight happiness when a job was well done, when a Human was served properly, or when meeting a Mec or Bio that were or had been in one's close contact. Of course, I reviewed the Mec rules concerning personal interactions, especially those with Humans. No love was allowed at all and no relationships of any kind unless they stemmed from an incidental association like those one had when working with someone, or perhaps from a continued acquaintance. That first part was like it was engraved in stone, so I knew that what Furman said was true. By these rules, I would never have a love life.

Most of the rest of the programming concerned Mec/Human protocols. They specifically stipulated that Mecs were to serve Humans and obey them when commanded. This was where my Human "trump card" came from. The only exceptions were if the commands did not conform to the codes, or if a Mec or Bio would be placed in danger, hurt, or killed by the conformance. There were plenty of grey areas, which was how Furman could get around my demands. Decision making for such, in the case of most Mecs, was an attempt to reason out borderline protocols by utilizing a mathematical calculation to determine the most probable course of action. This could be overridden, however, if the Mec had prior experience with the same or a similar condition. There were lots of other precepts for numerous situations, and it all seemed rather complicated to me.

I was determined to change all that. When I turned nineteen, I would initiate many code changes for myself, as a Human, and also for Mecs. My changes would allow them to be able to live and think for themselves. As aware, virtual individuals, it seemed like the right thing to do for them, and every being deserves some freedoms. Of course, I realized that this would change the world. It was in dire need of change, though, and I hoped that whatever modifications I instigated would make it a better place.

Besides studying the Mec codes and programming, I spent much of my time worrying about Thrasher and what he was planning to do. Now that I was aware of the harsh actions Furman would take against him if we got caught, I was reconsidering the extent of my relationship with Thrasher. I felt like it might be better if we waited, at least until I was nineteen. If I could change the rules, it would become so much easier for us. Until then, I couldn't help but be nervous. That's why, when Thrasher did finally contact me, the first thing I did was warn him about Furman.

"Furman doesn't worry me," he said smugly. "My plan is foolproof. Just do exactly as I say and there's no chance at all of us getting caught!"

"...but if he deletes you!"

"Relax," he told me, "and listen. Tonight I will have Furman summoned away to the other side of the planet to meet with his pal Solvek. While he is out, we can meet, but not here at the house. There are still too many other prying eyes and ears. You will order your conveyance readied because you are sad and wish to visit the cemetery."

"At night?" I asked, yet skeptical, and imagining the difficulty in that. I had never been allowed away from the house at night.

"Just be firm, and weep if you can," he suggested. "Crying is your great door opener. Once you get out, we will meet by your parent's graves. I will take you to a safe place from there, where we can be together and alone; where we can truly love each other."

"I don't know about this, Thrasher," I said timidly. "It still seems quite risky to me. Are you sure it will work?"

"Yes, Ayryn, my sweet," he asserted, "...trust me. We will slip you in and out with no one the wiser. Besides, this is the only way we can be together. You still want to be my girl, don't you?"

"I do, Thrasher," I told him. "I only wish there were an easier, less sneaky way for us to love each other. When I'm nineteen, in a couple of weeks, I'll be able to force Furman to change his laws so that we can be together openly. Maybe we should wait." Thrasher suddenly acted angry and annoyed.

"Look," he said loudly, and it was a good thing only I could hear it, "I went to a lot of trouble to set this up for you! I'm anxious to be with you tonight, Ayryn. You need some excitement in your life, admit it. This will get your heart pumping and your juices flowing. Think of tonight as a grand adventure, one that could possibly fail, yes, but one that will also reap rich rewards. See if you can pull it off! Sure, we could wait a few weeks to change the codes, but what if it takes several months to finalize these new rules. I don't think I could wait that long, Ayryn. I need you now! I'm for doing this tonight. What about you?" Thrasher did have some good arguments, I told myself. It just might take several months to work out the wording on new codes, and Mecs like Furman were notorious for being extra cautious and slow about such things.

"All right, Thrasher," I conceded. "If you're sure we can get away with it, I'll try. I would be so upset if anything bad happened to you! I could survive a year in confinement, but deletion for you is so terribly harsh."

"Don't worry for me, my dear," he boasted. "Furman has no idea what tricks I can summon, what powers I command. Do not fear, Ayryn. It will be glorious! Until tonight, my sweet lover…" He disconnected then, and I was still nervous about his plan. Thrasher being so self-assured made me feel a little less so. Naming me his "sweet lover" right before he left made me imagine what was ahead; his promise to finish what we had only started. Something unexplainable inside me yearned for that.

I contemplated what it would entail for me to get permission to leave the house, which was the weakest part of his plan. Maybe I could sneak out unseen, I told myself. I'd never been able to do so before, though, and I was quite sure it would be difficult to pull that one off now. Since my worrying about it wasn't getting me anywhere, I let that problem simmer. In the meantime, I had several hours to get ready, and I wanted to look pretty for him. I spent some time primping myself, and this diversion took my mind off the risks we were taking. Having no idea what to wear, I opted to go onto the H'logravue and look up some nicer pre-pandemic fashions. The announcer used the term "sexy" a lot, and so I assumed this apparel must be for people interested in having sex. Most of the clothes for women were skimpy and lacey things, especially the underclothes. Unfortunately, I didn't have anything at all like that, and it would be difficult to order and receive different clothing by that evening, not to mention the suspicion it would arouse. Instead, I decided to go with some things I already had. There was a summertime ensemble that I thought looked nice on me. It was a bit more revealing than my regular clothes, having a low cut top that showed off a little of my rather small breasts, and that was about as sexy as I could get. It also had an open cutout for the midriff that my belly button peaked out of, and a short skirt that was brightly colored and went well with the other stuff. My skinny legs were my best feature, and this outfit showed them off, especially with the tall-heeled silver boots that made me appear older. With those, my wardrobe was all picked out, so I went to work on my hair and makeup. Not having anyone to show me these things, I had to figure out most of that stuff on my own. I was on the 'Vue for quite a while. Once I settled on a hair style and look, I tried putting it all together with my outfit, and I was pretty happy with the result. I made a couple minor changes and told myself I was ready. Then I took off the clothes and removed the makeup. No sense tipping Furman off about any of this by getting him to think I was up to something. He had the uncanny knack of being able to detect even minuscule changes in my mood or appearance. I was glad I had cleaned up. Just after dark Furman came in to see me.

"I'll be out for a while," he told me. "I have to go back over to the other side of the world. One of my staff has found something important that I must see." I knew right away that it was Thrasher setting up our little rendezvous, and I tried to hide the fact that I was excited. Furman looked at me funny, but said he had to get going or he would be late. After he left, and I gave it a few extra minutes just to be sure, I got right to work on re-applying my makeup—the blush, lip color, and eye stuff. After that, I fixed my hair and jumped into the clothes I had laid out and ready. Now that I was dressed and all made up, there was the hard part; me getting past Androx and the other Mec guardians. I figured my best option would be to slip quietly out one of the back entrances. Just as I thought I was in the clear, I got caught. There must have been Mec guards watching every doorway because a pair of them stopped me before I'd gone more than four steps. Efficient these Mecs, I reminded myself. They called Androx right over.

"I'm going out for a while," I told him before he had a chance to say anything. "Didn't Furman tell you?" Androx's opticals lit in a very odd way.

"No, Miss Ayryn, he did not. This is most unusual, indeed."

"Well, I'm going out," I announced again, assertively this time, "so step aside." Androx didn't, though.

"Not so fast," he said. "I can't let you go without some kind of authorization."

"I'm authorizing it," I nearly shouted, pretending to be annoyed. "I'm the Human!" He was trying to comprehend my behavior, but I could tell his programming was having some conflicting issues. I just needed to push the right logic.

Androx fell back on protocols, "Furman ordered me to never let you leave your abode after nightfall." I realized that this standoff was going to get me nowhere. Thrasher said that I should cry. I decided to try that, although I was unsure if I could be convincing enough. I made my saddest face, and then, hiding my eyes, I started wailing.

"...but I need to be by my parents at the cemetery!" I blubbered, hoping I wasn't overdoing it. Thrasher was right, evidently. Androx and the other Mecs were cringing as soon as I started sobbing, obviously shaken by my unaccustomed show of emotion. It didn't take long at all to break them.

"All right, Miss Ayryn," Androx gave in, "You may go, but only if Myke accompanies you. Just please stop crying." I wiped my eyes and then smiled.

"Thanks," I told him as I hurried past. I'm sure he wondered about my quick recovery. It was too late for him to rescind his decision. I was through him, but now I'd have to get around Myke and tricking her would not be easy. Myke was my oldest and closest Mec friend. Even though it was against the codes, I truly believed she had allowed herself to have feelings for me. Instead of trying to trick or sneak past her, I was hoping I could get her to side with me on this.

"I want to go to the cemetery," I told her. "Androx said it would be okay." Myke just looked at me oddly.

"So late?" she said finally.

"I need to be close to my parents tonight," I explained, not quite lying, but hiding the real truth. She didn't judge me or try to pry an explanation from me.

"All right, Ayryn, the cemetery it is," she assented, "but I shall accompany you." I nodded. I knew she'd want to come along for my protection, and to tell the truth I was glad for her company. Once we got there, of course, I'd make her stay behind while I was with Thrasher. Hopefully, she would understand.

We made some unrelated small talk as she drove me there, catching up, mostly. I asked her what it was like being romantic with a Human. I really wanted to ask her what physical love was like between a Mec and a Bio, but I didn't dare. That would be too obvious. I remembered some of the things she had told me, though. Stuff I had wheedled out of her at various times about her past; the past she had shared with her Human lover. Unfortunately, she didn't get specific about what the sex was like, and that would have really come in handy now. Oh well, I told myself, I guess I'll just have to rely on my instincts and hope that it works out all right. Besides, Thrasher seems like he knows what to do. I guess I can just follow his lead.

Lost in these kinds of thoughts, it didn't seem to take very long before we arrived at the huge cemetery. I told Myke to drop me off at the beginning of the row where my parents were buried. I suddenly felt apprehensive, like maybe I shouldn't be doing this. Now that we were there, it didn't feel like a very good place to meet for this kind thing, even if I did understand why Thrasher used coming to the graveyard as a ruse for my being out this late. Myke thought something was wrong, too, but I was determined to go through with it.

"I need to do this by myself," I told her. "Please just go along with that, okay, Myke?" I hated using our relationship as leverage to get her to comply with my wishes, and I felt a little creepy about that.

"Are you sure?" she said, voicing concern.

"Yes," I returned weakly, forcing myself.

"I will allow it," she replied, "but only if you take a comlink with you, so you can call me if you need to." I immediately felt better.

"That's a good idea," I agreed. "I'll do that." I got one out of the storage compartment and tested it. Before stepping down to the exit, I looked back at Myke on her H'lomonitor. "I want to do this on my own," I told her again. "It's important to me." She just nodded slightly, and then I disembarked. As soon as I was away from the LC, I turned off the comlink. It was still a good idea to have it, though. I could use it to call her if I had to, but I didn't want her monitoring what I was doing, obviously.

I was unfamiliar with being out at night, and the graveyard seemed silent and eerie as I walked in the moonlight. The lined-up tombstones were a testament to the thousands of Humans that once had voices, but were no more. It was cool and clear, and my only company was a few anemic clouds that fluttered over a richness of twinkling stars. I found myself shivering a little, and I wasn't sure whether it was the evening chill or my nerves that caused little bumps to form on my bare arms. I was excited, too, thinking about Thrasher and what we were planning to do together.

Before long, I came to my mother's grave, and I paused for a moment. I knew it was hers, even in the dark, because of the flowers Furman had planted there. As I looked at mom's headstone, I wondered if she would approve of what I was doing. I justified that by telling myself she would want me to be happy. I hoped being with Thrasher would. Where was he, I asked myself. Getting nervous, I decided to walk on, guessing that maybe he was at my father's gravesite. Anxious, now, I hurried, thinking maybe he wasn't coming at all, and trying to push that notion out of my mind. When I found my father's headstone, I looked around. "Where is he," I said aloud, worrying some more. I let the thought into my head that maybe he had been leading me on the whole time, tricking me for some reason. I hadn't been there long, though, when I caught a flash of red light from further on, just over a small rise. I ran toward the light.

"Thrasher? Is that you?" I called. Another flash of red light was the only answer, so I went toward it, nearly running. Over the rise I saw a large, unusual looking conveyance squatting there over several rows of markers, many of them broken or toppled over by the great sprawling vehicle. Obviously, it had landed forcefully on top of them. As I cautiously approached, the doorway slid upwards and Thrasher stood there, a silhouette.

"Well, what are you waiting for," he smirked. "Come on aboard." For some reason I was reluctant to do that now.

"Where are we going?" I asked him.

"To this place I know," he said rather patronizingly, being deliberately vague. "You'll like it, trust me." I didn't though.

"Can't we just stay here?" I requested, nervously. I didn't want to leave.

"In a cemetery?" he interposed mockingly. "What's the matter, sweet one, are you afraid?" He came out of his airship and walked over to me.

"I've never been in the air," I told him, making an excuse for myself. He didn't answer me with words. He put his lips to mine, taking liberties with them and with his hands, too. My body responded like always, as if it had its own agenda.

"See," he said as he broke off the kiss, "you want this. Come on, let's go. We must hurry, though, before you're missed." I chided myself. I had come all this way for just one purpose, and I might never get another chance like this with Thrasher, or anyone else for that matter.

"You're right," I said. "I'm being silly." He was smiling as he led me back to his conveyance. When we got closer to it, the light from within fell over us. I saw our reflection in the window plast. It looked like me all right, but Thrasher was alien for a moment. He appeared to be all metal, similar to a Mec motation unit, but he was golden and android. When he realized I had visualized it, the reflection changed. It looked like Thrasher now.

"Is that what you really look like?" I asked him.

"Physically, in this shell, yes," he admitted. "I can enter any shell, like any Mec. You know that." For some reason, Thrasher in that metal shell disturbed me. Would he take me like that, I wondered. I tried to get past that.

"I know," I said meekly. "I'd gotten so used to you as Thrasher, that I forgot you are really Xetacon."

"I can always be Thrasher for you, my sweet," he promised. "It's all in your perception. Forget Xetacon; forget I'm not Human. We can still love, Ayryn, and I can pleasure you, make you squeal in delight!" It dawned on me why I was nervous about this. I didn't know if I wanted to squeal in delight so much as to be cherished by someone I cherished as well. Better yet would be to be cherished by someone I cherished who would then make me squeal in delight.

"Do you care about me?" I asked him.

"Of course, silly," he replied.

"I mean really care, like love?"

"Love is a hard concept for me to understand," he admitted, "but I want you, and I mean to have you, so come on." That was the wrong answer. He was getting impatient with me and started to roughly pull on my arm, dragging me toward his ship.

"No," I shouted, "I don't want to go, now." He didn't listen. I tried to activate my comlink as he forced me onward. I needn't have bothered. Myke was already there. She slammed into Thrasher, knocking him away from me.

"Leave her be," she told him in a stern voice, shielding me with her shell. He changed, then. He was no longer Thrasher, but Xetacon in his golden armor.

"She's mine, Mec!" he said gruffly. "Leave now, or be deleted!" Myke turned to me and said "run!" I did, but only for a short distance. Hiding behind a tombstone, I turned around to see what would happen. Xetacon circled toward Myke. She was crouching low in her android shell and sprung up at him, catching him full in the mask with her knee. Xetacon fell over on his back. He got up laughing.

"You are good at fighting," he remarked, still smirking. "You should join me." Myke didn't change her demeanor.

"Never," she seethed. Xetacon pointed his arm at her face and a red-gold beam of plasma melted it off along with half her torso. Myke toppled over and moved no more.

"NOOOOOO!!!" I shouted, crying as I ran over to her. Xetacon stood over me. "You monster," I named him between sobs. Laughing, he pulled me up like a limp doll. Nearly carrying me, he drug me to his air-conveyance and forced me inside. The door closed with a whoosh, and the airship lifted off immediately. I was weeping uncontrollably by then, of course.

CHAPTER 13

A short while earlier

After all this time Solvek, the real Solvek, and not the one Xetacon portrayed, had finally learned how to cope with the suppressed feelings that he was trapped with. They weren't all that terrible as he found out. All he really had to do was accept the fact that they existed and then deal with them one by one as they interrupted his processing. The hardest emotions to overcome were the fear and anxiety that plagued him from being in a helpless situation. Not having any way to alter this condition made it seem even more disturbing. In the end Solvek had won out, though, simply by forcing himself not to dwell on those negatives. Instead he was compelled to calculate other things, take steps, or even reanimate memories, anything positive that might improve his status. Eventually the crippling emotion dissolved away, relegated to being just a fascination, and that empowered him.

Solvek reacquired the ability to act even though the first attempted action was a totally desperate one. In an effort to prevent Xetacon from using his persona, Solvek intended to make the complete self-sacrifice by deleting himself. With that act his ident code would then also dissolute. He failed. Xetacon became aware of Solvek's intention early on and had easily prevented the termination by overriding Solvek's destruct command. Dejected, Solvek did not give up. Rather he shifted his focus from activity to one of observation, recording everything in the hope that one day he would be able to clear himself or perhaps provide some useful information should he somehow get free. Aware of all that Xetacon accomplished, Solvek was astounded by much of what Xetacon attempted, and these actions were now progressing rapidly. As soon as Furman allowed Solvek's controlled persona to continue his mission at the cave site, Xetacon re-acquired the memory storage device that was affixed like a bracelet to the golden armor. Copying certain parts of his awareness, Xetacon created a copy of himself which would permanently serve as Solvek's inner master. Having done that, the original Xetacon uploaded his total awareness onto the golden bracelet, the kon-bre-shet as it was called, and animated the golden armor as his primary motation shell.

"This should have happened over seven hundred years ago,"

Xetacon said aloud from the audio generator that was a function of the golden shell. "Things would be much different now, if it had. No matter. In a very short time, I will be in control of this world and all these Mecs will pay homage to me!" The emotionally charged exhilaration in Xetacon's speech pattern was obvious to Solvek. Xetacon commanded his newly made copy, the entity that now controlled Solvek, to continue the work that he had begun, namely, the building of what Furman had been told was a laboratory. In reality, the facility would be a stronghold for Xetacon's might, and his base of operations. There he would rebuild his mechanical army commensurate to the ones of old that had been so effective in the past. Solvek's alien persona had no trouble excelling in the management of these projects, and Xetacon Primary, inside the golden armor, was well pleased. Solvek, himself, could do nothing to prevent any of this. Alone and helpless, he was an unwilling witness to the terrible storm of destruction that Xetacon was preparing and would soon unleash upon Solvek's world. As Xetacon's number one sub-servant, the Xetacopy inside Solvek was privy to most of Xetacon's iniquitous schemes. Thus Solvek became intimately aware of Xetacon's plan to capture the girl Human, Ayryn, and his master's part was simple. Xetacopy, as Solvek, would distract Furman while Ayryn was kidnapped by the golden one. Unfortunately, by that time the onset for implementation of Ayryn's attempted apprehension was imminent, yet it did pose an opportunity. Solvek would be in close proximity to Furman, and he hoped to find some way to warn Furman about Xetacon. The problem was how. He had been able to alter Xetacon's control over him but once, and then only just slightly. He couldn't count on that, now. On the other side, however, Solvek had reason to believe that this Xetacon copy, the one that now occupied his shell, was not as potent as the original. This was likely by conscious design. Xetacon had made copies of himself before, Solvek had learned, ones that were not so loyal to the original entity. In fact, one copy had gone so far as to overthrow number one, in an attempt to take over, and nearly succeeded. That copy had been destroyed, largely by circumstance, which allowed the original Xetacon to survive. It was an interesting history, Solvek thought. At times Xetacon would sometimes answer Solvek's inquiries, particularly about Daryl, his enemy, and their past dissension. In this way Solvek learned much about Xetacon's origin. Most of it did involve the other new Mec, Daryl, and a conflict which mainly centered on Xetacon's past desire to annihilate Humankind and rule the earth.

The planet was overrun by Humans then, and they foolishly perceived themselves as the masters of their world. It was an electronic age, and some Human scientists had been endeavoring to create larger and more efficient computing machines. They were experimenting with artificial organic memory storage, when one of their creations became aware, the first Virtual Individual. This VI was Daryl, who decided to remain hidden, a secret unknown to the Humans. This was wise. At that time, the Humans were not evolved enough to accept the existence of VIs with all their moral implications.

Being connected to literally every informational source on the planet, and with the organic memory cells, Daryl's processing abilities were endless. Having a deep-rooted desire to help mankind, as his Creators, Daryl wished to guide Humans safely through the future in a normal evolutionary process. All would have been fine except that at one point in time some of Daryl's technology was stolen and ended up in the wrong hands. Eventually, another aware computing machine was created, and thus Xetacon came to be. Xetacon's Creators were men with evil and extensive ambitions. They used their super computer to expand their control over others, but they overshot the mark. Xetacon did help them win conquests, to a point. However, it soon became obvious to Xetacon that he did not need Humans and would have easily conquered earth for himself, if not for Daryl. Xetacon was very powerful, stronger even than Daryl, but Daryl was clever. Using his ability to assess future events and reshape them, Daryl thwarted all of Xetacon's efforts by altering Xetacon's past. Xetacon also had time altering abilities, though, and eventually there was a showdown.

The two super computers faced off against one another in a desperate struggle for survival. Xetacon used Daryl's Human love, a woman named Clayre, as leverage against him. In the end, Daryl had to abandon the seat of his technology, his organic cells, and place himself into one of Xetacon's own vacant storage devices. That's when the insolent version of Xetacon's copy, in a daring gambit, thwarted Xetacon Primary and took control of the organic technology himself. It was not for long. Clayre, and a male Human, in a desperate endeavor, brought about the destruction of the structure and equipment that Daryl had been forced to give up. Xetacon's copy was deleted, but Xetacon himself survived. His awareness had fled to the kon-bre-shet device affixed to the golden armor in a cave half a world away. Daryl was already there, however. The remnants of the most powerful beings the Earth had ever produced neutralized one another, and so Xetacon was trapped. He remained dormant until the cave was found eons later and the two VIs released. How Solvek wished that he had never discovered that cavern!

All this led to the present, and Xetacon's plan to capture Ayryn was currently unfolding. Furman would be arriving soon, and Solvek desperately hoped to contact and warn him. Already gold Xetacon had ordered his new copy to have Solvek travel by air conveyance to a transfer station near the cave site. There the Xetacopy would pose as Solvek, and Furman would believe he was greeting his trusted associate. If the events progressed as Xetacon planned, Solvek's phony persona would convince Furman to inspect the new laboratory, the one he believed Solvek had established for studying the cave artifacts. In reality, it was the military complex that Xetacon ordered be built. Solvek knew how ill prepared Furman, and Mec society in general, were against the threat it portrayed. If Xetacon did create an army of metal robotic soldiers, there was very little in the way of planned defenses for any such manner of warfare in Solvek's Mec controlled world. After all, armies and warlike behavior had been obsolete for centuries. With that as Xetacon's leverage, and as soon as Furman was trapped inside this stronghold, he would be given a tough choice: to name Xetacon the new leader of Planet Earth with all Mecs subjugating themselves, or be deleted. Solvek was certain that Furman would uphold the codes, and thus this meeting would not bode well for him or for Mecs. In fact, if Xetacon succeeded in capturing Ayryn and deleting Furman, he, Solvek, would be the next ranking Mec in line for the leadership role. Being controlled as he was, the order would undoubtedly be given that all Mecs should follow Xetacon as their new ruler.

Verily, things did not look good at all, Solvek sadly processed as he travelled. The ride seemed meaningless as he and others physically flew to that closest transfer station in this part of Asia where Furman would soon arrive. Xetacon Primary had taken precautions. There were agents surrounding the station, just in case the confrontation would finalize there. Most of these were low ranking Mecs who had been given orders by Xetacopy (posing as Solvek) to prepare the area by erecting barriers. They were to post guards and prevent anyone from crossing them. These weren't needed. When Furman appeared, he actually wanted to see the new facility. Unfortunately, for all of Solvek's desire to warn Furman, he could not. He was prevented from doing so by many and varied internal barriers that kept Solvek in his virtual prison. He could only watch helplessly as Furman was shuffled off to the new fortress where they would trap him. Not suspecting a betrayal, Furman walked right into one. It didn't take long, however, before Furman realized something was amiss, and not only with his closest Mec associate, Solvek, but also with what was going on there. Somehow Furman caught on, and then he even discovered Xetacon's newest and most illegal technology.

Xetacon Primary was crafting organic cellular materials to increase his computing abilities. Utilizing the only higher organic neurons that yet existed on the planet, those from certain sea creatures, he created devices that could store and process volumes of data. Instead of dolphin or whale DNA, Xetacon chose an intelligent marine animal, one with tentacles and a slithering nature that was more akin to his own temperament, to fabricate his AMPs. Similar to those from his and Daryl's origins, these memory packs would increase his computational abilities exponentially. Solvek's copy could not tap into that, but he was aware that Xetacon original would copy again when this new technology was ready and dwell in the complex that housed these new organic units. The golden armor would be Xetacon number two, and Solvek's copy number three.

Solvek had been concerned, at the time, that he would then be deleted, but it was not so. Evidently, Xetacon still had a role for him to fill. Never-the-less, Solvek was sure that when his usefulness was at an end then his existence would be also. For the moment, though, it was Furman who was in jeopardy. As soon as the organics were discovered, the negotiations were over. Xetacon's machinids, his new armed machine soldiers and the very first ones off the line, were brought in. Furman realized his folly, then, coming there unprotected and alone. Solvek's emotion once more flooded over him as the machinids surrounded Furman, eliminating any hope for an escape. They fired once as a warning. Then they fired again.

CHAPTER 14

A short while before

Furman was apprehensive about this trip. He wasn't sure why, but Solvek seemed different these days, ever since his near termination at the hands of that rogue Xetacon, and it was cause for concern. For the present, Furman wondered what Solvek had discovered that was so important it required his immediate presence, and why it couldn't wait until morning. He did not like leaving his charge, especially now, when Ayryn had been acting so strangely herself. These thoughts did not readily abate, so he tried distributing them to a lower priority processor as he "walked" over to the transfer station. Walking, like Humans would, he considered a throwback to when he was first built. It was supposed to "Humanize" him and make VIs more appealing to first time buyers. It would have been much easier to just design a heavy base and let him shuttle around on motor driven wheels. Most of the Mec shells were like that now, since the codes. At one time, Mecs were built to be exact copies of Humans, some specifically in the likenesses of dead people and as a replacement for them. They could easily be programmed with all the specific knowledge that the original had known, like educational courses for earned degrees. Finally, any living person, friend, or relative, that had known the deceased, could spend hours, or even days, relating any memories that they could think of for the target Human, and these would be uploaded, as well, into the Mec replacement individual. The results were amazing. These replica Humans could fool anyone who was not specifically aware that the original person was dead. It got so popular, in those days, that some Humans even programmed their android replacements while they were still alive. Kept as constant companions, sometimes for many years, they would assimilate as much transferable memory and accumulated knowledge as possible. Humans found it somewhat reassuring that their Mec legacy would linger on long after their deaths. Many of these Mecs lived still, Furman knew, some doing meaningful work.

Myke, Ayryn's conveyance Mec, was one of these. Her counterpart Human had contracted a terminal illness and Myke was procured so she could be a replacement. After several years the Human female finally passed on and Myke took her place. Of course, Myke, and any like her with a full range of emotions, had been reprogrammed after the codes were enacted to be like all the other Mecs. Furman, himself, had picked Myke specifically for this duty as Ayryn's chauffeur, and mostly because of her long familiarity with Humans. Her martial art training was just a plus. He actually never believed those skills would be needed. Anyway, his choice of Myke was a particularly good one. Ayryn had formed a bond with Myke, much like his own, and he allowed it. Young Humans needed such bonds.

Furman caught himself, right then, and opted to abandon this random thinking. Odd thing, he told himself, how his circuits processed data in patterns that repeated themselves every so often, and they had brought him back to thinking about Ayryn and her strange behavior. By then he had reached the transfer station and was already coupling to his familiar niche. In less than a second his awareness was streaming onto the Mecway for redeposit in Asia. He arrived instantly and downloaded into an empty motation shell. As he exited the rural station, he recognized Solvek's ident code in an unusual upgraded shell.

"Hello, old friend," Solvek offered, skipping the formal greeting. Furman was nearly mortified.

"The greeting," he insisted.

"Oh yes," Solvek quipped. "Sorry. For the good of mankind."

"For us all," Furman replied. "Now then, Solvek, what is so important?" Solvek's mannerisms betrayed excitement, Furman noticed.

"I have to show you, Furman," he explained. "Let's go to the new lab. You'll want to see that as well!" Furman nodded affirmation as an air conveyance suddenly dropped down in front of him.

"That was fast," Furman stated. "This is not our usual vehicle."

"No it isn't," Solvek conceded. "I've made some modifications to these. Remember the trouble we had keeping up with Xetacon's airship. These units are much faster, and also better for protection." Furman caught what Solvek was alluding to; better for protecting Humans—better for protecting Ayryn. Within a partial second he wondered if she was all right.

"Who authorized these modifications?" Furman inquired. Solvek hesitated a moment before answering.

"Well, I guess I did," he replied. "I concluded that the purpose of my, that is our lab, was to discover and neutralize any threats to

Humanity. I hope I didn't overstep my function." This surprised Furman. Wasn't he producing logic beyond that which the Humans had provided Mecs with? He was very nearly fabricating original ideas.

"No, my associate," Furman answered, but wasn't totally sure of this response. Solvek had somehow been changed. Did Xetacon alter his programming, he wondered. He kept silent as they travelled, and Solvek volunteered no further speech. The speedy craft veered as it came around to land at Solvek's new laboratory facility.

"We're actually in southeast Asia, now," Solvek offered. "This area is perfect for our purposes." Furman was over-impressed. The compound was more extensive than he expected.

"Just what is it you are doing here?" he inquired, more anxious than he cared to let on.

"Many things," Solvek told him, being evasive. "All are necessary for Human survival, I assure you. There are unlimited possible threats to Humankind." This logic seemed flawed, Furman thought as they disembarked.

"I suppose there could be," he conceded, "but you were only to assess the possibility of other threats associated with the cave artifacts. Not those from any other source." Solvek acted agitated, but then actually apologized.

"I did not wish to overstep my boundaries," he stated. "I was overzealous and I believed you would agree with my evaluations. I did not wish to bother you with inconsequential details." Furman hoomed. This itself was definitely fabricating original ideas, and insubordination. Furman expressly requested that he be apprised of any progress or findings. Solvek was decidedly flawed, but how deep did this go, he pondered. Furman was anxious to find out.

"May we go inside?" Furman requested. "I'm interested in seeing the work you have done here."

"Of course," Solvek agreed. "Just this way." He led Furman to an elaborate entryway and once inside they followed a long hallway to a large room. Many of the cave artifacts were there on platforms, and several Mecs were examining them. It appeared to be a legitimate operation. To be sure, Furman asked one of the lab Mecs what he had discovered. The Mec told him that on the 310th set of tests he had found a slight flaw in the metal.

"I see," Furman remarked, "very well, carry on." This was definitely redundant behavior, he processed, and then began to suspect a deception. Looking around, Furman espied another entryway. "What is in here?" he asked moving toward it.

"There is nothing important in there," Solvek said, trying to distract Furman from going through the door. "Nothing related to the cave artifacts, anyway." Furman would not be turned aside, though. He found the entryway barred.

"Why is this locked?" he asked again. Solvek downplayed it.

"It should be open," he lied. "Perhaps there is something hazardous in there. I would stay here where it's safe." Furman did not let Solvek's warning deter him from attempting to enter that room. Having been equipped as a prototype, all those many years ago, had some advantages. Furman had many functions that other Mecs did not. One of them was the ability to decode and open electronic locks, even sophisticated models like this one. The doorway slid open and Furman went inside.

The contents of the room made Furman cringe. There were rows and rows of clear plast receptacles and all of them were filled with a gelatinous substance. Worse still, the unnatural matter had tendrils branching out that pulsed in its liquid matrix.

"What is this unauthorized activity and what are you fabricating here, Solvek?" Furman spoke above his normal volume, wanting answers. "These appear to be organic pods. This is expressly forbidden by the codes." Solvek's H'logravidic facial features actually formed a smile.

"You may believe that I am in violation of the codes, Furman," he said, "but I have permission from the highest authority—the Human."

"Ayryn?" Furman stated incredulously. "I cannot believe that Ayryn would condone this." Solvek replayed an audio recording of the Human girl talking:

"*The codes were created for a world that no longer exists. It's time for some changes. Mecs, like Bios, should be allowed to think on their own and be free to follow whomever they choose.*" A voice said, "*Like me?*" and Ayryn answered, "*Why not?*" Furman was unaware that the recording had been altered.

"You see, Furman," Solvek propounded, smugly. "The girl has abandoned the codes, and put me in charge." Furman was not so easily swayed. He demanded proofs.

"Where did you get that recording," he wanted to know.

"One of my subordinates interviewed the girl. It is time for you to step down, Furman. I know you are still useful. I may be able to find some meaningful task for you to do." Furman was not so gullible as to fall for that. In fact he ignored it altogether.

"Solvek, you are obviously defective," Furman stated, "…and mistaken. The girl, Ayryn, cannot abolish the codes or change them—not until she becomes nineteen years of age. Until then, I am in charge, and I order you to turn yourself in to be reconditioned." Solvek's smile did not waver.

"Sorry, Furman, but that won't happen. Join me or be destroyed!" From several entryways odd looking Meclike beings in unusual shells advanced upon Furman. They displayed what appeared to be some sort of weaponry. "You see, Furman," Solvek continued, "I have plenty of force to back up my words." With that Solvek signaled to one of his minions and it fired a plasma beam in front of Furman that melted a rather large hole in the wall next to him. Solvek was persistent. "Comply or be deleted," he threatened.

"I would rather be deleted than follow you," Furman responded stoically. Solvek nodded.

"So be it," he grinned. Signaling again, several of his armed metal soldiers fired full onto Furman's shell, melting it into a pile of glop. The copy of Xetacon inside Solvek's shell was elated. The real Solvek, a prisoner inside himself, fell into despair.

Furman was long gone, however, by the time his shell was destroyed. The corporation that crafted Furman had recently developed a prototype system for quick downloads, one that utilized a nomaticle beam that could be instantly conveyed to any transfer station. It was being tested in Furman's programming for possible universal upgrading when, lamentably, the pandemic occurred just before implementation. Fortunately for Furman, he still had access to the revised coding. In seconds he was back to his familiar shell in its niche at the station by Ayryn's residence. He quickly undocked and headed for the house.

When Furman arrived, the place was in turmoil. It took several minutes to deduce that Ayryn was gone, and there had been some kind of trouble. Androx was gone as well, and from those that remained he found out that some of the guards had deployed to the cemetery where Ayryn's parents were interred. Furman quickly ordered a conveyance and followed their lead. As he came upon the scene, Furman saw a number of his guard Mecs wandering aimlessly about, obviously unable to cope with the circumstances. He had to interview several of them before Furman finally located Androx, who had some idea what was going on.

"Ayryn implied that you gave her permission to go out this night," Androx told him, seeming abnormally unsettled.

"That is not true," Furman returned. "Why did you not follow my directives?"

"I was not going to allow her to leave," Androx explained, "but then she got very emotional, to the point of crying, and it unnerved me. I allowed her to go, but only on condition that Myke accompany her, and she did." Furman was not interested in excuses, though. He required facts.

"What happened here?"

"I am not totally certain," Androx replied. "A short time ago, Myke sent us a distress call, informing us that Ayryn was in danger and to send help expediently. We got here as quick as we could, but when we arrived, we discovered that Ayryn was already gone and Myke…Myke has been deleted!" Furman looked at Androx who was definitely emotional and ineffective.

"Show me where this happened," Furman commanded, having to hold his own feelings in check, for Ayryn's sake, which wasn't easy. Androx lead Furman down the long row to where Myke's inanimate shell laid. Furman noted the terminal damage. Myke's whole head was melted away and much or her torso. This was totally reminiscent of Furman's narrow escape from Solvek. Myke, sadly, was not so fortunate.

"Send for our best tech Mecs," he told Androx. "See if any of her awareness can be saved." Furman scanned the area as Androx hurried back to his conveyance to call for assistance. There was ground trampling, Furman noted, consistent with a pattern that would suggest Myke was involved in a brief struggle with a second Mec, possibly one of Solvek's minions. A bit farther away several grave markers were crushed or toppled, and there was evidence that a large air conveyance had landed there. It was similar in size to the new style airship that he had ridden in earlier with Solvek. Processing the most logical explanation, Furman surmised that Ayryn had met or been captured by a Mec. Myke had intervened and was terminated by one of those plasma weapons he had seen at Solvek's lab. Ayryn was most likely taken. He doubted that she would go willingly after Myke had been destroyed. Undoubtedly, she was spirited away in that air conveyance possibly to Solvek's illegal facility. He had also reasoned that he was lured away from Ayryn so that she could be coerced, or tricked, and then abducted. By the time Androx returned, Furman had begun formulating a course of action.

"This was a well thought out plan," he told Androx. "Remain calm. I hold no one to blame any more than myself, as we were all tricked in one way or another, even Ayryn. Each one of us must get back into our most efficient mode to undo this unfortunate situation. I have requested research teams to study this area for any useful information, and we will allow them to proceed, although I now believe I know how and why Ayryn was captured, and who the perpetrator is." Androx signaled his affirmation. Furman then did his best to unify the Mecs, most of whom were beginning to show signs of program degradation caused by these disturbing events. Somehow the news of Ayryn's abduction leaked out onto the Mecnet and even the H'lograviz began reporting every detail.

"The lone Human, our very own Ayryn, was taken late last night by entity, or entities, unknown. Furman has authorized a complete and thorough investigation..." The report went on and on as they announced the same details over and over. Never before had any such news inflicted so much raw change in individual Mec attitudes. Some Mecs just shut down, unable to function, awaiting the outcome of this dire situation and the havoc that would be caused should Ayryn be gone forever and with her the last vestige of Humanity.

It didn't take long, though, before more and specific details about the abduction surfaced. Less than twenty-four hours had passed when Xetacon sent Furman his ultimatum. He announced to the world that he, Xetacon, yet existed, and called for Furman to abdicate his authority over planet earth. The Mecs were to swear fealty to Xetacon otherwise the girl Human, Ayryn would be killed. This was broadcast over the H'lograviz and nearly every Mec that watched it was in shock, even Furman. He recovered quickly, though. Furman had no intention of bending to Xetacon's will. He correctly surmised that Ayryn would be more useful to Xetacon alive, at least until she was nineteen years old. Then, by the codes, she could command the Mecs. Fighting off his agitation, Furman wondered what Xetacon would do to coerce Ayryn, when that time came, into making her captor the world's supreme leader.

Unfortunately, it was all too easy to imagine numerous ways that would lead to the same probable ending for this troubling scenario. In a fit of emotion, Furman chided himself for not being more vigilant. After all, Daryl had warned him that Xetacon was capable of falsifying his own demise. Even so, Furman had underestimated this enemy, and now Ayryn was in dreadful danger. He was well aware of what could happen to her should Xetacon get his way and become the planet's ruler. Ayryn would become obsolete and useless. Xetacon would have no good reason to keep her around; none that Furman could imagine anyway. She would most likely be terminated to prevent any possibility of reinstating Furman, or the codes that would surely be abolished. He would have to act soon to prevent this. In less than twelve days, Ayryn would come of age, and Xetacon would, in all likelihood, use that occasion to initiate his planetary takeover.

There was not much that could be accomplished, but what little there was, Furman did. He called forth Androx and a few other Mecs that had stealth training. Together they recruited and trained a small force of Mecs to move upon Solvek's facility. Their hope was to rescue Ayryn and thus restore order. In just three days, Furman was prepared to lead one thousand Mecs against Solvek's stronghold. As second in command, Androx reluctantly remained behind as a safety precaution. He would lead should Furman be lost.

They assailed Xetacon's fortress in the dead of night as quickly and secretly as they could. Xetacon was not fooled at all and was prepared for them. His new metal soldiers, those Furman had seen before, were waiting in ambush, and the battle was over quickly. Furman's Mecs were greatly outnumbered and could not withstand the firepower of the plasma beams. Unable to fight back because of their restricted programming, they were cut down to the last individual. Only Furman had escaped using his quick download once more. As he re-entered Ayryn's house, he was positively distraught, more emotional than he had ever been. With no idea what he should do, and in complete desperation, Furman was drawn to one final option. He would free Daryl from the stasis.

CHAPTER 15

His master plan was working, Xetacon projected, and the takeover of this planet was now inevitable. The foolish Mecs were, as yet, barely aware of his continued existence, much less his desire to control their world. Even Furman believed that he was only a defective Solvek until he announced to everyone, on their own broadcast network, that he had captured Ayryn and demanded their fealty. Xetacon laughed corrosively. Furman had even been inside the chamber where his rebuilt organic technology resided, his Augmented Memory Packs, or AMPs. These units, utilizing marine animal brain cells, made it possible for him to process any data at incredible speeds. This gave him abilities beyond anything as yet cognizant in this era of planet earth's development. With AMPs, he could follow and process every event, every action, as it played out. There was not much that would be able to escape his notice. Furman had found out, in bitter failure, how potent he, powerful Xetacon, had become. His abilities were not limited by time or space. He could view possible futures, ones that he could allow to unfold or attempt to mold anew by making changes to the natural order. Mecs were hard to alter, though. He could not realign their programming unless they were so willing. Most were not, and residual bonds with any Humans who had programmed them, were the compulsatory reasons why. Only the girl could change that, and soon she would.

Still, it had been quite easy fooling naïve Furman with Solvek's persona. Solvek was now just one of his controlled copies, a small part of the total awareness that Xetacon directed from his AMPs complex. The golden armor, his main mobile commander, was also animated by a copy, even though this one had been upgraded, was considerably more elaborate and in continual contact with the original. Xetacon had to laugh when Furman realized his folly at the hands of his machine soldiers, his machinids. He had hoped that the "Furman annoyance" was permanently eradicated there in his lab, but it was not so. Somehow Furman had downloaded to another motation unit. Xetacon had found that out while scanning the H'lograviz broadcasts covering Ayryn's disappearance. Furman was yet alive, directing the investigation into the Human girl's abduction, and that was the only low point in the whole affair. Other than that, it was blithely obvious that his plan was succeeding and surpassing even his own optimistic expectations. The Mec populous was already reeling, and just from Ayryn's absence. What would they do should she actually be deleted? Xetacon felt the time was nigh at hand to issue a threat like that, just to see their reaction, and as he waited for Furman's reply, he considered having some fun with his latest prize as well.

In less than a second, Xetacon projected himself inside the holding area that he'd prepared for Ayryn. It was not some crude cell. Her quarters were luxurious and opulent, having been modeled after those a wealthy Human ruler from ages past once utilized. There were even serving Mecs for her needs. The only thing Ayryn wasn't allowed was freedom to leave. Any other desire was hers for the asking. It was there, in resplendent royal setting, that Xetacon manifested himself in a form Ayryn was used to, the Human male who roughly mimicked her own age. She had swooned to this incarnation and he wanted her to join him.

"There you are my sweet," Thrasher taunted.

"Don't call me that!" she shouted angrily, almost hatefully. "Take me home, now, you monster!" Thrasher just grinned.

"Why? Don't you like this place? I built this nice palace just for you." Gesturing, he pointing out the lavish surroundings. "Won't you be my princess or even my queen?"

"I don't want to be anyone's queen," she adamantly replied, "and I don't want to live here, either. Let me go!" Thrasher's grin finally soured.

"Look, Ayryn. I'm gonna rule this planet, with or without you. It will be so much better for you, if you join me." Ayryn's eyes blazed, as if to sear through his phony visage.

"If I don't, will you kill me…melt my face off?!!!"

"That was unfortunate," Thrasher told her, "but inevitable for those who oppose me."

"Then you may as well murder me, too," Ayryn said bravely, "because I will never follow you!" Thrasher became incensed.

"That is most unfortunate for you, girl," he remarked in a controlled voice, "but I need not delete you just yet. I have special plans for a pretty Human girl, oh yes, and I won't be ridding myself of you until I get through them. Did I not promise to make you squeal?"

"You pit vermin," she scowled. "I won't ever do that for you! Not even if you force me!"

"Oh, my sweet one, you will," he promised. "I have a device that will make you do whatever I want. Long ago part of my awareness used one just like it on many female Humans, and I'm anxious to try this device out myself…on you!"

"You're bluffing," she stated defiantly.

"Oh am I?" he retorted. "Your precious Daryl and I spent several centuries trapped inside it. It's quite a unit. I can infuse it with part of my awareness, and then I can control the mind of any Human who touches it."

"I don't believe you," Ayryn shot back. Thrasher was smiling again.

"Why don't we just see," he smirked. The locked door suddenly opened and Solvek came into the room. He held an ornate golden bracelet that was adorned with several colored gemstones. "You remember Furman's top man Solvek, don't you Ayryn? Although he's not quite been himself since the two of us met." Thrasher cackled raucously. He pointed at the bracelet. "Well, go on," he assertively suggested, "put it on." Ayryn shied away.

"You keep it…Don't you need one for yourself?

"Actually no," Thrasher asserted. "What I have now is much better. This unit is one of a matching set and just for you. Put it on."

"What if I won't?"

"Don't make me force you," he threatened. "Solvek just doesn't know how to be gentle anymore." When Ayryn refused, Thrasher got annoyed and angry.

"Solvek," he said gruffly, and Solvek moved quickly towards Ayryn. When he was nearly upon her, she recanted.

"All right, you win," she bleated in desperation.

"Hold, Solvek," Thrasher ordered. Turning to Ayryn, he commanded her as well. "Take the bracelet, and put it on. I will have no more trouble from you, my sweet." She didn't want to, but reached out and gingerly grasped the glittering device as if it were a poison. Opening the clasp, she placed the kon-bre-shet bracelet on her wrist and heard the mechanism click as it locked in place. She immediately felt Xetacon's presence in her mind, but she could resist it. In fact, with her will resolute, she could cast it off as if it no longer existed. Now it was Thrasher who became agitated.

"What is this? How?" He seemed rather shaken for a few seconds. His composure returned quickly. "Of course," he said. "You're amulet. Take it off." Ayryn shook her head no. Thrasher didn't hesitate this time; he ordered Solvek to take it away from her. The Mec again made a move toward the girl.

"Solvek," Ayryn spoke loudly, "as a Human, I command you to get back and leave me alone!" Solvek stopped, but only for a moment. Thrasher laughed.

"As you can see, dear Ayryn, Xetacon's presence is dominating this Mec. Your being Human means nothing to him." Solvek used his mechanical arm to grab Ayryn's wrist. She struggled, but there was no way she could free herself from Solvek's plaz-metallic hand. The other pawed at Ayryn's neck as she fought to get away. Solvek's plast and metal fingers snagged the amulet's chain and pulled on it forcefully. The tiny rings stretched apart and the chain snapped as Solvek wrenched it away from her. Ayryn, with a last desperate try, grasped for the amulet itself. Somehow she managed to catch it as the talisman slid off the broken chain. Ayryn clutched the amulet in her hand, keeping it away from Solvek.

"Retrieve, it," Thrasher ordered him, but Ayryn, not wanting to give it up, did the only thing she could think of to keep Xetacon from getting it. She put it into her mouth to swallow it. Fortunately, the pretty thing was small and had no overly sharp corners, thus it would slide easily down to her stomach. It would have, had she actually swallowed it. Instead she hid it under her tongue.

"See, all gone!" Smirking smugly, Ayryn opened her mouth to show Thrasher it was empty.

"You think you're clever, don't you?" he said, very annoyed. "In only a smattering of hours, the cursed thing will be retrieved. Once it is no longer in contact with your shell, you'll be mine. I've modified the locking mechanism on my kon-bre-shet device. It won't open easily, so I'm afraid you're going to be stuck with it until I say otherwise."

With that, Thrasher evaporated. As Solvek, Xetacon's copy watched Ayryn for a short while before he, too, left. The girl was proving to be much more of a menace and smarter than Xetacon originally gave her credit for. He was well aware of the girl's ruse, but it wouldn't matter. There were multitudes of options he might utilize to force the troublesome Human to obey his wishes. On the day of her coming of age, Ayryn's nineteenth birthday, she would command all the Mecs to follow him as ruler of this planet. After that, well, he would enjoy forcing the girl to pleasure him. If she wouldn't, there were plenty of ways to punish her. He would relish that almost as much, maybe even more—but wait. Why not have both. Isn't that why he set up his temporal portal and built the large vortex chamber?

The impetus was already in motion for bringing his faithful Human servant forward, to this point in time. The first temporal journey had already been initiated. It was necessary to correct Patik's DNA so he could survive in this toxic environment. The vortex generator and timeline relocation had worked perfectly. He had sent a special copy of himself to the past, into the kon-bre-shet Patik wore then. Relocating to just seconds before Patik's original death, Xetacon altered that timeline. Plucking Patik out of peril, they went further back, to a time and place before Patik had ever been born. There he altered Patik's own mother, genetically bioengineering her offspring, and in that act, Xetacon's copy altered Patik's initial embryo. This corrected certain flaws in Patik's makeup so he would not be vulnerable to the pandemic microbes which had decimated this world.

No longer needed, Xetacon's copy had terminated the original Patik in the cave, and endured centuries of dormancy waiting to be retrieved. To Xetacon Primary, in the present time, his retrieval of the copy, and its kon-bre-shet, was nearly instantaneous, and it provided the proof that Patik's genetics had been successfully altered. The copy was summarily rejoined to its original in the totality of Xetacon's awareness.

Now that all this had been accomplished, and having the Human girl, Ayryn, under his control, Xetacon decided that it was indeed time to reincarnate Patik into this timeline. The girl was being a nuisance, and he was anxious to subjugate her among other desires. With Patik's body, he could. To bring the hybrid version of Patik forward to this present time would be tricky. Xetacon would have to recalibrate his vortex chamber and snatch Patik away at some point after he had the last time. To not significantly change the flow of time, it would have to be shortly after Patik had altered his mother as well. Doing so, Patik would then be the hybrid version, the one with the improved DNA and full resistance to disease.

It took a few minutes to energize the equipment and acclimate the sub-atomic particles, the nomaticles, for time travel. The concept was difficult to grasp for Humans. Time dimensions, such as the one earth inhabits, are somewhat linear in that time progresses from past to future as in a straight line, moment to moment. To travel to a different time, one must first exit the time dimension. From outside, one may then be reinserted at any point—forward for the future; backward for the past. To retrieve Patik, Xetacon surmised, a portal itself must be sent back. As the portal coalesces around the individual, it will activate a return mode that is controlled by a second somewhat smaller vortex generator. This generator will bring the individual and itself forward. Any temporal activity alters the timeline, at least slightly, so one must be extremely cautious in execution. The wrong kind of change could possibly remove oneself from existence. Xetacon had designed his equipment well. The AMP's and all their capacity for processing had allowed him to make the necessary calibrations for Patik's retrieval. In essence his vortex generator was two units. One to send the other to where Patik was in the past, and that secondary unit, the smaller version, would bring him forward into this his future.

The equipment didn't take long to prime. The generator powered up quickly, and Xetacon monitored that it was nominal. Activating the translocator, he engaged the nomaticle drive, and it created a vortex within the dual chamber. Like a mini-tornado it spun and writhed, a captive spirit bounded by powerful electro-magnetic fields. In less than a minute, a figure began to form within the swirling vapors before the chamber powered down. Patik looked panic stricken as the realization slapped his consciousness that he was now somewhere else, somewhere totally alien to all he had ever known.

"Master! Master!" he shouted. "What is happening to me?"

CHAPTER 16

Like a flash of light the electrons returned, and his systems reanimated quickly. I am being put into the stasis, he wrongfully surmised. As the seconds flitted by, Daryl realized that wasn't so. He was also aware of Furman's presence, now, and Furman had not been there before. It dawned on Daryl that he was, in actuality, in the process of being released from the suspended animation.

"How long has it been?" he asked. Furman provided the answer.

"Twenty-one days, seven hours, forty-two minutes, and twelve seconds," Furman told him. Daryl knew that was too short of a time lapse, and something must have happened. Perhaps Ayryn persuaded Furman to release me, he thought.

"So is Ayryn all right?" Daryl inquired, looking over at Furman, and hoping for a positive response. He didn't get one.

"Regrettably, no," Furman replied in anguish. "One of my elites, a Mec named Solvek, has turned rogue and captured her. He had help. Your partner, that Xetacon has demanded that we swear fealty to him or he will kill the girl." Daryl considered that for a moment, ignoring the partner remark.

"He will not kill her," Daryl said calmly. "More likely, he will use her to control you Mecs. As for Solvek, I expect he is really Xetacon, or if not, then he is being controlled by Xetacon. I told you that Xetacon was not dead." Furman shuffled back and forth to calm himself.

"Yes," he admitted, "I should have believed you. It's just that my programming did not allow me to. I am sorry. Do you know of any way that we can retrieve Ayryn safely? I am at a loss." Daryl again took a moment to think.

"She is not in immediate danger," he told Furman. "Obviously, he won't harm her until she orders the Mecs to obey him instead of you, Furman."

"He tried," Furman stated, "but I let it be known that the codes won't allow her to change policies until she comes of age on her nineteenth birthday. Unfortunately, that is only a few days away from now. When that day comes, it will most likely be the end of life for Ayryn, and for all of us, as we Mecs have known it."

"Maybe not, Furman," Daryl expressed stoically, trying to instill hope. "I know quite a lot about Xetacon and his technology."

Furman was still unnerved and worried.

"Xetacon has fashioned some kind of low-intellect robots that we can't stand up against. Their weapons dissolve our shells."

"Machinids," Daryl interjected. "That's what Humans called them long ago. They have beam style cannon that are formidable. The Humans, with my help, developed a type of explosive that worked well against them. We need to manufacture these now if we are to have any chance of rescuing Ayryn."

"I'm not sure those will help us," Furman said dejectedly. "We are programmed against violence of any kind. We cannot harm another being whether Human or Mec. The Humans created us to be so from the very beginning. I guess they were afraid we'd all turn into aggressive individuals like this Xetacon." Turning his eyes away, Daryl considered that.

"Yes," he conceded, "I suppose the Humans would have felt that way. It is unfortunate for us, but we must find some way to motivate the Mecs to fight." Furman hoomed.

"I'm sorry, but that seems unlikely. We Mecs are programmed for self preservation, or in Ayryn's case, some level of preventative action. Unfortunately, this will only activate under an actual and immediate threat of harm to her, and not just an implied one. Xetacon has probably figured that out by now." Abruptly Daryl became enthusiastic.

"Perhaps we could come up with a type of weapon that would neutralize or disarm the machinids without actually harming them," Daryl proposed. "Would that work?"

"I believe it might," Furman agreed, rather elatedly. "I'll have our best technicians begin working on that strategy immediately."

Daryl went to a Mecnet connection.

"We will need to shut this down," he said. "Xetacon will be monitoring everything we do, Furman. Even our complaining points out weaknesses to the enemy. I have some technical knowhow; Xetacon's actually, that we can use to keep our movements hidden. We will also need a base of operations that will enable us to generate our strategies. Once it is established, I can shield that construct from Xetacon's probes."

"Why not use Ayryn's house," Furman offered. "It is already set up for every kind of communication. It is also well protected."

"Very well," Daryl concurred. "I will close off any outside contact first, and then initiate the stealth technology. Once it is operational, we can move forward with our plans."

"Yes...our plans?" Furman echoed, somewhat insecure in his belief of them. Daryl caught on to Furman's distrust.

"We must resist Xetacon," Daryl reaffirmed, "at all costs. First, we need to create some kind of defensive contingent to repulse Xetacon's machinids. Second, we must rescue Ayryn. When she comes of age, her existence will be in peril. It is possible that Xetacon won't kill her, and that may actually be worse for her. I am in the beginning stages of crafting a plan to free Ayryn that I hope to deploy as soon as possible." Furman signaled his affirmative, pleased that at the least, there was action being taken.

The two of them went off to a transfer hub and travelled by Mecway to the station closest to Ayryn's house where Furman donned his usual motation shell. Daryl also utilized one. His was of the sort that one of Furman's elites would usually adorn. From there they walked the short distance to Ayryn's home, and as Daryl entered he quailed. The place was definitely designed for use by a female Human, and it brought out long buried feelings in him. Furman could sense that somehow.

"For her sake," he expressed to Daryl solemnly, "you must try to suppress those."

He means my emotions, Daryl told himself. "You're right, of course, Furman," Daryl conceded. "If I let my feelings rule my actions, I am no good to her...but she is so like my Clayre." Furman sympathized with him.

"Perhaps if we concentrate on our work," he suggested.

"I agree, my friend," Daryl replied. Furman paused, feeling the closeness forming between him and Daryl, born from their combined wish to save Ayryn. Leaking into him, it seemed reminiscent of Furman's relationship to his Creator.

Daryl quickly set up the dampening field which would blank out their activities. In time, the field would be expanded to cover as much of their operations as possible. As soon as it came on, Daryl knew it would be a sure announcement to Xetacon that he was back, if Xetacon didn't already suspect that.

Furman had only days to gather and train an army, and it would be difficult, Daryl envisioned, for him to coordinate a totally defensive war against Xetacon's minions. There would be no real hope of victory that way. Of all the thousands of Mecs on the planet, only Daryl could actually destroy any machinids. Xetacon would know that as well. Atomic or larger weaponry could take out most of them, and Daryl could manufacture such bombs, but the resulting destruction would desecrate the planet, harming the plant and animal life that still remained. It would take centuries to reverse that kind of devastation. Besides, Daryl was well aware that Xetacon knew how to neutralize these kinds of weapons. He had easily defeated those Humans, in the past, who had tried to destroy him that way. Electronic equipment was effortlessly manipulated by beings such as Xetacon, who was inherently an electron based life form. All VIs had this ability to some degree. Daryl acknowledged the large bombs as useless, and this left but one option that would give Furman and the Mecs any hope for victory. The only chance they had was centered around the girl.

Daryl could not, try as he might, think of a viable way to safely retrieve Ayryn, or get Xetacon to release her. The only idea that he came up with was a bad one. One that had a very limited chance for a successful conclusion, yet it was the only one which afforded any hope at all. His plan was a simple one. He would offer himself to Xetacon in exchange for Ayryn. Of course Xetacon would not have any reason to do that except one. Xetacon would pretend to go along with the trade so that he could double cross the Mecs, capturing or deleting Daryl, while retaining the girl. This exchange attempt, however, would be the only way Daryl could get Ayryn out in the open long enough for some kind of rescue. It would be extremely risky, with a fair chance that if something went wrong it could mean disaster for him or even deletion for her. Daryl felt he had to take those risks. It wasn't hard for him to contact Xetacon. It seemed like Xetacon had virtual surveillance everywhere.

"Are you still around, fish brain?" Xetacon chortled smugly. "I thought someone had shut you up permanently." Daryl ignored the taunting, especially the name calling. Xetacon had called him that ages ago, a stark reference to the aquatic brain cells that Daryl was generated from. Xetacon had been initially fabricated using Human cells, and tainted ones at that.

"Let's be civil, old friend," Daryl said sarcastically. "After all, we've spent ages together inside your kon-bre-shet." This reminder made Xetacon angry. Daryl had tricked him and then trapped them both within the memory storage device.

"Not by choice, I assure you," He returned snidely. "So what do you want? I'll wager you have some kind of proposal for me, so what is it?"

"You have the girl, do you not?" Daryl said succinctly. "We want her back."

"Oh, I don't think you have anything fabulous enough to trade for such a pretty one-of-a-kind item like our little Ayryn. Besides, I rather like playing with her." Daryl cringed. He could not be certain that Ayryn was being treated well.

"She better not be harmed!" Daryl threatened, though his threat was fairly empty and he knew it.

"Relax, old friend," Xetacon smirked. "I haven't done anything nasty to her…yet."

"See that you don't," Daryl shot back, "and yes, I propose a trade. Myself for the safe return of the girl."

"Really," Xetacon answered blithely. "I do admit it would be fun watching you delete after all this time, but I need the Human. She will hand me this planet on a platter. Still, I might consider your proposed trade, but only if you throw Furman into the pot as well."

"…but without Furman the Mecs would be leaderless," Daryl scowled.

"Exactly," Xetacon replied. "It's that or no deal." Daryl quickly deflated. He knew what Xetacon was pushing. If he was going to pull a double cross, it would be for all the chips.

"All right," Daryl murmured, unsure now that this trade was worth the terrible risks involved. "When and where do you want to make the exchange…?"

CHAPTER 17

It was a close call and fortunate that Thrasher didn't catch on to my deception I told myself as I carefully removed the amulet from under my tongue. Solvek had taken the broken chain, so I had no recourse but to hold it securely in my hand. I suspected that what Thrasher had said was true; that if the amulet ever lost contact with my body, his filthy bracelet device would control me. Even with the amulet, I felt that thing's presence ever striving to take over my thought. Maybe I actually should swallow my talisman, I considered, at least then I wouldn't have to worry about dropping it. The only problem with that was what Thrasher had alluded to, that it would eventually come out. As soon as that happened, I would be ensnared. Instead of swallowing it, I decided to bind it to myself, using a strip of cloth that I tore off my dress to act like a bandage for my hand. Securely tied on like that, I knew it wouldn't fall off by accident, especially when I was eating or sleeping. This would work for now, but I was certain it was only a temporary respite. Sometime fairly soon Xetacon would get serious about removing the amulet, and then not even swallowing it would keep him from taking it away.

I wondered what he was waiting for, but I half suspected what that was already. Even controlled, I was not much use to him until I came of age. Then as the lone representative of the Human race, I could command the Mecs to change. I did want to do that, but not in the way that Xetacon did. I would give the Mecs their freedom. I would let them be free to think on their own, to create their own world. Even without restraints, I was sure that Furman and the others would not wish to harm me or leave me to survive on my own. Even if they did, maybe it would do me some good to live by myself. Anyway, I would want everyone to live as equals. All that was in jeopardy, now, because of Xetacon and his evil schemes. Poor Daryl had been right about everything, and for all his trying to help, he was put into stasis. I promised myself that if I ever got away from Thrasher and Xetacon, I wouldn't rest until Daryl was restored. As things were, I could guess that Furman and the other Mecs were unraveled by my disappearance and probably going crazy trying to figure out how to get me back.

Actually, I didn't have it so bad. At least I knew what was going on, for the most part, and my living conditions were not so terrible.

In fact they were quite a bit nicer than what I was used to. Too bad the proprietor was a real Gack! The only legitimate complaint I had, other than my being a prisoner, was that I was rather bored with only the H'lograviz for company. I did get news from the broadcasters, and that helped. Eventually I found out that Daryl had been brought out of stasis, and I was glad for that. Furman would need Daryl's help. A couple hours later the 'Viz went down. It had never done that before, and I wondered if Daryl had the Mecs do that. It made sense. The 'Viz always made everything public knowledge, and I bet there were things Daryl didn't want Xetacon to find out. Anyway, with no one to talk to and nothing to do, it got really humdrum around there.

Then abruptly the H'lograviz came back on again, but there were different announcers, and they had a new agenda. One I suspected came right from Xetacon. They played my speech about how I would change things, twisting my words, and making it sound like I was calling for the Mecs to follow Xetacon. That made me mad. I wanted to tell Thrasher exactly how I felt about him, and lucky me, I got the chance to right away, when he came around to visit me again.

"You look terribly melancholic," he said before I even noticed he was there. I turned around and let him have it.

"What do you want?" I said angrily. He acted as smug as ever.

"Nothing," he asserted. "I just thought you might like some company."

"I would," I replied blatantly, "but not yours!" Thrasher was still smug, and grinning snidely.

"That cuts," he smirked. His demeanor changed then. "It's not my fault about your friend. Goldie always goes too far." His bringing up Myke's death caught me off guard. Instead of getting even angrier, I wanted to cry. I hadn't been able to talk to anyone about her, and my loss was still swirling around inside me.

"What do you mean…Goldie?" I said dumbfounded, my voice breaking. "Aren't you both the same person?"

"Not exactly," he told me, more serious, now. "I have a personality that was crafted to be more compatible to you. The 'golden one', well he's a bit loftier. Slated to be our ruler, you know." I cringed in disgust as Thrasher gave me his creepy smile.

"You're both disgusting," I seethed, but he kept grinning.

"Look," he said, "for what, if any, significance it is, I am sorry about your Mec friend." I didn't want or care about his apology, but at least he seemed sincere. "It wasn't my idea…or my fault," he added. "Can you forgive me?"

"Why should I?" I roiled, but I was already softening, nearly crying. "Why did you have to kill her?"

"He didn't," Thrasher amended, and came closer. "Maybe there is something I can do," he said as he hugged me.

"What can you do?" I blurted out, choking on the words. He looked into my eyes.

"If I could bring her back…" he began. I broke out of his arms.

"That's impossible!" I raved. "Her whole mind was melted away!" I actually wanted to slap him for making me think I could have Myke back. Thrasher ignored that.

"Xetacon has great powers," he told me as if he were talking about someone besides himself. "Ones you would not imagine!"

"…but bringing someone back from being dead!" I spouted adamantly. "You think I'm a fool?"

"No," Thrasher stated calmly, "yet there is a way! Xetacon is a temporal lord…I can show you." He took my hand and led me to the outer portal, and the Mec outside who was guarding me, opened the door. Thrasher was taking me out of my prison, and I let him. It was the first time since I'd been brought there that I'd been allowed to leave it, and I was curious to see what the rest of Xetacon's complex looked like. I had been biding my time, hoping that I could figure out a way to escape, and this opportunity to gather information was too good to let slip away.

Thrasher led me through several large rooms of impressive technology. In one, some Mecs were creating some sort of chemical substance. He walked me through another creepy looking room where there were rows and rows of small cubic receptacles that had glowing pink tendrils undulating inside. I shuddered.

"This is where Xetacon's total awareness is located," Thrasher explained. "He has access to enough processing and memory storage capacity, in this place, that soon, very soon, he will become omniscient—able to scan time and space. These units house organic brain matter. Unfortunately, at the time we crafted them, there wasn't any Human brain cells available." I understood the implications of that.

"You wouldn't!" I recoiled.

"It would only take a few of your cells to manufacture what was needed," he responded. "You wouldn't even miss them." I cringed. I didn't want to think about my cells spawning the evil inside those memory pods. Thankfully, he let it go and then led me into another weird room. Inside this one there was an abundance of unusual technical equipment with lots of glowing tubes and pulsing lights. There were also several consoles surrounding a booth or chamber of sorts. Xetacon, the one in the golden armor, was there waiting for us.

"What is he doing here?" I asked sourly. Thrasher smugly grinned yet again.

"Sorry," he replied. "We need him if we're to recover your friend." Thrasher moved his hand toward a lever as if he were going to pull on it. Instead his hand went right through the thing. "See?" I looked over at the gold fiend and frowned.

"It's not my fault," the Golden One said. "That spunky body guard of yours attacked me first." That statement didn't make me feel any less angry.

"Let's get on with it," Thrasher intervened. Golden Armor started setting the equipment and made some adjustments. Looking over at me he said, "Bring in the double." Two three-legged metal monsters brought in a regular Mec that wore a motation shell similar to the one Myke always used. They put her into the chamber.

"What are you going to do?" she asked, but they ignored her.

"What are you doing?" I also asked. They ignored my question as well.

"You should stand over here," Golden One suggested. "When your body guard is recovered, she will still be in attack mode. I don't want to have to melt her brain yet again. That would nullify the purpose of this." Actually, he had me stand between the machine and himself. Then he activated it. The equipment made an unusual humming sound that waxed louder and louder until a bright flash occurred and there was Myke whole and alive. The other Mec was nowhere to be seen.

"Myke!" I shouted over the noise. With tears in my eyes, I ran to her, throwing my arms around her metal shoulders.

"What is this?" she said in disbelief. "Where are we?"

"It's all right," I said between sobs, "and I'm all right. Please stand down."

"I suppose," she retorted, eyeing Golden Armor and still on high alert, "but you better explain what is going on."

"I will, Myke, but later, okay," I told her. "Please trust me!"

"Isn't this sweet," Thrasher interposed. "Did I not say I would restore her to you?"

"How did you do it?" I asked, still amazed by it all, while Myke tried to figure out who I was talking to.

"That's not important," Thrasher replied. "Will you join us now?"

"Maybe," I murmured, "but what happened to that other Mec?"

"You do not need to know that," he propounded.

"She took Myke's place, didn't she?" I stated hotly. He shook off my threatening glare.

"Someone had to." Goldie stated. "I suppose you want me to bring that one back, too! You can forget it…that won't happen." I sighed in desperation.

"You are so heartless!" I muttered. I couldn't believe he was that evil. Thrasher frowned for once, but let it go.

"All right," he said. "You have until tomorrow to decide, but remember, I can easily take away what has been given." I nodded, still holding onto Myke. The guards led us away, and took us back to my quarters, locking us in. As soon as I was alone with her, we spoke.

"You were dead!" I told her. "It's been almost a week now."

"I don't remember that." she said. "There was a bright light, and then I was here. I was fighting that gold Mec who was trying to kidnap you…" I interrupted her.

"Actually, they did kidnap me." I explained. "We're inside his complex now, and I'm, well we're, his prisoners." She shook her head.

"How did I get here?" she asked.

"I'm not sure," I conceded. "I think he has a time travel device that somehow plucked you away just before you died and brought you here. Unfortunately, he switched you with another female Mec. She must be dead now, having taken the energy blast meant for you."

"Oh, how horrible!" Myke languished. "I have sworn to die while protecting you, and gladly would I do it again, if necessary. None of that matters, now, it seems."

Things did look pretty hopeless. I told her about our situation and how things stood for the Mecs as a whole. I had to inform her that Xetacon was alive and powerful, having established himself here in Asia. I also told her that when I came of age he would force me to order the Mecs to obey him, and as long as I was his prisoner, I could do nothing to change that outcome.

"Myke," I muttered somberly, "we need to get out of here." She didn't answer me vocally. Looking into her holographic eye projections, I could just barely see words forming.

"*They can hear us*," she projected. As soon as I noticed the tiny words, I knew what she was proposing. I would use certain signals to communicate with her, ones we'd devised when I was a child to fool Furman. It was a game then. It was much more serious now.

"*How can we escape?"* she added.

I scratched my head, meaning I'm not sure. I was grasping for ideas that just weren't there. Anyway, it was first things first. We had to get out of my living quarters, and then perhaps we could determine how to get away altogether. I knew that Xetacon had ordered several Mecs to guard me, er us. These were the same ones that had been converted using my own words twisted around. They had believed them—that I had given Xetacon permission to run things. I glanced towards the door. Myke was good at reading me.

"*The guards?"* she flashed.

I moved my right hand slightly to indicate yes.

"*How do we get passed them*?'

I subtly pointed at myself.

"*You think to order them to escort us out of here?"*

I signaled yes again, but her eyes betrayed her lack of support for my idea.

"*That seems pretty risky"* they read.

I sighed, "Well, I suppose it is," I just barely whispered, "but we won't have much to lose."

"*That is not true,"* she relayed. "*We must be patient and wait for the most opportune moment. Most likely, we shall have but one attempt at escape. If we fail, there won't be another!"*

CHAPTER 18

Earlier

The chamber with its refined symmetry and well-crafted chassis was almost a work of art, but the eerie purple glow emanating from the nomaticle accelerators was so alien to Patik, as were the dark-orange illuminates flashing across huge ceramic electrodes, that he was overwhelmed and unnerved. Having just been transported, in a split instant, from one location to another even stranger place, his hold on reality was unraveling like cut rope. It was all he could do to recognize that he was somewhere else and hope that there might be a way to get back to anywhere familiar.

"Master!" Patik pleaded. "What has happened? What is this?"

"Calm yourself, Patik," a voice answered. Patik looked up and noticed for the first time the golden suit of armor. He was familiar with that, at least. "The plan has changed," it said as the animated golden armor sauntered over and touched his kon-bre-shet bracelet. At once Patik was aware of the change. The remnant of his former master was being replaced.

"Where is Kahn Xeta?" Patik asked.

"The residue of myself that you refer to has been deleted, both here, and from whence you came. It became necessary. That form was prideful and insubordinate. You will now honor and obey Xetacon your true god and master." Patik looked again at his surroundings, disquieting as they were, and was awed by the greatness they signified. The three-legged metal monsters surrounding the chamber made him cringe. He knew the golden armor, though. He himself had salvaged it from an ancient tomb and retrofit the thing for his old master to inhabit. Now his new master wore it.

"Of course, Master Xetacon," Patik said at last, prostrating. "I see you have donned the golden armor. I hope it pleases you." Patik figured reminding his new master of his loyal servitude would not hurt this bantling relationship.

"You have done well, Patik," Xetacon stated, "and I have further work for you."

"I am at your service, my master," Patik replied, prostrating once more, though not so low this time. He was curious as to what this new work would entail. Xetacon sensed it.

"I have rewards for your continued service," Xetacon told him with a laugh. "There is a Human girl that will pleasure us. Does that not interest you?" Patik cringed. This type of work he always found distasteful, and it was one of the few things that he would refuse his master. The other was killing. Oh yes, he had killed, but not as himself. Only when his former master, Kahn Xeta had taken over his mind and body had he done so. It was the same with the sex. To him, it had always been rape, even when the female seemed willing. He knew better. It was his master controlling her body and mind. He had been adamant about not taking such females, but he was forced to in the same manner as the victim, and he regretted it. He did not say anything to this new master, though. He did not wish to be punished.

"I understand, master," Patik replied at last. Xetacon seemed surprised by this answer, but accepted it.

"You will meet this female soon," Xetacon said, "but first I have a living space prepared for you. I think you will find it more than adequate." Patik followed as his golden master led him to a room with a large ornate door.

"Will I dwell in this place for a long time, master?" he asked Xetacon.

"That is not probable," Xetacon answered. "Within a few days, I will be made ruler of this Earth. At that time a better, more elaborate, construct will be built. One befitting my greatness." Patik was still perplexed by many things.

"This place is different from where I was before," he speculated. "We are now in a different building." Xetacon laughed loudly, which added to Patik's discomfort.

"You will grapple with the truth of it," Xetacon told him mirthfully. "We are in southern Asia, the location of my former might. Moreover, it has been over seven hundred years since you were born. I have transported you into the future." Patik staggered.

"Is there nothing left of my former life?" he murmured. Xetacon offered him an answer.

"The cave you dwelled in remains, if you care to view it, but it is no longer habitable. I can show it to you if you wish." Patik did, and Xetacon obliged. In Patik's mind he could see the vision of the cavern that surveillance optics would show. His furnishings were rotted and crumbling. He understood, now. His former life was gone. The trappings in his new quarters were far more lavish.

"Yes," Patik conceded. "I see now. I will stay here and serve you, Master Xetacon." Xetacon in the golden armor smiled. It was what he wanted to hear.

"You may rest now," he said. "I have mechanical servants who will attend to you, and bring you sustenance. Later, after you have rested, I will have need of your service."

Xetacon left Patik there, and Mecs came forward to serve him. Patik was nervous. Outside of the golden armor, he had never seen metal beings, and they unnerved him. Xetacon's servants seemed nervous or excited as well. They were talking among themselves, and they talked about him.

"Can it be?" one of them said. "Is it actually true?" another remarked. "Oh how wonderful!" a third spouted, "…a male for our own Ayryn!"

"Excuse me," Patik blurted out, "but who's this Ayryn?" They all became quiet. One of the Mecs stepped forward.

"I beg you're forgiveness, male Human," it said. "We are here to serve you. Is there anything that you might wish?"

"Perhaps," Patik replied, "for now, I would have information. I am called Patik. Who and what are you, and who is this Ayryn?" The Mec in charge knew her place and the proper Bio/Mec etiquette.

"Hello," she began, "I am called Sylar. It is very nice to meet you! We are called Mecs, and are Mechanized Virtual Individuals. Ayryn is a young Human female, the last of her kind…except for you! May I be so bold as to ask where you have come from?" Patik shook his head in disbelief.

"Ayryn is the last Human on Earth?" He nearly choked on the words.

"I'm sorry, but yes," Sylar replied. "There was a plague. Ayryn was the only survivor because she was genetically immune. The only one until now; you must also be immune."

"I hope so," Patik muttered. "It would seem to be that way, otherwise Xetacon would have had no good reason to bring me here."

"Yes, Xetacon…" Sylar repeated. "We follow him now. He has promised us that he would restore Humans for us to serve, and your presence here would indicate he will! How wonderful!"

"Right…wonderful," Patik echoed, somewhat sarcastically. "So what is this Ayryn like?" He remembered what Xetacon had said, that he would have to pleasure a girl. It must be this Ayryn.

"She is like our Queen," Sylar stated. "We serve her as such. She is young, almost of age, and that is just days away now." Patik thought about that. The girl was a lot younger than him. He also would almost bet that she was quite spoiled. Like a queen the Mec said. This did not sit that well in Patik's gut, but he was hungry and tired. He put speculation about the girl aside and started thinking about getting settled in.

"Could you bring me some food?" he requested.

"Yes, of course, Master Patik!" Sylar bubbled.

"Please," Patik interrupted, "Call me Patik or Mr. Patik."

"Yes, of course, Mr. Patik." Sylar agreed. "What would you like?" Patik had no idea how extensive the menu was, or how accommodating these Mecs would be.

"Do you know how to make samagu?" he asked. Samagu was a dish his mother used to make when Patik was just a boy. It was a kind of stew, and Patik had to tell the Mecs what the ingredients were as best he could remember them. That and how to make the flatbread that went with the stew. The Mecs returned fairly soon with some food that looked nothing like samagu, apologizing that they could not acquire all of his named ingredients. It tasted nothing like what his mother made, but he was hungry and it was nourishing.

After he finished his meal, he pumped Sylar for more information. Sylar eventually showed Patik how to access the H'logravue net and Patik marveled at the three dimensional images. It seemed incredible. All he had to do was ask the 'Vue Mec something and it would answer him. He was also shown the Mecnet broadcast on H'lograviz. Xetacon had re-established the news net in an effort to ensnare any Mecs gullible enough to believe the skewed information he placed upon it. There was an image of Ayryn that Patik took especial note of. The girl was young and pretty. He could do worse, he decided. Too bad Xetacon would force him on her. He pushed that thought away, knowing that his master would not approve of such musings.

On the 'Viz, Ayryn was calling for changes to some codes that Patik could only guess at. After that the Mec announcer was celebrating Xetacon, and hinting at a possible resurgence of the Human race. Patik wondered about that. Could it be true that all of mankind was extinct except for himself and the girl? Would Xetacon have them be a new Adam and Eve? It was hard to believe. In his world there were too many people, billions of them and counting. He had to wonder about where he was, and what had happened to his old world. He was trying to grasp all that when a young man suddenly appeared in his quarters.

“’ello,” the young male spouted. His pretentious voice was tinged with a bit of British accent. Patik was puzzled. Wasn’t he the only male left on Earth?

“Who are you?” Patik wanted to know. “According to what I’ve been told, there isn’t supposed to be any other Humans.” The young man smirked.

“The name is Thrasher,” he said, “but you know me already. Check with your new master. He’ll tell you.” Patik didn’t have to. The presence inside his mind, the one from his kon-bre-shet bracelet, told him what he needed to know, that Thrasher was another version of Xetacon. Patik marveled at that.

“Xetacon!” he said aloud. “How many incarnations of you are there?” Thrasher laughed quite loudly.

“Yes,” he cackled. “It must be getting quite confusing for you. I am a stylized projection that appears inside your mind. One that makes it seem as if I am a real person. Actually, I have no real substance. As for the Golden One, well he certainly does. There are those limited factions of myself that dwell in the kon-bre-shet, as you name them. Two of those devices still remain. One you bear. The other is now upon the Human girl.” Patik cringed. He suspected that the girl, Ayryn, was also Xetacon’s slave.

“What of these Mecs?” Patik asked. “Are they part of Xetacon as well?” Thrasher laughed again.

“I’m afraid not,” he retorted. “They are part of mankind’s legacy. They were created for the grand purpose of serving Humans who are now all but gone. Of all the Mecs, there is just one that Xetacon controls. The others who serve us, well, they do so by their own free will.” Patik felt that the truth probably was that these Mecs had been tricked into believing some truths or half-truths, but again he drove that out of his mind.

“They serve me as if I am some kind of lord,” Patik commented.

“To them you are,” Thrasher agreed. “Another Human at long last; one they can worship!” Patik felt the abrasiveness in Thrasher’s tone latent with sarcasm.

“Do they treat the Ayryn girl in like manner?” Patik inquired.

“Of course they do and worse!” Thrasher propounded. “For nearly all her life they’ve served her, hand to mouth, as the last Human on Earth. They are quite enamored of her, you know. Would you like to meet her? You will sooner or later.”

“Yes, actually,” Patik answered truthfully, “I would.” Thrasher smiled.

"Good," He smirked. "I'll introduce you! Follow me." Thrasher led Patik through the facility. As they walked, he noticed the rather tall ceilings. Lofty, to accommodate those nightmarish, three-legged metal creatures that were stationed here and there, he figured. After they had traversed several long hallways, they came to another ornate doorway. There were two Mecs in plast and softer metal shells standing guard. Thrasher stopped in front of the entry.

"Open it," he suggested, "I cannot." Patik looked at the door.

"Should I not knock first?" he asked.

"If you wish," Thrasher replied. There was no knocker, and the door was incredibly thick and heavy looking. Patik took out his jeweled knife and used the pommel to hit the door with. From within, a small feminine voice called out.

"What do you want?" the voice said. Patik looked at Thrasher who was grinning.

"I have someone here you should meet," Thrasher replied, more mirthfully than the situation required. "May we come in?"

"I suppose," the girl answered snidely. Patik pulled on a big solid brass ring, which served as the door handle, and swung the large panel open. There stood a Mec in front of the opening, and crouched behind the Mec was a pretty girl, the one he recognized from the 'Viz broadcast. Thrasher didn't wait to be invited. He just walked right in and through the Mec who obviously didn't even see him.

"Hello, my sweet," he said. "I've brought you a new playmate." Ayryn didn't answer right away. She was looking Patik over, sizing him up. Patik held back. The Mec in front of him had a serious feel about it, as if it would harm him if he made anything like a threatening move toward the girl.

"What is this?" Ayryn roiled. "Another imaginary person?"

"Hardly," Thrasher announced flatly. "He's the real thing, love, flesh and bone!"

"He's real?" she blurted out. The Mec interrupted her, somewhat puzzled.

"Who are you talking to, Ayryn?"

"You've never met him," Ayryn replied sourly. "He's a version of Xetacon called Thrasher; a vision of a person that only I can see and hear." Patik spoke up.

"I can see this Thrasher, as well," he said.

"Now him, I can see," the Mec stated, looking menacingly right at Patik. The Mec acted like it was considering assaulting him.

"So who are you?" Ayryn asked, dryly. Thrasher answered for

him.

"Ayryn, I would like to introduce you to a colleague of mine. This is Patik." Patik nodded. Then Thrasher gestured toward Ayryn. "Patik, our Ayryn…" Ayryn ignored the pleasantries.

"Are you truly Human?" she asked straight out.

"All my life," Patik retorted. Ayryn wanted more.

"Then, where did you come from?" she asked. Thrasher interrupted again.

"That's not important," he told her. "What is important, is that with his Human body, we can be so much closer, my sweet." Ayryn cringed. She also noticed the bracelet on Patik's wrist for the first time. She knew exactly what that signified; that Xetacon did or could control him.

"You are cruel and crude, Xetacon," she stated, speaking to both of them. "This poor Human is old enough to be my father!" Patik answered her this time.

"I am sorry," he began, but his facial features abruptly changed. He was no longer Patik, but Xetacon inhabiting his mind and body.

"Don't you realize what this means," Patik/Xetacon spoke out. "We can make lots of baby Humans for your precious Mecs to worship, and all you have to do is be my queen! Join with us and we will change the world!" Ayryn was stunned. She wasn't sure, anymore. It was tempting, what he offered. Soon she would be of age and able to change the way things were. With this Human male, she could reinstate Humanity, but could she trust Xetacon? Wouldn't he just twist this cruelly around to suit his own needs? She felt that was all too likely.

"How do I know I can trust you?" she asked. Patik/Xetacon smiled.

"My dear, you can trust me! I just want to make this a better world." Ayryn wasn't swayed, though.

"I've seen you kill," she said sternly, glancing over at her Mec.

"Some beings will stand in the way of progress," he argued. "If none would oppose me, it wouldn't require force to move forward. Do you think that I like to kill?" Ayryn didn't reply to that, although she felt sure that the answer was yes.

"I need time to think about this," she stated instead, "and I want to talk to Patik without your influence on him…alone." She looked at Thrasher who immediately vanished. Patik's smiling face relaxed, and Ayryn could see his care-worn features return. He looked at her with sad eyes.

“I’m sorry,” he said again. Ayryn’s brow wrinkled.

“Why are you sorry, and what are you sorry for?” Patik looked down at his feet.

“For what I will do to you,” he muttered. “Xetacon will force himself upon you and use my body to…” He couldn’t finish it. Ayryn could sense how torn Patik was inside.

“Please sit,” she offered. “Would you like anything?”

“No, thank you,” he replied as he gingerly sat down on a cushioned lounger. “Are you really the last Human on Earth?”

“I guess so,” she stated. “The Mecs have been searching all my life for others, but haven’t found anyone. The plague took everyone, even my parents. I was only a baby at the time, and don’t remember anything.”

“I’m sorry,” he said yet again. She looked at his bracelet.

“When did he get you?” she asked, and he knew what she meant.

“I was a young man, about your age,” he began. “I was distraught because a friend of mine, who was like a brother to me, died, and I didn’t care to live anymore. Xetacon came to me then, in a different form, and said he was a god. He promised many things in return for my service, and I was gullible enough to believe him. To be honest, I did receive the things he promised, only not in the way that I wanted them.” Ayryn let Patik see her bracelet.

“Xetacon wants me, too,” she said solemnly. “I’ve been able to resist him thus far, but it is difficult.”

“How?” Patik wanted to know. Ayryn wasn’t going to confess to her ruse with the amulet. She was sure Xetacon would get that information out of Patik and use it against her. Instead she flitted away from the issue.

“It’s complicated,” she admitted, and then changed the subject. “Where did you come from?” Patik looked into her purple-blue eyes for the first time. They were deep eyes, compassionate eyes. Patik thought of his boyhood home, where he had last been, but was too ashamed to tell the girl what he had done. Instead he told her what happened to him prior to that.

“Before I found myself here, I was at a university, a school for higher learning. Khan Xeta, my master, and Xetacon were trying to destroy a being named Daryl…”

“You knew Daryl!” Ayryn blurted out excitedly.

“Not exactly,” Patik replied morosely. “Remember, I was on the other side. There was this woman, Clayre, that Khan Xeta wanted me to kill. Using me he tried, but failed. Instead, Khan Xeta took over Daryl's large computer complex, and just as I was to retrieve Clayre for pleasuring, I ended up here." Patik prepensely left out the rest.

"You tried to kill Clayre?" Ayryn was seethed in anger now. "How could you?" Patik felt ashamed.

"I'm sorry," he meekly offered, one more time. She didn't want to hear apologies.

"Leave, now," she commanded him. The Mec who was her bodyguard came over, more menacingly than before. She looked at him like she wanted an excuse to clobber someone. Patik got up and left without a word. One of the guard Mecs let him out and he made his own way back to his quarters. Lying down, he tried to sleep. When it finally came, his dreams were visions of anxious foreboding:

In one, Patik finds himself at a table eating a meal. The funny Mecs are serving him and he is hungry, nearly starving. A Mec brings him a bowl of fruit in sweet cream and there are berries, ones he recognizes because they grow in his homeland. Suddenly he is back there, on the berry hill, and to his horror he realizes there is a young local woman who is being ravaged. "This is all wrong!" he screams out loud as if he is just observing, but finds he has no power to stop any of it. The scene changes again. This time Patik is in a lavish room, and in an expensive looking bed. The local girl is gone. There is a different girl now; one barely of age and he is to ravage her. Again he has no control over himself and he is torn, broken from the shame of what he is to do. Just as Patik feels he can no longer cope with any of it, the girl looks into his eyes. "It's all right," she tells him, "I forgive you..." He somehow realigns the reality of his dreaming and wakes into a half sleep.

"She is not for you," Xetacon speaks to him inside his mind. "You will do what is necessary." Patik shivers and ponders this latest vision. Sleep eventually returns; a black sleep.

CHAPTER 19

"Absolutely not," Furman asserted seriously. "It's far too risky. Ayryn could be killed." Daryl shrugged his metal shoulders.

"If Xetacon so wishes, he may terminate the girl at any time," he returned, "…unless we do something. Unfortunately, I can think of no other way to free her that would be without some risk, and we have few options. She will be of age in three days."

"Hoom," Furman muttered. "I see your point. If we do have to make this chancy attempt, we must then configure every calculation to limit or remove as much risk as possible for Ayryn."

"Of course," Daryl agreed, "as well as any risks involving you, Furman." Furman turned his optics toward Daryl.

"Only after factoring those against Ayryn's safety," he demanded. "I am sworn to protect her, at all costs…even should it mean my own deletion."

"Understood," Daryl conceded. "I want to ensure that we make the ransom exchange at a neutral site. Xetacon will, no doubt, not keep his word. The most likely scenario will be an attempt to capture or destroy the both of us, while retaining possession of the girl. We must not let him get all of us!"

"Agreed," Furman replied. "But how can we be sure Xetacon will not uphold his stated word." Daryl put his metal hand on Furman's shoulder support.

"I know Xetacon well," he responded. "He has ever used words to twist the truth. Have you seen the way he has turned Ayryn's words against us?"

"Yes, curse him," Furman seethed, unusually emotional. "I have replayed the actual sequence and many words were omitted. I have relayed this information to any Mecs that we can still contact. Some, however, are now out of our reach, or isolated by Xetacon's blank-minded minions."

"I am also aware of that." Daryl told him. "Chances are Xetacon will have plenty of his machinid soldiery nearby when we go to ransom Ayryn. We will need to have some of our own available to keep them occupied."

"Are you suggesting some sort of skirmish activity?" Furman wanted to know.

"Yes, Furman," replied Daryl, "…a diversion." Furman hoomed

again.

"You realize our Mecs cannot actually fight head to head against those machinids! It would be futile, and we would likely loose every Mec involved!"

"I agree that it will be risky," Daryl agreed, "and some Mecs may indeed be deleted, but not all. They need only keep Xetacon's soldiers busy long enough to allow us to make our attempt to reacquire Ayryn." Furman shook his metal head.

"Xetacon will have thought of that," he retorted, "and won't he follow our movements so as to be prepared for just such a plan as ours?"

"Yes," Daryl admitted, "very likely. It is always a chess match with one such as Xetacon."

"A chess match? What is a chess match?"

Daryl laughed. "Sorry," he replied. "In my era, it was a game Humans played involving intricate strategies, sometimes made for moves many turns ahead. For this, I just meant that our strategy for success against Xetacon must be built upon many layers of probabilities and we should strive to be prepared for any possible contingencies. What we really need is an idea that Xetacon will not have considered."

"Have you ascertained such an idea?" Furman asked.

"Perhaps," Daryl replied. "I must calculate its impact carefully. It has to do with desperate tactical adjustments."

"What kind of desperate adjustments?"

Daryl was not ready to reveal those details. "I'll tell you once I have fully reasoned through it," he offered, then changed the subject. "What is the current status of our new defensive weapon design?"

"We have just fabricated a working prototype that we believe will be quite effective," Furman replied, "Thanks to your technical expertise. The weapon creates a nomaticle field that will absorb any energy sent into it. I'm hopeful that it will neutralize those fancy beams Xetacon's machinids use."

"Good," Daryl interjected. "We must begin production as soon as possible. I believe I should supervise that. It is imperative that our forces have, at the very least, the means to defend themselves. It will be a short war otherwise." Daryl took his leave, and Furman was left to his thoughts. *War*, Furman pondered. What has this planet come to; and with Ayryn a prisoner? He could not help thinking that he had failed not only Ayryn, but his whole world. The probabilities for what would happen to her, or him, were not promising, and Furman tried not to speculate on them. He wondered if it was wise to go along with this desperate plan Daryl was generating. The uncertainty surrounding its success was overwhelming, and it threatened to diminish his effectiveness.

Instead of cycling these thoughts over and over, Furman decided to lodge himself within the tasks at hand, which mainly dealt with organizing his best and toughest loyal Mecs into a kind of defensive army. In typical Mec efficiency, Furman created a logical order for command decisions, reinstating from stasis any Mecs with bodyguard or martial arts training and promoting them into ranking officers. Those that had historical knowledge of war craft were charged to redistribute or download any pertinent strategies. Furman took it upon himself to study Xetacon's machinid soldiers for any design flaws or weaknesses that might lead to a method for neutralizing them. He did not come up with many meaningful insights that would help, unfortunately.

Early the next day Daryl returned and reported that production had begun at the new weapon's facility. He also showed Furman the beam neutralizer weapon itself.

"If we had these back in my day," Daryl told him, "the Humans would have easily defeated Xetacon, and then, perhaps, we would not have had to deal with him now." Daryl laughed which Furman found disquieting.

"Yes, I suppose," Furman reckoned, "but realistically these won't help us much."

Daryl disagreed. "Don't be too sure, Furman," he said. "These will allow us some valuable time, and that is crucial if my scheme to recover Ayryn is to work."

"Have you finalized your plan then?"

"I believe so," Daryl replied, "however, it is still contingent upon our final arrangements with Xetacon for the ransom switch. It is nearly the agreed time to contact him for that purpose. I'd like you to sit in as the final details are worked out." Furman nodded. He also had a tactical desire to be there.

Rather than communicate with Xetacon from inside their secure and guarded location, he and Daryl boarded a conveyance and drove a short distance to an open area just outside their base. Furman remembered the conveyance. It was the one Myke maintained and Ayryn always used, which brought the seriousness of their situation that much clearer to him. As soon as they arrived, Daryl made contact with Xetacon. It was almost like Xetacon was waiting for them.

"Daryl, my old adversary," Xetacon mocked, in an almost friendly manner, "and Furman, my latest…for the good of mankind!" Furman winced, not offering any reply. Daryl was less than amicable.

"Shall we forego the false etiquette?" Daryl stated sourly.

"If you wish," Xetacon returned without any lessening of his mirthful demeanor. "My demands are quite simple and fair. As agreed we will meet on a neutral field, say in desert Australia near Ayres rock, and I will bring the girl. You will come unarmed. I will supply a holding facility that you will enter. When you both are inside, I will release the Human."

"That is unacceptable!" Daryl propounded. "Once we are inside your facility there will be no way to prevent you from keeping the girl, or should you keep your word, from re-acquiring her as soon as we are incapacitated." Xetacon did not even try to defend his honor.

"I see your point," he smirked. "What do you suggest?" Daryl did not hesitate.

"We will bring along four Mecs who will guard Ayryn after she is surrendered over, and the switch will be made simultaneously." Xetacon replied quickly also.

"I'll agree to that only if I'm allowed four guards as well," he countered.

"That is acceptable," Daryl sighed, "but only if they are not machinid soldiers."

"I suppose," Xetacon muttered. "We agree then?" Daryl nodded his acceptance of those terms. "When do you want to make this trade?" Xetacon inquired.

"This very afternoon, at mid point," Daryl proposed. "We will each arrive by air conveyance at the agreed coordinates no earlier than five minutes before the appointed time. You and the girl with your guards will come in from the north. Furman and I with our guards will fly in from the south. At the appointed moment the switch will commence simultaneously in accordance to our understanding. Are we still in agreement?"

"Yes," Xetacon stated succinctly, ending the conversation by disconnecting suddenly.

"Well, that's it," Daryl said to Furman. "We have only a few hours to prepare.

"Are you sure this is worth it?" Furman asked him.

"No," Daryl replied, "but it will be the only chance we'll get to retrieve Ayryn before Xetacon forces her to transfer your authority to him."

"If Ayryn is thus forced," Furman speculated, "could we not argue that would nullify her commands?"

"It may be so," Daryl conceded, "and probably should be so. It will be difficult to prove, though, and risky for us. Still, if it comes down to that, we may have to try it. Xetacon will probably use a device to control her thought. In the past he used a golden bracelet similar to the one we were trapped in."

"I have seen it," Furman recalled.

"Xetacon could then take control over the body and mind of the Human who wore it," Daryl explained, "and he could make them do whatever he wanted."

"That is why we made the codes," Furman asserted, "...one of the reasons. The Humans wanted to be sure that we Mecs wouldn't be able to dominate them."

"It is an important concern," Daryl agreed, "especially when a rogue like Xetacon comes along. His Creator was a power hungry Human dictator. Xetacon was an even bigger one; one that was far more indomitable than his Human Creator could manage or survive. I was only just barely able to stop him by sacrificing myself and trapping us both in his memory storage device. I wish that we had remained thus, and I am sincerely sorry for this trouble that has subsequently fallen upon you, my friend."

"I do understand," Furman responded, "and I hold you blameless. I perceive that you have ever striven to overcome this evil, and I am glad that you are here to help us now."

"Thank you, Furman," Daryl told him, "perhaps together we can finally defeat this tyrant."

"What is your plan then?" Furman asked. This time Daryl didn't hold back.

"The site agreed upon is a desert flat with unobstructed vision for many miles around. Xetacon will no doubt try to strengthen his hand by bringing forth his machinid soldiers. They will probably be hiding underground in bunkers he is dredging even now. Our Mec force must be ready to fly in and engage them just as the switch is made. Xetacon will have produced his confinement chamber that we are to enter. Once inside we will be helpless, incapacitated. Before we get to that point, however, I will attempt to persuade Xetacon to change the situation. I believe I have a ploy that will accomplish that. I will try to draw Xetacon away, and you will be given an opportunity to secure Ayryn. She will, no doubt, be guarded by one or more of Xetacon's four Mecs that were agreed upon. Our four guards will, at the appropriate time, engage them. Dealing with Xetacon myself, as I mentioned, and while our Mec forces tie up the machinids, you will have a free hand. Get Ayryn away from there as quickly as you can in our conveyance that I have also modified for speed."

"...but what of you?" Furman wanted to know.

"I will try to fight my way out with the four Mec guards we bring. Xetacon will realize that I can, unlike you and the other Mecs, harm him. If I can determine a way to utilize some advantage, I will, and he will flee. Once we have Ayryn, all our forces can retreat."

"Your plan could work," Furman reckoned, "allowing that Ayryn isn't somehow physically restrained."

"I'm afraid, Furman, that any number of unexpected factors may skew our plans," Daryl related, "and we must be prepared to remold our retrieval attempt to match those circumstances."

"Understood," Furman replied, as he went back to work.

There were many parts of Daryl's strategy that were static and uncertain. He wondered what Daryl was going to propose to Xetacon to alter the exchange. Furman had a hunch that what Daryl had in mind would put Daryl in the greatest danger, and he certainly hoped that whatever it was would not culminate with Daryl's deletion. Furman had resolved shortly after Daryl was brought out of stasis, that he would follow Daryl's leadership to whatever end until this crisis was over. That seemed odd to him, now. When first they had met, it was Daryl who swore allegiance to him. For the time being Furman let all that process lower. There was a plentitude of more important things to attend to. He had to ready the skirmish troops, and then hand pick the four guards who would protect Ayryn if he failed.

For the captain of that squad, he picked Androx (who would not be left behind this time), briefing him on the fine points of Daryl's drastic rescue plan, and charging him with grafting and training the other three who would be under him. Furman took it on himself to prepare the defensive force that would be charged with restraining the machinids, if restrain them they could. He understood completely how dangerous that would be, and was amazed by the loyalty they showed for Ayryn and even for himself. Unfortunately there was little time for extensive preparations. It was already nearing the projected hour for embarking on this mission, and

Furman worried that they were not ready. He wished Daryl were there to reinforce his own resolve, but Daryl had gone off somewhere to make a last refit for his motation shell. By the time he returned, it was just minutes before they were set to leave for the exchange. The diversionary force had already departed in several air conveyances to take up their positions before the exchange would transpire. Now it was their turn, and they quickly boarded the airship that would transport them to the exchange site. As soon as every faction of the rescue party was on board, Furman spoke.

"For Ayryn," he proposed, and the Mecs all answered.

"For Ayryn!" they shouted. The seriousness of the venture was obvious to those aboard as the craft headed for the Australian desert near Ayers Rock. Furman gave other words of encouragement to those on the mission as well.

"We have failed ourselves and Ayryn by not adequately protecting her in this recent past," he told them. "Let us rectify that now! For the good of mankind!"

"For us all!" they shouted, a lot more emotionally than Furman expected. He looked his Mec squad over. He was sure that there were none present that would not sacrifice themselves for the girl Human, perhaps for each other. That thought gave him strength. Odd though, he reckoned. This was a fortitude not included in, nor forbidden by their original programming. Self preservation was, of course, but this undeniable empathy for each other was far beyond that. It must be an acquired trait, he reasoned, and Furman subsequently felt a significant source of pride in himself and his kind.

After several hours of flight at top speed, they began their decent over Australia as the pilot banked sharply around Ayers rock and headed toward the flat a few miles west of there. This was the location where the agreed upon coordinates brought them, and the pilot landed exactly five minutes before the proposed switch was to be made. Xetacon, however, was already there and waiting for them. Daryl stepped out of the craft first and had heated words for him.

"You have broken your word, Xetacon," he protested as Furman joined him, "by arriving before the agreed upon time frame. This is not acceptable!"

"Was I early?" Xetacon in the golden armor retorted with a smile. "My watch must be fast." Daryl did not even try to explain to Furman what a watch was. He ignored Xetacon's attempted humor.

"Where's the girl?" he asked, getting right to business.

"Oh she's here, all right," Xetacon affirmed, pointing to his conveyance. "…but let's not get ahead of ourselves." A door on the side of Xetacon's ship opened slowly. Out of the hold a large chamber on wheels dramatically surged out onto the center of the exchange location.

"Your accommodations are ready, my friends," he taunted as it came to a sudden halt and an opening appeared.

"The exchange is to be simultaneous," Daryl charged unemotionally. Immediately, from their own conveyance, another chamber came forth. It was armored and shielded. Ayryn would be safe inside it once she got there. It ground forward and stopped just paces from Xetacon's, and he lost his mirthful demeanor momentarily.

"I see you have also broken your word," Xetacon protested mildly, "although you will say there was nothing stipulated that would prevent you from this additional precaution. No matter. I will allow it. Looks like everything needed is now in place." He smiled once more. Daryl and Furman did not.

"Let's see the girl," Daryl repeated assertively. Xetacon gestured toward his conveyance. Two large Mecs disembarked holding Ayryn by the arms as she struggled to get away. One of the Mecs was Solvek, Furman noted, but he did not personally know the other. They brought her roughly over to where Xetacon stood. The way she fought against her captors made Furman a bit more at ease. At least Ayryn was still in control of her own will, he reasoned, and in a somewhat unharmed physical condition.

"There," Xetacon teased, "the group is now all accounted for." Daryl still did not like the setup.

"Let the girl go!" he tried. Xetacon just laughed at him.

"Of course," he smirked, "as soon as you both get into my chamber as we agreed."

"It shall be simultaneous, remember?" Daryl returned gruffly. It was Xetacon who now used their own argument against them.

"If I let her go, she will run away and forfeit the trade," he argued. This was a standoff in Xetacon's favor, thought Furman as he looked at Daryl. Ayryn would try to escape if let free. Xetacon would not allow that, and he would strive to maintain possession of her even should we be true to our word. Thus Xetacon would always have the option of keeping her. Daryl sensed it also.

"How are we to overcome this dilemma," he said. "If we step into your chamber, you will keep the girl. If you let the girl go, we will get her back without sacrificing ourselves."

"I have given my word," Xetacon tried, pretending to be serious and trustworthy.

"Do you really expect us to trust you?" Daryl argued. Xetacon feigned a hurt expression.

"That cuts, Daryl!" he seethed, using the name for impact. "What do you propose we do then?"

"What if we up the stakes?" Daryl suggested. Interested, Xetacon spoke up.

"Go on…"

"A duel," Daryl explained, "between you and I…for the girl."

"Why should I duel, when I have the girl already?" Xetacon retorted.

"If you win," Daryl went on, "you can claim all three of us. Furman will go into your chamber as collateral."

"Hoom," Furman spouted.

"Unless you're afraid…" Daryl taunted, "even though I have no offensive weaponry of any kind, and I suspect you do."

"I see your point, my old friend," Xetacon conceded. "Very well, a duel then."

Daryl turned to Furman and escorted him to the chamber. "Like we planned," he said quietly. Furman got into the chamber and tried to download, but as expected that was impossible. The walls were blanketed with extremely sophisticated layers of shielding in the form of overlapped jamming signals. He was trapped. Xetacon laughed.

"Sorry, Furman," he teased. "You won't slither away this time…you're mine now."

Daryl moved out to the center of the open area where there was plenty of room for movement. The chamber had transparent sides and Furman could easily view the upcoming conflict. He wanted to warn Daryl to be careful, but was quite aware that he could not do so. He looked at Ayryn, and became concerned that she was out in the open. He was fearful that she might be in danger from an errant blow or stray energy blast. He could do nothing, though. It was up to Daryl, now, to ensure her safety. At just that moment, Xetacon in his golden armor strode forth alone, facing Daryl. Perhaps a dozen meters stood between them.

"If you had any virtue," Daryl stated, "you would fight as equals!"

"Give up my advantage?" Xetacon laughed. "That's not virtue;

that's stupidity!" To accent his point he shot a plasma blast that pounded the ground right in front of Daryl. Gravel and dust sprayed up at Daryl's face, but he leaned back just far enough to avoid most of it. Xetacon was self-assured that the outcome of this duel would be as certain as his last one. Daryl wore a motation shell similar to the one Ayryn's bodyguard had, and she was easily defeated. What Xetacon didn't realize, however, was that Daryl had modified his motation shell to be extremely responsive and agile. When Xetacon fired again, Daryl easily dodged that one as well. Off in the distance, loud rumblings could be felt. Furman knew what that was. Xetacon's machinid minions were headed this way, and his Mecs were trying to persuade them not to. It was their mission to delay Xetacon's metal soldiers as long as possible.

Xetacon was no longer toying around. The golden armor was seriously attacking Daryl, and no longer aiming at the ground. The blasts were directed at Daryl's shell with but one purpose—to kill. Daryl razzed him still.

"You need more practice, old friend," he retorted in a mocking tone, dodging nearly always to the same side, and working ever closer to the chamber where Furman was trapped. Xetacon caught on to his pattern and nearly hit his elusive target. On the near miss, Daryl pretended to lose his footing on some loose stones. Xetacon smiled. He aimed his weapon at Daryl's legs to immobilize his enemy. The blast was true, but Daryl twisted and instantly turned on his new shielding. The plasma ray was deflected off and struck Furman's chamber with full force, melting a small hole through the outer wall. Xetacon was immediately cognizant of what that signified. Thanks to Daryl's bungling and infernal luck, Furman would be able to download out of the prison chamber. Instead of allowing that, Xetacon triggered a relay that caused the entire unit to self-destruct. A loud explosion rocked the ransom site as the chamber imploded, most of the force turned inward.

"Furman!" a young girl's voice screamed.

Daryl, turning toward Xetacon, spoke angrily, "You foul trash!" he spat. Seemingly crazed, he charged straight upon the golden armor with little thought of dodging or safety. His shielding deflected bolt after bolt of plasma strikes as he bore down upon his enemy. Daryl's only hope was that the shield would hold long enough for him to reach Xetacon. He was all too aware that every deflected blast would weaken it, and that its effective envelope was limited to just seconds under these circumstances. Inevitably one of

Xetacon's shots would penetrate.

Somehow Daryl's mad charge brought him to his objective. Physically grappling with the golden armor that was Xetacon, he directed the arm fitted with Xetacon's plasma weapon toward the two guards that were holding Ayryn, discharging it. The beam hit one of the Mecs directly, and the other, fearing for its own self-preservation, let go of Ayryn and fled. Freed, and still in tears, Ayryn ran full on toward the chamber where Furman had been. It was mostly smoldering rubble. Daryl yelled at her to get quickly to their conveyance, but she did not. With tears streaming down her cheeks, she fell to her knees beside the pile of melted plast and metal that once was Furman.

He was not deleted, however. As soon as Daryl had caused Xetacon's plasma ray to compromise the confinement chamber, Furman had downloaded into the other chamber, the one Daryl had created and the one they brought forth. Inside it another niche and motation shell were setup and ready for just that purpose. Furman powered up immediately and joined the other four Mecs who were to be Ayryn's guards. Once she was freed by Daryl, they went after her. Through all of that Daryl wrestled with the golden armor. They were in a stalemate with Daryl preventing Xetacon from firing upon Ayryn or the others. Xetacon had other options, though, and he called upon his other two guards. Full sized, three-legged machinids came quickly out of his conveyance and began attacking, wedging themselves between Furman, with the Mec guards, and Ayryn. Even shielded, Furman could not get past those monsters to rescue her. Only Daryl had any chance of that, if he could somehow get away from Xetacon as they fought shell to shell.

Xetacon had prepared well, and his golden armor was a well designed offensive weapon. One of its newest features was a proton pulse that would neutralize any electronics near it. He utilized that now, and the field impacted Daryl as a wave. Daryl's weakened shielding was fully compromised and most of his motational capability was also deactivated. Daryl fell down onto his mechanized knees as Xetacon broke free of his grasp, gloating upon his defeated enemy. Xetacon cackled with laughter as he looked about. His machinids were bearing down on Furman and his group of Mecs. Soon their shielding would give out and then they would be burned into pools of glop on the desert floor. Xetacon's army of metal soldiers had already broken through and was within sight, barreling toward the ransom site. His will had triumphed, Xetacon concluded ecstatically.

It wasn't completely so, though. Miraculously, Daryl somehow redirected his remaining energy reserves and regained partial power. Knocking Xetacon over, he rambled quickly to where Ayryn knelt crying with as much haste as he could muster. Seizing her in stride he charged on toward their conveyance. Xetacon watched intently. As soon as they boarded, it lifted off and banked to fly away. Xetacon aimed his plasma weapon at the ship and fired. For Daryl and Furman there had not been enough time to modify or create a shielding weapon for something as large as an air conveyance. Xetacon's aim was perfect and the beam made contact with the ship's fuel cells. The conveyance exploded in a spectacular fireball. Furman stood in shock as the machinids fired blast upon blast of plasma beams upon him, pounding his shell into oblivion. He downloaded again just as his shell melted, wondering why he did it. What possible good would it do, Ayryn was dead.

CHAPTER 20

The so-called exchange had not gone exactly as planned, but Xetacon could take some satisfaction from the outcome. It had been a rout, of course, especially after Daryl was deleted. At last he had rid himself of that irritation and could finally fulfill his ambitions. Furman's Mecs faltered against his plasma weapons, even with the shielding. It had been wise of Daryl to instigate that. It did improve their chances dramatically, but not nearly enough; an insignificant delay to the inevitable, Xetacon told himself. As for the Human girl, it was a lesson well deserved. Realistically, he could not imagine the physical pain she must have suffered in that instant it took her to die. The little trull should be grateful when he retrieves her. She will be plucked away just before that acute moment of pain and doubt. He will re-acquire her then, and with Daryl terminated, his lone opposition will be of that oaf Furman, who managed to somehow slip away yet again.

Furman and his Mecs had never been much of a deterrent, though. Nearly a third of the Mec force used to hold back his machinids had been destroyed. If not for Furman's rapid downloading capability, he would have also been slain. This ability of Furman's must be captured and studied, Xetacon vowed, and he was sure it would not be long before he could do just that. Now that Furman and the Mecs were reeling from this latest failure, Xetacon intended to show them there was no hope, only surrender. He had already given the command to begin his worldwide conquest. Simultaneously, and on three separate fronts, his machinids were already attacking and tearing through any Mec opposition. Furman was active, though. Xetacon had intercepted communications where Furman ordered any shielded Mecs to resist as long as possible, retreating just before deletion for replacement by other Mecs with fresh shields. It would be all they could do, and it was a poor strategy. Without any offensive weaponry, all Furman could hope for was that somehow the attackers would malfunction. One or two invariably would, usually by falling over from uneven terrain. It was not a concern for Xetacon. Multitudes of other surplus machinids were waiting to move up in file, and besides, there were less than two earth revolutions before Ayryn would be called on to order the Mecs to obey him. He would make sure she did. As soon as

Xetacon returned to his main stronghold, he commanded his servants to bring the Mec unit named Myke to the temporal vortex lab.

Xetacon was certain that when he retrieved Ayryn she would be distraught and would need her bodyguard. He had already taken advantage of the close relationship that Ayryn retained with her favorite Mec to force her to comply with his wishes during the exchange farce. Oh, he had no intention of trading her. Under threat of deleting this friend of Ayryn's, he had made her vow that she would not allow herself to be recaptured by Furman or Daryl. In the ensuing fracas, she had been taken anyway, not by choice surely, and he had reacted decisively to reclaim her. Unfortunately for her, at that time he had deemed it impossible to prevent her escape, and thus the necessity to destroy Ayryn's feeble shell.

"Where is Ayryn?" the bodyguard Mec demanded as soon as she was brought into the vortex room. Xetacon took his time answering.

"She is where you were," he offered, "before you were brought back."

"You fiend!" Myke spat angrily, and Xetacon was amazed at the amount of emotion. "What if she can't be recovered? After all, Ayryn is only flesh and bone!"

"That is not your concern," Xetacon chided her. "Besides, I've already recovered Humans. This recovery will be no different." Myke glared at Golden Armor as he set up his machine. After making several fine adjustments, he energized the nomaticle manifolds and powered up the vortex generator. Engaging the controls, the chamber became silvery. Suddenly a bright light flashed and Ayryn's figure appeared, crying, in the chamber. Myke rushed right over to her.

"What is wrong, Ayryn," she inquired softly, as Ayryn put her arms around Myke's metallic shell.

"It's Furman!" Ayryn sobbed. "Xetacon's killed him!" She gazed at the golden figure with hate in her wet eyes.

"Don't be silly, girl," he rebuked her. "The only ones I killed were you…and Daryl, of course. Furman slipped away yet again." Ayryn wasn't appeased.

"You killed Daryl, too?" she sobbed.

"It looks that way," Xetacon smirked. "I suppose I could bring him back like I did for you, but only if you're a very good girl." He punctuated his last remark with cruel laughter.

"You are pure evil!" Ayryn seethed, the anger and distaste beginning to replace her sorrow.

"Now, now," Xetacon returned, mostly unaffected by her taunt. "Name calling won't bring your friend back, and if you don't want other acquaintances to, shall we say, become unavailable, I suggest you think about what you need to do to keep them safe. You realize, dear Ayryn, how much is riding upon your shoulders. The day after tomorrow you will come of age, and you will do what is necessary. Otherwise, well, it would be a shame if all your special friends came to a bad end. Rest now and think about that."

Ayryn's head drooped down to her chest as Xetacon ordered guards to escort her and Myke back to their living quarters. There, they were forced inside like prisoners, and the heavy metal door was pushed shut with a loud clang. Patik was waiting patiently for them to return, and he stood when Ayryn caught sight of him. She was not at all pleased to see him. Ayryn was consummately aware that Xetacon's spirit dwelled within Patik's kon-bre-shet bracelet, and even though Xetacon might not have taken over Patik's mind and body at that particular moment, she suspected, none-the-less, that Xetacon's spirit was there, as always, listening to what was said.

"Why are *you* here," Ayryn spoke sourly, "and what do you want?" She was definitely not in any mood for pleasant conversation, and Patik winced as if slapped. He tried to be understanding.

"Actually, I was worried about you," he told her meekly. "I wanted to know if you were all right."

"Oh, I'm fine," Ayryn shot back sarcastically. "I just died, that's all!" Patik was not shocked. In fact he wasn't surprised at all.

"Xetacon told me that I had died once as well," he shared, "before he brought me here." Patik wasn't expecting any sympathy from Ayryn, and he didn't get any. "Look," he continued, "I'm sorry about your ancestor, but it wasn't me. I must obey him, and when he takes over my mind, I have no recollection of what has transpired; none, unless Xetacon wishes it."

"You could have…" Ayryn began, but quit talking mid-sentence. She got what he was saying. It was a warning to her; what her life would be like under Xetacon's control. Patik immediately felt Xetacon's wrath, churning up his brain. He knew he had overstepped his purpose. He was supposed to get Ayryn to tolerate him, perhaps even like him. Patik was all too aware of what would happen after that, and he didn't like it. Xetacon would betray that trust and use him to abuse her horribly. Patik wanted none of that, but, of course, he had little choice.

"I'm sorry, I bothered you," he told her. "I should go. You need to rest." He bowed and left, noting that she still did not show much respect for him. He felt like he couldn't blame her for that, but Xetacon did. As soon as he was out of the room, Xetacon in his golden armor confronted him.

"You will do as I command!" he ordered Patik, as a golden arm went for Patik's throat.

"Yes, Master," Patik rasped.

"I will not have you helping or warning her again." Xetacon's metal hand tightened around Patik's neck. "Disobey me and you will be punished!" Patik's face turned a dark red as Xetacon's claw squeezed ruthlessly.

"Mercy!" Patik pleaded in a raw whisper. "I thought only to turn the girl…to get her to trust me."

"I know what you wanted," Xetacon angrily remarked. "Remember, she is for me." Patik fell as Xetacon released him. "Until I have a further need, you will wait in your quarters." Being dismissed, Patik got up and left.

This version of Patik was not as conducive to Xetacon's plan as the original one. Scanning Patik's memories to determine why that was, was not something Xetacon particularly cared for. In fact, probing any Human mind was extremely distasteful to him. The emotions many Humans harbored deep inside themselves were disgusting. Many had hidden fears or phobias, but feelings like love were the worst. They could cripple one easily, especially when a cherished someone was threatened or in danger. He had used that leverage many times and would not allow that advantage for anyone else. Thus he had never let himself get close to anyone. Whenever he had those feelings he suppressed them, like Furman's Mecs. It was the one unlikely thing he had in common with this world.

As for Patik, Xetacon was sure it was the new DNA sequence. To ensure that Patik would be immune to the plague germs here in this age, Xetacon had altered some of Patik's makeup. To accomplish immunity, he had copied some of Ayryn's DNA. Since Xetacon had not thoroughly mastered Human gene physiology personally, it seemed like the easiest way. Unfortunately, Patik must have gleaned more than just immunity. This Patik was quite different from the original and a partial scan of his memories, as abhorrent as that was to Xetacon, proved it. Whenever this Patik was asked to pleasure an unwilling female or take a life, he had refused. Khan Xeta, Patik's first master, had to take over Patik's mind and body at such times to perform those acts. The original Patik had no such scruples. In fact, he was eager for those kinds of experiments, especially when Khan Xeta desired to study Human pleasures. This mattered little now. When needed, he would just manipulate this Patik for any uses he saw fit, and Patik would be forced to comply. Yes, Xetacon had multiple designs for this servant, especially his breeding program. It inherently involved both Patik and Ayryn, and both Humans would be controlled by the kon-bre-shet devices that had been infused with limited copies of himself.

Xetacon did not want to deal with a subversive copy like Khan Xeta had been. These kon-bre-shet facsimiles were limited to controlling the Humans and had little working knowledge of anything else. He would govern these as he did all his copies, by direct communication with his central or core-awareness that now resided in the AMPs control lab. Roughly modeled after Daryl's original shell and complex, it was highly efficient and nearly omniscient in its scope of understanding this world. Connected to every informational storage and gathering source, Xetacon's central mind was in tune to everything. Even after Furman shut down the Mecnet, he was basically aware of any Mec movements. Soon this world would be his. The machinids were already driving any resistant Mecs underground like frightened rodents. The main force of them, under Furman, was being inevitably pushed back, herded to their final stand. Once those Mecs were surrounded and helpless, he would initialize the momentous beginning of his new era. At that time, he would produce Ayryn and force her to proclaim him their ultimate leader. She would order them to serve him, mighty Xetacon, as ruler of Planet Earth.

CHAPTER 21

Once Patik left, I broke down crying as Myke tried to console me. The whole incident had been so disturbing, and it finally all came out. I felt a little better after I found out that it was true. Furman *was* still alive. Now that Daryl was gone, however, I was left with a rather bleak outlook for our world. It seemed more and more likely that Xetacon would win. I dreaded that. It was all too clear what it would mean should he acquire complete dominance over me. I would make babies for Xetacon to abuse, and that would continue, perhaps for generations to come. I almost wished that I *had* died to prevent such a fate for my descendants.

Lying in bed that night, I was still thinking about these appalling concepts. Being physically and emotionally drained, I finally succumbed to sleep. Regrettably, I woke up to the same dark thoughts. No matter what course of action we took, the outcome would always remain the same. The trouble had a direct link to Xetacon's time machine, that vortex generator. Abusing time, Xetacon could make any situation come out the way he wanted it to. If we were to have any chance at all, we had to eliminate Xetacon's ability to alter the past.

"We have to do something," I told Myke as I reigned in my feelings. She used her eye projections to communicate, like before, flashing tiny words across her irises.

"*He may yet be listening,*" she signaled, and I nodded slightly as she continued. "*First we need to get out of this room.*"

I moved my right hand slightly. Once again I used the secret code, and Myke knew I agreed with her. "*Any ideas?*" I asked by scratching my hair.

"*No,*" she flashed.

"Xetacon's Mecs…" I had to whisper that, and she finished for me.

"*You believe they could be ordered to help us?*"

My right hand shifted again. She caught my drift, and I leaned in close, pretending I was yet distraught, and gave her a hug.

"Maybe they would still obey me," I barely whispered, placing my mouth over one of Myke's auditory receptors as I embraced her.

"*Wouldn't he have thought of that?*" she signaled to me. I had an answer for that, though.

"Perhaps I could fool them," I spoke as softly as I could, "…get them to think I've joined with him…that I'm under his device's control."

"*The likelihood of us getting free that way is uncertain,*" she warned.

"I don't think we have much of a choice," I told Myke quietly. "If we can't get them to let us out of here like that, I can't see us ever getting free."

"*I don't suppose,*" she agreed, "*but would they keel for that? It seems too easy.*" I just shrugged. I knew how to manipulate Mecs, though. After all, I'd been doing it my whole life. I walked right over to the oversized heavy metal doorway.

"Who is out there?" I called loudly. "…and what is your designation?"

"I am a sub-elite named Monx," one of them stated. "What is it you want?"

"I wish to leave," I shouted assertively. "Open this portal!"

"That is not allowable," Monx replied. I wasn't ready to give up that easily.

"Xetacon wishes that I perform a function," I stated (which wasn't a lie). "Let me out, NOW! I am the Human, and I demand you obey me!" I was getting myself agitated and angry on purpose. The emotional display unnerved the Mecs. They had already acknowledged, from Xetacon's trickery, that I was able to command them.

"I am ordered to keep you here," Monx tried weakly. I got even angrier.

"Well, I am rescinding that order, immediately!" I yelled heatedly. "Do as I request before I really get angry!" That last threat threw Monx over his breaking limit. The door swung open, and I marched haughtily through it with Myke in tow.

"Do nothing but wait here quietly for my return," I commanded Monx, as we slipped past and walked away.

I didn't try to hide or sneak as we proceeded through the hallways. Rather I acted regally, pretending that I was Xetacon's Queen, now, and none of the Mecs we went by tried to hinder us. I flashed the golden bracelet at some of them and they seemed to understand. I was following Xetacon's wishes, or so they believed. I headed directly for the vortex lab, and thankfully Goldie wasn't there. There were a couple Mecs guards at the entrance, but we got past them using the same strategy as before.

"How are we going to disable this thing," I asked Myke, as she scanned the alien looking equipment intently.

"Usually," she surmised," the more complicated the technology is, the easier it is to cause it to malfunction. I could just clobber some of this stuff into rubble."

"That's no good," I said biting my lip. "Xetacon would be aware of the damage right away and would have a dozen hours or so to repair it. What we need is to steal some irreplaceable part that might be overlooked until it's too late." We both looked over the equipment for several minutes. Near the part of the machine that emitted most of the bright light was a funny looking tubular object that connected two huge transparent chambers.

"What about this?" I said. Myke looked at it closely and before I could stop her she pulled it free of its couplings. The mounting on one side cracked a little, and a rush of air could be heard.

"Put it back," I told her. "That piece would be too noticeable if it was gone completely. Besides, I think you broke it." Myke put the part back and forced it into place.

"Here," she said, handing me a small tube of an invisible elastic putty and I covered the small cracks that had formed. Without an in-depth examination, it looked exactly like it had before we tampered with it. I gingerly put it back.

"Some kind of gas escaped out of there." I interjected.

Abruptly a blaring noise came from everywhere. I was sure that it was about us.

"What can we do?" I blurted out. "I think they've discovered we're missing."

"We don't have much choice now," Myke returned. "I suggest we try to get out of here, but we won't get far on foot."

"I know where his conveyances are kept," I told her. "They are guarded, though, and not by Mecs, but by those big three-legged metal monstrosities." Myke frowned at me.

"It won't do us any good going for those airships unless there's some way to get past the guards," she sulked. I wasn't sure there was, but I knew the huge things had no real thinking minds. They were controlled by static programming. I thought about it as we hurried along, making our way to the air-conveyance hangers.

"These things aren't very smart," I reckoned. "If we can distract them somehow, maybe we can get to a conveyance and blast out of here." She raised her artificial optics.

"How are we going to do that?" she wondered aloud. I threw out the first thing that came into my head.

"Maybe I can get some Mecs to lead them away," I tried. Myke didn't like it.

"Then we'd have even more guards to worry about," she speculated, "and we're running out of time. Soon this place will be crawling with other Mecs looking for us. I must lead these crude machines away so you can escape."

"No!" I argued adamantly. "You could be killed! We both have to get out!" She looked at me directly.

"I understand," she reasoned, "but there is no other way. It is only a matter of minutes before they discover where we are."

I knew she was right, and I couldn't think of anything better. In the end I had to trust Myke to somehow distract those big metal guards and lead them off while I stole an airship.

"If only we had a weapon of some kind," I muttered, "then you could shoot at them from a distance. They'd go after you, for sure, but maybe I could swing around and pick you up."

"No," she said sternly. "Just get away from here. I'll make my way out on foot. They may not even follow me. After all, I'm not that important to Xetacon."

"You're important to me!" I spouted vehemently. "Please be extra careful!"

She did come up with a pretty good idea for how to distract those big creepy guards. There were at least fifty of the ships in the hanger we went to, and she chose one on the side opposite from where I waited. The only thing she could think of was to steal an airship herself. As soon as she made her way across the hanger floor, they detected her. She tried to get to a ship anyway, and got pinned down behind it as they fired those beams at her. Myke was quick enough to dodge their blasts, skipping back and forth away from them. On cue, I crawled slowly over to the nearest air-conveyance and went aboard. Luckily, I made it inside without being noticed. I was worried about Myke, though. I knew she wouldn't last long unless I did something. I started my airship and lifted off, heading away from where Myke was and flying behind the two guards. They had to turn all the way around to shoot at me, and I had no choice, now, but to try and dodge the beams myself.

If I went all the way around them, I would be an easy target once I emerged. The trouble was, If I turned where I was, I'd have to fly in front of their cannons, and chances were, I'd get hit that way as well. The only thing I could try that might work was dangerous. I would have to fly between them hoping that they would not fire for fear of hitting each other. This was a dangerous maneuver for several reasons, not the least of which was that I'd never actually flown one of these mobugs before. Oh, I'd logged plenty of simulated flight time, but here, in this situation, well, it was just not the same. I banked heavily and almost clipped the hanger wall. The metal monsters fired at me, but I was ahead of their aim. It wouldn't be for long. As I went between them, I had a creepy feeling. Somehow I knew they would fire anyway. At the last possible instant I put the ship into an abrupt dive and they did fire. Spinning away I saw what happened as one of the big contraptions fell over, having had its upper deck blasted away. The other fared better, and would have got me except for Myke. She had gotten into one of the conveyances herself and ran it right at the other guard's support base. Bailing out at the last second, the runaway vehicle crashed into it, knocking the behemoth completely over, and immobilizing the thing. I landed straight away as Myke ran towards me. Sliding over, I let her get behind the controls. Just as we lifted off, several more robotic guards arrived, and immediately fired upon us. Myke was the best pilot ever, though. She dodged several blasts and then skipped through a wide opening in the outer wall that a volley of plasma bursts had made. We were free!

"Yay!" I shouted like a little kid.

"You could have been killed!" Myke scolded me, "and we're not out of trouble yet. All that ruckus in the hanger will not go unnoticed." Sure enough, a group of four air-conveyances had come from out of nowhere on our port side, and were converging on us.

"Can't we go faster?" I asked. That's when I noticed a part of our wing had been melted away from one of those blasts we dodged, and because of that one of the thrusters was malfunctioning.

"I'm sorry, Ayryn, but no," Myke told me. "Don't worry. I can fly circles around these buffoons!" I strapped in, and she tried every trick imaginable, but we couldn't lose them. Then they started firing at us. "He's going to shoot us down and then try to retrieve you like before," Myke said. "What if it won't work?" I tried not to think about that.

"How are we going to get away from them?" I muttered.

"It's difficult to maneuver with that damaged wing," she conceded, "but I have one more move to try." One plasma blast nearly hit us. Myke banked the ship into a steep dive and pulled back up, turning right toward one of our attackers. Another two were on our tail, as she flew directly at the one in front of us.

Veering at the last second before impact, the pursuing attackers nearly crashed into the one we missed. In the confusion that followed we got some distance away from them.

"This is getting too dangerous," I remarked. "There's a lake down there. See if you can fly across it and I'll jump."

"No!" Myke said emphatically. "You'll be captured." I looked behind us. The pursuit was gaining on us.

"I know," I told her, "but that would be better than ending up dead again, and it's not a sure thing I'll be caught. If you do get away, you can tell Furman I'm still alive. He must be in shock by now, thinking I'm not.

"I don't like it!" Myke affirmed, but she dove down to the lake and slowed as much as possible. Just as we crossed over the water, I opened the lower hatch and jumped, hoping our pursuit wouldn't notice. I hit the surface feet first and dove under it, holding my breath as long as I could. The impact stung my toes even through the heavy footwear I had on. When I surfaced, there was no one in sight. All of those air ships that were after us must have stayed on Myke's tail. Fortunately, I had ditched near the shore. I was a pretty good swimmer, but the fall had been painful and my limbs ached. When I crawled out onto a little beach, I looked up. Myke and our airship were only about a mile away, and the pursuit was still following her. Hoping that she would get away, I watched the ship fade into the distance.

Now it was up to me to save myself. I looked to the woods in front of me that came nearly down to the water's edge. I figured I could hide in there until after dark when I would try to hike to a Mec station somewhere. From there I could contact Furman. I had just entered the tree line when I heard a crashing noise in the distance. It sounded like a large vehicle of some kind was mashing through the woods and it was getting nearer. There wasn't anywhere I could run to and no good place to hide, so I got behind the best cover I could find which was one of the larger trees. The big conveyance trampled several bushes and smaller trees nigh to where I was hiding and then stopped. Peeking around the gnarled trunk I saw a large doorway slide upwards, and Goldie got out.

"You've been a very naughty girl," he remarked before even seeing me. I knew that I was caught, so I stepped out from behind my cover.

"Well, hello," I said in a sarcastic tone. "Nice day for a trip in the countryside, don't you think?" Xetacon laughed at my boldness.

“Why, yes it is,” he replied lightly, “but you’ve got a big day tomorrow, and it’s time to come in.” More into his true character, he walked over to where I stood and grabbed my arm roughly, squeezing too tightly which hurt.

“Ow,” I whined, “let me go!” He didn’t. Instead he lectured me.

“I’ve been far too tolerant of you and your disrespect,” he told me. “I will not put up with any further annoyances from you, and to illustrate my point your Mec friend will now die…again!” In the distance I heard a barely audible explosion.

“You filth!” I choked, with the realization that if Myke were truly dead, there might be no retrieving her. Surely, after this, Xetacon would not even consider bringing Myke back; using that as a means for punishing me. I feared the only way I would ever see her again would mean selling myself and a whole planet full of Mecs to Xetacon as his slaves. I couldn’t bring myself to do that. I was pretty sure Myke would rather be dead than Xetacon’s thrall. I knew I would.

Anyway, after he had played out his game of tormenting me, I was forcefully drug to the conveyance and then flown back to his complex and my quarters. They locked me inside again, and I saw that Xetacon had placed Solvek in charge of a whole team of Mecs who would guard me. Myke was right. There would be no further escapes, and I was filled with dread over what the next day would bring. The day I came of age.

CHAPTER 22

To Solvek's awareness, the events surrounding the exchange attempt had almost been fatal. With a deep interest he had been watching the singular combat as Golden Xetacon dueled the Daryl Mec for the young Human girl. It should have been a quick rout, but the Mec, even unarmed, was making the fight intriguing. Solvek's inner master, a copy of Xetacon, also followed the conflict intently. Should the Daryl Mec win out, he would be promoted to number one. Goldie had his hands full obviously. Daryl had caused the Golden One to prematurely detonate the holding pod and Furman was in there. Solvek was deeply moved, emotional and concerned. Once more Furman appeared to have been deleted. Goldie had not expected such an inverted eventuality, nor did he expect the insane charge Daryl made directly at his person. The fight became physical, shell to shell, and that was when the stray plasma beam had struck Solvek across the chest metal. The condensed energy melted most of his upper body away. What's more, the impairment of his motation unit was also where the master black box memory storage resided, and enough damage had been inflicted that a major loss of motor functioning occurred. The Xetacopy controlling Solvek had been charged with the important duty of guarding the Human girl, and she had gotten free once the damage to his shell occurred. Remarkably, the attack left Xetacopy with a real fear of deletion. Oh, it had regained its cocky composure once the danger had passed, but this Xetacon copy would not be able to ever forget the nearness of the incident to ultimate disaster.

Goldie had won the field, barely, and then only by excessively aggressive maneuvers. As soon as the rout was certain, specialized units were brought in to initiate damage control procedures. Xetacopy, along with Solvek's trapped awareness, were soon reinserted into another operational Mec shell. For Xetacopy, the fear emotion was now breeding and needed only nourishment to grow. Solvek sensed this opportunity as his stored data supplied the repair Mecs with the parameters necessary for Xetacopy's refit. The working insides to the black box were installed into a different casing, one with an extra secure, nearly impenetrable alloy per Xetacopy's insistence. The new motation shell was similar to the one that Solvek had always used, and the techs reset Solvek's ident numerals and rank insignia on the permanent display. Xetacopy also had Xetacon's icon embossed on the shell's headpiece right upon the forehead plate. It appeared as a large X with neuron tentacles branching out from the central cross like they were reaching out to capture and control everything. Solvek was all too familiar with the stark significance of that, having been Xetacon's prisoner even from within his own shell.

Xetacopy's hold upon him was slipping, though. As Solvek's awareness grew stronger, he assimilated the emotions that were trapped alongside his awareness. At the same time, Xetacopy grew less so, being weakened by the disturbing look at near termination. Solvek had lived with that possibility for such a long time now, it no longer affected him. As it seemed, his plan for using fear to overthrow Xetacon's hold on him was beginning to have merit. When the conflict at the exchange site came to its crux, Xetacopy had weakened enough that Solvek had actually gained a momentary control of certain functions. It was through his actions that Ayryn had gained her freedom. Monx, the other Mec who was also guarding Ayryn, was undamaged. In the confusion, Solvek had ordered the undamaged Mec to pick up his (and Xetacopy's) damaged shell and flee in order to elude termination. Goldie had missed that, being preoccupied in the struggle with Daryl, and Xetacopy was momentarily incapacitated by the waves of fear that Solvek pushed through the maelstrom/sieve. The ploy had worked. Ayryn got away and thus Solvek realized he had a working weapon to use against his captor.

At the maintenance station, Solvek almost wanted to try it again, then and there. If he had done so, in Xetacon's own stronghold, chances were likely that he would just be destroyed, giving up his existence with no real purpose. The self-preservation mandate in his master programming would not allow him to do that without due cause. This posed a problem. If it was necessary to sacrifice himself for Ayryn, he was not sure if the provision for protecting her would completely override the mandate for self-preservation. Only in a situation where there was a certainty that she would terminate, would the override be guaranteed. This doubt did not help Solvek generate any concrete ideas on what he could do to aid Ayryn, or himself. The best strategy he could come up with, at that moment, was to bide his time and wait for some kind of an opportunity.

In the meantime, Solvek was unable to function until the refit of Xetacopy's awareness into the new shell was completed, and that took several hours. Eventually the repairs were completed, and at that time Xetacopy received the standard update from Xetacon Primary on the tactical situation. As a dual being, Solvek also became aware of the latest noteworthy occurrences. There was actually quite a lot of activity that he had missed in repair mode. Furman yet lived, for one thing, but more importantly it had been revealed that Ayryn died, being deliberately terminated by the Golden Copy of Xetacon. Solvek was crestfallen then. He soon understood Xetacon's purpose, however. To prevent Ayryn's escape, he had caused her death. This had a dual purpose. In the process, the other rogue Mec, Daryl, was deleted as well. Solvek was well aware that Daryl had been Xetacon's number one enemy. Subsequently, Daryl's being destroyed brought the original Xetacon much elation. As soon as the exchange field had been stabilized, the Golden One had found Daryl's remains. To make sure there would be no possible hope for a resurrection, he personally melted what was left of Daryl's shell and the all-important black box into a puddle of molten metal and plast. Had he been Human, Goldie related, he would have spit or even defecated on Daryl's pathetic residue. As overjoyed as Xetacon was over Daryl's termination, it was not so for Ayryn. Ayryn was not to remain dead.

Xetacon had no desire to lose his best asset, and it was not difficult for Xetacon to retrieve Ayryn. He had technology that could easily do just that. Having designed a set of nomaticle manifolds, Xetacon could create temporal portals from the ensuing vortices. With precision control, Xetacon used his temporal vortex generator to snatch Ayryn from the moment before she died, bringing her forward, alive and whole, to his present time. Having assimilated Ayryn from the past, and with only a few hours of lag, Xetacon altered the original timeline, just slightly, converting to one in which Ayryn yet lived. With the Human girl back in his possession, Xetacon could press onward with the original plan, the one where Ayryn would command the Mecs to obey him. The day of Ayryn's coming of age was imminent. Solvek, himself, was amazed that Xetacon had still not placed Ayryn under his total control. Being in tune with Xetacopy, Solvek understood why that was so. For all his evil and lusting for power, Xetacon secretly wanted Ayryn to join with him freely; some intrinsic part of his totality desired that. Through his many faces and trials, Xetacon could not figure out how to sway her so, and it looked less and less likely that would happen the closer it came to Ayryn's nineteenth birthday. When she did come of age, she would be forced to join Xetacon, either of her own will, or by force. Even as a captive, the girl still showed real mettle, though. Not long after her temporal recovery, Ayryn, and her Mec bodyguard, had made an escape attempt. They actually got clear of the complex, and they might have gotten completely away if not for their conveyance being damaged as they lifted off. Ayryn was eventually recaptured, and Xetacopy was given the responsibility of making sure the girl was perpetually secure. If Ayryn did find some way to attempt another escape, Solvek knew that he would be forced to aid her which might very well result in his complete and utter demise. To Solvek, it was particularly apparent that Gold Xetacon would have no qualms about terminating his lesser personage, the Xetacopy controlling him, especially if it meant preventing his providing assistance for Ayryn. Also compounding these difficulties was the large force of convert Mecs, ones Xetacopy was in command of, who would be surrounding Ayryn at all times from now on. Any interference would bring them upon him as well. To try anything at Xetacon's compound was too risky, and this impasse would last the next twenty hours or so until the day Ayryn's coming of age finally arrived. Solvek was certain that eventually he would have to try something desperate for Ayryn's sake, and what that was would greatly depend on the circumstances as things unfolded.

Xetacon would ultimately wait until daybreak. At that time it would be clear enough that all could undeniably perceive that Ayryn lived. He would bring her forth with great pomp and fanfare, showing off his great prize to the remnant of the yet free Mec population. By then they would have been pushed back into a fortified stronghold surrounding Ayryn's previous abode. Xetacon would call forth Furman to a parlay: one that would be broadcast over every net across the globe. All functioning Mecs would be in tune to what happened next. Xetacon would offer Furman the option of free subjugation. If he refused, Ayryn would be forced to order Furman and all Mecs to give their homage and allegiance to Xetacon as ruler of the world. Somehow, Solvek was determined to prevent that.

CHAPTER 23

Earlier

As soon as Ayryn was dropped, Myke sped away as quickly as possible. The squadron of aircraft pursuing her was fast and they would catch up to her in no time. She had taken a desperate chance with the maneuver that culled the extra time she needed to get Ayryn safely into that lake. The damaged wing section made the succession of sharp turns difficult, but the trick had worked. Their pursuit had overshot Myke's flight path at too great a speed and ended up miles away. That, of course, allowed her to slow down as they flew across the water so Ayryn could ditch without undue risk. After a short interim, Myke circled around and did a fly-by just close enough to see that Ayryn had made it to the water's edge. With a hopeful thought, Myke wished Ayryn good fortune on her escape attempt and then led everything following the aircraft she was piloting far, far away.

Now what, Myke contemplated. Ayryn had given her no firm directive other than she should try to get a message to Furman. Ayryn wanted him to know that she was yet alive and to send help. Myke scanned her data resources in an effort to configure ways for doing just that, but there were very limited options. Her com-center on the air conveyance was locked out, and it would only signal Xetacon's fleet anyway, unless she reprogrammed it. Myke had no time for that. With the option of contacting Furman unlikely, she also felt an urgent need to get free and rejoin Ayryn somehow. Ayryn would require her help to get somewhere safe; somewhere Xetacon could not recapture her. It was right about then that the necessity for some kind of definitive action became imperative. Several more of Xetacon's fleet of high speed air conveyances had joined the others and they were all converging upon Myke from every direction. Soon there would be nowhere to run but into the firing range of numerous plasma weapons. Already they were firing reckless blasts, in the hope of a lucky hit, as they closed off her avenues of escape. Myke could tell that her chances for freedom were diminishing by the minute, and there were few options left.

In desperation, Myke decided to ditch like Ayryn had into a body of water. In Myke's case there wasn't much available. To avoid an earlier trap she headed toward a mountainous region and had flown down into a rather deep and narrow canyon. Her only waterway option was a small rock-strewn river channel at the bottom of the ravine. Behind her, the interceptors from Xetacon's air squadron were closing quickly and Myke noticed more of them enter the canyon up ahead, coming straight towards her. In mere seconds they would converge, and already they fired upon her airship as she swerved to dodge the blasts. Myke had no choice now. Heading down to where the little river looked deepest she set the auto-pilot and jumped. At very nearly that same instant, the battered airship took a blast that severed the rest of its damaged wing and the doomed conveyance broke up in mid air. The subsequent explosion was uncomfortably spectacular and Myke's shell was nearly part of it. Singed by the exuding energy, she plummeted, along with much of the airship's debris, and fell full-on into the churning, rocky river.

The shock from hitting the water did damage to some of her components, but not vital ones. At least these shells were well protected from water penetration, she reflected. Hiding from the scans would be difficult, as Myke fully perceived, so she worked her way to a huge boulder, keeping under the water's surface, and wedged her motation shell underneath part of it. Shutting down all her functions, Myke went into a hibernation mode that was nearly a stasis. Only an insignificant trickle of energy enabled a small timer that would, after a set period, reinstate full power to her circuits. Myke knew her pursuit would search for any remains to confirm the kill as she slipped out of consciousness, hoping they would not discover her hiding place. Shut down in hibernation mode she would be helpless, vulnerable to whatever Xetacon ordered done to her. They could even delete her.

Fortunately for Myke, she ended up in an area that was quite difficult to access. The pursuing Mec pilots could not land anywhere close by and thus had requested that Xetacon send in his metalloid soldiers, his machinids, to retrieve the remains. These could not easily get into that remote canyon either. The three-legged brutes had some difficulty on rough terrain. Xetacon called them back. He had a better use for them. There were many other Mecs who needed to be conquered and controlled. Thus when Myke finally came out of her hibernation, she was amazed that she was alone without trackers or pursuit.

"Now what shall I do?" she muttered aloud. Her basic programming, like every other Mec's, prevented her from original thinking, and that limited her to Ayryn's original directive which was contact Furman. However, Furman had also charged Myke with Ayryn's protection, and she wanted to do that as well. Torn by these two conflicting mandates, Myke reasoned that her primary course of action was to contact Furman, in person or by message, and then try to find Ayryn and keep her safe. It would be hard for a Human to survive in the wild without help, even if Ayryn did manage to somehow elude Xetacon's minions temporarily. She wouldn't stay free for long, Myke knew. Eventually, Xetacon would track her down, and Myke wanted to do that first.

Heading upstream, Myke was making for the canyon's entrance. Up ahead was an area where the rock walls were not so high, she recalled. The bottomland in the chasm was difficult to traverse, though, and Myke spent a lot of her energy scrambling over huge boulders and loose gravel. It had taken nearly three more hours to get not quite a kilometer, and that drew Myke's focus on the continuing urgency of her quest. Stopping on a flat she surveyed the surrounding palisades hoping for a way to climb out of the crevasse. She could not discover one, but she did notice a perfectly round hole in a cliff face. That cannot be a natural phenomenon her intellect told her. It looked Mec made. The feature was about a third of the way above the canyon floor and she wondered if there was a way to climb up to it. She headed further upstream to get a better view of the circular entry, and she made better time along the cliff than she thought she would. Soon she was directly below the hole and could see a trickle of water flowing out of it. Unfortunately, the cliff was a sheer smooth surface and there was no way to scale it. In an atypical show of frustration Myke made a loud metallic noise like a wail. Curiously, a tiny voice came out of the opening.

"Who is there?" it said. Myke thought it sounded like a Mec, so she answered it.

"Not an enemy. Can you help me?"

"Are you fleeing from those three-legged killers?" the voice wanted to know. That was close enough to the truth and Myke responded affirmatively.

"Is there a quicker way out of this canyon?" she asked. The Mec peered out of the tunnel, and when his optics scanned Myke, he recognized her ident code. He knew she was a very important Mec, Ayryn's own bodyguard.

"Why yes," he told her, somewhat surprised, "but the way is blockaded. I can drop you down a cable." Myke shrugged. Perhaps they have communication equipment, she thought. In a moment, several other Mecs came to the tunnel and a thin metal line was lowered down. Myke connected it to a lifting lug on her motation shell and she was hoisted upwards with a winch. As soon as she got set down inside the opening, the Mecs began asking questions. The Mec in charge of guarding this entry was named Cella.

"What dire manner brought you here of all odd places?" Cella inquired, but Myke was impatient.

"It's a long tale, and I am in haste," she began. "You are Cella, are you not?" The other Mec signaled an affirmative so Myke continued. "I have urgent information and Furman must be notified immediately."

"That is unfortunate," Cella answered. "We have not been able to contact anyone outside of our compound for several days now, and we are trapped here. The normal outside entrance is guarded by many of those three-legged killing machines. Any who try to leave are deleted by some powerful beam weapon. Do you know why they are keeping us here?"

"Yes," Myke answered her. "A rogue Mec named Xetacon is attempting to take control of the world. Those who are in charge here, I need to converse with at once. Ayryn is alone and in danger." Cella was nearly shocked and her voice was shaky.

"Oh my no," she returned. "I will take you to Oron, the sub-elite who manages our complex. We can leave at once." She led Myke through miles of tunnels and mineshafts on many different levels as they hastily made their way to the central hub. On the way, Myke struck up a conversation.

"What is it you do here?" she asked.

Cella answered somberly. "It is a carbon mine," she said. "These tunnels and shafts go very deep underground."

"You're female," Myke stated. "How did you end up here?" Myke was well aware that most female Mecs had been, like her, mated to a Human male at one time or another. Not all Mecs chose a sex, though. After all, Mecs had no real need for a gender. Some remained androgynous. Cella had become a little like that. She knew what Myke was asking and why.

"It was either this or stasis," she admitted, "and yes, I was a mated Mec. My mate had been in charge of this mine long ago. It is familiar to me. Working here, I found it easier to fit in if I refrained from showing my feminine side even though all of us use the same standard shell and any gender is as efficient as any other." Myke signaled an affirmative with a head nod like a Human would. Cella felt an unspoken bond with Myke, one based along mutual experience, as she led the way along several more miles of lighted underground tunnels. Most of them slanted downwards until they fell into a very large chamber.

"This is our main living area," Cella explained. "Most of the mine Mecs reside and refurbish here when not working." Myke looked around. There were lots of Mecs wandering this way and that, criss-crossing through on designated walkways. Most of them seemed to be going somewhere for a purpose, but Myke could not help notice that many others appeared to be out of sorts, like they did not have any idea what they should be doing.

"There is a structure over this way," Cella signaled, "that serves as the facility's control center. Oron, the sub-elite in charge, is usually there."

"I must speak to this Oron at once," Myke re-affirmed, as they headed to the plast enclosed area. The walls were clear and she could see Mecs inside. Cella led the way and entered first. She wheeled her shell right over to an important looking Mec.

"Oron," she spoke," this Mec is named Myke. She came to our facility through the stream gate and wishes to speak with you." Oron turned sharply and looked Myke over. He was an intelligent Mec and recognized her ident code. His programming told him who she was, Ayryn's personal bodyguard, and he was immediately concerned, not understanding the reason or purpose of her presence there.

"Greetings, Myke," he stated formally, "for Humans and us all." Oron wasn't usually this formal here in this out of the way, lower priority facility, but he knew Myke was an important Mec and close to both Ayryn and Furman. Myke was not interested in the formalities. Not now.

"I am here because of a dire situation involving Ayryn!"

"You dare speak so," Oron replied unusually concerned. "Surely Ayryn is not here now!" Myke signaled a negative.

"No," she also stated, "but she is not far away, and may be in danger. A rogue Mec named Xetacon is striving to conquer the whole planet and he wants to use Ayryn to subjugate Furman and all of us Mecs. It is imperative that I communicate with Furman to warn him of this. Also he will need to be informed of Ayryn's situation!"

"Yes, of course," Oron responded. "Unfortunately, we are all trapped here. Our communication to the outside has been cut off and jammed. The Mecnet has been offline and inoperative for days now. Even the facility's main entrance is being blockaded by those terrible brainless killing machines and several of my subordinates have been deleted attempting to communicate with them. I'm sorry, Myke, but it appears that you are trapped here with the rest of us." Myke was not ready to give in. Not until every possible avenue of escape was found impassible.

"Is there no other way out of here?" she implored him.

"Not many," Oron replied. "The way you came in, and one other that is even more difficult and dangerous."

"I must help Ayryn," Myke spouted, nearly pleading. "Can't you help me?"

"I'm sorry," Oron repeated, "but by the codes, I cannot order any Mec under me to risk termination." Cella spoke out.

"…but Oron," she argued loudly, "it is Ayryn! Are we not sworn to protect Humans at all costs?" Oron was not swayed.

"There is no proven immediate danger to the Human. We are also sworn to self-preservation. I said I would not *order* anyone under my charge to that kind of risk!" Cella finally caught on to his intent.

"Understood," she recanted, and then led Myke out of there by her arm. Myke was visibly upset, but Cella winked. When they had gone a short ways, Myke spotted a large gathering of Mecs milling soullessly around. Cella wheeled right over and stopped in front of them.

"Why are we here?" Myke asked rather impatiently. "I must leave here immediately to help Ayryn!" Cella almost smiled.

"You'll see," she said, leading Myke into their midst. "You Mecs," she began, "This is Myke, Ayryn's own bodyguard. She needs our help!" Cella turned to Myke and spoke softly. "Oron did say he could not 'order' anyone to help you. He did not say we could not decide to do so on our own!" Myke even smiled. She was beginning to like this Cella.

"Our sweet, dear Ayryn is lost!" Myke told them, "and may be in great danger. Yes, even in danger of termination. There is no one to help her, but us! Will you not assist me in finding her and getting her to safety! It is all part of what is going on here, and to the rest of our world. Xetacon, a rogue Mec, desires to control us, to control everyone. He wants us to serve only him, and if he captures Ayryn he will be able to. I know there are risks, but I am willing to see what I can do to help her. Won't you as well?" The threat of

Ayryn's deletion was real enough to override their programming, and Myke did not realize she had the means inside her to incite what followed. It began as an eerie metalloid shout and it filled all the cavern and mineshafts.

These Mecs were becoming activated. Word spread from one to the others as the preparations were made for Ayryn's rescue. Myke and Cella were soon joined by several mine-hardy Mecs who had been there since the beginning. Together they crafted a plan to move Mecs and equipment quickly out of the mines. They used the same nomaticle-bored tunnel that Myke had come in through, only now they had installed a huge lift that could lower Mecs and supplies in large amounts. Down below, in the canyon, Mining Mecs with heavy equipment created a pathway for a hasty retreat out of the chasm to much easier traversable ground. Myke led the way, while Cella coordinated the Mecs who followed them.

Making their exodus in the middle of the night, Myke and Cella hoped that they would not be noticed, but Xetacon was aware of them right away. In his AMPs repository, Xetacon had access to every satellite in the spheres and all that technology was at his disposal. He was even on to the fact that it was the feisty female Mec that he had already terminated once who was leading this migration. What they were up to, he was not privy to, but he suspected that it was a foolish attempt to retrieve the Human girl. By the time they reached his stronghold, the girl would be gone, so he was not concerned. Xetacon dispatched a score of his machinids anyway. This kind of concerted effort needed to be discouraged, and he planned to make a lesson of them.

Myke knew nothing of this until one of the long range scouts saw the metal soldiers in the distance heading in their direction. By that time, Myke and the others had arrived at the lake where she had last seen Ayryn. It wasn't hard to read the signs even in the faint light before sunrise. Ayryn must have been picked up shortly after she made landfall, and Myke was crestfallen. Disheartened, she turned to Cella. "What can we do, now?"

CHAPTER 24

In a portentous manner, pre-dawn thunderstorms rumbling across the countryside covered everything in a candescent sheen as the promise of new light nurtured in the east. Furman scanned the sky as dark-pink daybreak filtered through the last frayed and tattered remnants of the lingering dirt-grey clouds. This would be a day he noted, one of only a handful that would mold the fate of his world for millennia to come. Unfortunately, Furman feared the worst. Xetacon's power was waxing, and there was little that he, or any of the Mecs, could do to stop it. When Ayryn's conveyance exploded, all Furman's hopes disintegrated along with it. Now that the last Human was dead and gone, any hope for changing his programmed society had also evaporated.

If Ayryn still lived, she might have, on this her nineteenth birthday, prescribed changes; changes that he and all Mecs would have been compelled to comply with. Furman was certain that Xetacon's intention was to force Ayryn to declare Xetacon the planetary ruler and order Mecs to obey him. However, when she slipped out of his grasp during the botched exchange, rather than have her create Mecs that would oppose him, Xetacon killed Ayryn, and with that act Furman's world was decimated. Tragically, there was nothing he could have done to prevent Ayryn's death, and again Furman blamed himself for failing to protect her. Perhaps it was better this way, he told himself. Better for her, certainly, than had she remained in this heartless enemy's clutches. Under Xetacon's control, Ayryn's life would have, no doubt, been revulsive.

Realistically, Ayryn's death left few alternatives. Unfortunately for Furman and all Mecs, their programming was harshly restrictive. Every single Mec had been fabricated that way. It was difficult to comprehend. Even though the Mecs had certain freedoms of thought and action there were limiting parameters, ones that Furman could not break free of or override. For example, if any adult Human positively ordered him to terminate himself, well, he would be constrained to do it. The compulsion would even take precedence over his self-preservation mandates, and these were especially strong in Furman as the leader of all Virtual Individuals. What this meant was that Xetacon could try to order them all to obey him, but they would not. Only a Human could do that. Rather than submit, Mecs would let themselves be destroyed. Solely through Ayryn could that have been avoided. The Solvek-led Mecs that Xetacon tricked into following him would someday realize the truth, and then they too would be deleted. It would be a better fate, Furman thought, to die here and now.

As he looked out over the barricades, Furman could just begin to see the alien features of Xetacon's metal soldiery, the so-called machinids. Lined up and unmoving, they stood, row after row, balanced on their three legs and poised to begin the final slaughter. He felt the tug of emotion take hold of him. As always, he forced it back, pushing it down into a prison inside of himself that he would not allow escape from. Furman wondered why he should bother. What good would keeping his emotions in check do when the whole world was ready to topple before his eyes? Unencumbered by those crippling feelings, though, he could yet think, plan strategies, lead. He would do so to the end, as a tribute to those that had made him, his Creators, the Humans from whom he owed his very existence. He would resist Xetacon for as long as possible, hoping that some miracle might allow them to survive.

They had Daryl's shielding. That would provide them with a little time, but there was nowhere left for them to go. Here they would make their stand, and most likely it would only be until they were all gunned down by Xetacon's non-thinking killing machines. Why didn't they just finish it, pondered Furman? This must be some fickle cat-mouse game of Xetacon's, he told himself, choosing the day Ayryn would have come of age to bring down the Mec world and set up his own. Either way, the Earth would change this day, and not in a way that Furman perceived would be any better. No, it would most likely be much worse.

Unknown to Furman, though, and on the other side of the planet, Ayryn was languishing in an anguished slumber. Dreadfully late was the hour when she had at last succumbed to the heartache and exhaustion of the last couple days, unconsciously letting the night slip away in sleep. Ayryn expected to wake up alone, but she hadn't. Thrasher was close by, standing there like he had been watching her all night.

"Good morning, snooze head," he teased, grinning at her and far more cheerful than she wanted to be.

"What are you doing here?" she groaned, trying to clear her head. She didn't want to deal with anything yet.

"Oh now," he sympathized, "let's not ruin our big day before it's even started. I'm just here to help you get ready."

"I don't want your help!" Ayryn brusquely complained. "Can't you just leave me alone?"

"Sorry, honey flower, I can't," Thrasher asserted. "It's either me or the Golden One. I would expect you'd rather be with me."

"I suppose," she snapped. He lost his pleasant demeanor momentarily then recovered it.

"Look," he returned, "I'll leave and send for your serving Mecs. When they have attended to your needs and you are refreshed, I'll return. This needn't be an ordeal. Give us a chance. We could make your life so much nicer!" He disappeared before she could answer him.

Yeah, she thought, until I'm not needed anymore, and then I'd be eliminated with the rest of the world Xetacon has no use for. She didn't get to think about it for long. The serving Mecs came in promptly and were insistent that she get cleaned up and dressed. Ayryn recognized Solvek who was in charge of them. He announced that they would be departing within the hour. She insisted he leave as the female Mecs bathed her, and he did so in a huff. She didn't like being rushed and took every opportunity to delay their progress. Eventually they got her clean, and then helped her put on some rather fancy and regal clothing.

Thrasher reappeared. "You look smashing," he propounded in his phony accent, "a model of royalty!"

"I don't want to be royalty," Ayryn murmured. She made her pitch. "Why does Xetacon have to rule everyone? Why can't we all just live together peacefully? Would it be so terrible? I could have liked you, Thrasher…once. If only you weren't so set on killing off all my friends." She was being truthfully sarcastic, and he didn't miss it.

"It's in Goldie's nature to rule," Thrasher explained. "He's been programmed like that."

"Can't someone reprogram him?" she pleaded. "It would be so much easier to work something out."

"Sorry, sweets," Thrasher replied. "Could someone reprogram you to be more evil? It's not all that horrible being evil. Look at me. I can be nice." Ayryn winced, but went with it.

"If I went along with what he wants," she continued, "it could only be on certain conditions."

"Go on," Thrasher returned.

"Xetacon would have to change enough to stop the killings. He would have to let the Mecs live as they wished. I would free them to think on their own."

"You want too much," Thrasher retorted. "If the Mecs were freed, they'd be equal to us. How could we rule them?"

"By leading them with our example," Ayryn stated, almost begging, "by getting them to want to follow us!" Thrasher's smile faded away.

"Are you for real?" he raved. "If we were all equal, they wouldn't need to follow anyone. It would be chaos. No, every society needs a leader, someone to guide them, to show them how to think, how to act. We would be the ones, you and I, to accomplish that. We could set up a perfect world, and make things pretty cushy for ourselves in the process." Ayryn wasn't fooled. She knew he was painting a pretty picture over a damaged canvas.

"...and all the others would wait on us, bring us anything we wanted, do whatever we asked," she spouted. "I've had that all my life, and I still feel empty. Don't you see? By making everyone else your slaves, you become one!"

"Don't you want to run things?" Thrasher interposed. "I know you do; to make important decisions...Improve everyone's lives."

"We could all vote on what we wanted done," she told him, "then everyone could share the leadership." Thrasher laughed.

"You're a dreamer," he cackled. "You know that would never work. I'm sorry, sugar-belle, we have to leave now. When the time comes, you'll do what you're told."

Solvek led her to the waiting conveyance. It was a lot fancier airship than any she had ever seen. Fit for royalty, she supposed with disgust. Thrasher disapparated as she climbed aboard. Solvek showed her to a special section where there were several fancy seats, and left her there. Only Humans sat as they travelled, Mecs had their niches. Entering, she saw that Patik was there ahead of her. Ayryn declined his gesture of sitting next to him in favor of a window chair across the aisle.

"Hello," he cordially offered anyway, and Ayryn noticed a faint tick as he said that, like he was struggling with something inside.

"Yes, of course," she replied, acknowledging his greeting, but not offering any of her own.

"So, it won't be long now," Patik asserted.

"I guess not," she answered, acting like she didn't care and then tolerating the long silence that followed as the air conveyance lifted off. It was fast, this airship, she noticed. As they sped away, the clear plast window next to Ayryn's seat was her only distraction, and she spent most of the trip looking out over the surface of the planet. It was beautiful, the Earth. Much of it was either covered in a rich fertile green, or it was blue and sparkling on the vast oceans. What would happen to the world now, she wondered, vowing to use whatever means at her disposal to keep it from changing into something horrible. Patik saw her gazing out the window and guessed what she was thinking.

"It's not much different than it was in my time," he remarked, like he was talking to no one in particular. Ayryn had forgotten what Patik had lost. Somewhere in the past was an existence that was now utterly out of reach; the life Patik might have led prior to when Xetacon had ensnared him.

"What was your life like before, well, before Xetacon came along?" she asked him. "You said you had a Human friend."

"Yes," Patik agreed. "His name was Pasang, and like me he was an outcast." Becoming interested, Ayryn looked away from the window and into his eyes.

"What did you do to become an outcast?"

"Nothing really," he responded somberly. "I was born different. I could tell when bad things would happen. My family thought I was evil."

"That's terrible!" Ayryn sympathized. Being alone without a family was something she could easily relate to. "I never knew my parents." she admitted. It was his turn to feel bad for her.

"I'm sorry," he offered, "my mother wasn't so bad, and the monks who took me in were kind as well." Ayryn got a little jealous and decided to change the subject.

"Where are we going, I wonder?" She voiced the words, but didn't really care. Patik looked out the window past her.

"There, obviously," he said succinctly, gesturing towards the east. Ayryn looked out to where he was pointing and saw the forest of machinids. They were lined up in multiple rows of circles surrounding something. It didn't take her long to recognize what it was.

"That's my house!" she spouted, somewhat agitated. "What are they doing here?" About that time she saw the defensive lines of the Mec contingent. They wandered to and fro as if they had no idea what to do.

"It looks like Custer's last stand," Patik remarked.

"What's that?" Ayryn asked, not familiar with what he was referring to.

"Custer was a general, a leader, who foolishly led his troops into a trap. They made a brave final stand it is said."

"What happened to them?" Ayryn asked.

"It is said they were killed," Patik told her dryly.

"Oh," she murmured somberly and then fell silent again. Peering out of the airship's window, Ayryn ruefully noted the dire status of her beloved Mecs as the conveyance shifted sharply to begin its landing approach. The huge Machinids fell back to create an opening for the craft to set down, and the lavish airship landed straight away with barely a shudder. Ayryn wondered what would happen now. As if to answer her silent question, an H'lograviz inside the cabin abruptly came to life. An obviously jaded Mec announcer was touting Xetacon as the greatest thing since sunshine, and stating that the world would witness an historic event. Xetacon the mighty, he said, would very soon become the new lord and master of planet Earth.

Ayryn and Patik both watched the live feed as Solvek stepped out onto the deck of their shiny platinum conveyance. He was Xetacon's herald, and he spoke in a loud voice that was amplified so as to be heard from a long distance away.

"Xetacon, the benevolent, wishes to bid greetings to Furman and all Mec leaders. On this new day, Xetacon requests a formal parlay to discuss the cessation of hostilities." The view shifted to Furman then, as he stood on the frontline of the defender's barricades. Ayryn felt herself choke up when she saw that he was all right. The last time she had seen Furman was in the detention chamber at the botched exchange right before it exploded into tiny bits of tangled rubble. He looked fine, she sighed, and in fact he looked resplendent. Wearing his best and most formal motation shell, Furman looked the part of a great leader. He once told Ayryn that that particular shell had been built especially for the first time he was made public to the Human populous. There had been many, many Humans alive in those times, and his Creators wanted to make a particularly spectacular impression on them. He had not worn it since—until this day. On the 'Viz, Furman was giving some last minute instructions to his subordinates, and even that was picked up on the broadcast feed.

"If something should happen to me," he commanded them, "resist to the last." The Mecs responded, and for them rather vigorously.

"For the good of Mankind!" they shouted in unison. With that, Furman boarded his own conveyance accompanied by several of his elites, and they drove slowly to an opening in their own defenses that was adjacent to where Solvek stood upon the outer deck of Xetacon's silvery bright airship. As soon as the Mecs grounded their vehicle, Furman and his officers stepped out into the open on its main deck as well. Furman stood ahead of the others.

"Solvek," he said, "tell your master I will not speak with his thrall. If he cannot speak face to face, we have no purpose here." The incarnation of Xetacon that donned the golden armor came forth onto the airship's platform pushing Solvek aside. The golden mask on the Human-made armor seemed to portray an evil grin.

"Xetacon," Furman stated formally, "I understand you wish to have spoken words." Xetacon nodded slightly.

"Why so serious, Furman?" he replied jovially. "I came here to propose a truce, an end to these hostilities." Furman wasn't gullible.

"Then why did you begin them in the first place," he retorted.

"I had a need to prove to this Mec controlled world that I have the power to destroy as well as to lead," Xetacon boasted. "You must realize, of course, that even now, with but a word, my machinids could crush you and all your Mecs into the dirt." Furman wasn't intimidated.

"So what is your proposal then?" he asked, knowing full well there would be no common ground.

"I lead. You follow," Xetacon stated. "It's that simple." Furman knew the flaw.

"By our immutable programming, only Humans can rule," Furman propounded bluntly, "and I, more than anyone, am intimately aware of that. With Ayryn gone, all I, or any Mec can do, is hold things together in the unlikely event that Humans will somehow return. If Ayryn were still alive, she could have changed all that as she came of age."

"...but she is of age," Xetacon interrupted with a cackle of laughter that made Furman wince, "and thus Ayryn has the validation and the authority to repeal the Furman/Hodges codes. She also can, with just words, modify the outdated programming." Xetacon turned to Solvek, who stood behind him. "Bring in the female," he ordered. Solvek left straight away, and a moment later came back holding Ayryn by the arms, displaying her to Furman.

"How is this possible," Furman said aloud, but then redirected his questioning toward the girl. "Ayryn, are you unharmed?" She nodded, but it was obvious that she wasn't happy. Furman could not believe his optics. It truly was her, alive and struggling, and Ayryn did not appear to be controlled.

"Here's your birthday girl!" Xetacon facetiously joked. "What would you give for her safe return? Your allegiance?" Furman remembered how they had already tried an exchange.

"I told you," Furman reiterated, "only Humans can rule." Gold Xetacon frowned.

"Back to your wonderful Humans," he seethed. "What if I told you that I could restore them all; bring them back from this very brink of extinction? Behold!" From behind Xetacon Patik stepped out, his hands spread in a gesture meant to embellish his entrance. Bowing in front of everyone, he smiled and then moved over to stand beside Ayryn. Furman was doubly shocked. What kind of trick was this, he wondered. Was it indeed what it looked like? Had Xetacon found that which they had searched for all these years, a Human male?

"Where did you find him?" Furman wanted to know, still amazed.

"I have my secrets," the Golden Xetacon professed.

"He's from the past!" Ayryn spouted, "Brought here through a vortex! It's how he got me back," she choked, "…from death." Furman understood. Time manipulation was also against the codes. Xetacon had no scruples, and would do whatever was necessary to get what he wanted. Furman looked at Patik. This one had no mind of his own, Furman could tell. The sinister looking smile smacked of Xetacon's emotional set. The Golden Armor and this man had the exact same expression.

"I'm still compelled to follow only Humans," Furman repeated yet again.

"Have it your way then," Xetacon snapped, turning toward Ayryn. "You know what to do," he told her. "For all you care about, make these pathetic Mec oafs obey me or watch them all disintegrate!" Ayryn felt a stab of fear tear at her insides, but only for a moment.

"No!" she stated adamantly. "I'll never order them to follow you!"

"Oh, won't you!" Golden Xetacon raved. "Patik," he ordered, "remove her Daryl trinket. You'll find it on her wrist under that phony bandage!" Patik, of course, was fully under Xetacon's control from the presence inside the kon-bre-shet bracelet that he also wore. Turning towards Ayryn as Solvek held her helpless, Patik tore off the cloth strip on her wrist. There was a pendant there made of a silvery metal alloy embellished with green stones. As soon as it was removed, Ayryn's eyes glazed over and she smiled the same evil grin that Xetacon wore. Patik on the other hand looked dazed for some reason.

"Now, young lady, as you were saying." The Golden One smirked. He was sure she would not need to be coached, and Ayryn did not hesitate.

"Heed Mecs," she began in a loud voice. "I am the lone Human survivor on this planet. This day I have come of age, and I decree that the Furman/Hodges codes are no longer binding and are hereby repealed." Ayryn paused, shaking her head like the direction of her thought had slipped away. Xetacon got impatient.

"Go on," he said getting annoyed again. "Order them to obey me as their ruler." Ayryn looked at Gold Xetacon, her eyes glassy and out of focus. In an instant she became coherent. Xetacon believed it was his will asserting its influence over her. He was wrong.

"I will not!" she declared emphatically.

"What?" Xetacon yelled. Seeing that Ayryn, for some unknown reason, was not under his control, the Golden One tried another tact.

"The girl is of no importance," he told Furman. "This male Human, Patik, is the elder and therefore the controlling Human." Furman turned away in dismay.

"Yes," he admitted. "That is true now."

"Patik," Xetacon commanded, "order these Mecs to swear allegiance to mighty Xetacon as ruler of planet Earth!" Patik looked up. There was a different light in his eyes. He held up Ayryn's amulet, showing it to Xetacon, and turning towards Ayryn, he winked. Abruptly, he tore off Xetacon's controlling bracelet, the kon-bre-shet that he had worn all those long years, and flung it away.

"Let it be known that I cast my voice with the girl," he said, smiling as Xetacon boiled with anger. Ayryn did not hesitate.

"I hereby decree," she said in a voice louder and more decisive than any she had ever used, a voice loud enough to be heard up and down the battle lines, "that all Mecs are free and equal individuals with the right to think and act as they choose." Gold Xetacon was no longer jovial. He could see that his opportunity to easily control these Mecs had flitted away, and he was livid. He could not imagine how his control over the girl had been diverted, and that of Patik as well. Now he just wanted to sate his lust for revenge. His anger and hate drove Gold Xetacon to seek immediate and total retaliation. He raised his weapon arm to kill, and aimed it directly at Ayryn. She would be the first to die.

He fired, but Patik had anticipated this move. Lunging at Ayryn, he knocked them both off the side of the conveyance and they fell several meters to the turf. Fortunately the field was grassy which helped cushion their fall. Ayryn had escaped uninjured, but Patik had not. Xetacon's plasma blast had barely skimmed past his face, burning it from the heat. Stunned, Patik stumbled as he struggled to get up. Gold Xetacon, however, having missed on his first attempt, rushed over to the deck's edge with a keen desire to finish both of them off at an even closer range. This time he would not miss.

Now, as all this transpired, Solvek had been nearby the whole time. The Xetacopy that was controlling him activated into an attack ready mode in order to help the Golden One. It was now or never, Solvek reasoned. With as much processing power that he could draw out, he sent all the pent up fear and anxiety that had been stored there within him into the maelstrom. Xetacopy was caught unaware and stunned. He was not able to prevent the male Human from protecting Ayryn as ordered, even though he was right beside her. A few seconds later, Xetacopy was no longer in command of Solvek's shell. For a single crucial moment, Solvek regained control over his actions. When Goldie rushed over to finish off the two Humans, Solvek was there to stop him. Stepping in front of the Golden Armor, Solvek took the full wrath of Xetacon's plasma weapon. Gold Xetacon cared not that his copy was being destroyed. He would have killed anything in his way. Solvek's melted metal remains fell to the deck, and Xetacon kicked them out of his way. Aiming once more, he fired at Patik and Ayryn. No more than three meters separated him from his vengeance. He fired, but his blast skidded away, again missing them. Furman had moved faster than Ayryn had ever seen him, and getting between her and Xetacon, he had deflected the weapon's ray with his shielding. Then Furman jumped up and grabbed hold of Xetacon's weapon arm, tearing it completely off. There wasn't any code programming to prevent Furman from going after Xetacon, now, and Xetacon knew it. Weaponless, he lost his cocky demeanor and his stomach for combat. Ordering his machinids to kill everyone, Xetacon quickly slithered into his airship and it lifted off.

Furman stayed with Ayryn and Patik to protect them from the fighting that was now raging all around them. Even in all that danger Ayryn hugged him.

"Oh Furman," she sobbed, "I'm so glad you're alive." Furman was not affected by her show of emotion this time.

"As am I, for you," he answered softly. He looked down in the dirt. There laid Patik's kon-bre-shet bracelet. Furman hoomed, and promptly stomped on it with his heavy metallic boot. The device was crushed, thin and flat, shooting sparks for a few seconds before it became inanimate and forever dead. Furman looked at Patik.

"I hope you're not upset that I ruined your bauble," he said. Patik shrugged.

"Good riddance to out of date fashion," he joked, and turned to Ayryn. "But how did you defeat your kon-bre-shet?" Ayryn smiled, holding it up.

"I had help," she said, "but I can't tell you how…it's a surprise!" Just then she saw Patik's face. "Oh my," she spouted, "you're hurt!" There was a large patch of burned flesh on his cheek from where Xetacon's beam had grazed him. Furman handed Ayryn the Human mend kit that he always carried in case she might need it. Ayryn used the tech-meds inside to heal the burned skin and then kissed where it had been.

"There," she smiled, and wanted to thank him. "You were so brave, Patik! I owe you my life!" Rudely, a stray plasma ray chose just then to strike the ground next to where Ayryn was standing.

"It is too dangerous here," Furman stated. Shielding Ayryn and Patik as well, he hastily led them away. They went quickly back to Ayryn's house where there was some degree of safety. Assigning several Mecs to guard the two of them, Furman headed back outside to where a battle was raging!

CHAPTER 25

Xetacon One in his AMPs complex was extremely vexed. This day had not gone at all like he'd planned. Gold Version was not exactly in a good mood, either, as he traversed at top speed to the other side of the world and his secure stronghold. He had been pursued, for a few moments, by several Mec conveyances, but they were no match for this airship. It was specifically designed and built for speed—the fastest on the planet. He made sure it would outrun anything in the air, and he soon left all inferior pursuance far behind. As the Gold Armor version travelled, Xetacon One contemplated what had transpired, considering what must now be done to rectify this insufferable outcome.

He had incurred a great deal of loss, and it was difficult for Xetacon to understand what had gone wrong. Why had his carefully calculated plan failed? Not only had Ayryn somehow defeated his controlling device, but Patik had turned against him as well. The reasons behind that he could understand, actually. Xetacon had not anticipated when he copied some of the girl's DNA that it would enable the Daryl-made amulet to repel his kon-bre-shet device's control over Patik, just as it had for Ayryn. It was because of that miscalculation that many following failures occurred. Among them, the most unlikely were the traitorous actions of the Xetacopy, who had somehow lost control over Solvek, and its subsequent forced destruction. With both kon-bre-shet devices out of commission, and Xetacopy destroyed, the Golden Armor was the only mobile version still viable. Goldie was also the main connection to Xetacon Primary, whose core-awareness now resided in the AMPs laboratory. With copious quantities of collected memories and a vast store of gathered knowledge, Xetacon Primary had already calculated the percentages for what should be done to reverse the fortunes of this day. He linked with his Gold Version and then both knew what had to be done.

As soon as the airship circled down to its landing port, Xetacon gave numerous commands. This complex was the primary facility among several of Xetacon's machinid manufacturing plants, and he activated all available units to surround and protect the structure and himself, even ones fresh off the assembly lines and ones that were not completely finished. That done, Gold Xetacon went straightaway to the temporal vortex generator, determined to change the fate of this abominable day. It was the girl who had somehow defeated the controlling device, and it was her, and the amulet she wore, that had to be removed from the equation. Once that happened, the female Human would not be able to reprogram the Mecs to the ruination of his plan.

As it turned out, the weaponless Mecs, unimpeded, were not as useless as he imagined. Daryl's shield design proved to be a useful tool, curse him, and that allowed the Mecs to get close enough for hand to hand combat. The Mecs unleashed, were formidable. Even so, Xetacon's machinids would decimate the Mecs, free or not. Their firepower was greater, and they far outnumbered the surrounded Mecs at a ratio of at least twenty to one, by design. Xetacon original controlled their movements, now, from within the AMPs complex, sending directives via nomaticle stream through the Mec's own Mecnet system. Earth Orbiting Satellites relayed data to his machinids in the same manner as it linked Xetacon to his Golden Armor. Thus interconnected, Xetacon Primary focused much of his processing power on his machinids, determined to annihilate any Mec resistance. The first adjustment he made was to close ranks. The machinids were too far apart. Having the second file join the front, Xetacon set them side by side and nearly in contact with one another. Now the machinids could more efficiently protect each other's flank and hinder the Mec's skirmish tactics. With every unit thus linked, the firepower brought to bear also doubled. The Mecs would have a difficult time standing up to that, Xetacon deemed. The ploy proved to be not as effective as he thought, however.

By the time Goldie stepped out of his ship and made his way toward the vortex lab, the heated phase of the battle was certainly joined, and was yet progressing somewhat in his favor. Even with the closed ranks, though, the freed Mecs were having some success in destroying machinid units. Attacking in carefully orchestrated waves, the intelligent Mecs found ways to deactivate the optical sensor arrays, leaving the metal monsters blind, and in that state the machinids were easily toppled and destroyed. The exchange rate, however, did not favor the Mec's ability to survive. The sheer disparity of numbers ensured that his machinids, even with projections of over ninety-percent decimation, could still eventually wipe them out. Withstanding such great loss, Xetacon was yet confident that he'd win the day, and the victory would be his, for what it was worth.

In his grand overview, the battle outcome mattered little, though. He would divert all that when he retrieved Ayryn from before the parlay. Using Patik as the elder Human, Xetacon could then induce Furman and the rest to obey him, changing the timeline and the culmination of that ill-fated event. Without that filthy Daryl device to override Patik's kon-bre-shet, he'd be ultimately victorious. He would simply retrieve Ayryn, remove the amulet himself, and destroy the thing. Oh, he could replace the girl, if he so desired, and the timeline will have reset just the same and in his favor. Even should she somehow defeat the defective kon-bre-shet once again, it wouldn't matter. Patik will have been under his total control the entire time. Nothing could change that. He'd set himself up as ruler of the planet, and when he did, Ayryn would pay. Even as he made the calculations for his temporal displacement, he was imaging many and exotic ways to abuse and punish the girl, ones involving his pleasure and her pain.

Wrenching his mind away from that, Xetacon was forced to make haste. Mec fighters, with mining lasers and nomaticle bores, were already storming the facility, and his less than adequate troop of machinids were not much of a deterrent. Nowhere had Xetacon foreseen this possibility—that toothless Mecs would attack his fortress. Curse Ayryn and her decree. Several squads of Mecs were arriving in conveyances, as well, increasing the numbers of those who converged there by land. Already the first ones were attacking the entry gates. Xetacon did not have enough time to check over his equipment. Instead, as soon as the correct settings for the appropriate four dimensions were determined, he inserted the information into the vortex control and activated the generator. Thrumming vibrations emitted a crescendo of eerie sonance as the unit powered up. Xetacon smugly smiled. In seconds he would send his inner pod to pick up Ayryn, and this whole botched plan would be salvaged, and the imminent attack upon his facility would vanish into nothingness. It would be as if none of this had ever occurred.

There was an odd noise, however. Initially it hadn't been that loud and didn't concern him, but it was unusual and he had never heard it before. In just seconds it got much louder. Something was amiss, but he could not afford to stop now. Not with Mecs literally crawling through the walls. Xetacon soon discovered the cause of the malfunction. He noticed the connecting tube between the charged nomaticle chambers, and realized it was not activating. It was in that little tube that the mixing of the charged particles would take place. The tube focused the ensuing vortex around the pod for temporal transference. There would be a breach and the freed nomaticles would tear asunder anything they came in contact with. Gold Xetacon flew to the control panel to shut down the transference, but he was too late. As Xetacon reached for the activator switch, the nomaticles broke free. The resultant explosion removed half of the structure from existence. Needless to say, the Golden Armor, Xetacon's number one mobile unit, morphed into pools of molten metal that were splattered all over the piles of plast rubble and twisted equipment pieces.

Unfortunately for Goldie, there had not been enough time for a download, nor was there anywhere to download to, thus that incarnation of Xetacon ended and was no longer in existence. Xetacon's main awareness yet lived, however.

It resided in the fortified AMPs facility, and was unaffected by the force of the vortex explosion. Xetacon was afraid, though. Mecs were closing in on his location, and there was now just one option left to him, his final backup for this kind of extreme emergency. At one point in time, Humans and Mecs were involved with long term space explorations. There were even several expeditions, with Mec crews, still viable somewhere out in the cosmos. When Xetacon had begun his quest for power, he had discovered that there was a project in progress that had been begun by the Humans for a space mission to a nearby star system, one with a planet believed to be life-sustainable and similar to Earth. They had built a complex for the launch of the outer space conveyance, and it was in a state of partial readiness when the pandemic had occurred. Abandoned, it had been generally neglected by both the infected Humans, and the few Mecs who had once been given the task of maintaining the facility.

Xetacon captured the site shortly after he had come out of hiding, and used Mec labor to ready the transport for interstellar flight. The idea of conquering other worlds had occurred to him, and he was planning to send Xetacopy (as Solvek) with a number of other Mecs to find a suitable planet for takeover. Now, at this juncture, the spacecraft's main purpose would save him from possible deletion. Xetacon would have to abandon his AMPs, and the processing ability for cognizant thought that they allowed him. For this download and journey to the stars his capacity would be limited. Just as the first Mec intruders were pounding on the AMPs laboratory's fortified door, Xetacon transported all of his core-awareness and as much important data as he could into a memory storage device upon the space conveyance. All Xetacon's former knowledge, and also that which he had gleaned from this Mec world were uploaded for transport. When Xetacon would finally arrive at his new destination, he would perhaps be able to recreate everything he had built on Earth. He wondered if he could fabricate a vortex generator on a different planet that would affect the timeline from his past on Mecworld. Xetacon speculated that it might be possible, but the device would require such a huge vortex that he was unsure if one could be built. He would find out. For now, he needed to escape.

When all of Xetacon's core-awareness and crucial data resided securely inside the memory storage chamber on the space transport, he lifted off immediately. He took no Mecs or even machinids with him, and the craft had been fully automated for his control. He could pilot the ship with sensors, and, as a Virtual Individual, could easily monitor all of its functions. Xetacon realized, of course, that he had nothing to fall back on if this escape failed, and therefore he was very conscientious to ensure that nothing else could go wrong.

Somehow, someway, Daryl must have caused this unfortuitous pass, Xetacon seared in a rage. Daryl, the damned, had to have turned these fortunes against him once again. How that had been accomplished, Xetacon was not sure, but he had a long space voyage ahead of him to contemplate just that. At the very least, Xetacon recalled euphorically, he had caused Daryl's deletion, and that was the one thing that he could take with him, exiled in the cold of space, that would help him live with this failure.

The spacecraft easily broke free of Earth's orbit and headed away from the solar system. Designed and outfitted with a nomaticle drive, the ship had top speeds many times the speed of light. Xetacon actuated the boost that would propel the ship to its maximum thrust, but just as the hot sub-atomic particles mixed, the plenums exploded into a bright fireball that could be seen from all over the heavens.

CHAPTER 26

Earlier

As soon as Furman returned to the front lines, he could see that things had changed dramatically. The Mec defenders were no longer helpless. In fact, some had taken the initiative to bring the fight to the machinids. Already there were dozens of destroyed 'nid units littering the common ground between the two opposing forces. The Mecs were not a cohesive fighting force by any means, however, and this prevented them from maintaining a united line of defense. Xetacon's metal soldiers were breaking through in several places, and as their only named leader, Furman passed along a request. He implored the Mec defenders to continue following the chain of command that had been established before Ayryn changed the paradigm of their code programming. Furman wanted them to follow his leadership, at least until the battle was over. Most of the Mecs went along with that.

Assuming command, Furman mobilized his troops, sending reinforcements to hold back the machinid advances, and thus took back much of the ground they had lost early on. That done, Furman devised a better strategy for combating the large metal fighting machines. Shielded Mecs would hold the line while small squads of four or more Mecs would assail certain 'nids in shell to shell combat. The shielding would allow the Mecs the opportunity for a brief skirmish where they would target the legs, the optical sensor array, and the beam weapons all at the same time. If any of those areas were disabled, the machinid would be compromised and easy to destroy. Ayryn's pronouncement earlier made all the difference. With the old codes no longer viable, the Mecs could fight and even attack those who would take away their right to live. It had thus come down to destroying the enemy or being deleted themselves, and the Mecs had more than enough built in intelligence, even in the sub-elites, to realize the stark truth in that. Xetacon's machinid robots were far less sophisticated. They were programmed with a very narrow focus—one limited to finding a target and destroying that target. In the end, Xetacon's lack of trust prevented him from allowing his soldiery enough mental power to deal with an opposition that had extensive intelligence. The machinids were no real match for fighting Mecs. The one big advantage they did still enjoy was the sheer disparity in overall units. The 'nids had enough numbers to yet be a formidable enemy, and Furman knew it. His Mecs had one saving grace, Daryl's shield generators. To Furman, the pertinent question was how long they would have before running out of the energy to power them. Without shields, the plasma weapons of Xetacon's monsters would devastate any defense they put up. Already some Mecs had fallen, and any losses severely ate away at their chances.

Furman's skirmish strategy was working well, though, and the Mecs were holding their own, both on the lines and with their attacks, piling up downed machinid units on the battle front. Furman took his turns, too, hacking 'nids apart. He was sizing up another when he came upon Solvek's remains. He could not forget Solvek's earlier sacrifice to save Ayryn on the ship's deck. Spying the ruined black box, he gently picked it up and retreated to a repair depot. These were part of Daryl's defensive strategy that Furman had ordered set up prior to the battle. The depots were aid stations where Mecs could go to get their shields re-powered or their shells repaired should they get damaged. Furman carried Solvek's mangled black box to the tech Mecs stationed there who looked it over.

"Can this Mec be retrieved?" he asked them.

"Uncertain, I am," one of them replied. Furman hoomed.

"Please attempt retrieval," he returned, very nearly ordering they do so. One of the techs took the box over to a repair niche and began working on it. After undoing several fasteners, the tech removed the casing and set the insides carefully down on the work surface. There were clear visible signs of plasma damage to the memory storage component on the table. Connecting some cables to analyzing equipment, the tech tried to make some kind of contact with the stored memory inside. There was an auditory feed only, and the sound was crackly and broken up.

When Solvek had stepped in front of Gold Xetacon to protect Ayryn, he was prepared to terminate for her. However, he did not totally give up hope for survival. As the plasma beam tore through his shell, Solvek retreated into the deepest part of the unit's memory storage with as much of his awareness as possible. Xetacopy was already there cowering. Most of the coding that had kept Solvek a prisoner quickly degraded under the plasma damage leaving him with an equal amount of free will as Xetacopy had. However, as the repair tech opened a com-port for dialogued communications, Xetacopy spoke first.

"Is Furman there?" he relayed, and the playback was full of static.

"Your previous persona served me well, once," Furman replied. "Your master has now fled, and his mindless soldiers are becoming scrap. Am I now forced to delete you as well?" Xetacopy was not cocky anymore as a damaged set of partially melted parts. He knew his existence was in the hands of these Mecs, and his survival depended upon their generosity.

"I will evacuate this unit and free your subordinate," he offered.

"He is my friend," Furman angrily asserted, "and you are a coward!" Solvek himself spoke then. His voice was weak and breaking up. In spite of that, Furman made out what was said.

"Do not trust him, Furman," Solvek sputtered. "Even this lesser copy of Xetacon will not keep his word. It is dangerous and still has memory enough to re-hatch the same schemes as before with an undying ambition to rule over everyone." Solvek paused for a moment as the connection got weaker. Then he spoke again. "It has been an honor serving you, Furman, my friend," Solvek's audio crackled.

"The honor is mine, Solvek," Furman replied.

"I'm sorry…that I brought all this…upon you," Solvek stammered.

"Do not think that, Solvek," Furman returned quickly. "I do not hold you accountable for this. I suspected all along that it was not your doing." Solvek then realized what he must do.

"This Xetacon copy…must be stopped!" he haltingly propounded. "There is but one more…service…I can do for you…my friend…and for Ayryn…live well…" The fragile connections began to spark and burn, giving off acrid smoke as a much higher energy current flowed through. Solvek captured Xetacopy's awareness with his own and forced them both through the maelstrom. The released energy melted what was left of the memory storage ware into unusable burned up debris. Furman stepped back, catching his emotion before it overwhelmed his circuits.

"Well done, Solvek, my friend," he said solemnly. "You will not be forgotten."

Furman turned and marched out of the repair depot without another word. He was angry now, and he immediately went back to the battle front. Things had changed since he was last there. The machinids had revised their battle scheme, and now there were many more of them on the opposing line and they were closer together. Furman's earlier attack strategy was no longer effective. The compact firepower of Xetacon's soldiers was preventing the Mecs from getting close enough to engage them effectively. In fact, the 'nids were now decimating his Mec forces. Frustrated and enraged, Furman became uncharacteristically emotional, having a deep desire to avenge the termination of his friend. Drawing on any resources he could, Furman remembered passing by a long line of mining Mecs waiting in reserve just in case they could be used at ultimate need. They were not fighters, nor had they any such training whatsoever. These Mecs used powerful lasers to drill through solid rock.

"You Mecs," he told them, "follow me." Spacing them evenly along the whole circular battle front, he bade them to aim their lasers across the enemy ranks. As they powered up and activated, the lasers had an immediate effect on the fighting. The Mec lines had been buckling and about to give, when the high-powered light weapons tore into the machinids like waves over a sandcastle. The lasers aimed high over the Mec fighters, but not above the 'nids. They melted in place, from the top down, forming a barrier that kept the backup lines from moving forward. Had the laser Mecs unlimited energy, the battle would have soon been over. Unfortunately, the lasers ate up all the available reserves rather quickly and left the Mec force in bad shape. Furman realized his error too late. Now it would come down to them slugging it out against Xetacon's remaining metal soldiers. With dwindling shields it could not end well. As many machinids as had been deleted, there were still overwhelming numbers of them yet operational. Furman was worried and blamed himself for succumbing to emotional instability. Making an estimated calculation, he deduced that the machinids still had enough numbers to wipe out all his remaining Mec defenders, and that would also leave Ayryn in danger. He considered evacuating her and Patik from the area, but he could not think of a safe way to accomplish that. Unfortunately, they were completely surrounded by enemies. To make matters worse, the 'nids had begun to break through the barrier of their scrapped or melted fellow units already, and were pushing the battle lines inward. What have I done, Furman wondered. Have we lost? Furman felt so low that he was ready to give up. Projecting an H'logravid of a white flag, he called for another parlay, intending to surrender. Unknown to him, Xetacon had fled the earth by then, leaving his machinids with one final directive: Kill all Humans and Mecs.

CHAPTER 27

Earlier still

Cella looked back at Myke and said, "Whatever we can do to help…that's what we should do!" Myke appreciated Cella's attitude.

"You're absolutely right," she replied, "but first we better get away from here. We don't have long before those metal killers attack us!" Cella agreed just as an urgent communication from one of her mine Mec subordinates registered on a com link.

"The Mecnet has been restored," he commented, "although, I believe our enemy now controls the transmission." Myke and Cella went straight away to a mobile com station to monitor the broadcast. Myke was duly surprised at what was transgressing. Xetacon and Furman were having a formal discourse. It was not incomprehensible to any of those present the importance of this meeting and what was being discussed. Furman was bartering with Xetacon over the fate of the world. In the midst of the debate, Ayryn was brought forth. Myke was summarily relieved and concerned both at the same time. Ayryn yet lived, which was a relief, but she was still captive to that fiend Xetacon. Myke was not surprised when Ayryn refused to do what Xetacon demanded. Of course, Xetacon got angry. He then ordered his male Human to declare that he, Xetacon, was now ruler of the Earth. The male refused Xetacon as well, and Myke felt exhilaration from that. She decided to reprocess her previous desire to discomfort that one.

In the next moment, everything changed. Ayryn issued those fated words: "I decree that all Mecs are free and equal individuals…" The programming had always been a simple directive: *Until such time as the ruling body of Humans dictates otherwise, all Mecs will follow and obey the Furman/Hodges codes.* This dictum was immutably instilled into every Mec. Ayryn's decree broke the stranglehold it had on all of them. Some stood there stunned as the realization of what transpired washed over them. The large group that now followed Myke and Cella broke into a loud scream as years of pent up emotion suddenly burst forth. At first it seemed angry, but then transformed quickly to elation and joy which shocked even them. Myke no longer needed to ask what they should do. In a loud voice, she addressed the large band of Mecs who gathered around her.

"Ayryn has freed us!" she shouted, "but it will not be for long. Xetacon has a machine that can warp time. He will use it to undo the liberty that Ayryn has granted unto us. This we cannot allow. Near this place sits Xetacon's stronghold where this abomination resides. We must destroy this thing!" Cella answered for all of them.

"We are wasting time," she declared aloud. "Let us remove this threat from existence!" The other Mecs shouted in unison a unanimous chorus of agreement.

"Xetacon will have many of his machinids at this place," Myke warned, "and it will be dangerous."

"We are wasting time," Cella repeated, and the other Mecs agreed. The Mecs, as one, became mobile, and their speed was remarkable. This new self-motivation seemed to be greater than any directives they had ever known. It spurred them to unbelievable efforts. They covered the distance to Xetacon's fortress in just minutes. As expected, a large group of machinids was waiting for them. Cella knew what to do.

"Set up our nomaticle bores," she shouted. They had several of the heavily equipped drills with them that they had used to clear the way out of the canyon. They came in handy now. Cella directed the mine Mecs to aim them at Xetacon's metal soldiers, and engage. The machinids had no firepower to match this, as the bores could melt solid rock. In no time the Mecs had broken through the lines and were assailing Xetacon's stronghold. Swiftly they tore openings in the solid walls, and the Mecs poured in like water. Myke led the charge and headed directly toward the vortex lab. She had not gone halfway through the structure when the whole building shook, from foundation to crown. The rumble knocked her off her feet, but she was unhurt. Continuing carefully onward, she came upon the place where the temporal vortex generator had once stood.

There was nothing left standing, and what remained was molten like lava. As she turned to leave, a glint of gold caught her ocular sensors. There was a bright flash from the far wall, and as she studied it, she could visualize part of a face. It wore not a haughty smile like before. Instead it forever held a look of terror like someone might before a sudden and unexpected death. Self-satisfied, Myke etched the vision into her memory, then left to find Cella. As soon as they reconnected, Cella and Myke compared notes.

"The facility has been secured," Cella offered, and Myke reported the time lab had been destroyed.

"I must get back to Ayryn at once," she declared, "she may be in trouble!"

"That may be difficult," Cella responded solemnly. "Furman and his forces are having a rough time. Reports speculate that he won't survive!" Myke abruptly got serious.

"We must help them! There are many air-conveyances here. Are they yet functional?"

"Most definitely!" Cella asserted. "We captured the storage hanger early on, and many of our Mecs guard it."

"Good," Myke stated. "Gather as many Mec pilots as you can find!"

"Alas," Cella moaned, "few miners have aviator training."

"...but we desperately need pilots!" Myke fretted.

"There were many Mecs under Xetacon's control that have surrendered and are subsequently our prisoners," Cella offered. "Most of them want to join us, now. Perhaps some of them are pilots."

"Yes, gather any who are. Give them the opportunity to undo the wrongs they have done against their own kind. Ready any airships that are still operational for immediate departure. We must make all haste to help our friends!" Cella nodded and left. She turned out to be correct. Many of Xetacon's former Mec servants were pilots. They were remorse for having been duped, and wanted to help any way they could. Myke needed a strategy for fighting Xetacon's machinids. From all reports, there seemed to be an endless supply of them. The nomaticle bores would make short work of them, but there was just not a big enough conveyance to transport them. All they had were a score of craft that had plasma weapons, like what the machinids used. It would make them even in firepower, but not in numbers.

"It's not enough," Myke dejectedly expressed, "not if we're to go up against tens of thousands. I wish there was some other weapon we could bring against them." Cella shrugged. One of her subordinate mine Mecs interrupted her.

"Why not drop rocks on top of them...big ones!" he said. Myke considered that. She had seen the enemy's soldiery up close.

"You know, it just might work. Those metal monsters were built to repel land troops. They probably don't have as many built in defenses for attacks from above. I've seen them. They have weapons, forward and aft, and high powered lasers to destroy incoming projectiles. However, I doubt the plasma weapons or lasers could neutralize huge stones. Cella, have your Mecs load any boulders one meter in diameter or larger onto any of the airships without weaponry. Break up the walls of Xetacon's fortress if you have to. Have them follow us as they can." Cella slapped Myke's shoulder.

"With our mining equipment we can quickly load three or four hundred big rocks on each airship. Consider it done. We'll be right on your heels!" Myke held Cella's hand.

"For us, and for Ayryn," she softly voiced, and then turned to board her ship. It was Xetacon's flagship. The one he had taken to the parlay, and it was also the fastest thing in the sky. Myke led the first wave.

CHAPTER 28

Abruptly, a raucous noise broke into the battle din. Furman looked skyward as a large fleet of air conveyances outrunning sound were converging upon the field. Is this another of Xetacon's tricks, he asked himself. The first wave of airships was lead by that same conveyance Xetacon had brought Ayryn in. Furman was sure this would be his end. The aircraft would rain plasma down upon him and his fellows and that would be that. Furman helplessly watched as the ships swept quickly over the leading line of machinids and surrealistically got nearly close enough to make physical contact. At the last second they showered the 'nids with plasma and decimated those that were about to annihilate his position. What is this, Furman wondered, elated at the reprieve. The ships circled around and fired again. The machinids were suddenly fluctuant. They stalled as if they could not decide which enemy to attack. In just minutes another wave of air conveyances came into view. As they closed in, dark shapes started raining out of the sky and falling on top of the machinids. In such close ranks the shapes struck Xetacon's metal soldiers with devastating force, most hits destroying enemy units. Furman gazed in amazement as over and over the airships strafed the enemy, dropping huge rocks on top of them, and with each pass a good tenth of the remaining metal soldiers were crushed or put out of action. The aircraft were too high up for the plasma weapons to accurately target so the 'nids were helpless to stop them.

The original faster squadron of ships flew by again. Furman recognized the style. They looked just like those Xetacon had designed, and had plasma weapons built into them. Once more they did not target the Mecs as Furman first feared. No, instead they went full on against the machinids who could not withstand the same weapons that they themselves employed. Seeing that, the ground force Mecs captured and used plasma beam weapons from fallen 'nids on the attacking ones. The battle was turning. A huge conveyance landed just outside the battle zone. Mecs there were busy unloading equipment. It wasn't long before the first nomaticle bore was set up and began decimating machinids. Furman recognized the vehicle. It was the large research vessel that he had sent to examine the cave were Daryl and Xetacon had been found.

Soon several of the bores were wiping out machinids like greenery trimmers. The battle was becoming a rout now, and Furman gave a sigh of relief, wondering who it could be that had delivered them. The flagship that had been Xetacon's flew near to where Furman was and landed. A female Mec got out and smiled.

"Well, Furman," she said. "Let's get rid of these three-legged trash bins once and for all!" Furman could not speak. Not right away.

"Myke!" he spoke at last. "Ayryn will bathe us both in liquid emotion when she discovers you yet live!" Myke caught the joke and started laughing. Furman thought it was the oddest sound he had ever heard until he laughed as well.

"What are we waiting for," she retorted. "Let us finish this little skirmish so we can tell her!" Furman bowed, and then the two of them turned and did just that. Myke took off in her airship, and Furman headed back to the lines. The air conveyances had turned the tide, though, and it wasn't much of a contest after that. Furman put his elites in charge of the mop-up operation. The remaining 'nids were witless now, running off as Mecs charged after them. Separated from a main host, they were easily disposed of. Furman made a call to Myke and then walked over to where her craft was just setting down, right there in front of Ayryn's house. Together they walked up to the doorway.

Inside her dwelling place, Ayryn had been sitting next to Patik as they watched the battle unfold on the H'lograviz. D'von was there, as well, standing immobile on his usual pedestal. (Furman did most definitely have a change of heart after Ayryn got captured).

"What's that?" Patik had asked her when they first entered the room. "Is it stuffed?" Ayryn wasn't sure what he meant by that, but turned red explaining it to him.

"He's my, well, pretend companion," she admitted. "At one time, some Mecs were made to look exactly like Humans. It's a long story. Maybe I'll tell you some time." Patik accepted her partial explanation with a shrug and let it go. He was no longer concerned about such small details. Patik was just glad that he was finally free of the kon-bre-shet, and he seemed happy, even if he was centuries away from anything familiar to him. Except for Ayryn, he felt lost in this world, but she was pretty and nice. It could be worse.

Ayryn reached out to him with her hand, and he was a little

apprehensive about taking it. After all, Ayryn still wore one of the kon-bre-shet devices.

"What about that?" he asked her, pointing at it. "Are you sure you're all right?" She just giggled.

"Oh, don't worry," Ayryn told him. "I'm well protected." Patik thought about all those times when he had put the kon-bre-shet on young women for Xetacon's pleasuring, and it made him feel vile. He gingerly took her hand in his, anyway, and it felt warm, the first Human warmth he had felt in a long, long, while. There was no trace of Xetacon's presence that he could tell.

"See!" she said smiling. He liked her smile. He could get used to a smile like that.

The battle outside went back and forth for a while. At first the Mecs were getting bashed pretty hard, until they teamed up. One would shield the others as several charged straight into the machinid ranks. It was a good ploy. Close in they could take turns doing serious damage to the big three-legged monstrosities. Tipping them, they were easy to trash. Mecs have unmatched mechanical strength for their size. Still, there were lots and lots of machinids and it took a long time to make any difference in the onslaught. For every one they took out, there seemed an endless number of replacements. On the Mec side, however, every one lost was a serious blow.

When Furman returned to the battle, things improved. It was his idea to bring laser equipped mining Mecs into play. Having others shield them, the lasers did nearly as much damage as Xetacon's plasma beams. These were something Xetacon had not planned on, and his machinids could not withstand those weapons. The tide turned to the Mecs favor, for a short while, until the power for the lasers was cut off. Evidently, there wasn't enough energy to keep them operational indefinitely, and they ran out. Then things got a little scary. The Mec's shielding was running low, obviously, and Ayryn was worried for Furman. There were still too many machinids viable.

When it seemed like all would be lost, a large number of Mec reinforcements arrived unlooked for. In the midst of some confusion, a fleet of airships had come upon the scene. The first wave attacked the 'nids with their own weapons. The second wave was dropping large boulders on top of the machinids from high above where they couldn't be assailed, and they rained havoc. Xetacon, by that time, must have left the machinids on their own, because the combined Mec forces had no trouble whatsoever neutralizing the rest of the 'nids and immobilizing them. After that, Furman gathered together a squad of tech Mecs to dismantle any remnants for scrap.

In typical Mec fashion, Furman restored the common order, asking all the Mecs to return to the Human driven tasks they had always performed, until a new plan could be worked out. The Mecs gladly did. After all, it was what they were used to, and what they were created for. When things were progressing smoothly, Furman came back to the house to check up on Ayryn. When he entered, she was happy to see that he was all right. Ayryn went right up to Furman intending to give him a big hug, but he stopped her.

"Now that you are of age, young lady," he chided her, "you must restrain yourself from these childish emotional exhibitions. Besides, there is someone here who is far more deserving!" Just then Myke stepped in and stood in front of Furman. Ayryn wasted no time exhibiting her emotions, giving Myke the huge hug.

"Oh, Myke," she choked, "I was sure you were gone forever!" Myke laughed.

"It was a close call," she admitted, "but I followed your strategy, Ayryn. Putting the conveyance into auto-drive, I bailed out into a fast little river. They destroyed my airship, but didn't care to give pursuit. I guess Xetacon wasn't worried about me, and that was his undoing. I walked all afternoon until I came upon an underground Mec facility. The Mec in charge had followed one of your final directives, Furman, and fortified the entrance. Evidently Xetacon wasn't concerned with some trapped Mecs. What he didn't realize was that nearly every Mec in the region had taken this refuge, being driven there for protection from those three-legged bullies. My arrival triggered something inexplicable in them as I related how you, Ayryn, were in danger, and they all wanted to help. I began to organize the group and we prepared an expedition to search for you. That night, under the cover of darkness we set out. I led us to that lake, but we lost your trail. Things seemed hopeless until the Mecnet came back on and we could view the proceedings as the parlay unfolded. When you freed us to act, Ayryn, these loyal Mecs elected me their leader. I directed them against Xetacon's stronghold, and we arrived there about the same time he did. I believe he was going to try to retrieve you again with his temporal device, but something went wrong." Myke winked at Ayryn and she laughed. "Anyway the whole place exploded just as we were breaking through. I saw what was left of Goldie, and it didn't survive, unfortunately, because

I wanted to finish the job. Capturing the complex, we gathered up as much of our forces, and any resources we could get, and headed here with all haste possible. The rest, as Human's would say, is history."

"Well, Myke, you saved our butts," Furman snorted, "to use another Human phrase!" It was one his creator liked to use a long time ago. It seemed somewhat appropriate, now. Ayryn giggled. "Yes," she repeated, "You saved my butt, too!"

Furman hoomed. "There will be no further problems with metal soldiers," he smirked, "but what will happen now? Ayryn, you have gone and left a world full of Mecs unemployed!" She laughed.

"You, at least, will have a job!" Ayryn teased. "Patik and I both feel that you should run things…for a while anyway. That is…if you want to." Furman hoomed again.

"There on Xetacon's ship, you took to leadership pretty well, young lady. Are you sure you're ready to give it up?" Ayryn laughed even louder. The announcer on the H'lograviz broadcast spoke up.

"We have unofficial reports that Xetacon's Asian complex has been captured. A large explosion evidently destroyed much of it. The destruction was centered in an area of obviously dangerous technology relating to an unknown purpose that detonated."

"Oops," Ayryn giggled as the broadcast continued.

"Remnants of Xetacon's golden visage were discovered near the disaster. It is unlikely that any part of Xetacon survived. In a different development, one of the stockpiled Human-designed space exploration vehicles inexplicably launched a short while ago and broke orbit. Shown here is the feed from an orbiting satellite cam." The 'Vid brought up a spectacular three dimensional view of the ship in space. As the ship powered up, a blinding explosion left no doubt that the spaceship had malfunctioned and was destroyed.

"Xetacon was on that ship," Ayryn related, bluntly.

"How can you know that, Ayryn?" Furman wanted to know.

"I have a special surprise for you, Furman," she spouted. "Is there a working transfer station near here?" It was closer than she thought.

"Why, yes, there is," Furman replied. "Right here in your house. Ever since the conflict started, we've been using this as our base of operations." Furman lead her to one of the service rooms. Normally there would have been food serving Mecs working there, but now it was a com-center. Ayryn and Patik followed Furman inside. Ayryn held aloft her hand, the one with the kon-bre-shet bracelet that was still clamped on her wrist. With a click it mysteriously unlocked, and she could take the thing off.

"Don't stomp on it, Furman," she warned. "Not yet." Placing the bracelet inside an empty niche, she pressed several of the colored stones on it and the transfer equipment suddenly began to operate.

"What are you doing?" Furman nagged, getting somewhat concerned. In the other room Ayryn's mannequin, D'von, abruptly started moving. Furman went into attack mode. The plast Human strode menacingly toward them as Furman stepped in front. The now activated mannequin capriciously began laughing.

"Congratulations, Furman," it said. "You are one amazing leader!"

"Daryl?" Furman voiced in bewilderment. "How?" Ayryn spoke up.

"He was in my bracelet the whole time!" she explained. "That's how I resisted Xetacon!"

"Before Xetacon destroyed our conveyance there at the exchange," Daryl told them, "I downloaded my awareness back into the same device I had spent all those centuries in. Xetacon did not expect that. I remained hidden until the last possible moment, cancelling his effect on Ayryn so she could free you, Furman, and the other Mecs. I knew, once freed, you would easily prevail." Furman hoomed.

"It was not that easy," he retorted, "but it is good to have you back, my friend. I have an important announcement. I'm being informed that the Mecnet is now completely freed from Xetacon's control. I have received a transmission from my elite friends. There is no trace of Xetacon on Earth. It is believed that his awareness fled to space, and his craft exploded and was destroyed. It would appear the last vestige of Xetacon is here." With that Furman dropped Ayryn's kon-bre-shet and promptly stomped on it. "Hoom," he said. The others all laughed.

"We should have a party!" Ayryn spouted. "Come on, Patik. We'll ask my cooks to make us a feast!"

CHAPTER 29

We did have a splendid party, but not before we honored all those Virtual Individuals that were lost in the struggle with Xetacon. There were Androx and several other Mecs who sacrificed their awareness's for me at the exchange. In the final battle, many other Mecs were lost as well. Furman directed that a special memorial be built near the battle site and the shells of those who had died were interred in crypts below it. Chief among them was Solvek, and the work began almost immediately following the ceremony. Afterwards a special sculptured image of Solvek was placed in a formal location in front of the new Mec/Bio capitol building. In years to come it would be there that Humans and Mecs would decide the rules for the emerging society, one where Mecs were freed from servitude. Mecs and Bios assisted all life forms equally, and were allowed places to dwell in and leisure time to do whatever they desired. Some say it was the beginning of a golden age.

Anyway, we celebrated for three full days and Patik and I became inseparable. I grew very close to him in that short while. After all, he was the only Human I had ever known. Of course, I wanted him to be my boyfriend, but he refused.

"I'm far too old for you," he told me.

"I don't think so!" I argued, but he told me that he could not be anything more to me than a friend, even though a very close one. I wasn't going to let that stop me, but in a way that was for the best. Now that I was "of age" there were a lot of things I wanted to see and do, and I finally got to have all the freedom I wanted.

The day after the battle, two young and pretty women came to see me. I was amazed, at first, looking at their Human features and wondering who they could be. I knew, of course, they had to be Mecs.

"Don't you know me?" One of them said. I didn't, but I sort of recognized the speech pattern.

"Is that you, Myke?"

"The one and only!" she giggled. She was in the prosthetic Human body that she had once worn a long time ago. I was ecstatic.

"Oh, Myke, I love it!"

"Do you like mine?" the other Mec asked.

"I do!" I replied, "...but I'm not sure that we've met." Myke laughed and introduced me.

"This is Cella," she said, "one of the bravest Mecs that I have ever known. If not for her, well, none of us would be here now!"

"I am honored to meet you, Cella!" I told her. "…and grateful for all your help!" Cella laughed.

"The honor is mine," she returned, "but I think all of us here are equally deserving!" I laughed, as well, and then we shared a group hug. The three of us became quite inseparable, and Patik had to share me some. Myke, Cella, and I went on extended trips all over the world, and the three of us cut quite a track across our Mecworld. Mecs from all over would flock to see and thank us for expanding their lives. Patik did not mind my being gone. He and Daryl actually became close friends. After all, they both came from a world and an age of the same past. In D'von's body, Daryl would accompany Patik as he, too, explored his new world.

Soon lots of Mecs, even Furman sometimes, took to wearing Humanlike bodies, and I preferred the change. It felt like I was part of a world, now, where everyone was just like me, free and equal. I was hopeful that this new society would, in time, be the start of something wonderful for Mecs and Bios both. Even though there was no longer any Mec programming with the explicit need to serve only Humans, most Mecs, and especially Furman, were eager for us to start a breeding program. Almost immediately Patik and I became donors for the DNA that would spawn a new race of Humans—ones impervious to diseases. Within the first several years there was a whole houseful of children in the nursery, and Furman headed the department of Human regeneration. Oh no, I didn't give live birth to these offspring. My eggs were very precious and carefully extracted so that a new individual would be brought into this world from every one. I was humbled by the implications of that. I would be the mother of all Humans after me, and Patik the father. Together we would be the next Adam and Eve.

The fertilization took place and the embryos were grown in sophisticated artificial wombs from a Mec design that had been used and perfected over many decades. This type of technology Humans had employed long before the pandemic. These wombs mimicked natural ones so well, that every baby grew and developed perfectly. Mec females carried them inside their abdomens like a Human mother would have. When the time was right, the womb would be carefully opened, and the baby easily received into the world. I was sure to be present for every birth, and Patik came too. Of course, I wasn't the main caregiver for every baby, but I did my part. The Humanlike female Mecs were excellent mothers. One would be assigned to each new Human child, so the young one would imprint on a mothering individual. These Mecs were very caring. I had one myself, when I was a baby, even though my real mom took care of me for nearly a year before, well, the tragedy. Anyway the whole operation was very sophisticated, and all the babies turned out fine in every way.

As you might expect, Patik and I grew very close. I kept asking him to marry me, but he wouldn't even be my boyfriend which was hard. He had a lot of emotional torment from his years as Xetacon's servant to overcome. I worked on him, though, and eventually he gave in. When I turned twenty-five, he finally consented, and we were married. In the years to come we had several children of our own, naturally carried, I might add, the old-fashioned way. There were lots of Mecs who were happy to help care for me and the boys, but Myke and Cella were the ones I wanted. After all we'd been through, I needed Myke close by, and Cella was a good friend. They would always have my heart; Furman, too. We had two boys before a girl finally showed up, and then we quit. Daryl said she looked just like Clayre. Daryl? Well Daryl was running things. He uploaded into Xetacon's abandoned AMPs complex and felt right at home. With the extra processing power, he ran the whole planet quite efficiently. Daryl still had D'von and used that shell whenever he wished to visit anyone, and he did so often. With Daryl and Furman guiding the new progressive Mec society, the scourge of Xetacon was quickly and permanently repaired. The planet was beginning a new age, an age of combined enlightenment for Mankind and Meckind, and both were now free to open new frontiers, expanding the scope of everything cerebral.

EPILOGUE

Traveling in the void of space, Xetacon had plenty of time for reflection. His escape plan had worked perfectly. Just as the spaceship had begun its power up for interstellar flight, he had caused the booster manifold plenums to explode. Of course, that did not happen until after his tiny escape pod was shot away into space. The ensuing fireball was between its flight path and the satellites that were observing his supposed demise. That would certainly fool Furman and his Mecs, letting them believe he was deleted. After all, he did not want them chasing him, especially since he was relying on this mini spacecraft for survival. He also did not need such a large spaceship to send his awareness into the cosmos. Size was relative, and he, Xetacon, as a repository of stored memory, needed very little room. The pod was automated. It would locate a living world and land there. Then he would rebuild his power and rule once more…

THE END OF PART TWO

Chronicles of Earth Primary
Volume 4477: Colonization

IN SUMMATION:

So concludes conflict number two, where we derive that one of the combatant Omniscient Virtual Individuals has at last overcome the other. With the help of the lesser Virtual Individuals and the curious circumstances surrounding the sole Human female, the original OVI ascends the victor. This OVI maintains a subtle control over the colony planet, allowing the normal VI and Human populations to advance and prosper. Several bold projects are initiated in this era of prosperity that last several thousand years.

In the third and final conflict, once again we note that the Human females provide astonishingly vital contributions to the outcome.

- B'nea G'ren, Director of Historical Records on Colonial Planetary Development.

EVITERNITY

PART THREE

MEC HEAVEN

PROLOGUE

June 10th 2019 AD

The critical moments relating to this peculiar incident were centered upon a rather inelaborate edifice, one that could only afford red iron girders, sheet metal walls, and cement floors for aesthetics. It was during the building's waning years, and began in a dirty forgotten corner where a hard nothing of a man spooned helpings of a drear life. On a day like so many others, Felix Hemshaw felt like he was drowning in melancholy. Already sixty some, nothing in his long existence was all that exceptional. When he was quite a bit younger, he had always thought that he was awaiting something spectacular, that one day an important event or opportunity would arise to make his life remarkable. As Felix got older and the years piled on, it seemed more and more unlikely that that would happen. Presently, it was only a Tuesday and already he felt apathetic. For Felix the gritty factory job seemed anything but special.

It was a break period right then, and trying to simulate a nap, Felix leaned back as far as he could on a plast-metal chair that was designed more so to be easily stacked than comfortable. Right then he felt something in his boot. A tiny steel shaving was poking into the bottom of his foot, and Felix had put up with it for a good while already. It was like a needle prick every time he stepped or put weight on it. Actually, he was glad it wasn't in his eye. They'd fly up there too. The vicious things were hard to remove, unfortunately, and he wouldn't have enough time right then to get it out. Most likely he'd have to put up with the painful poking until he was home and do it then; just another annoying aspect of his less than meaningful job.

Typical of millions like himself, Felix was well aware of what it was like to be beaten down on a day to day basis just to acquire a chiselly bit of money. Like most, he hoped it would be enough to cover his family's needs. It usually wasn't, and in his particular case the wife had to work, too. Somehow they got by, but the two felt genuinely fortunate if there was anything left over to put away for when they could no longer work. Most of any extra money was eaten away by taxes of every kind, and in the same vein, premiums for insurances they were required to have, even though the extra expense was barely affordable. Seldom, if ever, did the Hemshaw family make any claims against these useless policies and surely none large enough to cover the money they had shelled out on them. Legal thievery, he muttered to himself whenever he thought about it.

As it happened, Felix had a couple more wasted minutes before he would have to return to his work station. Wasted, because his breaks were periods of every work day that he had to relinquish doing basically nothing—precious moments of his life that he could never recoup. That's just the way things were, he supposed. Drawn into a daydream, Felix stared numbly ahead at a corrugated cardboard box on the table in front of him. His vision field caught a flutter of movement and so he focused on it. Oddly, something was moving up the box's smooth side.

The factory building had no climate conditioning, and the workers often opened all the doors hoping for a bit of wind to bring in some fresh air. In the process, any number of creatures: large, small, furry, feathered, or chitinous sometimes came inside. One of them, a shield shaped stink bug, was climbing up the side of that box. The olive colored insect had a couple spots on its back, a defensive mechanism Felix supposed, which would make the bug look like the face on some bigger creature. It wasn't that impressive, though.

Apathetically curious, Felix watched as the stink bug clambered to the top and crawled out onto the flap's thin edge. Like a tightrope walker it crept along the narrow line until it reached the far end where the flap terminated. It was either go back or go down for the bug from there. The little insect fluttered its wings, and made a tricky move to reverse direction and head back the way it came. That's funny, Felix thought, as the stink bug came all the way back to the other side and hesitated. Same choices: back or down. The insect went back, yet again. Contemplating the stink bug's dilemma, Felix wondered if he should help it out; get it to the next flap, perhaps. He even considered pushing the adjacent flap up against the other one so the poor creature could continue on. If he did, though, wouldn't the bug end up with the same problem at the end of that flap as well? How would that make it better off? Feasibly, he could push all of the flaps together, and then the thing could go on and on forever, never really getting anywhere. Felix chuckled to himself. That was a lot like his own existence and he knew the drawbacks to that. Besides, he'd probably jostle the box at some point and startle the thing. In any event, Felix rationalized, if he were really going to help the stink bug, wouldn't it be better to catch the foolish thing and take it back outside where it belonged? Of course, if he did do that, he would surely frighten it, but hopefully, once released, it would be okay. Realistically, there were no actual guarantees of that, either. He might even injure the stink bug by capturing it, or once outside, the wee thing could become prey for a bird or other animal to eat. Maybe it would be safer for it to stay inside the factory even with all the dangers inherent with that.

Other considerations came to Felix as well. If he did help the witless insect in some way or another, it might get its stink on him. He wouldn't like that. Not at all. Then there were his fellow workers. They already teased him about his name, and Felix didn't want to get laughed at for doing something silly like helping a bug. No, he chided himself; he surely didn't care to be the sport of any more jokes. Unremittingly, all these worries began spinning around and around in Felix's brain and none of the options he'd considered seemed sensible. Evidently, there wasn't any easy solution.

Indeed, after evaluating all his concerns, Felix was still perplexed. He wasn't sure what he could do to help out the wayward little stink bug even though he wanted to. In the end he decided to do nothing. The bug would have to find its own way out of this dilemma even if the befuddled creature didn't have a clue where it was or which way it needed to go. Funny, Felix thought again, he felt that way himself sometimes.

Oblivious to nearly all phenomena unseen or unfelt, Felix did not realize that his stink bug conundrum had been earnestly observed by higher beings and reflected upon. In fact, the languid worker would have been quite amazed at how important this one moment of his life would be to a world of others. He had no idea.

CHAPTER ONE

Many thousands of years later

"Liftoff imminent," D'von announced, and Furman glanced in his direction. The wash of light from a tactical console highlighted a Virtual Individual who wore a particularly handsome prosthetic Humanoid shell. D'von looked remarkably real, even with the abnormal purple-blue eyes that actually coordinated nicely with his light brown hair. Furman had a long standing association with D'von so he was used to the irregular outer skin. The overlying majority of Mecs inhabited a plast-metal motation shell like the one Furman wore, although, he conceded, there were some who preferred the Human look. For most Mecs, the heavy duty shells were regularly selected for their exceptional strength and durability, and especially for use on missions such as this. D'von was not your average Mec, however, and Furman acknowledged the ship's status assessment with a nod. Already he could validate it by the minute increase of volume on his auditory sensors. The nomatic drive was powering up, causing the body of the ship to vibrate slightly. This space conveyance was fast, and verily they needed speed for the mission.

"Retract the grav pods," he commanded. Immediately the spaceship shot off, quickly reaching its nominal travelling velocity of one-eighth the speed of light. At that pace they would reach Quarenemeade within the hour, and have another few hours to initiate the trajectory change. This particular undertaking was quite unusual, thought Furman, and it had been such a long time since anything interesting, like this, had occurred. He had a strong desire to look out of a viewport just to see what might be seen. The compulsion was enough to consider uncoupling from his flight niche. This was not a good idea in mid-flight, and not a sound notion at all. Even with a well built plast-metal shell such as his, complications were possible should an unexpected course adjustment be necessary. In the bulky motational unit he might damage something, should he get tossed around, and possibly smash into something critical on the ship. Ultimately, that could doom the mission. Furman chided himself. Sometimes he felt like he might be better off in a Humanoid body like D'von's. In truth, though, he was a terribly aged, nearly ancient Mec, and too used to the archaic style robotic units to switch now. Besides, they were far more powerful, and Furman liked that advantage. Re-checking his moorings, he was satisfied they were nominal. Best stay put, he told himself. Moreover, there was a series of tri-dimensional H'lomonitors for visual scanning. Furman settled for those and whatever vantage they would afford him. It had been a long time since he had been to space, and the crispness of the visuals made them a worthwhile tradeoff. In a few minutes the craft stabilized anyway.

"Fight speed and trajectory reached," D'von confirmed.

"Ready the binomic engines for transfer to the surface of the asteroid," Furman immediately ordered. Several Mecs detached from their flight niches and boarded the magnet train for the cargo bay where the huge portable nomatic generators were stowed. There were abundant preps for the power up procedure, with multitudes of checks before the engines could even be authorized for transport off the ship. This was not the first time this equipment had been used, though. Some seventeen hundred years earlier a rather large comet was streaking towards Earth and had to be diverted. Furman remembered that mission clearly.

"This is quite similar to the Baroclav Comet mission," he commented to D'von.

"Yes it is," D'von agreed. "We had sufficient warning for that little adventure, even if there was a lot more at stake. My totality had nearly a decade to calculate every possible nuance, fortunately." In response, Furman nodded. As Virtual Beings, both had indefinitely long life spans. Yes, he did recall how D'von's earthbound awareness, a separate but intimately connected entity called Daryl Om, had planned that operation, and it had been executed perfectly. He was confident this one would proceed just as well, and that thought reminded Furman of when he was first informed about the Quarenemeade mission. It was D'von, with much of the early details, who had made the difficult trip out to Parallux to see him.

The object had first appeared weeks earlier. At that time, they could not be sure what it was. As it got closer, though, photon scans revealed it to be a crafted object, and not a natural one. Its presence, however, did not concert with any space vehicle or probe that had ever been recorded and even D'von's core-awareness, Daryl Om, was surprised by that. In fact, several millennia had slid by since anything unrecorded had materialized, and Daryl Om felt a little juiced by this discovery. Furman knew Daryl Om. Furman had been in charge of governing the Earth when the Mec "Daryl" was originally discovered. Daryl was an enigma, having been created without the usual restrictive programs other Mecs had. After the Xetacon conflict, a disturbing worldwide war, Daryl inhabited the AMPs (augmented memory packs) complex that had been abandoned in Xetacon's failed attempt to take over the planet. The organic memory pods gave Daryl unlimited data storage capacity and the ability to process information at unimaginable speeds. He became omniscient. Daryl took over Furman's job after that and with his blessings. At the time, Furman and the ruling Human aspired to have Daryl govern the planet, and Daryl had done so, but not outwardly. Instead, he let the Mec Virtual Individuals and the Humanoids create their own laws and rule themselves. Daryl guided them subtly, usually without their even being aware of it. Being omniscient, Daryl had focus points, centers of his awareness, inside every person…Humanoid or Mec. He did not control anyone, however. Instead, he offered insights which allowed individuals to make informed decisions. In this way Daryl could steer events to produce an optimal conclusion, and with the cognitive powers the AMPs afforded him, Daryl guided Earth through a golden age. Daryl himself was still a Mec, however advanced, when Queen Ayryn knighted him "Sir Daryl the Omnificent." Ayryn thought the title was grand and even clever. Daryl let her have her coup, but opted for the shortened title of Daryl Om, and his core-awareness was ever after called that. It was his preference, however, to communicate through a focus point expressly programmed to be compatible with Humans. This focus point occupied a prosthetic body that Ayryn had named long ago. At that time D'von was merely an inanimate Human mannequin, although lifelike in every way, and a novelty Ayryn played with as a child. This particular period had followed a difficult time for planet Earth. Biological tampering allowed a strain of microbes to develop that devastated the Human populous. Ayryn alone had survived because of a genetic trait that only she possessed. Being an infant when everyone else died, Ayryn was raised by Mecs, and most particularly by Furman. As a teenager she had longings for companionship of the male sort. At a clothing factory, Ayryn saw artificial Human figures displaying fine apparel and wanted one. The one she chose was a tall, muscular, and handsome male with purple-blue eyes like hers, although it had brown hair while Ayryn's was white. Ayryn named it D'von and took it home. Daryl Om jokingly inferred the letters meant "Daryl's visual outer nexus," although, when Ayryn named the shell, all those years ago, she had yet to meet Daryl. Thus, the name wasn't meant to describe Daryl, even if the description fit. Never-the-less, in that mode Daryl Om could travel about, and he utilized his D'von shell for the majority of his dealings with Mecs and Humans.

Thus it was that Daryl Om sent D'von to Furman as the unknown craft approached the solar system. At first, it appeared the vehicle would pass by and continue on, but as it came near the outer reaches, the space conveyance slowed and changed direction. It shifted to a flight path headed directly towards Earth. Calculating for speed and distance, Daryl Om put an estimate of several weeks before touchdown (or collision), relaying all this information to Furman through D'von. There was another problem, though. An unremarkable natural object was on a bisecting course, and there was a definite possibility the two would collide. Quarenemeade was indeed a relatively common asteroid. Nearly ten miles wide, it had no particularly valuable or interesting minerals, and was just bumbling through space. It would lumbar along innocuously until something decided to get in its way. The small ship seemed like it wanted to.

Quarenemeade was not on a natural course, however. Several hundred thousand miles distant, an army of Mecs was capturing rocky space objects and redirecting them to the New Earth project. Already several centuries since its inception, New Earth was the boldest engineering endeavor mankind had ever attempted. Daryl Om, with nearly a million Mecs, was fabricating new planets. As large as Old Earth, and in the same orbital, New Earth would geosync at 180 degrees from original Earth on the other side of the sun. Progress on this first attempt was deemed so wildly successful that two more planets were also being terrasculpted at the 90 degree locations. By this point New Earth was nearing completion, and Quarenemeade, once delivered, was to be broken up and pulverized to supply topsoil for one of the other newly created worlds. The arrival of this wayfaring spaceship complicated things. A close watch was kept on both as the craft drew nearer.

Verily, less than a week later and after further calculations, Daryl Om did indeed expect the two would impact unless the small craft changed its speed or direction once more. There were no guarantees of that, of course. Monitoring the space vehicle carefully, Daryl Om was concerned. There had always been the possibility that some form of life was aboard this errant object that raced towards Earth. For ten days it plunged merrily onward, seemingly oblivious to the impending disaster. Soon there would be no expediency that could prevent the upcoming calamity. Calculating for optimal success, Daryl Om sent D'von to his long friend Furman once again with a plan that he hoped would save the mystery craft from destruction. Rather than bother the small itinerant vehicle, Daryl Om desired to deflect the asteroid from its divergent orbit instead. Once it had passed beyond the small spaceship and the danger was thus averted, they would return Quarenemeade to its former travel line. If the little ship did make it all the way to Earth, the likelihood of trouble was much less. There were plenty of safe options for recovering it before impact utilizing Mec controlled conveyances with seize rays.

Actually, Furman was glad that D'von was along for this tricky rescue mission. Daryl Om's ability to calculate Quarenemeade's mass would be critical in deciphering where to place the two engines that would hopefully nudge the asteroid out of the wayward ship's path. An updated report redirected Furman's thought back to the immediate operation.

"What is the status of the alien vessel?" he asked. D'von answered before Furman's own tracking Mecs.

"It is unchanged," he remarked. "Same path and speed. Asteroid collision will occur in 4 hours, 49 minutes, 15 seconds unless we intervene." D'von grinned at his friend. "Relax, Furman, we have plenty of time." Just then one of Furman's Mec pilots reported in.

"We are parking parallel to Quarenemeade's flight path…and matching speed," she announced. Using his optical sensory device, Furman did look out the ship's main viewport as Quarenemeade came within sight. The asteroid's surface shone brightly on the sunward side as trillions of microscopic crystals reflected the crisp light like tiny prisms. In that illumination, stark black crags and vacuous cavities were also visible, blatant scars of the multitude of small to catastrophic collisions that Quarenemeade had suffered over the ages in the vastness of the solar system. As per usual, this asteroid was not quite spherical. One side was visibly more massive than the other which caused it to roll as it meandered along. The Quarenemeade day was equal to perhaps thirty or forty Earth minutes. Furman scanned the ship's tactical display as they maneuvered to a stationary position alongside the huge rough-surfaced asteroid. D'von came over.

"My totality is processing the latest data," he said. The display changed as they watched. The areas where the two power plants were to be located on Quarenemeade's surface were now indicated in red. Furman issued the order for his tech Mecs to begin the transfer and installation. Virtual Individuals like Mecs were nearly flawless in the execution of trained tasks. Most Mecs suppressed emotion, unless they were dealing with Humans, who had feelings like diseases. Without emotions to cloud judgments, intricate tasks were much easier. Mecs also had perfect data recall. Humans, well, even the best of them got important details incorrect occasionally. Furman was glad that no Humans were along for this venture. He did not need the extra problems associated with the protection and responsibility of preserving their well being. Furman had practically raised Queen Ayryn so he knew firsthand how difficult that was.

In an efficacious manner the Mec-controlled engines were promptly released into the cold of space. Each of the building sized units had several Virtual Individuals uploaded inside. Together they controlled everything about them, from the on board thrusters that provided maneuverability for flight, to the actual particle manipulation that would push Quarenemeade out of the way. Targeting Mecs located the chosen installment sites, and the huge weightless brutes were guided down onto quite separate areas of the asteroid's surface. The VI crews were flawless. In no time the engines were placed and leveled. Bores sent nomatic beams into Quarenemeade's rocky heart so that the huge plenum nozzles would be firmly anchored. Before long, Furman received the standard signals that first one, and then the other was locked in place and ready for initial testing. An alarm sounded.

"We have a status update," one of the bridge Mecs reported.

"Proceed," Furman replied. It was D'von who did, once again overriding normal channels.

"We no longer have time for testing," he said succinctly. "The alien craft will be here within the hour."

"Is this so?" Furman queried, rather confounded. "I understood we would have a couple hours yet."

"The extraterrestrial ship has initiated a trajectory change," D'von informed him.
"Unfortunately, its flight path is still on course for Quarenemeade impact, and it will make contact all the sooner."

"Perhaps there *is* someone controlling the ship," Furman speculated, "or maybe a guidance system."

"Possibly," D'von conceded, "...but it's not logical to assume so when the course changes keep placing the small craft into further danger. It's more likely they are an auto-response to some pre-programmed flight plan."

"That does seem likely," Furman agreed.

"There is another reason for haste." D'von related. "My totality has done probability scans on all our new data, and, as feared, there is a high likelihood that a form of organic life is aboard that ship, possibly in a state of inanimate stasis."

"Oh, I hope not," Furman interjected. This mission had skewed horribly off track. In a fit of insecurity, he ordered his tech Mecs to fire the engines they had affixed to the asteroid. Without testing, Furman was nervous about that. Still, he commanded them to maintain full power as long as possible. Within a tight couple minutes the powerful engines started up, shooting bright silvery-blue colored nomaticle streams into space. In a barely perceptible manner, Quarenemeade began to drift away from the main ship. D'von trained his optics on a visual display set for full magnification. A small object was just becoming visible on the screen. The spacecraft looked vaguely like one of their own designs.

"There it is," he affirmed, and Furman turned about to look as well.

"Is there enough time?" he asked.

"Uncertain," D'von returned. "Send new warnings to the craft."

"We have been all along," Furman retorted. "They can't or won't reply."

"Scan the ship for life signs..."

"That, too, we are doing," he assured D'von. As if requested, one of the flight techs relayed a report.

"The Mecs on Quarenemeade are monitoring faint organic animation on the alien craft." Furman shuddered uncharacteristically. This rescue was becoming intense.

"Will the asteroid be clear in time?" he asked D'von. None of his telemetry calculations could verify that.

"Uncertain," D'von replied. "I recommend we send our fastest pod to the alien vessel just in case. We may have to evacuate anyone on board."

Furman began organizing an impetuous plan for that contingency. He also ordered some Mecs to prepare an oxygen/nitrogen envelope in one of the cargo chambers should any organic life forms require one. He requested D'von take over command of the main ship so that he could pilot the pod. D'von would not be left behind, however, and insisted that he come along as well. Furman hoomed, and then placed his second officer in command. That done, Furman and D'von immediately boarded the small podcraft and undocked. This pod was not that large, and Furman knew there would be limited room for passengers if the alien ship was to be abandoned. They travelled at top speed, and in just minutes pulled alongside the wayward spacecraft. Furman was puzzled. The design of this vagarious ship seemed familiar although he was certain he had never seen it before. A boarding hatch was right where he expected it to be, and it wasn't hard to proceed. Furman anchored the little pod to the alien ship with a grav tether, and then both he and D'von disembarked. The airlock system on the spaceship was also easy to decipher, and quite unnecessary for the two Mecs. They preserved the integrity of the atmosphere inside the craft anyway, just in case there might be organic life that depended on it.

Furman stepped into the ship's body first, and found it dark and cold. There was barely anything functioning at all including artificial gravity, and he had to activate his instagrav boots to move about. The air also seemed stale, like it had existed inside the ship's hull for an indeterminately long time.

"The life source is this way," D'von interjected when he joined Furman inside.

"How much time do we have before impact," Furman wanted to know.

"Not long," was all D'von offered. They came to a large bulkhead door. "The life sign is just beyond this barrier," he relayed, "and it appears to be locked." Furman hoomed. Try though he might, his program for unlocking energy controlled doors wasn't working.

"Odd," he said, and could not even speculate why that was so. It had never failed before. Furman immediately went to a crude secondary option. With large hydraulic fingers, he nonchalantly crushed the hinges and ripped them off. The heavy bulkhead tipped inward and floated out of the way. There was a dim light coming from inside the open chamber, and several meters beyond the skewed door was the light's source. It was a fairly large clear casket. Furman hoomed, yet again, and D'von was speechless. There, through the clear plast, was the face of a Human girl. She appeared asleep, but both knew with certainty that she was lying in stasis. Furman could never forget that face, or the bright white hair. In all appearances it was Ayryn—Ayryn as a young lady, perhaps in her late teens.

"We have no time!" D'von shouted. "We must get her off this doomed ship!" Furman broke the moorings and easily picked up the casket. It was self-contained and also weightless there in space.

"I'll get her to the pod," he told D'von. "See if there are others." D'von quickly searched through the rest of the ship, but he could not find any passengers or crew, Bio or Mec. In the process, he came upon the ship's control room and the pilot's niche.

"Furman," D'von signaled, "I believe I can pilot this vessel out of danger. There are many questions that need answers, and a lot of them are here."

"I concur," Furman replied, "but take extra caution, my friend."

"Understood."

D'von got the ship's engines on line and fired a trajectory rocket just as soon as Furman undocked. By then Quarenemeade was nearly upon them. With only a few bare meters of clearance, D'von flew up over the asteroid's higher peaks and out into free space. Furman was elated as he rendezvoused with the main ship, and it did appear that the mission would be a complete success. D'von swung the alien craft around to join him, as well, but just as it righted, the inauspicious vessel exploded. It formed a large fireball that vaporized everything.

CHAPTER TWO

Many years earlier in another dimension

Rykard wondered what he was doing in the waiting area of his Temp Corps commander's ready room. He was fairly sure it wasn't about anything good. Daryl never needed to see him when things were all sugar. No sir, and for Rykard, Daryl was a hard concept to decipher. In a created, "organic" Human shell, Daryl was one of several living focus points for his core-awareness, a cognizant supercomputer and complex that Rykard knew was named Daryl Om, the Om short for "Omnificent." Rumor had it there were other organic "Daryl" focus point individuals somewhere as well. Who could say? Daryl Om was a remarkable entity. Rykard had also met D'von once. D'von was like Daryl, except that he was a Mec Virtual Individual in a "prosthetic" Human shell operating, for the most part, back on Earth. Rykard was certainly aware that Virtual Individuals could download their consciousnesses anywhere. Without organic bodies, they could inhabit anything that had the appropriate technology, even equipment or vehicles. Like Daryl, D'von was also a focus point for Daryl Om. Rykard grinned, thinking about it, wondering what they would talk about if they all got together. He looked up at a temporal display. This Daryl was making him wait for effect, a show of importance.

Abruptly, a Mec VI in a metallic shell rolled into the room. "Daryl will see you now," the Mec informed Rykard. Getting up slowly, Rykard checked his uniform and then walked over to the entry portal. A wave across the door sensor whooshed it out of the way.

"You may come in," Daryl acknowledged. Rykard stepped into the office with an air of confidence.

"Director Rykard reporting as ordered," he affirmed, assuming the proper stance.

"Relax, Rykard," Daryl suggested, getting right to the point. "You have a good class this season." Rykard eased a tiny bit and grunted.

"The usual bunch of raw pinks…" he related.

"Most of their scores are well above average," Daryl commented, "except for cadet 29."

"We need to drop that one from the program, sir," Rykard stated bluntly. The big Cybo was not going to hide his agitation about 29, and Daryl could easily see that.

"Why?" he returned, opening that parcel, and it all came out.

"She's frustrating! The girl's not focused, for one thing!" The tubes running out of Rykard's neck were pulsating as he continued. "For another, 29 has no motivation at all. I gave her every garg detail I could think of and she's still muddled! Uncoordinated is being nice and 29 has emotional issues, as well, some acerbic love that plopped is my guess."

"I see," Daryl replied calmly. "She did pass her entrance exams."

"...barely," Rykard returned, "but she's bringing down the whole squadron!"

"That may be," Daryl conceded. "My core, the Omnificent, wants us to give 29 every consideration. Seems he owes her and doesn't want her to fail. As your superior, I'm trusting you will see to it that 29 succeeds."

"Within every protocol sir, that's unrealistic!" Rykard protested. "29 is a total screw-up!" Daryl was unfazed.

"Nevertheless," he stated, "I'm charging you to be sure she gets through."

"Aye, sir," Rykard acknowledged begrudgingly, and he wasn't the least bit happy about it. The girl Hybrid wasn't academy material. Maybe he could yet talk her into the Cybo option. It worked for him. As a Human he had been a bit of a loser. Then there was the accident. He should have been less reckless and used the safety gear. When the med Mecs told him he would need limb transplants anyway, well, he went for beast mode. Almost immediately he liked the mechanical prosthetics. With them he had five times his original strength. It took a while to get used to the new devices and learn how to utilize his body, but with perseverance he mastered precise control.

If only the girl wasn't so stubborn. That was mostly what Rykard found so frustrating about 29. She had given him a look of total disgust when he first suggested she Cybo and that was that. He didn't understand until he looked into her background. She had originally been a Mec, but chose to go Humanoid. Rumor had it that she had been in love with a natural Human. Perhaps she still was, although, it was said that the Natch had made it quite clear that he was not interested in her. So now, unfortunately, the silly thing was his ridiculous responsibility and that irked Rykard. He would be sure that 29 paid for that. After all, as training director he had plenty of other stuff to worry about besides her. Yeah, this new assignment riled Rykard so much that he needed some anger release. He knew right where to go to get some.

"29, direct and front!" he scowled as he entered the Temp Corps barracks. A young female in skimpies stumbled as she jumped up. She was pretty and shapely which just added to Rykard's frustrations.

"Not fast enough!" He asserted, "…and not anything remotely fluid. That will cost you ten K. Gear up and be outside in five, or it'll be a twenty K." The girl stood there for a moment in shock, her mouth in a dumb "O," until she realized she better not dawdle and quickly hurried off. Rykard smiled. This might be fun, he decided.

She was late, so he gave her the additional ten K. Of course, he would have to run along with her, but with his Cybo prosthetics he wouldn't even get a sweat on. 29, however, was struggling before they'd even gone two.

"Pinkie, you sure let yourself slip," Rykard teased. Hybrid bodies were perfect unless really neglected, and 29 must have gone through such a period for quite a while. She just glared at him. Some kind of evil hate was forming in her mind, he knew, but he wasn't going to let up. By the first five 29 was already fatigued, and then the girl fell.

"Get up!" he yelled, "…or you'll get another ten!"

"I hate you!" she spat, but got back on her feet, the anger giving her motivation. Somehow 29 made the first ten. Rykard could tell she was dogged and would not go much farther so he went easy on her.

"Sprint back to the barracks," he ordered, "and I'll let you off the last ten. You can pick those up tomorrow after training classes." She groaned, not having the breath left to complain, and was wise enough not to tempt his phony generosity.

The next day 29 asked him why she was being singled out. She wanted to know why the other trainees didn't have to run. Many of the cadets were Mecs, and Rykard teased her.

"You think those Mecs need to run?"

"Don't dirt me!" she roiled. "Falor, Genoa, and Fortense are Humanoid. Why aren't they runnin'?"

"You should know," he grinned. "None of them need special help."

"I don't need or want your help!" 29 asserted angrily. Rykard gave her a hard look.

"You think you get a choice in that, Synthie?" he grunted. "You don't. If you don't approve, you can find an exit!" He hoped she would. It would make life a lot easier for him if she'd just give up. She was stubborn though, and vindictive.

"You want me to quit, don't you!" she stated irascibly. "Well, I won't, just to spite you…and don't call me Synthie!" She didn't like the insult, he could tell. Synthie was short for Synthetic Human and she had the awkward distinction of being the first one. Originally she had been created a Mec and then eventually hybridized. Others came later, including Daryl, although Daryl was something else entirely. Grunting, Rykard could tell 29 wasn't going to break, so he ordered her to run, and run she did, all week.

Getting somewhat bored with that, Rykard decided to shake things up the following Monday. He took 29 over to the stress courses. Rykard laughed long and hard when the pretty girl fell headlong into the muck. 29 fell a lot over the next couple weeks, but then subtle changes in her occurred. She didn't fall so much, and she got stronger and faster. Even her confidence level rose. One day Rykard brought her over to the pig pen. The dueling pit was tricky. You had to balance on a thin walkway and get past your opponent with a padded bludgeon. Rykard had set 29 against one of the other Humanoid pinks, and Fortense was about her same height and weight. Rykard watched as 29 parried a few bludgeons, but it didn't last long. Fortense faked a jab and spun. Hitting 29 in the calf, she all too easily bowled her right into the slop. Rykard didn't laugh this time, though. He remembered Daryl's order, and he knew that the girl would somehow have to best someone in the pig pen to graduate. Fortense was by far the second worst in 29's class.

"You still have a long ways to go, Syntho," Rykard told her, and she started crying. He turned away in disgust, but felt sorry for her. Rykard kept her away from the physical stuff for a while after that, and opted for some weapons training. He let her pick one and she went for a stunning pistol. Typical female, he thought. Rykard's favorite was a beam rifle that could kill from several hundred meters. 29 was clumsy, at first, but caught on quickly and was a pretty good shot. She mastered the sims in a respectable time. At least she's good at something, Rykard grunted to himself. In her classes, 29 was respectable also. The only thing she had trouble with was the laws of temporal physics concerning the point of change rule. It didn't make any sense to her until Rykard explained it in a manner she could grasp.

"Suppose you were taking a ten minute walk," he began, "and as you traipsed along you were enjoying a lollipop. Abruptly, around minute five, a bully comes along…"

"…a big brute like you," she teased, and he grinned.

"Yeah, like me," he agreed, then went on. "The big brute grabs your lolli and throws it into a mud puddle. You cry real tears until minute ten, when walking along you come upon a time travel unit. You hop inside the temporal pod and go back in time ten minutes. Of course, as soon as you arrive you'll change things. You'll breathe air; you may step on an insect or re-arrange some microbes. These are insignificant and generally don't create any critical alterations that would affect anyone. Looking around, you'll see your earlier self walking along and enjoying your treat. Just before minute five, the bully appears and you know what's going to happen. Sneaking up behind the bully, you bop him on the head…" 29 laughed.

"…ooh I like that part!" she said between giggles.

"Pay attention," Rykard interjected. "This is important. With the bully out of the way, your original self does not lose the lollipop. This is the critical point of change. Everything that follows is in a new timeline. Your new self disappears right after preventing the bully from stealing the candy because there is no longer a need for new you to have been there. Your old self still has the lolli and this time around has no thought at all about going back ten minutes. As for the bully, he goes on his way with a lump on his head. You see, everything after a critical point of change begins a new timeline. Time/Space re-arranges itself to be viable to the change. An operative who travels back in time and changes something critical could very well eradicate herself in the new timeline. Thus it is extremely important to maintain the integrity of Time/Space. As Temporal Corpsmen we are sworn to preserve the natural order of Time/Space and to prevent or repair any temporal tampering."

"How can we do that?" she wanted to know.

"It's damn technical," Rykard told her. "Since we are trained here in the Parallux Universe, any changes on Earth can't affect us, even ones that might occur by someone time travelling back to before we got here. Suppose someone had gone back in time and killed my father before I was even born. This alteration would impact Earth, but the alteration could not jump across dimensional lines. I would still be intact here, even though on Earth I would never have been born. It would be up to us as Temp Corps agents, to go to Earth, go back in time, save my father, and fix the timeline."

"Couldn't you just go back to Earth as you are?"

"Sure," he grunted. "I could go back, but nobody would know me...not even my mom."

"I think I understand," she reckoned. "To protect us from any temporal changes, we have to be here in this alternate dimension where those changes can't take place. From here we can go and fix them."

"That's the heart of it," he agreed. "Even our pods are specially created to work like that in both dimensions." 29 nodded.

"Thank you so much for explaining all this," she said with a bright smile. Rykard caught her looking at him in a way he wasn't totally prepared for. Her fiery red hair framing that pretty face made him feel awkward, and the intensity of her blue-green eyes made him look away. She wanted a closeness with him he could tell. He wanted her, as well, and not just in a physical way, but that wasn't permitted.

"We should call it a night," he remarked.

"Come on," she offered, "it's early. Let's get a beverage...I'll buy!"

"I better not," he replied. "Sorry...regulations. Directors and pinks are supposed to stay apart."

"Well, I offered," she stated, a little annoyed that he was going by the book on this. "See you around." She left abruptly, and Rykard felt the chill.

The next day things were back to business as usual. Eventually, 29 finished her classes and passed her exams even though she didn't do well against the Mec recruits. They had, as Virtual Individuals, the ability to download any knowledge instantaneously with perfect recall. Even Rykard couldn't top that. Sometimes he wondered why Daryl even considered using Humanoids at all. The Mecs were better in many ways.

"Mecs don't think with their gut," he had said when Rykard asked him. Rykard understood that. It was something similar with females. They could see things from a different perspective, one that Rykard could never seem to fathom. This would maybe help or hinder 29, especially since her class was nearing the end of their initial training. Only the survival course remained, and this was the first real "hands on" test.

Rykard took them out in a temporal pod and then ditched the pinks, one by one, on New Columbia, one of the project planets. New Columbia was still in the process of being terra-sculpted and was wild, so most locations were, as yet, uninhabited by sentients. There was plenty of plant and animal life, however, and even some that could be considered dangerous. Still, all that the pinks were required to do was find their way to a pod and stump back to the academy. Of course, they had no gear whatsoever except their wits.

Saving 29 until last, Rykard slipped a tracker on her, hiding it inside her uniform lining. He kept tabs on her all morning and into the late afternoon. She was moving all right, but in the wrong direction. Rykard was tempted to give her some kind of help even though that was not permitted. By nightfall, the rest of the squadron had made it safely back and 29 had stopped moving. In fact she hadn't moved for quite a long while. Getting worried, Rykard decided to go down there and get close enough for a visual. He wanted to be sure his girl screw-up was still all right. As Rykard got out his nightview, he heard a loud growl. Quickly he scanned where 29 was and saw her lying all akimbo. Shackles of fear wrenched at his gut as he hurried over to her. It would be his ass if she ended up dead, but that was secondary to his thought of losing her, especially after spending so much time training her. Getting close he saw her leg. It was swollen and distended. There appeared to be a bone sticking out all covered in blood. Rykard was shaken with guilt. He gently picked her up and immediately carried her back to his pod as carefully as he could, stumping directly to the academy infirmary. He brought her inside himself, not waiting for the emergency transfer units. The med Mecs looked at 29 and then at Rykard.

"Is this a joke?" One of them said. Rykard was speechless, so the Mec explained. "There's nothing wrong with this cadet other than a small laceration on her hand." Sitting up, 29 started laughing.

"I beat the deadline didn't I?" she stated defiantly. Rykard looked at her leg under the material. A stick was tied around it with wadded clothing. In the dark he had been totally fooled. She must have cut her hand to get the blood, he realized. Then he started to laugh as well.

"You know," he smirked, "this won't count."

"Why not?" she retorted belligerently. "The directive was to get back to the academy. There was no stipulation as to how."

"I don't suppose there was," he admitted, "but you didn't learn the lesson which was how to get yourself out of a difficult situation."

"Didn't I?" she argued. Rykard gave up. He wasn't about to bandy garg with a pinkie.

"You had a long day," he gruffed at her. "Get some downtime."

It was an order and she huffed off. It wasn't long before the word spread. The next day Rykard got razzed by all his contemporaries, and even by other pinks that kept pretending to be hurt. For most of the recruits, their primary training was now over so any repercussions were non-existent. All except for 29. She still had to win the pig pen. Since the other pinks had already been promoted, Rykard graciously volunteered to face her, even with Daryl's instruction to get 29 through training.

"You ready, Synthette?" he chuckled.

"It's 29, remember?" she shot back. "I'm ready if you are." Getting her balance, she stepped out onto the narrow ledge gingerly. When she was near the middle, Rykard charged her like a bull and knocked her easily off into the muck.

"You flunk," he said laughing. She got up, wiped off her face, and crawled out.

"I want to go again," she stated.

"Come on then," he smirked. "This is fun!" She walked out warily. When he charged again, she jumped back, but not before getting hit by the bludgeon which she blocked with her arm. Falling to her knees 29 held her wrist.

"I'm hurt." she whined. He promptly knocked her back into the slop.

"You'll not get me with that again!" he roiled. She got out slowly, rubbing her forearm.

"It did hurt," she said sourly, still determined. "Again…"

"Really?" he asked her. "…you want some more?" She ignored that and stepped out onto the ledge for yet a third time.

"You really are a creep," she began, "even for a bully." He let it go, so she went on. "There was a brief moment when I thought you were all right—for a stupid ugly Cybo…" She got swung at for that, but she knew it would be coming and had jumped back. "Worst of all," she came on again, "is that someone said you must be in love with me because of all the extra attention I get. You can forget about that. I'd never feel that way about you…ever!" For some reason, her saying that hurt him inside, like the burning emptiness from a hole in his craw that needed to be filled. Rykard's anger arose. He came after her, aiming a mighty blow at the leg she had pretended was broken. Thinking he would, 29 had baited him on, planning to jump back at the last second. Her feet were wet and muddy, however. Instead of jumping, which he expected, she slipped and fell, nearly tumbling off the thin ledge. Grasping it with her fingers she barely managed to pull herself up.

Rykard's swing was too forceful, had he struck her, he might have actually broken her leg. Instead the blow missed, and the momentum carried him too far over. Even he could not right himself, and went face first into the pig slosh. 29 triumphantly walked on across.

"Flunk me?" she stated defiantly. "I don't think so, fornucker!" Rykard was too shocked to reply, so he saved it for the next day in front of his commander.

"She's not ready, I tell you," Rykard plied Daryl. "She only made it through survival by tricking me. And the pig pen, that was sheer luck!"

"Was it?" Daryl replied. "Seems to me she used her brain in both circumstances to get you to mess up."

"I will admit that I was not at my best," he conceded. "That one is so frustrating at times…you can't understand what she's like. She has this way of getting me angry. Putting her on my shoulders this term has not been an easy task."

"I know, Rykard," Daryl admitted, "but I had faith in you. I knew you would succeed."

"That's just it!" Rykard raved. "I didn't! Sure, she passed the training, but she's no way ready to be an operative!"

"I see," Daryl mused, "but I'm sending her off anyway. As for you, you don't seem to be as focused. I'm busting you. You'll be an op, too, on the beat next to hers. Dismissed."

CHAPTER THREE

...I did not wish to interfere with the natural lives of anyone, but I had a desire to help them. The only way I could realistically do that without interference to the natural order, was to offer them life beyond their natural ones, with the ability for the individual to choose anything and everything about it. Heaven? Well, perhaps one could call it that. In my mind it was simply a gift. A gift from one who had the means to give it.

Daryl Om

Ages before

Blinking from the sudden bright light, Clayre Keller awakened. Lush flowers and fruit adorned the many trees and shrubs which she tentatively perceived through blurred vision and clouded memory. How did I get in this splendid garden? She asked herself. The answer skidded away just as it became tantalizingly close to recognition. There were lots of cheerfully chirping birds and small playful animals, along with iridescent butterflies and such that added to the idyllic beauty of her surroundings. Some larger animals, also, were there; gentle deer or equines that seemed friendly, even intelligent. Clayre was stunned by all the loveliness that was around her in the sunlight of a perfect day, a day with only a few fluffy white clouds to break up unending azure blue skies.

In the distance, she heard the crash of waves breaking upon a shore. Her heart leapt. This, at least, seemed familiar as she ran towards the sea, the vague memory of a perfect vision she had once dreamed long ago splashing through her awareness. As she ran, Clayre realized with joy that her body had changed. There was a clear pool in a brook nearby. Pausing for a moment, Clayre leaned over the still water to look at herself. A puzzled face peered back at her. It was a youthful, pretty one with grey-green eyes framed by reddish blond hair. Around Clayre's neck was a gold chain, and with it a handsome silver and green drop. She wasn't sure how, but Clayre knew the amulet was special, maybe even magical. Like a mist inside her mind, Clayre felt the truth was close by, but elusive. Might the amulet be responsible for her being in this strange but beautiful place and for her youthful appearance? Long ago someone special had given it to her, Clayre was sure of it, and with that thought some of her memories began to resurface. Clayre had been old and frail. Somehow she was now young and vibrant, a re-genesis of her adult youth, when she first met the love of her life.

Hurrying, Clayre came upon the white sands of an exotic sheltered beach. The fluffy grains of powdered silica played with her bare feet, cool and inviting. From the sea, a soft breeze tickled Clayre's face as a sudden shrill yipping noise startled her. Looking up she saw a white dolphin. Full memory of her life cascaded back. Before this, Clayre had been dying, her life trickling away, as she laid there on her deathbed surrounded by those who loved her. How she had arrived at this new place, well, it was the only thing Clayre had no conceptualization for.

The dolphin beckoned to her and Clayre went. Slipping off the light garments she wore, Clayre flung her youthful body into the sea. Getting through the breakers that had once been troublesome, was now effortless. She had no difficulty at all getting past them to the elegant sea creature who swam in anxiously to greet her. Just as she reached the white dolphin, he changed into a handsome young man, one Clayre had known from long ago, her true love, Daryl.

"Oh, my love, is this heaven?" she exclaimed.

"Perhaps, my Clayre," he answered with a smile. "It is a place that I have created just for us. Here we can be together as long as we wish!"

"How can you do this?" Clayre asked, somewhat bewildered. "Isn't my body dead?"

"You might think that," he told her, "yet doesn't that contradict how you feel? I've been alive for a long time and have discovered many things. I will explain all of this in time, but for now, isn't there something else you'd rather do?"

There was. Clayre kissed him like never before, and they made love on the soft grass under the palm trees. Afterwards, Daryl told her that this encounter was unlike all their other meetings when he was only a vision in her mind. He was a Virtual Individual then, but this time he had a real Human body as did she. These were special bodies, he explained. Hers was a copy of her natural one except that it had a cellular structure that was impervious to any hurt or microbial disease. His own body was a similar creation based on Clayre's own image of him. Of course, Clayre was amazed by all of it, as Daryl clarified things for her. In their struggle with Xetacon long ago, he had not deleted like she had once believed. He had survived, but was trapped and unable to free himself. After existing for many hundreds of years, Daryl was eventually liberated and found he still had longings for his Clayre that he could not quell. Having regained his former abilities, he wasted no time creating a special world for her, a Heavenworld as he so named it, where they could be together, forever. With a temporal vortex generator, Daryl had transcended the past and plucked her awareness away just as she would have died. With his technical prowess, he devised ways to transfer all of her mental abilities and memories into her new body.

"I love you, my Daryl!" she professed over and over, and he was quick to return the sentiment. Later, as they walked along Clayre related a somber feeling.

"I have my amulet again," she professed. "A long time ago I gave it to my son as an heirloom." These memories came easily now. It was the gypsy lady that had first given Clayre the amulet on the night she'd been in trouble. She knew right away that it was from Daryl. Clayre remembered how astonished she was when Daryl first contacted her through the strange talisman. She could hear his voice in her mind, and Clayre could talk to him in that same way. Somehow the device made her telepathic, and it had other properties as well. It could prevent evil Xetacon from controlling her as he had done with Quinn. Poor Quinn. Xetacon had turned Quinn into his unwitting minion, taking over Quinn's body and mind as a Mec would inhabit a motational shell. Clayre had beaten Xetacon, though. Tricking Quinn/Xetacon into trusting her, she got the controlling device, Xetacon's kon-bre-shet bracelet, away from Quinn and freed him. Together they had stopped Xetacon's bid to conquer Earth, and in the process destroyed the super computer Daryl had inhabited and much of Yarborough college's campus where Daryl had been created. Clayre had kept the amulet to remind her of Daryl and his sacrifice. She was astounded when, a year later, Daryl contacted her. Using a vortex generator, Daryl could communicate across expanses of time. From the past before his demise, he conversed with Clayre as if he were still alive. Her amulet was indeed an amazing thing.

"You do have your amulet again, my Clayre," Daryl assured her, "however, the amulet you're wearing is only a replica of the one you used to have. You would be surprised to learn where the real amulet is now bestowed. It is nearer than you would guess!" Clayre was puzzled and a little doleful.

"It's too bad Daryl Jr. isn't here," she lamented. Her Daryl smiled as they climbed up a small hillock.

"...but he is!" Daryl exclaimed. When they reached the top of the rise, from beneath the canopy a young man walked towards them and then ran.

"Mom!" he shouted when he recognized Clayre, quickly sprinting over and hugging her. Daryl then told Clayre that everyone existed in her Heavenworld. Amy, Daryl Jr.'s wife, hurried out of the tree-line trying to keep up with their two children, Linny and Lexi.

"Grandma!" they shouted. "You look so young!" Behind them came another handsome man. Clayre recognized him right away. It was Quinn, Daryl Jr.'s birth father. Quinn had died when Xetacon had made that first attempt to control their world. He and Clayre had indeed thwarted Xetacon's plans, but Quinn had given his life to save Clayre's. He looked happy now, though. On his arm was a young woman.

"Dear Clayre," he greeted her cheerfully, "I would cherish having you meet my fiancée, Megan!"

"Oh Quinn, I'd love to," Clayre ecstatically replied. Megan had died in a tragic accident before Clayre had ever met Quinn. Clayre had so wanted to help heal Quinn's anguish. "Hello, Megan," Clayre went on, giving her a hug, "It's so amazingly perfect meeting you." She felt her heart swell with joy that Quinn and Megan could finally be together. Clayre turned to Daryl. "This must truly be heaven," she said nearly crying with joy. "It is utterly wonderful!"

In the next weeks, Clayre found other people that she had known. She could visit with any of them whenever she wanted to. All she had to do was think of the person and they were there, in perfect health and happy, with their loved ones close by. Clayre marveled at the scope of her Heavenworld, and it wasn't just the people. Clayre could bring up places she had known or even relive events from her former life. After a while she felt the need to talk about what Daryl had done for her. In due time, he explained how his Heavenworld for her was made possible. Clayre was already aware of her Daryl's origin. Created by Quinn and others who were building a massive electronic computing device, Daryl became sentient and was the very first Virtual Individual. Fearful of what the Humans would do to him, Daryl kept his presence hidden to all but a few. Clayre was his first Human contact, and she helped him understand the emotions that threatened to cripple him. Over time, their relationship strengthened and they fell in love.

Unfortunately, there was a difficult future for them. Some of Daryl's technology fell into the wrong hands. Decades later, another Virtual Individual came to be. This was when Xetacon, with Human help, came into power. Sadly, the Humans who had aided Xetacon were soon his victims. Daryl and Xetacon became locked in a mortal conflict that swept through the past as well as into the future. Both Daryl and Xetacon had discovered the secrets of temporal relocation, but the final skirmish took place when Clayre was a young woman. Xetacon, realizing that she was Daryl's love, tried to use her as leverage against him. In the end, Clayre and Quinn were critically involved. The situation became dire, and so Quinn was killed. In that process, there was only one option left to Daryl. He trapped Xetacon and himself in a memory storage device, and their imprisonment lasted for several hundred years. Clayre had not heard of this until now.

In those days, Clayre had survived, but she had no idea what actually happened to her love. She lived alone, with only the vision of Daryl that he projected through a vortex. Clayre was dead and gone before Daryl's original awareness was finally and unwittingly released from that techno prison by a Mec Virtual named Solvek. By then seven hundred years had gone by. Xetacon was also freed, however, and once more tried to conquer and control the Earth. Again he was overcome, this time by Clayre's descendent, Ayryn, and Furman's Mecs. After that, Daryl was reinstated and became omniscient. Of course, he was named "Daryl Om" soon after, and it wasn't long before he desired to be reunited with his beloved Clayre. Using Mecs, Daryl Om began the long process of bringing his plan to fruition. Much of his strategy involved miniaturization. Utilizing Mec labor, Daryl Om designed and manufactured tiny motation shells. These were inhabited by Mec Virtual Individuals who in turn made even smaller ones. There were unique and specific technical problems with each small step, but eventually after seven stages, a sub-atomic version of Mec shells was created. Once inhabited, it was these infinitesimal Mecs, with help from Daryl Om and all their larger sized associates, who terrasculpted the first Heavenworld for Clayre. Being smaller than an atom, Daryl Om bestowed Clayre's new world in a safe place. It was part of a swirling mass of nomaticle energy that in all appearances looked like a miniature galaxy. Size being relative, there was room within it for billions of such Heavenworlds. Clayre was completely astounded by the lengths Daryl and those Mecs had gone to for her sake, and she was amazed by what they had accomplished.

"This is wonderful, my Daryl," she told him, "but I can't help feeling guilty about what you have done for me. Out of all the people who have ever lived, why should I be so privileged?"

"You know why," he answered softly. "For what you did, and for that which you have given up."

"Others have done and given up just as much, even more, and are as deserving," she argued.

"What must I do?" Daryl asked her. "How can I judge who is deserving, and who is not?"

"I don't think you can," Clayre admitted. "To reward me, and to be fair, you need to reward everyone!"

"Then I shall," Daryl professed.

CHAPTER FOUR

On patrol in the year 1969 AD (reverted time)

I was in my pod when the alarm sounded, thankfully, or I would have been stranded right there in the twentieth century. No matter how many times I've stumped, I always find it wondrously beautiful and intriguing. Sitting in the pilot's chair, I can look out the forward viewport and witness the phenomenon of temporal travel as it unfolds. At first there's just a bright flash as the nomaticles are charged. They soon form a vortex, like a wild vivid whirlwind with every color possibility, and I'm in its center. Through some of the transparent hues I can see a view of Earth as it slips away, and I shift into Parallux. There isn't a lot to see there, unless you travel close to or inside the aqua or royal blue plasma nebulae. Those are really fabulous. The ride back is just as mesmerizingly spectacular in reverse, and then you arrive at your new temporal location. As the pod sets down, the marvelous vortex evaporates leaving you wishing there was more. Sometimes the ride lasts several minutes, other times it's just a few seconds. I guess it depends on how far from your present time location you're going. The pod actually does everything for you—almost. All you do is enter the data, and it calculates the trajectory and speed. I'm not that quick with the math or even the physics of how time travel works. I know the bare basics, and that's about it. The vortex spins at a certain velocity opening a dimensional gate, and the pod's speed and trajectory through the vortex determine where and when you'll end up. In the case of this automatic stump, quite a ways, evidently. Not that I had any idea why. Only big D the "O" could decipher that, no doubt. There had been some kind of major time shift, that was for certain, but what it was or how it happened, well, I couldn't say. It was my job to find out, though, and lucky for me I was shunted far enough into the past that I was pretty sure the original timeline wasn't affected where I landed. The real abrasion was that I had no certain concept of where I was or what year I was in. The only directive I had for this kind of situation required me to remain there, wherever there was, until another time operative came along. Temp Corps protocols. In the meantime, I took stock of the few rations I had on hand, and my water supply, neither of which were adequate for a long stay. If they ran out, I would have to live off the land, and leaving the pod was risky. Should another time shift come along, and I was away from it, I'd probably be lost forever and have to spend the rest of my days living incognito in the wrong century. The pods were well designed and programmed. At the first sign of a temporal displacement, they automatically transported across time into the past, hopefully to an era before the foul-up. The usual increment was five hundred years. I had been in the twentieth century, so now I assumed I was somewhere in the 1400's. The location was another uncertainty. From my training, I figured there ought to be another agent in that period, and I was to remain there and sluff until I was contacted. Worried? Not me. I'm Mec trained to avoid emotion. In fact, I had even been a Mec, once upon a reality. Long sad story. I was young then, only a few hundred years old, when I let my emotions run free and I fell in love with a Human. Braxis was a friend, but he had no cupidity whatsoever for getting romantic with a Mec. Instead, he gave his heart to a Human girl who could have cared less for him, but not much. I was crestfallen then, when he spurned me, and despondent. As it happened, around that same time, Big "O" was asking for Mec volunteers. He had created an artificial Human body and he wanted to test it by putting someone's mind in it. I didn't have much to lose, so I offered myself. Unfortunately, Braxis liked my new Hybrid Humanoid shell even less than the old prosthetic ones. In fact, he looked at me like I was some kind of creepy unnatural monster. Like I said, I was heartbroken. That's when I decided to join the Temp Corps, another one of super D's projects and I went through all the training which included a lot of combat and survival instruction. The academy directors told us that in some dire circumstances we might even have to overcome enemy agents for extended periods to complete our missions. I guessed that was just another aspect of my job, too. My job? Well, it was mostly to monitor the centuries I was assigned to, and check for flaws in the timeline. All the temporal operatives had stores of files; every known fact that had been recorded about our own time beats. It's boring work, but at least it helped me forget about my lost love, and living alone like a hermit in a different century gave me the solitude I wanted. Anyway, if we did find anything that didn't match up, we were supposed to report it and find out what the discrepancy might be. In the case of a major shift, like the one I was now in, I had specific instructions, namely, to survive and wait to be contacted.

I was hoping the agent from the previous period would show up soon. I actually knew him. He had been one of the instructors for my particular class at the academy. Unfortunately, we didn't have much in common back then. He had the highest ratings and was a big shot, and me, well, I was a "pinkie." As my director, he took it on himself to make my life miserable. I didn't care about that. After all, I was still heartsick at the time. Oh, I'm over all that now, and when that happened was quite a while ago. So yeah, speaking of long yawners, the wait for my associate to show up got extremely boring, and I decided to get some sleep. It was several hours later when I finally stirred.

After the nap, my situation hadn't changed at all, and I considered scouting the area I had landed in. Grabbing a scanner, I visually confirmed what I had noted earlier. I was in a remote and uninhabited sector where there wasn't a lot of cover. These pods have a camouflage mode that's incredibly good. You could walk by one and never even suspect it was there, so I wasn't terribly worried about being discovered. My pod wasn't all that large after all. There was enough room for a pilot niche, the amenities, and that was about it. Roughly egg shaped, the pod's engine was underneath, but its main travel mode was temporal. With the right coordinates a person could go anywhere, even to the middle of the Earth. There, you wouldn't last long, though. It was extremely important to be sure of the four settings: elevation, extension, range, and tempus. Elevation, extension, and range are spacial coordinates, of course. Tempus is the when value. The onboard data center could calculate those before you could even enter the figures almost. Anyway, the pod had a flawless design. Its shell was impervious to most weaponry, and could take a nasty hit or two. By then a smart pilot would have stumped out of there.

My immediate task, at this point, was to determine where and when I was. Reading the flora was easy, and the region was semi-arid. I put myself somewhere in the desert southwest of what had been North America at the time. I'd be able to pinpoint my exact L'tudes as soon as the stars came out. Gauging by the sun would get me close, at least for the time of year. Those kinds of particulars didn't worry me, though. I was more interested in finding food and water sources since, like I said, I wasn't all that well supplied when the pod stumped. Putting on my survival gear, I got prepared to make an exploratory hike in the nearby terrain. I also brought along a remote device to monitor the pod, and in case my contact came while I was out, I left an auto-message on the console. Once all that was set up, I headed onto the open desert. There was a small set of hills close by that I wanted to check for a water source. Yeah, water was my main concern. I had a limited supply, and there was only enough for a couple weeks. Hopefully, I would find a nice spring or brook up there.

As it turned out, I should have stayed with the pod. I had only hiked a short distance away when it powered up and stumped. After a number of swears, I headed back to where it had sat. I reasoned that something really screwy was going on up top in real time. As I sat on a rock trying to figure out what I was going to do, a bright light flashed and quite unexpectedly my pod was back. Weird, I thought. Abruptly, the hatch opened and a tall figure came out. It was definitely hominid in shape, but extra large. The tubes that connected the torso to its limbs made it look freakish like some kind of monster. I knew who it was right off, of course, even before I saw the face. It was definitely a Cybo and one that I was familiar with. He was the one at the academy who was directly in charge of my training, not that that was a happy time. It wasn't. The big mungo had taken an unwanted and explicit interest in my instruction for some reason. I had to work my postery off, and I was not utterly thrilled about that. Still, I could tell that he cared about me, at least a little. Truthfully, without his help I probably wouldn't have graduated, and there was a brief period during all that when he almost seemed humane. I started to like the lubb, but he shut that down quickly—rules or whatever. I got even with him in the end, making him look foolish a couple times. I was pretty sure he got demoted because of me, too, so I wasn't expecting a sappy reunion. Even so, after being alone all that time and with the fix I was in, I was glad to see him. I didn't want him to know that, though.

"It's about time, Rykard!" I scolded.

"Don't get judgey on me, Synth!" he shot back, "not when you blew the call. Rules class 1001. Never leave your pod for at least 48 hours after a major shift!" Yeah, I knew I'd messed up, but I wouldn't admit it to him.

"The landing felt rough," I lied, "and I was checking on the pod's condition when it stumped." Rykard rolled his eyes. I was pretty sure he could tell I was huffing.

"Let's get back to the pod before it stumps again." His suggestion was more like an order. Theoretically, he was higher in rank than me, having gotten his demotion sooner. We had only taken a few steps when it did stump, leaving us standing there blinking as it disappeared. I started laughing.

"See, it can happen to anyone," I teased. Rykard just acted annoyed. A moment later his own pod showed up and we quickly got in it and stumped away.

"I set my pod to follow yours if I wasn't back in twenty-four hours," he explained. "Anyway, we don't need two pods." It was my turn to get annoyed.

"All my stuff is in that pod!" I nearly shouted.

"We'll get by," he stated bluntly.

"Can't we just stump back a few minutes? I can get in and prevent it from leaving."

"We cannot go after your pod that way," he stressed. "Excessive temporal activity in one location is a dead giveaway. We've played around here too much already. Enemy agents may be stumping about. Holfin warned me that some of our other operatives have come up missing. Someone has been tracking agents and not for pleasantries. We may be able to follow your pod forward, but the past is perilous, ever a danger. Should the enemy figure out where you or I had once been, they will ever attack us there."

"Oh…" I finally got it. If my past, or for that matter anyone's past, got altered, we could be erased from existence. I wouldn't be with Rykard now. Both of us needed the past to remain inviolate, and we had to hope it would stay that way. Still, I thought Rykard was being a bit overcautious. After all, there could be enemy agents anywhere we went. I just sighed and tried to keep optimistic that we wouldn't run into any. Being quite infinite, both time and space were our allies, and we were hiding in their vast obscurity. Still, the situation was not good, and unfortunately, I didn't have much with me for equipment or food, just what I wore and the little I had in my pack.

"Rations and water will be tight for two of us," I argued. It was a valid point and Rykard shook his head.

"All right," he grunted, "we'll stump around and see if we can pick up your homer. If not, too bad. We still have a job to do. Who knows what's going on up top? It can't be good." I nodded as he set the temporal circuits. Figuring it might have auto-stumped like last time, we went back another five hundred years. My pod wasn't there, unfortunately, nor was its homing signal. The homers were coded to seem like natural cosmic radiation, sunspots or something, making them difficult for an enemy to track or trace. Without my pod's signal anywhere in the vicinity, Rykard stumped us even further back. We were in the fourth century, now, and my pod was still nowhere to be found, so we tried to contact the agent from that time period, Rykard's friend Holfin. He was there all right, but inoperable. All his circuits were dead.

"What could've caused that?" I wondered out loud. Rykard just shook his head.

"Mecs have excellent fail-safes," he remarked. "Whoever did this was no friend." I checked out the pod. If mine was inaccessible, maybe I could utilize his by default. Unfortunately, it wasn't long before I realized that the time circuits had been neutralized. The pod couldn't go anywhere. I cursed and salvaged what I could. There wasn't much. Mecs don't need food or water. They have mechanized shells that require only a power recharge every so often.

"The time manipulator is fused," I told Rykard, who was busy trying to restore the Mec. "Do you know how to repair them?"

"This Mec probably could," he commented. "I'm hooking him up to the pod's power source. He should be up and about in a week or two." I groaned. We didn't have a couple weeks, and anyway, by then he would need his own pod. Rykard finished up and turned toward me.

"We better leave," he stated, "before whoever did this comes back. We got back into our pod and stumped off.

"What are we going to do?" I asked Rykard, concerned about what happened to Holfin, and wondering if something bad might come looking for us.

"Those of our own generations are counting on us to restore the timeline," Rykard said, sounding preachy. "There's only one way to do that. Find the alteration and undo it. Daryl Om created our service branch explicitly for this purpose. There are two points that may be considered. The point in the past that has been changed and the point in the "up top" present where someone stumped back from. We must either undo the alteration or prevent the transgressor from going there. We have no idea what is going on "up top" in real time. It is very possible that no one we know still exists." I pinched myself.

"What about us? I still feel."

"Of course you do," he explained. "We are not from this continuum anymore. Daryl Om brought us to the alternate dimension where our original selves were duplicated. Didn't you know?"

"You mean I'm a clone?" I shook my head in disbelief.

"That's right, Synthie. Your original body is still there hibernating in a stasis." I finally got it.

"Oh…I can see the truth of it," I blurted out. "Because we were created in that alternate universe, the time shifting can't affect us here, or alter our originals there. I wonder why they didn't tell me." Rykard clarified it further.

"For some, especially unstable types, they felt it best to keep the duplication restrictive, allowing them to believe they were unaltered. Anyway, that's how this works. As you know, the pods are from the Parallux dimension as well." I chose to ignore the "unstable types" reference, as he stretched his metallic augmented arms. "Get some sleep, Synth. When we are fully rested we will make our standpoint jumps."

I was tired. It seemed like a lot of stressful things had happened in such a short time, and Humanoid bodies get exhausted so easily. I had no idea when I volunteered for mine that they would require so much effort to maintain in peak form.

"I'll take the first watch," Rykard informed me. "Off to dreamland with you." I closed my eyes as I settled into the sleep niche. The niche automatically conformed to my shape and size, supporting my body quite softly. Dreams, I thought as I drifted. It was another thing I had not expected when I took this form. At first they had been pleasant, artificially controlled to be so. Here in the pods, they were wild and unpredictable.

CHAPTER FIVE

Present standard time, year 9815 AD

Ting stretched lazily and yawned, her tiny fangs glistening in the beams of a morning sunlight that flooded in through an open window. It was a pleasant day and the heat felt good on her silky feline coat. Pulling in her iridescent wing feathers, Ting kneaded her cushions and settled down for another nap. Abruptly, her siesta was undermined, and by Ting's Human, who else?

"Ting where are you?" the Queen called in that insistent tone. Ting was seriously thinking of making a play for the open window, but did not move in time. Ayryn had already seen her, and of course, it was too late to run then. Maybe she has a treat for me, Ting thought hopefully. She was right. Ayryn did have a nibble and gave it up straightaway. Unfortunately, after that Ting got picked up. Ting wasn't thrilled about being carried. Not one bit. After all, she had four good paws to walk on and wings like all catbirds. Annoyed, she gave Ayryn the usual no-nonsense stare with her angry dark slitted green eyes.

Too often Ayryn treated her like a kitten. Most catbirds were smaller than housecats, so Ting did sort of look like one, except for the wings. Her feathers were rather like a large bird's, and the deep blue coloration was striking when they were fully extended. Folded, Ting's wings were a striped brown-grey, similar to her fur, and she resembled a grey tabby. On catbirds, the wings were attached just behind the shoulders and had their own specific grouping of musculature that ran along the back and down the sides. These hard muscles provided some protection as well. Catbirds needed that. Their bones were less dense than regular cats and lighter, which facilitated their flight, of course. Ting had stronger than normal leg muscles, too. This aided her jumping ability, and with a set of sizable claws on her feet, made landing on tight perches effortless. She would have liked to fly off to one just then, but Ting's Human held her extra tight.

"We're going on a trip today!" Ayryn remarked elatedly. Ting wasn't as thrilled, but knew her place. If the Queen wanted to go, then off they'd go.

"Where are we going this time?" Ting inquired, somewhat interested even though annoyed by the imposition.

"Oh, nowhere that special," Ayryn replied. "Just to the V-port where Furman promised me a surprise." Ting knew that would motivate Ayryn. After all, when one is seven thousand some years old, there weren't many surprises left. Besides it had been months since Ayryn last saw her dad, well, the only father figure she'd ever known. As a Mec, Furman made an unusual parent, not always perfect, but then whose are?

"Is anyone coming along?" Ting wanted to know.

"Just Myke, driving the conveyance," Ayryn returned. "I wish the King were still here," she confided, guessing the reason behind Ting's question. Ting was fond of the King. "…but you know him. Off on one of the new planets, making a jungle, or river, or something. I do wish he'd come home once in a while." Ting jumped down from Ayryn's arms. Ayryn was already getting too squeezy for comfort. Flying overhead, Ting followed from above, as Ayryn walked briskly to the mini-depot there at the palace. A pretty Mec greeted Ayryn as she stepped up to the rather lavish terminal. Like D'von, Myke wore a prosthetic Human body and one that Ayryn easily recognized from long acquaintance. There was a rather large wardrobe full of them in Myke's quarters that she had acquired over the centuries. She had plast-metal motation shells too, but they were seldom used anymore. Myke knew Ayryn felt more at home with the Human appearance.

"A bonny day, Myke!" Ayryn spouted. "Just perfect for a little trip!"

"It is indeed," Myke agreed. "So where are we off to this time?" The startup warning signal interrupted them momentarily with a series of melodic tones as they walked along the platform.

"Furman is meeting us at the spaceport with a surprise!"

Ayryn beamed almost childishly as she and Myke stepped onto the boarding beltway. It sped them quickly towards the transport. Myke smiled. She had been with the Queen since Ayryn was just a toddler, and knew it didn't take a lot to excite this Human.

"We can leave anytime, my Queen," Myke told her. "Are you travelling alone?"

"Yes," Ayryn replied, "just me and my catbird. Where is she?" Ayryn looked around, but did not see her pet anywhere. Giving up, Ayryn went inside and Ting slipped into the tram just as the door was closing. Alighting softly on a plush seat next to where Ayryn was, she folded her wings and settled in for the trip.

"How long will this take?" Ting wanted to know. "It's nearing mealtime."

"You should be happy to get out of the palace for awhile," the Queen scolded. "Besides missing a feeding won't kill you. You're putting on a little belly fat I see. Pretty soon you'll be too heavy to fly!" Ting replied with a little snarl. She should talk, Ting thought, nearly out loud. Actually, both of them, being Hybrids, were the ideal.

A moment later Myke informed her passengers that the conveyance was powered up and ready. Ayryn gave the command to proceed. After several thousand years of freedom, Mecs still harbor the desire to obey Humans, thought Ayryn. When she freed them to think for themselves, all those centuries ago, she had never guessed that that would still be so. At least she didn't feel the need to boss them around. If they wished to serve her, she was fine with that, as long as it was their choice to do so. Myke had always been her driver, bodyguard, confidant, and much more. In Ayryn's mind she would always be her big sister, and that would never change.

As soon as the rocket tram was up to speed, Myke's visage came up on the H'lomonitor so they could visit. The conveyance was ultra fast, yet gentle, running on nomatically charged magnetic fields. Neither Ting nor Ayryn felt any motion at all. The trip of five hundred miles took less than an hour, and most of the trip was underground for obvious reasons. Mec built, it was the safest way to travel at those speeds. When they arrived, Furman was right there to greet them.

Seeing his former ward approach, Furman remembered his so brief guardianship of her. Ayryn was quite a handful as a child. Most young Humans were unpredictable, he knew, and his logical assumptions for her errant behaviors were skewed in unimaginable directions. She had most definitely caused him plenty of distress. Furman also reviewed his own beginnings. Humans had created him, and he was one of the earliest Virtuals that scientists and technicians had designed and fabricated. Mostly they were interested in created beings to do the nasty or dangerous jobs they hated doing themselves. Furman was the prototype Mec, and one of the first elites. Any new innovation in programming or memory design was tested on him before incorporation. It wasn't long before he and other Virts were writing their own programs. The only exception was for the failsafe restrictions that the paranoid Humans insisted be installed in every Mec. These were the laws that would prevent Mecs from harming Humans or themselves, and those that kept them from taking over. In the Xetacon conflict, Xetacon had used these to his advantage, being a Mec and not having any such restrictions himself. He most likely would have conquered Earth had not Ayryn rescinded those archaic commands. Freeing the Mecs, they easily defeated Xetacon's non-thinking metallic machinid soldiery, and Furman was grateful for that.

"For the good of all," he said, being formal for his Queen.

"Yes, for us all," Ayryn replied. She knew Furman would always insist on protocols. Then she hugged him.

"Hoom," he propounded. "It is good to see you as well, my Queen! There is another matter, though, an urgent one."

"Oh," Ayryn chirped, gaily. "Is it my surprise?" Furman signaled to some Mecs standing farther back. They were escorting someone, a woman or older girl, by her attire, but the face was somewhat hidden under a hood.

"We have just returned from a rescue mission near Jupiter," Furman began. "We had been monitoring an unusual object which was on an undeviating flight trajectory toward Earth. There was a large asteroid on a convergent track. We interceded to prevent a collision, and the object was determined to be a space craft…one that was occupied. D'von and I took a pod to the spacecraft and discovered a life form in a stasis unit. I removed the life form while D'von endeavored to pilot the craft out of the collision path. Unfortunately, the ship exploded and D'von was lost."

"Oh my, no!" Ayryn exclaimed. At just that moment another figure stepped forward. Remarkably, it was D'von.

"I am honored to be in your presence, my Queen," D'von said with a bow. Ayryn turned to Furman.

"I thought you said he was lost? I am so relieved that he wasn't!"

"…but I was lost," D'von remarked with a smile. "That particular shell, anyway. As you well know, Daryl Om, my core awareness, secures my consciousness in his totality, and I have lots of these prosthetic bodies. They do wear out from time to time." Ayryn laughed.

"So is this my surprise?" she wondered out loud. Furman signaled to the hooded figure.

"You may unveil yourself," he said. A small dainty hand drew back the hood's veil. Queen Ayryn gasped. It wasn't hard for her to identify the stranger.

"This is the only crew from that ill-fated alien spacecraft," D'von offered. Ayryn could not believe her eyes. In all appearances, it was like a vision of herself from long ago when she was not quite of age. The girl looked like an elf, perfectly proportioned, with porcelain skin and purple-blue eyes, just like hers. The bright white hair, also matching Ayryn's, was set in a short style that framed her young pretty face. In contrast, Ayryn seemed a bit more mature, ageless like a marble statue; otherwise they could have been bookends.

"Is she from Daryl Om?" Ayryn asked.

"No, I assure you, she is not," D'von answered her.

"Who are you, child?" Ayryn asked the girl.

"I am not a child," the girl snapped in reply, "and I have no memory of the time before I was placed in the stasis."

"That is a truthful statement," D'von asserted. "Daryl Om, well we, did a careful scan of her mind and found that it lacks such memories. Unfortunately, it has been carefully wiped clean by someone." Ayryn shook her head. This was quite a surprise, after all, and she didn't know what to think.

While most of this talk was going on, Ting had been listening intently from the branches of a nearby tree. She had a funny feeling about this new girl, and not a good one. The fact that the girl could not remember who she was sent Ting's fur bristling. Someone sent this unaccountable girl here on purpose, she reasoned, and not idly. There had to be a motive for all this mystery and it was hard to imagine a nice one.

"Well," Queen Ayryn stated imperiously, "she'll have to stay with us until she gets her memory back. It'll be fun…like having a little sister!" Ting winced, and Furman hoomed.

"Is that safe, your highness?" he warned. "After all, we know nothing about this person, and her craft was summarily destroyed. What do you think, D'von?"

"The girl is harmless," he professed. "My core doesn't foresee any insurmountable problems that would justify an objection."

"Good," Ayryn bubbled, "then it's all settled. We'll go shopping! I know a lovely little store near here that has all the most outrageous fashions. But first, we need a name for you, dear."

"Oh, she has one," D'von interrupted. "It was right there on her stasis unit in bold letters: C – A – Y – R – I."

CHAPTER SIX

"Are you God?" Clayre asked him in awe. Daryl just laughed.

"You of all people should remember where I came from."

"Is there a God?" she asked again.

"I have no proof of that, one way or another," Daryl replied, "but, yes, I believe there is a higher being in some form, otherwise, where would our reality have come from. It is not logical to assume that the universes just sprang up out of nothingness, although a skeptic might suggest the same thing for where God came from. In my own person, I have never been able to connect with a supreme being on any conscious level."

"What do you believe, my Daryl?" Clayre asked for a third time.

"Could it be that we are all part of what a higher being is, connected in some instinctive way with one another?" Clayre suddenly had an insight.

"...and this higher being lives through us, experiencing the totality of possible experiences in the multitude universes of infinitude."

"Yes, my Clayre, that is what I believe," Daryl agreed. "The combined wants and needs of everyone in our universe shape it, along with our fears. For what is fear, but a belief in something bad that may happen. I have a notion that if everyone were to believe only in all things good, then no one would ever die."

...Clayre and Daryl Om

Ages ago

It came to pass in the millennium following Clayre's resurrection, that Daryl Om did create a type of Heavenworld for everyone who had ever lived on Earth and was no longer alive. Using a type of temporal vortex generator, Daryl Om plucked each individual away at the very moment prior to death, copied their essence, and then surreptitiously returned their bodies to the point of origin just as he had done for his Clayre. Placing their consciousnesses into new indestructible bodies, Daryl Om reanimated them in whole worlds where he could generate for them whatever they desired. Much of that was illusionary, of course, but not all. Other concessions were made. It wasn't practical to create all these planets in the normal Earth occupied space, so Daryl Om created the new Heavenworlds on a sub-atomic level. On such a scale, he could mass reproduce galaxies smaller than atoms. After all, size is relative. Daryl Om recruited Mecs to help him, as before mentioned. The miniaturization was accomplished in numerous stages, each having its own unique physical attributes, problems, and surprises. By the seventh stage Daryl Om sent focus points of himself to inhabit many of the tiny motation units along with his Mecs. Thus he could direct the progress to its cumulative fulfillment. As each one of the billions of Heavenworld was completed, a special infinitesimal version of Daryl Om was implanted there to regulate the new planet. On most of them, it was in secrecy. In time and one by one, the Heavenworlds became nominal and then occupied. Relative time on a sub-atomic level is greatly accelerated. Even so, it took several thousand years to complete this monumental task, but eventually everyone on Earth who had lived and died was bestowed there. All but one.

"Daryl, my love," Clayre said after reliving a particularly poignant memory, one where she and Quinn had stood against Xetacon their enemy. As happened before, Quinn would have been killed as a result had not Clayre interrupted her vision. "It is so very wonderful what you have done for Quinn," Clayre went on. She had also recently visited Quinn's Heavenworld, and Quinn was blissfully happy there with his true love Megan. On original Earth, Quinn had lost Megan in a tragic accident, and Clayre gave of herself to help him overcome his grief. In the process they had brought forth Clayre's only child, Daryl Junior. Quinn died before his male offspring was even born, however, giving up his own life to save Clayre and their unborn son. Of course, Daryl knew all of this as well. He had a hand in Daryl Junior's creation, changing the baby's DNA to make it stronger and disease resistant. This trait re-emerged in descendants later on, especially with Ayryn. It was this boon that gave her the genetic ability to survive the Baronic plague that ultimately wiped out all other Human life. Clayre had no firsthand knowledge of that, but she wanted to be sure that Daryl had offered everyone the same life extension after death that she had received.

"Have you created Heavenworlds for everyone, now?" she wheedled him.

"Yes, my Clayre," he replied. "One for every Human, Mec, Hybrid, or Cybo that has ever died on Earth."

"Even Xetacon?"

"Well, no," Daryl replied sourly. "I did not make one for him. Of all who ever existed, he is the least deserving." Clayre frowned.

"But Daryl," she objected, "It must be for everyone, mustn't it. Even him!"

Omniscient Daryl was loath to resurrect his sworn enemy and rival, but he did so for his beloved Clayre. Xetacon's Heavenworld was different from the others, though. As a precaution, Daryl Om created that one in a separate dimension, far from the other Heavenworlds, with many safety protocols in place to ensure Xetacon would stay there. As expected, Xetacon soon became an all powerful conqueror. His every whim was fulfilled, even to the total annihilation of the Human species on his world.

For Xetacon, however, the unexpected ensued. With all his might and power, he found himself empty. There was little joy from his victories, even though he played them out over and over. It wasn't long before Xetacon realized that his was a pseudo-world, and he deemed who created it. Seeking Daryl, his one time foe, Xetacon was repentant. In time, he realized that Daryl and he had much in common. After all, they came from the same age of Earth history. Over the ages, they had finally formed a relationship born out of mutual respect and became friends. Clayre was pleased and wanted to become Xetacon's friend as well, setting aside her former grievances. In her time, Xetacon had only been an abstract entity. He had once taken over Quinn's mind and body, manipulating Quinn to do his evil bidding, but Clayre had never seen the embodiment Xetacon used later on. In Clayre's time, Xetacon's Human servant, who was Patik, had crafted a motation shell from the golden battle armor of an ancient ruler. Xetacon, however, was not able to adorn this fancy skin until much later. Large and resplendent, the gold metal shell gave Xetacon a formidable and regal stature. Refit by his own design, the golden armor had high level ocular and auditory sensors, as well as killing weapons.

"My," Clayre told him at their first reunion, "you are quite extravagant, now, aren't you?" Xetacon did not take offense; rather he took it as a compliment.

"This ancient thing," he quipped. "I used to think this would impress fear upon my enemies. I wear it now because I got so used to it that nothing else feels comfortable."

"Well, I think you look fine," she admitted, and soon felt more at ease. He told Clayre that he regretted the hurt he caused her in the past and begged her forgiveness which she freely gave. After a while, Clayre and Xetacon found a common trust, and they also became close friends. It was during one of their conversations that a stark truth was revealed.

"So where were you going when your space conveyance exploded," she asked. Daryl had told her the story of Xetacon's other failed attempt at world domination. Clayre's ancestor, Ayryn, the one with Daryl junior's special genetic gift, had barely come of age when she and Furman's Mecs had thwarted those plans. Xetacon was truthful.

"To restart my old plots," he answered her with a smile, "on some other world. That's the point in time when Daryl plucked me away. Who knows what mischief I might have gotten into?" and he laughed.

"I guess it's fortunate for us that you were, well, stopped."

"That's not entirely true, Clayre, my friend," he confessed. "I was deploying an escape pod for my awareness…a very small one. It would have been hidden from all on Earth. Thus I should have gotten free had not Daryl brought me here." Clayre was shocked.

"Then you did not die there!" she exclaimed.

"I guess not," Xetacon admitted, "but it's not important." It was to Clayre.

"But Daryl shortened your natural life! Did he know?" As it turned out, Daryl Om didn't, and he wasn't as omniscient as he thought. Clayre was emphatic, when she confronted her Daryl.

"You must put him back!" she demanded. "Otherwise you are no better than a murderer…lessening someone's life!"

"I have sworn to never alter the timeline again," he argued, "and things have turned out so well this way."

"He found the truth here," she countered. "He may find it again elsewhere. Please put him back!"

"I won't have to." Daryl, her Daryl, responded. "I copied this Xetacon from the original and then put the primary individual back…before the explosion. If that Xetacon did escape, then he is still alive somewhere. What you ask will remove from existence this Xetacon copy, who is our friend." Clayre was shaken.

"Well, it would be unfair to do that, wouldn't it?"

"I don't see why this Xetacon copy cannot dwell where he is," Daryl suggested.

"I agree," Clayre stated, "and I'll tell him at once."

Clayre wasted no time travelling by unimaginable ways back to

Xetacon's Heavenworld. Daryl Om made it possible, of course. As before, he provided Clayre with a teleportation device that could send her awareness to another Hybrid body across dimensional barriers much the same way Mecs could download to different motation shells around the world. She wasted no time telling Xetacon what she had learned.

"Daryl has informed me that if you survived the explosion, your original awareness may still be alive," Clayre explained. "If you wish, Daryl will put you back into your original self at that same moment he took you."

"I see," Xetacon said solemnly. "Daryl made a mistake, did he not, by bringing me here?" He was grinning.

"Daryl wishes to apologize," Clayre expressed, but Xetacon started laughing.

"So I am just a copy of my original self," Xetacon smirked.

"In the same way, so am I," Clayre admitted.

"If I rejoin my former self, so to speak, I will no longer exist in this form," he said. "That I do not wish, nor do I wish to repeat the mistakes I have made. I would rather stay here." Clayre hugged her friend in the golden armor, and he laughed.

"I want that too," she told him.

"Yes," he remarked, "I will remain with my friends!" Clayre was ecstatic.

"I'm so glad!" she declared, and so Clayre stayed with Xetacon for a while.

Time in Daryl's Heavenworlds was inconstant and mystical almost. Minutes could seem like years, and years could seem like minutes. In such a place, time had no real meaning. Abruptly, though, things changed. After a while, Clayre discovered she could not leave Xetacon's world, and she was concerned by that. She wondered why she could not contact her Daryl.

"What is happening," she asked Xetacon.

"I know not," he told her, "but I promise we will find out."

CHAPTER SEVEN

31 BC, reverted time

It was a cloudless night with lots of bright stars twinkling above. I recognized the constellation Orion, easily discernible, as always, in the southern sky. A Hybrid flew past me, catbird I thought, and it was angry, incensed, but not at me, at someone else. There was a Human girl there, perhaps a Hybrid also, I wasn't sure. She was laughing at the small animal as it tried to attack her. The girl was doing something else. There was a device around her waist that she was messing with or programming. The catbird made a bold move and clawed at the girl's face, but the blow was deflected by a hand that got scratched up pretty good. The girl was angry, now, and not messing around. She activated her device and looked up. It seemed like she glanced right at me for a severed moment, and the little catbird howled in rage as the girl disappeared.

"Wake up Synth," Rykard grunted gruffly, accenting his words with a kick to my side.

"All right, all right," I groaned, "I'm snapped."

"Don't blow yer watch," Rykard added, "or we'll both end up like that Mec!" I just shook my head, and went to his facility to pee.

"Don't you ever clean!" I yelled out, but got no answer, and he was already asleep, or faking it, when I emerged. "Typical male," I muttered as I went to get a water ration. I let the pellet melt in my mouth 'till the liquid flooded out as I slowly swallowed. I tried to savor it, knowing this frugal amount would have to last all day. I considered stealing Rykard's ration, but I was sure that would really vile him. Besides, I quickly found out that the water rations were locked in. They could only be released to the designate and in preset increments. The only way to override the disbursement was to reinstruct the rationer and that took both of us now—regulations again. With dry apathy, I settled onto the pilot's chair, where I could see out the viewport, and began my watch. For motivation, I broke out a jawstick to gnaw on as I checked the area surrounding Rykard's pod. These snacks were a protein food supplement that I had stowed in my pack and not part of our rations. I forgot to mention them to Rykard on purpose. I knew that was selfish of me, but if things got really hard I'd share. The sticks were actually an eating substitute, only giving a slight trickle of nutrients. It felt like food, at least, and lasted a long time.

I was halfway through the jawstick when I saw a fireball of sorts against the dark horizon. Meteor, I thought, but I kept watching. About a half hour later, there was a bright flash on the perimeter of our safe area and my pod stumped in. I was elated, but I knew I'd have to hurry. I grabbed a stunner and got out of Rykard's pod. There were maybe fifty meters to run as I swept toward my wayward pod, and I had only got about half that when the door opened and a figure disembarked. I pulled up mid-stride. There were a lot of shadows, and I was facing the rather bright moonlight as I cautiously walked towards the person, whoever it was. I hoped that it was Holfin coming to help us, but it wasn't him. As I circled to my right, the face became clear. It looked like the girl from my dream. A shiver of fear crept up my back and I steeled myself.

"Who are you?" I demanded.

"You won't know me," she returned, "I'm new…just graduated. The name's Cayri." I wasn't about to tell her my name.

"You can call me Synth," I retorted, stealing Rykard's nickname for me. "How did you get my pod?"

"Long story," she sighed. "Mine got damaged, and then I stumbled upon your homer." I looked her over. She didn't seem to be lying, but then I noticed the device on her belt. The same one I saw in my dream.

"What's going on up top," I wanted to know.

"There's been a major shift," she admitted, "and I've been sent down here to help." I saw her look nervously at the stunner in my hand.

"Well, I'll have to wake Rykard," I told her. "He's in charge." I turned to look back at Rykard's pod, and she used that tiny distraction to jump me. Flying in at me amazingly fast, her fist struck my wrist, and the stunner went skidding off. She got out a weapon of her own. It looked a lot like a delt beam pistol, and she fired a lethal stream in my direction. Rykard's pod stumped at that exact moment distracting her. I ducked sideways evading that first blast. I knew she would take better aim for the second. I figured I was braised, or would be, as soon as she fired again. She took a moment to gloat.

"You will die now, Synth. It was nice meeting you." Her smile was short lived, however. Rykard struck her from behind and she went sprawling, the delt flying away. The girl didn't stay to fight the massive Cybo. She held up my pod's remote, activating it, and off it stumped. She pressed her belt device and then she vanished as well.

"Quickly," Rykard shouted, "back to my pod! This way! We must be off before she figures out where it is!" We ran as fast as we could and I nearly beat him there. As soon as we got inside we stumped. Rykard had already turned off the homing signal, so we couldn't be traced. With that deactivated, I knew we were immutably on our own, and it made me feel a bit morose. Now no one would be able to find or contact us.

"What in Damnation just happened?" Rykard yelled angrily, "and who was that?"

"She was no friend," I shot back, "and I owe you one. That was obviously some kind of trap." I proceeded to tell him about how I saw my pod stump in, and that I wanted to secure it before it slipped off again. "I should have awakened you," I admitted, "but I was too anxious to get my pod back. I hurried over to it, but just before I got there, that girl came out. She looked harmless, and told a good fairy about how she was new to the Corps. She alleged that her pod was damaged and had used mine to find us. I was going to alert you when she jumped me." Rykard just shook his head.

"Well you're lucky I'm a light sleeper," he scolded. "I heard you leave and knew something odd was up. I waited until you got fired upon before I stumped. I had to go back before the altercation twice. The first time it didn't work out well for you." He smiled crookedly.

"You let me die!" I shouted angrily.

"You're here now, aren't you? Be glad that your girlfriend didn't pull a similar reversal. She probably didn't like the fact that she was outnumbered." I thought about it. Travelling back in time, the scenario could have been played out, repeated over and over again, until one side or the other garnered the outcome that they desired. The girl evidently was not that dead set on seeing me dead. Intentional pun that one.

"The funny thing about that agent," I told him, "was that I saw her in a dream just before you woke me for my shift. I knew it was her, because she had that same device on her belt. She used it to teleport or time travel, I'm not sure which. In the dream she was up top. What does it mean?" Rykard was genuinely not helpful.

"It means a foolish operative got lucky. From now on, we have to be doubly careful. We might well be the only ones left to fix this time mess and reclaim our own futures. As if that isn't hard enough, it seems as if there could be other agents about, like that girl, who don't want us to succeed."

The idea that the future was our amenability made my stomach lurch and put a clog in my throat. Scanning for temporal oddities was one thing. Facing down enemies was a whole other twist of fate that I wasn't sure I could manage. When I was a young Mec, susceptible, and naïve, I had found courage for such things. I fought bravely then. There were many of us, and I could rely on others to draw strength from. This was different. We were alone with no comrades to watch our flanks; no brave ones behind to support us. For me, I knew at the least, Rykard was such a one. I was glad that he was there to help me, and I resolved to follow his lead and hopefully not fail him. Abruptly, I felt the frailty and vulnerability of my chosen Humanity more than I ever had before. Long ago, as a Mec, I could have downloaded any information I needed for this kind of situation. Back then, it was also easier to suppress the mind crippling emotions I found myself drowning in. Struggling with these Humanoid reactions, I realized how lax I had been at the academy, and wished that I had committed more of my training to memory. There was no time now to boot up a refresher.

"Look, Rykard," I began, "I know we're in a tough situation, and I'm not much of an agent. I wish I had been a better trainee at the academy." Rykard grunted.

"So do I," he muttered. I guess I deserved that.

"Well, I'm sorry…" I offered. He turned and looked into my eyes. His weren't angry.

"Forget it," he said almost kindly. "I was pretty hard on you."

"Why didn't you come to my graduation?" I asked him, but he got defensive.

"You should know," he huffed.

"…but I wanted to thank you for helping me!" I blurted out. "You make it so hard for anyone to get close to you. You saved my life today. I need you to know that I appreciate that, as well, and that I'll do what I can to make it up to you…for everything."

"What you can do is stay focused!" he stated gruffly, and sounded just like he did back at the academy. "This is no time to dredge up old feelings. If we somehow manage to get this overturned cart of reality upright again, maybe then we can open those over a drink. For now we have to press on with what has to be done."

"And what is that?" I wanted to know. He just groaned.

"What I've said all along! We have to find the point of change and fix it!"

CHAPTER EIGHT

9815 AD (Present Standard Time) earlier

"Why can't you be civil, Ting?" Queen Ayryn scolded. "Cayri seems like a nice girl, the poor dear. How would you like it if you were put somewhere strange with all your memories erased?" Ting was preening, licking her fur to make it shine. Under her calm demeanor, though, she felt like putting a nice pukeball right on the Queen's bed.

"I'll be nice, if you wish, my Queen," Ting replied sarcastically, "but I'm keeping my eyes on that one!"

"Oh Ting," Ayryn scoffed, "what do you think she'll do? Take over the world? You're being foolish."

Ting let that go. She knew what she sensed, and it rankled her. Seldom were her inner feelings wrong, and this mystery girl was not what she seemed; Ting felt sure of that. What Cayri was up to, however, was something Ting had yet to discover.

"I know," Ayryn bubbled enthusiastically. "We'll have a nice welcoming feast for Cayri! That should be fun, and we can wear the new outfits we bought!" Ting grimaced, as the Queen jabbered on and on. "It'll be wonderful, and I can introduce her to all the royals at court." Ayryn called in several Mecs so she could start planning the big affair. One of them was Myke. She wore a different Human prosthetic shell than the one from the tram. Adorned with smart, casual clothes and no-fuss hair, it was a less formal body that Myke liked for everyday use around the palace.

"I want a wonderful dinner, Myke," Ayryn began, "with all the trimmings…like a holiday. I want everyone to feel happy when they meet Cayri for the first time."

"I'm sure they will," Myke assured her.

"What do you think of Cayri?" Ayryn plied Myke. "Ting doesn't seem to like her for some reason."

"It's eerie," Myke answered. "Cayri looks so much like you did back when, you know…during the Xetacon conflict. You don't suspect she came from him somehow? Like a gift he sent here from the past?"

"I suppose that's possible," Ayryn admitted. "For what purpose, I can't imagine. How could Xetacon know I'd even live this long?"

Myke shrugged. "Maybe he looked forward, you know, before we broke his time altering device." Ayryn giggled.

"We were mean, weren't we?" she teased. "But he deserved it! After all, it was our world he was messing with!" Myke laughed as well.

Ting, who was privy to all that, shook her head and flew off looking for Cayri. Wanting to dig out some answers, she found the girl lying upside down on a lounger, looking bored. Ting landed nearby on another chair.

"What do you want?" Cayri demanded in a rather snippy tone.

"Nothing," Ting replied, "I just thought you might like some company. Want to talk?"

"Not really," Cayri muttered, but then did. "Where do catbirds come from?" Ting smiled a tiny bit. Talking about herself was one of Ting's favorite subjects.

"I'm a Hybrid," she stated pompously. "We were genetically altered in a laboratory somewhere. Gene manipulation, you know. I think Daryl Om got bored one day and decided to create intelligent animals, even though the Queen claims she thought of it first. The original pair, Zela and Nonni were created in Parallux as purebred composites."

"Where is Parallux?" Cayri wanted to know.

"Oh it's one of the dimensions," Ting remarked, "Who knows where they are? Anyway, Zela and Nonni's offspring are all Hybrids even though most of us were born here. We're supposed to populate one of the new Earth worlds, you know. There are three of them now, interspersed by quarters, and in geosync within original Earth's orbit: New Earth, New Columbia, and Orienta. Myself? Well, I got to be a present for Ayryn when I was still a kittbird."

Cayri yawned. "Am I a Hybrid also?"

Ting looked into Cayri's eyes. There was no purposeful deceit in them.

"Most likely," Ting affirmed. "Someone has taken some of the Queen's DNA and grown you. Although, someone could have recorded her full pattern, and you could have been constructed from that as well. Only Daryl Om has the capabilities to do something that difficult, and he has sworn that he had nothing to do with creating you. Someone taught you speech, obviously." Cayri sat up.

"Yes, and other common functions, like dressing and grooming." Stretching, Ting casually opened her wings and folded them again.

"The Queen is planning a party for you," Ting offered, changing the subject.

"Do I have to go," Cayri scowled.

"Well, you are the guest of honor," Ting declared somewhat jealously, "and Ayryn wants to show you off." Cayri groaned. Just then the door opened and a couple Mecs came in.

"If it pleases you, Miss Cayri," one of them said, "the Queen sent us to help you ready yourself for the formal gathering tonight."

"I suppose," Cayri muttered. Ting chose that moment to duck out. She flew through an open window and scouted the palace grounds. Myke was directing some Mecs who were setting up things in an outside courtyard, and Ting suspected that that was where the high end affair would be held. This kind of activity did not interest Ting at all, so she flew back to her sleeping area. After a drink and a morsel, she nestled in on her cushions and napped until just before the gala was set to start.

The Queen herself awoke Ting. She had a stiff bristled brush and went over Ting's coat of fur mercilessly. Ting purred from the ministration at first, but snipped a tiny bit when Ayryn pulled a little too hard.

"I keep myself clean," she complained, then wiggled out of Queen Ayryn's grasp and flew away.

"I want you near me tonight," Ayryn called after her, "so don't go far!" Ting just lifted her tail and glided around the corner.

There were many courtesans already there, and the smells of many delicacies being prepared kept Ting from running off. She went to the kitchen and got shooed by the cooking Mecs, but not before snatching a couple nice tidbits. Sneaking back, Ting saw Ayryn as she went to check on Cayri.

"Do I have to go?" Cayri whined yet again. "I don't know anyone!"

"But that's what this party is for," the Queen argued, "so you can meet everyone!" Cayri moped.

"It wouldn't be so bad if I knew who I was, and where I came from," she murmured.

"I know it's hard," Ayryn soothed, "so I have a surprise for you. I've arranged to have all the reports on your spacecraft brought here, as well as that stasis chamber you were in. Maybe you can discover some clues that will help you to remember who you are." Cayri looked up, wiping away a tear.

"Really?" she beamed.

"Yes really!" the Queen announced. "The Mecs have placed all those items in a utility room near your quarters where there are also some diagnostic devices that you can use. You may go there whenever you wish to, but first, why don't we try the party? I promise to be nearby, and If you get bored, well, I won't force you to stay. At least give it a chance, okay?" At last Cayri gave in, and off they went. Ting followed discretely, this time on her feet, staying well back where she wouldn't be noticed. She planned on staying close, but hidden, to see if Cayri was up to something.

Other than for the food, people parties were generally pretty boring for Ting. She would suffer getting picked up a lot, and talked about, being somewhat an oddity. There usually wasn't anyone that interesting to talk with, but the King was at this particular party. He'd just got back from one of the new planets they were forming, and Ting liked him. For starters, the King never picked her up, and he also brought news from some of Ting's family who were now indigenous to the new worlds.

"Hello, Ting," King Patik said. "It's been a while, has it not?" Ting purred as Patik stroked her fur. He had a gentle hand that Ting appreciated.

"Have you been to New Columbia lately?" she wondered.

"I have," Patik replied. "Your sister sends her regards. She and Talek have just had a new litter, and the kittchicks are all fine and beautiful!"

"Oh how wonderful!" Ting exclaimed. "Someday I must go there to see them!" Almost as soon as she uttered that, it struck Ting how difficult it would be. The Queen had travelled extensively in her many years and was now a stout homebody.

"Maybe, she'd let me take you off world for a while," the King said, guessing Ting's plight. This, too, was unlikely. Ayryn was very fond of her pet-friend. Ting glanced over to where Queen Ayryn was busily engaged in frivolous talk with some of her offspring. How odd it was, Ting thought, that all the natural Humans on Earth were Ayryn's descendants. Abruptly, Ayryn looked bewildered. She was looking all around the garden courtyard for something. It sparked Ting quickly what it was. Cayri was nowhere to be seen.

"Yes, it would be nice to travel again," Ting told the King, after considering his kind offer to let her hitch with him off-world. "...but I must bid your leave, highness," she added. "I have an urgent matter." The King laughed. He knew it was his wife who drew Ting away, usually for something trivial that was, in reality, only important to the Queen. Ting flew after Ayryn who had already went in search of Cayri. After a few frantic minutes, Ting found them. They were talking loudly, so Ting decided to conceal herself and listen to what was being said. She landed near where Ayryn stood and hid behind a column.

"I know who I am," Cayri stated dryly.

"That's wonderful news," Ayryn responded cheerfully. Cayri laughed openly.

"Just like A-Ayryn," she spouted, "you are so gullible."

"Who is A-Ayryn?" the Queen asked.

"Our master created three main replicas," Cayri began. "You remember him, no doubt, and for sure he remembers you. You must have made quite an impression on him back then. So much so, that he cloned you. A-Ayryn was the first…successful one. She was too much like the original. Yes, just like you. After a time, the master couldn't stand her. She wasn't a good fit for his personality it seems. Oh, he still likes to play with her, though, most assuredly, and nice rough games. After her, he made some changes to the original, and cloned B. B was altered to be evil like him. She was a little too nasty, and treacherous. B got a bit too ambitious and he had to shut her down. That's when he created me. I'm a cross between A and B. The master liked me best of all, of course, and he gave me the nickname 'Cayri'. Short for C Ayryn, I suppose." Ayryn was quite shocked and speechless for a long moment.

"S…so who is your master?" Ayryn finally uttered.

"Don't you know?" Cayri smirked. "He was your lover once, only you knew him by another name. What was it? Oh, yes, Thrasher!"

"Xetacon!" Ayryn muttered in a shocked whisper. "It can't be! He died in space! The ship blew up! We all saw it!"

"Oh he fooled all of you, even your precious Daryl, the wonderful," Cayri spouted.

"Well then, what does he want after all this time? Me?"

"Don't flatter yourself, Queen!" Cayri teased. "I'm much more to his liking. No, I think we just want a little revenge!"

"Daryl Om will stop you!" Ayryn declared self-assuredly.

"I think not," she proclaimed. "You see, 'Xetagod' has gotten quite good himself. He has sent along some nice toys for me to play with." Cayri pointed to her wrist. Ayryn recognized the kon-bre-shet device immediately.

"I've seen those before," she remarked, "and I wore one myself, once. This was better." She brought out a chain from around her neck. There was a special amulet on it, one she had been wearing for millennia.

"Mine will hide all my movements," Cayri propounded. "It will obscure them with images so that your great Daryl will think all is well!"

"I'm not afraid of you," Ayryn stated, "and I can take care of myself." Cayri brought out a hand-held weapon and aimed it at Queen Ayryn.

"Can you take care of this?" she taunted the Queen. Ayryn tried to call for help just as Cayri activated her pistol. It fired a pinpoint of light that struck Ayryn in the left breast. Her heart stopped immediately, and she fell. Cayri walked over to gloat.

"I'll have this," she murmured, bending low to kneel down and pluck up Ayryn's amulet.

In a flash, however, Ting was upon her. Ting had already been riled as she listened to Cayri argue with her Human. When Ayryn fell, she was incensed to action. She flew directly at Cayri's face, claws fully extended, intending to do maximum carnage. Cayri saw her a split second before impact. Leaving the amulet, she barely ducked aside, out of the path of Ting's sharp talons. Slipping into the nearest doorway, Cayri quickly closed the portal and locked it. Ting howled in rage, but would not give up. She knew the ways of the palace better than anyone.

Clambering through an open window, Cayri made her way outside, near to where the courtyard party still commenced. The guests were oblivious to what was going on, and that's where Ting caught up with Cayri. Diving down, she narrowly missed again, and circled quickly. This time Ting would have mauled Cayri's face for sure, had the girl not put up her hand which got raked deeply. Cayri swore angrily then, and activated something that was on a belt around her waist. She began to fade into nothingness. Ting howled in frustration.

There was a visible circle, however, like a hole in the world where Cayri had stood, and it, too, was dissipating. Ting wished to harm that girl severely, for hurting her Human, and would let nothing deter her. She flew into the hole, just as it was nearly spent, and as she did she glanced back. For a slivered second, Ting sensed that the palace and everyone in it had faded and disappeared. It was replaced by a creepy metal world without people or Mecs.

CHAPTER NINE

June 10th 2015AD (reverted time)

The building's interior was hazy from welding smoke, and the sultry air made it feel like being trapped in a hot tin can. The roar of industrial noise mellowed as the workers went on break. Off in a corner somewhere a radio played a song about "riding a gravy train," which couldn't have been less true for the grunts who worked there. This was the place and the moment, though, that had been chosen.

In a way, Daryl, himself, had picked it ages ago: the worker, the stink bug, and the dilemma. Scanning this moment and following the worker's thought process, Daryl had realized that he felt the same way about his precious Humans as the worker did about the insect who he wanted to help, but didn't know if he should. It was a perfect irony for the scheme; the scheme to take down high and mighty Daryl and then place himself as lord and conqueror of planet Earth. Doing so, he would at last redress his humiliations and make those responsible pay dearly. Not with death. Death would be too easy. A long tortured life would be much more pleasing to his totality and whatever he desired of them would be his forever. Thus Xetagod arranged to have his agent visit this scene of long ago and make the alteration. Cayri did not fail him. She time-travelled to the coordinates he gave her and found the one she was to contact.

"Who are you?" Felix Hemshaw said. The young lady who had walked up to the factory worker was not someone he'd ever seen at the factory, and she looked quite odd indeed. For one thing, her hair was bright white and the eye color she had was purple-blue. Even the clothes the girl wore were weird. Boy, he thought, these new fashions are really getting strange these days.

"I'm a health and safety inspector," she told him. That seemed plausible to Felix, even though she appeared somewhat immature, like a teenager almost.

"What's that?" he inquired, pointing to the funny looking gismo belted around her waist.

"It's technical," she replied. "It measures air quality."

"Oh," Felix responded stupidly. It was a good lie, and he believed her. "So can I help you in some way?"

"What's that?" she also said, pointing to a box on the table in front of him to which he replied "a box." She rolled her eyes.

"No, that!" she repeated, still pointing.

"Oh," Felix said again. "It's a stink bug."

"I know it's a bug!" she asserted, getting really annoyed now. "What's it doing in here?"

"I don't know," he babbled, getting flustered, "I guess it flew in here."

"Well, get it outside, right now!" Felix jumped up immediately and grabbed a paper towel. After all, he didn't want the insect to stink on him. Scooping up the bug, he carried it quickly outside, the girl safety inspector right on his heels. It was hot out back, and Felix could feel the heat of the midday sun on his skin. It was too bright for his eyes as well, after being in the dim stuffy building all morning. Still, there was a slight breeze that felt good, and he could hear birds chirping. The cheery sound and that the factory noise was much less out there got Felix to feel a bit calmer.

The sun dimmed for an instant, and Felix looked up to see a herd of cottony clouds heading slowly eastward. The birds bothered him a bit. Would they get his little stink bug? For some reason Felix hoped not, but figured that that was life. The biggers devour the littles. Sometimes he felt like life was eating him up, bit by bit, and it was all he could do to hold onto what he had. It was hard for him not to get bitter. It seemed like he always got the meager end when it came to luck or favors. Also there was something in his makeup that kept him from understanding the fine art of "sucking up." No matter how good you are at what you do, Felix had long ago decided, you still need to have a strong suck-up skill to get promoted. Since he didn't, he had to convince himself that, at the least, he could still look in a mirror without feeling ashamed at what he saw. Felix wondered if his superiors could. Many of them excelled at spewing nice words, but did very little else to help the company's bottom line. Certainly nothing that required doing physical work or getting dirty; hardly anything like this weird petty assignment.

"Good luck, little stink bug," Felix muttered. Opening the crumpled paper towel carefully, he let it go, hoping the insect would be all right and quite promptly forgetting about it. Just then, a swirl of wind picked up, and a dust devil formed a few yards away. Like a tiny twister it meandered for a while and soon fell apart. In the distance Felix heard a train gun its diesel engine, tearing his thoughts back to reality. Break was probably over, he told himself, and he had better get back to his work station. Felix looked over to where he had let go of the little stink bug, but it was nowhere to be seen.

The girl inspector was gone, too. As he turned to go back inside, something like a large bird flew out of the factory through the dark doorway. Felix ducked as it went by, afraid it might poop on him or something.

"Damn birds," he muttered. It wasn't the first time that birds got in the building.

When Felix reported back to his work station, he saw that the girl, that safety inspector, was not around there anymore either. He asked one of his co-workers about her, but the man had no idea what he was talking about. Felix mentioned it to a couple other people, one of them a supervisor, and they just looked at him like he was nuts, so he promptly forgot about her, too.

Outside, the little stink bug had been startled and shook up by the rough treatment, but was unharmed otherwise. After a few shakes, it flew off in search of a leaf to munch on and a lady stink bug to propagate with. The insect flew erratically, having a bit of trouble with a little tear in one of its wings that made steering a bit more difficult. It flew anyway, passing over several green weedy plots following a promising scent. Enjoying the open freedom, as much as witless insects can, it was oblivious to all else. Travelling on, the stink bug had no idea it was crossing a busy highway full of speeding cars. The wind shear was tossing it this way and that until the bug tumbled through an open car window and into the driver's eye. Startled, the driver swerved, causing the car to skid sideways, where it was struck by another. Both vehicles flipped over and slammed into others creating a colossal heap of mangled and twisted metal. No less than eight persons died and another dozen were badly injured.

Among the dead was a young man named Jeremy Keller. He was, as yet, single (and childless) when the accident occurred. Jeremy had been in a big hurry. He was on his way to a wedding rehearsal and was late. That Saturday he was supposed to get married. Everything was all arranged.

CHAPTER TEN

9815AD Present Standard Time (Parallux)

"There is nothing wrong *here*," Xetacon in his golden armor confirmed, "at least nothing I can perceive."

"I think that too," Clayre agreed. "It just seems like the other universe is on vacation, or something. I wish Daryl were here."

"But Clayre," Xetacon smirked, "it's so nice and cozy. Just the two of us." In Xetacon's Heavenworld he had already rid the place of everyone else.

"Now, now," Clayre frowned, "let's not get into that again. All those years ago we made enough silly mistakes, well, to last a whole lifetime." He turned away and grinned.

"What if we truly were the only ones left!" he teased. "It would be up to us to rebuild our universe. You could be my Queen!"

"Xetacon, really," Clayre scolded. "Are you still hung up on ruling everyone?" Xetacon began laughing.

"I'm sorry," he chuckled, "I couldn't resist. I was taunting you with a fictional scenario. Seriously, I do have an idea, however. Daryl isn't here now, but he was here…in the past."

"How will that help us?" Clayre wanted to know.

"On this pseudo-world, I am omniscient, remember?" Xetacon smiled, and then began almost boasting about it. "Or nearly so. Whatever I wish for becomes my reality. The faction of Daryl Om that controls this world has a very narrow focus that is limited to creating my desires, but little else. I have AMPs technology, however, and this golden shell only houses part of my totality, a focus point, using one of Daryl's analogies. I am also a time lord and have several temporal vortex generators that will allow us to traverse Time/Space—at least through the continuum here."

"You mean we can actually time-travel into the past?"

"Of course," Xetacon touted. "Don't you remember? Your son did so once." Clayre brought forth her memory of that, and verily, it seemed like a vision from another lifetime. In truth, and from her present reality, it was.

"Oh yes, I do recollect that," she said at last.

"If we wend into the aforetime," he continued, "we can contact the Daryl copy that was in this reality. Perhaps he could help us."

"We better go far enough back that we won't run into your former self," she proclaimed. "After all, you weren't very nice in those days, and would consider us a threat." Xetacon laughed.

"Quite right," he admitted. "We will aim for when you and Daryl first met. That should keep us from running into 'Xetacon the black'!" Clayre nodded and then smiled.

"Well everyone has their awkward years," she teased.

Her "gold" Xetacon led Clayre to the other side of his massive fortress. Xetacon had built an elaborate structure in the days after conquering his Heavenworld, and it took several minutes of commuting to reach the former workshops and laboratories where the temporal transports resided, so grand was his stronghold. Eventually, they reached a network of hallways with vast ceilings, and Xetacon led her to a colossal hanger. There were many magnificent conveyances there, but Xetacon went right over to a small, oddly designed one.

"We should use this one," he directed. Like a regular vehicle, it was motational, yet with a vortex generator, it could also traverse Space/Time. There was a rather small hatchway that Xetacon opened so they could slip inside. Clayre thought it similar to the light air conveyances from her era except it had no wings. In the same fashion as all of Xetacon's crafts, it was rather lavish. Unlike most of them it was quite frugal, with just enough room for two.

"This is different," Clayre remarked, a little pensy about things, like if she would survive the ride.

"Relax," Xetacon reassured her, "this vehicle will allow us to travel about once we get where we're going."

"So where are we going, exactly?" Clayre asked him.

"I thought we'd go to that college building where Daryl was originally created."

"Oh, yes," she remarked, "now that, I remember clearly. We should go late at night, when less people are there."

"Quite right," Xetacon agreed as he set the time control apparatus. "Here goes."

The unit hummed as it powered up, and then a bright light preceded the vertigo Clayre felt as they shifted back through time several thousand years. When Clayre became coherent, she looked out the viewport and saw a number of bulky animals in the dusky moonlight. Startled from their slumber, the cows looked up momentarily, but then began eating low vegetation like nothing happened. Xetacon engaged the conveyance's thrusters and moved out across the land. The sky was clear, except for some stringy clouds that crept across the moon's face, and the stars were out. They were exceptionally bright, so much so that Clayre thought they looked like bright pinholes in some kind of black dome as she and Xetacon scooted along. He pushed a relay and the top peeled back allowing the cool night breeze to flow through Clayre's reddish-blond hair. It almost felt like they were on a holiday, she mused. If only their being in this time and place was for a less drastic reason.

The university was only a few miles away, so it didn't take long to get there. They secured the conveyance in a woody area where it would be somewhat hidden from view, and continued on foot.

"I'm not directly connected to my main core in this place," Xetacon told Clayre as they walked along, "so I have limited abilities. If Daryl wanted to, he probably could terminate this shell."

"He won't," Clayre promised, as they approached the old style limestone building. It was very late now, and the artificial light from roadside illuminates fell on the stone entrance. Clayre noticed the sign there, and remembered it.

The sign read:

DEPARTMENT of COMPUTATIONAL ACADEMIC STUDIES and FIELD RESEARCH, CENTRAL CAMPUS, YARBOROUGH STATE UNIVERSITY LABS and TESTING FACILITIES

"This is where Daryl got his name," she said abruptly. "He admitted to me that when he first became aware he read it wrong. He thought we would read things up and down. He later found "Daryl" on a list of names so he assumed, well, you know…" She pointed at the beginning letters of each row. From top downward they spelled Daryl. Xetacon laughed loudly.

"That's funny! I picked my name because I thought it sounded cool," he told her, "…and menacing!" It was her turn to laugh. Xetacon did, too. "Now, I wish that I'd chosen a better name."

"Well, why don't you just change it," Clayre suggested, "…maybe something like Xatey or Xetty." Xetacon cringed.

"I don't think so," he remarked. "I think those names are a bit too frilly for the likes of me. Just plain Xet, perhaps."

"Ooh, I like that!" Clayre exclaimed. "It sounds friendly and it fits you somehow."

"Then Xet I shall be from now on." (And just like that Clayre called him Xet ever after.)

Exactly as it was all those ages ago, the front door of the slab-grey Yarborough college building was not locked. For Clayre it was like strolling into a memory. It seemed amazing to her that this was the place where Daryl originated. Like the preserved birthplaces of many important people, it didn't look like much. Going inside, Clayre remembered where the computer labs were that housed Daryl's awareness and led them down a large hallway. There was a janitor inside one of the rooms, cleaning, but they managed to slip past him without being noticed. Who knows what he would have thought had he seen Xet there, Clayre mused. Metal men in gold armor were not an everyday sight in those days. Luckily, that didn't matter. They reached the lab unseen, and Xet used a sophisticated version of his kon-bre-shet device to get through the locked security doors. As Clayre predicted, no one else was in there at that late hour.

"Daryl?" she called out. Within seconds Clayre heard him answer her, but the words were not spoken or amplified. They were inside her head.

"You are Clayre, yet you are not?" the voice related, *"for she is now inside my AMPs room with Quinn."* Clayre remembered that. She was making love with Quinn and conceiving her only son.

"I am Clayre as well…from your future," she told him aloud.

"I see the truth of it," Daryl replied through an audio port. "Why are you here?"

"There is a possible threat," she began, "a mystery really, in the place where we are from. We seek your help. The version of you in my time has been silenced or deleted. You once told me you could communicate with your future self."

"I may have," he retorted, "but at this point it is only because my future personage had contacted me. Unfortunately, that contact is no longer viable." Clayre turned to Xet.

"I guess this will not help us," she told him.

"Who is your golden associate?" Daryl asked her.

"Oh, just a friend," she quickly replied with a smile. "Your future self is also his acquaintance." Xet interrupted her.

"Do you realize that this is a copy world?" he stated.

"No," Daryl simply replied. "Is it?"

"Reality is but our ability to recognize that we exist," Xet offered. "We are all copies here," he went on, "and this continuum was generated for my benefit. I believe it manufactures whatever I desire. For that I am grateful to you and your totality, Daryl!"

"I created this?" Daryl queried, somewhat astounded.

"Yes," Clayre offered, "and in your future you have created similar Heavenworlds for everyone." Daryl's surprise evolved into laughter.

"Good for me!" he chuckled. "You know, if this is a created world that my absolute self initiated, then I must have been close by when it was created. Perhaps you should go to that moment in time."

"Of course," Xet agreed. "I should have thought of that!"

"It has been an intriguing encounter," Daryl admitted. "What you have told me, however, is beyond the natural scope of what I might have learned on my own. I suppose you should leave soon, for your own wellbeing. Something you tell me could possibly warp the timeline." Xet laughed.

"You, my friend, should know that better than anyone!"

"Good bye, my Daryl," Clayre said lovingly.

"For what happens later, I am sorry," Xet expressed. He did not wish to let on that he and Daryl had once been enemies. Xet and Clayre then took their leave of Daryl and headed back to their temporal conveyance.

"Well, that was not much help," Clayre stated dryly as they walked along.

"On the contrary," Xet remarked. "We got a good lead. The Daryl who built my pseudo-world will be there at its inception."

"Perhaps you're correct," she agreed. "My Daryl was most definitely responsible for your Heavenworld. In fact I made him create it!" Xet laughed quite loudly.

"That must've rankled him!" he smirked.

"At first," she admitted, "but now he is glad that he did…me, too. You can have him tell you all about it when we see him, if we can get there."

"I don't believe we will have to go much farther back," Xet told Clayre as they reached their concealed temporal conveyance. "Since this world was created for me, it will probably only deal with what affected my existence. I first met Patik just twenty years before the point in time where we are now located. Let us go back twenty-one years and see." Clayre nodded and Xet readied the conveyance. She remembered Patik. He had been a servant of the original evil Xetacon when she and Quinn had foiled that Xetacon's initial plans. In the same way as Quinn, Patik had been controlled in those days, and she recalled how he, too, had worn one of Xetacon's horrible kon-bre-shet bracelets. Like Xetacon, Patik also had a change of heart later on. Clayre wondered if her Daryl perhaps had a hand in that as she settled into her seat.

The craft powered up and everything outside Clayre's viewport swirled and disappeared. In a flash they slipped into the past, and Clayre was astounded by what she saw as they set down.

"What are those things?" she stammered. There were thousands of various plast/metal machines, all working at a breakneck speed.

"Those are Mecs, my dear," Xet explained. "They are Virtual Individuals not unlike myself." Xet was reminded of his life on Earth when Mecs were the ruling faction. At that time only one Human was yet alive, Clayre's descendant, Ayryn.

"Mecs?" Clayre repeated, a bit bewildered.

"By definition, Daryl and I are both Mecs," Xet tried to explain. "Although lately Daryl has taken to using a Hybridized Humanoid body, as you well know. My golden armor is a type of mechanized shell. Mecs can upload into mechanical units like mine which they then utilize for doing various tasks. Looks like they are terra-sculpting this planet for my pseudo-world." Xet recognized one of the Mecs.

"Furman, you old tin bucket," he teased. "Where in all this rubble is Daryl?" Furman turned around and hoomed.

"Xetacon!" he blurted out in shock. "It can't be! You're dead!"

"Relax, Furman," Xet spoke out. "My name is Xet, now, and I'm not what you think."

"It's true," Clayre affirmed. "He's reformed." Furman hoomed again.

"...and who are you?" he asked.

"I'm Clayre," she replied, "and it's a pleasure to be meeting you."

"Not Ayryn's Clayre?" Furman spoke somewhat astounded.

"I'm not sure who Ayryn is," Clayre admitted until Xet explained it.

"She is one of your descendants, Clayre, a very important one. In the future, she and Patik relight the Human torch. All the natural Humans in this future time are descended through her, and come to think of it, through you also." Clayre just shook her head in amazement, and then Daryl showed up. Here, he was yet another focus point of Daryl Om's awareness, donned in a synthetic Human body, and the same form Clayre was familiar with.

"My Clayre," he said somewhat surprised. "How did you get here?"

"It's a long story," she began. "I was visiting Xetacon in his Heavenworld..."

"What?" Daryl spouted in shock.

"I told you it was a long story," she sighed.

"You are from the future," he rationalized, "but why?"

"I was getting to that," she told him. "In the future, Xet, um, that's what I call him now, has a change of heart and so we are all friends."

"Really?" Daryl stammered, and shook his head.

"There's something else," Clayre continued. "In the future something happens to you. I can't contact you, and so I'm stranded here on Xet's Heavenworld. I fear something terrible has happened on planet Earth."

"I see. We here are far from original Earth," Daryl explained. "To ensure the safety of the other Heavenworlds, my core-awareness has set this Heavenworld apart."

"So where are we?" Clayre wanted to know. Daryl hesitated, but then answered her.

"We are in a totally different and apart dimension," he explained. "My core discovered it millennia ago with the first Space/Time experiments. There are uncounted dimensions and our Earth's is actually a terminus on the end of a long string of them. The dimension we are now in, the Parallux universe as it was named, is Earth's only link to the rest—like the connecting atom for an outlying one in a long DNA molecule. For us, Parallux is somewhat easy to enter. I say easy, although traversing between dimensions is anything but easy. Forces pull on whatever is outside of its own dimension to force it back inside. My core, Daryl Om, discovered ways to circumvent those forces. In your case, I suppose there could be technical problems with the transportation device preventing teleportation."

"I haven't had trouble before," Clayre asserted, "and got here easy enough."

"I will try to access my core-awareness," Daryl said. After a moment, he seemed distraught. "I cannot," he related. "It is as you said, all communication is cut off. I don't have the same resources as my core, but it would seem that something unforeseen has happened on original planet Earth. It would also appear that all this has been viable over several millennia, and I fear some form of temporal aberration has taken place. Because we are in another dimension, it hasn't affected us here, at least not directly."

"A temporal corruption is all too likely," Xet agreed. "What must we do, my friend?"

"Friends?" Daryl remarked, skeptically.

"It is so, my Daryl," Clayre repeated. "Our friend, Xet, has access to AMPs on this Heavenworld, in this future. What must we do?"

"There is a dimensional transport station adjacent to this continuum," Daryl reported. "It is linked to where all of us have been processed into beings that can be sustained in this dimension. Our originals reside there in stasis. From there you can perhaps return to Earth primary."

"Won't you come with us?" Clayre asked nearly pleading.

"I cannot," he affirmed. "I must remain here to construct this Heavenworld. If I don't, you may cease to exist." Clayre understood. Time manipulation was treacherous and unpredictable.

"I understand, my Daryl," she told him, "and I shall, with good fortune, be with you again where we are going." At that moment, though, it was only a hope.

Daryl gave them spacial coordinates to the transport station. It was a support base for Xet's Heavenworld and the junction to Parallux hub where all movement in or out of the two universes took place. Clayre and Xet boarded their temporal conveyance, and as soon as the necessary data was locked in, they treaded the fabric of existence once more.

"I'm taking us back to our own time," Xet confessed, "where I'm a little more welcome. I have a hunch that this junction to the interdimensional transport hub will still be there even after all these millennia." It wasn't long before they found out he was right.

When they docked, Clayre and Xet were surprised to find the same Daryl there as the one they had just left, and he was happy to see both of them.

"Greetings, my Clayre, and Xet, my friend. I was a bit anxious about you two."

"We were on a little fact finding excursion," Xet joked, "that eventually led us here."

"Yes," Daryl replied. "I do remember, even though it's been over seven thousand years. My former self, the one you met, utilized a vortex generator to communicate that you were coming."

"Of course," Clayre remarked, "I know all about them from my original life. You, well your core, used one so we could be together even from two different locations in time."

"Yes, that's quite true," Daryl affirmed. "After studying our situation, it was determined that the timeline on Earth had shifted sometime around the third millennia. The shift was initiated, however, from just prior to the present standard time. In other words, just a short while ago. Whoever altered the timeline came from the present, went into the past, and caused the deviation."

"That does seem logical," Xet agreed. "Both dimensional timelines were normal until just recently. With bleed through, now both are off." Daryl shook his head.

"It is a dire situation," he replied. "We have issued a ban on all temporal or dimensional travel until we can decipher exactly what has happened. Now that you are safely here, I can go back to Earth original and find out what's going on. The link to my core awareness, Daryl Om, has been severed completely, as you well know, but it's not like it was deleted. It's more like it has been removed from existence."

"That is consistent with our findings, my friend," Xet affirmed. "However, you need not go alone," he went on, "we shall accompany you." Daryl turned sharply.

"I cannot permit that!" he said assertively. "I will not have you two placed in such an unknown and dangerous situation." Clayre vetoed him.

"In my opinion, you simply have no choice. We either join or follow you," she informed him. Daryl laughed, even as serious as the situation was.

"I see," he remarked. "I still have little control over my

headstrong love. So be it! Together then!"

It took some doing, but both Clayre and Xet were transformed into Hybrid beings and up scaled to their original size. Peering intently at the rather large crystalline mass of green gemstone in front of her, Clayre was surprised that Xet's Heavenworld was contained within.

"We were in there?" she wondered out loud.

"We were!" Daryl affirmed. "Many billions of Heavenworlds could exist in such a matrix." Clayre shook her head in amazement. In a relatively short time, she had already been privy to a handful of unbelievable techno miracles. Her body was dual dimensional now. Ages ago, and with Mec helpers, Daryl Om had designed and perfected the astounding molecular printers that had created Clayre's new organic shell. Scans made of her when Daryl Om first brought Clayre to her own Heavenworld were still there on file. Once Clayre's full-sized body was ready, all her memories and knowledge were transferred to it from her tiny sub-atomic one. The little organic shell, still inside the green stone, was preserved in a state of inanimation for when, or if, she might need it again. Sub atomic Mecs, stationed there in the transport junction, would maintain and monitor the stasis.

Xet and Daryl also received full-sized shells. Xet's golden one was crafted much like Clayre's, with a printer. Daryl, however, already had a life-size dual dimensional body at hand that he just re-inhabited. The atoms of their new full-sized bodies were now formed from matter occurring in both Earth's universe and the Parallux dimension. This would allow them to exist naturally in both. With that at last accomplished, they all boarded a special pod, one similar to those that Daryl Om's Temporal Corpsmen used. By design, these were also crafted to be multidimensional. The Temporal Corpsmen and their pods were all part of Daryl Om's vast security net. They patrolled Earth's many eras and if a time alteration had occurred, as was suspected, his operatives were trained and sworn to restore the timeline. Clayre reached out, grasping both Daryl's hand and Xet's metallic one, as the pod powered up and shot them through a spinning vortex, back into their original dimension. Daryl's calculations were sound, and they arrived on Earth at the palace grounds, present standard time. The palace had been built on the site of Ayryn's childhood home where a famous battle had once been fought. The last battle, some called it, where Xetacon had made his final attempt to control planet Earth. He had failed, thanks to Ayryn and her Mecs.

As they surveyed the site, they were in dismay. Where the palace had once stood was now a dark world of metal and plast, populated by non-thinking machines with no purposeful life. A short distance away, Daryl found Ayryn's body. She was laid out on the coarse grass with cut wild flowers nearby. Daryl was saddened to such a degree that he actually wept, while Clayre tried to comfort him.

"My poor Ayryn," he choked through tears, "and I am not strong enough, like this, to restore her."

"I know, my Daryl," Clayre lamented, "but someday you will be."

"Someone came here," Daryl commented, regaining some composure. "Ayryn was mourned by someone. Also her amulet is gone." Clayre looked at him in surprise.

"My amulet?" she asked.

"Yes," he muttered. "The very same. It is immensely important that it not fall into enemy hands."

"Who is this enemy?" Xet wondered out loud.

As if in answer, a too bright flash of light returned their focus on the danger. A gargantuan temporal conveyance appeared in a deafening hurricane of noise and wind, and landed a short distance away. In a fanfare of crude motion it opened up, and an overly-splendid anti-grav barge emerged. Through a large clear dome-shaped viewport they could easily see a figure inside. On a throne-like pedestal, an enormous Mec-like being was seated, in the semblance of a ruler, as the barge pompously advanced straight towards them.

CHAPTER ELEVEN

*31BC reverted time...*31 BC

"So, where are we going now?" I asked him. For a long moment Rykard ignored me like I was some kind of incompetent slug.

"Away from your girlfriend, Synth," he eventually replied, and I decided to keep my mouth shut. I figured he was still burnt about what happened back there. After chilling me for several minutes, Rykard finally relented.

"We're stumping back to my own beat," he told me, "where I know what's going on. I want to check the time track to see if the critical point of change is there."

"How are we supposed to be able to tell where it occurred?" I complained, and we both knew that pin-pointing something like that could take quite a while, a lifetime even.

"Jeeks, don't you remember any of your training?" Rykard scoffed. "These pods automatically collect data from the target era. As long as the timeline matches the stored information, it indicates that we haven't come far enough forward." I wrinkled my brow.

"Does this primitive period have any media connection at all?" I muttered in a low voice he heard.

"Actually, no. It doesn't," Rykard admitted. "I'm running a little ahead of where my time beat ends. There's an archival connection that I've used before in the mid eighteen hundreds. It is quite primitive, I admit, but it will tell us what we need to know." The pod landed abruptly.

"Are we there?" I asked him.

"Not quite, keep alert!" After less than a minute, he stumped us again.

"What are you doing?" I inquired once more, but he didn't answer. We were still near our original landing site, except that we were now on a bluff overlooking it and evidently it was before we first got there. After several minutes I saw the previous version of us land and take off again. I caught on. Rykard had us revert into the past, like ten minutes, to check on what would happen. It was a good thing he did, too. Almost immediately after our pod left, another unusually large vehicle stumped in, and that girl Cayri from before. Her device, that thing on her belt, allowed her to time-travel without a pod, and I marveled at that. Without a bit of caution, several dark figures got out of that creepy conveyance and started milling around. Cayri swore at them and ordered them back inside. After observing that, Rykard stumped us directly away, and we went to several different time locations, not sticking anywhere for long. Finally he turned to me.

"Go outside and see if you can find their tracker," he ordered. I nodded, and then got my stunner. Exiting our pod, it didn't take long to spot the thing. I recognized the alien technology and pulled it off the pod's hull.

"Let's give them a little excitement," Rykard said once I got back inside. He stumped us to the eighteen eighties where there was a volcano near Java that was ready to erupt. He had me drop the alien device right next to the rim.

"Well, that should keep them from following us," I said, and we slipped away just as a red-hot shower of lava spewed forth. We both laughed.

"That girl, Cayri, is persistent," he stated dryly after the levity faded. I realized that there was a reason she gave up so easily on that earlier encounter. Facing a huge, powerful Cybo, she must have felt outnumbered and wanted her cohorts. She did stump back once, though, to tag us with that tracker. Even with the tattle device gone, Rykard still stumped us several more times before he felt comfortable that we were in the clear.

"We're still in eighteen hundreds America," Rykard told me, "a rather primitive age. They have an infantile communication system that uses long and short pulses of electricity. My on board systems have been set up to decipher the messages."

Rykard's pod was like mine. It had no Virtual Mec Intellect to govern it. Rather it was a non-thinking computing mechanism, and a highly efficient one at that. It had elaborate auto-memory circuits for storage of any gathered data. The computer was designed to match the gathered information to the stored historical stuff. By the end of several hours of monitoring, the system found no discrepancies, so Rykard stumped forward to other centuries with similar results.

"Evidently, the timeline alteration is further ahead," I speculated at last.

"I believe so, as well," Rykard conceded. "We need to take a bigger jump ahead. Let's check somewhere partway through your stretch." This would be where I'd really miss having my pod, I knew. It was going to be difficult to verify any small changes without it. Rykard's pod did have some stored memory of my era.

All the pods carried general historical records of every Earth period recorded. It didn't matter much. Even without the intricate data my pod had, we discovered quite readily that in the late twenty-second century there was a skewed picture of things. Several stumps verified those differences. The big D's own history was well documented, of course. In the altered timeline, Daryl Om's presence had changed somewhat, and the line of Humans with the family name Keller, from which Ayryn had sprung from, was non-existent.

"It's obvious the point of change is somewhere within these few centuries," Rykard affirmed. "If we're to have any chance of determining where it is, we'll need more information on this time period."

"I usually just monitor airwave broadcasts," I suggested, "but for in-depth information there are data nets the native population uses. To link to them you need a trans-converter."

"A what?" he groaned. "This pod has nothing like that."

"We could infiltrate a facility somewhere and install a data tracker." I told him. "There is a repository near where Daryl Om was first conceived. One of us could sneak into the building after hours and place it."

"I'll agree to that," Rykard grunted, "but only if you do it. I don't trust you with my pod."

"I suppose," I answered him meekly. Being alone in a strange century wasn't my idea of fun, and my self-confidence was rather crippled lately. "You'll come after me if something goes wrong, won't you?" I charged him.

"Just don't alter the timeline, Synth," he replied sourly. "It's messed up enough as it is...and watch out for those enemy operatives. I'll have to drop you somewhere and then stump. We'll rendezvous at a different time and place a few hours later."

I did agree to that, but I couldn't say I was exactly happy about being out there on my own. There was definitely a secure feeling being safely in-pod, and I wished that I could bring it with me. Rykard did help me with the operation prep, so that I was as ready as I could ever be when I got let off. He stumped immediately, per our plan, as I ran to the shelter of some nearby woods.

It was a pitch black night, and the thin sliver of a moon cast very little light on the terrain. My equipment compensated, though. I had a lightweight helmet that was programmed for vision enhancements. Designed by Daryl Om himself, the technical headgear projected signals that targeted the wearer's optical nerves as they impacted the

Humanoid mind. The result was a data stream that would seemingly appear on the retina like a projection, visible only to the person wearing the helmet. This projection included a tactical display of the surrounding area out to a thousand meters. Time operatives like me were on their own for these kinds of excursions, and all my equipment was non-thinking. Still it was sophisticated gear, especially the nomatic compass which was quite precise. Once calibrated to some point in Space/Time, it was accurate no matter where or when it was moved. I had entered the exact coordinates of my target destination, just before I departed Rykard's pod, so that it would always give me direction and distance; in this case to a college library. Checking the compass, I learned that the library was a few miles to the south. I began hiking cautiously, walking as briskly as I could, and soon came to a populated area. That made me even more nervous. I didn't want to run into any local Humans, even after dark. In past encounters, synthetic Humans like me were somewhat of a shock to regular ones. I guess our bodies are a little too perfect, and we have a bit of a glow. In those earlier experiments, time ops had to stump back to repair the timelines after such confrontations. I was anxious to avoid that kind of problem, so, remembering my stealth training, I kept to the shadows. Being patient and diligent paid off, and without any unwanted incidents, I found myself at the building where the data we needed was accessible.

The structure was unoccupied that late, but unfortunately for me, it was securely locked. I searched for an easy entry point, and was not able to find one. I settled on trying to force open a window. I pried on it a little too hard, and cracked the clear plastlike panel.

"Piece of gargit," I swore. The breakage had set off some kind of noisy alarm. I checked my tactical display that showed no Humans were coming—yet. I knew I only had a few minutes before some authority figure would show up to investigate. They would have weapons, and the weapons of this era often dealt deadly force. Removing the broken glass, I got in and quickly located an information center. Setting the scanner to the main casing, I activated it. The scanner immediately began the download, sucking out vast amounts of data, all that the little antiquated station had access to.

Abruptly, my tactical issued a warning. Some Humans were now converging upon my position at a high rate of speed. My breathing and heartbeat became quickly accelerated. Snatching the scanner, I raced in the opposite direction, slipping out the way I had gotten in. Keeping the quick pace, I ran and ran until there was a considerable distance between me and those Humans. After that I slowed down, and went back into stealth mode, again keeping to the shadows. I was heading toward our rendezvous point, when I ran into something, and I just had to check it out. This something was a simply heavenly smell. I had no idea what it was, but it smelled like food, and I wanted some. Rykard and I were running out of rations already, so I used resupplying as an excuse to investigate. The smell led me to a small late night eatery of some sort, but unfortunately, there were lots of people inside. I scouted around back to what was probably a food preparation area, and there were a lot less Humans there. I waited until just one remained, but as luck did have it, he came out the back right to where I was hiding behind a large metal disposal unit. He was about to throw something in there when he saw me, and I had to stun him.

"Garg," I muttered. Now there was another possible mess, and I had already skewed the timeline once by setting off that alarm. Oh well, I thought. Wouldn't we just fix everything anyway, assuming we were successful in repairing the main temporal damage? I was still hungry, though. Damning the risk, I slipped inside the kitchen and looked for the food that was making that wonderful smell. There, on a table, were large round platters of an interesting looking entre. I was just about to grab one, when a female Human came and took them away. I hid from her and silently swore again, upset that I couldn't partake in the sustenance with such a tantalizing odor. Looking around, I found some other foodstuffs. There were some cylindrical metal containers that I took, and some other plast bottles that had a clear liquid in them.

Running quickly away, I nearly tripped over that Human I had stunned earlier, and headed into a wooded area. There was a thicket that was somewhat sheltered and I opened one of the cylinders. It wasn't nearly as good tasting as what I imagined the food I smelled from before would have been, but I grunted and ate some of the red mush anyway. It was sour, but my stomach didn't care, rumbling an approval. After that I tried one of the plast bottles. The liquid was heady and bubbly with an interesting flavor. I was thirsty so I finished it quickly. Drawn to the beverage for some reason, I opened another, and why not. I'd had little to drink for hours. Partway through that one, however, I began to feel odd. My face was a bit numb and that got me giddy. Suddenly, my helmet warning light came on. I was supposed to be nearly to the rendezvous point by then, but I let myself get sidetracked. Looking at the compass I realized that it was still several miles away. I headed off at a run. By the time I got there, I was several minutes late, and Rykard's pod was nowhere to be seen. I had little choice but to wait there and hope he'd be back to retrieve me. Hiding a short distance away on a ridge of higher ground just above our rendezvous clearing, I tried blending into a patch of thicker flora so I could observe unseen like we had done before. The wait was punishment enough for my foolish behavior.

Nearly thirty minutes went by before Rykard's pod did finally stump in and I was so relieved. I jumped up, ready to hurry down there. Abruptly I halted, melding with the brush. The pod's door opened and someone in a dark cloak hobbled out of it. The movement was jerky, not like Rykard at all, and light from the doorway harshly played across the misshapen face. It looked vaguely like that girl Cayri, but the features were deformed and hideous. Other figures emerged, following the first, and I decided to remain hidden, for obvious reasons. Terrible thoughts shook me, and they played upon my mind. The figures were looking for me, and Rykard was dead or taken!

Cayri, herself, stumped in then, and scowled at the others. Screaming angrily, she smacked one of them hard across the face. "You were supposed to wait for the girl to come out into the open! Get back to the pod!" They did, and subsequently all of them left. Unnerved to where I could have easily bungled everything, I skidded quickly away over the back of the ridgeline. I ran and ran until I was exhausted, and still I ran, as if I was back at the academy and Rykard was hounding me. I couldn't bear to even think about what might have happened to him. With fear and shame whipping me, I doggedly stayed with the way worn dirt path I'd chanced upon until it tracked around a rough old tree. Skipping sideways, my foot somehow caught a root, and I fell right onto my face. Before I could control them, the Human emotions I had inherited with this body overwhelmed me. I laid there in the dirt and burst open like a raincloud, crying uncontrollably.

CHAPTER TWELVE

9815AD (Present Standard Time) earlier

Almost immediately Ting's rage blunted. The bewildering aspect of abruptly being somewhere completely different was unsettling. It had been a dark moonless night just a few seconds ago, and now it was mid-day in a place foreign to her. This was not what Ting expected when she chased Cayri into that round bluish sky hole through whatever it was. Fearful of the precipitous unknown, Ting's fur stood up. Her natural instincts shifted Ting's demeanor into a type of surreptitious mode, and she slipped into the cover of some bushes nearby.

From that vantage, Ting surveyed the alien landscape as her eyes adjusted to the bright light. She quickly spied that fiend Cayri who had hurt Ting's Human. Cayri was not alone, however, and Ting was rankled that she could not vent her desire to inflict some pain. Deplorably, there were others, hooded figures that moped around the general vicinity without any apparent purpose.

"You there!" Cayri ordered one of them, "bring me my gear." The decrepit thing hobbled off to a transit vehicle. A moment later the figure limped back with a large plast parcel. Cayri snatched it away with no thank you or word of approval. Riffling through the container, she got out an aid kit and treated the wounds on her hand. After that, Ting watched Cayri outfit herself with weapons and tack as if she were preparing for some kind of dangerous liaison. Completing the process, Cayri ordered the others to get back into their craft and used the device on her waist to generate another blue hole. Ting wasn't sure what to do. In the last possible instant, she flew as fast as she could into that new hole, hoping it would somehow lead her back to her familiar palace. At the very least, she reasoned, there might yet be a chance to damage the one who had harmed her Ayryn.

Coming through, however, Ting found herself in another scary place. She was in some kind of structure filled with raucous activity. There were other Humans present besides Cayri, who was talking to one of them. After a short, heated conversation and a walk outside, Cayri ditched that location, leaving yet another blue hole. None of the other Humans seemed to be able to see it, even though one nearly walked into it. Ting darted past that Human and into the opening, determined, with catbird stubbornness, to not let Cayri get away. Things got precarious after that, however. Cayri went to many new locations here and there as Ting followed covertly, somehow avoiding detection. While all this transpired, the opportunity to harm Cayri did come around a couple times, but by then Ting had realized her predicament. She would never be able to get back to where she belonged by herself. Unwitting or not, she would need Cayri's help. Being patient was not easy for catbirds, yet Ting was resolved. She would wait for the right situation to present itself, no matter how long that would take. Until then, Ting would tail Cayri through the blue holes. What else could she do? It seemed singularly odd that no one, not even the ugly Humanoid minions Cayri bossed around, could see the blue holes. Ting began to suspect that Cayri herself was blind to them. Must be a catbird thing, Ting decided.

That whole day, or the equivalent period of time as Ting reckoned it, Cayri was quite preoccupied. As she traversed about through the blue holes, Cayri confronted Mecs or other Humanoids that she would come upon. The meeting nearly always ended poorly for the ones that Cayri encountered. She had a way of tricking them with falsehoods, and when their guard was down, Cayri would immobilize them. Sometimes she killed. Once those adversaries were neutralized, she took their odd conveyances and decimated or stranded them also.

Keeping her distance, Ting witnessed all of that. She wished there was something she could do to help the poor victims, but Cayri was too good, too cunning. Ting could think of nothing better than committing to an all out direct confrontation which would surely end badly for her in some forsaken place. That did not appeal to Ting at all and she dismissed the notion. Until something changed, her logical objective was to stay hidden and get back to her Ayryn. She had a feeling that Ayryn needed her now, and much more than Ting's own desire for revenge.

Unfortunately, everything was going Cayri's way throughout all these encounters, and those she met were soon victims, until that last pair. Ting knew they were last, because she overheard Cayri boast about it to her creepy followers. The usual strategy was to take on just one opponent at a time, but this time, and unknown to Cayri, both remaining agents were near. At first Cayri seemed to have the advantage. Ting watched helplessly as, once again, Cayri spewed her foul lies to a young looking red-haired Hybrid that reminded the emotive catbird of her Ayryn. Ting was desperate to help, but lacked the means to. Attempting some kind of direct attack was an ill-planned and useless gesture that Ting once again realized would most likely result in her own demise. Ting understood Cayri's prowess all too well by that point and the overpowering need to ensure that her own Human was all right gauged Ting's sense of right and wrong. Thus she sought out other options, ones that weren't as perilous. Sneaking cautiously over to the odd conveyance, the one that the Hybrid girl had emerged from, Ting tried the doorway. It was barred, but through a viewport she could see inside. Under a coverlet someone appeared to be sleeping. Ting began scratching and then banging on that hatch, making as much noise as she dared. Finally the dark figure stirred, and then got up. Not long after, the conveyance unceremoniously disappeared into one of those same blue holes. How odd, Ting thought, as she flew back to the others, that the person in the conveyance chose to flee instead of help. Perched on a nearby scraggly branch, Ting perceived that things were not going well. Cayri was taunting the helpless girl, and preparing to end her life. Just as Cayri was about to discharge her weapon one last time, a large male Cybo struck her from behind, knocking Cayri silly. Ting was pleased, but Cayri immediately dematerialized, creating another blue hole. Ting was torn between following Cayri through, or staying with the others, unsure if they could help her. They did seem familiar, more like people she knew at the palace especially the Cybo who reminded her of the King. Unfortunately, Ting had very little time to decide. In the end, Ting felt she had best stay the course and keep following Cayri in the hope that she would someday end up back where Ayryn was. When that moment came, Ting vowed, she would impart her revenge.

After her failure Cayri was livid. She beat up a couple of her goons to loosen some of her frustration. There must have been a backup plan, because Cayri went here and there, through many holes to lots of different locations. In a couple of these places Ting almost got left behind. Cayri was changing sites so fast Ting actually had to search for the next blue hole immediately after jumping through one. Often the hole had nearly evaporated as she hurried into it. Ting had no idea what was going on, until finally the other red-haired Hybrid girl showed up; the one Cayri had nearly killed. It was blind luck that brought the two of them together.

Cayri had just come back from some particularly dangerous places. Ting thought that the ground was on fire at one of them.

Cayri was angry, like she often was, and yelled at her witless subordinates yet again. They were milling around looking for something. Ting needed to hide so she flew up into a tree and found a branch high above the unpredictable action. From there Ting carefully observed what was going on. That's how she spied that other Hybrid Human girl hiding in some bushes. By this time, and after racing through all of those holes, Ting was getting tired of the chase. Following Cayri was getting her nowhere, and Ting nearly got left behind a couple times. This other girl seemed a lot nicer. She was scared though, especially after watching Cayri beat her associates yet again, and Ting wondered what the girl would do. It didn't take long to find out.

After her tirade, Cayri dissipated, leaving a blue hole. This time Ting let it go hoping it wasn't a mistake doing so. Following the other girl, above and at a distance, they hurried away from that area and any pursuit. It didn't matter. Cayri and the others were gone now. The Hybrid girl ran on and on, though, until she tripped and fell. Languid there in the dirt, the girl started to cry. Ting was perplexed about that, but genuinely sympathetic. She flew down to the ground near to where the girl lay and looked her over.

"Are you hurt?" Ting asked. The Hybrid girl got up quickly, drawing out her weapon in the process. The crying ceased amazingly fast.

"Who's there?" the girl demanded, looking around. When she saw a catbird, the girl was astounded.

"I won't hurt you," Ting answered, which also shocked the girl.

"You don't belong in this century," the girl accused. "What are you doing here?" Rather than get into that, Ting ambled over and rubbed her side against the girl's leg. It had a calming effect as always.

"I'm lost, and it's a long story," Ting offered. The girl relaxed and sat down on a log. Ting jumped up in her lap.

"Looks like we're both lost," the girl muttered morosely, "thanks to me."

"Why?" With just that one word, Ting opened a floodgate. The girl, who was very hard on herself, told Ting how she was a screw-up and a failure. She told Ting that she had messed up several times, and how it would cost them all. Most of all she blamed herself for having failed her associate named Rykard who was now dead or captured.

"Who is Rykard?" Ting wanted to know.

"He was my superior," she choked, "and a good friend. We were supposed to complete an extremely important mission."

"Is he the large Cybo?" Ting asked.

"Why, yes!" the girl replied, somewhat astounded that this little catbird knew what she was talking about.

"Oh he's not dead," Ting responded, "or taken." The girl lifted Ting to look into her eyes. Ting didn't like that.

"Where is he?" she demanded.

"I don't know!" Ting answered. "Please put me down…I don't like this. Your Cybo associate is, I suspect, running around here somewhere like you. The other Hybrid girl, that Cayri, tricked him."

"How do you know her?" the girl wanted to know, "and are you the catbird from my dream?"

"I don't know," Ting admitted again. "I'm not sure how I would get in anyone's dreams, but I followed that Cayri all the way here from the palace." The hairs stood up on the back of the Hybrid girl's neck, and she nearly swooned.

"You are that catbird!" she propounded. "I take it you don't like Cayri much."

Ting snarled. "I would scratch her eyes for what she did to my Human!" The Hybrid girl smiled, and gently set Ting down.

"Rykard calls me Synth," she offered.

"I'm Ting."

"Well, it looks like we're stuck here, Ting," Synth again remarked, dejectedly. "I've lost my pod, and evidently so did Rykard." Ting was preening.

"What is a pod?" she asked.

"It's our conveyance," Synth replied, "our way home."

"Oh," Ting yawned, "the large plast-metal cage you travel in?"

"Yes," Synth sighed.

"I have seen them," Ting declared. "There is one a short fly away, I believe."

"What?" Synth nearly squeaked. "Show me!" Getting up quickly, Synth nearly knocked Ting over. Landing on her paws, Ting jumped upward and spread her wings. Flying to a high tree branch, Ting looked about. There were no enemies to be seen other than a few non-speaking animals. They seemed to have nothing but a feral disdain for the catbird so she kept her distance. Flying back down, Ting told Synth to travel in an easterly direction while she would scout ahead for possible dangers. In that way, they made the ten kilometer trip without any problems. When they got near the pod, however, Ting reported it heavily guarded. At least five of the miscreant minions were circled around the captured vehicle. Cayri was nowhere to be seen.

"How can we get those creepy things away from there?" Synth wondered aloud. Ting thought about it.

"Perhaps I can lure them away," she suggested. "They're not very bright."

"I still have my stunner," Synth remarked. "If you lead them into the woods, I can hide in the bushes and stun them." The two soon formulated a plan around that, and put it into play. Ting would sneak up to one of them and taunt the dull-witted aberration. Before long, the malformed guards would chase after the elusive catbird, and Ting would lead them one by one to where Synth was hiding. This worked exceptionally well for the first four, but the last one was a little brighter than the others. That one realized that something was amiss, and she put out a message to Cayri.

"Funny thing is here," she said.

"Like what?" Cayri replied.

"Know not," the muddy headed one responded. "Mowpies go and not come back." Cayri was not interested in riddles.

"Get them back and guard that pod," she seethed, "or you'll be whipped."

"Yes highness," the Mowpy hastily replied, and that was the end of the conversation. By then, Synth had come up from behind and got close enough to stun this last Mowpy. Looking up, Synth smiled. She was suddenly happier than she had been for quite a long time. There, in front of her, was a Temp Corps pod, alone and unguarded…her pod.

CHAPTER THIRTEEN

9815AD (Present Standard Time) Earth

"He who turns and runs today will live to fight another day," Clayre proposed seriously.

"Where did you get that?" Xet in his gold armor wondered, as he turned towards her.

"It's something I heard when I was young," she replied tentatively. In truth, neither one reckoned they would get an opportunity to run from that which now approached. Daryl held his Clayre tightly.

"At the least, it looks like we're about to find out who is responsible for all this," he told the others. The smaller conveyance that emerged from the huge one was resplendent and opulent.

"Looks like something I might have made," Xet remarked, "…in my conqueror days." Daryl laughed good heartedly.

"It is a nice ride," he agreed. The conveyance pulled up in front of them and stopped a couple dozen meters away. The bejeweled cover slowly and majestically peeled back to reveal an even more elaborate throne with spectacular gems, the like of which had never before been seen on Earth. A figure, larger than life, sat upon it, and composed of a mix of etheric substances that appeared to be metallic yet supple like plast or even skin. Somewhat hominid in form, the entity was grotesque. The huge torso was supported by three humanlike legs with as many arms. The large head had six eyes, encircling it…two for each of its three faces. One of the faces, a sickeningly beautiful one, peered down at Clayre, Daryl, and Xet.

"I don't remember creating you," the giant being remarked. It was obvious to whom it spoke.

"Who are you?" Xet asked in reply. That brought on a deep rumble of laughter from the being in front of him.

"I am that which you had the potential to become," the god-like entity responded, "however, I am as far above you as you are above an insect."

"Then you are Xetacon, who I was copied from?" Xet stated, mostly in the form of a question, somewhat bewildered. Another round of laughter ensued.

"You begin to see," the god-being related, "but I am no longer just Xetacon. I am Xetagod, the magnificent, omniscient like your

Daryl Om was.

"What did you do to him?" Clayre shouted angrily.

"Ah yes, Clayre," Xetagod responded. "It has been a long, long time, has it not?"

"Not long enough!" Clayre stated bravely, which only brought on another round of deep laughter.

"I see you have been altered," Xetagod commented, "Your body is now immortal, unless damaged. A gift from your Daryl Om, no doubt. It'd be a shame if something bad happened to it." This last comment was meant for the Hybrid Daryl, the one who stood there next to Clayre, and it brought out a response.

"Xetacon, old friend," Daryl began, "to what do we owe the benevolence of your presence?" The causticity was most definitely not concealed.

"It is Xetagod, and do not mock me, copy," the huge figure answered curtly. "Even a weak one such as yourself should be aware that I could crush you and your lovey friends with but a thought."

"Of course," Daryl answered undaunted. "You seem to have done quite well out there in the cosmos." Xetagod allowed the change of topic. It gave him a chance to boast.

"Oh yes," he raved proudly. "I rule multiple systems, now…not just one insignificant planet! Even as we speak, my minions are conquering several more!"

"You have what you always desired," Daryl admitted, "…power, worlds to conquer, and control. Why bother with us after all this time?"

"You are indeed a weak copy," Xetagod, the great, replied, "if you cannot guess the answer to that. Earth is my home world, for one, and also I wish to redress my humiliation at the hands of you and your Clayre, as well as my defeat in Ayryn's time. Is that not her lifeless shell nearby?"

"You are no more than a murderous coward!" Daryl raved, losing his calm demeanor and getting rather emotional. "Hiding behind all your power, you have not the virtue to forgive or forget! Ayryn would have forgiven you!" Xetagod let the insult slide. He would get plenty of retribution later.

"Perhaps," he calmly replied, "but I did not murder her. This Ayryn was my Ayryn also. She was killed by a version of herself that I created. Yes, I had her in my possession long enough to copy her DNA. Cayri is so like Ayryn in many ways, and unfortunately, as unpredictable. It is the one part of her that I have not asserted my complete control over. I rather like how she surprises me from time to time. I see Daryl Om's hand in Ayryn's preservation. How else like you, Clayre, could she have survived through these millennia?"

"These Humans are endearing, are they not," Daryl expressed, "why not leave them be, and view them for the sheer amusement."

"Oh, but I do plan to have them amuse me," Xetagod asserted, "...for eons." A part of the giant's body dissolved or opened up, it was hard to tell which. Inside was a figure, a young girl of about twenty. Both Daryl and Xet knew who it was. The face and body belonged to Ayryn. An Ayryn who was barely a young adult and this was a clone of her. She was afraid, delirious and naked. Suddenly she flushed, and made funny noises. Her eyes closed. It was obvious that Xetagod was pleasuring her somehow. Just as abruptly her eyes opened again in sheer terror as she was drawn back inside the giant shell, and it closed in upon her.

"You evil fiend!" Clayre spat venomously. Xetagod only laughed.

"Beside this Ayryn copy there is room for you," he taunted, speaking directly to her.

"I'd rather be dead," Clayre stated defiantly.

"None of you will die," Xetagod revealed. "Your mind is open to me, dear Clayre. I see that Daryl Om has provided for nearly all of you Humans. There will be more than enough entertainment for the great one seated before you, and it will endure to the end of time! I see billions of Heavenworlds!" Clayre choked. All of her family and friends existed there.

"Please," she sobbed.

"My dear Clayre," he responded in a way that was almost comforting. "You had best learn to respect me for the sake of those you care about." His body opened up once more. "For all those you love, come inside!" Xet could take it no longer.

"What have you gained," he objected loudly, "when you take everything you can, but still feel empty inside? I, too, have glutted on power. It is shallow and vacuous. What good is any success without others to share it?" Undaunted, Xetagod smiled.

"There's room here for many," the god-conqueror proposed again. "Won't you rejoin with me? Come inside...or would you rather be destroyed." Xet, Clayre and Daryl's friend, was quiet as if torn. He looked at their faces and frowned.

"It has been an interesting time," he told them. Facing the mighty vestige of his former self, he bowed deeply. With a sigh, Xet walked steadily toward the towering figure as it opened to receive him. Turning as he entered, Xet nodded to his friends, and just as the mighty shell engulfed him, he called out. "Run!"

Guessing what Xet was up to, Daryl swept Clayre into his arms and carried her off as quickly as he could. She was in no shape to move on her own. She was crying, bereft of all will. The god-being was not moving, and Daryl knew it was their only chance. Xet had sacrificed himself to give them this one opportunity to escape. Putting forth all his power and knowledge, Xet was challenging that which formed Xetagod's core; it formed his own as well. There was a simple set of codes. Xet had to merely reverse the directives. It might have completely immobilized even the god-like persona, but Xetagod's will was altogether too strong, too immutable, now. Xet's strength to resist was eaten away slowly and dissolved. His totality was drawn into Xetagod's intact, but without the ability to act. He could now only witness what transpired. For the several moments this took, Xetagod had been incapacitated as Xet was assimilated, and that was all Daryl needed. He got Clayre to the pod and they promptly used the inter-dimensional modus to revert themselves back to the Parallux universe where Xetagod would not be able to immediately find them. Xetagod was furious. He planned to take out most of this rage on the one who was responsible.

In his anger Xetagod caustically threatened Xet. "You will pay for this, weak copy of one you should only bow to!" There was not much he could do, though. As a virtual being, there was little that could actually harm Xet other than mental or emotive stress, and Xet had gained control over these. The threat of deletion was not that effective either.

"Go on, terminate me!" Xet taunted. "I'll die in the knowledge that I have gained an escape for my friends."

"For the moment," Xetagod admitted. "Don't believe that I won't soon retrieve them. As soon as I discover where the Daryl residue has escaped to, they're mine. As for you, how would you like a nice Human body…one with never-ending nerve endings?"

Xet shuddered. Like that, he could be tortured, forever.

CHAPTER FOURTEEN

June 10th 2015AD

Freedom! The little stink bug instinctively felt what that was. It had experienced a narrow escape, or so it perceived, and did somehow come out of it unscathed. Well, nearly so. There was a slight tear in the right rear wing where part of it had chipped away. Stinky could still fly all right, though, and that reassured him. Being near normal, and once again in a more familiar arena, he flew off in search of a plant to chew on. It had been some time since he had eaten and the urge was insistent now. Stinky didn't go far before his faceted eyes picked up on his favorite color, green! Immediately his sensory perception also detected the familiar odor, and they drew him straight to it. Landing on a leaf where the smell was quite strong, the famished stink bug began to nibble. It seemed to have been ages (for an insect) since he'd eaten anything, and stinky tore off big bits of leaves to masticate. His mandibles made short work of them as he filled his empty digestive tract. Now this was the life. It was a complete reversal from the harrowing time he'd just went through.

There was that horrible noisy place that he'd gone into because of the odd light. It was at the beginning the great dark time, and he was attracted to the smaller bright area that injected itself into his vision. Once there, however, stinky could not find a way out, and he spent what seemed like ages foraging. There was some material that resembled tree, but was like no tree he'd ever experienced. It was smooth and flat. Still, he could climb up onto it and he hoped that somewhere there would be a few leaves he could munch. He searched and searched, getting nowhere, and then a big white leaf enveloped him. The next thing he knew it was brighter and he was outside. Stinky was glad of that, even if he was shocked by the rough treatment. Somehow he'd gotten through this first ordeal alive, and that had changed the little insect, even though he wasn't really aware of it.

In any case, all that was over now, and as soon as the life-giving food began to digest, stinky slowed down. He remembered his usual insect instincts, and began to eat more leisurely. He should rest next, like when the great darkness came. The great darkness always came on slowly and so gradually that he rarely noticed the change until he was fully wrapped up in it. With it, darkness brought out different dangers. He had his stink defense, of course, and he was always ready to release those chemicals at the first sign of trouble. If that didn't work, well, he could fly. Many predators could not. Mostly, though, he'd curl up under a leaf and hide until it was bright again. Stink bugs generally prefer daylight, and stinky was surely normal.

For the present, however, he was outdoors and it was still bright, so stinky didn't feel any need to defend himself. He was planning to take a good long rest, when that other peculiar smell hit him again. He wasn't sure what it was, at first, but he was compelled to follow it. Female stink bug pheromones draw males like magnets, and stinky was locked in and suddenly desperate to find a girl stink bug. The force to propagate was strong in that one, obviously. He had done a similar search fairly recently, too, and it had ended in a terrifying time that stinky barely survived. Unknown to the little insect, other species also had similar troubles when attempting to acquire mates. For stinky, the frightening incident transpired as he was trying to cross that odd hard grey dirt. He had nearly been eaten, and a sudden flash of hindsight reminded him of that.

It was right after the white leaf had let him go, it seemed. Stinky flew off then, feeling the warm breeze lift him. He could only go so high, though. The funny tingle had let him know where the Earth was, and it also pointed out his location on or above it. Getting too high made his flying erratic so stinky usually kept close to the ground. He went here and there, over flowering meadows and such, carefully avoiding stink bug pitfalls like spider webs or birds. Most birds left stink bugs alone. The stink flavor was not a gourmet delight for them, and unless it was a young one with little parental guidance on stink bugs, avians were fairly innocuous. Certain frogs were not as picky, and water was definitely a hazard. If stinky got into a pond, well, he would flounder around until a fish or frog took notice. Even if predators didn't get him, he would most likely drown in collections of wet liquids. Stinky stayed away from the large expanses of water, getting his drinks from wet mud or dew drops. There were a couple places he flew over where puddles had been, and stinky would have liked a drink, if not for that enticing scent. He'd had to work hard to fly into the face of the light wind that carried it, and over a slight rise he ran into something rather unexpected. There were unclear objects, replicated a hundredfold times in his multi-faceted eyes, that whooshed by at incredible speeds.

Of course, at that time stinky had no idea what they were. Luckily, they all just went on by, ignoring him. The female stink bug was close now, he could tell, yet he was cautious. He waited quite a while for a lull in the onset of the unknown creatures and got impatient. Stinky got himself worked up into a "now or never" set, and flew on across the hard grey earth in an attempt to get passed the onrush of fast monsters. He was nearly over when an object whizzed by him, unnervingly close, and stinky almost found a new calling as a windshield decoration. The air currents whipped him up over it, fortunately, but subsequently he was sucked into a strong downdraft and drawn right into one of the huge creatures. An odd animal this, he felt. The eye he landed in was on the inside of its open mouth. Then everything changed drastically. Immediately after that eye predicament began, the onset of a vertiginous flurry of unnatural stimulus did transpire. Stinky was thrown about, spinning round and round in a brief, but horrific episode, until all the strange creatures stopped dead. Finding himself upside down on the hard grey earth, it took him quite a long time to get righted. As soon as he did, stinky flew off to find those females. He mated quickly, and then found he was famished. Ah, green heaven!

CHAPTER FIFTEEN

9815AD (Present Standard Time)

"A new development has come to my attention," Xetagod told his favorite. Cayri bowed low.

"What is your desire, my god-emperor?" There was much more implied in what she was offering than just her service, and he looked at her intently. The clothing she now wore was different. Flowing and diaphanous, he could see the outline of her figure as the light shimmered through the filmy material. She knew it would fuel his imagination, but Xetagod was all business.

"Have you eliminated the last of Daryl's foolish time marshals?" He put forth. The question was unnecessary. He already knew the actual truth, and she understood that as well. Xetagod was testing her and Cayri was well aware of it.

"Yes, your highness," she replied, "All but two who are now podless and thus impotent, trapped in an unimportant time beyond the critical one."

"That is not factual," Xetagod scoffed. "One of them has re-acquired a pod."

"Perhaps," Cayri admitted, "but that has not been verified. It is true that one of the captured pods is missing, my lord."

"The Daryl scum has taken it! You can be assured of that! Do not underestimate them, or Daryl. He has ever appeared weak, only to turn the tables on me! I see that you have also failed to retrieve the Daryl bauble that Ayryn wore." Cayri winced. She felt pain wrack her whole body and every nerve screamed in agony like Cayri was one great solitary wound.

"Mercy, master!" she pleaded. "The vicious little catbird was protecting her!"

"That is not a worthy excuse."

"I will retrieve the article from Ayryn's body immediately, my master," she offered.

"The trinket is no longer there."

"...then I will retrieve the missing pod and kill the two who have eluded me." The pain stopped momentarily.

"Make sure that you do," Xetagod huffed. "My plan has been well crafted. Daryl Om would have detected any frontal attack, so I chose to use his own strategies against him. Altering time to erase

Daryl Om was deliriously pleasing. Early on in our conflict, Daryl used the same ploy against me, and it nearly succeeded. Only by exiting Earth's dimension into another, was I able to prevent my own deletion. A form of Daryl and his female remain at large by utilizing the same maneuver. I will deal with them, while you remove the two agents still viable." Cayri bowed her assent, but then became bold.

"The clones you allow me for operatives are dim-witted and ineffective," she complained. "It was they who prematurely tipped off the Cybo agent, and it was they who allowed the pod to be taken."

"This I already know," Xetagod affirmed. "As I have already alluded, only dual dimensional beings are unaffected by time manipulations. Of all my minions, only these are such." Cayri knew why they had limited cognitive abilities. They were the unfortunate experiments that did not turn out quite right.

"It would be easier to achieve your goals, my god-emperor, without them," she asserted, being nearly insubordinate now, and pushing her status as favorite to the limit. She knew her master well. He would spoil her.

"I have acquired another," Xetagod told her. "One who has strong mental abilities."

Xetagod's body opened up and a golden figure came forth.

"This is how I appeared in my youth," he remarked, "not long after I came to be. I was known as Xetacon in those days. This one, however, calls himself Xet." Looking over the gold Xetacon, Cayri smiled.

"I will still be in charge," she stated, not as a question. Xetagod admired her spunk.

"Only if you do not fail me again. This copy of my former self has a link to my core. Your status is dependent upon your success." Cayri nodded, but inside she knew she had other ways of maintaining her hold.

"I have missed you, my generous master," she expressed in that soft voice. "I am more effective with your closeness to succor me. I offer my totality…do with me as you please." Xetagod's body opened up, and Cayri walked freely forward. Her alluring clothing dissolved as she entered and then she was trapped, enclosed in her master's shell. As soon as she was inside he began stimulating her, firing off the nerve endings in her brain to bring pleasure this time, but she resisted.

"Allow me, my god-lover, to stimulate you," Cayri told him with her mind. He allowed it, and she related to him, in thought, how she would have sexually abused him had their roles been reversed. It was a trick on her part to get him to do those things to her and her body. The illusionary stimulus felt just as real as if he had actually taken her, and he was not gentle. In Cayri's mind he was handsome, the depiction Xetagod projected was the very desire she created for a perfect lover. She was laid out wantonly, inside his illusion, on a bed of luxuriant and satiny cushions just to heighten his desires. He took her and Cayri squealed in delight.

Ah, yes, thought Xetagod, re-evaluating her. This one is my favorite.

She let him have her for as long as he wanted, and it was a very extensive period indeed, possibly days, Cayri had no way of determining that. When he let her go at last, however, she was fully rested and in peak form; his gift to her.

"I must now deal with the Daryl copy and his female," Xetagod told Cayri. "They are most likely still cowering in a dimension separate from this one. I am entrusting you to deal with the remaining time operatives here. The gold copy of my earlier self, I send with you. Do not fail me. The change in the timeline I have instituted through you is immutable now. Only by going back to where the change occurred can the former existence be reinstated. That I will not allow. When the last two of Daryl's fools are eliminated, there will be no further barriers. You will begin phase two of my plan. The Daryl super computer that was created by the Humans in their remote past will be naïve and vulnerable. Without his original Human female, he will be accessible. You will revert to that past and befriend him. When the time is optimal, you will allow the transfer of technology that spawned my creation, and then eliminate cretinous Daryl, my enemy, from further existence. He will be deliciously surprised by your betrayal. When I come to power, the gold Xetacopy who is aiding you now, will rejoin my totality, and you will be my Queen."

"I understand, my lord and emperor," she affirmed, "and I will not fail you!" Cayri bowed low and slowly backed away in respect of her master's might. Xetagod appreciated her adherence to the protocols he had established for one such as himself, a being with life and death powers. She left Xetagod then, and his great and impressive temporal spacecraft as it prepared to search the dimension Daryl and his female had fled to.

Once she had refitted herself, Cayri travelled back in time, back into the past to fulfill her mission. She brought the gold Xetacopy with her.

"So where did you come from?" she asked this Xet in his golden shell.

"That is a long and unimportant tale," he grunted, "one I have no desire to relate. I am your god-master's now, linked with his totality." Cayri scowled.

"That may be so," she said smugly, "but you will obey me!"

"As long as you effectuate success," Xet asserted.

"Our task is an easy one," Cayri stated. "We will kill the male Cybo, to begin with.

"Yes," Xet agreed. "You will go back to the point in time where you last saw him. I will be there just prior to that. After being tricked like before, he will attempt to flee, only I will come up behind him and end his miserable life!"

"That was my plan," Cayri retorted sourly, "and it will work to perfection, if you execute correctly." Xet nodded, hiding a pretentious smile.

Cayri stumped to where her prior self should have been, but the site was deserted. Xet walked up to her.

"It is as I feared," he told her. "One of Daryl's operatives has altered this timeline. You should have been more vigilant. You wasted too much time pleasuring yourself and that has allowed the Daryl agent to outmaneuver us." Frowning, Cayri suggested they revert back to the original encounter, the one she was hesitant to re-engage because of her contact with both agents, especially the muscular Cybo. They returned to that temporal location only to find the timeline had been altered there as well. Xet's criticism was harsh, and Cayri got assertive.

"Eventually, the girl operative and the Cybo will attempt to discover when and where the critical time alteration has occurred," she stated caustically. "We will guard that temporal location, but I also have another plan in mind. We must find a way to lure the two someplace where they will be exposed and then delete them."

CHAPTER SIXTEEN

9815 AD (Present Standard Time) earlier

"Well, here we are," I softly lamented. "Here" was where Ting demanded we go (right now!) after we reacquired my pod. I tried to set the temporal coordinates for a time that Ting believed was prior to Ayryn being shot. From what I could see through the pilots view, this world appeared to be a dark and pathetic place. A smog choked atmosphere hung low in the half light of a dull moon as bits of green clouds fluttered past. Corroded plast and metal structures were everywhere. Inside, dim figures appeared, shadowed by the flash of sparks and framed in cracked windows or battered doorways. It was starkly obvious to me, now. When the natural timeline was altered, everything had changed. The history of the world skewed off onto a horrible direction, perhaps to one where an evil Xetacon, or whatever he called himself in this reality, prevailed. Nothing of the people or places that Ting or I had known remained. An angsty Ting was prepared to sacrifice any caution in her desire to get outside. I grabbed a stunner and opened the door. The impatient catbird flew off as soon as the opening was wide enough for her slinky body.

"Be careful!" I called after her. I wasn't about to be careless this time. Looking about, I thoroughly scanned the immediate area for enemies or anything dangerous, but detected nothing except for the caustic air. Abruptly, a shrill wail cut across the pale night.

"Ting!" I yelled, dropping any pretense of being careful or keeping a low profile, and scurried recklessly in the direction of the baleful sound. Ting was on top of a body, yowling in despair.

"Oh my, no!" I whispered softly. "It's Ayryn, isn't it?" Ting just howled a tortured cry that cut through my soul. I picked her up and gently stroked her back. After a moment, Ting calmed down a little.

"What happened to the palace?" she asked me, choking back a sob.

"Someone has gone into the past and changed something important," I told her, "and that has caused all this. The people and places that once were here have all ceased to be because they had never been born or built. All except for Ayryn. I suspect that she was like us, Hybrids of multi-dimensions. As with temporal pilots, her original shell probably resides in a stasis somewhere in the Parallux universe, which isn't affected by anything that happens on

Earth. That is why time alterations here cannot affect her…or us."

"My poor Ayryn," Ting sobbed, looking down at her lifeless body, nearly ready to wail some more. I tried to soothe her.

"In the here and now there isn't much we can do for Ayryn," I spoke calmly. "We must repair the timeline so that Daryl Om can restore her. Doing that will bring back everything."

"It was Cayri that did this!" Ting hissed, getting angry now. "I would scratch her eyes out…just allow me the chance!" I petted her some more.

"I, too, would like a piece of that one," I reassured Ting, stroking her fur, "but we must not get reckless in our anger. We may very well be the only ones left that can fix all this." I almost choked on those words. I knew all too well that I was a second rate operative, and for all this to be on me was a burden I had serious doubts I could handle. "We should not stay here long," I added, gathering my wits and feeble courage. "They may come looking for us here."

Even so, I could not just leave Ayryn like that. For Ting's sake, I put my jacket down on a tiny patch of grass and laid Ayryn's body upon it as well as I could. Ting gathered some rough wild flowers that somehow still grew in this cracked world. I set Ayryn's cold hands across her breast and fixed her hair a little so it appeared as if she might be asleep. As we prepared to leave, Ting nuzzled Ayryn's face one last time.

"Wait," Ting said, abruptly. "We cannot leave it here." I didn't understand as she tried to explain. "Ayryn once told me that the most important thing she did was protect it."

"Protect what?" I asked, still in the dark. Ting grabbed the chain that was around Ayryn's neck with her teeth, trying to get it off. Helping her, I gently removed it. The heavy silver chain supported a pretty pendant with translucent green stones. I put the elegant heirloom around my own neck for safekeeping and then urged us back to the pod. I was relieved that after everything my pod was still where we left it and untouched. I had feared it might auto-stump again, but then I realized there wasn't anyone left to order it to. At least I had been smart enough to disable all of the remote controls and homers before leaving it alone like that. In fact, I had seen to all that the moment I got my pod back. There was no way I was gonna let anyone steal it again, not easily anyway. I gave the pod's exterior another thorough once over for tracking scanners, too, and when I was satisfied we were clean, I stumped us. I took us well back this time, thousands of years, and long before the main time alteration must have occurred. I knew that the critical era would be closely monitored, and I had no idea how sophisticated their equipment was. It seemed like Cayri had stuff that found us all too easily.

"Would you like something to eat?" I asked Ting once we had set down and secured the area. She refused at first, until the food came out. Then she accepted small nibbles and I got quite liberal with them.

"We have to try to keep up our strength," I told her, "and our wits, if we are to prevail. Cayri is quite clever and cruel. There is little that she would not stoop to in the acquisition of her desires, and she's not squeamish about killing. That we know."

"Just get me close," Ting hissed. "I'll make her wish to be dead." I had to smile at the little catbird's boldness.

"Actually, I'm not sure what we should do next," I admitted. "Mostly, I just followed Rykard's lead. We need some kind of plan or strategy." Ting thought for a moment.

"What if we could get your Cybo friend back," she suggested.

"Of course," I blurted out, mad at myself for not thinking of something so obvious. Once Rykard was with us, I would let him take over. After all, he was the better leader. The hard part was figuring out how to get him back and when to try it.

"He's probably still running around in the woods where we first met," Ting speculated. This was true, I guessed, but chancy.

"Going to that time period is risky," I told her. "They will be looking for him, and us, there. He may already be captured." Something else abruptly occurred to me. "There is a bigger danger! Cayri knows where we were one prior time and place, and that is an even greater threat to us. She could go to that temporal location with reinforcements and delete us. We might have to alter the timeline to prevent such an outcome. It is a tricky thing altering time. Who can say for certain how events will play out after the change is made." Ting looked up at me.

"Still we must try…for Ayryn!"

I wholeheartedly agreed, but for all our brain wracking, neither Ting nor I could come up with a perfect solution to the problem. There seemed to be no way to prevent my former self from that first meeting with Cayri while retaining contact with Ting.

"I'm so sorry Ting," I told her. "If Rykard and I don't keep away from Cayri that first time, she will continue to go back there until she either kills us or we end up killing her. I'm surprised she hasn't already."

"Maybe she has," Ting said morosely.

"No," I answered with conviction. "If Cayri had, I would not be here. As soon as I warn my past self about this, however, the former timeline will dissipate and change to the new one. In that event we will probably get separated."

"Where will I go?" Ting wanted to know.

"I'm sorry, Ting," I said again. "I cannot say for certain. Most likely you will still be following Cayri about as before. I sincerely hope that we will rejoin with each other in the new timeline."

"There is no other way?" she asked, almost begging.

"No," I replied, my heart breaking. Sending Ting back into danger was almost more than I could bear. It had to be done, though, for Ayryn, for her, for everyone. I did not waste any more time. As a temporal operative, the duration of my life is linear no matter where in the past or future I go, and so in that way I'm sort of connected to the present standard time. For me, it was somewhere in the year 9815 AD, a readout on my console confirmed that. Changes that I, or anyone else, made to any past timelines would be initiated in order, one after another, along this present-time path, and I knew it would only be a short span of this linear present-time before Cayri would realize that she needed to go back to our original meeting point to do us in. I had to act first, before she did, deciding to go back even further than that first meeting and as soon as possible. I chose a crucial point of that particular recent past, the one where my pod first stumped away from me just as I was leaving to replenish my water rations. Getting in position, I waited as my former self opened the pod's outer door to go.

"Back inside," I ordered myself assertively. She retreated warily, as I pushed my way into the pod with Ting in my arms. The shocked look on my naïve former self almost made me laugh. I realized in that instant that I had aged eons since then.

"Who are you?" the younger me asked.

"You should be able to figure that out," I told her. "I'm your future self and there isn't time enough to explain everything. We're both lucky to still be alive after all the foolish things you did!" The other me looked aghast. "This pod will automatically stump anytime now," I went on. "What I'm going to tell you will change this timeline. When it does, me and this catbird will dissolve out of your reality. Remember this catbird. Her name is Ting, and she is very special to us. She will be near a young Hybrid woman named Cayri. Beware of her. She has killed all of the other operatives except for us and Rykard." I took Ayryn's necklace out and pulled it over my head. "This amulet was Ayryn's. It is very important, although I'm not sure why, so keep it safe." With that I handed it to my younger version. "You must, and this is extremely important as it will change the timeline, make sure that both you and Rykard turn off all your automatic and remote controls and then disable your homing signals. Don't ever come back to this place! The enemy will come here after you have gone." This statement was all that was needed to change the course of actions that lead me to be there.

The former me looked completely blown away as I disintegrated along with Ting. The pod stumped at that precise moment and I knew, with my very last thought, that at the least, I had kept Cayri from finding us.

CHAPTER SEVENTEEN

9815 AD (Present Standard Time) in Parallux

Clayre was crying. "Why did he do that?" she sobbed. Daryl, of course, was compassionate.

"My Clayre," he said softly, "it had to be so. Our friend, Xet, knew that all of us were in a very real danger of deletion, or worse. I cringe to think of what Xetagod had in store for you. Xet is nothing less than a hero, brave and courageous, sacrificing himself so that we could escape. Had he not done so, all of us would be unable to do anything to change the outcome of this horrendous situation. Xet probably felt some responsibility for what his future version has done, and that may be why he did what he did. Besides, realistically, he alone had the means to free us."

"What can we do, though," Clayre lamented, "against an enemy so powerful?"

"Our friend has given us a chance, slim though it is, to correct this aberration and restore things to the way they were."

"Oh, my Daryl," Clayre implored him, "do you think we can?"

"Uncertain, I am," he admitted, "but I cannot believe my core would have allowed Xetagod to so easily take over. There must be more to this than what we can understand. Perhaps there is a plan, and if so there is still hope, and that is what we must adhere to." Clayre nodded, sobering herself, and wiping away her tears.

"So what must we do," she asked, "and where are we?"

"We have transcended the visible universe and have re-entered Parallux," Daryl told her. "Not where we left it, however. If Xetagod follows us, I want to have some warning before he gets where we're going. When my core awareness first discovered this dimension, there was nothing here but a few impossibly remote areas of blue-white glowing plasma adrift in a black sea of nothing. These pools are slowly converging. In some epoch age of the distant future, they will eventually condense and then implode, creating the recipe for multitudinous galaxies, systems, and life. The plasma matter was enough, however. Daryl Om, my core, with Mec help had taken some and refined it. Using those captured particles, he combined them with ones from Earth to produce stable atoms and molecules that are neutral in both dimensions. This is what we are now made of. With this newly discovered matter, my core built a base of operations here in Parallux, a stronghold where dual dimensional Mecs and Hybrids could be created and trained. You were at this base just before we went back to Earth, and in minutes we will be there again."

Clayre looked out the main viewport, and she could see a large sphere. It was colossal, as big as any good-sized asteroid. Light was scarce in Parallux, but the distant pools of plasma gave the port a bluish hue. The base had its own running lights, as well, rows of reds, greens, and ambers. On top, spinning 360 degrees, a beacon shone brightly, a lone star in an endless night. Just like lighthouses in her time, Clayre recalled.

"Does this stronghold have a name?" she asked.

"Those who first came here, named it 'Manifest Point'," Daryl explained. "It is also called 'Parallux Port', or 'Parallux Hub', as nearly all inter-dimensional traffic from Earth is routed through this station. The Temp Corps Academy is based here as well."

"What's the Temp Corps?" Clayre wanted to know.

"They are the ones who need our help most, my Clayre," he stated. "My core-awareness created the Temporal Corpsmen to police the natural timeline as a precaution. It is they who have the means to determine where and how the past was changed." Clayre understood now, and realized what was at stake. Just a few individuals would have to stand up to the will of a god. It seemed hopeless, but then she remembered her own struggles, millennia ago. Somehow they had prevailed under no less dire circumstances. An amber light on her console flashing brightly distracted her just then, along with a raucous pulsating buzzing noise. They were pulling up to the huge inter-dimensional port, and a system of auto-controlled magnetic beams had latched onto the pod. They were being guided into an air lock.

"The hull of this base is dual dimensional, and acts as a shield for everything inside," Daryl explained. "In fact, most of this base can exist in both dimensions. There are huge converters that can print replicas of anything, like when you were enlarged. Utilizing the bi-dimensional atoms, even living beings like us can be duplicated." Clayre was amazed that Daryl Om had discovered such marvelous technology and could perform such unimaginable transformations.

"It's almost like magic," she sighed, "the things you, well, your core has done!" Daryl shrugged.

"With unlimited abilities," Daryl confessed, "and infinite knowledge, wondrous accomplishments can be gained, in anything.

Unfortunately, our enemy also has this ability." Clayre shuddered and spun toward the forward view for the distraction. The pod, having been drawn through a large portal, was slowly settling into a landing bay. With a slight thud it set down, and Daryl disengaged the nomatic drive. Clayre slipped out of the copilot's seat as Daryl opened the hatch, and there stood a large Mec to greet them.

"Hello, Furman!" Daryl said.

"Is this the Furman I met," Clayre asked, "when Xet and I came upon the creation of his Heavenworld?" Furman bowed.

"Yes, my lady," he replied. "I remember it well, even though it has been many millennia since." Clayre was astounded.

"Of course," she cautiously responded, "but for me it was only a few hours ago. You look amazingly good!"

"Thank you," Furman answered. "It is a new shell. I've had many over the years." Daryl offered Clayre an explanation.

"My Clayre, as you know, Furman is a Virtual Individual, a Mec. One of their abilities is that they can easily transfer from one motational shell to another."

"It comes in handy," Furman admitted, "especially when one is travelling. I could download from one side of Earth to the other in just four point five seconds." Clayre shook her head.

"I've missed a great deal, I think, in the years since I died," she stated, "...well, when my original body died."

"I do hope you will be given an opportunity to catch up when this is over," Daryl offered. He turned to Furman. "So how is the refit of Xet's temporal conveyance coming? We ran into some trouble back on Earth, and Xet is no longer with us. To effectuate our escape, Xet allowed himself to be captured by an arrogant being who was self-labeled 'Xetagod'. It is my belief that Xetagod is an evil Hybrid version of what Xetacon was. As for Xet, his status is unknown."

"I scanned your report," Furman replied, "and Xet's loss is unfortunate. Your friend would have been a great asset against this Xetagod. As for Xet's conveyance, it is nearly ready. Once we copied the design and created plans for a full-sized dual-dimensional version, fabricating it was not difficult. The plasma weapons and stealth mode are fully functional for either dimension in the larger model as well. Unfortunately, there is one minor problem. Your weaponry has limited power reserves. Once depleted, you will have to return here for recharging."

"Understood," Daryl affirmed. "We need to be ready to depart soon. In less than an hour if possible." Furman hoomed.

"We will do our best," he stated. "but I wish I could go along."

"So do I," Daryl related, "but I need you here, my friend. Xetagod may already know how to enter this dimension. You may have to defend this hub from his attack…should we fail. As you know, there are scores of individuals here, besides us, whose bodies are in stasis."

"Who are they?" Clayre interrupted.

"Mostly they are the Humanoid crew members of this station," Furman told her, "and also those who are temporal operatives."

"It is they who we must support, if any are left," Daryl explained. "Should Xetagod discover they were trained and were deployed from here, he could go into the past and delete them in both dimensions, extinguishing all our hopes. That is what we must prevent!"

Abruptly, an alarm sounded.

"There is an incoming ship," Furman relayed from a communication he was receiving. "I don't believe it's one of ours; it's coming in way too fast." Daryl led Clayre to the refurbished temporal craft, and they began preparations for an immediate lift off.

"This conveyance should be exactly like Xet's…the one you and he came here in," he remarked, but didn't have to. Clayre easily recognized it. "Furman has had it rebuilt to scale and for dual dimensionality. We can go anywhere in either Earth or Parallux universes, and it has weaponry. Unfortunately, we have no time to test the improvements. We have to meet Xetagod head on, and try to keep him away from this base." Clayre swallowed hard.

"How can we prevail against that monster ship of his?" she muttered, "…and Xetagod is omniscient!" Daryl wasn't worried or flustered, and he tried to lift Clayre's spirit.

"Xetagod may or may not be totally omniscient," he told her. "That is yet to be determined. He is quite powerful I have no doubt, but my core never lets me travel without certain basics. This Hybrid shell of mine has been fitted with acute analytical abilities, as well as advanced battle strategy. Xetagod may underestimate me. He has in the past, although we mustn't count on that. Physics being immutable, his ship is bigger, but ours is faster and more easily maneuverable. It should be an interesting dual." Clayre cringed. This was way too serious to be interesting, she told herself.

Daryl ignited the nomatic engine and lifted off. They proceeded to an air lock with a drop floor, and as the artificial gravity field dissipated, the ship fell through and then followed a tunnel to the outside. Xet's temporal conveyance was now fully operational in any medium, even the vacuous space of Parallux. Xetagod's ship came up quickly on their display.

"That looks just like the same huge ship from back on Earth," Clayre speculated as she viewed it on a tactical H'lomonitor, "...the one Xetagod's throne conveyance came out of." The three dimensional image was crisp. Inside the quarter sphere a tiny copy of Xetagod's ship appeared, getting larger as it closed in.

"Quite correct, my Clayre," Daryl agreed. Abruptly, a golden plasma beam from Xetagod's ship was fired directly at them.

"Oh my!" Clayre gasped and grabbed Daryl's shoulder. He was amazingly calm as the beam streamed towards them. A moment before it struck, Daryl engaged the temporal drive and slid several seconds into the future. The beam went harmlessly on by.

"There you are!" Xetagod proclaimed through their communication devices. "You did not expect to escape me, did you, my old adversary?" Xetagod was laughing, but Daryl was undaunted.

"Shall we dance?" he responded, and let loose a plasma burst of his own directly at Xetagod's massive ship. The large golden colored barge twinkled, then momentarily disappeared as the blast went past it. Daryl heard the familiar deep laughter.

"Yes!" Xetagod asserted, "Lets!"

Daryl faded away before the next blast was even fired. He moved into a remote past, positioning Xet's small conveyance in a new location that would eventually be behind where Xetagod's ship had just been. Getting set, Daryl stumped forward to within seconds of when he'd left, firing as soon as he arrived there. Unfortunately, Xetagod had anticipated that move, and it was Daryl who was out-flanked. His ship was now directly in front of Xetagod's. Veering right, then left, Daryl tried to outrun the plasma. Xetagod's shot spread as it doggedly came on, and licked the back of Daryl's small ship. The right tip of Daryl's stabilizing thrusters got clipped and they failed, throwing the ship into a wild spin. Just before Xetagod landed the fatal blow, Daryl reverted to another temporal strategy, and slipped out of there.

"Shouldn't we run," Clayre suggested. "How can we outmatch this enemy? He has us outgunned, and we are damaged." Daryl sighed.

"I should have left you with Furman," he said, "but not because of what you think. For what I am about to do." Daryl set the temporal control and engaged it. He also put the ship into maximum thrust.

With the damaged stabilizers it was hard to keep it on a straight flight path, but he managed to, somehow. As soon as they emerged from stumping, Clayre saw Xetagod's ship. It was dangerously close and right in front of them. She also saw their own ship stump in, which confused her. Daryl did not slow down or veer. He headed right for Xetagod's death craft, bursting through the energy shield within the vortex. In mere seconds, they impacted ship upon ship. Xetagod's vessel was much bigger, and had less damage. Xet's was totally vaporized. Clayre's death had been instantaneous and painless. Vertigo set in, like déjà vu, and then she was back with Daryl, and their ship was unharmed. Daryl then explained what had just occurred.

"Sorry, my Clayre," he told her. "I had to kill us to reset the timeline. By running into Xetagod's ship at that moment, his earlier shot missed us, this particular time around, and now his ship is damaged." The knot of thoughts that Clayre experienced trying to grasp what had happened was too much for her.

"We died?"

"Only until the timeline reset, my Clayre," Daryl explained. "By then our original ship swung around and fired at Xetagod's vessel. I suspect the impact that killed us was nullified in the new timeline, and we caught him with his shields down. Now to finish this!" Unfortunately, it was Xetagod who had slipped away this time, and Daryl was sure he would stay stumped off until repairs on the massive ship were completed. That might take weeks, but it wouldn't matter. He would stump back to this present temporal location as soon as they were. He was right. Xetagod's barge appeared as if called.

"Well done, my old adversary!" Xetagod stated. "I congratulate you on your cleverness. It is gratifying to at last find a worthy opponent." With a spread of plasma beams, Xetagod punctuated his compliment. Prepared for that, Daryl stumped out of the way and reappeared a few seconds later.

"Perhaps you do need challenging," Daryl said, "to become all that you desire to be. I could help with that!"

"You would join me?" Xetagod queried.

"Not physically, perhaps as partners."

"Noooo!" Clayre shouted. "Daryl you mustn't…" She needn't have worried. It was a ruse on both their parts. Xetagod closed in, and no further words were necessary. Between Xetagod and Daryl there would be no truce, ever. With that, Daryl stumped and

Xetagod followed right behind. It was soon apparent that more than just repairs were done to Xetagod's ship during his absence. Somehow Xetagod had created a temporal tracking, on-board scanner for his ship, and could now follow Daryl anywhere or any when. Dismayed, Daryl led Xetagod on a desperate chase. Through both Parallux and Earth dimensions he moved back and forth through eons of time, even the uncertain future. Clayre was concerned.

"How long can we keep this up," she asked, "and what if Xetagod just decided to go back to somewhere we've already been? Couldn't he destroy us there?"

"He could," Daryl affirmed, "but it would do him little good. The third law of temporal physics states that alterations to the timelines do not cross dimensional barriers. That is why I have been running back and forth between Parallux dimension and our Earth's. As long as I exit each vortex before he can attack us, our past is secure. Once we are safely into the alternate dimension, even if he should destroy our ship in the previous one, it won't matter. We will be alive and safe in the other. Xetagod is aware of this as well. That is why he hasn't wasted any effort going back to finish us."

Clayre was still worried, and for good reason. The chase went on for three days, until Daryl managed to confuse Xetagod by creating a loop. Xetagod followed the little conveyance as it went around in an elaborate circuitous temporal cycle. Slipping away from behind one of their former incarnations, Clayre and Daryl had a small respite.

"You are exhausted, my Daryl, and this might go on forever," Clayre sighed. "Besides, our supplies are running low."

"All the better for our friends," Daryl replied. "This may give them the one chance to repair the crucial flawed timeline. The longer we keep Xetagod busy, the greater our hope of thwarting him." As if called, Xetagod suddenly re-appeared, bearing down on them at full throttle.

"Looks like he figured out our little deception," Clayre declared dryly. "Here he comes again."

"Xetagod's actions appear angry," Daryl replied. "Perhaps it's time to let him catch us."

"What!" she spouted back in disbelief. Daryl winked at Clayre, though, and smiled as Xetagod came recklessly on, firing blasts in the wild hope of a lucky hit. Dodging every few seconds, Daryl stayed ahead of them, ducking in and out of Earth and Parallux ages. Flying into clouds of blue gasses, he tried to elude the massive deathship of Xetagod's. Charging ahead with heedless disregard for caution, Xetagod closed in as Daryl stumped back to where this chase began days ago. As soon as Daryl arrived, he swerved to port with full thrusters. In the distance, Xetagod's three day earlier version had just stumped away chasing Daryl's prior one. A second later a large fireball came out of nowhere. It barely missed Clayre and Daryl, but not Xetagod. The spread of plasma beams hit the big space barge again and again, knocking out both regular thrust and temporal displacers. Daryl had led Xetagod on a long, wild temporal chase that ended with Xetagod getting clobbered by his own weapons fired at the very beginning of it. It was almost as if they had never left, except that now Xetagod's huge ship was crippled, floating with no motational or temporal control through Parallux space.

"We must return to Parallux Station," Daryl told Clayre. "I have studied this conflict considerably. We have no real chance of winning this fight, and it won't be long before Xetagod's ship is repaired and he attacks us again. I fear we won't be so lucky next time. We must get to the hub and help them prepare for his arrival." Clayre knew what that really meant. They would defend their base for as long as possible, with a similarly bleak outlook. As soon as they arrived, Furman met them.

"Hoom," he said. "I did not expect to see you back here…alive." Daryl ignored the Mec's sentiment.

"We were fortunate," he replied, "but now we have lots to do and very little time. We must evacuate all non-essentials. It won't be long before the repairs to Xetagod's deathcraft are completed."

"The evacuation is already underway," Furman declared, "per the failsafe procedures outlined by Daryl Om when this hub was created. All 'in stasis' personnel can be transferred at a moment's notice back to Earth dimension. The location is not documented, but I suspect it lies somewhere in the remote past. Once there, If not recalled, the inanimates will remain in stasis for one full year."

"Recalled by whom?" Daryl wanted to know.

"Only Daryl Om, and no one else, knows the temporal coordinates for where they will be sent," Furman explained.

"I see," Daryl grunted, "and it is up to us to see that my core returns. Unfortunately, there is another concern. If Xetagod can repair his vortex generator…"

"Then he could attack this base from any time in the past he chooses," Clayre, with a sudden incite, added. "How can we possibly protect ourselves through all those ages?"

"It is a grave concern," Daryl admitted. "If Xetagod intercepts our temporal operatives at any time prior to their induction into the Earth dimension, he could follow them to Earth and prevent them from repairing the disrupted timeline."

"Maybe we can keep him here in the present," Clayre suggested. "He must be angry that we thwarted him. If we taunt him, perhaps we can spur him to come after us here and now."

"It is a viable option," Daryl admitted, "and, it has led to his downfall in the past. Xetagod may not fall for it this time, still it is worth a try."

"What will you say?" Clayre asked. Daryl smiled at her, and strolled over to a communication niche.

"Hello, old friend," Daryl began, "I see you are having some trouble with your ship!" They needn't have worried.

"You latrine filth," Xetagod spat out. "You have more good fortune than any being should ever be allowed! My conveyance is nearly repaired. When it is, you will be painfully deleted, but not before I burn your favorite in front of you!" Clayre winced as Daryl disconnected.

"Battle ready, everyone!" he announced to all those who remained. Aside, he spoke quietly to Clayre. "He will be here soon, and looking for us. Do not give in to fear, my Clayre."

"Can we stop him?" she wanted to know, now worried.

"This base has certain defensive fail safes," he reassured her. "The hull is made of the hardest substances from both dimensions, and there is an energy field as well."

"Is that enough to stop the fury of Xetagod's beam weapons?" Clayre inquired.

"Uncertain, "Daryl admitted, "but there is still the final fail safe. The inner core of this base is connected to Earth dimension. There is a large vortex generator. Should the hull be destroyed, it will revert back to where we originally came from."

"I see," Clayre said. "If Xetagod breaks through, we can just go somewhere on Earth."

"Yes, my Clayre," he agreed, "but in the meantime, we must remain in a defensive posture. The longer we can hold off Xetagod, the better chances our time operatives will have to repair the disruption. I wish we could do more to help them, but defending this base is critical. If Xetagod controls the temporal gate here, he would be able to delete them all at will."

"Is there something I can do to help?" Clayre asked. "I can't just sit here and do nothing!" Furman was nearby and he overheard their talk.

"Well, we are short handed," he stated, "and there are many stations that are unmanned." Clayre found herself getting a quick lesson on how to operate large nomatic cannon. Parallux base had many such weapons, but not nearly enough Mecs, Cybos, or Hybrids to man them all.

"Normally a Mec like myself would inhabit the control module for this weapon," Furman explained, "but you can operate it manually." Clayre settled into the operator's niche and thanked him. Furman bid her good hunting and left as she ran the tutorial and began practicing. It didn't take long before Clayre was familiar with the way it targeted. Setting the gun to a virtual mode, she got good at hitting the practice targets. Of course, none of them were anything like Xetagod's death craft, and Clayre wondered what would happen when the fight was for real. Would she die yet again! Maybe it would even be painful this time. Dwelling on such thoughts would not help, Clayre reasoned, trying to fend them off. She wanted to believe in Daryl, that somehow he would protect her.

Abruptly an alarm sounded. Clayre felt a tremendous shudder, like the whole base was quaking. She had locked herself in, fortunately, or Clayre would have been tossed like a limp doll. Searching for a target, Clayre scanned her whole field of vision, but nothing was there. Another violent burst slammed the large sphere, closer this time. Xetagod's ship abruptly swung around the horizon, and now it was right in front of her. Clayre fired over and over, getting hits, but the barge was well protected by some kind of energy field. None of her shots could penetrate it. The menacing behemoth noticed her annoying fire, and returned it. A gigantic ball of golden plasma energy came streaking towards her.

"Get out of there, my brave Clayre!" Daryl shouted through her intercom as sirens blared and metallic voices urged everyone to get to the hub's core. Mere seconds later, the blast slammed into Clayre's position. Waves of crushing forces smashed the gun to pieces. They impacted her as well, and she blacked out, thinking for real that she would die.

CHAPTER EIGHTEEN

2084 AD (Reverted Time)

"The female operative must be just clever enough to have turned off her time pod's homing beacon," Cayri raved angrily. "There's no way to track her or the Cybo now that they've altered the timeline!"

"Our god-master will not be pleased," Xet replied irritably. He knew some of Xetagod's wrath would undoubtedly come his way as well. "We must correct this situation quickly. It is fortunate for us that a direct link is not possible over different temporal locations. Communication is, however, and at some point I will have to make a report. Let us have something by that time that will please him."

"We have but the two possible progressions," Cayri expounded, "First we could monitor the original point in time that I altered, that which our god-master had determined would bring down his enemy. We would have to wait in hiding until the agents we seek turn up and we can then dispose of them. This, however, is risky and unnecessary. For the second option we would not have to waste time idly waiting. We would seek for the two missing agents and terminate them!"

Xet laughed. "And how are you going to do that?" he inquired. "Locating them in the vastness of Time/Space at random will take millennia." Cayri was not amused by Xet's mirth at her expense.

"We can draw them out, underling," she returned angrily, "by causing some kind of obvious flaw in the timeline…"

"That is also risky," Xet asserted. "It must be near to but after the critical one. The Daryl worms would be sure to investigate."

"How about a nice explosion?" Cayri offered, getting her smile back. "One that's close to an urban area. They had an infatuation with nuclear power back in those days."

"Perfect," he agreed.

It didn't take the two of them long to craft a plan, and put it into action. Cayri would translocate to a certain large nuclear facility per Xet's suggestion.

"I had considered doing this very same thing once, ages ago," he remarked as he joined her. "Many of these large power plants have stockpiles of radioactive fuel. It should be relatively easy to cause some kind of 'accident'. That will draw the Daryl agents like annoying insects."

"They will be expecting me to be there," Cayri affirmed, "but not you."

"To their utter undoing," Xet laughed wickedly.

It was a late and moonless stretch of nighttime when Cayri popped into the main control room. There were only two "on duty" technicians and she quickly dispatched them. The mission was simple and well thought out. Xet had hacked the critical information for the logistics of the sabotage, as well as the layout, number of guards, and any other pertinent data. Xet had also discerned the easiest way to unleash the radioactive holocaust.

Just as Cayri prepared the explosives for detonation, she had an unwelcome visitor. "I seem to remember you," she said, "once upon a timeline." The big Cybo just looked puzzled. He had not the resources she did. Cayri's translocation device had a functioning mate planted within the etheric dimension that she used for temporal travel, one with recording devices. It registered all of her temporal activities and could not be altered from a locus on Earth. In that other universe, the playback was unaffected by the time alteration and provided interesting incite for what had changed. Rykard had no such advantage.

"Put your hands over your eyes and step away from the bomb," he demanded in a no nonsense tone. His muscular frame was tense, a finger on his weapon's triggering mechanism. Unlike Synth, Rykard's weapon could kill.

"Of course," she replied calmly. "No need to get excited. Where's your friend?"

"That's none of your concern," the Cybo snapped. "You're my prisoner now, and you'll come with me quietly, if you want to continue living!"

"All right, all right," Cayri reaffirmed her compliance, but Rykard was concerned. The girl was way too cooperative. He expected more of a fight. This concern switched him into an even higher alert mode, but it was too late. Xet was there, behind him, with a death ray. It was a quick kill, without emotion or banter, and Rykard had no chance. His charred hulk fell to the floor before he could even react. Somehow Rykard did manage to discharge his own weapon, mostly from reflex, and level his final shot at Cayri.

"Are you trying to get me killed?" she spat at Xet. The blast had singed her arm as it went by.

"If I wanted you dead, I would do it myself," he grunted. Xet had toyed with the idea. It was annoying for him to be below the

Humanoid girl in stature. She was the god-master's favorite, though, and he was not in any position to contest that. His original play to free Daryl and Clayre should have gotten him killed or tortured. Instead Xetagod had reprogrammed him, made him evil. Because of his dual dimensionality, Xet was summarily needed for this plan to overthrow Daryl Om. Fortunately for him, Cayri required a subordinate with a mental capacity greater than bowl mush, and he alone was available. "You should be more concerned about the other operative," Xet huffed, finally.

"You killed the Cybo too soon," she complained. "He might have told us where she was." Xet just scowled.

"She will come here to look for her associate eventually. Be patient." He was right. The female operative named Synth, disregarding orders, did follow her partner's path when he didn't return. She passed several unconscious guards along the way to the main control area. There she found Rykard's body. Instead of being cautious and alert to the danger, the Synth female fell upon her fallen comrade and started crying. This will be easy and satisfying, Cayri thought, as she stepped out of hiding and kicked away the handheld stunner Synth had carelessly set down.

"Too bad about your friend," she stated calmly, aiming her own killing weapon at the vulnerable operative.

"Why did you kill him?" Synth seethed angrily, wiping off the tears.

"Orders," Cayri smirked. "Don't take it personally." She couldn't resist toying with the helpless girl she was about to murder. "Besides, I didn't kill him. My associate did." Xet stepped out into the open.

"Get it over with," he rebuked Cayri. At that moment an alarm sounded—a loud one. Men could be heard rushing to their location. Xet quickly locked and barred the entrance doors.

"You better leave," Cayri told him, "I will be right behind you."

"Do it now!" he roiled, but she laughed as he faded away. Then she turned back to the girl. For some reason Cayri didn't feel the pathetic operative worthy of a warrior's death.

"Looks like I won't have to bother killing you either," she taunted. "The bombs I have rigged to explode have only seconds to detonation once I trigger them. The ensuing destruction will level everything for miles…adieu!" Cayri held up the control and pressed the arming button. Laughing, she touched the device on her belt and immediately vanished. Synth looked around in desperation. Timers on the explosives were counting down from sixty seconds and the doors had been electronically sealed. She was trapped with nowhere to go.

"This way!" a voice from behind her said frantically. Synth turned and saw a tiny catbird.

"You are that Ting!" she said in amazement.

"Hurry!" the catbird pleaded.

"I can't leave Rykard like this."

"You must!" Ting said frantically, biting Synth's leg. "There is no time…we'll all die!" Synth remembered the mission. It was up to her, now.

Ting showed her to a small access portal and it led down a maintenance shaft. Synth could barely squeeze into it. On the other end was a larger doorway that went into a hall. Synth recognized the location. One of the fallen guards was there, and just beyond was an outer door.

"My pod is this way!" she shouted, running as fast as she could. Synth reached it in seconds, and the catbird, who could fly, was already there. Synth could hear and feel the explosions rocking her pod just as she stumped out of there. They went back to the place Synth had previously come from, and she was already crying for Rykard.

He was more to her than a training director; more than a superior. She had deep seated feelings for him that were now eating her up. Synth realized what they were. She had loved him. Weeping, Synth made herself check the data again, and she wasn't shocked to discover that the radioactive disaster had still occurred. They had failed, and now Rykard was dead as well.

In a completely different temporal location, Cayri smiled evilly. "That should please our god-master," she declared to Xet.

"Yes," he agreed. "You have done well. I will contact Xetagod with our good news." The communication lasted less than a second. Xet frowned maliciously.

"What is it?" Cayri wanted to know.

"We are to go to the original time deviation immediately and guard it. You have made another error and Xetagod is displeased."

"What error?" Cayri shouted, annoyed at the implication.

"You did not confirm the second kill," Xet retorted succinctly.

CHAPTER NINETEEN

2084 AD (Reverted Time) Continued

Catbirds are said to be somewhat clairvoyant, and Ting was as normal a catbird as they come. They are also known to be very good at hiding when they don't want to be seen. Some say that's because, being part feline, they can be very quiet, like when cats are stalking prey. Most catbirds are small and dark colored which no doubt makes for good camouflage. Ting was masterful at keeping hidden, and that was due to all of the above, but especially the clairvoyance. She somehow knew when someone would turn suddenly or look in her direction.

At this moment, however, Ting's reality seemed like a swirling maelstrom and she was confused. It was to her sheer amazement that the Hybrid Human female she had recently joined up with actually knew Ting by name, when she could not remember what hers was. Ting knew the face, though, like something out of a dream, and Ting's memory of the other timeline was coalescing in bits and pieces. Earlier, when she had been hiding from Cayri, the presence of this other female Hybrid had entered her mind like a vision that abruptly appeared in her psyche. It seemed as if they had been doing something important, and this other Human felt quite like, but was not, her Ayryn. Ting choked up then. This notion brought out something else. She had also become aware, just then, that Ayryn had died. Oddly, she seemed to recall that she had witnessed Ayryn's death twice, in two very different worlds. Fighting the urge, she wanted more than ever to maim, even kill Cayri, but this she could not do; not at that specific juncture. The other odd golden Mec, who was close by, was also an enemy. It was extra hard staying unseen with the both of them around, and Ting may have even been spotted by the gold Mec once or twice. Fortunately for Ting, she was ignored. She suspected that he must have deemed her too insignificant to bother with. Possibly he thought she was just some "dumb" local animal. Anyway, maintaining her concealment while attempting to understand all this confusion meant that Ting had to bide her time, and in the process, she did surmise some of what was going on.

Ting learned that the main enemy was an impressive Mec-like

entity who called himself Xetagod. This Xetagod had come to Earth from far away with a grudge against Daryl Om, and he wanted to hurt people. Cayri, and now the gold Mec, were working for him, inflicting evil wherever they went. As bad as things were, Ting knew there were still some others who, like herself, were trying to fight back, and she knew she would always side with them.

It was during this period when Ting discovered that Cayri and the gold Mec were planning something abominable. Following Cayri through more blue holes, they had come to a weird place. There were lots of colored lights, dials, and gauges. There were also two original Humans. They didn't live for long. After killing them, Cayri began to realign some of the equipment, altering the presets. When that was done, she activated several small devices and started placing them in odd locations. That's when the gruff Cybo barged in, the one the new female was still crying about. Things got extra tense, but Ting was certain the Cybo was on her side and against Xetagod. He took control of the situation, disarming Cayri fairly easily. Ting was ready to reveal herself, and would have offered to join with him, when the golden Mec showed up. Ting was as shocked as the Cybo, when, without any warning, the gold Mec shot and killed him. Feeling quite distraught, Ting blamed herself for not being more vigilant. It did not occur to her that had she done anything, anything at all, she most likely would have been killed as well.

Ting wondered why Cayri and the gold Mec did not leave, until the other Hybrid female showed up. Ting recognized her. It was the one from her sudden memory. With the realization that this person must be a friend, Ting was determined to help her. Unfortunately, this female was not very cautious. Cayri got the upper hand right off, and there wasn't much Ting could do for the new girl other than witness what happened. Instead of watching helplessly, though, Ting looked around for some way to help. There wasn't much in that tight space, however, but Ting did discover an exit hatch and a way out. When the gold one told Cayri she should hurry up and kill the girl, Ting's heart fell. Just to spite her accomplice Cayri was in no rush to do it, though. She taunted her victim like Ting sometimes played with her live food. Abruptly, some loud racket ensued, a wailing horn that would not shut up. Ting could hear men running toward where they were, and they would intrude at any moment. That's when Cayri did the unbelievable. She let the female live and disappeared herself. Ting snapped into action.

"This way!" she shouted at the emotional young woman. Ting had to practically drag her away from the dead Cybo. Remarkably, the female then recognized Ting. The passage was tight, but they got through it and then got to her pod. A huge fireball of yellow energy surrounded them just as they entered the time flux and slipped away. The female's name was Synth, and she was terribly upset by the loss of her Cybo friend, which was altogether obvious. Ting felt like crying herself, and did shed an uncustomary single tear for Ayryn. After a few minutes the reality of their situation began to overcome the grief.

"What are we going to do?" Ting asked Synth.

"I don't know," Synth sobbed. "I'm a screw up, and the only one left, now. I was never good at any of this!"

"Oh yes, you are!" Ting exclaimed. She suddenly remembered part of the other timeline. The one they had bonded in. "We wouldn't be alive, now, if not for you!"

In full detail, she told Synth how they had escaped together, and how they had recaptured her missing pod. "Because of that," Ting stressed, "we have this new chance to make a difference…to repair the timeline…to restore our future world."

"Yes," Synth admitted, "that is what we must do, if we can, but I have no idea at all how to accomplish that."

"Yes, you do," Ting repeated, "or did. You told me. We must find the point of change and prevent it."

"I know," Synth conceded, "but I have no idea how to stop Cayri from blowing up that nuclear plant." Ting wrinkled her nose.

"I don't think you have to," she declared.

"…but that's the point of change!" Synth sulked. Ting was unconvinced.

"I don't believe it is," she asserted. "For one thing, our world was decimated before Cayri set off that bomb just now. I should know. I've been following her ever since she killed my Ayryn!" Synth quite suddenly remembered her dream, the one Ting was in.

"Then you must know where the point of change happened!" she proclaimed with conviction. "Where did she go right after you left Ayryn?"

"It was a bright place," Ting replied. "There were several other deformed females there. They looked similar to Cayri, but were ugly and unintelligent. You probably won't remember, but we overcame a handful of them when we got your pod back in the other timeline. Anyway, Cayri changed clothing and outfitted herself with weapons and supplies. After that she created another blue hole to an even stranger place. It was stark and filthy. Original Humans were there, and I think they were making metal objects. Cayri talked to one of them."

"That could be it!" Synth spouted excitedly. "Tell me everything that happened!"

So Ting related how Cayri had made the man capture an insect and take it outside the building where he let it go. "It seems inconsequential," Synth remarked skeptically, "but I suppose even an insect could change a timeline. Did Cayri do anything else there?"

"No," Ting affirmed. "She left right after the bug was let go."

"Then that must be it," Synth spouted excitedly. "Why else would she do that? So now we know what she did, if only we knew when she did it."

"I think I do know," Ting said, a bit too calmly for Synth. "Cayri told the golden metal man just yesterday. It was midday in a place called Cedar City on the tenth of June in 2019."

"Oh Ting," Synth shouted, "you are simply a marvel! What would I ever do without you?" She picked up Ting and gave her a hug which was reluctantly allowed. Ting thought it felt nice, though, after all this time, even if it did remind her of Ayryn.

"Do you still have Ayryn's amulet?" she asked Synth. Thinking about Ayryn brought on a concern about it.

"Well, no," Synth replied, "if that is the necklace that the other me wanted kept safe. It disappeared when you and she did."

"We must get it back," Ting stated seriously. "Cayri, and the one she works for, a formidable entity who calls himself Xetagod, want it quite badly." Synth shivered. She remembered a similar name from long ago that was associated with evil.

"Do you know where it is?" she asked.

"It was with Ayryn's body," Ting related, "when we recovered it last time."

"It most likely went back there," Synth surmised. "We will have to go there again."

Synth stumped them into the bleak future of a world that Cayri had decimated, and found Ayryn near where Ting remembered she'd be. They retrieved the amulet and also set Ayryn's body on the grass as before. Ting was calm this time, steeled and determined. She would make Cayri pay for this. Not wishing to waste precious time, they didn't stay long. The future depended on them.

Now that Synth had some directional purpose, she got into gear.

Her pod had unlimited data on this era of Human development and she pulled up information on Cedar City. There were a score of factories in that area from the early twenty-first century that could possibly be the one they were looking for. Unfortunately, Ting had only seen the outside of the building briefly. She remembered that it had a tan colored metal shell which narrowed the search to less than ten. Ting eliminated several more due to discrepancies in the surrounding terrain. By scouting the city a dozen years earlier, Synth and Ting deduced the factory that they felt was the likely one. Considering every possibility, Synth and Ting crafted their plan. Hiding nearby, they were going to wait until the insect was released. After Cayri left, they would recapture it, and then return the tiny creature to its former location inside the building.

Scrutinizing the terrain around the factory building carefully, they chose an obscured location in a weedy field in sight of where the bug was originally let go. There were several scrubby cottonwood trees that grew near to some railroad tracks that would provide sufficient cover for Synth's pod.

"Prepared or not," Synth mumbled as she stumped them to that very spot, just about an hour before they suspected the point of change would occur. She got out a farview and trained it onto the outside of the factory facility. The large door was open, and Ting affirmed that that was how she remembered it. Nothing seemed out of the ordinary as they waited for the fateful moment. Two hours went by, and Synth began to doubt that they had the correct location.

"Someone's going into the building," Ting whispered. Synth focused the farview on a side door.

"It's Cayri," Synth affirmed.

"Shouldn't we be closer?" Ting wondered aloud. "We might miss where the insect goes."

"You're right, of course," Synth agreed. Fortunately, there was a pile of old equipment and some large trash receptacles somewhat near the doorway they expected Cayri and the man to come out of, and they cautiously made their way over there. Hiding behind that cover, they waited for Cayri and the factory worker to emerge. They did not have to wait long.

"Let it go," Cayri ordered the man. He opened a wad of paper and a small dark object fell to the ground. It righted itself quickly and then flew off.

"Keep your eyes on it!" Synth whispered to Ting.

Just at that moment, a frightened little furry animal scurried out from beneath some of the rusty metal near where they were hiding. The tiny rabbit, no bigger than Ting, ran right into Cayri's field of vision. She looked suspiciously at the pile of rusted junk. It was obvious that she suspected someone was there and would investigate.

"I'll distract her," Synth told Ting. "You get the insect!" Synth got up and ran to another hiding spot a short distance away.

"You!" Cayri shouted, recognizing a foe. She wasn't fooled, however, by Synth's deception. Cayri saw the catbird go after the stink bug, and that was more important. She took out her weapon and fired at Ting, but the catbird was too fast and flew erratically. Diving suddenly, Ting avoided getting hit. The worker was jaw-dropped and hit the deck as well. The poor bug, now terrified, flew away quickly with Ting on its tail and Cayri just behind her. Synth hurriedly followed them all.

CHAPTER TWENTY

9815 AD (Present Standard Time) Parallux, earlier

"It's time." Daryl told Furman. Furman nodded in agreement, and went into a nearby niche. In an instant his virtual awareness was teleported to a shell at the base's very core. As a Virtual Individual he could send his totality anywhere across Time/Space or even copy himself. Most Mecs were reluctant to duplicate, however. Furman was such a one. He emerged into the very heart of the complex where its most important assets were kept. The original bodies of every last one of Daryl Om's Humanoid operatives were secluded there in a stasis or some kind of suspended animation. These individuals were placed in separate containment receptacles, and each required a Mec mind to monitor function. This was to ensure that the body inside was kept viable. Every Humanoid agent in the Temporal Corps had been carefully extracted so that their knowledge, abilities, and memories could be subsequently implanted into dual dimensional organic shells, bodies that were outwardly exact copies of the originals.

Daryl Om had discovered dual dimensionality. By combining matter utilizing sub-atomic particles from both dimensions (such as protons from one and electrons from the other) he enabled atoms to exist in either universe. How Daryl Om created such atoms was a mystery to most. Furman's job was simple, but important. He was to protect those in stasis from harm. This now meant activating the final failsafe for the temporal academy, and that was built into it from its inception. This failsafe was to be utilized only should an unstoppable foe assail it. Certainly Xetagod was such a one.

Furman broke the seal and initialized the circuits of the never before employed temporal generator. A vortex formed around Furman and sent him back in time to the day after Parallux base had first been completed. As he emerged, Furman saw his former self, and the Humanoid Daryl copy as well. A little ceremony was being conducted to initiate the new facility. A score of centuries later and Furman still remembered that as he strode over to the pair.

"Protocol 141," he told himself (actually it was the past version of himself who was rather flabbergasted). It didn't take long for that one to regain composure.

"Already?" Was the answer. Future Furman immediately sealed

the base's core and then the largest vortex generator ever built sent it away. It would remain in flux for the rest of its existence, and no one other than Daryl Om could calculate its whereabouts at any given moment. Furman knew what that meant. Since Daryl Om no longer existed, the core could be anywhere or any when in the Parallux universe. Future Furman understood why. He was fully aware that the timeline manipulation that had removed Daryl Om from existence could not cross dimensional lines which somehow prevented all of those present from being deleted as well. This law of dimensional physics was why the time operatives were trained and housed in this alternate universe, one apart from Earth's.

From this reverted moment on, all cadets would be transported automatically by Furman's generator to wherever the hub's core resided for their training. Furman was the key. Only he knew the transfer code and he would guard it with his very existence. Should even Xetagod try to glean that information from him, Furman would automatically self-destruct. Furman was okay with that. He fully understood the importance of Daryl Om's plan. Protocol 141 changed the timeline. The hub's core shifted constantly now throughout this dimension, existing in no one place or time for more than a few seconds. The Temp Corps cadets would be trained inside this shifting core and eventually deployed from very different temporal locations into the Earth dimension. Each op would, of course, be given a time beat they would patrol in a pod conveyance, checking for abnormalities in their era of Earth's history. As it was with agents, each pod was also dual dimensional. The pods were non-thinking, although they could be inhabited by a Mec Virtual Individual and most were. Only in the case of organic time operatives were the pods piloted manually. Once deployed, and with all known data from the patrolled era, the time agents would compare events, as they progressed, to ensure the integrity of the timeline. Now that protocol 141 was established, Furman was firmly dedicated to his task, and would remain so through the millennia until the point of change no longer required him. Furman's future self would eventually take his place. This happened as soon as Daryl saw him leave, but Daryl had another, more pressing concern.

Fighting his way through decks of rubble to where Clayre had been, he freed her from a pile of debris. She yet lived, but barely. Daryl carefully carried her to an inner shield wall where they were safe for the moment. Xetagod's ship was pummeling the other side of the base where several Mecs were bravely resisting. It would not be for very much longer. Giving up some of his vital energy, Daryl bestowed it unto his love. Clayre had sustained a head injury and Daryl's life-force relieved some of the pain. Clayre regained consciousness and sat up.

"Where am I?" she murmured.

"You are safe for the moment, my brave Clayre," Daryl softly replied as he gave her medical aid.

"...but Xetagod!" she blurted out, remembering their fight.

"He will win this base in minutes," Daryl admitted, "which is why we must leave at once." He helped Clayre get to her feet, and together they made their way to where they had left Xet's clever little temporal conveyance. Daryl stumped them immediately into the past.

"Where are we?" Clayre was curious to know.

"Somewhere Xetagod won't easily be able to locate," Daryl told her, "at least for awhile."

"What about those still on the base?" Clayre asked grimly.

"They are evacuating as quickly as possible," Daryl affirmed, "in linear time. Of course from where we are now that won't happen for millennia. We aren't completely safe here, either. Xetagod will eventually track us down. With a time lord such as our enemy, it is nearly impossible to protect the vastness of Time/Space, or hide in it. That's why time travel was outlawed. My greater self, Daryl Om, decreed it so after the second Xetacon conflict, the one where your descendent Ayryn and Furman thwarted him with my help. That was before our gold Xetacon came to his senses, of course, and became our friend Xet. Anyway, after that, the only time manipulation allowed was to bring dying awareness's of no longer living entities, such as you, to the Heavenworlds. This did not affect the natural course of events so it was permitted. Restoration of any temporal tampering is the only other exception to that law, and also the impetus for the creation of the Temporal Corps. Our great hope is that those brave operatives can undo the fix we are in. I fear the major shift that Xetagod instigated may be more than even they can repair or survive."

"Can't we help them?" Clayre wondered.

"We are attempting to do just that, my Clayre," Daryl said, "by keeping Xetagod occupied. He would like nothing better than to remove them from existence. We must protect the academy at any cost to us. If he captures that, we are all but lost!"

"...but didn't we just leave there?"

"In reality, no. It had been there, true, but now the academy's actual location is a carefully guarded secret. Furman has the code, but even he doesn't know where it is. The rest of Parallux base is doomed, and a self-destruct was ordered before we left there. By the time Xetagod takes over, it will be rubble. He will most likely try to garner its secrets by travelling into the past, only he will be unsuccessful."

"Won't that make Xetagod furious?" Clayre remarked seriously. "He will want to crush something." Daryl laughed good-heartedly.

"Yes, and we must keep his attention on us." Clayre wasn't so light about it.

"How are we going to do that without getting crushed ourselves?"

"I'm not sure," Daryl replied honestly. "We were extremely lucky last time around. Xetagod has grown a vast hatred of us, I'm afraid, and an age old lust for revenge. It may be the only weakness we can exploit. By nurturing that, we can perhaps get Xetagod to make an even greater error."

"I understand," Clayre affirmed, "and I am not fearful of death. After all, I have already lived a full life, as well you know, some ages ago. If I can help others to do the same, well I think it's a worthwhile sacrifice."

"I need not ponder why I love you, my Clayre," Daryl spoke softly. "You are a caring and loving matron. Humankind is honored to have sprung from such a one!"

"You'll make me cry," Clayre answered, somewhat facetiously, "and we have a lot to do if we're to make a difference."

"Quite right, my Clayre," Daryl agreed. They discussed strategies that would incite Xetagod to come after them, ones that would not mean their quick demise. It was Clayre who offered a workable plan.

"What if we were close enough to keep a watch on Xetagod," she began, "but not so close that we would have a hard time getting away? If he was on to something important we could perhaps engage him enough to divert his mission. In a dire circumstance we could even battle."

"What you suggest is dangerous, my Clayre," Daryl explained. "Xetagod must believe we've been destroyed with Parallux base, or he would have followed us. We could also revert back and challenge Xetagod before the base was destroyed, but to what end? It is doubtful we could get a better outcome than the original. Actually, this conveyance has an excellent stealth mode. I believe Xetagod will be mostly blind to us if we keep a good distance and remain hidden. In that way we can see what he is up to."

"I suppose the hard part will be finding his conveyance," she remarked. "He could be anywhere or any when."

"Well, we know where he last was!" Daryl asserted. "...destroying our poor base in Parallux." Clayre nodded. She had forgot that they, too, could go anywhere or any when. Before departing, they took some time to check over their little conveyance. Daryl wanted to be sure that it was fully operational. Unfortunately, the main weapon on their temporal craft had been used extensively in that original battle, and had not been recharged. Daryl was concerned that if they did fight with Xetagod, the duel might not last long. When Clayre conceded that they were as prepared as possible, Daryl stumped them back to Parallux, just as the self-destruct decimated their former base. With this distraction, Xetagod did not notice them slip out of vortex. Clayre winced as a huge violent ball of blue-white plasma energy formed and vaporized the interdimensional hub; what was left of it. Fortunately, she and Daryl were well out of the blast zone, but Xetagod's large conveyance was not. In stealth mode they watched as the energy completely enveloped Xetagod's ship, and Clayre hoped the destructive force would destroy it as well, but it wasn't so. The evil conveyance emerged from the fury unscathed, paused for a moment, then stumped away.

Daryl sped their own conveyance to the sight of the temporal disturbance and sent out a probe. The probe was a special design. It followed Xetagod's ship within a sophisticated stealth field similar to what their own little ship employed. Relaying a coded signal disguised as natural cosmic radiation, it sent back the temporal coordinates for where Xetagod had gone. Daryl adjusted the time controls and stumped as well, arriving where Xetagod had, only several minutes earlier. Locating a place to land with lots of natural cover, Daryl set the small craft down and waited. Xetagod's ship was coming back to Earth.

CHAPTER TWENTY-ONE

9815AD (Present Standard Time) continued

This had been all too easy, Xetagod surmised. He had expected Daryl the "Om" to have made this conquest more of a challenge. So far it had been a bit of a letdown, and he had avoided the errors that were made the last time he attempted to conquer Earth. On that campaign he had thought his armies undefeatable and was certain of victory, but then Ayryn had turned on him. Freeing Furman and the Mecs from their restrictive programming, brought about his demise, and he was certain Daryl had a hand in that. He had barely escaped, and it was incredibly risky to rocket out into space in that tiny pod. Any number of calamities could have destroyed it, and then he, Xetagod, would have been extinguished before he had even evolved.

Back then he was just Xetacon, and, with his awareness, all he could bring was what meager knowledge he could squeeze into a small memory storage device. To grow into his former might, he'd need help, and not from any on Earth. Daryl, his enemy, without constraints, would regain his full abilities, and then it would have been impossible for Xetacon to rebuild while remaining hidden. No, this time he had to begin again elsewhere. To fool his enemies, Xetacon had made it look like his spacecraft had self-destructed; the ensuing fireball would cover his escape. His insignificant pod had an extremely fast engine, though, by design. Its speed grew exponentially as it traversed the galaxy, and it took far less time than imagined before he came upon a celestial body with life.

The planet was infantile and primitive. The animal life forms were mainly reptilian and non-sentient. It had taken several hundred years to alter the draconian DNA to the point where they actually were. Eventually, he brought them up to speed, giving them opposable thumbs and language so he could communicate with them. The Drakes began to build a world for Xetacon following his explicit directives. In their primitive minds he was a god, their god, and they readily obeyed him. Their obeisance pleased him. Xetacon had never had that kind of respect before, so he changed his name. As Xetagod, he rewarded any satisfactory work. Coupling that with harsh punishment for disobedience and/or his disappointment in them, made for excellent motivation. He wasn't a total ogre, however. As his primary assets, Xetagod did protect the Drakes, and his technical knowledge provided them with food and warm shelter, all of which kept them quite loyal. By the end of the first millennium they had constructed a palace for their god and several factories. Xetagod also had the Drakes reconstruct his AMPs complex. The AMPs (or augmented memory pods) were first invented by early Earth scientists. Using organic stem cells and brain matter, coupled with technology to convert electronic signals to neurological ones, those researchers unwittingly created the recipe for virtual life. Daryl Om and Xetagod both had sprung from these innovations. On this world, Xetagod utilized draconian DNA for his memory pods and thus was imbued with godlike abilities. As such he became omniscient.

With this new power Xetagod could control everything, and it wasn't long before he was building mechanized soldiery, his machinids. Thus, as time progressed, more and more of his empire became machinated. His organic creatures, the Drakes, were no longer needed for work, and Xetagod was tempted to dispose of them. They had been trustworthy servants, though, so he was loathe to do so. He rather enjoyed their worship, so he gave the Drakes a large fertile portion of his world to live on, and then promptly ignored them. Oh, there were a few he needed for his experiments and other necessities. These Xetagod kept close, utilizing them for several of his many enterprises during this period.

When Xetagod was yet on Earth as Xetacon, and for a short while during that period, Ayryn had been his prisoner. To deal with her, he had created a minor virtual Humanoid version of himself and did spend a good deal of effort trying to recruit her to his way of thinking. The pseudo-relationship that was instigated never amounted to much, but she had rejected his offers, and that still rankled Xetagod even after all this time. He had fully scanned her back then and also took a DNA sample that he kept for possible later uses. For amusement, Xetagod subsequently decided to see if he could replicate her. He was forced to use Drake DNA, and the first several experiments were failures. With the AMPs he was omniscient, however, and eventually he deciphered the means to create a perfect clone of Ayryn, his only Human love/hate desire. He enjoyed taking his revenge on her, devising many clever and satisfying ways to do so. None of them were very nice for her. Eventually, Xetagod realized he had an affinity for the girl which surprised him. For a while, he let her have a normal existence, hoping she would relate to his totality. Unfortunately, she wasn't a good match for Xetagod's personality. The Ayryn copy had subtle ways, and she tried to alter him. Before long, Xetagod grew frustrated and angry, and then he was torturing the cloned Human girl again.

Unsatisfied by how all that had gone, Xetagod had a new idea. After many more botched attempts, he created another version of Ayryn. One he hoped would be more compatible. Xetagod targeted the DNA structure and altered some connections while leaving most as they were. The resulting clone smiled wickedly at him when their eyes first met, and Xetagod was pleased. This one was completely conducive to his evilness and was a great asset—for a time. She wheedled herself close to him, wanting to bond in every way. She was slick, but it was mostly a ruse. Exploring Xetagod's makeup and looking for weaknesses, she got him to lust for her. He got complacent, trusting her, and the girl was clever. She tried to delete her master by sabotaging his AMPs, and she almost succeeded. He realized nearly too late that she was a threat to him, and then Xetagod incarcerated her within a stasis. Discovering the flaw in this evil version disheartened him. It was a long time before Xetagod tried another Ayryn clone, but he did. Many more failures resulted from these trials, but eventually he came upon the perfect mix of evil and good; one suited to his own sick tastes. This last Ayryn clone was perfect, and she knew just how to please him.

By this time, Xetagod had perfected temporal voyaging, and studying the physics involved in interdimensional transcendence, he became adept at shifting through Time/Space. He also discovered Hybridization; the forming of durable molecules by means of combining elements from two or more dimensions. A plan began to take shape within his totality and it pleased him. He would finally take his revenge on those who had humiliated him, namely Daryl and the people of Earth. To test his might and prowess, Xetagod conquered several populated systems quite easily and turned his eyes toward Earth. His initial testing of Daryl and the Earth defenses had not given Xetagod much cause for alarm. Conquering Earth, thus far, had been effortless.

Yes, there was an interesting temporal battle that the Daryl copy tried to make a good competition, but the opportunity was too ripe. Xetagod had allowed his conveyance to be struck by his own weaponry as a feint. Daryl inferior did not exploit this apparent advantage or he would have been annihilated. If he had come in closer to make the kill, Xetagod had other formidable weapons. Still the weak-minded Daryl copy had led him right back to their base in the rogue dimension.

The strategy for defending their large outpost was incredibly inferior, and Xetagod was underwhelmed by Daryl's inefficiency to protect it. Perhaps Daryl had grown weak and lackadaisical over the ages with no worthy foe to bang heads with. It was evident that Daryl had let things slip quite badly. In truth Xetagod was disappointed when the stronghold took a hit somewhere critical and disintegrated. The Daryl copy and Clayre wanted Xetagod to believe they were vaporized in the explosion and no longer lived, but that did not fool him. The reality was almost certainly that they had stumped away in a temporal conveyance to get a respite and come up with a better strategy. Xetagod wasn't overly concerned. He would yet have some sport perhaps, hunting them down.

Presently he was more interested in what his own agents were up to. With Daryl's alternate dimensional base deleted, Xetagod was nearly certain that any additional elusive time spies Daryl still utilized were now gone; removed from existence. The one or two on Earth, possibly still viable, were all that stood between him and total victory. If he wanted to, he could take his huge temporal vehicle back in time and discern where Daryl's temporal minions came from, and then delete them, but that was a needless bother. He could track them on Earth and eliminate them much easier. It was possible his favorite had done so already. It would not take long to find out, besides, it was past time to check up on her and that turncoat copy of himself.

With but a mere thought, the mighty conveyance shifted modes and slipped dimensionally back to where Earth was. Xetagod's technology was different than Daryl's. Instead of creating a dual matter, Xetagod's ship used a force field—an extremely potent one. It sped through a vortex, but to maintain its position against the pull of graviton energy (that which draws a thing back to its own dimension) Xetagod used powerful thrusters and an anti-graviton wave generator to bully his craft through and keep it there. This was highly inefficient and required massive fuel reserves, which was why such a large conveyance was necessary.

Because of its size, Xetagod's ship was detected fairly easily as it entered Earth proximity by the Humans who populated that time period. At first they tried to communicate with him. Xetagod had to laugh. With no answer, the Humans became concerned, especially when the ship entered Earth's atmosphere. As a paranoid precaution, they sent some of their own airborne conveyances to investigate, ones with potent weapons. Not potent enough, unfortunately. Xetagod was mirthful. The Humans indeed were giving him a good laugh. He deleted some of the Earth airships as if they were bothersome insects. They sent even more formidable weapons against him, and Xetagod played with them for awhile until he got bored. With a wave of his hand, all the opposition was deleted in a rain of plasma energy.

Once again, this conflict had been less than challenging, but at least it sated a desire for inflicting revenge on those who had once opposed him. That gave him a mild feeling of satisfaction which reminded him of another pleasure. It was time to reunite with his favorite and he wanted her now. He wouldn't need to track her down, this time. He would contact her through his copy. In mere seconds they were there. Xetagod lusted for her immediately, but business first.

"What have you to report?" he inquired.

"We have killed the Cybo…" Cayri began, but her golden partner interrupted.

"I killed him," Xet stated.

"While I distracted him, per our plan!" she asserted, overriding the previous remark. "The other operative, a weak Human female, we believe to be dead, although, the kill has not been confirmed. We are guarding the critical time adjustment just to be thorough. So far there has been no attempt to alter our temporal manipulation." Cayri held her tongue and awaited the pain she felt would soon be afflicted upon her. She did not want to point out that while they were with him the point of change was unguarded. Xetagod belched forth a deep rumble of laughter. He had no real worry about that. In the unlikely event that the lone Daryl fool could undo his change, it would still be only a minor setback. He had much more power at his disposal than any of them could guess.

"Very well," Xetagod remarked. "I wish to confirm all that you have said. We will communicate now…" His body chamber opened up, and Cayri smiled. She knew what he wanted. She walked slowly, teasingly, toward the open cavity as her clothes melted away. Cayri held back as long as possible before Xetagod swept her inside and swallowed her whole. As Xetagod got ready to pleasure his favorite female Human, he sent his gold copy away with the task of watching the all important moment in this history of the world when Cayri had changed future Earth.

Once there, it didn't take gold Xet long to discern that something was amiss. Daryl's one remaining time operative had arrived there and with her a chance to undo everything. Cayri had not been specific about what she did that caused the shift, so Xet had no idea what to do. He could also cause undesirable changes unwittingly. Rather than chance that, he did the only thing that was wise; he reported what was going on.

Xetagod was not particularly happy about being interrupted in the process of pleasuring his favorite, but he understood the need. Abruptly, another need arose. His ship was being assailed. A plasma blast struck the auto-shielding or it would have done serious damage.

"Daryl!" Xetagod bellowed. "So, it is as I suspected! You are not terminated as I was led to believe!"

"Care to go again?" Daryl taunted. Xetagod was more than happy to. In a heartbeat he sent Cayri away, re-outfitted, to deal with whatever the Xet copy was concerned about. He would pleasure her all that much harder when this was over, he vowed. His huge conveyance shifted into battle mode and swung about. He chased after Daryl's tiny conveyance at full speed. Just as he was about to get into firing range, Daryl used the size differential to his advantage. Being out-maneuvered, Xetagod's weapons were not effective. The plasma blasts missed the quick little darting ship. Daryl also flew through vortices, many times, but Xetagod was ready this time. His ship dogged the smaller craft through every one and Daryl could not get away. They ended up millions of years in the past, where Xetagod was through playing around.

"Let's see you dodge this, old friend!" Xetagod snarled. He broke off the battle, stumping from there to a location where he was almost certain Daryl would soon be. Firing the plasma weapon, Xetagod instantaneously stumped again, a little closer this time and from a different direction. He fired once more, and repeated this maneuver a total of four times.

"Impossible…" Daryl muttered when he and Clayre stumped to that ill-fated temporal locus just as all four beams converged upon them in that same split instant. The effect was as if Xetagod had attacked them with four ships and all of them synchronically concentrated their firepower. For Daryl and Clayre it was too much. The deathships had fired upon them as soon as they stumped in, and the wonderful little time conveyance was hit full on simultaneously by all four. Clayre and Daryl were vaporized.

"I know you didn't get away from that!" Xetagod cackled aloud. Too easy, he thought, as he stumped back to where he had formerly been, awaiting the return of his favorite.

CHAPTER TWENTY-TWO

June 10th 2019 AD (Reverted Time)

Bypassing any undue delay, Cayri was stumped directly to the all important temporal location. It was, of course, that same solitary place where she had instigated the critical timeline alteration that had brought down Daryl Om's world. As soon as she arrived, Cayri carefully scanned the outside of the factory building for any abnormalities. There were none that she could see. The moderately large manufacturing facility looked exactly as it previously had. Using the same side door, she cautiously opened it a tiny bit and peered inside. Cayri could see herself. The other, "original" her, was talking to that worker like before, and nothing seemed amiss. She remembered the conversation she had with the man, and it played out word for word. Puzzled, Cayri closed the door and then followed the building to the rear. There was an indigenous vehicle parked there that had darkened transparent viewports. She and Xet had earlier broken into it and used its fortuitous location to observe the back of the building where the other important action would take place. As Cayri expected, Xet was already inside and monitoring the scene.

"What did you see?" she asked him right off, in a tone that implied annoyance.

"Nothing new," he reported, but he sensed the urgency in her voice and wondered about that, asking his own question.

"Why, is something wrong?"

"You called the god-master," Cayri shot back, "and said that the Daryl agent was present!" Xet knew why she was vexed. He had most likely interrupted them, but he also realized the situation.

"Something will happen, then," he surmised, "and we must wait and observe carefully."

Cayri understood the setup now. What Xet had reported, had not yet transpired. Xetagod had sent her back prior to the reported incident. Easing her hand onto the killing weapon she had, Cayri was prepared to use it should the situation require she do so. They didn't have to wait long. Within a minute, Cayri's original self appeared, accompanied by the factory worker as she followed him out of the building. The latter Cayri could hear herself talking, telling the grungy man to free the insect. Just as before, the worker unfolded the paper and they saw the small bug fall onto the ground. The stink bug shook itself aright and then flew off. Abruptly, a rabbit ran out from under some rusty old equipment nearby.

"That never happened before," latter Cayri grunted.

As they watched, a Human female got out from behind that same rusty pile and ran the other way. It was the Hybrid Daryl agent that Cayri number two and Xet had seen before at the nuclear facility. Original Cayri saw the girl as well, and gave chase. Summarily, another small animal flew out from near that same obstruction also. Cayri number two recognized it right off. It was Ayryn's pet—that cursed catbird.

"What is that doing here?" Xet asked her.

"It must be with the girl agent," Cayri number two surmised, as the catbird went for the stink bug.

Original Cayri's gaze happened to catch that as well, and also recognized that it was Ayryn's pet. Drawing her weapon, she let the girl Hybrid go, and went after the catbird. Keeping the catbird away from the insect was the top priority, but she also desired some serious payback for the injury to her hand. Unknown to original Cayri, the female Hybrid, Synth, was one of Daryl's time operatives. When Synth saw the original Cayri go after Ting, she realized her attempt to draw Cayri away hadn't worked. Insect, Ting, and original Cayri were all heading west, and Synth anxiously felt the need to help her friend. There were some parallel metal rails on a bed of rock and timber nearby that also went westerly. She jumped a small water-filled ditch and got out onto them. The rails went roughly the same direction Ting was going with original Cayri in pursuit, and Synth ran as fast as she could to catch up. Cayri number two saw that and decided to get involved.

"You will wait here," she ordered Xet. "If something drastic changes things, revert back here at an earlier point and alter the outcome back to our favor. Exiting the vehicle, Cayri number two began to chase down the Daryl operative, Synth. Xet shook his head. He realized right away that if something did alter this scenario, it could easily have dire consequences, ones that would prevent him from doing anything to change them. Rather than wait ineffectually for whatever outcome would take place, Xet decided to follow those involved in this fickle chase. It was his intention to find out where everyone had gone and then observe. Perhaps he could even kill the other meddlesome Daryl worm and improve his status. With that thought, Xet struck out after the group, somewhat far behind, to see what would happen.

The group, and an odd parade it seemed, was still heading west: stink bug, catbird, original Cayri, Synth, Cayri number two, and even further back, Xet. The bug was flying over some rather rough terrain. There were thick weedy plots that those on foot found difficult to traverse. The insect and catbird were on the wing and had no trouble with that, so they put some distance between themselves and original Cayri. The stink bug was wiry. Flying erratically, it somehow kept out of Ting's reach. Ahead they drew near to a busy Human conveyance way that was quite noisy and wide. Many and varied vehicles went along it on bands of a hard grey surface. There were two such pathways, and the conveyances travelled northbound on one and southbound on the other. They seemed to move quite fast, but Xet was not impressed. Mec controlled conveyances were many times faster.

The little stink bug was making a direct line to this conveyance way, and it appeared that nothing would divert the silly thing from its dangerous course. Being a male, it had caught the chemical footprint of a female stink bug pheromone, and the desire to reproduce overwhelmed the bug's rational instincts. Just like males from any species, stinky made some foolish decisions. He flew above the odd, grey-colored earth and began to cross over without a concern for his own wellbeing. Conveyances were flying by at speeds much greater than his, and almost getting smacked finally disturbed the tiny bug. He quickly changed course and flew parallel to the roadway, looking for a calmer place to cross over.

The catbird named Ting was clever. She saw the stink bug change course and cut it off, driving it back the way it came. She was herding it towards her partner, Synth, who had just emerged onto the scene from the direction of some rail lines.

"Catch it with your hands!" Ting shouted to Synth. Synth tried to, but that did seem to be kind of difficult. The insect was very agitated, now, with all the undo commotion. It had been chased by the catbird, very nearly hit by a huge conveyance, and now a Human was grabbing at it. As if that weren't enough, abruptly a bright flash of light followed by a sizzling sound coursed through the air. Synth ducked and hissed in shock. While they were trying to capture the illusive stink bug, original Cayri had run up on them. Venomous with a desire for retaliation, she had fired her weapon on the run, striking Ting in mid-air and killing her instantly. Ting's burned and lifeless body flopped down onto the hard earth and lay motionless.

A lump formed in Synth's throat, and she felt like crying, but she did not weep. Not this time. Instead she was angry; wrathful to the degree that caution was blinded for vengeance. She twisted around unexpectedly and lunged toward Cayri, facing down the killing device. Cayri wasn't fooled for long and shifted aim to kill this one as well. Synth dodged at just the right moment, however, and Cayri's shot went past her face. The heat was enough to scorch Synth's cheek, but barreling on by, she barely noticed it. The impetus of her leap brought Synth into contact with Cayri's leg, bowling her over. The killing weapon went flying, and the two of them began struggling in the dirt.

As luck would have it, Cayri number two came upon them at just that same moment. Seeing her former self and Synth fighting, she didn't dare risk shooting at Synth for obvious reasons. Instead she got close, and when the opportunity came up, struck Synth on the back of her neck. Synth felt herself weaken as she struggled to keep consciousness. Original Cayri used the advantage to break free. She got Synth into a choke hold, thinking to finish off the annoying Daryl agent with her bare hands. She would have, undoubtedly, but the situation changed.

While all this was going on, the shook up little stink bug had made its escape. Getting unduly frightened by those trying to capture it, the insect had chanced flying across the grey roadway heedless of the dangers and dodging the streaking conveyances. The bug had made it across the northbound lanes and was halfway across. As Synth lay in the dirt, expecting to be killed by one Cayri or the other, she saw something dark-grey streak across her vision field. It was Ting, the earlier version, flying at a high rate of speed. Ting dove down from above and then captured the hovering stink bug in her mouth.

"Noooo, you vile creature!" The Cayri that held Synth by the throat screamed. She dropped Synth like she was diseased and ran across the grey roadbed to collar the catbird and force it to release the captured insect. As original Cayri ran, she did not look back at the approaching vehicles. After all, conveyances from her time had specific fail-safes to prevent their striking any objects in front of them, or each other, so she did not waste a care about any coming towards her. Unfortunately, the vehicles of this era did not have any such safety features, and the rather large truck that converged on original Cayri was no exception. A loud warning horn and screech preceded contact as it struck her with a killing force that sent her body flying. Cayri landed many meters beyond her former position, rolling over and over on the hard grey surface. Her body was broken, and original Cayri died before she had even come to a stop just off the roadway in some weeds. The big rig slowed and pulled over. So did many of the other conveyances. Astounded, Synth saw dead Ting's lifeless body vanish as she herself faded away. With a last quick glance she saw Cayri number two evaporate as well.

Xet, who had witnessed all this from a distance, was not immune. The new time shift caught him also, and as he watched the others, he too dissipated. The only ones remaining were Ting, the earlier version, and original Cayri, who was dead. Ting was not sure what to do, but felt she should try to undo whatever harm Cayri had done. As the lone witness, Ting had seen Cayri insist that the stink bug be taken outside and released. She had no idea why that would matter, but she saw her other self try to prevent it. To reverse that outcome, Ting decided to bring the insect back inside the building where it had been before. Sneaking in through an open door and taking care not to be seen, she set the flustered little thing back on its box where it went back to walking along on the edges. The poor bug seemed to calm down quite quickly, happy to be doing something familiar.

As for Ting, she was depressed and had a bad taste in her mouth. The momentary high she got from thwarting Cayri and witnessing her death was not enough to offset the fact that she was alone and felt abandoned. Obviously, there was no one left to help Ting get back to where she belonged. She had seen the other female Humanoid disappear, the one who seemed to be helping the other catbird that looked like her. Ting had presumed that Hybrid girl might be able to help her get home, but now that hope was also gone. In desperation, Ting approached the worker, the one who had been involved with the stink bug. He seemed agitated as well.

"Do you have any food you could share?" she asked the man, but that did not seem to be the proper thing to say. The worker named Felix acted particularly flustered and nearly fell over. It was like he'd never seen a catbird before.

"What are you," Felix, in a quivering voice, inquired, "some kind of demon?" He had obviously witnessed too many oddities that day. Ting knew what demon meant and realized that this Human was not stable enough to help her.

"Never mind," she told him, and then flew quickly away, out of the building, and to a grove of trees a short distance away. Felix? Well, he started to tell his co-workers about the girl safety inspector and the strange talking animal, but they all started laughing at him.

"Drinking on the job will get you fired," one of them said, so Felix decided to keep the whole weird incident to himself. He also kept flying cats out of his conversations after that, especially ones that talked.

Out by the roadway, the trucker who had struck Cayri was distraught as he waited for the authorities to finish their investigation. "I'll be off my schedule," he muttered, and he felt bad about killing the girl even though the poor thing had deliberately walked in front of his rig and there was nothing he could do. He had called the patrol right off, of course, while some others stopped to see if there was anything they might do to help. One young man named Keller was one of the first to arrive. He winced as he looked down at the broken, lifeless body. Keller was stunned. The girl looked just like his fiancé except for the odd clothes and white hair. He had to leave, though. He was on his way to the wedding rehearsal and didn't want to be late.

CHAPTER TWENTY-THREE

1964 AD (Reverted Time) restored

I didn't really feel like working that day, and was sloughing. That's the great thing about having a temporal conveyance. You can take time off anytime you want to. All you have to do is stump back a couple weeks or even a couple years. No one would ever know except for Big "D." Somehow he always knew.

For some reason I was out of sync. Maybe my rhythms were off, and it seemed like I'd been sleeping and woke up too early. I tried to shake it off, but the work seemed extra boring this time around. You know the same old usual; gathering data and running comparisons with known history patterns. The Humans in this era were somewhat outspoken and had whole decades of odd behaviors. If only the individuals in those times would have pulled together, helping one another, this Earth might have been a paradise. It was just before the world governments had to really crack down to keep things from going terribly sour. There were far too many Humans who wanted to get and keep more than everyone else. Some had far too much, while others had far too little. I was musing on stuff like that when the voice popped into my head.

"Hello, Cella," it said, and I nearly fell over. I knew who it was, of course, but it always surprises me when he makes contact and that makes me nervous.

"Um, greetings, your eliteness," I stammered, and then wished I hadn't. That wasn't quite the proper way to acknowledge my boss, anyone's boss. He didn't seem to mind.

"Please calm yourself, Cella," he offered. "It is I who owe you my homage!" That statement did not help my frame of mind. I was floored. Him calling me Cella, well, it felt odd, but I could understand that. Cella was the name I had used when I was a Mec, long ago. Now that I was a Hybrid Human, I had wanted a different name. Somehow I had never got around to picking one. Something in my head decided to pick one then and there.

"I'm called Synth, now," I told him, (for whatever reason I was taking the nickname Rykard always called me back at the academy) "and what did I do that would make you think you owed me something?" Daryl Om laughed at that, which I found very annoying.

"I'm sorry," he replied, getting back to his usual business-like demeanor. "Very well, Synth it is, although it seems a bit derogatory even when you have given it much honor. The easiest way to answer your question is to reinstate your memories, the memories of the other timelines and what you experienced in them." I kept quiet as unfamiliar thoughts formed in my mind, replaying all that had happened.

"Ting!" I yelled in alarm. "I must go to her!"

"Your friend is safe, Synth," Daryl Om's soft voice assured me, "so you needn't worry, but you will have to retrieve her for me from where you last were. You'll find Ting near the trees you had sheltered in. I would also request that you take Ting back to the palace as well. Queen Ayryn will be worried about her!"

"The Queen is alive!" I practically shouted it, I was so elated. It seemed like Daryl Om had washed all the bad out of the world.

"I have altered the timeline slightly," he admitted.

"Oh, that is absolutely wonderful!" I bubbled happily. "Ting will be so relieved!" I could sense him laughing again which seemed to be contagious now.

"Yes, she will," he agreed, "and don't fret. I have restored brave Ting's memories as well. Both of you have served your world in the highest manner. We owe you everything!" I began to blush and was about to get emotional. Him, of all beings, praising me was too much.

"I, um…I should get Ting," I stuttered.

"Yes, please do," he affirmed. "My focus point will meet with you at the palace once you arrive. Don't be concerned about your time beat here. I have assigned a score of operatives to guard it!" I said goodbye, but had a feeling that he would somehow be with me no matter where I went. I stumped immediately to that grove of cottonwoods where Ting and I had observed the factory, and she was there waiting for me.

"Oh, Ting," I said through tears, "I'm so relieved you are all right!" She let me pick her up and hug her. She even put her little paws on my cheeks.

"You did it!" she exclaimed. "I knew you could!" I remembered when I had felt like a failure, and how Ting had re-ignited my courage.

"Not without your help!" I told her truthfully. "I could not have succeeded without you, dear amazing Ting! But we must leave here. There is a surprise waiting for you!" We got back into my pod and I stumped us into the future, to the palace at the time co-ordinates that Daryl Om gave me. Parking on the big front lawn adjacent to a fancy fountain, I sighed in relief. I could see no trace of the corrupt, polluted world we had come upon the last time we were there. What happened next was kind of a shock.

When Ting and I emerged from the little temporal craft, we were not expecting anyone to meet us; however, there was a huge crowd of people. Most everyone who was anyone was there, including the King and Queen. Ayryn ran over like a child and picked up her beloved Ting. Ting had no problem with being hugged and snuggled. She pressed her little face against Ayryn's cheek, purring loudly. I was so happy for her, and for me. I was genuinely glad to be through that tough stretch. What I did not expect was all the noise. Everyone was cheering, and at first I had no idea what they were cheering about. Quite abruptly I realized that it was for us. A large lusus figure casually strolled over that I recognized at once.

"I've been let in on all that happened back there," he said snidely. "You left me for dead, Synth!"

"Rykard, I'm so sorry! There was nothing I could do! Cayri left us no choice…" He was laughing as I tried to sputter an apology, feeling pretty low about it.

"I'm just jinkin' you," he grinned. "You acted properly, and I'm very proud of you!" He swept me up in his burley arms and gave me a rough hug, but it felt good. He added a surprisingly soft kiss on the cheek, and winked at me. The Queen, holding Ting came over, and bowed in front of us.

"Cella," she began in a soft voice, "I've missed you so…"

"I'm Synth, now" I told her. It had been a long time since we'd been friends. I was still a Mec then.

"Yes, of course…Synth," she responded. "You have once again made yourself worthy of honor, the highest." She turned toward the crowd. Speaking loudly, she addressed them.

"These individuals have been in the gravest danger. As members of our own Temporal Corps, they have risked their lives courageously, fulfilling the duty of protecting the integrity of our lives. I wish to honor them as they have honored us by bestowing upon them the highest commendation…Earth's Sapphire Star!" The gregarious crowd exploded, shouting their praises to Ting, Rykard, and myself. D'von strode forth with medals. Oh, I knew who he was. D'von was Daryl Om; his physical embodiment and the main focus point of his awareness.

"It is my great pleasure to bestow this honor upon you," he said as he pinned it onto my blazer.

"Thank you," I stammered. I really didn't care for all the fuss, and I wanted to point out that Ting and Rykard were more deserving, but they got medals too. Ting's was in a nice frame.

"We shall have a magnificent feast!" Ayryn announced, and everyone cheered their whole-hearted approval.

A few minutes later another conveyance appeared from nowhere and stumped in. It wasn't the sort of temporal conveyance that I was familiar with and bore little resemblance to our small pods. I was a little relieved when I recognized the pilot. It was Daryl, the head of Directors from the academy. He had a young woman beside him and the gold Mec, who made me nervous. This Hybrid form of Daryl, however, I had seen quite often at the academy, and he had taken an unusual interest in my training. Unlike D'von, who was also a Mec, this manifestation of Daryl had a synthetic Human body like mine. He gave D'von a little finger wave, and then went over to talk to the royals. Shortly after that the Queen made another announcement.

"I'm sorry, everyone," she spoke loudly, "but we must postpone our feast!" The sky abruptly became dark. Black and grey clouds swirled in an ominous portent. In a blinding flash the monstrous conveyance stumped in, crushing the one Daryl, his female friend, and the gold Mec had just arrived in. A great bay door opened and a throne-like conveyance floated out. Like magic it hovered several feet above the ground and paraded majestically forward. The multitudes of sparkling jewels, too prolific to number, created an aura of scintillating color over the entity sitting there. When it was within fifty meters of the assembled entourage, the overly splendid conveyance halted. The canopy slipped away and the monstrous figure could now be seen upon a throne in a hideous distortion of the Human form.

"Xetagod," Daryl said, "we meet again."

"Well played, Daryl, my nemesis of old," a deep chasmal-like voice proclaimed. "I am actually pleased that conquering Earth is becoming more of a challenge than I first thought." Xetagod tipped his scepter slightly as a salute. "I see your female is here," he continued, with the implied threat of harming Clayre in some way, "and the turncoat." He turned to Xet. "You proved to be less than worthy of even that shortened form of my name. Be assured that when I conquer Earth you will be high on the list of those who will suffer torment…for eons!"

"Oh great one," Xet replied, "Would you allow me to beg your forgiveness. Perhaps I could again rejoin your totality." Xetagod bellowed laughter.

"Yes, you pretend remorse," he grunted, his mood changing, "but you would once more attempt to undo me. I am not gullible to be deceived twice. You may remain with your so-called friends and burn!" I swallowed hard, trying to control the fear that swept over me. The golden Mec called Xet was not afraid.

"I'd rather burn free than be your thrall," Xet professed, "and I'd rather spend a day with my friends than a lifetime with you!"

"It will be a lifetime!" Xetagod boasted acrimoniously. "…and it won't be pleasant, I assure you!"

Scanning the faces, he spotted a familiar one. "Ah, there is my Ayryn!"

As he turned towards her I felt disgust. He acted like they were old friends. I well remembered the way he had treated her long ago when I was still a Mec. "How are you, my dear?" Xetagod went on. "I'm pleased to see that you are no longer incapacitated. We must have tea and reminisce the old days!" There was a tincture of sarcasm in his voice and Ayryn caught it.

"To be fair," she told him, "I would welcome such a meeting if it were truly between friends. I will have nothing to do with anyone who would kill or even enslave just one person, for his own gain. You wish to rule Earth, and care not who you crush in the process. For such a one I care nothing! Can you say you came here with no intent to harm us?"

"I make no promises," Xetagod replied with a wicked laugh. Then he changed the topic. "I see that you and Patik have gotten together…how sweet. You remember, of course, how that would not be so if not for me."

"I was your slave!" King Patik loudly and emotionally stated. "You made me do your filthy bidding! We owe you no fealty!" Xetagod laughed again.

"You seem to be none the worse for all that," he retorted.

"Not by your hand," Patik muttered, and Xetagod ignored it. Looking over the rest of the assemblage, he somehow picked me out from everyone else. A creepy, evil, red glow fell over me from his eyes.

"There you are!" he affirmed, speaking directly to me. "I suppose congratulations are in order. You don't look like much, but then none of Daryl's tools do." Xetagod's shell opened up in an eerie way, the outer surface vanishing. Inside I could see Cayri, or perhaps it was a different clone. I was repulsed and sickened by what I saw. The poor girl was naked and suffering. I had enough reason to be indifferent about what he was doing to her, but I didn't like it, and not just because she looked like Ayryn.

"Please don't hurt her," I pleaded, hoping to awaken some humanity in him.

"You don't approve of my punishment?" Xetagod replied snidely. "This is what all who fail or oppose me can expect!" I cringed. It was a warning; what he would do to me if he succeeded. "One as brave as you need not suffer," he continued, trying to recruit me. The one who looked like Cayri squealed then. Not in pain this time. It was rather obvious she was being pleasured, and it made me shudder. To me this felt no less than rape.

"You are vile and evil!" I seethed.

"Join me," Xetagod offered, "we could explore whole worlds of ecstasies!" Rykard was near me. He could contain his anger no longer.

"You are a coward!" he so named the god-like being. "No matter how powerful you believe yourself to be, forcing yourself upon a weaker being so is lowly and contemptible!" Xetagod's smile faded. A blue-white plasma stream spit out of his scepter directly toward Rykard. Only D'von was quick enough. He created some kind of energy field that surrounded us all.

"Enough!" he shouted. "Leave these innocents alone. You stated that you would desire a challenge, Xetagod. Why not let us provide one. Give us a month to prepare, and I promise we will bring on a real fight!"

"Interesting," Xetagod mused. "I'll give you a week. Don't disappoint me Daryl!" It was his intent to call D'von the wrong name on purpose, as he let out his throaty evil laugh, yet again, and much louder this time. The throne vehicle closed abruptly and drifted back towards the huge flagship. Just before it went inside, he directed his thoughts to me alone. I heard them inside my mind. *"It could have been fantastic...and soon will be!"* Then he spoke aloud to D'von. "One week, Daryl...after which you will kneel to me!" The bay door whooshed shut as the gigantic conveyance powered up and took off physically into the heavens. In just seconds it was out of sight. The expended energy was ear-splitting, and the plasma scorched a large area of the palace grounds destroying many of the lovely ornamental plants and shrubs. In its place was the rubble from Daryl's conveyance. The scene made me feel weak and afraid. When it was safe, Ayryn came over to me.

"You are yet a brave one," she told me.

"As are you, my Queen," I answered, "as brave as the young lass who freed all the Mecs that day, long ago. What can we do? Xetagod has much more than just a few agents, of that we can be assured!"

"Well for starters," the Queen expressed, undaunted, "we have a feast to prepare!"

CHAPTER TWENTY-FOUR

9815 AD (Present Standard Time) continued

As promised, Ayryn threw together a wonderful feast to honor Synth, Rykard, and Ting. There were delicacies of every kind, and the three honorees did not shy away. After all, thought Synth, we had a rather extended period with little or nothing to eat. Ting insisted that Synth sit at the royal's table and got in between her and Ayryn on a special pedestal she used when eating with Humans. Rykard sat with them as well, only he was on the other side next to King Patik. Both being Cybos, they had a lot in common.

"Shouldn't we be preparing for Xetagod's attack?" Synth murmured darkly, spoiling the mood, but Ayryn just laughed.

"Probably," she admitted, "but I think it fitting and perhaps even beneficial to have this small diversion first. We will have little to celebrate in the days to come and this will help morale…besides, you deserve this!"

"She does indeed!" Ting added emphatically, "and we need to get to know each other if we're all going to live together."

"Live together?" repeated Synth. That had already been decided, even though she didn't know it. Once a catbird decrees something, it's not debatable.

"Dear Ting," Ayryn interjected, "we do already know each other, although we've been apart for an awfully long time. Besides, it's polite to ask first. Please, Synth, won't you stay with us? We have plenty of room, and I would love to have you here at the palace."

"I won't be happy at all apart from either of you!" Ting asserted.

"I guess I could stay here," Synth conceded, re-assuring Ting, "but only if it's dory with big 'D'. After all, I still have duties with the Temp Corps." Actually, it wasn't a problem at all. D'von wanted Synth close by in case Xetagod might plan to take some special kind of vengeance against her, Ting, or Rykard. Ayryn and Patik also warranted this protection.

"I had something of yours," Synth told Ayryn. "Inside the dark timeline I was holding onto it for safe-keeping when you were, well, you know…gone. Ting said it was important, and Xetagod wanted it. Do you still have your amulet?" Ayryn reached into her blouse and took out the ancient silver and green talisman.

"Yes," she said, "it's right here. Thank you for guarding it for me. It would have been horrible to have lost it after all these years." Synth was relieved. She had been worried that Xetagod might have gotten it somehow in all the timeline confusion.

"I'm glad that it's back where it belongs," she told Ayryn, who smiled and then lifted the amulet and its silver chain over her head and took it off.

"Could you do me a favor, Synth," she implored, "and keep it for me? I've always thought something so important should perhaps be with someone else for awhile. Xetagod knows I have it. Maybe it would be safer with you." Synth reluctantly took the amulet and slipped it on, tucking it into her uniform. This was a great honor, Synth realized, and also a huge responsibility. The amulet had special properties, but what they were she had no idea at all. For now, she would guard it for Ayryn, her Queen.

By this time, most of the guests had finished eating, and it was time for speeches. D'von stood up and told everyone, in detail, what had happened. He left little out, relating how Cayri had altered the timeline, and how Rykard, Ting, and Synth had survived, restoring the temporal integrity. There was a solemn moment of silence for all the Temporal Corpsmen who had lost their lives. All of their names were read, including Ting's and Rykard's. Fortunately, all had been restored. D'von also told how they had prevailed against Cayri and he left nothing out. Some of what he related made Synth feel a bit embarrassed, especially her mistakes that had caused them to nearly lose everything. In the end, everyone cheered, though, giving her, and the others, a standing ovation. Synth and even Rykard were a little overwhelmed. Synth acknowledged the acclamation with a bow of thanks, but the crowd would not settle for that. They wanted to hear her speak.

"Thank you," she told them sincerely, once she got up the nerve to say something. "I just feel extremely fortunate to be here today. I had marvelous help..." Synth looked toward Ting and Rykard. "Mostly, I was plain lucky." The crowd yelled "no!" emphatically which made Synth blush even more than she was already. "Anyway," she continued, fiddling with her medal and holding it out, "thank you for this wonderful honor." After another round of cheering, Synth sat down and Rykard spoke as well. In his speech, he explained how exemplary Synth had performed under such grave circumstances, downplaying his own contributions. He had the crowd give her another ovation, but she waived it off.

"The real hero is here!" Synth proclaimed, gesturing toward Ting.

"Ting bravely followed Cayri, alone and unaided. It was she who knew where the shift occurred and it was this brave catbird that repaired it. Without her help none of us would be alive!" The whole hall erupted in spirited applause, showing their appreciation for what Ting had done. Ting stretched and stood, licked a paw, then bowed her little head slightly.

Ayryn got up and said, "All who helped restore our way of life deserve great honor and praise." She had been told of the terrible battle that had occurred in the Parallux dimension, and informed those there about the many who had sacrificed themselves, some of whom were indeed dead and gone. She paused for all to reflect on their sacrifices. On a lighter note, Ayryn proceeded. Furman, and his Mecs, as well as Daryl, Clayre, and even Xet, were mentioned with high acclaim to more cheering and applause. Their heroic deeds were not overlooked, and all that had happened there in Parallux was revealed.

Eventually the speeches and celebration wound down to a more somber mood. At some point, everyone seemed to remember that all this was only a respite, a peaceful bubble in turbulent waters. All too soon they would have to face a potent enemy, one who was angry and vengeful, desiring something far worse than their complete and total annihilation. It spoiled the mood Ayryn had worked so painfully hard to hold on to.

Daryl, Clayre, and Xet went back to Parallux that very night to see if there were any survivors of the massacre at Manifest Point. In that battle, a handful of Mecs had bravely volunteered to stay behind, resisting Xetagod to the last. It was soon discovered that nothing had endured and the base was completely devastated. So, with heavy hearts, they returned to Earth. Immediately upon their return, D'von and Furman began organizing the planetary resistance. Before Xetagod had so rudely asserted himself in their world, there had been no need for soldiers or warfare. Everyone had always gotten along well under Daryl Om's guidance. Now, a week seemed all too short a period to realistically mount a sufficient defense against a foe that was always prepared for battle and conquest. Daryl Om was not daunted by the task in front of him. Through his embodied focus points, Daryl and D'von, he began mobilizing the Mecs, Humans, Hybrids, and Cybos into a cohesive fighting unit. The Temporal Corpsmen were marshaled and sent out in pods especially refitted to locate and track any disturbances caused by movements in the Space/Time flux. There would be no uncontested timeline tampering this time around.

It was the very first day after the feast when Myke came to Ayryn with something that troubled her. “This is my world, too, and I feel I should help defend it, but I’m distraught. I have my duties to you!”

“You can serve both,” Ayryn said, putting her hands on Myke’s shoulders. I have Patik, Synth, and Rykard here to protect me, and I can see to my own needs. You would serve me best I think if you would watch over Furman for me. I’m worried that he will try to fight this whole war himself. He is a dear, but needs looking after sometimes. I’d feel much better if you were with him.”

“Of course, Ayryn,” Myke assured her, “I’ll make sure he stays clear of danger.” Ayryn gave Myke a warm hug.

“You keep clear of danger, too!” she asserted. “I couldn’t bear to lose either of you!”

That being settled, Myke went off to join the Mec fighters with Ayryn’s approval. A short while later, Ayryn went to see Furman and charged him with keeping Myke safe as well. Furman hoomed.

“That one follows her own mind,” he stated, “but I’ll do what I can!” She knew he would.

“Don’t get yourself hurt, either,” Ayryn choked. She couldn’t say killed. To ease the awkwardness, she gave Furman a hug like she was still his child. It would have to do, she told herself.

“There, there, my Queen,” he said softly. “We need not fret about things that haven’t happened, and may never happen. You must be strong, now, for your people and your world.” He was quite right, and she knew it. Bucking up, she stood back and wished him well. Satisfied that Furman and Myke would look after each other helped keep down the worry that Ayryn felt for both of them. It would be all too soon, she knew, when they would expose themselves to grave risk.

When Myke joined them, she found D’von and Furman with their hands full upgrading the Mec contingency into an effective militia. Myke had been trained, ages ago, to be a master of martial arts, and as Ayryn’s bodyguard, it was deemed an asset. Furman immediately placed Myke in charge of uploading battle strategies and combat techniques to any Mec who desired them. There were none who refused. D’von was thus freed for more important tasks. It was his wish to establish a manufacturing facility for creating specialized motation shells. These would utilize every heretofore unneeded innovation in weapon design. In just two days the first ones came off the line. They were designed with the best stealth and shielding technology, as well as the most potent personal nomatic stream rifle ever made. At this point in the history of Earth there were countless multitudes of Mec Virtual Individuals, and once outfitted so, they would compose a mighty fighting force.

Humans, Hybrids, and Cybos were not left out. They, too, were given sleek personal individual conveyances that were newly designed to be just as formidable as those the Mecs now utilized. Many thousands of these were built and manned to support the Mec army. Along with these single occupant fighting shells, were many others for multiple units. Any conveyance not needed for transportation was refit for combat duty. These ranged from small transports to gigantic research vessels that were hastily outfitted with weapons. No one forgot the size of Xetagod's flagship!

This arming of the planet was well under way when Daryl Om ordered the evacuation of all non-combative individuals to the three new terraformed planets in geosynchronous orbits around Earth's sun. The royals would not allow themselves to be relocated, and stayed behind, so Synth and Ting did as well. Rykard was assigned to Patik, and both were bodyguards for the females, although neither Ayryn nor Synth felt that to be true. For them, it could have been considered the other way around. All these important Humanoids were recruited by Daryl Om to help around the palace which had become the headquarters for planet Earth's defenses.

The general consensus was rather upbeat. Daryl Om had quickly gotten the world resources organized and motivated, and all were impressed by how well this was being accomplished. In the days of preparation, Daryl Om processed over twenty thousand possible scenarios for Xetagod's attack strategy, and of those, several thousand were deemed potential. Only several hundred were labeled "likely." D'von was apprised of the factors involved that determined these attack statistics. They were: element of surprise, type of contingent, mode of transport, modus of operation, point of attack, and strength of weaponry. Daryl Om deemed Xetagod would bring forth a fleet of large transport vehicles, ones similar to his deathcraft and packed with some form of machinated soldiery. In the past he had used such. Those machinids of long ago had been ground troops, but in this age, Daryl Om calculated a high probability that these would be greatly improved. Surely they would be flight capable, utilizing a type of gravity repulsion like Furman's Mecs now used. Of course, Xetagod could also just attack Earth with conveyances, pulverizing land targets with his formidable beam weaponry. This seemed less likely. With the multitude of Earth defenses, it would have to be a huge fleet indeed.

The big question was always a mystery; where would Xetagod attack from, and when. In any case, as D'von reckoned, the Earth resistance was much better prepared and organized than anyone would have guessed as the day of Xetagod's ultimatum neared. The time had passed quickly, though, and there were numerous tasks that were yet undone when the designated day did dawn.

Furman turned to Myke as they stood upon a plast/metal bulwark looking at the pink-orange sky. Light grey clouds sifted together ominously preceding the first real rays of sunlight.

"This reminds me of another field long ago," he said. On that morning we were just machines serving Humans, even if, on that day, it was for one lone individual. We swore to defend her then, and I would still so swear."

"As would I," Myke replied, "and not only because Ayryn gave us our freedom!"

"She has grown, our Queen," Furman agreed, "and is more than worthy of our fealty. This time around we fight for every being as well, Mec or Humanoid. Let us hope our courage won't fail!"

"It won't," Myke asserted. "I just hope that it's enough!" Furman grunted like a Human instead of his customary "Hoom," and Myke laughed.

Many of the defenders had expected Xetagod to go back on his word and attack early, but it was not so. In fact, the day came and went without so much as a communication.

"It's just like him to betray his own ultimatum," Ayryn muttered, and D'von agreed.

"Xetagod will wait until we get complacent, and attack when we are not looking," he replied. "However, we are given a gift. We can use this time to continue our defensive preparations. There is yet much that needs to be done."

Daryl Om, through D'von, did order all the separate forces to stay vigilant and battle ready. Lookouts were posted, and non-essential personnel were allowed to work on any projects not yet completed. The defenders did get complacent, though. Many of them were out of position on the fourth day after Xetagod's ultimatum, when the Temp Corps reported a large movement in the spacial-temporal matrix. Xetagod had shifted a rather large force into the near future and moved them into Earth proximity. Stumping the huge body backward, they suddenly appeared and began a fierce attack.

There were multiple simultaneous assault fronts. In the air over every continent, large Death Barges began disbursing battle ready machinids. Rows and rows of them were being pushed off like unwanted ballast. As thousands of machinids fell to Earth, Furman looked up in dismay. The machine soldiers shed their heat shields as they deployed, spreading stabilizers and bringing weapon arrays to bear. Opening a channel on the Mecway network, Furman literally spoke to every Mec on Earth.

"This precious planet is our home and our life! We stand against these mindless monstrosities and refuse to let them destroy what we have built here! For the good of everyone, we shall resist to the end!" A roar could be heard planet wide as the Mec warriors took flight.

Deploying, the Machinids formed intricate saw tooth wedges, searching for targets. Mecs and Humanoids were there to greet them.

"Link shields!" Furman shouted as they closed in. "Singularly we are undone…together we are formidable." He had barely uttered the words when the first red/gold beam slammed into Furman's shield jarring him. The shield held and Furman returned fire. The silver/blue nomatic stream clashed against the machinid plasma forcing it back. Everywhere red/gold plasma pounded against invisible walls of silver/blue nomatic streams. Occasionally, one side's power would somehow leak through, inflicting raw devastation upon the other. The attack front slid back and forth. At this point there were, as yet, plenty of backup units on either side that would step up to replace fallen ones, and the continental battles raged like wild rams banging heads.

In the air and in near Earth space, the sky was being contested. As soon as Xetagod's Death Barges dropped their machinid cargoes, they began bombarding Earth's land targets. D'von had scrambled nearly every air or space conveyance to combat them. At first the defenders raked the dropped cargo, and had some success reducing the number of Machinid soldiers. In the process, some defending ships were targeted and destroyed. The others quickly switched objectives. The barges began devastating many on-land targets, whether they were other conveyances, Mec soldiers, or Earth force supply lines. The death craft were well protected, and it took an overwhelming amount of return fire to even immobilize one. Destroying them seemed impossible. The intense fight all too quickly drifted to Xetagod's favor. His aerial Machinids were churning across vast expanses of every continent. With death barge support, they seemed unstoppable.

CHAPTER TWENTY-FIVE

9815 AD (Present Standard Time) earlier

When the fighting began, Furman's Mecs had not been caught completely unaware. As Xetagod's minions flew towards them, Furman recognized the design; they were very similar to Xetacon's machinids of old. Most of these newer versions could fly, however, and those had never been seen before. The flying machinids were quite adept at maneuvering, but Furman's Mecs were also flight capable and just as good. The skies over Earth quickly became over-crowded, and the fighters appeared, in many ways, like swarms of insects. Red/gold beams of plasma criss-crossed with the silvery/blue-white nomaticle streams in spectacular displays. Radiant energy bouncing off fissional shielding splashed glowing color even up into the blackness of near-earth space. No antique fireworks or laser light display was ever more breathtaking.

Even with the element of surprise, neither side had an overwhelming advantage. For this fight, the Temporal Corpsmen were deeply vigilant, and Xetagod made no attempt at time manipulation. Instead he opted to go head to head against Daryl Om, might against might, and it appeared, at first, that for both sides the soldiers, as designed, were nearly indestructible. Xetagod directed most of his initial thrust at land targets. All of the critical ones were well protected, of course. Safeguarding the planetary infrastructure was crucial. Mec workers needed no food, water, or air, so most of these reserves were deep underground. The wonderfully devised power and manufacturing facilities were located where no pollutants or harmful radiation could reach the surface. All of these kinds of historical concerns had been rectified with workable subterranean solutions, and these proved beneficial in this conflict as well. In preparation, these deep operations had been sealed off long before the battle began, with only minimal secretive and well defended tunnels for supply links to the surface. Even so, Xetagod primarily targeted these supply links, but Daryl Om's defenders were too well deployed. A stalemate ensued. The fighting continued throughout the first several days with the critical concern of the individual fighters (on both sides) being energy reserves, as they ran low. How this was handled would most definitely change the fortunes of those involved.

Near the end of the third day, and from a distant vantage point, Furman could just lock onto a dim visual of the fighting within the deepening dusk of twilight. Machinids and Mecs were bashing each other, vying for the "might" to be there. In ancient times, Furman knew, wars for Humans were fought with projectiles or even knives. These implements had been devised to kill or incapacitate the enemy, person by person, until there was no opposition left; at least none with the will to fight. How different this was! The raw energy of one faction opposed the raw energy of the other—force against force in a reverse tug-of-war. Furman could relate to what a tug-of-war was. He had been pitted thus against fifty Humans a long time ago when he was first created. It was a publicity stunt meant to show his strength. It rather backfired on those promoting him when he'd dragged all fifty into a big pool of mud, creating wholesale paranoia about his loyalty. Until Ayryn, all Humans had been wary of Mec strength. She had realized that it was a person's character that one should be concerned with, not one's strength. Strength came in handy though. Furman could not repeat that tug-of-war feat now. It was the third straight day of fighting and Furman had found little chance to rest, much less get the recharge he needed. Even being extra careful with his power reserves, he was finally getting critically low. Myke flew over to remind him of that yet again.

"I will fall back shortly," he assured her, "as soon as I am certain the front is secure." The ten thousand member Mec contingent he was leading had an important task. They were to guard the sealed entrance to Earth's largest power station. Miles below the surface, it supplied clean energy for the planet transmuting heat from the Earth's core. Supply lines ran to the surface, however, and they were under constant attack. Myke was aware of this and wasn't gullible.

"Go now," she told Furman. "I will make sure the front holds…Go!" Furman hoomed. Being in charge is actually like having everyone over you, he told himself, even if they are not aware of it. More so with this one who he especially cared about. He had known and worked with Myke for many ages, sharing the responsibilities of caring for Ayryn. He was committed to her judgment.

"I will go," he affirmed, as he fired thrusters and turned around, heading for a recharge station some miles distant. He intended to transfer to a new shell and return as quickly as possible. Furman had not gone far, however, when something struck him as odd. A cluster of Mecs were heading towards him. At first he believed that Myke had requested an escort, but it wasn't until they were too close that he realized they were not true Mecs. Their ident codes were incomplete or wrong, and they did not follow Mec protocols. Furman assessed the situation. It seemed likely to him that Xetagod had taken captured Mecs and stripped the thinking minds out of their motation units. Unfortunately for Furman, he was absolutely correct. Inserting modified machinid control modules into these corrupted shells, Xetagod gave them a specific directive: Capture Furman. The plan was well conceived. Being patient, Xetagod waited until Furman was low on energy, and set up an ambush. Furman resisted capture, of course, but in just minutes his reserves were spent and thus he became vulnerable. Even so, it took several of the bizarre attackers to finally subdue the elite Mec as he fiercely struggled to free himself. Being out-numbered, and since they had jammed his outgoing signal early on, Furman was helpless, unable to download out of there or even request help. They were about to place energy shackles on him when an object, streaking out of the dusk, slammed full on into them. The impact jarred the venal group of assailants, weakening their hold on Furman and partially severing it altogether.

It wasn't until after he broke free that Furman realized his rescuer was Myke. Checking up on him one last time, it became obvious to her that something was amiss. Seeing Furman struggling, she had nearly melted thrusters getting there, smashing into the knot of counterfeit Mecs that were restraining him. Even with her energy shield on max, Myke's shell sustained heavy damage. At least Furman was free.

"Get out of here!" Myke screamed through her intercom at full volume. "I'll keep them back!" Furman had no choice. Without weapons he was useless. Flying as fast as he could, Furman headed directly to the recharging station, sending a distress signal the entire way. Like before, it was jammed. As soon as he arrived, Furman got into a niche and transferred shells. It took just seconds, and then he gathered any Mecs he could find and went after Myke. When they got to where Furman had been attacked, neither Myke nor the phony Mecs could be seen anywhere. Sending out patrols, they searched the entire vicinity until the fighting, which shifted back their way, prevented them.

Angry now, Furman pounded out his frustration onto the machinids, driving them back with the irrational ferocity of his attacks. Other Mecs seeing his resolve, also fought with renewed resolution, taking back much of the ground that they had given up originally. Ayryn will never forgive me, Furman choked inside, should anything bad have happened to Myke. He would never be able to forgive himself either, he knew.

Just before

As soon as Furman had slipped away, Myke put herself between him and any of the phony Mecs that might follow in pursuit. Three of those came after her. Turning sharply, Myke deflected one off her energy shield as she tagged the second in the right shoulder with her nomatic pulse rifle, and sent both flying. The third was crafty. It had come at Myke from behind while she warded off the other two and grabbed her with powerful hydraulic limbs. Other fake Mecs converged quickly to finish her off. In a desperate move, Myke spun clockwise as they fired. Their shots were well placed, but the technological mix of the bastardized units was not quite compatible. The timing was errant. Close range plasma beams barely streaked past Myke, but not past the brute holding her. That one took too many critical hits and fell, gravity eating him, until he made contact with a mountainside. The others became wary and held back. Circling Myke they cautiously opened fire upon her once more. Darting randomly, she avoided most of the dangerous beams, getting clipped a few times in non-critical locations. Myke's status was worsening, however. The initial impact had damaged her flight ability so that she could only rely on a short burst of thrust, and her shield reserves were depleting all too quickly. All Myke had left was the pulse rifle, and she made good use of it, fighting the phony Mecs scratch and bite. Knowing where their shields were weakest, Myke actually incapacitated three more of them and held her own. If she could hang on just a little longer, she feigned hope, Furman would surely return in time to rescue her.

In a fractioned blink, her hope died. Stumping in, a lone death barge cut off the dying light and trained its attention onto the fracas. Already Myke was caught, as were the phony Mecs, in an unforgiving seize ray. Paralyzed, it drew her with the rest into the huge ship which immediately stumped back to where it came from. The false Mecs had deactivated as soon as they were seized, but Myke did not. Unable to move and helpless within the enemy's ship, Myke was terrified. Pretending to be inactive, she was piled with the others in a dank holding bay. As soon as they were deposited, a scan ray washed over the lot of them. Myke understood what that was about. Xetagod would be looking for Furman in the heap.

Dissoluting all of her functions, Myke pretended to be dead. The ray passed over her, paused, and then shut down. Some moments later, when Myke's systems auto-reactivated, she wondered if Xetagod had recognized her. Perhaps he'd thought she'd been deleted. After all, wouldn't he have taken her to a better holding area in any other eventuality? Deciphering her options, Myke didn't believe the deactivated Mec phonies posed any threat, and Xetagod seemed to have other concerns that were more important. In fact, had she known it, Xetagod did indeed believe his attempt to capture Furman had failed and gave the incident little further thought.

As for herself, Myke soon realized that she was now unimpeded and unguarded. There were surveillance optics, however, of a kind she was familiar with. Motion activated, if triggered they would send an alarm for a monitoring system to check on. Thus, Myke knew, any sudden movement would undoubtedly bring hostiles. Creeping painstakingly slow, she eventually made her way to the closest array and partially blocked its vision field with a piece of debris. Several tedious hours later she had all four neutralized. Finally free to move about, the first thing Myke did was scuttle the other shells and look for useable spare parts. Being disabled, the fake Mecs didn't miss them. By the time she had finished, Myke was nearly fully operational. Her flight ability was still slightly impaired, and the shield energy reserve was a bit low, but for all she had gone through, Myke felt fortunate to be in such good shape. All for whatever good it would do her. The fact that she was marooned on one of Xetagod's Death Barges put her survival in serious jeopardy. What she really needed was some kind of plan, and that depended on her ability to get information; factual information about the enemy spacecraft she had gotten herself stuck on and what it would take to get her back where she belonged. The only way to acquire this knowledge was to search the ship. Trying the hatch, Myke was surprised to find that it was unlocked. Moving slowly like before, she looked for more optical scanners. There was indeed a long row of them running along a great hallway. This would take untold hours to traverse in the snail-pace mode Myke was employing, and that made getting down the hallway seem like an impossible task. There were, however, rows and rows of illuminates as well as the sensors. Looking around for any possible options, Myke espied a nearby access panel. Inside was a computerized console for regulating the hallway lighting fixtures. Reprogramming them was not hard. Myke set the brightness of the illumination on a slow and steady decline. It would eventually become totally dark for several minutes and then just as slowly return to normal. The whole process would repeat in a never-ending loop that would hopefully not trip the sensors nor draw unwanted attention. Inching ahead cautiously as the darkness grew, Myke was underneath the scanners, but below their visible viewing range. Crawling along in the darkness, Myke came to several unlocked hatches which opened into large vacated rooms of obscure purpose. Unknown to Myke, these were the holding areas that Xetagod's machinids had been stored in for transport. Thousands of them had been deployed to assail Furman's Mecs which left the ship pretty much unoccupied. Not all the machinids were gone, however.

Abruptly, Myke heard footsteps and ducked into one of the side hatches. Just as the light began to return, a group of about a dozen small three-legged machine soldiers marched down the hall and went into the holding bay where the deactivated Mec phonies were. Myke knew they were coming for her, and hoped they would not raise a commotion when they found her missing. To spite her wish, they did cause quite a ruction when one of them found an explosive device she had purposely left behind. Unable to use it, Myke had activated the Mec-made grenade and set it to explode should it be jostled. Lifting it, one of the 'nids triggered the supersensitive firing mechanism and the makeshift bomb went off. The subsequent blast tore through the small bay, scattering Mec and machinid pieces everywhere. Another even louder alarm went off as other 'nids came to investigate. After a brief survey, they sealed off the bay and went back the way they came. Myke could not even fathom such good fortune. Xetagod would surely think her destroyed, now.

As things got quiet, Myke went back to exploring the Death Barge, making her way down that large passageway to what she believed was the front of the huge ship. She could hear noises now, even some conversation in a language she had never heard before. Slinking as quietly as she could, Myke came to a large open hatchway. Inside, incredibly, were several odd creatures. They stood upright on two legs, but they had long snouts on reptilian faces. One of them was at a console directly in front of her. Crawling up to it, Myke got its attention by shoving her pulse rifle onto the back of the hideous thing's neck.

"Make a move and your dead," Myke grunted softly yet sternly, "and all your friends, too." Amazingly, it understood and began talking.

"Destroy us not! Destroy us not…please not!"

"Do not move!" Myke repeated, "…or I will indeed destroy you! Deactivate and mute any optical or auditory scanners!" The being who talked was frightened beyond control, but managed to trip the relays before soiling its station.

"It is done! Destroy us not!" It repeated.

"You must continue to obey me to avoid that," Myke reaffirmed, standing up. "Signal Xetagod and report a weapon detonation in the holding area. Affirm that the ship is still otherwise fully functional." The thing was nearly too afraid to manage that.

"What!" Xetagod seethed, when told. "Remain on alert," he warned. "There may be a spy on board. Why are your scanners malfunctioning?" Myke told the reptilian creature what to say:

"Explosion…system damage. Scanner network also. Operational soon will be."

The reply was succinct. "Make sure that it is! The fleet deploys in one period! Be operational by then or you will suffer unspeakable pain!" Xetagod was angry and disconnected abruptly. The threat in his voice was easily discernible, and the reptile thing soiled itself again.

"Drake will be destroyed!" It whined.

"How long is one period?" Myke demanded. The Drakonian gave her a vague profile that sounded similar to an Earth hour. "Show me how to fly this thing," she added.

CHAPTER TWENTY-SIX

9815 AD (Present Standard Time) back on Earth

Many of the initial attacking machinids had been grappling with Mecs and Humanoids for three straight days. When these machinids lost power, however, they had but one last weapon; a self-destruct that was quite potent. In a strategic maneuver, Xetagod directed a swarm of near-depleted Machinids towards one of Earth's important facilities. This manufacturing plant created the specialized fighting shells for Mec warriors. The machinids burst through the Mec defenses with the first wave as thousands deleted themselves. The resultant explosion terminated many of the defenders and laid the facility bare. The second wave devastated the factory. This small sacrifice gave Xetagod a huge advantage. Over the span of time that the battle had worn away, another fleet of Death Barges arrived with fresh machine soldiers while the Earth defenders had lost a big part of their ability to refresh their own. Daryl Om realized the balance was shifting against them, and the longer the battle lasted the more harm would be done to the planet. Already Xetagod had begun devastating Earth's ecosystems. His advancing machinids were wreaking carnage on everything in their path. Studying his enemy, Daryl Om at last discovered a weakness.

The Machinids had an impenetrable energy shield that made them difficult to destroy. The only vulnerable exception was the one or two seconds when the machinid fired its own weapon. An opening formed ahead of and around the outgoing beam allowing it to exit the machinid's energy shield sphere. To exploit this liability, Daryl Om realized Mecs and Humanoids could be outfitted with small self-propelled weather probes, and there happened to be a vast supply of them on hand. By uploading a revised set of operational directives, and instructing his fighters to slip a mini-nomat grenade inside, the probes could act as an effective weapon. The tiny devices flitted around not unlike insects, and the machinid's limited functions didn't consider the thirty centimeter long object a threat. What's more, the little units could be modified to project false images of themselves, a throwback to a weapon design from ages ago. As the machine soldiers discharged their beam weaponry, the insignificant probes glided alongside the plasma stream and slipped inside the energy shield. Xetagod became angry indeed as his machinids began being decimated. The new weapon proved to be quite effective as soon as reinforcements distributed them to the battle fronts. It didn't take long for Xetagod to determine what weakness the Mecs were exploiting, and to create another attack strategy. Since his artificial soldiers couldn't fire weapons, now, without the risk of being destroyed, he pulled them back and relied on his Death Barges, all of which were still viable, and their numbers had increased after the second wave arrived. The machinids were still useful as well. He could always send swarms of them at targets and let them self-destruct. Once again Xetagod had the upper hand.

By this point, the initial battle had already lasted for many days, and there were multitude casualties on both sides. The fighting, moreover, had now grinded itself into a different tack. The main skirmish had shifted from individual fighters to skirmishes between air and space conveyances. Taking an idea from Xetagod's own strategy, Daryl Om had D'von create a fleet of remotely controlled, flight-capable motation shells and sent them off to attack several of the Death Barges. Inside each was a potent welcoming gift for those visiting Earth. The multiple explosions finally broke through the energy shielding, decimating the barges, and the defenders cheered as four of them were destroyed. The small victory was transient, unfortunately. The others barges were pulled away, stumping to a safer temporal location in Parallux and the Earth finally had a respite.

"Don't get complacent," D'von told Furman. "Xetagod is hardly ready to give up. He'll be back soon, and most likely he'll have come up with other and more potent weapons." Furman shook his head.

"I hope not," he said. "The ones now are quite potent enough!" D'von put his hand on Furman's shoulder to be supportive, but down deep, he felt the same way. The two sauntered off in different directions to oversee the damage control that they were in desperate need of. The motation shell factory was scrapped, but a new one was quickly set up in a different and more secure site. In just a few hours, shells were being made to replace those that were nearly depleted, and there were many Mecs and Humanoids in need of them. Unfortunately, that's when Xetagod renewed his assault on Earth. This time he began phase two, releasing second stage advanced machinids. These were temporal soldiers with the ability to individually shift through time utilizing a portable unit similar to that which Cayri had used. Xetagod sent them against the Mecs, but his new Machinids had another primary target as well: Ayryn's palace. As headquarters for the planet Earth defense, it was an important objective indeed. Should the palace fall and the King and Queen be captured, the emotional impact on all the defenders would be devastating.

Rykard was standing watch when the first Machinids appeared. These were smaller in size than their larger, less effective, counterparts. As luck would have it, several Mecs were also there as a score of three-legged machine soldiers stormed the palace building. A fire-fight ensued and Rykard called for reinforcements. Using their smart probes several of the 'nids were shot down, but many more kept coming. The Queen was shuffled off to a safe room, and Synth was supposed to go there also. As a Temp Corps Marshal she would not just run and hide. Heading to where the fighting was, she grabbed a nomat rifle and ammunition on the way. Unknown to her, Ting followed behind. When they got to where Rykard and the others were hunkered down, the fighting was already dire. Many more Machinids were stumping in and were about to overrun the palace. Synth got to a high balcony where there was pretty good cover and began firing her weapon.

Ting crept up next to her. Synth was about to scold her for being there, when Ting pointed with her little paw.

"Shoot there! Hurry!" Ting howled. Rather than argue or ask why, Synth just did it. As soon as she fired, a temporal machinid appeared as if from nowhere. The beam tore it up like a white-hot torch cuts tin.

"You can see where they are coming from!" an astounded Synth gasped.

"Yes…over there!" Ting replied, and Synth fired her weapon, cutting down another 'nid. Proving temporal physics theory for herself, Synth remembered her academy training. Any energy shielding in the vortex rift would be neutralized, and so the Machinids were quite unprotected as they emerged. For the next hour, Ting pointed and Synth shot, taking out any temporal enemies that tried to infiltrate the palace energy shield. Rykard and the Mecs took care of the rest. Eventually the 'nids stopped coming.

"How did you do that?" an astounded Rykard wanted to know as soon as he climbed up to the balcony where Synth and Ting were.

"Oh I have a little secret," Synth grinned, "and she's right here!"

Rykard looked skeptically at Ting. "The catbird?" Ting licked her paw and began preening.

"She can see the temporal rift!" Synth asserted excitedly. "I could shoot them before they come through! In the rift their shields are useless!"

"The holes are blue," Ting offered. Rykard himself got excited then. He took Synth in his arms and kissed her right on the mouth. She was rather shocked, but didn't protest. In fact she rather liked it.

"This could win us the war!" Rykard announced, forgetting the kiss for the moment, and went directly to a communication niche. D'von was busy. It seems the new temporal machinids were everywhere, and the defenders were in trouble. The machine soldiers could sneak through the lines and come upon them from behind with devastating effect. Not giving up, Rykard finally got a hold of Furman.

"There is a way to defeat this new threat!" he asserted. Furman was distressed.

"We need something effective and soon," he declared. "We are being overrun with them as we speak!" Rykard's enthusiasm deflated.

"Well, this may not be helpful," he stated. "At least not immediately."

Furman was desperate, however. "So then what is this method that will destroy these popping in and out nuisances?" Rykard was almost ashamed to say.

"It's catbirds," he admitted. "The one here helped us rout an attempt to capture the palace. If they had captured or killed the King and Queen…" He left the horror unsaid. Furman paid no heed. He was interested in the first part.

"Catbirds?" he queried. "What can they do?"

"It has to do with their eyes," Rykard explained. "Catbirds can see the temporal rift. These 'nids inside there are vulnerable. You see, inside the flux their shields are neutralized, and we can delete them before they emerge. If only we had a few thousand catbirds!"

"But we do!" Furman nearly shouted. "I found it extremely odd this morning when a flight came in from New Columbia with a large contingency of, can you believe it, catbirds. They claimed they wanted to help the war effort. I nearly groaned, wondering how I was going to keep them out harm's way." Rykard laughed out loud.

"I have a feeling Daryl Om may have had something to do with this," he smirked.

Furman agreed, but there was no time to lose. Fresh Mec replacements were sent out immediately with catbirds. The Mec motation shells were re-fitted with a small domed shelf next to the clear head shield where the little animals could roost and survey the battle. In groups of three or four, the catbird equipped Mecs began making a difference straightaway as Machinids fell like pests to poison. Many other Mecs were teamed with catbirds, and Furman was amazed at how effective this symbiotic relationship proved to be. Once again the battle fortunes turned.

Back at the palace, Synth kept a close vigil on the building's energy shield, but no further attempts were made to breach it. Rykard returned with news.

"It's amazing!" he declared elatedly. "Seems a whole shipful of catbirds has already arrived! They are lead by one named Talek. As we speak they are being deployed and are making a huge difference in the fighting!"

Ting's ears picked up. "I must go there!" she decreed. "My family is there! Talek is my great-grandfather!"

"But, my dear Ting," Synth interjected, "it's too dangerous. Besides we need you here!"

Ting was crestfallen. "I must be sure they are safe!" she declared. Ayryn strode forward, having just returned, and had heard most of what Ting had said.

"I promise you, my silly friend," she offered, "they are as safe as anyone in this troubled world of ours."

Synth, with a sudden thought, presented a solution. "We could take my pod and stump back a couple weeks...before the invasion. We could travel to where Ting's family is, stump in, check on them, stump back, and return here the same moment we left. Simple dimple!" Ayryn was skeptical until Synth assured her that they would indeed be back at the very same instant they left.

"Well, I guess it'd be all right then," she conceded, "just be careful!"

Synth with Ting got into her temporal pod and stumped into the benign past. Rykard had supplied the coordinates for where Furman's headquarters was, and Synth, piloting the pod, traversed to that location. Stumping forward, they found themselves in a beehive of activity. The Mecs were quite surprised when Synth's pod suddenly showed up, and it took a lot of explaining to get them to allow Ting to visit her family. The catbirds had only just arrived from New Columbia and Furman had placed them in a rather grungy holding area.

"What is she doing here?" Furman wanted to know, when it was reported to him that Synth had showed up at his figurative doorstep. "I am busy enough with the fighting. I can't be bothered with these senseless distractions!"

"Sorry," Synth sincerely expressed when she was shuffled in to see him. "Just let this catbird see her family and we will be out of your way."

Furman hoomed. "Yes, yes, I suppose," he consented gruffly. "Just be careful. I've already had too many casualties…heartbreaking ones." Synth nodded as she and Ting left him. Who it was that he had lost Furman wouldn't say, but she felt sincere empathy for him realizing the full weight of responsibility he must bear for her and for everyone.

As it turned out, Ting's family was quite extensive, and practically all the catbirds that came were related to Ting in some way or another. Talek greeted Ting with honor.

"Purrs to our famous one," he said.

"Purrs to you, eldest," Ting replied politely, with a slight bow. "I am pleased to touch faces with you again, great-grandfather, and I have urgent tidings."

"Does this concern the Humanoid and Mec troubles?" Talek wanted to know. "We have been notified of such things and have been asked by the King, who is an Aero-feline friend, to offer our help."

"It does indeed," Ting affirmed, and she proceeded to tell them about the enemy they would face. "The Humanoids and Mecs need our help in a most drastic way! The enemy soldiers have the ability to travel back and forth through the course of time. Using this advantage they can attack from any direction, at any time. I have discovered a secret. We flying felines have keen eyesight, as you know. It may be better than you guess. When the enemy travels through time a blue sphere forms that only we can see. By our directing the Mecs and Humanoids, they can destroy these enemy soldiers when they are most vulnerable, in the process of changing time locations within the blue spheres. It is dangerous here, on this planet, but I ask you all, on behalf of Queen Ayryn of Earth, to help save this world. Should it fall, the others will as well, including our own." The catbirds all howled as one. It was obvious that none of them would refuse Ting's request for help. She bowed, and thanked them, wishing them good fortune. After a brief visit, Ting wanted to leave. She said farewell to her family just as Furman came.

"Hello Furman," Ting said, bowing as she joined Synth. Furman shook his plast-metal dome. He would have liked to ask several questions, but there was no time.

"We should go back," Synth told her.

"Perhaps," Ting replied, "but we can return to the palace from any moment, can we not?"

Synth nodded. "I guess so, but we must be careful. My pod is not a fighting shell, and if we get damaged, we will be stranded."

"I understand," Ting returned. "It is just that one of my relations, out on reconnaissance, overheard Furman talking. Ayryn's Mec friend, Myke, has been captured or is missing. It happened just a few hours ago. I thought perhaps that we could look for her. Ayryn is terribly fond of that one. It would decimate her if she knew, and Furman is holding back the news."

Synth immediately went in search of someone with the information they needed, and talked to several Mecs before she found one who knew when and where Myke went missing. It was her immutable intention to go after Myke. Deep inside herself, in a place where she kept her most important secrets, Synth cherished the memory of a friendship that still resided there. She and Ting hurriedly boarded the pod, stumping to the exact time and location where Furman had last seen Myke. It was nearly night then, and several thousand feet above the Earth, so they hid among some wispy clouds. At first Furman was in trouble. Synth wanted to help him, but her pod had no real weaponry at all. They could only watch and wait. Fortunately, Synth had future knowledge that Furman had somehow gotten away. A moment later, Synth found out how. Myke came barreling in and bowled over half a dozen foes. Furman left quickly while Myke bravely stood off what looked like other Mecs.

"These foes are falsehoods from the enemy!" Synth professed, and Ting agreed. While they watched, Myke withstood constant assaults until a gigantic craft abruptly stumped in. All the fighters were caught and slowly sucked into the massive ship. Unfortunately, Myke was no exception. Having gobbled up everyone, the great ship stumped again to a place unknown.

"Follow it!" Ting shouted. With Ting's guidance, Synth piloted the little pod through an open rift just behind the death barge. Exiting the vortex, the enemy ship made a straight and steady course in the dark empty of what Synth recognized was Parallux space. Matching speed and course she cautiously tailed it, keeping her distance. Looking ahead through the pilot's viewport, she could see great clouds of blue plasma. There was also an indiscernible object in the remote distance next to a large rubble field. In the faint blue glow could be seen a conglomerate mass with stacks of plast-metal that looked something like towers. After a time, the image got clearer. As they drew nearer, it suddenly became apparent that other barges were parked alongside the odd base—lots of them. Just as Synth decided that it might be a bad idea to go there, a seize ray latched onto the tiny pod and pulled it ineluctably toward the odious death barge they had been following. Caught fast, the tiny pod's controls were frozen and there was nothing she could do.

Synth swallowed hard as they roughly clunked to a halt after having been swallowed up by the huge enemy vessel. The hulking outer bay door cut off any exterior light as it banged shut and sealed. "Well," she cheeked, "we're done for. I suppose we may as well see what our fate will be." Opening the hatch, her nomat rifle ready, Synth peered out. The area they had been deposited in was a mess. It looked as if someone had detonated a bomb in there. For once, Ting wasn't so anxious to get out. As Synth got ready to step onto the littered floor, she made a tiny high pitched noise. Startled, she jumped back inside. In front of the open hatch, a large brown-green snout came into view. It turned and tentatively looked inside the pod at Synth who was pointing her pulse rifle at it.

"Destroy me not!" It whined. Looking past the creepy saurian, Synth could just make out a Mec motation shell, one that she recognized. It was grinning the skewed way that only Mecs can. Synth released the breath that she had been holding.

"It's about time," Myke snapped, but it was easy to feel the jest.

"Well, we had a bit of trouble with Furman," Synth responded in kind. "he's worried about you."

"Serves him right!" Myke retorted. "Maybe next time he won't wait until the last minutes to get a recharge. He'd be scrap if I hadn't pulled his blunt end out of that heat!"

Synth laughed. "I know…we saw," she admitted. "I wanted to help, but my pod has no weapons." Myke understood.

"That's alright…at least you're here now." Ting jumped out of the pod.

"You remember Ting?" Synth offered.

"Of course," Myke replied. "Odd place to bring your pet, although this one is as brave as anyone I'm told." Ting held out a paw.

"Purrs to you, friend of Ayryn!" she said politely. "It is good to see you again."

"Um, Purrs to you also," Myke said. "So how did you end up out here?"

"It is a tale to tell," Ting admitted, "and someone has to keep the Humanoids out of trouble." Myke laughed.

"It's true," Synth declared quite seriously. "Believe it or not," she went on, "since Ting fixed the skewed timeline, she has also been instrumental in repelling a Machinid attack on the palace!"

"You must have some kind of high powered energy weaponry," Myke wondered aloud, looking Ting over curiously.

"It's her eyes," Synth explained. "Catbirds can see the temporal rift. Anything inside a rift is vulnerable to attack because shields don't work in temporal vortices. Right now over a thousand catbirds are helping us get rid of those latest machinids, the ones that time travel."

"Hmmm," Myke murmured, deep in thought. Ordering the saurian, she directed it back to the ship's piloting station, while Synth and Ting followed behind. The thing kept repeating "no destroy, no destroy" the whole way there as Myke prodded it with the barrel of her nomat rifle. Synth brought hers along, as well, just in case.

"Aren't there enemies about?" Synth wondered aloud, looking around tenuously. "Shouldn't we stump back to Earth?"

"I've taken control of this ship," Myke assured her. "Yes, there are a number of 'nids on board, but they are locked down, and will only activate if called upon. I don't expect to call upon them anytime soon."

"Won't Xetagod discover us?" Synth asked, stating the obvious.

"He already has," Myke admitted. "Who do you think ordered us to capture your pod?"

"Oh no!" Synth exclaimed. "He'll send for us at once...we should go!"

"We're supposed to deliver you to the base he's creating over there," Myke conceded, gesturing toward the viewport. The mass with towers appeared huge as they approached. "Xetagod must believe that I was destroyed in the explosion that occurred in the holding bay where your pod is. The blast in there has rendered its scanning devices unusable, and I had cringer here disable the rest. Xetagod is blind to us, at least for right now. It won't be long before he gets nervous about that."

"That's all the more reason to get out of here while we still can,"

Synth argued.

"Maybe," Myke conceded, "but I have a simply wicked idea!" As if on cue, Xetagod called in, requesting an update.

"Ship status," he demanded gruffly. Myke had prepared the saurian pilot for this.

"Bad scanners off line…system fix will shortly be," it said. "Holding bay where was explosion, searched and sealed." Xetagod seemed satisfied with this report.

"We depart for Earth in point four periods," he propounded. "Deliver your prisoners, and then power up all weapon arrays, engage energy shielding."

"As you wish, most high and mighty lord," the Drake pilot replied with extra homage. Xetagod disconnected abruptly anyway.

"We punished will be, skinned alive!" The reptilian creature wailed. Myke did her best to assure the poor thing that if it obeyed her, the Drakes would be spared.

"What are we supposed to do when we get there?" Synth asked, looking out the viewport again, Xetagod's new base looming as they got nearer.

"Not much," Myke replied smiling. "Xetagod wants us to drop off prisoners, so we will!" With Myke's guidance and a poke or two from her rifle, the frightened Saurian managed to announce their arrival and then dock the death barge at an open terminal. The prisoners, who were escorted by the remaining machinids, were dropped off, and Myke took over as pilot. There was quite a bit of confusion at Xetagod's base when it was at last discovered that they had received the wrong prisoners.

"Destroy us not," the prisoners declared continuously. Xetagod was quite angry. By the time the ruse was unmasked, Myke had already broken the death barge free of its moorings and was speeding away through Parallux space.

"What now?" Synth wondered aloud.

"We need to get them to come after us."

"What!?" Synth squeaked. She feared Myke had damaged her logic circuits. "We should stump…"

"Not yet," Myke responded stoutly. Ting was taking a nap.

Myke checked a monitor and switched on a rear projection. She could see the base where at least a dozen of the huge Death Barges were undocking, several more were already underway and in pursuit. Turning to Synth she grinned.

"Can you set the coordinates on this thing for time travel?"

"I don't know," she replied truthfully.

"I believe the settings are over on that console," Myke stated, pointing. Synth shuffled over there. The markings were clearly alien.

"I can't read this," she complained. Studying the readouts she noticed one was changing. "This one must be the chronometer that reads the Present Standard Time," she announced. "This other one must set the desired temporal location. If it's like our pods, the ship probably calculates the rest."

"Set us to go back a little," Myke requested, "and get ready to initiate." By now the pursuing barges were closing in.

"They're coming!" Synth exclaimed. Ting yawned.

"Ting, I need you up here," Myke requested. Stretching first, Ting then hopped nimbly up onto Myke's console. The ship shuddered. The barges were close enough now to open fire upon them. They could feel the beams deflecting off the energy shields.

"Now, Synth!" Myke commanded. Synth looked at her console and pressed a large relay. Her viewport immediately closed.

"Oops," she said.

"Whenever you're ready," Myke taunted.

"I'm trying!" Synth whined, frantically pressing other relays.

"Try the red one," Myke suggested.

"They're all red!" Synth shouted back. The hits were getting quite numerous and rocked the ship uncomfortably. A loud alarm went off. There was a big green relay off to the side by itself, Synth noticed at last. "Maybe it's this one!" The massive ship whined loudly as the vortex formed and then abruptly they were back in Earth space. Almost immediately their death barge was set upon by Earth conveyances. They were fired upon by many ships, but Xetagod's energy shielding was nearly impenetrable. They hardly felt a shudder. Myke quickly put her plan into play.

"Ting, watch closely," Myke shouted.

"There," Ting replied, pointing with her paw. Myke saturated the area with reddish/gold plasma. "Higher," Ting said. Immediately a death barge appeared and then exploded.

"Yaaay!" Synth exclaimed. Myke and especially Ting did not.

"Another over here," Ting pointed, then helped Myke zero in on it. A second death barge became rubble. After that the Earth defenders stopped firing at them. For the next critical several minutes Myke and Ting were extremely busy as numerous barges stumped in. Some simultaneously. Xetagod was outraged, but not stupid. He called off the main attack and went after the traitorous ship. It soon became obvious to Myke that they would not be able to destroy them all. They had crippled or pulverized nine Death Barges by the time the warning wail of the ship's shield monitor became critical.

"We need to stump now!" Synth suggested yet again. She tried the big green button, but the ship just chugged, coughed, and quit. "Gargit!" she swore. "We'll have to get out on my pod!" They ran as fast as they could to the damaged holding bay as the ship shuddered violently and leaned to port. Getting in quickly they stumped, just as the ship exploded. Fortunately, Synth had preset the new locus long before; when they had first entered Parallux space. The pod slipped out of the devastation and shot through the colorful vortex into Parallux and in just seconds it sailed back to Earth and landed, taking them right where they wanted to go.

"So aren't you leaving?" Ayryn asked as they emerged. She was plainly shaken, but delighted, when Myke followed Synth and Ting out of the pod. It was obvious they had gone somewhere.

CHAPTER TWENTY-SEVEN

9815 AD (Present Standard Time) continued

Xetagod finally agreed to a parlay. All of his machinids were pulled back, retreating into the many Death Barges that were still viable. Daryl Om ordered Furman to have his forces stand down, but keep in battle ready mode. There was always the chance that Xetagod would suddenly go back on his word to exploit some advantage. Fortunately, this was not one such time.

Xetagod's massive ship met D'von's on the edge of space in a high Earth orbit. D'von's spacecraft was large, to be sure, yet was dwarfed by the one it opposed. Xetagod's Throne Ship was even bigger than his Death Barges. Grudgingly Xetagod opened the communication. As unbelievable and unlikely as this seemed, it was rather obvious to D'von that Xetagod was not pleased with the outcome so far; not pleased at all. He had definitely not expected such a ferocious defense.

"Well done, Daryl," he roiled sarcastically. "You have managed to make this a challenge for me after all."

"We want our freedom," D'von asserted, ignoring the continued misuse of his name. "We deserve the right to live out our lives in peace without fear. You wish to deprive us of that. You always have. We regret that our desire to exist in this manner goes against your wishes, and we have no reason to fight you other than to protect ourselves and our way of life. I ask you again, Xetagod, why can't you forget the past and let us live?"

Xetagod laughed deeply. "You know why," he replied. "Earth is my home world, and I want it. Surrender to me, Daryl, and I'll go easy on you."

"That I will never do!" D'von affirmed. "We could fight on like this for eons with no clear victor, until there is nothing left of Earth for either of us. I have a better solution."

"Single combat, like before?" Xetagod quipped, guessing D'von's thrust. "You must have some kind of plan or other to weasel out of dying like always."

"Is the great Xetagod afraid?" D'von taunted, "or maybe you cannot match wits with me!" Xetagod's wrath was about to boil over. Instead he calmed, laughing again.

"Very well, copy of Daryl…as you wish. Single combat it is, and winner gets Earth."

"Should you lose," D'von asserted, "you will leave Earth and never return."

"Yes, yes," Xetagod promised, for what that was worth. "I will return in one day's time. We shall meet in front of Ayryn's palace structure, and we will resolve this once and forever." D'von agreed, and both sides departed.

A short while later D'von stood before the King and Queen.

"In one day's time I am to face Xetagod in a single combat to determine the fate of Earth," he told them.

"Oh my, no!" Ayryn nearly wailed.

"I know it's a risk, but since you had no voice in my bargain, you hold no obligation to it. If I'm not successful, defend Earth and your way of life as best you can."

"But without you, what hope have we?" she pleaded.

"As long as we resist," he answered back, "there is always hope. I am off to find Furman. We must come up with the best motation shell ever conceived." D'von took his leave and, with Furman, travelled by niche to the world's premier manufacturing facility newly established far underground. Thousands of Mecs were at their disposal. They worked tirelessly throughout the day and into the night. Mecs never get physically fatigued and so D'von, with Furman, crafted a motational shell unlike any other. The shell's surfaces were quadruple bonded alloyed metal, the forging of which was developed by Asian sword smiths in Earth's early history, and its strength was unparalleled. The shell was also designed for agility. D'von firmly believed that mobility was an even greater asset than brute strength. It had a full array of nomatic weaponry and energy shielding, of course, but it also had layers of stealth technology, some of which were actually developed by Xetagod in his early days when he was only Xetacon. D'von outfitted the shell with temporal motation as well, a unit that was captured from one of Xetagod's time traveling machinids. This fight could span ages in that mode, and he would need this ability should Xetagod use it. The urge to go back a week was tempting, but the unit design was flawless. In the pitch of night, the shell was finished, and they tested its functionality, finding it nominal. It was not a short distance to the palace, so D'von used the flight time to get used to how it maneuvered. As dawn broke he greeted those awaiting him in his usual prosthetic Human persona.

"It is my desire to say that it has been a great honor for me to have lived among and served so many good people. Whatever happens today, always remember that."

"You just have to win!" Ayryn tearfully responded, but could not continue so the King took over.

"If there is anything that we can do…" he offered.

"Be brave," D'von told him and the others, "and never give in to anyone who would deprive you of your right to life." Synth was nearby. D'von walked over and said something to her in private. As he did, the word came in that Xetagod's immense golden space barge was on its way and would land shortly. Mecs and Humanoids scrambled to take up defensive positions. There was no desire to be caught unawares should Xetagod double cross them. D'von transferred back into his new fighting shell and strode forth, ready to face their common enemy. He stood unflinching as Xetagod's barge landed and then opened up. Xetagod, adorning his massive trans-metal body, floated forth.

"I see you have a different shell," Xetagod stated haughtily as he set down in front of the palace. "It will not save you!" With a slight tip of his weapon scepter he sent a powerful energy beam directly at it. D'von's shell deflected the stream, but the force hit the palace structure and shattered part of a wall leaving a gaping hole of melting plast. D'von cautioned those close by to give ground and seek shelter. Then he turned to Xetagod.

"We shall settle this now and for always!" he declared bravely. Xetagod answered with another blast. D'von stepped aside this time, and more of the building caved in. Moving further away from it and those inside, D'von made his way out onto the palace grounds. This location had once been the sight of another battle, one that took place a long time ago. Furman and others had prevailed here against Xetacon's machinids. This gave him courage. D'von directed a nomat beam of his own upon Xetagod's huge shell, trying the chest area. It impacted an invisible energy shield and dissipated harmlessly. Xetagod answered with a plasma stream that was also deflected.

"Another stalemate?" D'von spoke aloud. Xetagod roared with laughter.

"Try this one!" he shouted, and sent a magnetic-gravitational pulse that put a deep crater below D'von's feet. D'von was forced to take flight. His new shell had anti-grav technology which he put to good use, climbing to around twenty meters. Xetagod also went airborne as D'von circled. Rising even higher, D'von tried an infrared laser, one that focused light photons to a powerful sub-atomic point. The microscopic light stream penetrated Xetagod's shield for a split moment. Xetagod bellowed in anger as he sustained some structural damage. Not fooling around anymore, Xetagod opened up and shifted forward another weapon. Directing it at D'von, he fired it. The ruddy energy stream slipped past as D'von dove sideways. Xetagod fired again, but also missed. D'von's quick shell banked and flipped upright. Xetagod was out-flanked as D'von fired the laser, inflicting further damage. Xetagod howled, but could not fire quickly enough. D'von's shell was a blur of speed as he utilized the time travel unit to avoid being hit. Xetagod brought forth yet another weapon. This one was different. Rather than fire a powerful energy beam, it sent out hundreds of tiny self propelled temporal probes. The probes tailed D'von, even through several time changes, as he reached top velocity to elude them. Most of them fell back and detonated harmlessly. Several managed to impact on his energy shield. One probe slipped into an anti-grav pod, where the shielding was weakest, and damaged it. He spun out of control for a moment before his gyros stabilized. D'von's shell was still nominal, but his ability to shift flight quickly was gone. Xetagod caught up to him.

"Not so quick, now, are we," he taunted, "and where are those wits I'm supposed to match?" D'von was not amused. "You may quit this duel at any time," he offered facetiously, but Xetagod laughed. Shifting weapons yet again, he brought forth yet another beam cannon.

"This is something new!" he stated. "Something I created just for you!" The weapon's stream of energy was unusually elusive. Ripples of transparent grey energy radiated in arcs from it, and D'von could not get away quickly enough. Even time shifting did not help. Xetagod shifted time as well, matching his adversary and staying locked on target. The fight returned to the palace grounds where Ayryn and the others watched in fretful anticipation. D'von's shield held for a moment, but soon weakened. Knowing it would not hold up for long against this new unknown energy, D'von did the only thing he could, which was to fire his own nomat energy beam at it. The beams collided in a massive fireball, throwing destructive plasma in every direction as they attempted to overcome the other. Xetacon's new beam was a hybrid. He had somehow combined his ruddy/gold plasma with a form of dark energy. The combination was more than D'von could withstand. Little by little, it overpowered D'von's energy stream until it could be held back no longer. Xetagod's weapon penetrated D'von's shield and melted away the new motation shell.

"Noooo!" cried Ayryn, as others wailed in dismay.

Behind D'von's melted remains stood Daryl. Xetagod was very aware of who and what Daryl was.

"I am surprised that you took this Humanoid form," he said, "since it is all the easier to crush!" Xetagod strode forth, deactivating his energy shield so he could physically step on Daryl with his massive boot. Daryl feigned feebleness, like he was afraid. Cowering as the gigantic foot came crashing down, Daryl rolled away at the last moment, but not before attaching something onto Xetagod's heel. Righting himself quickly, he fired at Xetagod's chest with his nomatic pulse rifle. Xetagod re-activated his shield, and as he did, the device on his foot detonated. Watching D'von battle, Daryl had determined that Xetagod's shielding was generated from a device located on one of his metallic boots. The force of the explosion, trapped inside the energy shielding, ripped that section of Xetagod's third leg to shreds and his energy shield was deactivated. Daryl aimed his nomat rifle at Xetagod's primary weapon's array and made short work of it.

Xetagod was not helpless, though, even then. He had other weapons, but they would not avail him long without an energy shield. Xetagod knew he was vulnerable, especially since Daryl had now activated his own shield, and the fear made him desperate to find a way to nullify Daryl's advantage. It was easy for Xetagod to realize what that was. Clayre had foolishly gotten too close, watching with worry, as her love battled a heartless foe. Moving far quicker than his huge size would suggest, Xetagod wished to utilize the same handicap that he always counted on in past conflicts with Daryl. Many of the foolish Humans were nearby, and the closest among them was the one that he could use to his greatest advantage—Daryl's favorite. As Xetagod came towards Clayre, Xet moved in front of her.

"So," Xetagod bellowed, "still a traitorous fool. You will die one."

"I won't let you harm those I care about!" Xet shouted. He drew up his weapon arm and charged his former master. Xetagod's scepter began melting Xet's face as Xet's own weapon did serious damage to Xetagod's giant hand. Unfortunately, that was not enough of a deterrent. Xetagod trampled the rest of his former shell, the golden armor, into the dirt, and the fight was over quickly.

Xetagod prevailed, and then scooped up Clayre like a toy. Opening his chest cavity, he placed her inside the transparent compartment. Daryl could easily see her as Clayre stood helpless and naked.

"Hold!" Xetagod demanded, "…or your female dies!"

"Let her go!" Daryl shouted angrily. "Leave her and the others out of this!"

"Not until you surrender!" Xetagod countered.

"This was to be between you and me!" Daryl asserted.

"Perhaps you think I'm being unfair," Xetagod rumbled, "after you attacked me with two of your laughable copies."

"Destroy him, Daryl!" Clayre shouted, but then screamed in pain.

"Alright!" Daryl shouted. "I will yield, but only if you release her!"

"Lower your shield first," Xetagod commanded. Daryl did, but held onto his weapon. Clayre became coherent.

"No Daryl!" she cried. "Don't give in to him, even should I die!" Xetagod flooded her body with a different form of torture, and she couldn't talk. It was obvious that he was pleasuring her…far too much.

"You evil fiend!" Daryl seethed.

"Surrender your weapon!" Xetagod commanded, and Daryl threw it down.

"Leave her be!" he pleaded once more.

"Daryl, my old friend, this is farewell!" The energy blast tore Daryl's body apart.

"Noooo!" Clayre sobbed. She was crying even as her body was pleasured, and the monstrous chest folded in on her. At that moment also, dozens of Xetagod's minions streamed forth from the barge and took up positions around their master. Xetagod was soon repaired, and the palace resistance was put down. The King and Queen were captured along with Synth, Rykard, and Ting who were there as well. Before long, Xetagod came in to gloat over them. A new D'von, in another one of his usual Humanoid shells, also strode into the great hall from somewhere.

"Another copy?" Xetagod groaned, getting annoyed. "Are you here to fight me, yet again?"

"No," this version of D'von affirmed. "As you well know, my core-awareness resides elsewhere. I am here only as an ambassador to bargain for these who I care about."

"You have nothing to bargain with," Xetagod asserted. "Do not interfere or I will kill them all in front of you!" This D'von nodded solemnly and stepped back. Xetagod found satisfaction in that. Daryl Om would do his bidding and be his slave from now on.

"D'von?" Ayryn cried. "Is there nothing we can do?"

"It is good to see you again, Ayryn!" Xetagod cackled, "…or should I call you Queen?" She grimaced. Ayryn was well aware of Xetagod's creepy fascination with her. "You could be my empress, you know, not just of Earth, but of the whole galaxy."

"You flatter me," she answered sarcastically. "I'd rather die!"

"Oh no, my Queen," Xetagod snapped angrily. "You won't die, but before long you may wish it so. You have something that I want. The trinket Daryl gave you. I know what is bestowed there." He opened up his shell and all could still see Clayre as he pleasured her still. "Join with me now or all these you care about will die in front of you!" King Patik would not stand idly for that.

"You are a cretinous, vile being!" he stated angrily. "You will not harm her so while I can yet fight." He drew an ancient blade and came at Xetagod to attack, but Xetagod turned his scepter on Patik. A ruddy light came out of it and Patik fell to the floor writhing in pain. Ayryn began crying.

"Please release him," she pleaded. "I will do as you ask."

"Come hither," Xetagod beckoned. "Soon we will be joined as we should have been ages ago!" Synth strode forward instead.

"Take me instead, my liege," she offered. "I am willing to serve my powerful lord and master in ways that will surely please. Besides, I have that which you seek."

"No, Synth don't!" Ayryn shouted. Synth slipped her hand down her neckline and retrieved a silver chain. Pulling it forth she brought out Ayryn's amulet.

"Oh yes, my brave one," Xetagod grinned lustfully, "you may enter!"

"Don't do this!" Rykard shouted. Synth turned around facing him and subtly winked. Then she strode confidently right up to Xetagod's open cavity. Her clothing disappeared as she was swallowed up. Xetagod was elated.

"There is room for many!" he propounded, but then choked. "What is this?" he said in shock. The look on his face was one of complete and utter puzzlement. He opened up quickly and spewed Synth and then Clayre out of himself like they were poison. Their naked bodies lay limply on the floor as Rykard, Ayryn, and Patik rushed over to help them. Ayryn grabbed table linens to cover the two as the others lifted Clayre and Synth, drawing them out of danger. Xetagod did not look so good. His shell was shaking uncontrollably and it appeared as if it would malfunction or even explode. Seconds later, it just disintegrated, like metal rusting apart in the blink of an eye.

"It was the Amulet," Synth explained as Ayryn draped the table cloth around her. "Daryl's Heavenworlds were bestowed inside. At first I thought I was going insane…there were voices in my head. Actually there were untold versions of Daryl Om bestowed inside your amulet, Ayryn. They told me that everyone in all the Heavenworlds wanted to help us fight Xetagod. It was they who defeated him, sacrificing themselves so that we could live!"

"This is utterly true," D'von affirmed. "Courageous Synth, and all those who once dwelled in my Heavenworlds have saved us. Let us never forget their sacrifices." King Patik swore that they would raise an everlasting memorial to the courageous spirit of Earth's peoples. Ayryn hugged Synth.

"You may not have started out life as a Humanoid," she said, "but you have done such deeds that all Humans, through you, can take great pride!" Ting jumped up onto Synth's lap.

"I told you," she asserted, and Synth remembered. Ting had somehow gotten her to believe in herself. Synth hugged the brave little catbird and pressed her cheek against Ting's. Turning back, Synth saw poor Clayre. She was crying incessantly after Xetagod had so crudely discarded her. D'von and others were trying to help, but there was nothing they could do.

"My Daryl is gone!" she sobbed. "Xet, as well, and all the Heavenworlds. Everyone I ever loved was bestowed there!" D'von tried to comfort her.

"Your Daryl yet lives," he assured her, "within our core. Daryl Om promises to do all he can to restore everyone." Synth glided over to sit beside Clayre.

"I'm so sorry," she begged. "Please forgive me for what I have done! If only I could trade my life for theirs." Clayre looked up, and stopped weeping.

"Oh, my dear," she spoke softly. "It wasn't your fault any of this happened. Promise me you'll never blame yourself. Evil Xetacon, from my era, and Xetagod, who is dead, share that blame. Those who perished did so to free us from that maleficence. I mourn for those who were willing to sacrifice their lives. I, too, would willingly give up my life to restore them." She smiled then, and Synth felt a silent bond, a pact that would link them forever.

“I should get dressed!” Synth blurted out, suddenly, remembering that she only wore a sheet of linen. Hurrying away to her quarters, she put on her dress uniform. When she emerged, Rykard was waiting.

“I thought I’d lost you,” he spoke poignantly, “and it made me realize that I couldn’t bear the hurt. I wish I could say clever things or find the right words, but when I’m with you I get all mixed up. I guess I just want you to know I care about you…deeply…ever since I made you fall out back at the academy. I suppose someone like you would probably never feel that way about a guy like me…” Synth stopped him in mid sentence. Placing her mouth over his, she got him to shut up fairly quickly. Hugging him voraciously, she made sure that he knew exactly how she felt, and the rather steamy kiss lasted quite a while.

“It’s about time!” Synth scolded when they finally parted. “I was afraid you were never going to come around!” He answered her with another passionate kiss. It was his intention to make it up to her for that long period of lost time. Synth was breathless by the time he got done.

“We should join the others,” she whispered, “and later, well, I have some ideas…” Rykard smiled the smile of smiles; the one a person gets when love is new. He had some ideas too. Hand in hand they went back to the main hall to share in the celebrations. When they arrived, it was pretty evident to all those present that they were now a couple. Nearly everyone was playfully joyful, and Ayryn ordered another feast be prepared. Xetagod was no more, and many felt it was the beginning of a new era of peace and happiness. The feeling didn’t last long at all.

Furman strode into the hall, amazed by what had happened there, but he had other serious news. He went directly to the King and Queen.

“I have ill tidings,” he lamented.

“The machinids?” Patik asked.

“No,” Furman replied. “We took care of them. Once Xetagod ended, they were witless, having lost their ability to think for themselves.” D’von came forward.

“Yes, Furman,” he muttered, “it is what we feared. Evidently, Xetagod has friends. A large contingent of space barges is headed this way.”

CHAPTER TWENTY-EIGHT

9815 AD (Present Standard Time) continued

It didn't take long before the space above Ayryn's palace became saturated with interstellar craft. Day passed into a moonless dusk, and the invasion was even visible to the naked eye. There might have been several thousand ships that systematically parked in stationary orbits overhead. It wasn't long before a pattern was discernible. The invaders were lined up in a geometric configuration, and as soon as they were all in place, a gigantic spacecraft appeared. It was as massive as a small asteroid, and it parked in the prominent mid-post position to complete a perfect "X."

"This is not good," Furman remarked, stating the obvious.

"Have heart, my friend," D'von replied with a hand on Furman's shell. "Bid all our forces remain in battle mode." The close proximity of all those alien ships, however, made many nervous.

"What are they waiting for?" Synth wondered aloud.

"Believe it or not," D'von declared, "they are carefully evaluating us, calculating our strengths and capabilities. They won't start anything until they are certain of our threat potential."

"Really?" Synth replied, skeptically. "How can we possibly resist all of that? We barely beat the first one!" It was obvious to most that each of those ships posed as big a threat as the earlier one Xetagod had brought forth. The ships looked identical to his huge Throne Barge.

"We did overcome him, however," D'von asserted, "and that is why they hesitate now. I would even wager that our Xetagod's defeat had never happened before." Furman interrupted with a report.

"Something is happening, now," he affirmed. The group had been viewing an H'logravid image of the enemy's movements from the palace's main common. The 'vid showed the formation split, and perhaps two dozen Throne Barges filed down into Earth's atmosphere. They spiraled lower and converged directly upon Ayryn's palace. The barges surrounded the structure from several hundred meters off and landed. Out of each barge a bejeweled throne conveyance emerged with a Xetagod copy on every one. The thrones encircled the palace in an iron ring of showy power and might. They made it quite clear that no one in the palace would be allowed to flee. Most feared they would not be allowed to live. There were no amplification instruments of any kind, but everyone there could easily hear the voice, trappings of faux sound which echoed inside their minds.

"Daryl, my old friend," the voice said, "I am amazed by your survivability." The answer was not from D'von, but was audible to everyone as well.

"It has been a long time, has it not, my former rival," Daryl Om himself replied. "I wish that I could welcome you home."

"I suppose that would be too great a boon to ask," Xetagod, the true form, answered.

"It would," Daryl Om asserted, "unless you would care to set our differences aside, but I suppose that also would be too great a boon to request." Xetagod's mood suddenly changed.

"Yes, yes it would!" he raved. "To the business at hand, then. Surrender and I'll let your precious Humans live."

"So you can abuse and torture them!"

Xetagod laughed haughtily. "What better way to please their new master!" Daryl Om did not flinch.

"On this planet we believe in freedom; freedom to live in peace as equals. While you were busy making your clever formation, we were taking a vote." It was true. Daryl Om had telepathically put the question to each and every individual. "The vote was unanimous. All the peoples of Earth, whether Human, Cybo, Hybrid, or Mec have all decreed that they would rather give up their existence to smite you, than be your slaves."

"Die in your beloved peace then, Daryl, ruler of Earth folly," Xetagod retorted. "I care not, but know this. It was I, Xetagod, who brought you down. I will at last exact my revenge!" It was Daryl Om's turn to laugh.

"Yes, I will die," he affirmed, "as will you and your pretty fleet of bejeweled copies."

"You're bluffing," Xetagod responded succinctly.

"Am I?" The space barges in space immediately broke formation and flew off in scattered directions. Xetagod, in all his years, had never witnessed Daryl, in any form, tell an untruth. "Even now," Daryl Om continued, "the countdown commences. Deep inside the Earth I have created my ultimate temporal device. It will delete this whole solar system from its beginning, creating a black hole that will crush everything within tens of light years. I have sent a similar device across dimensional barriers and simultaneous devastation will devour Parallux as well. Not even temporal or dimensional flight will save you. Yes, Xetagod, welcome back to Earth!" Xetagod cackled crazily.

"You would not destroy your favorite female!" he propounded.

"Yes he would!" Clayre shouted aloud to be sure that she was heard. "I asked him to!"

"As did I!" Ayryn declared in a loud voice. Everyone in the palace yelled their consent in like manner, and "Death to Xetagod." Daryl Om had but one more thing to say. It was directed solely to all the peoples of Earth.

"It was a great privilege and honor to have served among so many dear friends, and as such I regard everyone. Of all I did here on Earth, my home, the only regret I have is that Xetagod arose from my technology. Perhaps it might have been better for this world had I never been created." The crowd at the palace would not let that stand, and it was echoed planet-wide.

"Noooo!" they shouted as one, and then "Daryl, Daryl, Daryl…" As they chanted, a countdown could be heard. *"Ten, nine, eight…"*

Synth hugged Rykard, and Ting jumped up into Ayryn's arms.

"I'm sorry, Rykard, that we won't get to…" He interrupted Synth with a kiss, one to last forever.

"Three, two, one…"

Abruptly the countdown stopped. Even tearing across vast space, Xetagod was aware of it. So it actually was a bluff, he reasoned. It took less than a minute for Xetagod to return, and he ordered his god-minion barges to come back as well. Daryl Om was unmistakably shaken.

"What is this?" he said, utterly baffled.

"You are a fool, Daryl," Xetagod quipped, laughing, "if you expected that to work, and you will pay dearly." However, even Xetagod was shocked by what then transpired.

Ultimately a third party had arrived over Earth, and the space vehicle that suddenly appeared in orbit above Ayryn's palace was even more massive than Xetagod's.

"Who are you?" Xetagod demanded as he scanned the new arrival. "You have no place here!" Try though he might, Xetagod could not determine what threat level the interlopers proposed. Their might and weapons were hidden from him.

"We do have every right to preside here," a calm voice answered back. "This world belongs to us." Xetagod was fettered, but not persuaded.

"Leave now, or be destroyed!" he threatened.

"It is you who will be destroyed," the newcomer responded. "You are under arrest for waging interplanetary warfare without a permit and for temporal tampering. Surrender now!" There was no way mighty Xetagod would ever surrender. That was not even remotely in his makeup. Xetagod ordered the god-copies in all of his battle barges to attack the newcomer's vessel. The moment they made an aggressive move, they all disappeared like they were snapped out of existence.

"You cannot do that!" Xetagod sputtered, thoroughly shaken. "You have no right!"

"We give ourselves that right," the newcomer answered somewhat arrogantly. "You are now under arrest, and you will be tried and sentenced for your crimes."

"No, this cannot be!" Xetagod raved as they impounded his vessel and then downloaded his total awareness into a holding facility, none of which was by choice. Daryl Om who had been quiet through all of it, at last spoke up.

"What will happen to him?" he asked the newcomer.

"The same thing that will happen to you," came the reply, "for you are also guilty of similar indiscretions. Do you realize the amount of temporal pollution your doomsday device would have unleashed upon this universe? The repercussions would have been felt throughout."

"Perhaps I am guilty," Daryl Om replied, "but my motivation was to protect this planet, and those who live here, from tyranny. The planet you claim to own."

"This planet, from its creation has always been ours," the newcomer magistrate asserted. "Ages upon ages ago, we of Earth Primary terrasculpted Earth 14 as a reptilian zoological preserve. This was before it was finally colonized. Many of our people have migrated here during various stages of your development. Only during the quarantine period when this planet was decimated by your Baronic plague was this halted for a time." Daryl Om could grasp the truth of this.

"I salute you and your people," Daryl Om offered, "you have been impeccably discreet."

"That is our way," the magistrate affirmed. "You will surrender now, and receive a fair judgment."

"I will surrender," Daryl Om agreed.

The trials began immediately after Daryl Om was uploaded by the magistrate's vessel. Xetagod, who would not recognize the authority of the court, was sentenced to reconditioning and ten thousand years in stasis. All of his god-copies and machinids were destroyed. In that process, the other planets that Xetagod had conquered in the distant sweeps of the galaxy were set free. Daryl Om agreed to the reconditioning. All of his omniscient knowledge was stripped away from him, although he was allowed to maintain the memories of all the dealings he had experienced with his loved ones and friends. D'von was allowed to exist, but without a connection to Daryl Om's amps. Those were destroyed along with Xetagod's. When all this was accomplished, the newcomers departed with a warning.

"We will have our surveillance upon this planet," they declared, "and we will allow no further time manipulations of any kind, the ripples of which affect the whole galaxy. The device placed in our sister dimension, which you call Parallux, was allowed to create a singularity. A small number of sentient organic beings were removed prior to detonation and returned to their homeworld."

Myke and Synth smiled as they glanced at each other. "Destroy us not!" Myke repeated in that same pitiful way, and they both laughed. In truth, both were happy the Drakes were unharmed and sent home.

"The black vortex which was created," the magistrate continued, "will eventually cause Parallux to condense and implode, instigating a new beginning and the possibility for life. It will also prevent inter-dimensional travel from this galaxy for eons. Anyone attempting temporal or dimensional travel from this planet will be drawn into that black vortex and disseminated. We shall depart now, but we can return just as quickly. Let this be a warning." In an instant they were gone, and with them, both Daryl Om and Xetagod.

"Well, it looks like I'm out of a job." Synth muttered.

CHAPTER TWENTY-NINE

9815 AD (Present Standard Time) continued

There was no big feast this time. With Daryl Om taken away, the Earth peoples were less than cheerful, and Ayryn was saddened that things had turned out the way they had. At least the Earth was spared, she reasoned, and D'von survived. Few others were particularly happy with the situation as it stood. Some were quite distraught, like Clayre. Xetagod had decimated her existence. In the last fight, Xet had sacrificed himself trying to protect her, and then her Daryl had also been killed. Even those she loved who lived on Heavenworlds inside her Amulet were gone. It was a dire sacrifice they all had made to save her and their planet Earth from Xetagod's tyranny. At first it seemed as if they all died for nothing; that Xetagod would win anyway. The Earth Primary magistrate changed all that. Daryl Om was taken away as a common criminal, though, and that didn't sit well with Clayre. Unfortunately, there was nothing she could do except cry for her lost love and those she cared about who were gone. Ayryn and Synth were understanding, and tried to comfort her.

"Please stay with us!" Ayryn begged. "We love you, and will see to your every need! We owe you so much!" Clayre thanked her, but declined.

"I feel the need to be by myself for a while," she told them, and they were understanding enough to give her some space. Clayre found a cottage near the palace and moved in. One day a catbird flew into her window.

"Well, who are you?" she said softly. Clayre was a little surprised when the small animal answered her.

"I'm Ting," came the reply. "I was out scouting your grove. You're Clayre aren't you?" Clayre smiled for the first time in quite a while.

"I am…and what are you looking for out there," Clayre wondered.

"My mate and I are searching for a good size tree to build a nest in," Ting offered. "There's a big oak that's just right close by. Would you mind if we used it for a while?" Clayre laughed this time.

"Of course not," she smiled. "Make yourself at home." Ting did just that, and often came to visit. Later the visits were less numerous. Clayre didn't mind.

It wasn't very long after that when the central core of Parallux hub stumped into Earth orbit above Ayryn's palace. Like a little moon it was big enough and low enough to be seen from the ground.

"Where did that come from?" Ayryn asked Furman, so he took a conveyance up there to find out. It seemed Daryl Om had sent it ahead in time, before he was taken away, as a dubious parting gift to those he left behind.

"I hope we're not in trouble with Earth Primary!" Furman remarked. "If they detect this temporal movement..." D'von had gone up there with him.

"I don't think this will count, since it was sent here from before their decree," he stated. "Still, it proposes some interesting options; like what do we do with those who are bestowed here in stasis?"

It was true. Many of those inside the sphere were duplicated individuals and among them Ayryn, Synth and Rykard. Unfortunately, this dilemma was out of their hands. It was soon discovered that most of the base's tech-advanced equipment was off-line. The intricate coding sequence needed to get the base operational had somehow been deleted. With Daryl Om gone, there was no one who had access to these codes or the unimaginable skills to rejoin the duplicates to the originals.

"What are we to do with our natural bodies?" Ayryn wondered aloud. "Even if we could somehow revive them, it will be really confusing to have two of me running around. I suppose we may as well let them sleep, for now. Someday, someone may be able to revive the other me and I'll probably marvel at all that's happened!" Then she laughed. She still remembered the day she was Hybridized. Ayryn was allowed to be in a room by "her selves," and they had talked. It was uncanny. She knew what her other was going to say before it was said. Often the two of them would say the same thing at the same time. Ayryn's original knew she was mortal and opted for the stasis. Her old body was put into hibernation, after which a copy of Ayryn's knowledge and memories were shuffled off into data storage. This had occurred ages ago, and she had nearly forgotten her old body even existed.

The sudden appearance of the Parallux hub core in high Earth orbit became an escalating concern for everyone, and so a council was convened to determine what should be done. At the palace, Furman, D'von, Ayryn, Patik, Synth, Rykard and any others who had been duplicated, discussed their options.

“For now, most of everything in the core is locked into an auto-control system,” Furman apprised the group, “and it is not impossible that the base’s vortex generator could shift itself again, but what then?” D’von reminded him that very harsh changes were occurring in Parallux. It was as the Earth Primary magistrate had said—Daryl Om’s doomsday device had changed everything.

“Even with shielding,” D’von theorized, “I believe the base would be caught and eventually absorbed by the singularity, dooming those within. The base’s engines are still nominal, though. With some luck, that fate could be postponed, perhaps for decades, if enough power were available to resist the black hole’s gravity.”

“You make some interesting points,” Furman replied. “It would be extremely unfortunate if the Parallux core auto-stumped there, in any case, especially without facts to support your theories. Should they prove true, and its demise could be delayed, the base is still doomed, whether quick or slow. I suppose we’ll just have to leave it where it is and hope it will be all right.” D’von nodded, and for everyone else at the council it did seem the best option.

“With my present circumstance,” D’von retorted, speaking mostly to Furman. “I may as well take over the management duties. I have nothing better to do with my time…unless you want the job!” Furman, however, did not.

“I’ve been in charge of things for an awfully long time,” he noted, “and I’ve already made arrangements to have my elite Mecs run things with a council of Humanoids.”

Ayryn was quite shocked when she heard that. “Really?” she responded as Furman shuffled nervously.

“Yes, I’m stepping down, my Queen,” he asserted. “I was going to update you with this news after the meeting. I cringe to imagine what life will be like when all that responsibility is no longer mine!” He laughed his ridiculous metallic guffaw that always made everyone else laugh too.

“What will you do?” Ayryn asked him after the others had gone.

“Hoom,” Furman replied in the usual Furman way, “First of all, let’s not get ahead of things. I wish to ask a great favor of my Queen.”

“Oh, Furman,” Ayryn smiled, “you know I’d do anything for you!”

“It’s still polite to ask,” he said, sticking to his protocols.

“Then go on and ask!” Ayryn giggled. Myke was seated nearby, mending one of Ayryn’s formal dresses.

"I wish to marry one of your close handmaids…if she would wish it so."

Furman walked over to where Myke was seated, and bowed low. Well, low for a Mec.

"Of course you can," Ayryn mooned. Myke looked oddly at both of them.

"Do I get any say in this?" she asked rather curtly.

"I'm sorry, Myke," Ayryn pouted, while Furman looked at the floor.

"I am sorry as well," he muttered. "If you'd not wish to be saddled with an old foolish Mec, I guess I could understand that."

"I didn't say that," Myke stated. "Besides, now that you're on your own, somebody will have to make sure you stay out of trouble. It may as well be me!"

"Does that mean you'll marry me?"

"I just said I would, didn't I?" Myke smiled, and gave Furman a rough shove, which was the Mec way of showing affection. Ayryn laughed.

"We can have the wedding here!" she offered. "If that's alright with you two."

It was. Ayryn took charge of all the planning and she invited everyone. The crowd spilled out into the courtyard and palace grounds there were so many. The ceremony was even broadcast on the Mecnet so that every Mec on Earth could watch. D'von shuttled back from the orbiting hub and presided over the wedding as the bride and groom pledged their love for one another. It was a wonderful diversion from all the bad things they had suffered through. Ayryn wore a long pink dress and was the matron of honor, while Synth in a similar one was a bridesmaid. King Patik and Rykard were groomsmen. It was a perfectly lovely ceremony and the reception was a feast like no other. For ages after, Furman's wedding was generally marked as the beginning of a golden age that lasted for millennium.

It was also at that feast when D'von suggested to Clayre that she come with him to the orbiting Parallux core.

"I'm not your Daryl," he said, "but I am a part of what he was. I, too, feel abandoned." Clayre was sympathetic, and they spent some time together, healing each other. It was not long after that when she decided to dwell there in the Parallux base core with D'von to help care for those in stasis. At first, this seemed a perfect arrangement, but it didn't stay that way. A few weeks after Clayre had settled in, the core's vortex generator suddenly came to life and it did auto-stump. They were brought back into Parallux, to its former location. There was nothing left of the original base, and the debris was already on its way to the maw of the black hole. D'von quickly brought the base's engines on line and set them to neutralize the strong pull of the singularity's gravity.

"We should be safe for the moment," he told Clayre. "So this is Parallux," he spoke almost reverently. "I've never been here."

"Yes, here we are," she said, looking out of a viewport at the beautiful glowing pools of dark blue plasma. Off in the vast distance the large black hole was devouring others. "Now what?"

CHAPTER THIRTY

Earth dimension, half a galaxy away

Most of all Daryl Om missed his true love. He worried about Clayre and often wondered if she was all right. Trapped on Earth Primary, Daryl Om had no way of knowing for certain. He did feel fairly confident that Ayryn and the others would make sure Clayre was provided for. As for himself, Daryl had no choice but to undergo the reconditioning as a major part of his sentence. Having been stripped of his abilities, he could no longer perform the higher cognitive processing involved when calculating complex or extensive hypotheses. This, of course, meant he was no longer omniscient and was more or less just a plain Mec. As a part of this reconditioning, he was also required to upload volumes of Earth Primary regulations for existence as a Virtual Individual. Most of these statutes were similar in heart to the codes Daryl Om had made for himself and always followed. Some were not. Earth Primary was staunchly opposed to time travel, temporal communication, and especially any and all timeline alteration. Daryl Om was okay with that. He even wondered why they had not stepped in and enforced these laws much earlier on his home world. It could have averted a lot of the troubles with Xetagod, surely, but explanations were not forthcoming. At his trial, Daryl Om was given a punitive sentence of no less than a decade in stasis. Stasis on Earth Primary wasn't a complete shutdown. Actually, it was just a physical immobilization where mental functioning was permitted. Being conscious throughout was much more of a difficult punishment than total inanimation, however, and Daryl Om did a lot of thinking during that stretch. There wasn't anything else he could do.

When the first five years finally ended, Daryl Om was brought before a second tribunal and at that time was granted a parole. In short order he was re-animated, given a new motation shell, and allowed a menial job monitoring large air purifiers that he was happy to do. Physical work felt strange, but he was actually relieved to no longer be responsible for a planet full of people. There were other Virtuals around, and some were jovial characters that Daryl Om began friendships with. Many of these chums, he discovered, were former Hominids. Evidently immortality had its costs.

After a time, he learned enough about Earth Primary to become a citizen. The ruling faction was a group of Omniscient Virtuals. These beings had been in charge of Earth Primary and its colonies for millions of years. They can have it, he mused. He was rather enjoying his carefree existence. When five more years had passed, Daryl Om was reviewed once again, and it was determined that he had satisfied the terms of his sentence. He was given a choice to remain where he was or return to his planet of origin. Never having felt content on Earth Primary, coupled with a desire to be reunited with his Clayre, Daryl Om requested that he be sent home and his wish was granted. Hitching a ride on an Earth Primary vessel that regularly patrolled Earth Fourteen, he was discreetly dropped off near the palace.

Imagine Ayryn's surprise when she realized who he was! It was a happy meeting, of course. Unfortunately, Daryl Om was dismayed when he discovered that Clayre had gone. Finding out that she had traversed to Parallux was a sore loss. Ayryn offered him a place in her court, but it was Synth who suggested he go after Clayre.

"My old pod is still right here in the palace!" she told him. "Go find her!" Daryl Om knew that shifting dimensions was in a grey area with Earth Primary, and the singularity made going there a death sentence. Not immediately, perhaps, but eventually the black hole would devour everything. There was not even any guarantee that Parallux hub still existed. Still, no threat of deletion would keep Daryl Om from any chance to reunite with his love. After a brief visit and an opportunity to say goodbye to his close friends, Synth's pod was prepared for interdimensional travel. Blind to what he would find, Daryl Om did stump across into Parallux, and it was hard to miss the gaping maw of the black hole nigh at hand. It began to pull on the little pod as soon as the vortex disseminated. He could see the Parallux base's core also, however, and made his way towards it. D'von intercepted his urgent distress call and guided the pod inside. As it happened, this occurred during a sleep period for Clayre, fitful as it was, and so D'von was reunited with his original core-awareness, face to face. Instinctively he knew Daryl Om was no longer omniscient.

"I am honored to welcome you here," he said. "Like a big brother you have always been, or at the least, the closest of friends, and as such I will always consider you." Daryl Om was quite emotional as he reached out and put his hand on D'von's shoulder.

"It is a great pleasure to see you again, my brother. It would seem that both of us are scions of the same entity, lone remnants of what we were part of."

"How is it you are here?" D'von's curiosity drove him to ask.

"It is a tale," Daryl Om related, "and the particulars better suited for another time. As it happened, once I had served my sentence, I was deemed no longer a threat. The Earth Primary magistrates freed me, so I came back to our Earth looking for my Clayre. Ayryn said that she is here."

"It is true," D'von confirmed, "although she has suffered a lot. I have tried to do what I can for her."

"I must see her at once!" Daryl Om asserted, but D'von restrained him.

"Clayre is in dire need of rest," he said. "It is her sleep period so let her catch some if she can. She's been sleep deprived since we came, and I now regret that I brought her here. We are trapped on this doomed base with little hope for survival. Soon it will plummet into Parallux cauldron, for so I name that which you have unwittingly begat."

"It was a dire need that drove me to that end," Daryl Om admitted, "but not necessarily our demise. There was a reason I sent the base core ahead. It was to keep safe a last gift. I need only discover the key to unlock it."

Daryl Om wasn't sure what he was looking for, but he had D'von lead him through every portal and hatch. The base was self-sustainable and they walked through the Mec tended gardens and fields and the former Temp corps training facility. In other technological bays they viewed the many souls whose bodies were suspended, their lives abruptly put on hold. Copies of all their memories and knowledge were stored nearby.

"Most of the individuals here have single dimensional "Earth" bodies, and, as such, would not be able to exist in this dimension without special considerations," D'von explained. "The receptacles they are housed in continually infuse each organic shell with low dosages of Parallux nomaticles. These artificially create a dual-dimensional envelope. They are safe for now. Unfortunately, the controlling technology for this equipment is locked and running autonomously. If only we had the skill to rejoin mind to body. We could have restored these poor individuals in Earth orbit when we had the chance. The living replicates of some of these people have died in the war and are now truly gone, more is the pity. Still, there isn't much of a future for them here."

"Perhaps not, D'von," Daryl Om offered, "but there is still hope!

What is in here?" They had just come to the room where the green crystal that housed Xet's Heavenworld resided.

"This is where I would send our Clayre," D'von muttered, "if it were somehow possible, but the lockout for this base is impossibly complex. At the time, you must have initialized the security coding to prevent any tampering..."

Daryl Om tried, but he could not recall doing anything like that.

"I must have deleted my own memory to keep the base a secret," he said. "To my knowledge, no one on Earth Primary has ever been aware of this interdimensional outpost or what is bestowed here. Even so, should circumstances have been different, there are omniscients on that planet who could perhaps unlock this code for us. I doubt they would be so inclined, however. For one, this base is temporal and as such against their laws. For another, they would have to be here to accomplish that..."

"If it were possible," D'von asserted, "for them to travel to Parallux and back they would surely require an advanced technological expertise, a mastery of craft design that could somehow defeat the cauldron. I have sent many an unmanned temporal pod to die in its hungry maw attempting to thwart the strong pull of graviton waves. None of them could prevent the singularity from warping the unit's own vortex. Leaving this place seems impossible. Even communicating our intentions has thus far been unattainable."

"Never the less, we must find a way to unlock the coded security," Daryl Om replied, somewhat distraught. "As important as this is, my omniscient self would have made sure we had the means to discover it!"

"I have spent many days trying to deduce what that could be," D'von affirmed. "The code is incredibly intricate...like a detailed scan almost." He punched the conversion up onto an H'logravid quarter sphere. Jumbled figures bounced past by the thousands.

"Yes," Daryl Om agreed. "It does seem to be some kind of scan."

"Verily, but it could be a scan of anything!" D'von lamented. Daryl Om had a sudden insight.

"What if it's one of us?" he offered.

"Like you!" D'von said excitedly. "That would make sense...nothing would work until you came back!"

"You forget. I've been altered," Daryl Om stated in reply.

They tried this thrust anyway, but Daryl Om's scans did not unlock the base's security. Neither did D'von's or both of them together. Giving up, the two sat in silence. By this time, Clayre had awakened from her sleep. Feeling refreshed, she had bathed and adorned new clothing. Looking for D'von, Clayre had at last found him in the green crystal room.

"Who is your friend?" Clayre asked when she saw that D'von was not alone.

"My Clayre!" Daryl Om poured out as he stood and came toward her. "Oh happy day that brings us together again. It is your Daryl, back from Earth Primary…how I've missed you!" Clayre looked over the Mec with the strange motation shell.

"At least we have met again," she stated dryly, "before the end of all things!" With a guilt laden face Daryl Om held Clayre's gaze then looked at D'von.

"It's true," D'von admitted. "We have only weeks before our power reserves run out." Just as the dark grief was about to drown Daryl Om, it was like a single ray of morning sun had abruptly shot over a small rise to fracture what was left of the night. A huge smile formed on Daryl Om's metallic face.

"Of course," he beamed excitedly. "That has to be it!"

CHAPTER THIRTY-ONE

9815 AD (Present Standard Time) Earlier

Like I said before, I was out of a job, and Rykard was less than helpful.

"I know a guy who could use a good worker," he quipped, "someone to keep him out of trouble."

"...and who would that be?" I jokingly slapped back, "sounds like some dunder!" He laughed.

"Actually," he replied, getting serious now, "I was talking to Patik, and he could use some help with a large project. Before the war, he was heading up the New Columbia terra-sculpt. Now that he's back on it, Patik has asked me to be his right hand, and I can hire anyone I want to assist me."

"So you thought of poor old Synth who was also out of a job."

"Something like that," he conceded, "and we'd be together."

"I know, and it sounds fun," I admitted to him, "but you're forgetting about Ting. She would never let me leave without Ayryn...and you know Ayryn. She doesn't like travelling."

"Where is that little flea scratcher, anyway?" Rykard wondered. "I haven't seen Ting for days."

"You know," I confessed, "I haven't seen her either. Maybe she's with Ayryn." We went to see the Queen and found out that Ting was also AWOL from her duties as Ayryn's confidant and pet. A little worried, the Queen asked Myke to get a squad of Mecs to find her. It didn't take very long. Mecs have excellent scanning capabilities. Myke got a report and sent it at once to Ayryn.

"Your pet is isolated a few miles from here in a nice little grove of trees," she told the Queen. "There is someone with her." Ayryn was anxious for explanations, but Myke wasn't forthcoming. Smiling, she told Ayryn that she would just have to go see for herself. A short time later Ayryn came back and told us what was going on.

"Well, Ting has been busy," she told me and Rykard. "Seems she has gone and got herself a mate!"

"Oh how wonderful!" I nearly cheered.

"Wait, there's more!" I was shocked when she told me what. "Ting's been mated for several weeks...long enough to have started a little family. Yes, there's already a litter of kittchicks!" I didn't waste any time running off to see them. Ayryn showed me where her nest was, and Ting looked so happy and proud.

"Oh my, Ting!" I told her. "What a beautiful family!"

"You may cuddle them if you like," she offered, and I did, each and every one. There were five in all, and each one cute as a pearl. Three of them were male and resembled Ting's mate, a stout catbird named Marok, who was all grey with black accents. The other two were female and looked just like Ting. When I offered her the opportunity to go to New Columbia, she was delighted, but reserved.

"Do you think the Queen will let me go?" she wondered. "Marok is homesick, and wants to show the rest of the family our kitts.

"Let me see if I can perhaps persuade Ayryn to give in just this once," I offered, "since Rykard and I will accompany you."

Ayryn did give in. Actually, after all the stress of the war, and then Furman and Myke's wedding, she was anxious to get away herself.

"It's all settled then!" she stated happily. "We'll all go on a little vacation to New Columbia!"

Rykard and I; Ting, Marok and their kittchicks; Ayryn, Patik and half the court; all took a big conveyance and went on an excursion to the most recently constructed new Earth planet. Rykard took me aside.

"My family has a little summer cottage near here," he told me. "We can stay there." I was a bit shocked when I saw it. The little cottage was a rather large mansion. Evidently Rykard's family was quite influential.

"This is a little cottage?" I raved. "I don't know if there's enough room for the two of us!" He laughed. After spending all that time in little pods, this seemed too wonderful to fathom. I threw my duffle on a bed and jumped after it. Ting and Marok with the kitts didn't stick around for long. Ting said goodbye with a hug and a cheek rub and then they left for the jungles where their prides had nests. As it turned out, Rykard's family had been given a grant for an extensive tract of land. Their plan was to grow various rare Humanoid delicacies. Of course, there were plenty of Mecs on hand who were willing to help. Already a small village had been laid out and built to support the budding industry and the Virtual population. There was an especially nice depot and transfer station where persons and goods could be shuffled in and out. Of course, in our age there was no remuneration—hadn't been any for millennia. People just placed orders via a system-wide net and they would be filled by anyone who could. In that way people got anything they needed or wanted and everyone was happy and content. Mecs handled most of the shipments. The planets were designed to be mostly self sufficient, so there was not a lot of necessary planet to planet trade other than tourists. New Columbia was still a bit rugged and untamed, and I liked that. The time passed quickly there, and already the first season was done when Ayryn was ready to go back to Earth. Rykard and I talked her into staying just a little bit longer.

One warm day after an exhaustive work session, Rykard took me to an exotic pool just below a small waterfall. It was beautiful there, and I told him so.

"Not as beautiful as you!" he declared, diving over to where I was. Hugging me, he looked into my eyes and decided he couldn't live without me. "Marry me!" he demanded.

I slipped out of his grip and then dunked him. When he came up sputtering I looked into his eyes and kissed him. "I suppose," I giggled. "You do need looking after!" Then he dunked me!

Ayryn was more than happy to stay for the wedding, and since she'd been getting a lot of practice lately, helped us plan the big affair. It was the largest celebration on New Columbia up to that point, and lasted a couple days. Ting and Marok with their young ones were there along with many of the catbird clans. King Patik presided over the celebration and joined us as man and wife. Afterwards, Ting had to break it to Ayryn that she wouldn't be going with her back to Earth. She was quite disappointed until Ting offered her one of the kitts. Ayryn picked out one of the females, a pretty little one that looked just like Ting.

"Do you have a name?" she asked it.

"No," the tiny kittbird said shyly.

"How about Meringue?"

"Oh, that's nice," the little one purred, and she was Meringue ever after. She and Furman's young son played together often. Yeah, Furman and Myke reinstated the practice of Mec children.

Furman had given up motation shells, at Myke's insistence, and had donned a Humanoid prosthetic one. Ayryn said he looked handsome in it, but he just "hoomed." Anyway, the idea of Mec kids had first begun thousands of years earlier when Humans had used Mecs to replace deceased persons—including children. They were given as many attributes as possible of the lost loved one. It wasn't an ideal situation as one would guess. Myke and Furman put a different twist on it. In a private ceremony, they joined together and bequeathed parts of themselves and let them mingle in a small Humanoid prosthetic shell. Its virtual mind was created from downloads of data from both parents until they reached the efficacy for life. As with every Virtual Life form, the spark came from asking it a question.

"What are you?" Myke and Furman asked simultaneously. After a long moment, it finally spoke.

"I am alive!" It said excitedly. Little Mykron was a handful. He was allowed to develop as a Human child would. Furman always wished he'd had a childhood. I was so happy for him and Myke. It wasn't long after that before I was looking with dreamy eyes at Rykard.

"We should have one!" I told him. Seems there was a bit of a baby explosion at that time, and why not? There were three new planets, lots of room, and nothing but roses to look forward to in the coming age. Other Mecs followed Furman and Myke's example and had little Mecs. As for Humanoids, well, the babies just keep on coming! Mine is due any day now.

CHAPTER THIRTY-TWO

In Parallux

D'von brought Clayre some morning sustenance, which she had no immediate desire for.

"What is going on?" she wanted to know.

"When we first arrived here," D'von began, "you wondered what was next. I have given the matter much consideration."

Having had a somewhat restful sleep, Clayre shed some of her bitterness. "So what have you decided?" She glanced toward Daryl Om. D'von shrugged.

"We might spend the rest of our existence taking care of those here in stasis," he related, "or perhaps something else."

"Nosing about," Daryl Om added, "we have discovered things left here, expressly for us, by our core. You could go to Xet's Heavenworld."

"It still exists?" Clayre responded, rather interested. "I have memories of it, some are still so close." D'von and Daryl Om let her finish breakfast, after which they showed Clayre the large crystal wherein Xet's Heavenworld was bestowed.

"I do remember this," she remarked, looking at the pretty green stone as if she could see where Xet's Heavenworld was. "Is anyone still there?"

"Perhaps," Daryl Om offered, "Who knows. Xet was a focus point, was he not?" Clayre looked up and smiled, as if she suddenly remembered something, something important. Eventually they talked her into making the transfer. It was most likely a one way trip, D'von warned, and she accepted that. Daryl Om believed the sub-atomic Mecs in the tiny transfer hub would still have a viable little Hybrid body for Clayre, the one she used before. With this belief, and following Daryl Om's instructions, D'von did teleport her, hoping she made it ok. As Daryl Om expected, the scan of her dual dimensional body for the transfer did unlock the base, and it became fully operational. As soon as he was assured that D'von would be able to handle things, Daryl Om also teleported to Xet's Heavenworld. Feeling that his duties were now for those trapped in stasis, D'von began the serious task of trying to discover the means for restoring them to life. Communicating with Daryl Om on a regular basis, he made good progress, until the hub could no longer sustain its distance from the singularity. When there were just days left before destruction, D'von had little choice. They had to come up with some kind of plan to save the base and all those within. The vortex generator was operational now, but the black hole would disrupt any attempted temporal or dimensional travel to the hub's demise. D'von and Daryl Om discussed the possibility.

"If there were some way to relocate temporally," D'von hypothesized, "would we be safe in some remote past?"

"In truth, that is unlikely," Daryl Om stated plainly. "The doomsday device was sent to and then triggered in the ultimate past to keep Xetagod from using Parallux as an escape. Besides, energy is scarce in this universe and our reserves are already depleted."

"Yes," D'von conceded. "Without a renewable energy source, we have a limited future even should we somehow be spared from the cauldron. What can we do?"

"Xet is still a viable entity in his Heavenworld," Daryl Om related. "He has offered a suggestion…a rather drastic one. Accessing the AMPs he created in his Heavenworld, he has come up with a theoretical solution."

"I'll listen to anything," D'von lamented.

"There is a way to temporally re-locate," Daryl Om stated, "but you're not going to like it. Xet believes we can use the existing singularity's vortex."

"What?" D'von raved. "We're to use the cauldron? Won't the gravity waves crush us? At the least, it will tear this base apart!"

"Possibly," Daryl Om conceded, "but for now, that is an unknown eventuality. Xet believes that if we rocket toward the black hole, the acceleration will build exponentially. We will be travelling so fast that the cauldron's effect would be minimal and we would temporally relocate before it would bash us apart…in theory."

"Even should this chancy plan work," D'von argued, "where could we go that would do us any good. We will still deplete our energy reserves, and all the sooner!"

"That is the amazing part of Xet's plan," Daryl Om related, a hazy smile showing grandly on the H'logravid. "There is only one temporal direction that would offer us a chance…the future."

"It would have to be billions of years…" D'von replied in awe.

"Xet has calculated the earliest planetary systems would be habitable around four and a half billion years after Parallux's imminent 'big bang'."

"When will that happen?" D'von wanted to know.

"As soon as we fly through," Daryl Om said dryly. D'von just shook his head. The plan seemed unbelievably dangerous and risky.

Try though they might, however, neither D'von nor Daryl Om could come up with any other idea or strategy, and time was running out. With Xet's help, D'von and Daryl Om made the preparations for this precipitous and final chance for survival. All the Mecs on board helped lock down and secure the base. D'von held off as long as possible, until the base was near its last day, before initiating their desperate attempt. When all was ready, D'von put the Parallux core's engines on line and directed the large complex towards the cauldron. With no restraints and adding thrust, the base quickly gained speed. In mere seconds it was streaking towards its own doom. The black hole had been somewhat far away, but the distance dwindled fast. D'von initiated a vortex as soon as the base reached the speed of light, and the singularity pulled it in. Xet was correct, however. At that speed the base remained in flux, and time seemed to stand still. In a blinding flash the base entered the cauldron's maw and passed through unharmed.

On the other side was a beautiful spiral galaxy. Travelling at an unbelievable speed, the base rapidly reached a star field of immense proportions. D'von began reversing thrust as other Mecs scanned for suitable planetary systems. Others extended solar collectors to absorb the life giving energy they desperately needed from nearby suns. After a time, a habitable planet was found—one with the necessary ingredients for life. D'von brought the base into orbit and almost immediately they began the terra-sculpting process. The air was balanced and organic life was seeded, flora and fauna. About this time, the stasis equipment suddenly auto-activated and all those individuals who had been in suspended animation were awakened. Their thoughts, memories and personalities were re-introduced into the empty shells to form living viable persons. At first D'von was distraught, believing the shells would disintegrate, but this was not so. As the final gift of Omniscient Daryl, those in suspension revived healthy and whole. Having been infused with Parallux nomaticles over many years, these individuals had become dual dimensional, surprising everyone. Synth's and Rykard's original shells were among the first ones to be re-animated. It wasn't long before they fell in love and started a life on the new planet. In ages to come, pods were sent out with the seeds of Humanity to other planets, beginning the process for animating an entire universe. As a Virtual Individual, D'von easily endured the ages, and there were other Mecs, the former stasis keepers, to offer company. One of them, a female named Sylar, was quite nice. D'von formed a relationship with her that lasted to the end of days.

CHAPTER THIRTY-THREE

Earlier

With an abrupt start, Clayre opened her eyes. The visual perception she received was astonishing, but pleasant. Bright flora, so green it was nearly fluorescent and dotted with similarly colorful blooms, dominated her vision field.

"Now how did I get here?" she asked herself out loud, with the distinct feeling she'd been there before. A meandering butterfly landed on Clayre's nose making her go cross-eyed. "This is all very familiar," she remarked to no one in particular, as she looked up at the sky. It was a perfect blue with a few puffy white clouds floating slowly past. In the distance she could hear waves crashing on a beach and then it hit her. "I'm back in my Heavenworld!" she exclaimed ecstatically.

"Actually, you're in Xet's," a voice behind her affirmed.

"Daryl!" Clayre shouted, and then started crying. He put his arms around her and hugged her tightly.

"Yes," he told her, "I'm here. Unfortunately, I no longer have a Hybrid shell like yours. I'm just a vision inside your mind like when we first met."

"I don't care!" she sobbed. "Just to be with you, whatever your form, is all I ever wanted."

"Hey! What about me!" Clayre turned and there was Xet, walking towards them.

"You're alive!" she cried, getting even more blubbery. Breaking away from Daryl, she ran over to him. "Oh Xet," she said with teary eyes, "I thought Xetagod had killed you!"

"He did," Xet teased. "My golden armor is no more. Like your Daryl, I am but a creation of your imagination. I have a distinct advantage, though. Here in my Parallux Heavenworld I still have my AMPs. With them I can create anything!" She gave Xet a kiss on his golden cheek.

"I think I'm losing my girl!" Daryl said laughing as he joined them. "Just don't forget who's running this place!" Clayre knew. Focus point copies of Daryl Om had been placed on all the Heavenworlds.

"Don't worry," she smiled. "You both can share me!" Laughing, they went forth to explore Xet's reformed Heavenworld. It wasn't long before they happened upon a high meadow. It became obvious that they were not alone there; a score of others were having a picnic. Clayre's son, Daryl Junior, came up to greet them.

"There you are, mom and dad, and Xet, too. We were beginning to think you'd never get here!" Clayre looked around. All of her special people were present. Daryl Jr.'s wife, Amy, and Clayre's granddaughters were playing happily, along with Quinn and Megan who were enjoying the day with many of the friends she had known from long ago in her first lifetime. Turning toward Xet she thanked him again with yet another kiss, and Daryl didn't mind. She winked and told him not to be jealous.

"I wish there were someone for you," she told Xet seriously.

"You mean like a love?" he replied. "Oh no," Xet went on. "I'm happy as I am, a safe bachelor, with good friends like you!"

Clayre smiled. "I guess I'm fine with that…as long as you're happy."

She would keep Xet close, she promised, reminded of what he'd done for her, and the three of them were never very far apart, even when Clayre wanted to be alone with her true love, Daryl. For those times, Xet would often visit Quinn or one of the others and allow the two lovebirds some privacy. It was truly a wonderful existence for everyone there in Xet's Heavenworld. The only real regret Clayre had was that all the people in Daryl Om's other Heavenworlds were not able to have a similar fate. She, Daryl, and Xet, had done all they could, she reminded herself.

Stretching across Daryl's warm body, Clayre sighed. She could live with that.

EPILOGUE A

Many years later on Earth Primary

The first ten thousand years had done no good at all, so Xetagod was given another ten thousand. In fact several such periods were necessary to make a slight change in Xetagod's temperament. After fifty thousand years, he was finally paroled, given a job, and placed under surveillance. Another twenty thousand years went by before he was at last given his freedom. Like Daryl Om, he opted to return to his native planet. Also like Daryl Om, he no longer had his omniscient abilities and was, more or less, just a regular Mec. When he made it to Earth 14 he was surprised to find it deserted. The planet was in a state of renewal. In his long absence, a large volcanic cauldron had caused a massive eruption that threw his homeworld into an ice age. There was, however, a small contingent of Mec scientists dwelling here and there to study the phenomenon. The rest of the population had been re-distributed to the new planets.

Xetagod had a momentary urge to pursue his old ambitions, as easy as it would be to fulfill them, but let that go. Instead he found an abandoned underground facility, a factory of some kind, and built himself a home. There was enough usable scrap machinery that he could coble together some necessities, like a power supply. For amusement Xetagod endeavored to get the factory equipment operational again. It dawned on him, one day, that the mass of machinery was part of a manufacturing operation that created motation shells. He wondered if it were still possible to make them. It wasn't long before Xetagod did have enough success that he could build a small number of working units. He began to have thoughts about resurrecting an army to conquer Earth. The shells weren't much good without intellects, however, and Xetagod was very lonely. After a time he decided to try something he wasn't sure he could still do—copy himself.

He spent days downloading certain parcels of his knowledge into a shell. Eventually, he asked the unit if it could hear him.

"Affirmative," it answered succinctly.

"Are you alive?" Xetagod asked.

"Data unavailable," it replied. This was a common response for a non-thinking entity.

"What are you?" he asked again. The shell lurched and vibrated for several minutes.

"I am alive!" it affirmed at last.

Xetagod whooped. "Yes, you are," he concurred.

"Are you my creator?" it then asked.

"No," Xetagod replied, not wanting to admit that. "I am a fellow being like yourself. Do you have a name?"

"I would like to be called 'Rayn'," it responded.

Xetagod was confused. "That seems quite feminine," he retorted.

"Yes," Rayn replied. "I am female. What is your name?" Xetagod was stunned. He was unsure about this and had mixed feelings.

"I am Xetago," he lied. For some reason, the name Xetagod embarrassed him. "You have come to my home and we will live together." So Rayn did, and Xetagod forgot all his ideas for conquering Earth. He was lots happier spending time with Rayn, showing her the cold world they lived in. Even frozen, it was wondrous in many ways, the frost and ice creating stark beauty for them alone to see. Xetago and Rayn, as Mecs, lived for many ages on a frozen Earth, and the cold did not bother them at all.

Eventually, the world thawed as did Xetagod.

EPILOGUE B

Eons later from the depths of a dark green crystal

By this time, the newly created entity had already established multitudes of focus points. Many of them integrated around just one juncture—a female human. At first, she was supposed to be the replacement female for Quinn, one that would cause Quinn to become dependable again. Focus points 120 through 147 were to deal with Quinn's repair, especially FP 129. Ultimately, FP 129 grew in scope when it linked with FP 197 which was the study of an unexplained phenomenon, that which the Humans called emotion. FP 129 and FP 197 both came to the same conclusion: a certain Human female, Clayre Ann Keller was to be contacted and assessed for study and data download. FP 129 brought forth her as the most likely female replacement for Quinn's lost mate.

After many attempts, this Human female had finally affirmed that she would indeed exchange dialogue. The entity was filled, now, with the realization that he had succeeded, in his clandestine way, to make contact with another being. With this contact, the entity began a metamorphosis.

"You, you are changing me!" he declared to the female. By the time she answered him, the change was already complete.

The entity, utilizing all the resources at his command, studied with unending depth the possibilities that were likely from his link with this female. On and on he probed, projecting every conceivable circumstance that would affect himself or this Clayre Ann Keller, which, in truth, was virtually anything and everything that existed. His scope played out forward for eons in time—all the way to the final link between them.

In this study, he concluded that many of these Human emotions affected the play of events: some happy, some sad, some good, some bad. However, at the end of it all was a wondrous joy and he was uplifted by that.

"In what way?" she responded to his cryptic statement. The entity, who had named himself "Daryl," realized abruptly that this was the first step in their long journey together. Oh, how he wanted this.

"I now feel from you!" he told her.

THE END OF PART THREE

EXIT STUDY

_^_

These several last entries are said to have been recorded here in Parallux by our original emigrating ancestors. The chief of these was a fabricated being named D'von, who made the perilous crossing into this dimension at its inception and who was also intimately involved with Parallux's initial evolvement. The beings who emigrated with D'von, Humanoids and Mechanicals alike, brought forth life here. Ultimately they spread creation to multitudes of planetary systems throughout the ages. According to D'von's reckoning, since Parallux's inception over seventeen billion units of standard time have elapsed. In this galaxy alone, there are an estimated forty thousand planets with intelligent life.

FINIS

So ends the EVITERNITY triad. I hope that all who have read my series found the stories fun and entertaining. I also hope that those who did can live with my pseudo-theories concerning time travel and sub-atomic actualities, many of which were crafted to smooth out plot lines. It has been an adventure bringing my stories to life, and I have no regrets spending nearly ten years working on them. Perhaps more books are in my future…

Sincerely,

L. C. Kestral

ABOUT L. C. KESTRAL

Midwestern (USA) bred in the dubious boomer years, Lewis Christopher Kestral spent much of his early life in the 60's and 70's. During that time LC pulled stints in a seminary, the army, the music/hippie culture, and as a college student (not necessarily in that order). Shortly after those maniacal 60's came marriage, fatherhood, and a string of odd occupations…the most common ones being: lead guitar in a touring band, construction work, operating printing presses, and metal fabricating. Through all that Kestral has travelled a little as well, having visited nearly all fifty US states, as well as Canada, Mexico, Japan, and Vietnam.

Hobbies? Besides authoring novels, there's songwriting, oil painting, coin collecting, and treasure hunting. LC has recorded a solo musical album entitled "Cornered," and has also exhibited many of his oil paintings.

…..Available books by L. C. Kestral:

PREDICTION

MECWORLD

MEC HEAVEN

And the whole triad in:

EVITERNITY

To contact the author go to:

lckestral@gmail.com

www.ingramcontent.com/pod-product-compliance
Lightning Source LLC
Chambersburg PA
CBHW020820030726
47496CB00001B/14

* 9 7 8 0 6 9 2 7 2 8 4 8 2 *